MENACE VEILED IN MIST

"That fog's moving straight toward us, and it's bringing the light with it. I don't like the feel of this, Sparhawk," Kalten said, drawing his sword.

The glowing fog-bank divided and flowed around the hill upon which they stood. And as it drew nearer, Sparhawk could make out the shapes of bodies within the blur of light.

Sephrenia shrieked, "Defiled ones! Foul and accursed!" But the lights in the fog never faltered as they continued their glowing, inexorable advance.

"Run! Run for your lives! It's the Shining Ones!"

By David Eddings
Published by Ballantine Books:

THE BELGARIAD
Book One: *Pawn of Prophecy*
Book Two: *Queen of Sorcery*
Book Three: *Magician's Gambit*
Book Four: *Castle of Wizardry*
Book Five: *Enchanters' End Game*
Book Six: *Belgarath the Sorcerer*

THE MALLOREON
Book One: *Guardians of the West*
Book Two: *King of the Murgos*
Book Three: *Demon Lord of Karanda*
Book Four: *Sorceress of Darshiva*
Book Five: *The Seeress of Kell*

THE ELENIUM
Book One: *The Diamond Throne*
Book Two: *The Ruby Knight*
Book Three: *The Sapphire Rose*

THE TAMULI
Book One: *Domes of Fire*
Book Two: *The Shining Ones*
Book Three: *The Hidden City*

HIGH HUNT

THE LOSERS

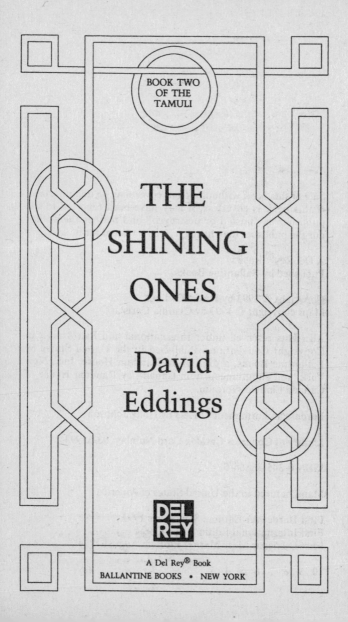

BOOK TWO
OF THE
TAMULI

THE
SHINING
ONES

David
Eddings

DEL REY

A Del Rey® Book
BALLANTINE BOOKS • NEW YORK

A Del Rey® Book
Published by Ballantine Books

Copyright © 1993 by David Eddings
Maps copyright © 1993 by Claudia Carlson

Borders and ornament © 1993 by Holly Johnson

Library of Congress Catalog Card Number: 93-54993

ISBN 0-345-38866-6

Manufactured in the United States of America

First Hardcover Edition: September 1993
First International Edition: April 1994
First Domestic Mass Market Edition: August 1994

10 9 8 7 6 5 4 3

For Pop,
The empty place in our hearts will be filled
by the beautiful memories we all have.
You played a good round of golf and a
helluva game of pool.
We'll miss you.

PROLOGUE

—Excerpted from Chapter Three of *The Cyrga Affair: An Examination of the Recent Crisis.* Compiled by the Contemporary History Department of the University of Matherion.

A compilation such as this is the work of many scholars, and thus inevitably reflects differing views. While the author of *this* portion of the work in hand has enormous respect for his eminent colleague who so ably composed the preceding chapter, the reader must be candidly advised that this writer differs from his colleague in the interpretation of a number of recent events. I most definitely do *not* agree that the intervention by the agents of the Church of Chyrellos in the Cyrga Affair was entirely untainted by self-interest.

I join my colleague, however, in expressing admiration and respect for Zalasta of Styricum. The inestimable services to the empire of this wise and faithful statesman cannot be overly praised. Thus it was that when the full import of the Cyrga Affair burst upon his Majesty's government, it was natural for our ministers to turn to Zalasta for counsel. Despite our admiration for this preeminent citizen of Styricum, however, we must admit that Zalasta's mind is so noble that he sometimes fails to perceive less admirable qualities in others. There were grave doubts in some quarters of his Majesty's government when Zalasta urged that we turn our attention beyond the borders of Tamuli in our quest for a solution to the problem which was rapidly approaching the dimensions of a crisis. His sug-

gestion that the Pandion Knight, Sir Sparhawk, was best suited
to deal with the situation troubled the more conservative members of the Imperial Council. Despite the man's military genius, he is nonetheless a member of one of the Militant Orders
of the Church of Chyrellos, and prudent men do not lower
their guard when compelled by necessity to have dealings with
that particular institution.

Sir Sparhawk had come to Zalasta's attention during the
Second Zemoch War between the Knights of the Church of
Chyrellos and the minions of Otha of Zemoch. Not even
Zalasta, whose wisdom is legendary, can tell us precisely what
took place in the city of Zemoch during Sir Sparhawk's fateful
confrontation with Otha and with the Zemoch God, Azash.
There have been some garbled hints that Sir Sparhawk may
have utilized an ancient talisman known as "the Bhelliom" in
the struggle, but no reputable scholar has been able to uncover
any details about the talisman or its attributes. However he
managed to perform the astounding feat, it is undeniably true
that Sir Sparhawk was successful in his mission; and it was
clearly *that* remarkable success which stampeded his Imperial
Majesty's government into turning to this Pandion Knight for
aid in the early stages of the Cyrga Affair—despite the grave
reservations of some highly respected ministers, who quite correctly pointed out that an alliance between the empire and the
Church of Chyrellos might well be fraught with danger. Unfortunately perhaps, the faction headed by Foreign Minister
Oscagne currently has the emperor's ear, and our prime minister, Pondia Subat, was unable to prevent the government from
embarking on a potentially dangerous course of action.

Foreign Minister Oscagne himself headed the mission to the
seat of the Elene Church of Chyrellos to petition Archprelate
Dolmant for Sir Sparhawk's aid in dealing with the crisis.
While no one can question Oscagne's skill in diplomacy, his
political views have been called into question in some quarters,
and it is widely known that he and the prime minister have disagreed violently in the past.

The politics of the Eosian continent are murky, for there is
no central authority there. Quite frequently, the Church of
Chyrellos finds itself at odds with the reigning monarchs of the
separate Elene kingdoms. As a Church Knight, Sir Sparhawk
would normally be under the command of Archprelate
Dolmant, but that simple and direct line of command was
clouded by the fact that Sparhawk is *also* the Prince Consort

of the Queen of Elenia and therefore subject to *her* whims. It was here that Foreign Minister Oscagne was able to demonstrate his virtuosity in the field of diplomacy. Archprelate Dolmant clearly saw the contiguity of interest with the empire in the matter, but Queen Ehlana remained unconvinced. The Queen of Elenia is young, and her emotions sometimes cloud her judgment. She clearly viewed the notion of a prolonged separation from her husband with a profound lack of enthusiasm. In a brilliant stroke, however, Foreign Minister Oscagne proposed that Sir Sparhawk's journey to the Daresian continent might best be masked by a state visit of Queen Ehlana to the imperial court in Matherion. As Prince Consort, Sir Sparhawk would quite naturally accompany his wife, and his presence would thus be fully explained. This proposal sufficiently mollified Sparhawk's queen, and she finally agreed.

Traveling with a suitable escort of one hundred Church Knights and various functionaries, Queen Ehlana took ship and sailed to the port of Salesha in eastern Zemoch. From there the royal party traveled north to Basne where an additional escort of horsemen from eastern Pelosia awaited them. Thus reinforced, the Elenes crossed the border into Astel in western Daresia.

The accounts we have received of the queen's journey have shown glaring inconsistencies. Objections have been raised that should we accept the word of these Elenes, we would clearly be faced with an absurdity. After some consideration, however, this writer has become convinced that these apparent discrepancies can be easily reconciled if those who so violently object will but take the trouble to examine the differences between the Elene and the Tamul calendars. The Queen of Elenia did *not*, in fact, pretend to have flown across the continent, as some have scornfully suggested. Her progress was quite normal, and it will be recognized as such if the learned gentlemen will but take note of the fact that *the Elene week is longer than ours!*

At any rate, the queen's party reached the capital of Astel at Darsas, where Queen Ehlana so charmed King Alberen that Ambassador Fontan humorously reported that the poor man was on the verge of giving her his crown. Prince Sparhawk, meanwhile, began to actively pursue the real purpose behind his journey to Tamuli, the gathering of information about what the Elenes had melodramatically come to call "the conspiracy."

The queen's party was joined at Darsas by two legions of

Atan warriors under the leadership of Engessa, the commander of the garrison at Cenae, and they journeyed to Pela on the steppes of central Astel to meet with the nomadic Peloi. From thence they set out for the Styric city of Sarsos in northeastern Astel.

A disturbing note emerges from the accounts of this journey, however. The foreign minister, either duped or willingly conspiring with the Elenes, reported that somewhat to the west of Sarsos, the royal party encountered *Cyrgai*! This clear evidence of an intent to deceive his Majesty's government has raised grave questions, not only about Oscagne's loyalty, but about the sincerity of the Elenes as well. As Prime Minister Subat pointed out, Foreign Minister Oscagne is, though brilliant, sometimes erratic, a common characteristic of the overly gifted. Moreover, the prime minister added, Prince Sparhawk and his companions *are* Church Knights, after all, and the Church of Chyrellos is widely known to be a *political* as well as a spiritual force on the Eosian continent. Dark suspicions began to arise in the halls of his Majesty's government, and many have expressed grave doubts about the wisdom of our course. Some have even gone so far as to raise the possibility that the disruption here in Tamuli might be of *Elene* origin, providing as they did a perfect excuse for an incursion onto the continent by the Church Knights, the acknowledged agents of Archprelate Dolmant. Could it be, they ask, that this entire affair has been contrived by Dolmant to provide his Church with the opportunity to forcibly convert all of Tamuli to the worship of the Elene God and thus to deliver political control of the empire into his own hands? It should be noted here that Prime Minister Subat has *personally* advised this writer that he is seriously concerned about this possibility.

At Sarsos, Queen Ehlana's party was joined by Sephrenia, who was formerly the tutor of the Pandions in the Secrets of Styricum, but who is now a member of the Thousand, the ruling council in that city. They were also joined there by Zalasta himself, a fact which has quieted some of our anxieties in regard to the motives of the Elenes. It was obviously through Zalasta's efforts that the Thousand were persuaded to pledge their aid, despite the long-standing and, many feel, fully justified suspicions all Styrics have of Elene motives.

The Elenes then moved on to Atan, where Queen Ehlana again charmed king and queen. It is clearly evident that the personality of this winsome girl is a force to be reckoned with.

Although Foreign Minister Oscagne's report of the encounter with the supposed Cyrgai is open to serious question, there can be no doubt about the veracity of the report of what happened after our visitors left Atana. *That* report came from Zalasta himself, and no sane man in the government could ever question the veracity of the first citizen of Styricum. It was in the mountains lying to the west of the border of Tamul proper that the party was set upon again, and Zalasta has confirmed the fact that the attackers were nonhuman.

There have been sightings of fearsome monsters in the Atan mountains in the past year, although many skeptics have dismissed these reports as being yet more of the illusory manifestations of the power of those bent on bringing down his Imperial Majesty's government. These clever illusions of Ogres, vampires, werewolves, and Shining Ones have been terrorizing the simple folk of Tamuli for several years, and the mountain monsters had been assumed to be no more than another of these illusions. Zalasta assures us, however, that these huge, shaggy beasts are Trolls, indigenous to the Thalesian peninsula in Eosia, which had migrated to the north coast of Atan across the polar ice, presumably at the behest of the enemies of the empire. Sir Sparhawk, once again reinforcing Zalasta's opinion of him, quickly devised tactics which routed the brutes.

Queen Ehlana's party then crossed into Tamul proper and shortly thereafter reached the imperial capital at fire-domed Matherion, where they were graciously welcomed by Emperor Sarabian. Despite the protests of Prime Minister Subat, the Elene visitors were given almost unimpeded access to his Majesty. The Queen of Elenia soon charmed the emperor, even as she had the lesser monarchs to the west. Candor compels us to admit that Emperor Sarabian has shown of late a lamentable tendency to interfere with the government, and to override the counsel of those far better equipped than he to deal with the day-to-day details of governing his vast realm.

The prime minister, acting on the advice of Interior Minister Kolata, had decided to place Prince Sparhawk under the command of the Ministry of the Interior. As Kolata correctly pointed out, Sir Sparhawk, an Eosian Elene, could not be expected to understand the myriad cultures of Tamuli and therefore would need guidance and direction in his efforts to counter the schemes of our enemies. Emperor Sarabian, however, rejected this approach and granted this foreigner almost total discretion in approaching such problems as arose.

Despite our reservations about Prince Sparhawk, his queen, and his companions, however, we must reluctantly concede that their presence in Matherion averted a disaster of the first order. Among the other structures in the imperial compound there is a replica of an Elene castle, which was specifically designed to make Elene dignitaries feel at home. Queen Ehlana and her entourage were housed in that castle, and the relevance of that fact will soon become clear.

In some as-yet-to-be-determined fashion, Sir Sparhawk and his cohorts unearthed a plot here in Matherion to overthrow the government. Rather than report their findings to the Ministry of the Interior, however, the Elenes chose to keep their discovery to themselves and to permit the conspirators to pursue their plot to its final conclusion. When an armed mob approached the imperial compound on that fateful night, Prince Sparhawk and his companions simply withdrew into their Elene castle, taking the emperor and the government inside with them.

We Tamuls had not fully understood the fact that architecture can be a weapon. Unbeknownst to his Majesty's government, Sparhawk's Elenes had modified the castle to some degree and had quietly brought in stores, all the while secretly constructing the brutal implements with which Elenes do war.

The mob, bent on the overthrow of the government, swept unimpeded into the imperial compound and found itself confronted by an impregnable castle filled with ruthless Elene warriors who routinely utilize boiling pitch and fire to defend their strongholds. The horrors of that night will remain forever etched on the memories of civilized men. As has long been the practice in Tamuli, many of the younger sons of the great houses of Tamul proper had joined with the rebels, more as a lark than out of any serious criminal intent. Always in the past these youthful offenders have been separated from the true criminals, severely reprimanded, and then returned to their parents. Protected by rank and family, they have had little to fear from the authorities. Boiling pitch, however, is no respecter of rank, and a high-spirited young aristocrat soaked in naphtha will burn as quickly as the foulest knave from the gutter. Moreover, once the mob had entered the compound, the Elenes closed the main gates, effectively sealing all inside, the innocent as well as the guilty, and further horrors were inflicted on the unfortunates by rampaging Peloi horsemen. The brutal suppression of the uprising was completed when the compound gates were opened once again to admit fully twenty legions of Atans, savages from the mountains who had received no instruction whatsoever in the customary civilities. The Atans systematically butchered all in their paths. Many young nobles, dearly loved students at this very university, were cut down even as they displayed their badges of rank, which should have guaranteed them immunity.

Although decent men the world around must view this unbridled savagery with horror, we must reluctantly congratulate Sir Sparhawk and his companions. The uprising was crushed, nay, annihilated, by these Elene savages and the unrestrained Atans.

His Imperial Majesty's government, however, made few friends on that dreadful night. Although the atrocities were clearly of Elene origin, the fact that Sir Sparhawk was here in Matherion at the emperor's express invitation has not been lost on the great houses of Tamul proper.

To further exacerbate the situation, the Elenes have seized upon the uprising as an excuse to send Patriarch Emban, a high-ranking member of the Elene clergy and ostensibly the spiritual adviser of Queen Ehlana, back to Chyrellos to urge the Archprelate to dispatch his Church Knights to Tamuli in force to aid in "restoring order."

Pondia Subat, the prime minister, has privately confessed that he is growing powerless, able only to watch helplessly as events move at an increasingly quickening pace. He has personally told this writer of his concerns. Foreign Minister Oscagne is clearly using his influence over the emperor to manipulate the situation. The invitation to Sir Sparhawk to come to Tamuli was obviously but the first step in some wider and more deadly scheme. Utilizing the present turmoil in Tamuli, the foreign minister has manipulated the emperor into providing the very opening Dolmant needed to justify an incursion in force onto the Daresian continent.

This writer is fully convinced that the empire faces the gravest threat in her long and glorious history. The willing cooperation of the Atans in the massacre within the imperial compound is clear evidence that not even *their* loyalty can be depended upon.

To whom can we turn for aid? Where in all this world can we find a force sufficient to repel the savage minions of Dolmant of Chyrellos? Must the empire in all her glory fall before the onslaught of the Elene zealots? I weep, my brothers, for the glory that must die. Fire-domed Matherion, the city of light, the home of truth and beauty, the center of the world, is doomed. The darkness descends, and there is little hope that morning will ever come again.

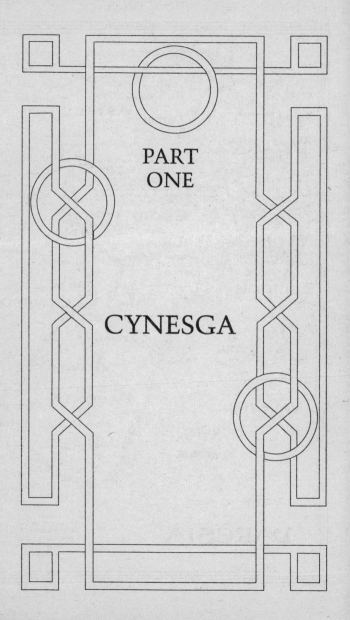

PART
ONE

CYNESGA

CHAPTER
ONE

The seasons were turning, and the long summer was winding down toward autumn. A tenuous mist hung in the streets of firedomed Matherion. The moon had risen late, and its pale light starkly etched the opalescent towers and domes and imparted a soft glow to the fog lying in the streets. Matherion, all agleam, stood with her feet bathed in shining mist and her pale face lifted to the night sky.

Sparhawk was tired. The tensions of the past week and the climactic events that had resolved them had drained him, but he could not sleep. Wrapped in his black Pandion cloak, he stood on the parapet looking pensively out over the shining city. He was tired, but his need to evaluate, to assess, to understand, was far too great to permit him to seek his bed and let his mind sink into the soft well of sleep until everything had been put into its proper place.

"What are you doing up here, Sparhawk?" Khalad spoke quietly, his voice so much like his father's that Sparhawk turned his head sharply to be sure that Kurik himself had not returned from the House of the Dead to chide him. Khalad was a plain-faced young man with thick shoulders and an abrupt manner. His family had served Sparhawk's for three generations now, and Khalad, like his father, customarily addressed his lord with a plain-spoken bluntness.

13

"I couldn't sleep," Sparhawk replied with a brief shrug.

"Your wife's got half the garrison out looking for you, you know."

Sparhawk grimaced. "Why does she always have to do that?"

"It's your own fault. You know she's going to send people out after you anytime you go off without telling her where you'll be. You could save yourself—and us—a lot of time and trouble if you'd just tell her in the first place. It seems to me that I've suggested that several times already."

"Don't bully me, Khalad. You're as bad as your father was."

"Sometimes good traits breed true. Would you like to go down and tell your wife that you're all right—*before* she calls in the workmen to start tearing down the walls?"

Sparhawk sighed. "All right." He turned away from the parapet. "Oh, by the way, you probably ought to know that we'll be making a trip before long."

"Oh? Where are we going?"

"We have to go pick something up. Have a word with the farriers. Faran needs to be reshod. He's scuffed his right front shoe down until it's as thin as paper."

"That's your fault, Sparhawk. He wouldn't do that if you'd sit up straight in your saddle."

"We start to get crooked as we grow older. That's one of the things you have to look forward to."

"Thanks. When are we leaving on this trip?"

"Just as soon as I can come up with a convincing enough lie to persuade my wife to let me go off without her."

"We've got plenty of time, then." Khalad looked out across moon-washed Matherion standing in pale fog with the moonlight awakening the rainbows of fire in her naked shoulders. "Pretty," he noted.

"Is that the best you can do? You look at the most fabulous city in the world and shrug it off as 'pretty.' "

"I'm not an aristocrat, Sparhawk. I don't have to invent flowery phrases to impress others—or myself. Let's get you inside before the damp settles into your lungs. You crooked old people have delicate health sometimes."

Queen Ehlana, pale and blonde and altogether lovely, was irritated more than angry; Sparhawk saw that immediately. He also saw that she had gone to some trouble to make herself as pretty as possible. Her dressing gown was dark blue satin, her cheeks had been carefully pinched to make them glow, and her hair was artfully arranged to give the impression of winsomely distracted dishevelment. She berated him about his lack of consideration in tones that might easily have made the trees cry and the very rocks shrink from her. Her cadences were measured, and her voice rose, then sank, as she told him exactly how she felt. Sparhawk concealed a smile. Ehlana was speaking to him on two levels at the same time as she stood in the center of the blue-draped royal apartment scolding him. Her words expressed extreme displeasure; her careful preparations, however, said something quite different.

He apologized.

She refused to accept his apology and stormed off to the bedroom, slamming the door behind her.

"Spirited," Sephrenia murmured. The small woman sat out of harm's way on the far side of the room, her white Styric robe glowing in the candlelight.

"You noticed," Sparhawk smiled.

"Does she do that often?"

"Oh, yes. She enjoys it. What are you doing up so late, little mother?"

"Aphrael wanted me to speak with you."

"Why didn't she just come and talk with me herself? It's not as if she were way over on the other side of town."

"It's a formal sort of occasion, Sparhawk. I'm supposed to speak for her at times like this."

"Was that intended to make sense?"

"It would if you were Styric. We're going to have to make some substitutions when we go to retrieve Bhelliom. Khalad can fill in for his father without any particular problem, but Tynian's decision to go back to Chyrellos with Emban really has Aphrael upset. Can you persuade him to change his mind?"

Sparhawk shook his head. "I wouldn't even try, Sephrenia. I'm not going to cripple him for life just because Aphrael might miss him."

"Is his arm really that bad?"

"It's bad enough. That crossbow bolt went right through his shoulder joint. If he starts moving it around, it won't set right, and that's his sword arm."

"Aphrael could fix it, you know."

"Not without exposing her identity, she couldn't, and I won't let her do that."

"Won't *let*?"

"Ask her if she wants to endanger her mother's sanity just for the sake of symmetry. Substitute someone else. If Aphrael's willing to accept Khalad in place of Kurik, she should be able to pick someone else to fill in for Tynian. Why is it so important to her in the first place?"

"You wouldn't understand."

"Why don't you try to explain it anyway? I might surprise you."

"You're in an odd humor tonight."

"I've just been scolded. That always makes me odd. Why does Aphrael think it's so important to always have the same group of people around her?"

"It has to do with the feeling of it, Sparhawk. The presence of any given person is more than just the way he looks or the sound of his voice. It also involves the way he thinks—and probably more important, the way he feels about Aphrael. She surrounds herself with that. When you bring in different people, you change the way it feels, and that throws her off balance." She looked at him. "You didn't understand a word of that, did you?"

"Yes, as a matter of fact, I did. How about Vanion? He loves her as much as Tynian does, and she loves him, too. He's been more or less with us in spirit since all this started anyway, and he *is* a knight, after all."

"Vanion? Don't be absurd, Sparhawk."

"He's not an invalid, you know. He was running footraces back in Sarsos, and he was still as good as ever with his lance when we fought the Trolls."

"It's out of the question. I won't even discuss it."

He crossed the room, took her wrists in his hands, and kissed her palms. "I love you dearly, little mother," he told her, "but I'm going to override you this time. You can't wrap Vanion in lamb's wool for the rest of his life just because you're afraid he might scratch his finger. If you don't suggest him to Aphrael, I will."

She swore at him in Styric. "Don't you understand, Sparhawk? I almost lost him." Her heart was in her luminous blue eyes. "I'll die if anything happens to him."

"Nothing's going to happen to him. Are you going to ask Aphrael about it, or would you rather have me do it?"

She swore at him again.

"Where did you ever learn that kind of language?" he asked

mildly. "If that takes care of our problem, I'm a little overdue at the bedroom door."

"I didn't quite follow that."

"It's time for the kissing and making up. There's supposed to be a certain rhythm to these things, and if I wait too long to soften Ehlana's displeasure, she'll begin to think I don't love her anymore."

"Do you mean her performance here tonight was nothing more than an invitation to the bedroom?"

"That might be putting it a little bluntly, but there was some of that involved, yes. Sometimes I get busy and forget to pay as much attention to her as I should. She'll only let that go on for so long before she makes a speech. The speech reminds me that I've been neglecting her. We kiss and make up, and everything's all right again."

"Wouldn't it be simpler if she just came right out and told you in the first place without these elaborate games?"

"Probably, but it wouldn't be nearly as much fun for her. You'll excuse me?"

"Why do you always avoid me, Berit-Knight?" Empress Elysoun asked with a disconsolate little pout.

"Your Highness misunderstands me," Berit replied, flushing slightly and keeping his eyes averted.

"Am I ugly, Berit-Knight?"

"Of course not, your Highness."

"Then why don't you ever look at me?"

"It's not considered polite among Elenes for a man to look at an undressed woman, your Highness."

"I'm not an Elene, Sir Knight. I'm a Valesian, and I'm not naked. I have plenty of clothes on. If you'll come to my chambers, I'll show you the difference."

Sparhawk had been looking for Sir Berit to advise him of their upcoming journey and he had just rounded a corner in the hallway leading to the chapel to find his young friend trapped once more by the Empress Elysoun. Since Emperor Sarabian's entire family was inside the castle as a security measure, Berit's escape routes had been seriously curtailed, and Elysoun had been taking advantage of the situation outrageously. The emperor's Valesian wife was a brown-skinned, sunny girl whose native costume left her unashamedly bare-breasted. No matter how many times Sarabian had explained to Berit that customary moral strictures did not apply to Valesians, the young knight remained steadfastly respectful—and chaste. Elysoun had taken that as a challenge and she had been pursuing the poor young man relentlessly. Sparhawk was just on the verge of speaking to his friend, but he smiled instead and stepped back around the corner to listen. He *was* the interim Preceptor of the Pandion Order, after all, and it was his duty to look after the souls of his men.

"Do you *always* have to be an Elene?" Elysoun was asking the knight.

"I *am* an Elene, your Highness."

"But you Elenes are so boring," she said. "Why don't you be a Valesian for just one afternoon? It's much more fun, and it won't take very long, you know—unless you want it to." She paused. "Are you really a virgin?" she asked curiously.

Berit turned bright red.

Elysoun laughed delightedly. "What an absurd idea!" she exclaimed. "Aren't you even a little curious about what you've been missing? I'll be happy to take that tiresome virginity off your hands, Berit-Knight—and it won't even hurt very much."

Sparhawk took pity on the poor fellow and intervened at that point. "Ah, there you are, Berit," he said, stepping around the corner and speaking in Tamul for the empress' benefit. "I've been looking all over for you. Something's come up that needs our attention." He bowed to the empress. "Your Imperial Highness," he murmured, "I'm afraid I'll have to commandeer your friend here for a while. Matters of state, you know."

The look Elysoun gave him had daggers in it.

"I was sure your Highness would understand," he said, bowing again. "Come along, Berit. The matter's serious, and we're late." He led his friend off down the opalescent corridor as Empress Elysoun glared after them.

"Thanks, Sparhawk," Berit said with relief.

"Why don't you just stay away from her?"

"I can't. She follows me everywhere. She even trapped me in the bathhouse once—in the middle of the night. She said she wanted to bathe with me."

"Berit—" Sparhawk smiled. "—as your preceptor and spiritual guide, I'm supposed to applaud your devotion to the ideals of our order. As your friend, though, I have to tell you that running away from her only makes matters worse. We have to stay here in Matherion, and if we stay long enough, she *will* get you. She's very single-minded about it."

"Yes, I've noticed that."

"She's really quite pretty, you know," Sparhawk suggested tentatively. "What's your difficulty with the notion of being friendly?"

"Sparhawk!"

The big Pandion sighed. "I was afraid you might look at it that way. Look, Berit, Elysoun comes from a different culture with different customs. She doesn't see this sort of thing as sin. Sarabian's made it quite clear that he wants some of us to accommodate her, and she's chosen you as the lucky man. It's a political necessity, so you're just going to have to set these delicate feelings aside. Look upon it as your knightly duty, if it makes you feel any better. I can even have Emban grant you an indulgence if you think it's necessary."

Berit gasped.

"You're starting to embarrass us," Sparhawk said. "Elysoun's been making Sarabian's life miserable about the whole thing. He won't step in and *order* you to do as she asks, no matter how much she nags him, but he quite obviously expects *me* to speak with you about it."

"I can't believe you're saying this, Sparhawk."

"Just go ahead and do it, Berit. You don't have to enjoy it if you don't want to, but do it. Do it as often as you have to, but make her stop screaming at the emperor. It's your duty, my friend, and after you and Elysoun have romped around the bedroom a few times, she'll start looking for new playmates."

"But what if she doesn't?"

"I wouldn't worry too much. Patriarch Emban's got a whole saddlebag full of indulgences if it should turn out that you really need them."

The failed uprising had given Emperor Sarabian the perfect excuse to escape from his government. Feigning cowardice, he had flatly declared that he felt safe only within the walls of Ehlana's castle, and then only if the moat remained full and the drawbridge raised. His ministers, long accustomed to arranging his every move, found that terribly inconvenient.

Sarabian had not been motivated entirely by a desire to breathe the air of relative freedom, however. Interior Minister Kolata had been revealed as a traitor during the coup attempt, but Sarabian and his Elene friends had decided that the time was not yet right to publicly reveal his treachery. So long as the emperor remained inside Ehlana's castle, Kolata's presence there as well was fully explained. He was in charge of the police, after all, and the protection of the emperor was his paramount duty. The interior minister, closely supervised by Ehlana's cohorts, directed the police forces of the empire from inside the walls. His meetings with his underlings were always just a trifle strained, since Stragen customarily sat beside him with one hand idly resting on the hilt of a dagger.

It was early one morning when Ambassador Norkan, the Tamul emissary to the court of King Androl and Queen Betuana of Atan, was escorted into the gleaming imitation throne room in the castle. Norkan wore his usual golden mantle and a puzzled expression. Though he tried to conceal the fact, he quite obviously disapproved of the fact that his emperor was dressed in western-style doublet and hose of a rich plum color. "Have you gone and stolen my emperor, too, Queen Ehlana?" he asked with a perfunctory bow. Norkan was a brilliant man, but he had an unfortunate tendency to speak his mind quite openly.

"What a thing to say, your Excellency," Ehlana protested mildly in nearly perfect Tamul. Ehlana was technically the hostess here, so she sat on her throne wearing her formal crimson robe and a golden crown. She turned to her imperial "guest," who sprawled in a nearby chair slowly twitching a string across the opalescent floor for the entertainment of Princess Danae's cat. "Have I stolen you, Sarabian?" she asked him.

"Oh, absolutely, Ehlana," he replied, speaking in Elenic. "I'm utterly in thrall to you."

"Has someone opened a school for modern languages here on the grounds while I've been gone, Oscagne?" Norkan asked.

"I suppose you might say that," the foreign minister replied. "His Majesty's proficiency in Elenic predates Queen Ehlana's visit, however. Our revered emperor's been keeping secrets from us."

"Is he allowed to do that? I thought he was supposed to be just a stuffed toy that we trotted out on ceremonial occasions."

Even Oscagne choked a bit on that, but Sarabian burst into laughter. "I've missed you, Norkan," he declared. "Have you had the chance to get to know our excellent Norkan, Ehlana?"

"I sampled his wit in Atana, Sarabian." The queen smiled. "His observations always seem so—ah—unexpected."

"That they are," Sarabian laughed, rising to his feet. He swore as the rapier at his side briefly caught behind the leg of his chair; the emperor still had difficulty with his rapier. "Norkan once made one of those unexpected observations about the size of my sister's feet, and I had to send him off to Atan to keep her from having him murdered." He cocked one eyebrow at the ambassador. "I really should make you marry her, Norkan. Then you could insult her in private. Public insults require public responses, you know."

"I'm honored more than I can say, your Imperial Majesty," Norkan replied. "The prospect of becoming your brother-in-law is quite likely to stop my heart entirely."

"You don't like my sister," Sarabian accused.

"I didn't say that, your Majesty, but I prefer to worship her from afar—at least out of the range of her feet. That's what precipitated my unfortunate remark in the first place. I was gouty that day, and she stepped on my toe. She'd be a nice enough girl, I suppose, if she'd only watch where she's putting those cattle barges she wears for shoes."

"It wouldn't be one of those marriages made in heaven, Sarabian." Ehlana smiled. "I've met your sister, and I'm afraid his Excellency's wit would be lost on her."

"You might be right, my dear," Sarabian agreed. "I'd really like to get rid of her, though. She's irritated me since the day she was born. What are you doing back here in Matherion, Norkan?"

One of Ambassador Norkan's eyebrows shot up. "Things *have* changed, haven't they, Oscagne? Are we supposed to tell him to his face what's *really* going on?"

"Emperor Sarabian's decided to take charge of his own government, my friend." Oscagne sighed mournfully.

"Isn't that against the law?"

"Afraid not, old boy."

"Would you consider accepting my resignation?"

"No, not really."

"Don't you want to work for me any more, Norkan?" Sarabian asked.

"I have nothing against you personally, your Majesty, but if you decide to actually meddle in government, the whole empire could collapse."

"Marvelous, Norkan. I love the way you start talking before you've saddled up your brains. You see, Ehlana? That's what I was telling you about. The officials in my government all expect me to smile regally, approve their recommendations without question, and leave the business of running things to them."

"How boring."

"Indeed it is, my dear, but I'm going to change it. Now that I've seen a real ruler in action, whole new horizons have been opened to me. You still haven't answered my question, Norkan. What brings you back to Matherion?"

"The Atans are growing restive, your Majesty."

"Are the recent disturbances starting to erode their loyalty?"

"No, your Majesty, quite the reverse. The uprising has them all excited. Androl wants to move out in force to occupy Matherion in order to guarantee your safety. I don't think we want that. The Atans don't pay too much attention to rank or position when they decide to kill people."

"We noticed that," Sarabian replied dryly. "I've received all sorts of petitions of protest from the noble houses of Tamul proper as a result of the measures Engessa took to put down the coup."

"I've spoken with Betuana, your Majesty," Norkan continued. "She's promised to shorten her husband's leash until I get some instructions from you. Something short and to the point like 'Sit! Stay!' might be appropriate, considering Androl's mental capabilities."

"How did you ever get to be a diplomat, Norkan?"

"I lied a lot."

"A suggestion, Emperor Sarabian?" Tynian offered.

"Go ahead, Sir Tynian."

"We don't really want to ruffle King Androl's feathers, so a hint to him that he's being held in place to meet a far greater threat might be preferable to just sending him to bed without any supper."

Sarabian laughed. "What a novel way to put it, Sir Tynian. All right, Norkan, send Engessa."

Norkan blinked.

"Pay attention, man," Sarabian snapped.

"That's something you'll have to get used to, Norkan," Oscagne advised. "The emperor sometimes takes verbal short-cuts."

"Oh. I see." Norkan thought about it. "Might I ask why Atan Engessa would be better qualified to carry your instructions than I would, your Majesty?"

"Because Engessa can run faster than you can, and he'll be able to put our commands to Androl in language far more acceptable to him. There's also the fact that using Engessa hints at a military reason for the decision, and that should smooth Androl's feathers all the more. You can explain our *real* reasons to Betuana when you get back."

"You know something, Oscagne?" Norkan said. "He might just work out all right after all—if we can keep him from making too many blunders at the outset."

Oscagne winced.

Sparhawk touched Vanion's shoulder and motioned with his head. The two of them drifted back to the rear of the throne room. "I've got a problem, Vanion," Sparhawk muttered.

"Oh?"

"I've racked my brains to come up with an excuse for us to get out of Matherion for long enough to retrieve the Bhelliom, but I haven't had a single idea that a child wouldn't be able to see through. Ehlana's not stupid, you know."

"No, that she isn't."

"Aphrael won't say anything definite, but I get the strong feeling that she wants us to sail on the same ship with Emban and Tynian, and I'm starting to run out of excuses to keep delaying their departure. Any ideas?"

"Ask Oscagne to help you," Vanion shrugged. "He's a diplomat, so lying comes second nature to him."

"Nice idea, but I can't really tell him where we're going and what we're going to do when we get there, can I?"

"*Don't* tell him, then. Just tell him that you need a reason to be out of town for a while. Put on a gravely mysterious face and let it go at that. Oscagne's been around for long enough to recognize the symptoms of official reticence when he sees them."

"Why didn't I think of that?"

"Probably because your oath keeps getting in your way. I know that you've sworn to tell the truth, but that doesn't mean that you have to tell the *whole* truth. You can leave things out, you know. Leaving things out is one of the perquisites of the office of Preceptor."

Sparhawk sighed. "Back to school, I see. I think I'm doomed to spend my whole life getting instructions from you—and being made to feel inadequate in the process."

"That's what friends are for, Sparhawk."

"You're not going to tell me, are you?" Sparhawk tried very hard to keep it from sounding like an accusation.

"Not yet, no," Princess Danae replied, carefully tying a doll's bonnet on her cat's head. Mmrr did not appear to care for the idea, but she endured her mistress' little game with a look of resignation.

"Why not?" Sparhawk asked his daughter, flopping down into one of the blue armchairs in the royal apartment.

"Because something might still come up to make it unnecessary. You're not going to find Bhelliom until I decide to *let* you find it, Father."

"You want us to sail with Tynian and Emban, though?"

"Yes."

"How far?"

"It doesn't really matter. I just need Tynian with us when we first set out, that's all."

"Then you don't really have any set destination in mind—with that ship, I mean?"

"Of course not. I just need Tynian to be along for a couple of days. We can go out to sea for a couple of leagues and then sail around in circles for two days if you want. It's all the same to me."

"Thanks," he said acidly.

"No charge. There." She held up the cat. "Isn't she darling in her new bonnet?"

"Adorable."

Mmrr gave Sparhawk a flat look of pure disgust.

"I can't tell you why, your Excellency," Sparhawk said to Oscagne later that same day when they were alone in one of the hallways. "All I can say is that I need a reason to be away from Matherion with a group of nine or ten of my friends for an indeterminate period of time—several weeks or so. It has to be significant enough to convince my wife that it's necessary, but not so serious as to worry her, *and* I have to sail on the same ship with Emban and Tynian."

"All right," Oscagne agreed. "How good an actor are you, Prince Sparhawk?"

"I don't think anybody'd pay money to watch me perform."

Oscagne let that pass. "I gather that this ploy is primarily intended for your wife's benefit?"

"Yes."

"Then it might be best if the idea of sending you off someplace came from her. I'll maneuver her into ordering you off on some inconsequential errand, and you can take it from there."

"I'd really like to see you try to maneuver Ehlana."

"Trust me, old boy. Trust me."

"Tega?" Sarabian asked his foreign minister incredulously. "The only superstition they have on the Isle of Tega is the one that says that it's bad luck not to raise the price of seashells every year."

"They never mentioned it to us in the past because they were probably afraid we'd think they were being silly, your Majesty," Oscagne replied urbanely. Oscagne looked decidedly uncomfortable in the blue doublet and hose Sarabian had ordered him to wear. He couldn't seem to think of anything to do with his hands, and he appeared to be very self-conscious about his bony legs. "The word *silly* seems to strike at the very core of the Tegan soul. They're the stuffiest people in the world."

"I know. Gahenas, my Tegan wife, can put me to sleep almost immediately—even when we're . . ." The emperor threw a quick look at Ehlana and left it hanging.

"Tegans have raised being boring to an art form, your Majesty," Oscagne agreed. "Anyway, there's an old Tegan myth to the effect that the oyster beds are haunted by a mermaid. Supposedly she eats oysters, shells and all, and that *really* upsets the Tegans. She also seduces Tegan divers, who tend to drown during the exchange of pleasantries."

"Isn't a mermaid supposed to be half-girl and half-fish?" Ulath asked.

"So the legend goes," Oscagne replied.

"And isn't she supposed to be a fish from the waist down?"

"I've been told so, yes."

"Then how—?" Ulath also looked quickly at Ehlana and then abruptly broke off.

"How what, Sir Ulath?" Ehlana asked him innocently.

"It's—ah—not really important, your Majesty," he replied with an embarrassed cough.

"I wouldn't even raise this absurd myth, your Majesties," Oscagne said to Sarabian and Ehlana, "except in the light of recent developments. The parallels between the vampires in Arjuna, the Shining Ones in southern Atan, and the werewolves, ghouls, and Ogres in other parts of the empire are really rather striking, wouldn't you say? I'd imagine that if someone were to go to Tega and ask around, he might hear stories about some prehistoric pearl-diver who's been resurrected and also find that some rabble-rouser's telling the Tegans that this hero and his half-fish, half-human mistress are going to lead the oysters in a mass assault on Matherion."

"How droll," Sarabian murmured.

"Sorry, your Majesty," Oscagne apologized. "What I'm getting at is that we've probably got some relatively inexperienced conspirator on Tega. He's just getting started, so he's bound to make mistakes—but experienced or not, he knows a great deal about the whole conspiracy. Since our friends here won't let us question Kolata too closely, we have to look elsewhere for information."

"We're not being delicate about the Minister of the Interior, your Excellency," Kalten told him. "It's just that we've seen what happens to prisoners who are on the verge of talking too much. Kolata's still useful to us, but only as long as he stays in one piece. He won't be much good if little chunks and globs of him get scattered all over the building."

Oscagne shuddered. "I'll take your word for it, Sir Kalten. At any rate, your Majesty, if some of our Elene friends here could go to Tega and put their hands on this fellow and talk with him before our enemy can dismantle him, they could probably persuade him to tell us everything he knows. Sir Sparhawk has some ambitions along those lines, I understand. He wants to find out if he can wring somebody out hard enough to make his hair bleed."

"You have a very graphic imagination, Sparhawk," Sarabian noted. "What do you think, Ehlana? Can you spare your husband for a while? If he and some of his knights went to Tega and held the entire island underwater for a couple of hours, God only knows what kind of information might come bubbling to the surface."

"That's a very good idea, Sarabian. Sparhawk, why don't you take some of our friends, run on down to the Isle of Tega, and see what you can find out?"

"I'd really rather not be separated from you, dear," he replied with feigned reluctance.

"That's very sweet, Sparhawk, but we *do* have responsibilities, you know."

"Are you ordering me to go, Ehlana?"

"You don't have to put it *that* way, Sparhawk. It's only a suggestion, after all."

"As my Queen commands," he sighed, putting on a melancholy expression.

CHAPTER
TWO

E mpress Gahenas was a Tegan lady of middle
years with a severe expression and tightly
pursed lips. She wore a plain grey gown, buttoned to the chin, and long-sleeved gloves of
scratchy wool. Her hair was drawn so tightly back into a bun
that it made her eyes bulge, and her ears protruded from the
sides of her head like open barn doors. Empress Gahenas disapproved of everything; that much was clear from the outset.
She had come to Sparhawk's study to provide background information on the Isle of Tega, but she did not come alone. The
Empress Gahenas never went anywhere without her four chap-
erons, a cluster of ancient Tegan hags who perched on a var-
nished bench like a row of gargoyles.

It was a warm day in early autumn, but the sunlight streaming in through the window of Sparhawk's study seemed to
grow wan and sickly when Empress Gahenas entered with the
stern guardians of her virtue.

She spent an hour lecturing Sparhawk on the gross national
product of her homeland in a tone that strongly suggested that
she was going to give a test at the conclusion of the lecture.
Sparhawk fought to keep from yawning. He was not really interested in production figures or labor costs. What he really
wanted from the jug-eared empress were little details of ordinary life on the Isle to flesh out the series of letters he was

writing to his wife—letters that were to be doled out to Ehlana to help sustain the fiction that he and his friends were tracking down ringleaders and other conspirators who were concealed among the general population.

"Ah—" He interrupted Gahenas' droning monologue. "—this is absolutely fascinating, your Highness, but could we go back for a moment to the island's form of government? That really has me baffled."

"Tega is a republic, Prince Sparhawk. Our rulers are elected to their positions every five years. It's been that way for twenty-five centuries."

"Your officials aren't elected for life?"

"Of course not. Who would want a job like that for life?"

"No one ever develops a hunger for power?"

"The government *has* no power, Prince Sparhawk. It exists only to carry out the will of the electorate."

"Why five years?"

"Because nobody wants to be away from his own affairs for longer than that."

"What happens if a man's reelected."

"That's contrary to the law. No one serves more than one term in office."

"Let's suppose somebody turned out to be an absolute genius in a particular position? Wouldn't you want to keep him there?"

"We've never found anyone that indispensable."

"It seems to me that the system would encourage corruption. If a man knows he's going to be thrown out of office after five years, what's to keep him from manipulating his official decisions to further his own interests? Later on, I mean?"

"Quite impossible, Prince Sparhawk. Our elected officials *have* no outside interests. As soon as they're elected, everything they own is sold, and the money's put into the national treasury. If the economy prospers during their term in office, their wealth earns them a profit. If the economy collapses, they lose everything."

"That's absurd. No government *ever* makes a profit."

"Ours does," she said smugly, "and it has to be a real profit. The tax rates are set and cannot be changed, so our officials can't generate a false profit by simply raising taxes."

"Why would anyone want to be an official in a government like that?"

"Nobody *wants* to be, Prince Sparhawk. Most Tegans do ev-

erything they possibly can to avoid election. The fact that a
man's own personal fortune's in the treasury forces him to
work just as hard as he possibly can to make sure that the government prospers. Many have worked themselves to death
looking after the interests of the republic."

"I think I'd run away from an honor like that one."

"That's really quite impossible, your Highness. Just as soon
as a man's name's placed in nomination for a public office,
he's put under guard, and if he's elected, he remains under
close guard for his entire term. The republic makes absolutely
sure that nobody evades his responsibilities to her."

"The republic's a stern mistress."

"She is indeed, Prince Sparhawk, and that's exactly the way
it should be."

Though his companions chafed at the delay, Sparhawk put off
their departure for two more days while he feverishly composed the letters to Ehlana. The progress of the fictitious inves-
tigation had to be convincing, certainly, and at least moderately
interesting. Sparhawk wove false leads, plots, and unsolved
mysteries into his account. He became increasingly absorbed in
the developing story, sometimes becoming so caught up in it
that he lost sight of the fact that the events he was reporting
were not actually taking place. He became rather proud of his
efforts, and he began to revise extensively, adding a touch here
and modifying a poorly phrased passage there, until he unwit-
tingly crossed the line between careful artistry and sheer fuss-
iness.

"They're good enough, Sparhawk," Vanion said to him after
reading through the letters on the evening of the second day.
Vanion was rather pointedly wearing the plain tunic and heavy
riding boots Pandions customarily put on before making an extended journey.

"You don't think it's too obvious?"

"It's fine just the way it is."

"Maybe I should rework that third letter. It seems awfully
weak to me for some reason."

"You've written it four times already. It's good enough."

"I'm really not happy with it, Vanion." Sparhawk took the
offending letter from his friend and ran through it once more,
automatically reaching for his pen as he read.

Vanion firmly took the letter away from him.

"Let me just fix that last paragraph," Sparhawk pleaded.

"No."

"But—"

"*No!*" Vanion put the letter back in its proper place, folded the packet, and tucked it inside his doublet. "Oscagne's sending Norkan along with us," he said. "We'll give the letters to him, and he can sort of dribble them back here to Ehlana. Norkan's shrewd enough to space them out just enough to keep her from getting suspicious. The ship's been ready for a week now, and Emban's getting impatient. We'll sail with the morning tide."

"I think I know what I did wrong," Sparhawk said. "I can fix that third letter in no more than an hour or two."

"No, Sparhawk. Absolutely not."

"Are you sure she's asleep?" Sparhawk whispered.

"Of course I am, Father," Princess Danae replied.

"The slightest sound will wake her up, you know. She can hear a fly walking across the ceiling."

"Not tonight she can't. I've seen to that."

"I hope you know what you're doing, Danae. She knows every tiny little mark on that ring. If there's the slightest difference between it and this new one, she'll notice it immediately."

"Oh, Father, you worry too much. I've done this before, after all. Ghwerig *made* the rings, and I still fooled him. I've been stealing those rings for thousands of years. Believe me, Mother will never know the difference."

"Is this really necessary?"

"Yes. Bhelliom's useless to you without both rings, and you may need it almost as soon as we lift it from the seafloor."

"Why?"

She rolled her eyes upward and sighed. "Because the whole world will shift just as soon as Bhelliom moves. When you were carrying it to Zemoch, the world quivered around like a plate of jelly the whole time. My family and I really don't like it when Bhelliom moves. It makes some of us queasy."

"Will our enemies out there be able to pinpoint our location from that?"

She shook her head. "It's too generalized. Every God in the world's going to know when Bhelliom starts to move, though, and we can be absolutely sure that at least *some* of them will come looking for it. Can we talk about this some other time?"

"What do you want me to do?"

"Just stand watch at the bedroom door. I don't like having an audience when I'm stealing things."

"You sound just like Talen."

"Naturally. He and I were made for each other. It was the Gods who invented theft in the first place."

"You're not serious."

"Of course. We steal things from each other all the time. It's a game. Did you think we just sat around on clouds basking in adoration? We have to do *something* to pass the time. You should try it sometime, Father. It's lots of fun." She looked around furtively, crouched low, and reached for the bedroom door-handle. "Keep a lookout, Sparhawk. Whistle if you hear anybody coming."

They all gathered in the sitting room of the royal apartment the following morning to receive their final instructions from Emperor Sarabian and Queen Ehlana. It was a formality, really. Everybody knew what they were supposed to do already, so they sat in the sunlit room making generalized small talk and cautioning each other to be careful, as people parting from each other do the world around.

Alean, Queen Ehlana's doe-eyed maid, was in the next room, and she was singing. Her voice was clear and sweet and true, and all conversation in the sitting room broke off as she sang. "It's like listening to an angel," Patriarch Emban murmured.

"The girl has a truly magnificent voice," Sarabian agreed. "She already has the court musicians in near-despair."

"She seems a bit sad this morning," Kalten said, two great tears glistening in his eyes.

Sparhawk smiled faintly. Kalten had preyed on maids since he had been a young man, and few had been able to resist his blandishments. This time, however, the shoe was on the other foot. Alean was not singing for her own entertainment. The brown-eyed girl was singing for an audience of one, and her song, dealing as it did with the sorrows of parting, filled Kalten's eyes. She sang of broken hearts and other extravagances in a very old Elenian ballad entitled "My Bonnie Blue-Eyed Boy." Then Sparhawk noticed that Baroness Melidere, Queen Ehlana's lady in waiting, was also watching Kalten very closely. Melidere's eyes met Sparhawk's, and she slowly winked. Sparhawk almost laughed aloud. He was clearly not the only one who was aware of Alean's subtle campaign.

"You *will* write, won't you, Sparhawk?" Ehlana said.

"Of course I will," he replied.

"I can virtually guarantee that, your Majesty," Vanion said. "If you give him just a little time, Sparhawk's a great letter-writer. He devotes enormous amounts of time and effort to his correspondence."

"Tell me everything, Sparhawk," the queen urged.

"Oh, he *will*, your Majesty, he will," Vanion assured her. "He'll probably tell you more than you ever really wanted to know about the Isle of Tega."

"Critic," Sparhawk muttered under his breath.

"Please don't be *too* vivid in your description of our situation here, your Grace," Sarabian was saying to Emban. "Don't make Dolmant think that my empire's falling down around my ears."

"Isn't it, your Majesty?" Emban replied with some surprise. "I thought that was why I was dashing back to Chyrellos to fetch the Church Knights."

"Well, maybe it is, but don't destroy my dignity entirely."

"Dolmant's very wise, your Majesty," Emban assured him. "He understands the language of diplomacy."

"Oh, *really*?" Ehlana said with heavy sarcasm.

"Should I convey your Majesty's greetings to the Archprelate as well?" Emban asked her.

"Of course. Tell him that I'm desolate at being separated from him—particularly in view of the fact that I can't keep an eye on him. You might *also* advise him that a little-known Elenian statute clearly says that I have to ratify any agreements he makes with the Earl of Lenda during my absence. Tell him not to get *too* comfortable in those pieces of my kingdom he's been snipping off since I left, because I'll just take them back again as soon as I get home."

"Does she do this all the time, Sparhawk?" Sarabian asked.

"Oh, yes, all the time, your Majesty. The Archprelate bites off all his fingernails every time a letter from her reaches the Basilica."

"It keeps him young." Ehlana rose to her feet. "Now, friends," she said, "I hope you'll excuse my husband and me for a few moments so that we can say our good-byes privately. Come along, Sparhawk," she commanded.

"Yes, my Queen."

* * *

The morning fog had lifted, and the sun was very bright as their ship sailed out of the harbor and heeled over to take a southeasterly course which would round the southern tip of the Micaen peninsula to the Isle of Tega. The ship was well-appointed, although she was of a slightly alien configuration. Khalad did not entirely approve of her, finding fault with her rigging and the slant of her masts.

It was about noon when Vanion came up on deck to speak with Sparhawk, who was leaning on the rail watching the coastline slide by. They were both wearing casual clothing, since there is no real need for formal garb on board ship.

"Sephrenia wants us all in the main cabin," the preceptor told his friend. "It's time for one of those startling revelations we've all come to love and adore. Why don't you round up the others and bring them on down?"

"You're in a peculiar humor," Sparhawk noted. "What's the problem?"

"Sephrenia's being excessively Styric today." Vanion shrugged.

"That one escaped me."

"You know the signs, Sparhawk—the mysterious expression, the cryptic remarks, the melodramatic pauses, the superior manner."

"Have you two been fighting?"

Vanion laughed. "Never that, my friend. It's just that we all have little quirks and idiosyncracies that irritate our loved ones sometimes. Sephrenia's having one of her quirky days."

"I won't tell her you said that, of course."

Vanion shrugged. "She already knows how I feel. We've discussed it in the past—at length. Sometimes she does it just to tease me. Go get the others, Sparhawk. Let's not give her *too* much time to perfect this performance."

They all gathered in the main salon belowdecks, a cabin that was part dining room and part lounge. Sephrenia had not put in her appearance as yet and after a few moments, Sparhawk understood what Vanion had been talking about. A familiar sound began to emerge from the lady's cabin.

"Flute?" Talen exclaimed in astonishment, his voice cracking in that peculiar adolescent yodel which afflicts human males at the onset of puberty.

Sparhawk had wondered how Aphrael intended to get around the rather sticky problem of explaining her identity. To have appeared to the others as Princess Danae would quite obviously have been out of the question. Flute was quite another matter. His friends all recognized Flute as Aphrael, and that would eliminate the need for extended explanations. Sparhawk sighed as a rather melancholy thought occurred to him. He realized sadly that he didn't know what his daughter really looked like. That dear little face that was engraved on his mind almost as deeply as Ehlana's was only one in a long line of incarnations—one of thousands, more than likely.

Then the door to Sephrenia's cabin opened, and the small Styric woman emerged with a smile that made her face look like the sun coming up and with her little sister in her arms.

Flute, of course, was unchanged—and unchangeable. She appeared to be no more than six years old—precisely the same age as Danae. Sparhawk immediately rejected the possibility of coincidence. Where Aphrael was concerned, there *were* no coincidences. She wore that same short linen smock belted at the waist and that same plaited grass headband as she had when they had first met her. Her long hair was as black as night, and her large eyes nearly as dark. Her little bare feet were grass-stained. She held a simple many-chambered set of goatherd's pipes to her bowlike lips, and her song was Styric, set in a complex minor key.

"What a pretty child," Ambassador Norkan observed, "but is it really a good idea to take her along on this mysterious mission of yours, Prince Sparhawk? I gather there might be some danger involved."

"Not *now* there won't be, your Excellency." Ulath grinned.

Sephrenia gravely set the Child-Goddess on the cabin floor, and Flute began to dance to the clear, sweet music of her pipes.

Sephrenia looked at Emban and Norkan. "Watch the child closely, Emban, and you, too, your Excellency. That should save us hours of explanation and argument."

Flute pirouetted through the cabin, her grass-stained little feet flickering, her black hair flying and her pipes sounding joyously. This time Sparhawk actually saw the first step she placed quite firmly on insubstantial air. As one mounting an invisible stair, the Child-Goddess danced upward, whirling as she climbed, bending and swaying, her tiny feet fluttering like bird's wings as she danced on nothing at all. Then her song and her dance ended, and, smiling impishly and still standing in midair, she curtsied.

Emban's eyes were bulging and he had half fallen from his

chair. Ambassador Norkan tried to maintain his urbane expression, but it was slipping badly, and his hands were shaking.

Talen grinned and began to applaud. The others laughed, and they all joined in.

"Oh, thank you, my dear ones," Flute said sweetly, curtsying again.

"For God's sake, Sparhawk!" Emban choked, "Make her come down from there! She's destroying my sanity!"

Flute laughed and quite literally hurled herself into the fat little churchman's arms, smothering his pale, cringing face with kisses. "I *love* to do that to people!" She giggled delightedly.

Emban shrank back even further.

"Oh, don't be silly, Emban," she chided. "I'm not going to hurt you. I sort of love you, actually." A look of sly mischief came into her eyes. "How would you like to come to work for me, your Grace?" she suggested. "I'm not nearly as stuffy as your Elene God, and we could have a lot of fun together."

"Aphrael!" Sephrenia said sharply. "Stop that! You *know* you're not supposed to do that!"

"I was only teasing him, Sephrenia. I wouldn't really steal Emban. The Elene God needs him too much."

"Has your theology been sufficiently shaken, your Grace?" Vanion asked the Patriarch of Ucera. "The little girl in your lap who's blithely trying to lead you off down the flowery path to heresy is the Child-Goddess Aphrael, one of the thousand Younger Gods of Styricum."

"How do I greet her?" Emban asked in a squeaky, frightened kind of voice.

"A few kisses might be nice," Flute suggested.

"Stop that," Sephrenia chided her again.

"And what are *your* feelings, your Excellency?" the little girl asked Norkan.

"Dubious, your—uh—"

"Just Aphrael, Norkan," she told him.

"That's really not suitable," he replied. "I'm a diplomat, and the very soul of diplomatic speech is formal modes of address. I haven't called anyone but colleagues by their first names since I was about ten years old."

"Her first name *is* a formal mode of address, your Excellency," Sephrenia said gently.

"All right, then," Aphrael said, slipping down from Emban's lap. "Tynian and Emban are going to Chyrellos to fetch the

Church Knights. Norkan's going to the Isle of Tega to help Sparhawk lie to my—uh—his wife, that is. The rest of us are going to go get the Bhelliom again. Sparhawk seems to think he might need it. I think he's underestimating his own abilities, but I'll go along with him on the issue—if only to keep him from nagging and complaining."

"I've really missed her." Kalten laughed. "What are you going to do, Flute? Saddle up a herd of whales for us to ride to that coastline where we threw Bhelliom into the sea?"

Her eyes brightened.

"Never mind," Sparhawk told her quite firmly.

"Spoilsport."

"I'm really disappointed in you, Sparhawk," Kalten said. "I've never ridden a whale before."

"*Will* you shut up about whales?" Sparhawk snapped at him.

"You don't have to get so touchy about it. What have you got against whales?"

"It's a personal thing between Aphrael and me," Sparhawk replied in a grating tone. "I won't win *many* arguments with her, but I *am* going to win the one about whales."

The layover of their ship at Tega was necessarily brief. The tide had already turned, and the captain was quite concerned about the inexorably lowering water-level in the harbor.

Sparhawk and his friends conferred briefly in the ship's main salon while Khalad directed the sailors in the unloading of their horses and supplies. "Do your very best to make Sarathi understand just how serious the situation here really is, Emban," Vanion said. "Sometimes he gets a little pigheaded."

"I'm sure he'll enjoy knowing how you really feel about him, Vanion." The fat churchman grinned.

"Say anything you want, your Grace. I'll never be going back to Chyrellos anyway, so it doesn't really matter. Make a special point of letting him know that the name of Cyrgon's been popping up. You might want to gloss over the fact that we've only got Krager's word for Cyrgon's involvement, though. We *are* sure about the Troll-Gods, however, and the notion that we're facing heathen Gods again might help Sarathi tear his attention away from Rendor."

"Was there anything else I already know that you'd like to tell me, Vanion?"

Vanion laughed. "Nicely put. I *was* being a bit of a meddler, wasn't I?"

"The term is *busybody*, Vanion. I'll do everything I can, but you know Dolmant. He'll make his own assessment and his own decision. He'll weigh Daresia against Rendor and decide which of them he wants to save."

"Tell him that I'm here with Sparhawk, Emban," Flute instructed. "He knows who I am."

"He *does*?"

"You don't really have to step around Dolmant so carefully. He's not the fanatic Ortzel is, so he can accept the fact that his theology doesn't answer all the questions in the universe. The fact that I'm involved might help him to make the right decision. Give him my love. He's an old stick sometimes, but I'm really fond of him."

Emban's eyes were a little wild. "I think I'll retire when this is all over," he said.

"Don't be silly." She smiled. "You could no more retire than I could. You're having too much fun. Besides, we need you." She turned to Tynian. "Don't overwork that shoulder," she instructed. "Give it time to completely heal before you start exercising it."

"Yes, ma'am," he replied, grinning at her authoritarian manner.

"Don't make fun of me, Tynian," she threatened. "If you do that, you might just wake up some morning with your feet on backward. Now give me a kiss."

"Yes, Aphrael."

She laughed, and swarmed into his arms to collect her kisses.

They debarked and stood on the pier as the Tamul vessel made her way slowly out of the harbor.

"They're sailing at the right time of year, anyway," Ulath said. "It's a little early for the hurricanes."

"That's encouraging," Kalten said. "Where to now, Flute?"

"There's a ship waiting for us on the far side of the island," she replied. "I'll tell you about it after we get out of town."

Vanion handed Norkan the packet of letters Sparhawk had so laboriously written. "We can't be sure how long we'll be gone, your Excellency," he said, "so you might want to space these out."

Norkan nodded. "I can supplement them with reports of my own," he said, "and if worse comes to worst, I can always use the talents of the professional forger at the embassy here. He should be able to duplicate Prince Sparhawk's handwriting after a day or so of practice—well enough to add personal post-scripts to my reports, anyway."

For some reason Sparhawk found that very shocking.

"May I ask a question?" Norkan said to Flute.

"Of course," she replied. "I won't guarantee that I'll answer, but you can ask."

"Are our Tamul Gods real?"

"Yes."

Norkan sighed. "I was afraid of that. I haven't led what you'd call an exemplary life."

"Don't worry, Norkan. Your Gods don't take themselves very seriously. They're considered frivolous by the rest of us," she paused. "They're fun at parties, though," she added. She suddenly giggled. "They *really* irritate the Elene God. He has absolutely no sense of humor, and your Tamul Gods are very fond of practical jokes."

Norkan shuddered. "I don't think I really want to know any more about this sort of thing," he said. He looked around. "I'd strongly advise you to leave town rather quickly, my friends," he told them. "A republican form of government generates vast quantities of paper. There are questionnaires and forms and permits and licenses for almost everything, and there have to be ten copies of every single one. Nobody in the government wants to really make a decision about anything, so documents are just passed around from hand to hand until they either fall apart or get lost someplace."

"Who finally *does* make the decisions?" Vanion asked.

"Nobody." Norkan shrugged. "Tegans have learned to get along without a government. Everybody knows what has to be done anyway, so they scribble on enough official forms to keep the bureaucrats busy and then just ignore them. I hate to admit it, but the system seems to work quite well." He laughed. "There was a notorious murderer who was appre-hended during the last century," he said. "They put him on trial, and he died of old age before the courts could decide whether he was guilty or not."

"How old was he when they caught him?" Talen asked.

"About thirty, I understand. You'd really better get started, my friends. That fellow at the head of this wharf has a sort of official expression on his face. You should probably be out of sight before he leafs through that pouch he's carrying and finds the right set of forms for you to fill out."

* * *

The Isle of Tega was tidy. It was not particularly scenic, nor did it have that picturesque desolation that sets the hearts of romantics all aflutter. The island produced no economically significant crops, and the small plots of ground under cultivation were devoted to what might be called expanded kitchen gardens. The stone walls that marked off the fields were straight and were all of a uniform height. The roads did not curve or bend, and the roadside barrows were all precisely of the same width and depth. Since the island's major industry, the collecting of seashells, was conducted underwater, there was none of the clutter one customarily sees around workshops.

The tedious tidiness, however, was offset by a dreadful smell that seemed to hover over everything.

"What *is* that awful stink?" Talen said, trying to cover his nostrils with his sleeve.

"Rotting shellfish." Khalad shrugged. "They must use it for fertilizer."

"How can they stand to live here with that smell?"

"They're probably so used to it that they don't even notice it anymore. They want the seashells because they can sell them to the Tamuls in Matherion, but people can't live on a steady diet of oysters and clams, so they have to get rid of the excess somehow. It seems to make very good fertilizer. I've never seen cabbages that big before."

Talen looked speculatively at his brother. "Pearls come from oysters, don't they?" he asked.

"That's what I've been told."

"I wonder if the Tegans do anything with them when they run across them?"

"They're not really very valuable, Talen," Flute told him. "There's something in the water around the island that makes the pearls black. Who would pay anything for black pearls?" She looked around at them. "Now then," she said to them, "We'll have to sail about fifteen hundred leagues to reach the place where Bhelliom is."

"*That* far?" Vanion said. "We won't get back to Matherion until the dead of winter, then. At thirty leagues a day, it's going to take us fifty days to get there and fifty days back."

"No," she disagreed, "actually it's going to take us five days to get there and five days to get back."

"Impossible!" Ulath said flatly. "No ship can move that fast."

"How much would you be willing to wager on that, Sir Ulath?"

He thought about that for a moment. "Not very much," he decided. "I wouldn't insult you by suggesting that you'd cheat, but . . ." He spread his hands suggestively.

"You're going to tamper with time again, I take it?" Sparhawk said to her.

She shook her head. "There are some limitations to that, Sparhawk. We need something more dependable. The ship that's waiting for us is just a bit unusual. I don't think any of you should get too curious about what she's made of and what makes her move. You won't be able to talk with the crew, because they don't speak your language. You probably wouldn't want to talk with them anyway, because they aren't really human."

"Witchcraft?" Bevier asked suspiciously.

She patted his cheek. "I'll answer that question just as soon as you come up with a definition of witchcraft that's not personally insulting, dear Bevier."

"What *are* you going to do, Aphrael?" Sephrenia asked suspiciously. "There *are* rules, you know."

"The other side's been breaking rules right and left, dear sister," Aphrael replied airily. "Reaching into the past has been forbidden almost from the very start."

"Are you going to reach into the future?" Khalad asked her. "People are coming up with new ideas in ship design all the time. Are you going to reach ahead and bring us back a ship that hasn't been invented yet?"

"That's an interesting idea, Khalad, but I wouldn't know where to look. The future hasn't happened yet, so how would I know where—or when—to find that kind of a ship? I've gone someplace else, that's all."

"What do you mean, 'someplace else'?"

"There's more than one world, Khalad," she said mysteriously. Then she made a little face. "You wouldn't *believe* how complicated the negotiations were," she added.

CHAPTER
THREE

E hlana and Sarabian had gone to the top of the central tower of the glowing castle, ostensibly to admire the sunset. Despite the fact that the castle was firmly in Elene hands, there were still enough Tamuls inside the walls to require a certain amount of care when the two wanted to speak privately.

"It all comes down to the question of power, Sarabian," Ehlana told the emperor in a pensive voice. "The fact that it's there has to be the central fact of our lives. We can either take it into our own hands, or leave it lying around unused; but if we choose not to use it, we can be sure that someone else *will*." Her tone was subdued and her pale young face almost somber.

"You're in a melancholy humor today, Ehlana," Sarabian noted.

"I don't like being separated from Sparhawk. There were too many years of that after Aldreas exiled him. The point I was getting at is that you're going to have to be very firm so that the people in your government will understand that things have changed. What you'll really be doing here is seizing power. That's an act of revolution, you know." She smiled faintly. "You're almost too civilized to be a revolutionary, Sarabian. Are you sure you want to overthrow the government?"

"Good God, Ehlana, it's *my* government, and the power was mine in the first place."

"But you didn't use it. You were lazy and self-indulgent, and you let it slip away. Your ministers have filched your authority bit by bit. Now you're going to have to wrest it back from them. People don't willingly give up power, so you'll probably have to kill some of your ministers in order to prove to the rest that you're serious."

"Kill!"

"That's the ultimate expression of power, Sarabian, and your situation here requires a certain ruthlessness. You're going to have to spill some blood in order to get your government's attention."

"I don't think I can do that," Sarabian said in a troubled tone. "Oh, I know I've blustered and made threats a few times, but I couldn't actually order someone killed."

"That's up to you, but you'll lose if you don't, and that means that *they'll* kill *you*." She considered it. "They'll probably kill you anyway," she added, "but at least you'll die for something important. Knowing that they're going to kill you in the end might help you make some unpleasant decisions at the outset. Once you get past your first couple of killings, it grows easier. I speak from a certain amount of experience on the subject, since almost exactly the same thing happened to me. Primate Annias completely controlled my government when I came to the throne, and I had to try to take my power back from him."

"You're the one who's been talking so freely about killing, Ehlana. Why didn't you kill Annias?"

She laughed a brittle, chilling little laugh. "It wasn't because I didn't *want* to, believe me, but I was too weak. Annias had very carefully stripped the crown of all its authority. I had some help from Lord Vanion and his Pandion Knights, but Annias had control of the army and the Church soldiers. I killed a few of his underlings, but I couldn't get to him. He knew I was trying, though, and that's why he poisoned me. Annias was really a very good politician. He knew exactly when the time for killing had arrived."

"You sound almost as if you admired him."

"I *hated* him, but he *was* very good."

"Well, I haven't killed anybody yet, so I can still step back from this."

"You're wrong there. You've already drawn your dagger, so

you're going to have to use it. You crushed that uprising and you've imprisoned the Minister of the Interior. That's the same thing as a declaration of war."

"*You* did those things," he accused her.

"Yes, but I was acting in your behalf, so it's the same thing—at least in the eyes of your enemies. You're in danger now, you know. You've let your government know that you're going to seize back the power you let slip away. If you don't start killing people—and soon—you probably won't live out the month. You'd be dead already if you hadn't taken refuge in this castle."

"You're starting to frighten me, Ehlana."

"God knows I've been trying. Like it or not, Sarabian, you're committed now." She looked around. The sun was sinking into the cloud bank building up over the mountains lying to the west, and its ruddy glow was reflecting from the mother-of-pearl domes of Matherion. "Look at your city, Sarabian," she told him, "and contemplate the reality of politics. Before you're done, that red splashed all over the domes won't just be the reflection of the sunset."

"That's blunt enough," he said, his jaw taking on an unfamiliar set. "All right, how many people do I have to kill in order to insure my own safety?"

"You don't have that many knives, my friend. Even if you butcher everybody in Matherion, you'll still be in danger. You might as well accept the fact that you're going to be in danger for the rest of your life." She smiled at him. "Actually, it's kind of exciting—once you get used to it."

"Well sir, yer Queenship," Caalador drawled, "it's all purty much th' way we wuz a-thankin' it wuz. That Krager feller, he wuz a-tellin' ol' Sporhawk th' ak-chool truth. Me'n Stragen, we bin a-twistin' the arms an' a-settin' fahr t' the feet o' them fellers ez wuz picked up durin' the koop—" He stopped. "Would your Majesty be too disappointed if I spoke like a human being for a while? That dialect's starting to dislocate my jaw."

"Not to mention the violence it's doing to the mother tongue," Stragen murmured.

The three of them had gathered together in a small blue-draped room adjoining the royal apartment later that same evening. Ehlana and Stragen were still dressed for dinner, she in crimson velvet and he in white satin. Caalador wore the sober brown of a businessman. The room had been carefully checked several times to be sure that no hidden listening posts lurked behind the walls, and Mirtai grimly stood watch outside the door.

"With the exception of Interior Minister Kolata, we didn't scoop up anybody of significance," Caalador continued, "and none of our other prisoners knows very much. I'm afraid we don't have much choice, your Majesty. We're going to have to go to work on Kolata if we want anything useful."

Ehlana shook her head. "You won't get anything out of him either, Caalador. He'll be killed as soon as he opens his mouth."

"We don't know that for certain, my Queen," Stragen disagreed. "It's entirely possible that our subterfuge has worked, you know. I really don't believe that the other side knows that he's a prisoner here. His policemen are still getting their orders from him."

"He's too valuable to risk," she said. "Once he's been torn to pieces, he'll be very hard to put back together again."

"If that's the way you want it, your Majesty." Caalador shrugged. "Anyway, it's growing increasingly obvious that this uprising was a pure hoax. Its only purpose was to compel us to reveal our strength. What concerns me the most is the fact that Krager and his friends obviously knew that we were using the criminals of Matherion as our eyes and ears. I'm sorry, Stragen, but it's the truth."

"It was such a good idea," Stragen sighed.

"It was, at first, but the trouble was that Krager's seen it before. Talen told me that your friend Platime used to have whole crowds of beggars, whores, and pickpockets following Krager around. The best idea in the world wears a little thin if you overuse it."

Stragen rose to his feet muttering curses and began to pace up and down in the small room with his white satin doublet gleaming in the candlelight. "It looks as if I've failed you, my Queen," he admitted. "I let a good idea run away with me. You couldn't really trust my judgment after a blunder like that, so I'll make arrangements to go back to Emsat."

"Oh, don't be an ass, Stragen," she told him. "And *do* sit down. I can't think while you're clumping around the room like that."

"She shore knows how t' put a feller in his place, don't she, Stragen?" Caalador laughed.

Ehlana sat tapping one finger thoughtfully against her chin. "First of all, let's keep this in the family. Sarabian's already getting a bit wild-eyed. Politically, he's an infant. I'm trying to raise him as quickly as I can, but I can only move him just so fast." She made a sour face. "I have to stop every so often to burp him."

"Now *that's* a picture for you," Caalador grinned. "What's he choking on, your Majesty?"

"Murder, primarily." She shrugged. "He doesn't seem to have the stomach for it."

Caalador blinked. "Not many do."

"Politicians can't afford that kind of delicacy. All right, if Krager and his friends know about our spy network, it won't be long until they try something in the way of penetration, will it?"

"You're quick," he said admiringly.

"Quick people live longer. Start thinking, gentlemen. We've got an exploitable situation here, and it won't last for very long. How can we use it to our greatest advantage?"

"We might be able to identify *real* conspirators instead of dupes, your Majesty," Stragen mused. "If they *do* try penetration, they're going to have to subvert some of our people. Let's say that we start passing out assorted fairy tales—this story to some pickpocket, another to some beggar or whore. Then we sit back to see which of those fraudulent schemes the other side attempts to counter. That will identify the turncoats in our own ranks, and we can squeeze useful names out of them."

"Surely we can get something a little better than that," she fretted.

"We'll work on it, your Majesty," Caalador promised. "If it's all right with you, I'd like to follow up on something else as well. We know that Krager's been busy here in Matherion, but we *don't* know how much information about our methods he's passed to his friends in other kingdoms. We might as well get what use we can out of our makeshift intelligence service before it becomes totally useless. I'll pass the word to the criminals down in Arjuna. I'd like to find out one way or the other if that silly scholar at the university has blundered across the real truth or if he's just weaving a theory out of moonbeams. I think we might all find a complete biography of the fellow known as Scarpa really fascinating reading. If nothing else, whether or not our spies in Arjuna succeed will tell us how much Krager *really* knows about the scope of our operations. If he thinks it's only localized, our apparatus hasn't been too severely compromised."

"Go after the others as well," Ehlana told him. "See what you can find out about Baron Parok, Rebal, and Sabre. Let's try to attach names to Rebal and Sabre at the very least."

"We'll do 'er jist th' way yer Majesty commands."

"I'd be happier'n a pig in mud iffn y'would, Caalador," she replied.

Caalador collapsed in helpless laughter.

"It's probably the change in the weather, your Majesty," Alean said. "It's getting chillier at night, and the days aren't nearly as warm as they were just a few weeks ago."

"She grew up in Cimmura, Alean," Ehlana disagreed, "and the weather changes there much more markedly than it does here in Matherion."

"It's a different part of the world though, my Queen," Baroness Melidere pointed out. "We're right on the seacoast, for one thing. That could be what's causing the problem. Sometimes children react more strongly to things like that than adults."

"You're both making too much out of it," Mirtai told them. "All she needs is a tonic. She's not really sick, she's just moping around."

"But she *sleeps* all the time," Ehlana fretted. "She even falls asleep when she's playing."

"She's probably growing." The giantess shrugged. "I used to do the same sort of thing when I was a little girl. Growing is very hard work, I guess."

The object of their discussions lay drowsing on a divan near the window with Rollo loosely clasped in her arms. Rollo had survived two generations of intense affection. He had been dragged about by one hind leg. He had been laid upon, crammed into tight places, and ignored at times for weeks on end. A shift in his stuffings had given him a slightly worried expression. Queen Ehlana viewed that as a bad sign. Rollo had never looked worried when he had been *her* toy. Mmrr, on the other hand, seemed quite content. An owner who didn't move around very much suited Mmrr right down to the ground. When Princess Danae was dozing, she was not dreaming up ridiculous things to do to her cat. Mmrr secretly felt that any day which did not involve being dressed up in doll's clothing was a good day. She lay on her little mistress' hip with her front paws sedately folded under her chest, her eyes closed and a soft, contented purr coming from her throat. So long as nothing disturbed her naps, Mmrr was perfectly at peace with the world.

The Royal Princess Danae dozed, her mind far more involved with the conversation Flute was holding with Sparhawk and his friends on the Isle of Tega than with her mother's concern over her health here in Matherion. Danae yawned and nestled down with toy and cat and drifted off to sleep.

Dearest,

We've reached Tega, and we'll be going out into the countryside for a while to see what's afoot. I'll be out of touch for a bit, so I thought it might be a good idea to let you know that we've arrived safely. Don't be too concerned if you don't hear from me for quite some time. I'm not entirely sure how long we'll be submerged in the population here.

The others are growing impatient to get started. There's no real point to this letter—except to tell you that I love you—but that's probably the most important point of all, isn't it? Kiss Danae for me.

All my love,
Sparhawk

"Oh, that's nice," Ehlana murmured, lowering the note from her husband. They were all sitting in the blue-draped sitting room in the queen's apartments, and the arrival of Caalador with Sparhawk's letter had interrupted a serious discussion about what they were going to do about the Interior Ministry.

Caalador, dressed again in sober brown and carrying a grotesque porcelain figurine from twelfth-century Arjuna, was frowning. "I think you might want to remind the people at the gates of the compound that they're supposed to let me in, your Majesty. I had a bit of an argument again."

"What's this?" Emperor Sarabian asked.

"Master Caalador's serving as my 'procurer of antiquities,' " Ehlana explained. "It gives him an excuse to come and go without interference. I've gathered a whole roomful of assorted bric-a-brac since I've arrived here."

"That brings us right back to the issue we were discussing before you got here, Caalador," Stragen said. Stragen wore black today, and Ehlana privately felt that the color didn't really suit him. He rose and began to pace up and down, a habit the Queen of Elenia found irritating. "The Interior Ministry's beginning to flex its muscles for some reason. We're sitting on the minister himself, so this onset of burliness is probably coming from some underling."

"Interior has always liked to throw its weight around," Oscagne told them. The foreign minister was wearing western-style clothes again, and he still looked distinctly uncomfortable in them.

"I think that reinforces the point I was trying to make earlier, Ehlana," Sarabian said. "Are you sure we shouldn't dissolve the Interior Ministry right now?"

"Absolutely," Ehlana replied. "We've got Kolata buttoned up inside the castle here and we've given the world a perfectly legitimate reason for his presence. He's still functioning—under our control—and that's of enormous value to us. We're playing for time, Sarabian. We're terribly vulnerable until Tynian and Emban come back from Chyrellos with the Church Knights—or at the very least until all the Atan commanders have been advised that they aren't supposed to obey the orders of the Interior Ministry anymore. We *definitely* don't want the Atans fighting on both sides if trouble breaks out."

"I hadn't thought of that," he admitted.

"Not only that, your Majesty," Oscagne added gently. "It's entirely possible that Interior would simply ignore a proclamation disbanding them. They have almost total power, you know. Queen Ehlana's right. We can't move against them until we're sure of the Atans."

Stragen had continued his pacing. "*Nobody* can subvert an entire branch of government," he declared. "There are just too many people involved, and all it would take would be one honest policeman to expose the entire scheme."

"There's no such thing as an honest policeman, Stragen," Caalador said with a cynical laugh. "It's a contradiction in terms."

"You know what I mean," Stragen shrugged that off. "We know that Kolata has dirty hands, but we can't be sure just how far that disloyalty goes. It could be very widespread, or it could be confined to just a few in the higher councils of the ministry."

Caalador shook his head. " 'Tain't hordly likely, Stragen," he disagreed. "Y' gotta have them ez y' kin trust out thar when y' start givin' orders ez runs contrary t' reg'lar policy.

They's gotta be *some* in th' hinterlands ez knows whut's whut."

Stragen made a face. "I wish you wouldn't use that vile dialect when you're right. It makes me feel inadequate. All right then. We can be fairly certain that most of the higher-ranking officials in the ministry are involved, but we can't even guess at how widespread the contamination is. I'd say that finding out gets to be a priority."

"Shouldn't take y' more'n a couple hunnerd years t' do that, Stragen," Caalador noted.

"Not necessarily," Baroness Melidere disagreed. She looked at Oscagne. "You once said that the Ministry of the Interior's very fond of paper, your Excellency."

"Of course, Baroness. All government agencies adore paper. Paperwork provides full employment for our relatives. Interior goes a little farther, though. Policemen can't function without files and dossiers. They write everything down."

"I rather thought that might be the case. The people over at Interior are all trained as policemen, aren't they?"

Oscagne nodded.

"Then they'd all be compulsive about writing reports and filing them, wouldn't they?"

"I suppose so," he said. "I don't see where you're going with this exactly, Baroness."

"Wake up, Oscagne," Sarabian said excitedly. "I think this wonderful girl's just solved our problem for us. Someplace over in that rabbit warren at Interior there's a set of files that contains the names of all the disloyal policemen and secret agents in the empire. All we have to do is get our hands on that set of files, and we'll know exactly which people to pick up when the time comes to move."

"Except for the fact that they'll defend those files to the death," Ehlana observed. "And there's also the fact that a move against their filing system would be the same as a frontal assault on the ministry itself."

"You really know how to burst bubbles, Ehlana," the emperor complained.

"There might be a way around the queen's objections, your Majesty," Melidere said with a slight frown. "Is there a standardized filing system here in Matherion, Minister Oscagne?"

"Good God, no, Baroness," he exclaimed. "If we all had the same filing system, anybody at all could walk into our offices and find anything he wanted. We'd *never* be able to keep any secrets from each other."

"I thought that might be the case. Now then, suppose that Queen Ehlana happened to mention to the emperor—just in passing—that *her* government had standardized the filing system, and that everybody filed things the same way. Then let's suppose that the emperor grew very excited about the idea— the enormous savings in the cost of government and all that. Then, still supposing, he appoints an imperial commission with extraordinary powers to examine *everybody's* files with an eye toward that standardization. Wouldn't that justify a search of the offices at Interior?"

"It's got possibilities, my Queen," Stragen approved. "Something like that would hide what we're really up to— particularly if we had people tearing up everybody else's files at the same time."

Oscagne's face went absolutely white.

"I'd sooner take pizen than insult y', little lady," Caalador drawled to the baroness, "but yer still a-talkin' 'bout a chore which it is that'd taken us a good twenty year 'er more t' finish. We got us a hull buildin' over thar t' take aport iffn th' furrin minister yere is kee-rect 'bout how miny tons o' paper they got over t' Interior."

"We can shorten that a bit, Master Caalador," Melidere replied. "All we have to do is question Interior Minister Kolata."

"Absolutely not," Ehlana said sharply. "I don't want him all torn to pieces—at least not until I don't need him anymore."

"We wouldn't be asking him any sensitive questions, your Majesty," Melidere said patiently. "All we want to know is how his filing system works. That wouldn't compromise the conspiracy he's involved in, would it?"

"I think she's right, Ehlana," Mirtai said. "There would almost have to be some sort of trigger—questions about certain subjects—that would make our enemies decide to kill Kolata. They wouldn't kill him if all we did was ask him about something as ordinary as a filing system, would they?"

"No," the queen agreed. "They probably wouldn't at that." Her expression was still dubious, however.

"It's all very clever, Baroness," Stragen said, "but we'll be sending Tamul officials into the various ministries to investigate files. How will we know that at least some of *them* aren't on the other side?"

"We wouldn't, Milord Stragen. That's why we'll have to

send our own people—the Church Knights—in to review those files."

"How would we justify that?"

"The new filing system would be an *Elene* invention, Milord. We're obviously going to have to send Elenes into the various ministries to evaluate the current methods and to instruct the officials on how to convert to the new system."

"Now I've got you, Baroness," he said triumphantly. "This is all a fiction. We don't *have* a new filing system."

"Then invent one, Milord Stragen," she suggested sweetly.

Prime Minister Subat was deeply troubled by the suggestion the Chancellor of the Exchequer had just placed before him. The two were alone together in the prime minister's ornate office, a room only slightly less magnificent than one of the imperial audience chambers. "You're out of your mind, Gashon," he declared flatly.

Chancellor of the Exchequer Gashon was a bloodless, corpselike man with sunken cheeks and no more than a few wispy strands of hair protruding from his lumpy scalp. "Look at it more closely, Pondia Subat," he said in his hollow, rusty-sounding voice. "It's only a theory, but it *does* explain many things that are otherwise incomprehensible."

"They wouldn't have dared," Subat scoffed.

"Try to lift your mind out of the fourteenth century, Subat," Gashon snapped. "You're the prime minister, not the keeper of antiquities. The world is changing all around you. You can't just sit still with your eyes firmly fixed on the past and hope to survive."

"I don't like you very much, Gashon."

"I'm not terribly fond of you either, Subat. Let me go through it for you again. Try to stay awake this time."

"How *dare* you?"

"I dare because I'd sort of like to keep my head where it is. First off: The Elenes of Eosia are absolute barbarians. Can we agree on that at least?"

"All right."

"They haven't caused much trouble in the past because they were too busy fighting among themselves about religion, *and* because they had Otha of Zemoch to worry about. Would it surprise you too much if I told you that Otha's dead and that the Rendorish insurgency's been almost completely crushed?"

"I have my own sources of information, Gashon."

"Have you ever considered listening to what they tell you? Now then, there was open warfare in the streets of Chyrellos preceding the elevation of this Dolmant to the Archprelacy. I'd say that's a fair indication of the fact that he's not universally loved. The best way I know of for a shaky ruler to consolidate his position is to contrive a foreign adventure, and the only real foreign ground for the Elenes of the Eosian continent is Daresia—the Tamul Empire. That's us, in case you hadn't noticed, Pondia Subat."

"I know that, Gashon."

"I just wanted to be sure, that's all. Are you with me so far?"

"Get to the point, Gashon. I don't have all day."

"Did you have an appointment with the headsman? All right, the Elenes are religious fanatics who feel that they're called of the Lord to convert everybody in the world to their absurd faith. For all I know, they also want to convert snakes, spiders, and fish. Dolmant's their religious leader, and they'd probably try to subdue glaciers and tides if he told them to. So, we've got a religious leader who has an uncertain grasp on power in his own church, and he has hordes of fanatic followers at his disposal. He can either use those followers to crush his opponents at home, *or* he can hurl them against a foreign power on some trumped-up excuse that will inflame the commons and stifle objections to his rule. Isn't it a coincidence that at precisely that time we have this 'state visit' by a silly female—a female who Foreign Minister Oscagne assures us is the Queen of Elenia. I hope the fact that we only have Oscagne's word for that hasn't escaped you. This so-called queen is obviously more accustomed to doing business in bed than she is on a throne. She clearly wrestled that silly ass Alberen of Astel into submission, and probably Androl of the Atans as well. We can only speculate about her adventures among the Peloi and the Styrics at Sarsos. Then, once she reached Matherion, she lured Emperor Sarabian to her bedchamber before the first day was out—you *did* know that Sarabian and Oscagne crept across the compound to that imitation Elene castle on the first night she was here, didn't you?"

Subat started to object.

"Yes, I know," Gashon cut him off, "that brings us to Oscagne. I'd say that the evidence strongly suggests that Oscagne has gone over to the Elenes—either for personal gain or because he's fallen under the spell of that blonde Elene strumpet. She had plenty of time to work on him while he was in Chyrellos, you know."

"It's all speculation, Gashon," Subat said, although his voice lacked conviction.

"Of course it is, Subat," Gashon replied with heavy sarcasm. "What would be the fastest way to get to Matherion from Chyrellos?"

"By ship, naturally."

"Then why did the strumpet of Cimmura choose to come overland? Was it to look at scenery, or to grapple her way across the continent? The girl's got stamina, I'll give her that."

"What about this recent coup attempt, Gashon? The government would have fallen if the Elenes hadn't been here."

"Ah, yes, the famous coup. Isn't it astounding that a group of Elenes who didn't even speak the Tamul language when they arrived were able to unearth this dire plot in about six weeks—when the agents of the Ministry of the Interior, who've only been in Matherion for all of their lives, hadn't come across a single clue about it? The Elenes crushed an imaginary coup, Subat, and now they've used it as an excuse to imprison the emperor in that cursed fortress of theirs—and Interior Minister Kolata as well, and Kolata's the one man in government who has the resources to free our ruler. I've talked with Teovin, Director of the Secret Police, and he assures me that no one from the ministry has been permitted to speak with Kolata privately since his incarceration. Our colleague is obviously a prisoner, and the orders he's issuing are just as obviously coming from the Elenes. Then, if that weren't bad enough, they've sent the so-called churchman, Emban, back to Chyrellos to lead the Church Knights back here to 'deal with the crisis.' We have all the resources of Interior *and* whole armies of Atans at our disposal, Subat. Why do we need the Church Knights? What possible reason is there to bring the most ruthless force in the entire world to Tamuli? Would the word *invasion* startle you? That's all that the famous coup really was, you realize—an excuse for the Elene Church to invade Tamuli, and quite obviously it's been with the emperor's full cooperation."

"Why would the emperor conspire with the Elenes to topple his own government?"

"I can think of any number of reasons. Maybe this so-called queen threatened to deny him her favors. Most probably, though, she's been spinning fairy tales for him, telling him about the joys of absolute power. That's a common fiction in Eosia. Elene rulers like to pretend that *they're* the ones who make all the decisions in their kingdoms rather than permitting the government to do it for them. We both know how ridiculous *that* idea is. A king—or in our case, the emperor—only has one function. He's a symbol of government, nothing more. He serves as a focus for the love and loyalty of the people. The imperial government's been engaged in a selective breeding program for the past thousand years. The emperor's Tamul wife—the one who produces the heir to the throne—is always selected for her stupidity. We don't *need* intelligent emperors, only docile ones. Somehow Sarabian slipped past us. If you'd ever really taken the trouble to pay attention to him, you'd have discovered that he's frighteningly intelligent. Kolata blundered there. Sarabian should have been killed long before he ascended the throne. Our revered emperor's beginning to hunger for real power, I'm afraid. Normally, we could deal with that, but we can't get at him to kill him as long as he's inside that blasted fortress."

"You weave a convincing story, Gashon," the prime minister conceded with a troubled frown. "I *knew* it was a blunder to invite that Sparhawk savage to come to Matherion."

"We all did, Subat, and you'll recall who it was who overrode all our objections."

"Oscagne," Subat spat.

"Precisely. Is it beginning to fit together for you now?"

"Did you devise all of this by yourself, Gashon? It's a little elaborate for a man who spends all his time counting pennies."

"Actually, it was Teovin, the Director of the Secret Police, who brought it to my attention. He provided me with very concrete evidence. I've summarized it for you here. Interior has spies everywhere, you know. Nothing happens in the empire that doesn't generate a report for those famous files of theirs. Now, Pondia Subat, what does our esteemed prime minister propose to do about the fact that our emperor's being held prisoner—willingly or unwillingly—not a hundred paces from where we sit? You're the titular head of government, Subat. You're the one who has to make these decisions. Oh, and while you're at it, you might want to give some thought to how we're going to prevent the Church Knights from sweeping across the continent, marching into Matherion, and forcing everyone to bow down to their ridiculous God—and butchering the entire government in the process."

* * *

"They're trying to stall, your Majesties," Stragen reported. "When suppertime comes, they escort us to the door, push us outside, and lock the door behind us. The building stays locked for the rest of the night—although there are always plenty of lights moving around in there after dark. When we go back the next morning, everything's been rearranged. The files migrate from room to room like ducks in the autumn. I wouldn't actually swear to it, but I think they move walls as well. We found a room just this morning that I don't think was there last night."

"I'll send in Engessa's Atans," Sarabian said darkly. "We'll chase everybody out and then tear the building apart brick by brick."

"No," Ehlana said, shaking her head. "If we make an overt move against Interior, every policeman in the empire will scurry down a rabbit hole." She pursed her lips. "Let's start to do inconvenient things to the other ministries as well. Don't make it obvious that we're concentrating all of our attention on the Ministry of the Interior."

"How can you possibly make things any worse than they already are, your Majesty?" Oscagne asked in a broken voice. "You've disrupted centuries of work as it is."

"Can anyone think of anything?" Sarabian asked, looking around.

"May I speak, your Majesty?" Alean asked in a small, timid-sounding voice.

"Of course, dear." Ehlana smiled.

"I hope you'll forgive my presumption," Alean apologized. "I can't even read, so I don't really know what files are, but aren't we sort of letting on that we're rearranging them?"

"That's what we're telling everybody," Mirtai replied.

"As I said, I can't read, but I do know a bit about rearranging cupboards and such things. This is a little like that, isn't it?"

"Close enough," Stragen replied.

"Well, then, when you're rearranging a cupboard, you take everything out and spread it on the floor. Then you put all the things you want in the top drawer in one pile, the things you want in the second drawer in another and so on. Couldn't we do that with these files?"

"It's a nice i-dee, little dorlin'," Caalador drawled, "but they ain't e-nuff floors in the hull buildin' fer spreadin' out all them there files."

"There *are* lots of lawns around the outside, though, aren't there?" Alean kept her eyes downcast as she spoke. "Couldn't we just take all the files from every government building outside and spread them around on the lawns? We could tell the people who work in the buildings that we want to sort through them and put them in the proper order. They couldn't really object, and you can't lock the door to a lawn at night, or move things around when there are seven-foot-tall Atans standing guard over them. I know I'm just a silly servant girl, but that's the way *I'd* do it."

Oscagne was staring at her in absolute horror.

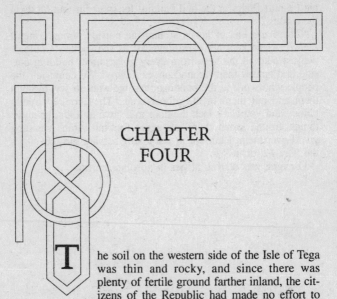

CHAPTER
FOUR

The soil on the western side of the Isle of Tega was thin and rocky, and since there was plenty of fertile ground farther inland, the citizens of the Republic had made no effort to cultivate the area. Tough, scrubby bushes rustled stiffly in the onshore breeze as Sparhawk and his friends rode along a rocky trail leading to the coast.

"The breeze helps," Talen observed gratefully. "At least it blows away that stink."

"You complain too much," Flute told him. The little girl rode with Sephrenia as she had since they had first encountered her. She nestled in her older sister's arms with her dark eyes brooding. She straightened suddenly as the sound of surf pounding on the western shore of the Isle reached them. "This is far enough for right now, gentlemen," she told them. "Let's have some supper and wait for it to get dark."

"Is that a good idea?" Bevier asked her. "The ground's been getting rougher the farther west we come, and the sound of that surf seems to have rocks mixed up in it. This might not be a good place to be blundering around in the dark."

"I can lead you safely to the beach, Bevier," she told him. "I don't want you gentlemen to get too good a look at our ship. There are certain ideas involved in her construction that you don't need to know. That's one of the promises I had to make during those negotiations I was telling you about." She pointed to the lee side of a rocky hillock. "Let's go over there out of this wind and build a fire. I have some instructions for you."

They rode away from the ill-defined trail and dismounted in the shelter of the hill. "Whose turn is it to do the cooking?" Berit asked Sir Ulath.

"Yours," Ulath told him with no hint of a smile.

"You knew he was going to do that, Berit," Talen said. "What you just did was almost the same thing as volunteering."

Berit shrugged. "My turn will come up eventually anyway," he said. "I thought I'd get it out of the way for a while."

"All right, gentlemen," Vanion said, "let's look around and see what we can find in the way of firewood."

Sparhawk concealed a smile. Vanion could maintain that he was no longer the preceptor as much as he wished, but the habit of command was deeply ingrained in him.

They built a fire, and Berit stirred up an acceptable stew. After supper, they sat by the fire, watching as evening slowly settled in.

"Now, then," Flute said to them, "we're going to ride down to a cove. I want you to all stay close behind me, because it's going to be very foggy."

"It's a perfectly clear evening, Flute," Kalten objected.

"It won't be when we reach the cove," she told him. "I'm going to make sure that you don't get too much chance to examine that ship. I'm not really supposed to do this, so don't get me in trouble." She looked sternly at Khalad. "And I want *you* in particular to keep a very tight rein on your curiosity."

"Me?"

"Yes, you. You're too practical and too clever by half for my comfort. Your noble friends here aren't imaginative enough to make any educated guesses about the ship. You're a different matter. Don't be digging at the decks with your knife, and don't try to sneak off to examine things. I don't want to drop by Cimmura someday and find a duplicate of the ship anchored in the river. We'll go down to the cove, board the ship, and go directly below. You will *not* go up on deck until we get to where we're going. A certain part of the ship has been set aside for us, and we'll all stay there for the duration of the voyage. I want your word on that, gentlemen."

Sparhawk could see some differences between Flute and

Danae. Flute was more authoritarian, for one thing, and she didn't seem to have Danae's whimsical sense of humor. Although the Child-Goddess had a definite personality, each of her incarnations seemed to have its own idiosyncracies.

Flute looked up at the slowly darkening sky. "We'll wait another hour," she decided. "The crew of the ship has been told to stay away from us. Our meals will be put just outside the door, and we won't see the one who puts them there. It won't do you any good to try to catch her, so don't even try."

"Her?" Ulath exclaimed. "Are you trying to say that there are *women* in the crew?"

"They're *all* females. There aren't very many males where they come from."

"Women aren't strong enough to raise and lower the sails," he objected.

"These females are ten times stronger than you are, Ulath, and it wouldn't matter anyway, because the ship doesn't *have* sails. Please stop asking questions, gentlemen. Oh, one other thing. There'll be a sort of humming sound when we get under way. It's normal, so don't let it alarm you."

"How—" Ulath began.

She held up her hand. "No more questions, Ulath," she told him quite firmly. "You don't need to know the answers. The ship's here to take us from one place to another in a hurry. That's all you need to know."

"That brings us to something we really *should* know," Sparhawk said. "Where *are* we going?"

"To Jorsan on the west coast of Edom," she replied. "Well, almost, anyway. There's a long gulf leading inland to Jorsan. We'll put ashore at the mouth of the gulf and go inland on horseback. Now, why don't we talk about something else?"

The fog seemed almost thick enough to walk on, and the knights were obliged to blindly follow the misty light of the torch Sephrenia held aloft as they rode down a steep bank toward the sound of unseen surf.

They reached a sandy beach and groped their way down toward the water. Then they saw other lights out in the fog, filmy, mist-shrouded lights that stretched out for what seemed an impossible distance. The lights did not flicker, and they were the wrong color for torchlight.

"Good God!" Ulath choked. *"No* ship could be that big!"

"Ulath!" Flute said sharply from out of the fog ahead.

"Sorry," he mumbled.

When they reached the water's edge, all they could see was a dark, looming shape lying low in the water several yards out, a shape outlined by those unwinking white lights. A ramp reached from the ship to the beach, and Ch'iel, Sephrenia's white palfrey, stepped confidently onto that ramp and clattered across to the ship.

There were dim, shrouded shapes on the deck, cloaked and hooded figures that were all no more than shoulder high, but strangely squat and blocky.

"What do we do with the horses?" Vanion asked as they all dismounted.

"Just leave them here," Flute replied. "They'll be taken care of. Let's go below. We can't start until everybody's off the deck."

"The crew stays up here, don't they?" Ulath asked her.

"No. It's too dangerous."

They went to a rectangular hatchway in the deck and followed an inclined ramp leading down.

"Stairs would take up less space," Khalad said critically.

"The crew couldn't use stairs, Khalad," Flute told him. "They don't have legs."

He stared at her in horror.

"I told you that they're not human." She shrugged.

The companionway they reached at the bottom of the ramp was low, and the knights had to half stoop as they followed the Child-Goddess aft. The area belowdecks was illuminated by pale glowing spots of light recessed into the ceiling and covered over by what appeared to be glass. The light was steady, unwinking, and it definitely did not come from any kind of fire.

The quarters to which their little guide led them were more conventionally illuminated by candles, however, and the ceilings were high enough for the tall knights to stand erect. No sooner had Ulath closed the heavy door to what was in effect to be their prison for the next five days than a low-pitched humming sound began to vibrate the deck beneath their feet, and they could feel the bow of the strange vessel start to swing ponderously about to point at the open sea. Then the ship surged forward.

"What's making it move?" Kalten asked. "There's no wind."

"*Kalten!*" Aphrael said sharply.

"Sorry," he muttered.

"There are four compartments here," she told them. "We'll eat in this one, and we can spread out and sleep in the other three. Put away your belongings, gentlemen. Then you might as well go to bed. Nothing's going to happen for five days."

Sparhawk and Kalten went into one of the cabins, taking Talen with them. Talen was carrying Khalad's saddlebags as well as his own.

"What's your brother up to?" Sparhawk asked the boy suspiciously.

"He wants to look around a bit," Talen replied.

"Aphrael told him not to do that."

"So?"

They were all staggered a bit as the ship gave another forward surge. The humming sound climbed to a whine, and the ship seemed to rise up in the water almost like a sitting man rising to his feet.

Kalten threw his saddlebags onto one of the bunks and sat down beside them. "I don't understand any of this," he grumbled.

"You aren't supposed to," Sparhawk replied.

"I wonder if they've got anything to drink aboard. I could definitely use a drink about now."

"I wouldn't get my hopes up too high, and I'm not sure you'd care to drink something brewed by nonhumans. It might do some strange things to you."

Khalad came into the tiny compartment, his eyes baffled. "I don't want to alarm you, gentlemen," he said, "but we're moving faster than a horse can run."

"How do you know that?" Talen asked him.

"Those curtains in that central cabin are hanging over openings that are sort of like portholes—they've got glass over them, anyway. I looked out. There's still fog all around us, but I could see the water. We passed a floating log, and it went by like a crossbow bolt. There's something else, too. The hull curves back under us, and it isn't touching the water at all."

"We're *flying*?" Kalten asked incredulously.

Khalad shook his head. "I think the keel's touching the water, but that's about all."

"I really don't want to know about this," Kalten said plaintively.

"He's right, Khalad," Sparhawk said. "I think this is one of the things Aphrael told us was none of our business. Leave those curtains closed from now on."

"Aren't you the least bit curious, my Lord?"

"I can live with it."

"You don't mind if I speculate just a bit, do you, Sparhawk?"

"Go right ahead, but keep your speculations to yourself." He sat down on his bunk and began to pull off his boots. "I don't know about the rest of you, but I'm going to follow orders and go to bed. This is a good chance to catch up on our sleep, and we've all been running a little short on that for quite some time now. We'll want to be alert when we get to Jorsan."

"Which only happens to be about a quarter of the way around the world," Khalad added moodily, "and which we're going to reach in just five days. I don't think I'm put together right for this kind of thing. Do I *have* to be a Pandion Knight, Sparhawk?"

"Yes," Sparhawk told him, dropping his boots on the deck. "Was there anything else you wanted to know before I go to sleep?"

They all slept a great deal during the next five days. Sparhawk strongly suspected that Aphrael might have had a hand in that, since sleeping people don't wander around making discoveries.

Their meals were served on strange oblong trays that were made of some substance none of them could identify. The food consisted entirely of uncooked vegetables, and they were given only water to drink. Kalten complained about the food at every meal, but, since there was nothing else available, he ate it anyway.

On the afternoon before they were scheduled to arrive, they gathered together in the cramped central compartment. "Are you sure?" Kalten dubiously asked Flute when she told them that they were no more than ten hours from their destination.

She sighed. "Yes, Kalten, I'm sure."

"How do you know? You haven't been up on deck, and you haven't talked to any of the sailors. We could have been . . ." His words sort of faded off. She was looking at him with a long-suffering expression as he floundered on. "Oh," he said then. "I wasn't thinking, I guess. Sorry."

"I *do* love you, Kalten—in spite of everything."

Khalad cleared his throat. "Didn't Dolmant tell you that the Edomish have some strong feelings about the Church?" he asked Sparhawk.

Sparhawk nodded. "As I understand it, they look at our Holy Mother in almost the same way that the Rendors do."

"Church Knights wouldn't really be welcome, then, I gather."

"Hardly."

"We'll need to disguise ourselves as ordinary travelers, then."

"More than likely," Sparhawk agreed.

Vanion had been looking at his map. "Exactly where are we going from Jorsan, Aphrael?" he asked Flute.

"Up the coast a ways," she replied vaguely.

"That's not very specific."

"Yes, I know."

He sighed. "Is there any real need for us to go on up the Gulf of Jorsan to the city itself? If we were to land on the north shore of the gulf, we could avoid the city entirely. Since the Edomish have these prejudices, shouldn't we stay away from them as much as possible?"

"We have to go to Jorsan," she told him. "Well," she amended, "Jorsan itself isn't that important, but we're going to see something along the way that will be."

"Oh? What's that?"

"I have no idea."

"You get used to that," Sparhawk told his friend. "Our little Goddess here gets hunches from time to time—no details at all, just hunches."

"What time will we make our landfall?" Ulath asked.

"About midnight," she replied.

"Landing on a strange shore at night can be a little tricky," he said dubiously.

"There won't be any problems." She said it with absolute confidence.

"I'm not supposed to worry about it. Is that it?"

"You can worry if you want to, Ulath." She smiled. "It's not necessary, but you can worry all you like, if it makes you feel better."

It was foggy when they came up on deck again, a dense, obscuring fog, and this time the strange ship showed no lights. Their horses, already saddled, were waiting, and they led them down the ramp to a pebbly beach.

When they looked back out toward the water, their ship was gone.

"Where did she go?" Ulath exclaimed.

"She's still there." Aphrael smiled.

"Why can't I see her, then?"

"Because I don't *want* people to see her. We passed a number of ordinary ships on our way here. If anybody'd seen her, there'd be wild talk in every sailors' tavern in every port in the world."

"It's all in the shape of the keel, isn't it?" Khalad mused.

"Khalad!" she said sharply. "You stop that immediately!"

"I'm not going to do anything about it, Flute. I couldn't if I wanted to, but it's that keel that accounts for her speed. I'm only mentioning it so that you won't make the mistake of thinking I'm so stupid that I can't put it together."

She glared at him.

He bent slightly and kissed her cheek. "That's all right, Flute." He smiled. "I love you anyway—even if you do underestimate me at times."

"He's going to work out just fine," Kalten said to Vanion.

The hillside rising from the gravel strand was covered with thick, rank grass, and by the time they had reached the top of the hill, the fog had entirely dissipated. A broad highway of reflected moonlight stretched out across the calm waters of the gulf.

"My map shows a kind of track a mile or so inland," Vanion told them. "It seems to run up the gulf in the general direction of Jorsan." He looked at Flute, who was still glaring darkly at Khalad. "Pending instructions to the contrary from higher authority, I suppose we can follow that track." He looked inquiringly at the Child-Goddess again.

She sank a little lower in Sephrenia's arms and began to suck her thumb.

"You'll make your teeth crooked."

She pulled her thumb out of her mouth and stuck her tongue out at him.

"Shall we press on, then?" Vanion suggested.

They rode on across a broad, rolling meadow covered with the rank salt grass. The moon washed out all color, making the grass whipping at the horses' legs seem grey and the forest beyond the meadow a formless black blot. They rode slowly, their eyes and ears alert and their hands never far from their sword hilts. Nothing untoward had happened yet, but these were trained knights, and for them the world was always filled with danger.

After they rode in under the trees, Vanion called a halt.

"Why are we stopping?" Flute demanded a little crossly.

"The moon's very bright tonight," Vanion explained, "and our eyes need a little time to adjust to the shadows here under the trees. We don't want to blunder into anything."

"Oh."

"Her night isn't going too well, is it?" Berit murmured to Sparhawk. "She seemed to be very upset with Khalad."

"It's good for her. She gets overconfident, sometimes, and a little too much impressed with her own cleverness."

"I heard that, Sparhawk," Flute snapped.

"I rather thought you might have," he replied blandly.

"Why is everyone mistreating me tonight?" she complained.

"They're only teasing you, Aphrael," Sephrenia assured the little girl. "Clumsily, of course, but they're Elenes, after all, so you can't really expect too much from them."

"Shall we move on before things start to turn ugly?" Vanion said.

They rode at a walk through the shadows, and after about half an hour they reached a narrow, rutted track. They turned eastward and moved on, riding a little faster now.

"How far is it to Jorsan, my Lord?" Bevier asked Vanion after they had gone a ways.

"About fifty leagues," Vanion replied.

"A goodly ways then." Bevier looked inquiringly at Flute.

"What?" she said crossly.

"Nothing, really."

"Say it, Bevier."

"I wouldn't offend you for the world, Divine Aphrael, but could you speed the journey the way you did when we were traveling across Deira with King Wargun's army?"

"No, I can't. You've forgotten that we're waiting for something important to happen, Bevier, and I'm not going to fly past it just because you're in a hurry to get to the taverns of Jorsan."

"That will do," Sephrenia told her.

Since it was still early autumn, they had not brought tents with them, and after about another hour's travel they rode back into the forest and spread their blankets on beds of fallen leaves to get a few hours' sleep.

The sun was well up when they set out again, and they traveled through the forest until late afternoon without encountering any local people.

Once again they moved back into the forest about a quarter of a mile and set up for the night in a narrow ravine where an overhanging bank and the thick foliage would conceal the light from their small cooking fire. Rather surprisingly, Ulath did the cooking without any of his usual subterfuge. "It's not as much fun when Tynian isn't along," he explained.

"I miss him, too," Sparhawk agreed. "It seems strange to be traveling without all those suggestions of his."

"This cooking business has come up before," Vanion observed. "Am I missing something?"

"Sir Ulath normally keeps track of it, my Lord," Talen replied. "It's a very complicated system, so none of the rest of us really understands how it works."

"Wouldn't a simple roster do just as well?" Vanion asked.

"I'm sure it would, but Sir Ulath prefers his own method. It has a few drawbacks, though. Once Kalten cooked every single meal for an entire week."

Vanion shuddered.

They had smoked mutton chops that evening, and Ulath received some hard looks from his companions about that. Flute and Sephrenia, however, complimented him on his choice. After they had eaten, they sought their makeshift beds.

It must have been well past midnight when Talen shook Sparhawk awake, laying a cautious hand across his mouth to prevent his crying out. "There are some people back near the road," the boy whispered. "They've built a big fire."

"What are they doing?" Sparhawk asked.

"Just standing around waiting for somebody, it seems—unless you want to count the drinking."

"You'd better rouse the others," Sparhawk told him, throwing off his blankets and reaching for his sword.

They crept through the forest in the darkness and stopped at the edge of a stump-dotted clearing. There was a large bonfire in the center of the clearing and nearly a hundred men—peasants for the most part, judging from their clothing—sitting on the ground near the blaze. Their faces were ruddy from the reflected light and from the contents of the earthenware jars they were passing around.

"Strange place to be holding a drinking party," Ulath murmured. "*I* wouldn't come out this far into the woods for something as ordinary as that."

"Is this it?" Vanion asked Flute, who was nestled in Sephrenia's arms, concealed by her sister's dark cloak.

"Is this what?"

"You know what I mean. Is this what we're supposed to see?"

"I think so," she replied. "I'll know better when they all get here."

"Are there more coming?"

She nodded. "One, at least. The ones who are already here don't matter."

They waited as the peasants in the clearing grew progressively more and more rowdy.

Then a lone horseman appeared at the far edge of the clearing, near the road. The newcomer wore a dark cloak and a slouch hat pulled low over his face.

"Not again," Talen groaned. "Doesn't *anybody* on this continent have any imagination?"

"What's this?" Vanion asked.

"The one they call Sabre up in Astel wore the same kind of clothes, my Lord."

"Maybe this one's different."

"I wouldn't get my hopes up too high."

The man on horseback rode into the firelight, dismounted, and pushed back his hat. He was a tall, gangly man with a long pockmarked face and narrow eyes. He stepped up onto a tree stump and stood waiting for the peasants to gather around him. "Hear me, my friends," he said in a loud, harsh voice. "I bring news."

The half-drunk babble of the peasants faded.

"Much has happened since last we met," the speaker continued. "You will recall that we had determined to make one last try to resolve our differences with the Tamuls by peaceful means."

"What choice did we have, Rebal?" one of the peasants shouted. "Only madmen would attack the Atan garrison—no matter how just their cause."

"So that's Rebal," Kalten whispered. "Not very impressive, is he?"

"Our cause was made just by Incetes himself," Rebal was responding, "and Incetes is more than a match for the Atans."

The mob murmured its agreement.

"There is good news, my friends," Rebal declared. "Our

emissaries have been successful. The emperor himself has seen the justice of our cause!"

A ragged cheer went up.

"I rejoice even as you," Rebal continued, "but a new peril, far more grave than the simple injustice of the corrupt Tamul administrators, has arisen. The emperor, who is now our friend, has been taken prisoner by the accursed Church Knights! The evil Archprelate of the Church of Chyrellos has reached half-way around the world to seize our friend!"

"Outrageous!" a burly peasant in the crowd roared. "Monstrous!"

The rest of the peasants looked a bit confused, however.

"He's going too fast," Talen whispered critically.

"What?" Berit asked.

"He's changing course on them," Talen explained. "I'd guess that he's been cursing the Tamuls for the last year or so—the same way Sabre was, up in Astel. Now he wants to curse somebody else, but he's got to uncurse the Tamuls first. Even a drunken peasant's going to have some suspicions about the miraculous conversion of the emperor. He made it all too fast—and too easy."

"Tell us, Rebal," the burly peasant shouted, "how was our friend, the emperor, taken prisoner?"

"Yes, tell us!" another man on the far side of the crowd howled.

"Planted henchmen," Talen sneered. "This Rebal's about as subtle as a club in the face."

"It was clever, my friends," Rebal declared to the crowd, "very clever. The Church of Chyrellos is guided by the demons of Hell, and they are the masters of deceit. The Tamuls, who are now our friends, are heathens, and they do not understand the guile of the heretics of Chyrellos. All unsuspecting, they welcomed a delegation of Church officials, and among those foul heretics who journeyed to Matherion were Knights of the Church—the armored minions of Hell itself. Once in Matherion, they seized our dear friend and protector, Emperor Sarabian, and they now hold him prisoner in his own palace!"

"Death to the Tamuls!" a wheezy-voiced old man, far gone in drink, bawled.

One of the other peasants rapped him sharply across the back of the head with a cudgel, and the slightly out-of-date demonstrator sagged limply to the ground.

"Crowd control," Talen sniffed. "Rebal doesn't want people making any mistakes here."

Other peasants, obviously more of Rebal's planted henchmen, began to shout the correct slogan, "Death to the Church Knights!" They brandished crude weapons and assorted agricultural implements as they bellowed, emphasizing their slogan and intimidating the still-confused.

"The purpose of these monsters is all too clear," Rebal shouted over the tumult. "It is their plan to hold the emperor as hostage to prevent the Atans from storming the palace. They will sit safe where they are until reinforcements arrive. And make no mistake, my friends, those reinforcements are even now gathering on the plains of Eosia. The armies of the heretics are on the march, and in the van come the Church Knights!"

Horrified gasps ran through the ranks of the peasants.

"On to Matherion!" the fellow with the cudgel bellowed. "Free the emperor!"

The crowd took up the shout.

Rebal held up one hand. "My blood burns as hotly as yours, my friends!" he shouted. "But will we leave our homes and families to the mercies of the Knights of the Church? All of Eosia marches toward Matherion! And what stands between accursed Eosia and fire-domed Matherion? Edom, my friends! Our beloved homeland stands in the path of the heretic horde! What mercy can we expect from these savages? Who will defend our women from foul rape if we rush to the emperor's aid?"

Cries of chagrin ran through the crowd.

Rebal moved quickly at that point. "And yet, my friends," he rushed on, "our defense of our beloved homes may yet aid our friend, the emperor. The beasts of Eosia come to destroy our faith and to slaughter the true believers. I know not what course you may take, but I pledge to you all that I will lay down my life for our beloved homeland and our holy faith! But in my dying, I will delay the Church Knights! That Spawn of Hell must pause to spill my blood, and their delay will give the Atans the time to rally! *Thus* may we defend our homes and aid our friend in one stroke!"

Sparhawk began to swear, half strangling to keep his voice down.

"What's your problem?" Kalten asked.

"We've just been blocked. If those idiots out there accept

what Rebal's telling them, the Church Knights are going to have to fight their way to Matherion foot by foot."

"They're very quick to exploit a changing situation," Vanion agreed. "Too quick, perhaps. It's almost a thousand leagues from here to Matherion. Either someone has a *very* good horse, or our mysterious friend out there's breaking the rules again in order to get word out to the hinterlands of what happened after the coup was put down."

Rebal was holding up his hands to quiet the shouting of the crowd. "Are you with me, my brothers?" he called. "Will we defend our homes and our faith and help our friends, the Tamuls, at the same time?"

The mob howled its assent.

"Let's ask Incetes to help us!" the man with the cudgel shouted.

"Incetes!" another bellowed. "Incetes! Call forth Incetes!"

"Are you sure, my friends?" Rebal asked, drawing himself up and pulling his dark cloak tightly around him.

"Call him forth, Rebal! Raise Incetes! Let *him* tell us what to do!"

Rebal struck an exaggerated pose and raised both arms over his head. He began to speak, intoning guttural words in a hollow, booming voice.

"Is that Styric?" Kalten whispered to Sephrenia. "It doesn't sound like Styric to me."

"It's gibberish," she replied scornfully.

Kalten frowned. "I don't think I've ever heard of them," he whispered. "What part of the world do the Gibbers come from?"

She stared at him, her face baffled.

"Did I say it wrong?" he asked. "Are they called the Gibberese? or maybe the Gibberenians? The people who speak Gibberish, I mean."

"Oh, Kalten." She laughed softly. "I love you."

"What did I say?"

Rebal's voice had risen to a near shriek, and he brought both arms down sharply.

There was a sudden explosion in the middle of the bonfire, and a great cloud of smoke boiled out into the clearing.

"Herken, Maisteres alle!" A huge voice came out of the smoke. "Now hath the tyme for Werre ycom. Now, be me troth, shal alle trew Edomishmen on lyve to armes! Tak ye uppe the iren swerd; gird ye your limbes alle inne the iren haubergeon and the iren helm! Smyte ye the feendes foule, which beestes derk do sette hom and fey in deedly peril. Goe ye to bataile ferse to fend the feendes of the acurset Chirche of Chyrellos! Follwe! Follwe! Follwe me, as Godes hondys yeve ye force!"

"Old High Elenic!" Bevier exclaimed. "Nobody's spoken that tongue in thousands of years!"

"*I'd* follow him, whatever tongue it is," Ulath rumbled. "He makes a good speech."

The smoke began to thin, and a huge, ox-shouldered man wearing ancient armor and holding a mighty two-handed sword above his head appeared at Rebal's side. "Havok!" he bellowed. "Havok and Werre!"

CHAPTER
FIVE

"T hey've all gone now," Berit reported when he and Talen returned to the camp concealed in the narrow ravine. "They spent a lot of time marching around in circles shouting slogans first, though."

"Then the beer ran out," Talen added dryly, "and the party broke up." He looked at Flute. "Are you sure this was supposed to be important?" he asked her. "It was the most contrived hoax I've ever seen."

She nodded stubbornly. "It *was* important," she insisted. "I don't know why, but it was."

"How did they make that big flash and all the smoke?" Kalten asked.

"One of the fellows near the fire threw a handful of some kind of powder onto the coals," Khalad shrugged. "Everybody else was watching Rebal, so they didn't see him when he did it."

"Where did the one in the armor come from?" Ulath asked.

"He was hiding in the crowd," Talen explained. "The whole thing was at about the same level as you'd find at a country fair—one that's held a long way from the nearest town."

"The one who was pretending to be Incetes gave a fairly stirring speech, though," Ulath noted.

"It certainly *should* have been." Bevier smiled. "It was written by Phalactes in the seventh century."

"Who was he?" Talen asked.

"Phalactes was the greatest playwright of antiquity. That stirring speech came directly from one of his tragedies, *Etonicus*. That fellow in the antique armor substituted a few words is all. The play's a classic. It's still performed at universities once in a while."

"You're a whole library all by yourself, Bevier," Kalten told him. "Do you remember every single thing you've ever read—word for word?"

Bevier laughed. "I wish I could, my friend. Some of my classmates and I put on a performance of *Etonicus* when I was a student. I played the lead, so I had to memorize that speech. The poetry of Phalactes is really very stirring. He was a great artist—Arcian, naturally."

"I never liked him very much," Flute sniffed. "He was as ugly as sin; he smelled like an open cesspool; and he was a howling bigot."

Bevier swallowed hard. "Please don't do that, Aphrael," he said. "It's very unsettling."

"What was the story about?" Talen asked, his eyes suddenly eager.

"Etonicus was supposed to be the ruler of a mythic kingdom somewhere in what's now eastern Cammoria," Bevier replied. "The legend has it that he went to war with the Styrics over religion."

"What happened?" Talen's tone was almost hungry.

"He came to a bad end," Bevier shrugged. "It's a tragedy, after all."

"But—"

"You can read it for yourself sometime, Talen," Vanion said firmly. "This isn't the story hour."

Talen's face grew sulky.

"I'd be willing to wager that you could paralyze our young friend here in midtheft." Ulath chuckled. "All you'd have to do is say, 'Once upon a time,' and he'd stop dead in his tracks."

"This throws a whole new light on what's been happening here in Tamuli," Vanion mused. "Could this all be some vast hoax?" He looked inquiringly at Flute.

She shook her head. "No, Vanion. There *has* been magic of varying levels in *some* of the things we've encountered."

"Some, perhaps, but not all, certainly. Was there any magic at all involved in what we saw tonight?"

"Not a drop."

"Is *that* how you measure magic?" Kalten asked curiously. "Does it come by the gallon?"

"Like cheap wine, you mean?" she suggested tartly.

"Well, not exactly, but—"

"This was very important," Sparhawk said. "Thank you, Aphrael."

"I live but to serve." She smiled mockingly at him.

"Stop that."

"You've missed me entirely, Sparhawk," Kalten said.

"We've just found out that not *everything* that's being reported back to Matherion is the result of real magic. There's a fair amount of fraud mixed in as well. What does that suggest?"

"The other side's lazy." Kalten shrugged.

"I'm not so sure," Ulath disagreed. "They're not afraid to exert themselves when it's important."

"Two," Sephrenia said. "Three at the most."

"I beg your pardon," Ulath said with a puzzled look.

"Now do you see how exasperating that is, Ulath?" she said to him. "This charade we watched here tonight rather strongly hints that there aren't many people on the other side who can really work spells. They're spread out a bit thin, I'd say. What's going on here in Edom—and probably in Astel and Daconia as well—is rather commonplace, so they don't feel that they have to waste magic on it."

"Commonplace or not, it's going to seriously hinder Tynian when he tries to lead the Church Knights across Daresia to Matherion," Sparhawk said. "If Rebal can stir up the whole kingdom the way he did this group tonight, Tynian's going to have to wade his way through hordes of howling fanatics. The Edomish peasantry's going to be convinced that our brothers are coming here to impose heresies on them by force, and they'll be lurking behind every bush with sickles and pitchforks."

"We still have a certain advantage, though," Bevier said thoughtfully. "There's no way that our enemies can possibly know that we're here in Edom and that we saw this business tonight. Even if they were to know that we're going to raise Bhelliom—which isn't very likely—they wouldn't know where it is, so they'd have no idea where we were going. Even *we* don't know where we're going."

"And even if they did, they wouldn't know that we could get here as quickly as we did," Khalad added. "I think we've got the jump on them, my Lords. If they're relying on hoaxes here, that probably means that they don't have any magicians around to sniff us out. If we can pass ourselves off as ordinary travelers, we should be able to move around without much hindrance—and pick up all sorts of information in the process."

"We're here to retrieve the Bhelliom, Khalad," Flute reminded him.

"Of course, but there's no point in passing up little treasures as we go along, is there?"

"Aphrael," Vanion said, "have we seen and heard everything we were supposed to?"

She nodded.

"I think we might want to move on to Jorsan rather quickly, then. If Khalad's right and we're one jump ahead, let's stay that way. What would it take in the way of bribes to persuade you to speed up the journey?"

"We could negotiate that, I suppose, Lord Vanion." She smiled. "I'm sure you could all offer me *something* that might induce me to lend a hand."

They kissed the Child-Goddess into submission and arrived in Jorsan late the following day. Jorsan turned out to be a typical Elene port city squatting at the head of the gulf. The question of suitable disguises had arisen during the journey. Bevier had leaned strongly in the direction of posing as religious pilgrims. Kalten had liked the notion of masquerading as a group of rowdies in search of constructive debauchery, while Talen, perhaps influenced by Rebal's recent performance, had thought it might be fun to pose as traveling players. They were still arguing about it when Jorsan came into view.

"Isn't all this a waste of time?" Ulath asked them. "Why should we play dress-up? It's not really anybody's business *who* we are, is it? As long as we're not wearing armor, the people in Jorsan won't know—or care—about us. Why go to all the trouble of lying about it?"

"We'll need to wear our mail shirts, Sir Ulath," Berit reminded him. "How do we explain that?"

"We don't. Lots of people wear chain mail and carry weapons, so it's not really *that* unusual. If somebody in town gets *too* curious about who we are and where we're going, I can make him get un-curious in fairly short order." He held up his hand and closed his fist suggestively.

"You mean just bully our way through?" Kalten asked.

"Why not? Isn't that what we're trained for?"

The inn was not particularly elegant, but it was clean and not so near the waterfront that the streets around it were filled with brawling sailors lurching from alehouse to alehouse. The sleeping rooms were upstairs over the common room on the main floor, and the stables were in the back.

"Let me handle this," Ulath muttered to Sparhawk as they approached the innkeeper, a tousled fellow with a long, pointed nose.

"Feel free," Sparhawk replied.

"You," Ulath said abruptly to the innkeeper, "we need five rooms for the night, fodder for ten horses, and some decent food."

"I can provide all those, good master," the innkeeper assured him.

"Good. How much?"

"Ah—" The man with the pointed nose rubbed at his chin, carefully appraising the big Thalesian's clothes and general appearance. "That would be a half-crown, good master," he said somewhat tentatively. His rates seemed to be based on a sliding scale of some sort.

Ulath turned on his heel. "Let's go," he said shortly to Sparhawk.

"What was I thinking of?" the innkeeper said, slapping his forehead. "That was *five* rooms and fodder for *ten* horses, wasn't it? I got the numbers turned around in my head. I thought you wanted ten rooms for some reason. A half-crown would be *far* too much for only five rooms. The right price would be two silver imperials, of course."

"I'm glad you got your mathematics straightened out," Ulath grunted. "Let's look at the rooms."

"Of course, good master." The innkeeper scurried on up the stairs ahead of them.

"You don't leave very many conversational openings, do you, my friend?" Sparhawk chuckled.

"I've never found innkeepers very interesting to talk with."

They reached an upper hallway, and Ulath looked into one of the rooms. "Check it for bugs," he told Sparhawk.

"Good *master*!" the innkeeper protested.

"I like to sleep alone," Ulath told him. "Bugs crowd me, and they're always restless at night."

The innkeeper laughed a bit weakly. "That's very funny, good master. I'll have to remember it. Where is it you come from, and where are you bound?"

Ulath gave him a long, icy stare, his blue eyes as chill as a northern winter and his shoulders swelling ominously as he bunched them under his tunic.

"Ah—no matter, I suppose," the innkeeper rushed on. "It's not really any of my affair, is it?"

"You've got that part right," Ulath said. He looked around. "Good enough," he said. "We'll stay." He nudged Sparhawk with his elbow. "Pay him," he said, turned, and clumped down the stairs.

They handed their horses over to the grooms and carried their saddlebags up to the sleeping rooms. Then they went back downstairs for supper.

Kalten, as usual, heaped his plate with steaming beef.

"Maybe we should send out for another cow," Berit joked.

"He's young," Kalten told the others jovially, "but I like the way he thinks." He grinned at Berit, but then the grin slowly faded, and the big blond Pandion grew quite pale. He stared at the young knight's face for quite some time. Then he abruptly pushed his plate back and rose to his feet. "I don't think I'm really hungry," he said. "I'm tired. I'm going to bed." He turned, quickly crossed the common room to the stairs, and went up them two at a time.

"What's the matter with *him*?" Ulath asked in a puzzled tone. "I've never seen him walk away from supper like that before."

"That's God's own truth," Bevier agreed.

"You'd better have a talk with him when you go up, Sparhawk," Vanion suggested. "Find out if he's sick or something. Kalten *never* leaves anything on his plate."

"Or anybody else's, for that matter," Talen added.

Sparhawk did not linger over supper. He ate quickly, said good-night to the others, and went upstairs to have a talk with his friend. He found Kalten sitting on the edge of his bed with his face in his hands.

"What's the matter?" Sparhawk asked him. "Aren't you feeling well?"

Kalten turned his face away. "Leave me alone," he said hoarsely.

"Not very likely. What's wrong?"

"It doesn't matter." The blond knight sniffed loudly and wiped at his eyes with the back of his hand. "Let's go get drunk."

"Not until you tell me what's bothering you, we won't."

Kalten sniffed again and set his jaw. "It's something foolish. You'd laugh at me."

"You know better than that."

"There's a girl, Sparhawk, and she loves somebody else. Are you satisfied now?"

"Why didn't you say something earlier?"

"I just now found out about it."

"Kalten, you're not making any sense at all. One girl's always been the same as another to you. Most of the time you can't even remember their names."

"This time's different. Can we go get drunk now?"

"How do you know she doesn't feel the same way about you?" Sparhawk knew who the girl was and he was quite certain that she *did* in fact return his friend's feelings for her.

Kalten sighed. "God knows that there are people in this world who are brighter than I am, Sparhawk. It's taken me all this time to put it together. I'll tell you one thing, though. If he breaks her heart, I'll kill him, brother or no."

"Will you at least *try* to make some sense?"

"She told me that she loves somebody else—as plain as if she'd come right out and said it in so many words."

"Alean wouldn't do that."

"How did you know it was Alean?" The big blond man sprang to his feet. "Have you all been laughing at me behind my back?" he demanded pugnaciously.

"Don't be an ass. We wouldn't do that. We've all been through exactly the same thing. You didn't invent love, you know."

"Everybody knows, though, don't they?"

"No. I'm probably the only one—except for Melidere. Nothing much gets past *her*. Now what's all this nonsense about Alean loving somebody else?"

"I just put it together myself."

"*What* did you put together. Try to make a little sense, Kalten."

"Didn't you hear her singing on the day we left?"

"Of course I did. She has a beautiful voice."

"I'm not talking about her voice. I'm talking about the song she was singing. It was 'My Bonnie Blue-Eyed Boy.' "

"So?"

"It's Berit, Sparhawk. She's in love with Berit."

"What are you talking about?"

"I just noticed it when we sat down to supper." Kalten buried his face in his hands again. "I never paid any attention before, but when I looked into his face while we were talking, I saw it. I'm surprised you haven't seen it yourself."

"Seen what?"

"Berit's got blue eyes."

Sparhawk stared at him. Then, being careful not to laugh, he said, "So do you—when they're not bloodshot."

Kalten shook his head stubbornly. "His are bluer than mine. I know it's him. I just know it! God's punishing me for some of the things I've done in the past. He made me fall in love with a girl who loves somebody else. Well, I hope he's satisfied. If he wants to make me suffer, he's doing a good job of it."

"*Will* you be serious?"

"Berit's younger than I am, Sparhawk, and God knows he's better looking."

"Kalten—"

"Look at the way every girl who gets to within a hundred yards of him starts to follow him around like a puppy. Even the Atan girls were all falling in love with him."

"Kalten—"

"I *know* it's him. I just know it. God's twisting his knife in my heart. He's gone and made the one girl I'll ever feel this way about fall in love with one of my brother-knights."

"Kalten—"

Kalten sat up and squared his shoulders. "All right, then," he said weakly, "if that's the way God wants it, that's the way it's going to be. If Berit and Alean really, really love each other, I won't stand in their way. I'll bite my tongue and keep my mouth shut."

"Kalten—"

"But I swear it to you, Sparhawk," the blond Pandion said hotly, "if he hurts her, I'll kill him!"

"*Kalten!*" Sparhawk shouted at him.

"*What?*"

Sparhawk sighed. "Why don't we go out and get drunk?" he suggested, giving up entirely.

It was cloudy the following morning. It was a low, dirty-grey cloud cover that seethed and tattered in the stiff wind aloft. It was one of those peculiar days when the murk raced overhead, streaming in off the gulf lying to the west, but the air at the surface was dead calm.

They set out early and clattered along the narrow, cobbled streets where sleepy-eyed shopkeepers were opening their shutters and setting out their wares. They passed through the city gates and took the road that followed the north coast of the gulf.

After they had gone a mile or so, Vanion leaned over in his saddle. "How far do we have to go?" he asked Flute, who nestled, as always, in her sister's arms.

"What difference does it make?" The Child-Goddess shrugged.

"I'd like to know how long it's going to take."

"What does 'how far' have to do with 'how long'?"

"They're the same thing, Aphrael. Time and distance mean the same thing when you're traveling."

"Not if you know what you're doing, they don't."

Sparhawk had always admired Vanion, but never quite so much as in that moment. The silvery-bearded preceptor did not even raise his voice. "All I'm really getting at, Divine One, is that nobody knows we're here. Shouldn't we keep it that way? I don't mind a good fight now and then, but would bashing our way through crowds of drunken Edomish peasants serve any real purpose right now?"

"You always take so long to get to the point, Vanion," she said. "Why didn't you just come right out and tell me to speed things up?"

"I was trying to be polite. I think we'll all feel much better about this when Sparhawk's got Bhelliom in his hands again. It's up to you, though. If you want the road from here to wherever it is you've got Bhelliom hidden awash with blood and littered with corpses, we'll be happy to oblige you."

"He's hateful," Aphrael said to her sister.

"Oh, I wouldn't say that."

"*You* wouldn't. Sometimes you two are worse than Sparhawk and Ehlana."

Sparhawk moved in rather quickly at that point. Aphrael

was coming very close to saying things that she shouldn't be saying in the presence of the others. "Shall we move right along?" he suggested quite firmly. "Vanion's right, Aphrael, and you know he is. If Rebal finds out that we're here, we'll have to wade through his people by the score."

"All right," she gave in quite suddenly.

"That was quick," Talen said to Khalad. "I thought she was going to be stubborn about it."

"No, Talen." She smirked. "Actually, I'm sort of looking forward to hearing that vast cry of chagrin that's going to echo from every mountain in Daresia when our enemies hear the sound of Anakha's fist closing around Bhelliom again. Just lean back in your saddles, gentlemen, and leave the rest to me."

Sparhawk awoke with a start. They were riding along the brink of a windswept cliff with an angry sea ripping itself to tattered froth on the rocks far below. Sephrenia rode in the lead, and she held Flute enfolded in her arms. The others trailed along behind, their cloaks drawn tightly around them and wooden expressions of endurance on their faces. The wind had risen, and it pushed at them and tugged at their cloaks.

There were some significant impossibilities involved here, but Sparhawk's mind seemed somehow numb to them. Normally, Vanion rode protectively close to Sephrenia, but Vanion didn't seem to be with them now.

Tynian, however, was. Sparhawk knew with absolute certainty that Tynian was a thousand leagues and more away, but there he was, his broad face as wooden as the faces of the others and his right shoulder as functional as ever.

Sparhawk did not turn around. He knew that another impossibility was riding behind him.

Their horses plodded up the winding trail that followed the edge of the long, ascending cliff toward a rocky promontory that thrust a crooked, stony finger out into the sea. At the outermost tip of the promontory stood a gnarled and twisted tree, its streaming branches flailing in the wind.

When she reached the tree, Sephrenia reined in. Kurik walked forward to lift Flute down. Sparhawk felt a sharp pang of bitter resentment. He knew about Aphrael's need for symmetry, but this went *too* far.

Kurik set Aphrael down on her feet, and when he straightened, he looked Sparhawk full in the face. Sparhawk's squire was unchanged. His features were rugged, and his black beard, touched with silver, was as coarse as ever. His bare shoulders were bulky, and his wrists were enclosed in steel cuffs. Without so much as changing expression, he winked at his lord.

"Very well, then," Flute said to them in a crisp voice, "let's get on with this before too many more of my cousins change their minds. I had to talk very fast and even throw a few tantrums to get them to agree, and many of them still have grave doubts about the whole notion."

"You don't have to explain things to them, Flute," Kurik told her in that gruff voice of his, a voice so familiar that Sparhawk's eyes filled with sudden tears. "Just tell them what to do. They're Church Knights, after all, so they're used to following orders they don't understand."

She laughed delightedly. "How very wise you are, Kurik. All right then, gentlemen, come with me." She led them past the gnarled tree to the brink of the awful precipice. Even though they were very high above it, the roaring of the surf was much like heavy thunder.

"All right," Aphrael told them, "I'm going to need your help with this."

"What do you want us to do?" Tynian asked her.

"Stand there and approve."

"Do *what?*"

"Just approve of me, Tynian. You can cheer if you'd like, but it's not really necessary. All I really need is approval—and love, of course—but there's nothing unusual about that. I always need love." She smiled at them mysteriously.

Then she stepped off the edge of the cliff.

Talen gave a startled cry and plunged after her.

The Child-Goddess, as unconcerned as if she were only taking a morning stroll, walked out across the empty air. Talen, however, fell like a stone.

"Oh, bother!" Aphrael exclaimed peevishly. She made a curious gesture with one hand, and Talen stopped falling. He sprawled in midair, his limbs spraddled, his face pasty-white, and his eyes bulging with horror. "Would you take care of that, Sephrenia?" the little girl said. "I'm busy right now." Then she glared down at Talen. "You and I are going to have a talk about this, young man," she said ominously. Then she turned and continued to walk out toward the open sea.

Sephrenia murmured in Styric, her fingers weaving the spell, and Talen rose with a curious fluttering movement, flaring from side to side like a kite on a taut string as Sephrenia pulled against the force of the gravity that was trying to dash him to the rocks below. When he had reached the edge of the cliff again, he scrambled across the wind-tossed grass on his hands and knees for several yards and then collapsed, shuddering violently.

Aphrael, all unconcerned, continued her stroll across the emptiness.

"You're getting fat, Sparhawk," Kurik said critically. "You need more exercise."

Sparhawk swallowed very hard. "Do you want to talk about this?" he asked his old friend in a choked voice.

"No, not really. You're supposed to be paying attention to Aphrael right now." He looked out at the Child-Goddess with a faint smile. "She's showing off, but she's only a little girl, after all, so I guess it's sort of natural." He paused, and a note of yearning came into his voice. "How's Aslade been lately?"

"She was fine the last time I saw her. She and Elys are both living on your farm, you know."

Kurik gave him a startled look.

"Aslade thought it would be best. Your sons are all in training now, and she didn't think it made much sense for her and Elys to both be alone. They adore each other."

"That's *fine*, Sparhawk," Kurik said, almost in wonder. "That's *really* fine. I always sort of worried about what was going to happen to them after I left." He looked out at the Child-Goddess. "Pay close attention to her now, my Lord. She's coming to the hard part."

Aphrael was far out over the surging waves and she had begun to glow with a brilliant incandescence. She stopped, hardly more than a glowing spark in the distance.

"Help her, gentlemen," Sephrenia commanded. "Send all of your love to her. She needs you now."

The fiery spark rose in a graceful little arc and then shot smoothly down through the murky air toward the long, lead-grey waves rolling ponderously toward the rocky shore. Down and down she plunged, and then she cut into the sea with no hint of a splash.

Sparhawk held his breath. It seemed that the Child-Goddess stayed down for an eternity. Black spots began to appear before the big Pandion's eyes.

"*Breathe*, Sparhawk!" Kurik barked, bashing his Lord's

shoulder with his fist. "You won't do her much good if you faint."

Sparhawk blew out his breath explosively and stood gasping on the brink of the precipice.

"Idiot," Kurik muttered.

"Sorry," Sparhawk apologized. He concentrated on the little girl, and his thoughts became strongly jumbled. Aphrael was out there beneath those endlessly rolling waves certainly, but Flute was there as well—and Danae. That thought caught at his heart, and he felt suddenly icy cold.

Then that glowing spark burst up out of the sullen water. The Child-Goddess had been an incandescent white when she had made her plunge, but when she emerged from the sea, she glowed a brilliant blue. She was not alone as she rose once more into the air. Bhelliom rose with her, and the very earth seemed to shudder with its reemergence.

All glowing blue, Aphrael returned toward them, bearing that same golden box Sparhawk had cast into the sea a half-dozen years ago. The little girl reached solid ground once more. She went directly to Sparhawk and held up the gleaming golden box. "Into thy hands, for good or for ill, I deliver up the Bhelliom once more, Anakha," she intoned formally, placing the box in his hands. Then she smiled an impish little smile. "Try not to lose it again this time," she added.

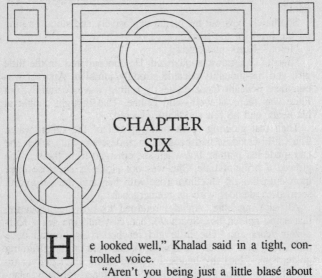

CHAPTER
SIX

H e looked well," Khalad said in a tight, controlled voice.

"Aren't you being just a little blasé about all this?" Talen asked his brother.

"Did you want me to go into hysterics?"

"You saw him, then?"

"Obviously."

"Where were you? I couldn't see you around any place."

"Lord Vanion and I were right over there," Khalad replied, pointing toward the far side of the trail. "We were told to just keep quiet and watch. We saw you all come riding up the hill. Why did you jump off the cliff like that?"

"I don't want to talk about it."

Sparhawk was not really paying very much attention to the others. He stood holding the golden box in his hands. He could feel the Bhelliom inside, and, as always, it was neither friendly nor hostile.

Flute was watching him closely. "Aren't you going to open the box, Anakha?"

"Why? I don't need Bhelliom just now, do I?"

"Don't you want to see it again?"

"I know what it looks like."

"Isn't it calling to you?"

"Yes, but I'm not listening. It always seems to complicate

things when I let it out, so let's not do that until I really need it." He turned the box over in his hands, closely examining it. Kurik's work had been meticulous, though the box was unadorned. It was just that—a box. The fact that it was made of gold was largely irrelevant. "How do I open this? When I need to, I mean? There isn't any keyhole."

"Just touch the lid with one of the rings." She was watching him very closely.

"Which one?"

"Use your own. It knows you better than Ehlana's does. Are you sure you don't feel some sort of—?"

"Some sort of what?"

"Aren't your hands aching to touch it?"

"It's not unbearable."

"Now I see why all the others in my family are so afraid of you. You aren't anything at all like other humans."

"Everybody's different in some ways, I suppose. What do we do now?"

"We can go back to the ship."

"Can you get in touch with the sailors?"

"Yes."

"Why don't you ask them to sail across the gulf and pick us up somewhere on this side? That way we won't have to ride all the way back to Jorsan again, and we'll be able to avoid any chance meetings with Rebal's enthusiasts. Some of them might be sober enough by now to recognize the fact that we're not Edomishmen."

"You're in a strange humor, Sparhawk."

"I'm a little discontented with you at the moment, to be honest about it."

"What did I do?"

"Why don't we just drop it?"

"Don't you love me anymore?" Her lower lip began to tremble.

"Of course I do, but that doesn't alter the fact that I'm put out with you just now. People we love *do* irritate us from time to time, you know."

"I'm sorry," she said in a contrite little voice.

"I'll get over it. Are we finished here? Can we mount up and start back?"

"In just a moment," she said, seeming to suddenly remember something. Her eyes narrowed and began to glint dangerously. "You!" she said, leveling a finger at Talen. "Come here!"

Talen sighed and did as he was told.

"What did you think you were doing?" she demanded.

"Well—I was afraid you'd fall."

"I wasn't the one who was going to fall, you clot! Don't you *ever* do anything like that again!"

Talen could have agreed with her. That would have been the simplest way, and it would have avoided an extended scolding. He did not, however. "No, Flute. I'm afraid it's not going to be that way. I'll jump in every time I think you're in danger." He grimaced. "It's not really my idea. I want to be sure you understand that I haven't *completely* lost my mind. It's just that I can't help myself. When I see you do something like that, I'm moving before I even think. If you're really serious about trying to keep me alive, don't do things like that when I'm around, because I'll try to stop you every single time— regardless of how stupid it is."

"Why?" she asked him intently.

"I guess it's because I love you." He shrugged.

She squealed with delight and swarmed up into his arms. "He's such a *nice* boy!" she exclaimed, covering his face with kisses.

They had gone no more than a mile when Kalten reined in sharply, filling the air with sulphurous curses.

"Kalten!" Vanion snapped. "There are ladies present!"

"Take a look behind us, my Lord," the blond Pandion said.

It was the cloud, inky black, ominous, and creeping along the ground like viscous slime.

Vanion swore and reached for his sword.

"That won't do any good, my Lord," Sparhawk told him. He reached inside his tunic and took out the gleaming box. "This might, though." He rapped the band of his ring against the box lid.

Nothing happened.

"You have to tell it to open, Sparhawk," Flute instructed.

"Open!" Sparhawk commanded, touching the ring to the box again.

The lid popped up, and Sparhawk saw the Bhelliom nestled inside. The sapphire rose was perfect, eternal, and it glowed a deep blue. It seemed strangely resentful as Sparhawk reached in and lifted it out, however. "We all know who we are," he told the stone and its unwilling inhabitants. "I'm not going to speak to you in Trollish because I know you can understand me, no matter what language I use. I want you to stop this nonsense with that cloud, and I want you to do it right *now*! When I turn around to look, your little patch of private darkness had better be gone. I don't care how you do it, but get rid of that cloud!"

The sapphire rose grew suddenly hot in his hand, and it seemed almost to writhe against his fingers. Flickers of red, green, orange, and purple, all interspersed with streaks of white, stained the azure petals of Bhelliom as the Troll-Gods trapped within the gem fought to resist. Bhelliom, however, appeared to exert some kind of overcontrol, and those ugly flickers were smothered as the jewel began to burn more brightly.

Then there was a sudden, violent jolt that numbed Sparhawk's arm to the shoulder.

"*That's* the way!" Kalten shouted with a sudden laugh.

Sparhawk turned in his saddle and saw that the cloud was gone. "What happened?"

"It sort of flopped around like a fresh-caught eel—" Kalten laughed again. "—and then it flew all to pieces. What did you do, Sparhawk? I couldn't hear what you said."

"I let our blue friend and its tenants know that the cloud was starting to irritate me. Then I sort of hinted at the fact that I get ugly when I'm irritated."

"They must have believed you."

Flute was staring at Sparhawk in open astonishment. "You broke all the rules!" she accused him.

"I do that sometimes. It's quicker to cut across the formalities once in a while."

"You're not supposed to do it that way."

"It worked, didn't it?"

"It's a question of style, Sparhawk. I'm technically in charge here, and I don't know *what* Bhelliom and the Troll-Gods are going to think of me after that."

He laughed and then gently put Bhelliom back into its box. "Nice job," he told it. They *were* going to have to work together, after all, and a little encouragement now and then never hurt. Then he firmly closed the lid. "It's time for some speculation, gentlemen," he said to the others. "What can we make of this?"

"They know where we are, for one thing," Talen offered.

"It could be the rings again," Sephrenia noted. "That's what happened last time. The cloud—and the shadow—were concentrating on Sparhawk and Ehlana right at first because they had the rings."

"Bhelliom's closed up inside the box," Sparhawk said, "and so are the Troll-Gods."

"Are they still inside the jewel?" Ulath asked him.

"Oh, yes," Sparhawk said. "I could definitely feel them when I took Bhelliom out." He looked at Aphrael, phrasing his next question carefully. There were still some things that needed to be concealed. "I've heard that a God can be in more than one place at the same time." He left it a little tentative.

"Yes," she replied.

"Does that apply to the Troll-Gods as well?"

She struggled with it. "I'm not sure," she admitted. "It's a fairly complicated business, and the Troll-Gods are quite limited."

"Does this box confine them in the same way that chain-mail pouch did, back in Zemoch?"

She shook her head. "It's different. When they're encased in gold that way, they don't know where they are."

"Does that make a difference?"

"You have to know where you are before you can go someplace else."

"I'll take your word for it." He made a face. "I think we may have blundered again," he said sourly.

"How so?" Bevier asked him.

"We don't really have any absolute proof that the Troll-Gods are in league with our enemy. If they're trapped inside this box with Bhelliom and can't get out, they couldn't be, could they?"

"That *was* Ghworg in the mountains of Atan," Ulath insisted. "That means that *he's* out and about, at least."

"Are you sure, Ulath? Those peasants around the bonfire were convinced that the big fellow in the ancient armor was Incetes, too, you know."

"All the evidence points to it, Sparhawk. Everything we've seen this time is just like it was last time, and it was the Troll-Gods then, wasn't it?"

"I'm not even positive about that anymore."

"Well, *something* had to have enough authority over the Trolls to make them migrate from Thalesia to the north coast of Atan."

"Just how smart do you have to be in order to be a Troll?

I'm not saying that it was something as crude as the hoax Rebal foisted off on those peasants, but . . ." Sparhawk left it hanging.

"That would be a fairly complex hoax, dear one," Sephrenia murmured.

"But not quite impossible, little mother. I'll drop the whole line of thought if you'll tell me that what I'm suggesting is impossible."

"Don't throw it away just yet," she said, her face troubled.

"Aphrael," Sparhawk said, "will this gold box keep our friend out there from being able to locate Bhelliom?"

She nodded. "The gold shields it. He can't hear it or feel it, so he can't just move toward the sound or the sense of it."

"And if I put Ehlana's ring in there as well? Would the box shield that, too?"

"Yes, but your own ring's still out in the open where he can feel its location."

"One thing at a time." He touched his ring to the lid of the box. "Open," he said.

The latch clicked, and the lid raised slightly.

Sparhawk removed Ehlana's ring from his finger and put it inside the box. "*You* look after it for a while," he told the Bhelliom.

"Please don't do that, Sparhawk," Vanion told him with a pained look.

"Do what?"

"Talk to it like that. You make it sound like a real being."

"Sorry, Vanion. It helps a little if I think of it that way. Bhelliom definitely has its own personality." He closed the lid and felt the latch click.

"Ah—Flute?" Khalad said a bit tentatively.

"Yes?"

"Is it the box that keeps Bhelliom hidden? Or is it the fact that the box is made out of gold?"

"It's the gold, Khalad. There's something about gold that muffles Bhelliom and hides it."

"And it works on Queen Ehlana's ring as well?"

She nodded. "I can't hear or feel a thing." She stretched her open palm out toward the box Sparhawk was holding. "Nothing at all," she confirmed. "I can feel *his* ring, though."

"Put a golden glove on him." Kalten shrugged.

"How much money did you bring along, Sir Kalten?" Khalad asked. "Gold's expensive, you know." He squinted at

Sparhawk's ring. "I don't have to cover his whole hand," he said, "just the ring itself."

"I'll have to be able to get at it in a hurry, Khalad," Sparhawk cautioned.

"Let me work on it. Does anyone have a gold florin? That would be about the right size."

They all opened their purses.

Kalten looked around hopefully, then sighed. He reached into his purse. "You owe me a gold florin, Sparhawk," he said, handing the coin to Khalad.

"I'm in your debt, Kalten," Sparhawk smiled.

"You certainly are—one gold florin's worth. Shall we move on? It's starting to get chilly out here."

The wind had come up, gusty at first, but blowing steadily stronger. They followed the trail on down the slope until they were riding along the upper edge of a long sandy beach with the wind screaming and tearing at them and the salt spray stinging their faces.

"This is more than just a gale!" Ulath shouted over the screaming wind. "I think we've got a hurricane brewing!"

"Isn't it too early for hurricanes?" Kalten shouted.

"It is in Eosia," Ulath shouted back.

The shrieking of the wind grew louder, and they rode with their cloaks pulled tightly about them.

"We'd better get in out of this," Vanion yelled. "There's a ruined farmstead just ahead." He squinted through the driving spray. "It's got stone walls, so it should give us some kind of shelter from the wind."

They pushed their horses into a gallop and reached the ruin in a few minutes. The moldering buildings were half-buried in weeds, and the windows of the unroofed structures seemed to stare down from the walls like blind eyes. The house had completely tumbled in, so Sparhawk and the others dismounted in the yard and led their nervous horses into what had evidently been the barn. The floor was littered with the rotting remains of the roof, and there were bird droppings in the corners.

"How long does a hurricane usually last?" Vanion asked.

"A day or two," Ulath shrugged. "Three at the most."

"I wouldn't make any wagers on *this* one," Bevier said. "It came up just a little too quickly to suit me, and it's forced us to take shelter. We're pinned down in these ruins, you know."

"He's right," Berit agreed. "Don't we almost have to assume that somebody's raised this storm to delay us?"

Kalten gave him a flat, unfriendly stare, a fair indication that he had not yet shaken off his suspicions about the young man and Queen Ehlana's maid.

"I don't think it's going to be much of a problem," Ulath said. "As soon as we get back on board that ship, we'll be able to outrun the hurricane."

Aphrael was shaking her head.

"What's wrong?" he asked her.

"That ship wasn't built to ride out a hurricane. As a matter of fact, I've already sent it back to where it came from."

"Without even telling us?" Vanion objected.

"*My* decision, Vanion. The ship's no good to us in this kind of weather, so there was no point in putting the crew in danger."

"It seemed well-made to me," Ulath objected. "The builders must have taken high winds into account when they designed her."

She shook her head. "The wind doesn't blow where that ship came from."

"There are winds everywhere, Flute," he pointed out. "There's no place on this entire world where the wind doesn't blow now and—" He broke off and stared at her. "Where *does* that ship come from?"

"That's really none of your business, Sir Knight. I can bring it back after the storm passes."

"*If* it passes," Kalten added. "And I wouldn't be at all surprised that when it does, this broken-down barn's going to be surrounded by several thousand armed fanatics."

They all looked at each other.

"I think maybe we'd better move on, storm or no storm," Vanion said. He looked at Flute. "Can you still—? I mean, will this wind interfere?"

"It won't make it any easier," she admitted glumly.

"I don't want you to hurt yourself," Sephrenia told her.

Flute waved her hand as if brushing something aside. "Don't worry about me, Sephrenia."

"Don't try to hide things from me, young lady." Sephrenia's tone was stern. "I know exactly what all this wind's going to do to you."

"And *I* know exactly what trying to carry it around will do to our mysterious friend out there. Trying to chase us with a hurricane on his back will exhaust *him* far more than carrying ten people on horseback will exhaust *me*—and I'm faster than he is. They don't call me the nimble Goddess for nothing, you know. I can run even faster than Talen, if I have to. Where would you like to go, Lord Vanion?"

The preceptor looked around at them. "Back to Jorsan?"

"It's probably as good as anyplace in a hurricane," Kalten said. "At least the beds are dry."

"And the beer is wet?" Ulath smiled.

"That *did* sort of enter into my thinking," Kalten admitted.

The wind shrieked around the corners of the building, but the inn was a sturdy stone structure, and the windows had stout shutters. Sparhawk chafed at the delay, but there was no help for it.

Sephrenia had put Flute to bed immediately upon their return to the inn and she hovered over the little girl protectively. "She's really concerned," Vanion reported. "I guess there *are* limits after all. Flute's trying to make light of it, but I know exhaustion when I see it."

"She won't *die*, will she?" Talen asked in a shocked voice.

"She *can't* die, Talen," Vanion replied. "She can be destroyed, but she can't die."

"What's the difference?"

"I'm not sure," Vanion admitted. "I *am* sure that she's very, very tired. We shouldn't have let her do that." He looked around the hallway outside the room where Sephrenia was tending the weary little Goddess. "Where's Kalten?" he asked.

"He and Ulath are down in the taproom, my Lord," Bevier replied.

"I should have known, I guess. One of you might remind them that I won't go easy on them if they're unwell when we set out, though."

They went on downstairs again and periodically checked the weather outside. If anything, the wind actually began to blow harder.

Sparhawk finally went back up and knocked lightly on the door to Sephrenia's room. "Could I have a word with Flute?" he asked when his tutor came to the door.

"No. Absolutely not," she whispered. "I just got her to sleep." She came out into the hallway, closed the door, and set her back protectively against it.

"I'm not going to hurt her, Sephrenia."

"You can make safe wagers on that all over Daresia," she told him with a steely glint in her eyes. "What did you want to ask her?"

"Could I use Bhelliom to break up this storm?"

"Probably."

"Why don't I do that then?"

"Did you want to destroy Jorsan? And kill everybody in town?"

He stared at her.

"You have no real idea of the kind of forces involved in weather, have you, Sparhawk?"

"Well, sort of," he said.

"No, I don't think you do, dear one. Whoever raised this hurricane is very powerful, and he knows what he's doing, but his hurricane is still a natural force. You could use Bhelliom to break it up, certainly, but if you do, you'll release all that pent-up force at one time and in one place. You wouldn't even be able to find pieces of Jorsan after the dust settled."

"Maybe I'd better drop the idea."

"I would. Now run along. I have to keep watch over Aphrael."

Sparhawk went back down the hallway feeling a little like a small boy who had just been sent to his room.

Ulath was coming up the stairs. "Have you got a minute, Sparhawk?" he asked.

"Of course."

"I think you'd better keep a close eye on Kalten."

"Oh?"

"He's beginning to have some murderous thoughts about Berit."

"Is it getting out of hand?"

"You knew about it? About the feelings he has for your wife's maid?"

Sparhawk nodded.

"The more he drinks, the worse it's going to get, you know—and there's nothing else to do during this storm *except* drink. Is there any real substance to those suspicions of his?"

"No. He just pulled them out of the air. The girl's very, very fond of him, actually."

"I sort of thought she might be. Berit was already having enough trouble with the emperor's wife without going in search of more. Does Kalten do this very often? Fall desperately in love, I mean?"

"So far as I know, it's the first time. He's always sort of taken affection where he could find it."

"That's the safest way," Ulath agreed. "But since he's waited so long, this is hitting him very hard. We'd better do what we can to keep him and Berit apart until we get back to Matherion and Alean has the chance to straighten it out."

Khalad came down the hallway to join them. Sparhawk's squire had a slightly disgusted look on his face. He held up Kalten's florin. "This isn't going to work, Sparhawk," he said. "I could cover the stone with it easily enough, but it'd probably take you a half hour to pry it open again so that you could use the ring. I'm going to have to come up with something else. You'd better give me the ring. I'm going to have to go talk with a goldsmith, and I'll need precise measurements."

Sparhawk felt a great reluctance to part with the ring. "Can't you—just?"

Khalad shook his head. "Whatever the goldsmith and I decide on will have to be fitted anyway. I guess it gets down to how much you trust me at this point, Sparhawk."

Sparhawk sighed. "You *had* to put it on that basis, didn't you, Khalad?"

"I thought it would be the quickest way, my Lord." Khalad held out his hand, and Sparhawk removed the ring and gave it to him. "Thank you." Khalad smiled. "Your faith in me is very touching."

"Well said," Ulath murmured.

Later, after Sparhawk and Ulath had carried Kalten upstairs and put him to bed, they all gathered in the common room for supper. Sparhawk spoke briefly with the innkeeper and had Sephrenia's meal taken upstairs to her.

"Where's Talen?" Bevier asked, looking around.

"He said he was going out for a breath of fresh air," Berit replied.

"In a *hurricane*?"

"I think he's just restless."

"Or he wants to go steal something," Ulath added.

The door to the inn banged open, and the wind blew Talen inside. He was wearing doublet and hose under his cloak, and a rapier at his side. The weapon did not seem to encumber him very much. He set his back against the door and strained to push it shut. He was soaked through, and his face was streaming water. He was grinning broadly, however. "I just solved a mystery," he laughed, coming across to where they sat.

"Oh?" Ulath asked.

"What would it be worth to you gentlemen to know Rebal's real identity?"

"How did you manage *that*?" Berit demanded.

"Sheer luck, actually. I was outside looking around. The wind blew me down a narrow lane and pinned me up against the door of the shop at the end. I thought I'd step inside to get my breath, and the first thing I saw in there was a familiar face. Our mysterious Rebal's a respected shopkeeper here in Jorsan. He told me so himself. He doesn't look nearly as impressive when he's wearing an apron."

"A shopkeeper?" Bevier asked incredulously.

"Yes indeed, Sir Knight—one of the pillars of the community, to hear him tell it. He's even a member of the town council."

"Did you manage to get his name?" Vanion asked.

"Of course, my Lord. He introduced himself just as soon as the wind blew me through the door. His name's Amador. I even bought something from him just to keep him talking."

"What does he deal in?" Berit asked.

Talen reached inside his tunic and drew out a bright pink strip of cloth, wet and somewhat bedraggled. "Isn't it pretty?" he said. "I think I'll dry it out and give it to Flute."

"You're not serious." Vanion laughed. "Is that *really* what he sells?"

"May muh tongue turn green iffin it ain't, yer Preceptorship," the boy replied, imitating Caalador's dialect. "The man here in Edom who has all the Tamuls trembling in their boots is a ribbon clerk. Can you imagine that?" And he collapsed in a chair, laughing uproariously.

"How does it work?" Sparhawk asked the next day, turning the ring over and looking at the underside.

"It's the mounting of one of those rings people use when they want to poison other people's food or drink," Khalad replied. "I had the goldsmith take it off the original ring and mount it on yours so that the cover fits over the ruby. There's a little hinge on this side of the mounting and a latch on the other. All you have to do is touch the latch—right here." He pointed at a tiny lever half-concealed under the massive-looking setting. "The hinge has a little spring, so this gold cap pops open." He touched the lever, and the half globe covering the ruby snapped up to reveal the stone. "Are you *sure* that the ring will work if you're only touching Bhelliom with the band? With that cap in the way, touching the stone to anything might be a little tricky."

"The band does the job," Sparhawk replied. "This is very clever, Khalad."

"Thank you. I made the goldsmith wash out all the poison before we installed it on your ring."

"The old ring had been used?"

"Oh, yes. One of the heirs of the Edomish noblewoman who'd previously owned it sold it to the goldsmith after she died. I guess she had a lot of enemies. She did at first, anyway." Khalad chuckled. "The goldsmith was very disappointed with me. He *really* wanted to be alone with your ring for a while. That ruby's worth quite a lot. I didn't think Bhelliom would respond to a piece of red glass, though, so I kept a close eye on him. You'd probably better find out if the ring will still open the box, just to be on the safe side. If it doesn't, I'll go back to the goldsmith's shop and start cutting off his fingers. After he loses two or three, he'll remember where he hid the real ruby; it's hard to do finely detailed work when you don't have all ten fingers. But I told him I'd do that right at the outset, so we can probably trust his integrity."

"You're a ruthless sort of fellow."

"I just wanted to avoid misunderstandings. After we make sure that the ring still opens the box, you'd better take it to Flute and find out if the gold's thick enough to shield the ruby. If it isn't, I'll take it back to the goldsmith and have him pile more gold on that cap. We can keep doing that until it does what we want it to do."

"You're very practical, Khalad."

"*Somebody* in this group has to be."

"What did you do with Kalten's florin?"

"I used it to pay the goldsmith. It covered *part* of the cost. You still owe me for the rest, though."

"I'm going to be in debt to everybody before we get home."

"That's all right, Sparhawk." Khalad grinned. "We all know that you're good for it."

"*That* does it!" Sparhawk said angrily after he had taken a quick look out the door of the common room. It was two days later, and they had all just come downstairs for breakfast. "Let's get ready to leave."

"I can't bring the ship back in this storm, Sparhawk," Flute told him. The little girl still looked wan, but she was obviously recovering.

"We'll have to go overland, then. We're sitting here like ducks in a row just waiting for our friend out there to gather his forces. We *have* to move."

"It's going to take months to reach Matherion if we go overland, Sparhawk," Khalad objected. "Flute's not well enough to speed up the trip."

"I'm not *that* sick, Khalad," Flute said. "I'm just a little tired, that's all."

"Do you have to do it all by yourself?" Sparhawk asked her.

"I didn't quite follow that."

"If one of your cousins happened along, could he help you?"

She frowned.

"Let's say that you were making the decisions, and he was just lending you the muscle."

"It's a nice idea, Sparhawk," Sephrenia said, "but we don't *have* one of Aphrael's cousins along."

"No, but we've got Bhelliom."

"I knew it would happen," Bevier groaned. "The accursed stone's unhinged Sparhawk's mind. He thinks he's a God."

"No, Bevier." Sparhawk smiled. "I'm not a God, but I have access to something very close to one. When I put those rings on, Bhelliom has to do what I tell it to do. That's not *exactly* like being a God, but it's close enough. Let's have breakfast, and then the rest of you can gather our belongings and get them packed on the horses. Aphrael and I'll hammer out the details of how we're going to work this."

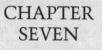

CHAPTER
SEVEN

The wind was screaming through the streets of Jorsan, driving torrents of rain before it. Sparhawk and his friends wrapped themselves tightly in their cloaks, bowed their heads into the wind, and plodded grimly into the teeth of the hurricane.

The city gates were unguarded, and the party rode out into open country where the wind, unimpeded, savaged them all the more. Speech was impossible, so Sparhawk merely pointed toward the muddy road that led off toward Korvan, fifty leagues to the north.

The road curved around behind a low hill a mile or so outside of town, and Sparhawk reined in. "Nobody can see us now," he shouted over the howling wind. "Let's try this and see what happens." He reached inside his tunic for the golden box.

Berit came galloping up from the rear. "We've got riders coming up from behind!" he shouted, wiping the rain out of his face.

"Following us?" Kalten demanded.

Berit spread his hands uncertainly.

"How many?" Ulath asked.

"Twenty-five or thirty, Sir Ulath. I couldn't see them very clearly in all this rain, but it looked to me as if they were wearing armor of some sort."

"Good," Kalten grated harshly. "There's not much fun in killing amateurs."

"What do you think?" Sparhawk asked Vanion.

"Let's have a look. They might not be interested in us at all."

The two turned and rode back along the muddy road a couple hundred yards.

The riders coming up from behind had slowed to a walk. They were rough-looking men wrapped in furs and armed for the most part with bronze-tipped spears. The one in the lead wore a vast, bristling beard and an archaic-looking helmet surmounted with a set of deer antlers.

"That's it," Sparhawk said shortly. "They're definitely following us. Let's get the others and deal with this."

They rode back to where their friends had taken some small shelter on the lee side of a pine grove. "We stayed in Jorsan too long," Sparhawk told them. "It gave Rebal time to call in help. The men behind us are bronze-age warriors."

"Like the Lamorks who attacked us outside Demos?" Ulath asked.

"Right," Sparhawk said. "These are most likely followers of Incetes rather than Drychtnath, but it all amounts to the same thing."

"Could you pick out the leader?" Ulath asked.

"He's right up front," Vanion replied.

"That makes it easier, then."

Vanion gave him a questioning look.

"This has happened before," Sparhawk explained. "We don't know exactly why, but when the leader falls, the rest of them vanish."

"Couldn't we just hide back among these trees?" Sephrenia asked.

"I wouldn't want to chance that," Vanion told her. "We know where they are now. If we let them get out of sight, they could circle back and ambush us. Let's deal with this here and now."

"We're wasting time," Kalten said abruptly. "Let's get on with it."

"Khalad," Sparhawk said to his squire, "take Sephrenia and the children back into the trees a ways. Try to stay out of sight."

"Children?" Talen objected.

"Just do as you're told," Khalad told him, "and don't get any ideas about trying out that rapier just yet."

The knights turned and rode back along the muddy track to face their pursuers.

"Are they alone?" Bevier asked. "I mean, can anybody make out the one who might have raised them?"

"We can sort that out after we kill the fellow with the antlers," Kalten growled. "Once all the rest vanish, whoever's responsible for this is going to be left standing out in the rain all by himself."

"There's no point in waiting," Vanion told them, his voice bleak. "Let's get at it. I'm starting to get wet."

They all pushed their cloaks out of the way to clear their sword arms, pulled on the plain steel helmets which had been hanging from their saddlebows, and buckled on their shields.

"I'll do it," Kalten told Sparhawk, forcing his mount against Faran's shoulder. There was a kind of suppressed fury in Kalten's voice and a reckless set to his shoulders. "Let's go!" he bellowed, drawing his sword.

They charged.

The warriors from the ninth century recoiled momentarily as the mail-shirted Church Knights thundered toward them with the hooves of their war-horses hurling great clots of mud out behind them.

Bronze-age weaponry and ancient tactics were no match for steel mail shirts and contemporary swords and axes, and the small, scrubby horses of the dark ages were scarcely more than ponies. Kalten crashed into the forefront of the pursuers with his companions fanned out behind him in a kind of wedge formation. The blond Pandion stood up in his stirrups, swinging his sword in vast, powerful strokes. Kalten was normally a highly skilled and cool-headed warrior, but he seemed enraged today, taking chances he should not have taken, overextending his strokes, and swinging his sword much harder than was prudent. The round bronze shields of the men who faced him barely slowed his strokes as he chopped his way through the press toward the bearded man in the antlered helmet. Sparhawk and the others, startled by his reckless charge, followed him, cutting down any who tried to attack him from the rear.

The bearded man bellowed an archaic war cry and spurred his horse forward, swinging a huge, bronze-headed war ax.

Almost disdainfully, Kalten brushed the ax-stroke aside with his shield and delivered a vast overhand stroke with his sword, swinging the weapon with all his strength. His sword sheared down through the hastily raised bronze shield, and half of the gleaming oval spun away, carrying the bearded man's forearm with it. Kalten swung again, and his sword struck the top of the antler-adorned helmet, gashing down into the enemy's head in a sudden spray of blood and brains. The dead man was hurled from his saddle by the force of the blow, and his followers wavered like mirages and vanished.

One mounted man, however, remained. The black-cloaked figure of Rebal was suddenly quite alone as the ancient warriors who had been drawn up protectively around him were abruptly no longer there.

Kalten advanced on him, his bloody sword half-raised and death in his ice-blue eyes.

Rebal shrieked, wheeled his horse, and fled back into the storm, desperately flogging at his mount.

"*Kalten!*" Vanion roared as the knight spurred his horse to pursue the fleeing man. "*Stop!*"

"But—"

"*Stay where you are!*"

Still caught in the grip of that reckless fury, Kalten started to object.

"That's an order, Sir Knight! Put up your sword!"

"Yes, my Lord," Kalten replied sullenly, sliding his blood-smeared blade back into its sheath.

"Take that weapon back out!" Vanion bellowed at him. "Wipe it off before you sheathe it!"

"Sorry, Lord Vanion. I forgot."

"*Forgot?* What do you mean, 'forgot'? Are you some half-grown puppy? *Clean* that sword, Sir Knight! I want to see it shining before you put it away!"

"Yes, my Lord," Kalten mumbled.

"*What did you say?*"

"*Yes, my Lord!*" Kalten shouted it this time.

"That's a little better."

"Thanks, Vanion," Sparhawk murmured.

"I'll deal with you later, Sparhawk!" Vanion barked. "Making him see to his equipment was *your* responsibility. You're supposed to be a leader of men, not a goatherd." The preceptor looked around. "All right," he said crisply, "let's form up and go back. Smartly, gentlemen, smartly. We're soldiers of God. Let's try to at least *look* as if we knew what we were doing!"

* * *

There was some slight shelter from the wind back in among the trees. Vanion led the knights through the grove to rejoin Sephrenia, Khalad, and the "children."

"Is everyone all right?" Sephrenia asked quickly.

"We don't have any *visible* wounds, little mother," Sparhawk replied.

She gave him a questioning look.

"Lord Vanion was in fine voice." Ulath grinned. "He was a little dissatisfied with a couple of us, and he spoke to us about it—firmly."

"That will do, Sir Knight," Vanion said.

"Yes, my Lord."

"Were you able to identify whoever it was who raised that party?" Khalad asked Sparhawk.

"No. Rebal was there, but we didn't see anybody else."

"How was the fight?"

"You should have seen it, Khalad," Berit said enthusiastically. "Sir Kalten was absolutely stupendous!"

Kalten glared at him.

Sephrenia gave the two of them a shrewd look. "We can talk about all this after we get clear of the storm," she told them. "Are you ready, Sparhawk?"

"In a moment," he replied. He reached inside his tunic, took out the box, and commanded it to open. He put on Ehlana's ring and lifted the Bhelliom out.

"Here," Sephrenia said. She lifted Flute, and Sparhawk took the little girl into his arms.

"How do we go about this?" he asked her.

"Once we get started, I'll be speaking through your lips," she replied. "You won't understand what I'm saying because the language will be strange to you."

"Some obscure Styric dialect?"

"No, Sparhawk, not Styric. It's quite a bit older than that. Just relax. I'll guide you through this. Give me the box. When Bhelliom moves from one place to another, everything sort of shivers. I don't think our friend out there will be able to locate Bhelliom again immediately, so if you put it—and your wife's ring—back in the box immediately and snap the cover down on your own ring, he won't have any idea of where we've gone. Now, hold Bhelliom in both hands and let it know who you are."

"It should know already."

"Remind it, Sparhawk, and speak to it in Trollish. Let's observe the formalities." She nestled back into the protective circle of his mailed arms.

Sparhawk lifted Bhelliom, making sure that the bands of both rings were firmly in contact with it. "Blue-Rose," he said to it in Trollish, "I am Sparhawk-from-Elenia. Do you know me?"

The azure glow which had bathed his hands hardened, became like fresh-forged steel. Sparhawk's relationship with the Bhelliom was ambiguous, and the flower-gem had no real reason to be fond of him.

"Tell it who you really are, Sparhawk," Flute suggested. "Make certain that it knows you."

"Blue-Rose," Sparhawk said again, once more in the hideous language of the Trolls, "I am Anakha, and I wear the rings. Do you know me?"

The Bhelliom gave a little lurch as he spoke the fatal name, and some of the steel went out of its petals.

"It's a start," he muttered. "What now?"

"Now it's my turn," she replied. "Relax, Sparhawk. Let me into your mind."

It was a strange sort of process. Sparhawk felt almost as if his own will had been suspended as the Child-Goddess gently, even lovingly, took his mind into her two small hands. The voice that came from his lips was strangely soft, and the language it spoke was hauntingly familiar, skirting the very outer edges of his understanding.

Then the world seemed to blur around him and it faded momentarily into a kind of luminous twilight. Then the blur was gone, and the sun was shining. It was no longer raining, and the wind had dropped to a gentle breeze.

"What an astonishing idea!" Aphrael exclaimed. "I never even *thought* of that! Put the Bhelliom away, Sparhawk. Quickly."

Sparhawk put the jewel and Ehlana's ring back into the box and snapped down the cover on his own ring. Then he turned and looked toward the south. There was an intensely dark line of cloud low on the horizon. Then he looked north again and saw a fair-sized town at the bottom of the hill, a pleasant-looking town with red tile roofs glowing in the autumn sunshine. "Is that Korvan?" he asked tentatively.

"Well, of *course* it is," Flute replied with an airy little toss of her head. "Isn't that where you said you wanted to go?"

"We made good time," Ulath observed blandly.

Sephrenia suddenly laughed. "We wanted to test our friend's stamina," she said. "Now we'll find out just how much endurance he has. If he wants to keep chasing us, he's going to have to pick up his hurricane and run along behind us just as fast as he possibly can."

"Oh, this is going to be *fun*!" Flute exclaimed, clapping her hands together delightedly. "I'd never have *believed* we could jump so far."

Kalten squinted up toward the bright autumn sun. "I make it just a little before noon. Why don't we ride down into Korvan and have an early lunch. I worked up quite an appetite back there."

"It might not be a bad idea, Sparhawk," Vanion agreed. "The situation's changed now, so we might want to think our plans through and see if we want to modify them."

Sparhawk nodded. He bumped Faran's flanks with his heels, and they started down the hill toward Korvan. "You seemed surprised," he murmured into Flute's ear.

"Surprised? I was stunned."

"What did it do?"

"You wouldn't really understand, Father. Do you remember how the Troll-God Ghnomb moved you across northern Pelosia?"

"He sort of froze time, didn't he?"

She nodded. "I've always done it a different way, but I'm more sophisticated than Ghnomb is. Bhelliom does it in still another way—much simpler, actually. Ghnomb and I are different, but we're both part of this world, so the terrain's very important to us. It gives us a sense of permanence and location. Bhelliom doesn't appear to need reference points. It seems to just think of another place, and it's there."

"Could you do it like that?"

She pursed her lips. "I don't think so." She sighed. "It's a little humiliating to admit it, but Bhelliom's far wiser than I am."

"But not nearly as loveable."

"Thank you, kind sir."

Sparhawk suddenly thought of something. "Is Danae at Matherion?"

"Of course."

"How's your mother?"

"She's well. She and the thieves are very busy trying to get their hands on some documents that are hidden somewhere in the Ministry of the Interior."

"Are things still under control there?"

"For the moment, yes. I know I've teased you about it a few times, but it's very hard to be in two places at the same time. Danae's sleeping a great deal, so I'm missing a lot of what's going on there. Mother's a little worried. She thinks Danae might be sick."

"Don't worry her *too* much."

"I won't, Father."

They rode into Korvan and found a respectable-looking inn. Ulath had a word or two with the innkeeper, and they were all escorted into a private dining room in the back where the golden sunlight streamed in through the windows to set the oaken tables and benches to glowing. "Can you keep anyone who might be curious from eavesdropping on us, little mother?" Sparhawk asked.

"How many times do you have to ask that question before you know the answer?" she asked with a weary sigh.

"Just making sure, that's all."

They removed their cloaks, stacked their weapons in a corner, and sat down at the table.

A squinty-eyed, slatternly serving-girl came in and told them what the kitchen had prepared for the day.

Sephrenia shook her head. "Tell her, Vanion."

"The lady and I—and the little girl—will have lamb," he said firmly. "We don't much care for pork."

"The cook ain't fixed no lamb," the girl whined.

"You'd better tell him to get started, then."

"He ain't gonna like it."

"He doesn't *have* to like it. Tell him that if we don't get lamb, we'll take our money to another inn. The owner of the place wouldn't like that very much, would he?"

The girl's face became set, and she stormed out.

"*That's* the Vanion we came to know and love when we were boys." Kalten laughed. The fight that morning seemed to have improved his temper.

Vanion unfolded his map. "We've got a fairly substantial road going east," he said, running his finger along the line stretching across the map. "It crosses Edom and then goes on through Cynesga. We'll cross the border into Tamul proper at Sarna." He looked at Flute. "How long a jump can Bhelliom make at one time?"

"Would you like to pay a visit to the moon, Lord Vanion?" She frowned. "There's a drawback, though. Bhelliom makes a very distinctive sound when it does something. It probably doesn't even know that it's doing it, but it *does* sort of announce its location. We might be able to teach it how to conceal itself, but it's going to take time."

"And that raises another point as well," Sephrenia added. "Sparhawk's holding Bhelliom's power, but he doesn't know how to use it yet."

"Thanks," Sparhawk said dryly.

"I'm sorry, dear one, but you don't. Every time you've ever picked it up, either Aphrael or I have had to walk you through it step by step. We're definitely going to need some time. We have to teach Bhelliom how to be quiet, and we have to teach you how to use it without having someone hold your hand."

"I love you, too, Sephrenia."

She smiled fondly. "You're holding tremendous power in your hands, Sparhawk, but it's not of much use if all you know how to do is wave it around like a battle flag. I don't think we should rush back to Matherion immediately. That story you cooked up for Ehlana will explain our absence for at least two or three more weeks. We'll want to avoid the traps and ambushes our enemies are going to lay for us along the way, of course." She paused. "They might even be useful. They'll give you something to practice on."

"Jump around," Ulath grunted.

"*Will* you stop that, Ulath?" she snapped at him.

"Sorry, Sephrenia. It's a habit of mine. After I think my way through something, I just blurt out the conclusion. The intermediate steps aren't usually very interesting. Our friends out there have been raising random disturbances to keep the Atans running back and forth across the continent—werewolves here, vampires there, Shining Ones off in that direction and antique armies in this. There's no real purpose to it all except to confuse the imperial authorities. We could steal a page right out of their book, you know. They can hear and feel Bhelliom— particularly when it's doing something noisy. I gather that there's no real limit to how far it can jump at one time, so let's just say that Sparhawk wants to see what the weather's like in Darsas. He has Bhelliom pick him up by the scruff of the neck and drop him down in the square outside King Alberen's palace. He stays there for about a half hour—long enough for the other side to smell him out—then he hops across the continent to Beresa in southern Arjuna and stays long enough to make his presence known *there*. Then he goes to Sarsos, then to Jura in southern Daconia, then back to Cimmura to say hello to Platime—all in the space of one afternoon. He'd get all sorts of practice using Bhelliom, and by the time the sun went down, they wouldn't know *where* he was or where he was going to go next. To make it even more fun, our mysterious friend out there wouldn't know which of these little jumps was the significant one, so he'd almost have to follow along."

"Carrying that hurricane on his back every step of the way," Kalten added. "Ulath, you're brilliant."

"Yes," the blond-braided Thalesian agreed with becoming modesty, "I know."

"I like it," Vanion approved. "What do you think, Sephrenia?"

"It *would* give Sparhawk and Bhelliom the chance to get to know each other," she agreed, "and that's basically what we need here. The better they know each other, the better they'll be able to work together. I'm sorry, Sir Ulath. Blurt out conclusions anytime you feel like it."

"All right then," Vanion said in his most businesslike fashion, "When Sparhawk's off on one of his little excursions, the rest of us will be sort of invisible—well, not really invisible, but if Bhelliom's not with us, our friend won't be able to hear us or feel us, will he?"

"Probably not," Flute agreed. "Even if he could, Sparhawk will be making so much noise that he won't really pay much attention to you."

"Good. Let's say that Sparhawk hops up to Darsas and rattles all the windows there. Then he hops back here, picks *us* up, and puts down in—" He frowned at his map. "In Cyron on the Cynesgan border." He stabbed his finger down on the chart. "Then he hops around to several other places, leaving Bhelliom and the rings out in the open so that our friend knows where he is each time. Then he rejoins us at Cyron and boxes up Bhelliom again. By that time, our friend will be so confused he won't know *where* we are."

"Pay close attention, Sparhawk," Kalten grinned. "That's the way a preceptor's *supposed* to think."

Sparhawk grunted. Then he thought of something. "I want to talk with you for a moment when we leave," he told his blond friend quietly.

"Am I in trouble?"

"Not yet, but you're working on it."

The slatternly serving-girl brought in their meal, glowering at Vanion as she did, and Sparhawk and his friends began to eat.

They did not linger after lunch, but rose immediately and trooped out.

"What's your problem?" Kalten asked as he and Sparhawk trailed along behind the others.

"Quit trying to get yourself killed."

"What are you talking about?"

"Don't be coy, Kalten. I saw what you were doing this morning. Don't you realize how transparent you are to people who know you?"

"You're unwholesomely clever, Sparhawk," the blond Pandion accused.

"It's a character defect of mine. I've got enough to worry about already. Don't add *this* to it."

"It's such a perfect solution."

"For a nonexistent problem, you jackass. Alean's had her eyes on you ever since we left Chyrellos. She's not going to throw all that effort away. It's *you* she's after, Kalten, not Berit. If you don't stop this nonsense, I'll take you back to Demos and have you confined in the motherhouse."

"How do you propose to do that?"

"I've got this blue friend here, remember?" Sparhawk patted the bulge in the front of his tunic. "I can pick you up by the hair, deposit you in Demos, and be back before Vanion even gets into his saddle."

"That's not fair."

"Now you're starting to sound like Talen. I'm not trying to be fair. I'm trying to keep you from killing yourself. I want your oath."

"No."

"Demos is nice this time of year. You'll enjoy it. You can spend your days in prayer."

Kalten swore at him.

"You've got *some* of the words right, Kalten. Now just put them together into a proper oath. Believe me, my friend, you're not going to go one step farther with us until you give me your oath to stop all this nonsense."

"I swear," Kalten muttered.

"Not good enough. Let's make it nice and formal. I want it

to make an impression on you. You've got this tendency to overlook things if they aren't all spelled out."

"Do you want me to sign something in my own blood?" Kalten demanded acidly.

"It's a thought, but I don't have any parchment handy. I'll accept your verbal oath—for the time being. I may change my mind later, though, so keep your veins nice and loose and your dagger sharp."

"Sparhawk?" Ambassador Fontan exclaimed. "What are you doing in Darsas?" The ancient Tamul diplomat stared at the big Pandion in astonishment.

"Just passing through, your Excellency," Sparhawk replied. "May I come in?"

"By all means, my boy." Fontan opened his door wide, and Sparhawk and Flute entered the crimson-carpeted study of the Tamul embassy.

"You're looking well, your Royal Highness." Fontan smiled at the little girl. Then he looked at her more closely. "I'm sorry," he apologized to her. "I mistook you for Prince Sparhawk's daughter. You resemble her very much."

"We're distantly related, your Excellency," Flute told him without turning a hair.

"Has word reached you about what happened in Matherion a few weeks ago, your Excellency?" Sparhawk asked, tucking the Bhelliom back into his inside tunic pocket.

"Just yesterday," Fontan replied. "Is the emperor safe?"

Sparhawk nodded. "My wife's looking after him. Our time's limited, your Excellency, so I'm not going to be able to explain everything. Are you cosmopolitan enough to accept the notion that the Styrics have some very unusual capabilities?"

Fontan smiled faintly. "Prince Sparhawk, a man my age is willing to accept almost anything. After the initial shock of astonishment that comes each morning when I wake up and discover that I'm still alive, I can face the day with an open mind."

"Good. My friends and I left Korvan down in Edom about an hour ago. They're riding on toward Cyron on the border, but I came here to have a word with you."

"An *hour* ago?"

"Just take it on faith, your Excellency," Flute told him. "It's one of those Styric things Sparhawk was talking about."

"I'm not certain how much your messenger told you," Sparhawk continued, "but it's urgent that all of the Atan garrison commanders in the empire know that the Ministry of the Interior's not to be trusted. Minister Kolata's working for the other side."

"I never liked that man," Fontan said. He gave Sparhawk a speculative look. "This message is hardly so earthshaking that it would move you to violate a whole cluster of natural laws, Sparhawk. What are you *really* doing in Darsas?"

"Casting false trails, your Excellency. Our enemies have ways of detecting my presence, so I'm going to give them a presence to detect in assorted corners of the empire to confuse them a bit. My friends and I are returning overland from Korvan to Matherion, and we'd prefer not to be ambushed along the way. This isn't a confidential visit, Ambassador Fontan. Feel free to let people know that I stopped by. They'll probably know already, but let's confirm it for them."

"I like your style, Sparhawk. You'll be crossing Cynesga?" Sparhawk nodded.

"It's an unpleasant country."

"These are unpleasant times. Oh, it won't really hurt if you're sort of smug when you tell people that you've seen me. Our side was definitely behind up until now. That changed a few days ago. Our enemy, whoever he may be, is at a distinct disadvantage right now, and I'd sort of like to grind his face in that fact for a while."

"I'll get word to the town crier immediately." The ancient man squinted up at the ceiling. "How long can you stay?"

"An hour at the very most."

"Plenty of time, then. Why don't we step over to the palace? I'll take you into the throne room, and you can pay your respects to the king—in front of his entire court. That's the best way *I* know of to let people know you've been here."

"I like *your* style, your Excellency." Sparhawk grinned.

It grew easier each time. At first, Bhelliom seemed impossibly dense, and Flute frequently had to step in, speaking in that language that Sparhawk strongly suspected was the original tongue of the Gods themselves. Gradually, the stone seemed to grasp what was wanted of it. Its compliance was never fully willing, however; it had to be compelled. Sparhawk found that visualizing Vanion's map helped quite a bit. Once Bhelliom grasped the fact that the map was no more than a picture of the world, it grew easier for Sparhawk to tell the jewel where he wanted to go.

This is not to say that there weren't a few false starts. Once, when he had been concentrating on the town of Delo on the east coast, the thought crossed his mind that there was a certain remote similarity between that name and the name of the town of Demos in east-central Elenia, and after the momentary grey blur where the world around him shifted and changed, he found himself and Flute riding Faran in bright moonlight up the lane that led to Kurik's farm.

"What are you *doing*?" Flute demanded.

"My attention wandered. Sorry."

"Keep your mind on your work. Bhelliom's responding to what you're thinking, not what you're saying. It probably doesn't even understand Elenic—but then, who really does?"

"Be nice."

"Take us back immediately!"

"Yes, ma'am."

There was that now-familiar lurch, and the moonlight faded into grey. Then they were back in bright autumn sunshine on the road a few miles outside Korvan, and their friends were staring at them in astonishment.

"What went wrong?" Sephrenia asked Flute.

"Our glorious leader here was wool-gathering," Flute replied with heavy sarcasm. "We just took a little side trip to Demos."

"Demos!" Vanion exclaimed. "That's on the other side of the world!"

"Yes," she agreed. "It's the middle of the night there right now. We were on the road to Kurik's farm. Maybe our stalwart commander here felt lonesome for Aslade's cooking."

"I can live without these 'stalwart commanders' and 'glorious leaders,'" Sparhawk told her tartly.

"Then do it right."

It came without warning. There was a certain desperation in the flicker of darkness at the edge of Sparhawk's vision this time, and a tinge of harried confusion. Sparhawk did not even stop to think. "Blue-Rose!" he barked to the Bhelliom, bringing up his other hand so that both rings touched the deep blue petals, "destroy that thing!"

He felt a brief jolt in his hands and heard a sizzling kind of crackle behind him.

The shadow that had dogged their steps for so long, which they had thought at first to be Azash and then the Troll-Gods, gave a shrill shriek and began to babble in agony. Sparhawk saw Sephrenia's eyes widen.

The shadow was crying out, not in Zemoch or Trollish, but in Styric.

CHAPTER
EIGHT

W ell now, yer Queenship," Caalador was saying, "I don't know ez I'd stort a-dancin' in the streets jist yit. Them fellers over t' Interior's bin a-doin' ever'thang but a-nailin' th' doors shet t' keep us from a-puttin' our hands on this yere pertic'ler set o' files, an' now they turns up sorta unexpected-like amongst a hull buncha others—which I'd swear a oath to that I already looked over 'bout four er five times my ownself. Don't that smell jist a bit like a dead fish t' you?"

"What did he say?" Emperor Sarabian asked.

"He's suspicious," Ehlana translated. "He thinks that our discovery of these files was too easy. He may just have a point."

They had gathered again in the royal apartment in what was by now generally called "Ehlana's Castle" to discuss the surprising discovery of a hitherto-missing set of personnel files. The files themselves were stacked in heaps upon the tables and the floor of the main sitting room.

"Do you always have to complicate things, Master Caalador?" The emperor's expression was slightly pained. As he habitually did now, Sarabian was wearing western-style clothes. Ehlana felt that this morning's choice of a black velvet doublet and pearl-grey hose was not a happy one. Black velvet made Sarabian's bronze-tinted skin look sallow and unhealthy.

"I'm a professional swindler, your Majesty," Caalador replied, dropping the dialect. "I've learned that when something seems too good to be true, it probably is."

Stragen was looking into one of the files. "What an amazing thing," he said. "Someone in the Ministry of the Interior seems to have discovered the secret of eternal youth."

"Don't be cryptic, Stragen," Ehlana told him, adjusting the folds of her blue dressing gown. "Say what you mean."

He took a sheet of paper out of the file he was holding. "This particular document looks as if it were only written last week—which it probably was. The ink's barely dry."

"They *are* still using those files, Milord," Oscagne said, "despite the inconvenience. It's probably just a recently filed document."

Stragen took out another sheet of paper and handed both documents to the foreign minister. "Do you notice anything unusual about these, your Excellency?"

Oscagne shrugged. "One of them's fairly new, the other's turned yellow with age, and the ink's faded so badly you can hardly read it."

"Exactly," Stragen said. "Don't you find it just a little odd that the faded one's supposed to be five years younger than the fresh one?"

Oscagne looked more closely at the two sheets of paper. "Are you trying to say that they falsified an official document?" he exclaimed. "That's a capital offense!"

"Let me see those," Sarabian said.

Oscagne handed him the documents.

"Oh, yes," Sarabian noted, "Chalba. Kolata's been singing his praises for the past fifteen years." He held up the suspicious document. "This purports to be his appointment to the ministry. It's dated no more than a week after Kolata took office." He looked at Stragen. "You think this has been substituted for the original?"

"It certainly looks that way, your Majesty."

Sarabian frowned. "What could there possibly have been on the original that they'd have wanted to conceal?" he asked.

"I have no idea, your Majesty. There must have been *something*, though." He leafed through the file. "This Chalba's rise in the ministry was positively meteoric. It looks as if he was getting promoted every time he turned around."

"That sounds a bit like the sort of thing one does for a close friend," Oscagne mused, "or a relative."

Sarabian smiled faintly. "Yes, it does, doesn't it? Your brother Itagne seems to have risen quite nearly as rapidly."

Oscagne made a face. "That wasn't my idea, your Majesty. Itagne's not a career officer of the Foreign Ministry. I press him into service in emergencies, and he always extorts promotions out of me. I'd rather not have anything to do with him at all, but he's so brilliant that I don't have any choice. My younger brother's intensely competitive, and I wouldn't be at all surprised to find that he has his eye on *my* position."

"This fallacious document Stragen found might give us a place to start," Caalador mused. Caalador frequently dipped in and out of the dialect like a leaping trout. "If Kolata took a cluster of friends and relatives into the ministry with him, wouldn't it stand to reason that they'd be the ones he'd trust the most?"

"It would indeed," Stragen agreed, "and we'd be able to tell from the dates on their appointments just *who* these cronies of his are, and his cronies would have been the people he'd have been most likely to confide in when he decided to take up treason as a hobby. I'd guess that anybody whose appointment coincided with Kolata's elevation to office is probably involved in this business."

"The ones ez is still alive, anyway," Caalador added. "A feller what turns down the chance t' join some friends in the treason business ain't got *too* much in the way o' life-expectancy after he sez no."

"May I speak, your Majesty?" Alean asked Ehlana timidly.

"Of course, dear."

The gentle girl was holding one of the files in her hands. "Does ink always fade and paper turn yellow as the document gets older?" she asked them in a barely audible voice.

"Indeed it does, child." Sarabian laughed. "It drives librarians crazy."

"And if there was something written down in one of these packages of paper that the people at the Inferior Ministry didn't want us to—"

Oscagne suddenly howled with laughter.

Alean blushed and lowered her head. "I'm just being silly," she said in a very tiny voice. "I'm sorry I interrupted."

"The place is called the *Interior* Ministry, Alean," Melidere told her gently.

"I preferred *her* term." Oscagne chuckled.

"May I be excused, my Queen?" Alean asked, her face flaming with mortification.

"Of course, dear," Ehlana replied sympathetically.

"Not just yet, Ehlana," Sarabian cut in. "Come here, child," he said to Alean.

She crossed to his chair and curtsied a bit awkwardly. "Yes, your Majesty?" she said in a scarcely audible voice.

"Don't pay any attention to Oscagne," he said. "His sense of humor gets the best of him sometimes. What were you going to say?"

"It's silly, your Majesty. I'm just an ignorant girl. I shouldn't have spoken."

"Alean," he said very gently, "*you* were the one who suggested that we take all the files of all the ministries out of the government buildings and spread them out on the lawns. *That* turned out to be an excellent idea. I don't know about these others, but *I'll* listen to anything you have to say. Please go on."

"Well, your Majesty," she said, blushing even harder, "as I understand what Milord Stragen just said, those people wanted to hide things that were written down, so they wrote new papers and put them in place of the ones they didn't want us to see."

"It looks as if that's what they've done, all right."

"Well, then, if new paper's white, and old paper's yellow, wouldn't that sort of mean that anybody whose package has white papers mixed in with yellow ones has something to hide?"

"Oh, good God!" Stragen exclaimed, smacking himself on the forehead with his open palm. "How could I have been so stupid?"

"And I went right along with you," Caalador added. "We both walked right over the top of the simplest and most obvious answer. How could we have missed it?"

"If I wanted to be spiteful, I *could* say that it was because you're men, Master Caalador—" Baroness Melidere smiled sweetly. "—and men just *adore* unnecessary complications. It's not nice to be spiteful, though, so I won't say it." She gave the two thieves an arch little look. "I may *think* it, but I won't *say* it," she added.

"It's very easily explained, your Majesty," Teovin replied calmly. "You've already touched on it yourself." Teovin, the

Director of the Secret Police at the Interior Ministry, was a dry, spare sort of man with no really distinguishing features. He was so ordinary looking that Ehlana felt him to be an almost perfect secret policeman.

"And what is this brilliant explanation that I've already discovered without even noticing it?" Sarabian asked acidly.

Teovin held up the yellowed sheet the emperor had just given him. "As your Majesty pointed out, the ink on this document has faded rather badly. The information in our files is vital to the security of the empire, so we *can't* let time erase the documents. The files are constantly reviewed, and any document that shows signs of approaching illegibility is copied off to preserve it."

"Why hasn't that one in your hand been updated, then, Teovin?" the emperor asked. "It's barely legible."

Teovin coughed diffidently. "Ah—budgetary considerations, your Majesty," he explained. "The Chancellory of the Exchequer saw fit to cut our appropriation this year. They're strange over at Exchequer. They always act as if it were their own personal money."

"They *do* rather, don't they?" Sarabian laughed. The emperor, Ehlana noted, was very fast on his feet, instantly adjusting to surprises. "Chancellor Gashon's hands start to shake every time I start talking about replacing broken tiles in the throne room. I'm glad we had the chance to straighten this out, my friend. I commend you for your devotion to your duty and your concern for the documents which have been placed in your care."

"I live but to serve, your Majesty." Teovin paused. "I wonder—might I have a word with Interior Minister Kolata? There are some matters—strictly routine, of course—that should be brought to his attention."

Sarabian laughed. "Afraid not, old boy," he said easily. "You wouldn't be able to keep his attention for very long today."

"Oh?"

"He got some tainted fish at supper last night, and he's been vomiting into a pail since just after midnight. We keep checking the pail, but his toenails haven't come out as yet. Poor Kolata. I can't remember when I've seen a man so sick."

"Do you think it's serious, your Majesty?" Teovin sounded genuinely concerned.

"Oh, probably not. We've all come in contact with bad food

before, so we know what to expect. *He* thinks he's going to die, though. I'd imagine that he rather wishes he could. We have a physician in attendance. He'll be all right tomorrow— thinner, maybe, and a little shaky, but recovered enough to look after business. Why don't you come by in the morning? I'll make sure that you get in to see him."

"As your Majesty commands," Teovin said, dropping to the floor to formally grovel before the emperor. Then he rose to his feet and left the audience chamber.

They waited.

"He's gone," Mirtai reported from the doorway. "He just went out into the courtyard."

"Quick, isn't he?" Caalador noted. "He didn't so much as turn a hair when your Majesty handed him that document."

"He was ready for us," Stragen said. "He had his story prepared well in advance."

"His explanation *is* plausible, Stragen," Sarabian pointed out.

"Of course, your Majesty. Secret policemen are very creative. We know that Interior Minister Kolata's involved in treason. He wouldn't be much of a threat all by himself, so his entire agency's suspect. We almost have to assume that every department head is involved. As Caalador so colorfully pointed out, anyone who didn't join in probably got himself defenestrated just as soon as he objected."

"De-*what*?" Melidere asked.

"Defenestrated. It means getting thrown out of a window—a high one, usually. It doesn't accomplish very much to push somebody out of a ground-floor window."

"There isn't really such a word, Stragen. You're making it up."

"No, honestly, Baroness," he protested. "It's a real word. It's a common solution to the problem of politically inconvenient people."

"I think we're straying here," Ehlana told them. "Sarabian, why did you make up that story about Kolata and the bad fish?"

"We don't want his underlings to find out that we're keeping him drugged into insensibility most of the time, do we, Ehlana?"

"No, I suppose not. Are you really going to let Teovin in to see him tomorrow?"

"Maybe we should. We've been stalling Kolata's underlings

for three days now, and I'm starting to run out of excuses. We'd better let *one* of them see him, or they'll start to get suspicious."

"I'm not sure it's a good idea, but maybe you're right. Alean, do be a dear and run down to the kitchen. Tell the cooks not to drug Minister Kolata's supper tonight."

"Yes, your Majesty," the girl replied.

"You might want to tell them to give him an emetic instead," Stragen suggested.

"Why would we want to do that?" Melidere asked.

"Emperor Sarabian just told the excellent Teovin that Kolata's been throwing up all day. We wouldn't want people to start accusing his Majesty of lying through his teeth, would we? Minister Kolata should show *some* signs of illness when Teovin visits him tomorrow. A good strong emetic should take care of that."

Alean giggled wickedly.

The Royal Princess Danae sat on a divan. She was carefully dressing Mmrr in a new doll's gown. Over the centuries, Aphrael had noticed that little Elene girls did that quite frequently. It didn't really make any sense to the Child-Goddess, but since it was a long-established custom— "Oh, quit," she murmured to her struggling cat. "I'm not hurting you."

Mmrr objected loudly, giving vent to a plaintive yowl filled to the brim with a heart-rending self-pity.

"Teovin was right about one thing," Stragen was saying to the rest of them. They had all gathered in the royal apartments again, and the Thalesian thief was holding forth once more. Danae liked Stragen, but the fact that he absolutely adored the sound of his own voice made him a bit tedious at times. "The Ministry of the Interior would die en masse before they'd destroy a single scrap of paper. The documents they pulled out of those files are *somewhere* in the building, and those documents would tell us things we haven't even *guessed* as yet about the conspiracy. I'd give my teeth to get a look at them."

"And spoil your smile, Stragen?" Melidere objected. "Bite your tongue."

"I was speaking figuratively, of course."

"He's probably right, your Majesties," Caalador agreed, forgoing the dialect. "Those original documents would be an absolute gold mine. I don't know that I'd give my *teeth*, but I *would* give a lot to browse through them."

Danae rolled her eyes. "Elenes," she said under her breath. "If it's all *that* important to you, Caalador," she said, "go look at them."

"We don't know whur it iz they got em hid, little dorlin'."

"*Look* for them, Caalador," she said with exaggerated patience. "You've got all night, every night, for the next month or two, haven't you? Talen told me once that he can get into any house in the world in under a quarter of an hour. You two are more experienced at it, so it probably wouldn't take you nearly as long. You're not going to *steal* the papers, all you're going to do is *read* them. If you put them back where you found them after you're finished, nobody will even know that you've seen them."

Caalador and Stragen looked at each other sheepishly. "Why didn't *we* think of that?" Stragen asked his friend.

"It seems to me I've already told you why once," Melidere said. "Shall we go through it again? It's really a very good idea, Princess. These two might not be much good at *thinking* sometimes, but they're probably very good burglars. They both have that shifty, unreliable look about them."

"They *do*, just a bit, don't they?" Danae agreed. She set Mmrr down on the floor. "There," she said, "isn't she adorable?"

The angry lashing of Mmrr's tail, however, totally spoiled the effect.

"The tail definitely detracts from the fashion statement, Danae." Sarabian laughed indulgently.

"Oh, I can fix that right up, Sarabian," she assured him. "I'll tell you what, Mmrr. How would you like to have me tie a big pink velvet bow right on the end of your tail to sort of set things off? You could wave it around like a parasol if you wanted."

Mmrr's tail stopped in midswish.

"I *thought* you might see it that way," Danae said.

"Shall we go down to the dungeon for your fencing lesson, your Majesty?" Stragen suggested. "Caalador and I are going to be busy being burglars tonight, I think."

"Not only tonight, I'm afraid," Caalador added. "I haven't been on a roof in years."

"It's like swimming, Caalador," Stragen said. "Once you learn how, you never forget."

"I'd really like to forgo the lesson today, Milord Stragen," Sarabian said. "I'm still sore from yesterday."

"Fencing is *not* like swimming, your Majesty," Stragen told him. "You have to practice continually. If you're going to wear that rapier, you'd better know how to use it. In a tight situation, that could be your last line of defense."

Sarabian sighed. "Sometimes I wish I'd never even *heard* of Elenes," he mourned.

"Because Ehlana *told* me to," Mirtai said as she, Engessa, Kring, and the two thieves crossed the document-littered lawn toward the Interior Ministry. "She wants to be sure that nobody interrupts you."

"Mirtai," Stragen said with a pained look, "I love you like a sister, but burglary's a fine art."

"I think my beloved can manage, friend Stragen," Kring said. "I've seen her walk through a pile of dry leaves and not make a sound."

"I just don't like it," Stragen complained.

"You are not required to, Stragen-thief," Engessa told him. "Ehlana-Queen said that Mirtai-daughter will go with you, so she will go."

Mirtai smiled up at the towering Atan. "Thank you, Engessa-father. It's so hard to make Elenes grasp reality sometimes."

"Engessa and I are going to relieve the two knights watching over the documents on the lawn," Kring told them. "We'll stay fairly close to the building, and we have other men nearby. Call if anyone surprises you in there, and we'll come and rescue you."

"I've never had a platoon of soldiers standing watch for me while I burglarized a building before," Caalador noted. "It adds a whole new dimension to the business."

Stragen grunted sourly. "It takes a lot of the fun out of it. A large part of the thrill of burglary comes from the danger of getting caught."

"I've never tried burglary," Kring admitted. "It's not much of a challenge among the Peloi, since we all live in tents. A sharp knife will get you into the stoutest tent in the world. If we want to ransack someone's encampment, we usually send in some men to run off his horses. He chases *those* men, and that gives us a free hand."

"Burglary's a crime of stealth, Kring," Stragen smiled. "You get to sneak around at night and climb over rooftops. It's a lot of fun—and really quite profitable."

"Be careful up there on that roof, Mirtai," Kring admonished his betrothed. "I went to a great deal of trouble winning you, and I'd hate to lose you at this point. Oh, speaking of that, friend Stragen—and you, too, friend Caalador—if anything happens to her, you *do* know that I'll kill you, don't you?"

"We wouldn't have it any other way, friend Kring," Stragen nodded.

Mirtai ran a caressing hand over her beloved's scalp. Stragen had noticed that she did that quite often. He wondered if the feel of the little fellow's shaved head might have had some bearing on her decision to marry him. "You need a shave," the giantess said. "Remind me in the morning, and I'll take care of it."

Then Stragen, Caalador, and Mirtai, all dressed in close-fitting black clothing, slipped through the shadows of a grove of trees near the Ministry of the Interior. "You're really fond of the little fellow, aren't you, Mirtai?" Stragen murmured softly, ducking under a tree limb.

"Kring? He's a suitable sort of man."

"That's a rather lukewarm declaration of passion."

"Passion's a private thing. It shouldn't be displayed in public."

"Then you *do* have those feelings for him?"

"I don't really see where that's any of your business, Stragen."

There was a filmy layer of fog lying on the lawns of the imperial compound. It was autumn now, and the fog crept in off the Tamul Sea every evening. The moon would not rise for hours yet, and all in all it was a perfect night for a burglary.

Caalador was puffing when they reached the wall surrounding the Ministry of the Interior. "Out of condition," he muttered.

"You're almost as bad as Platime," Stragen told him, speaking very softly. Then he squinted upward, swinging a heavy grappling hook in his hand. He stepped back and began to whirl the hook in a wide circle, letting out more rope with each circuit. Then he hurled it upward with the rope trailing behind it. It sailed up over the wall and fell inside, striking the stones with a metallic-sounding clink. He tugged down a couple of times to set the points in place. Then he sat down on the grass.

"Aren't we going up?" Mirtai asked him.

"Not yet. Somebody might have heard it. We'll wait until his curiosity's had time to wear off."

"Fellers what's a-standin' watch in the middle o' the night ain't really all *that* eager t' go lookin' fer where it is ez noises is a-comin' from, dorlin'," Caalador explained. "In my experience, they usually feel that a quiet watch is a good watch, so they don't go out of their way to investigate things. As long as nobody sets the building on fire, they're not overburdened with curiosity. B'sides," he added, dipping once again into the dialect, "fellers ez gits chose t' stand gord at night usual turns out t' be drankin' min, an' after a flagon er two, they can't really hear hordly nuthin' a-tall." He looked at Stragen. "Do you want to try the ground floor before we go up on the roof?" he asked in clipped Elenic.

"No," Stragen decided. "Ground-floor windows are always double-checked when people lock up, and watchmen pass the lonely hours of the night rattling door-handles and trying the windows close to the ground. I've always preferred attics myself."

"What if all the attic windows are locked as well?" Mirtai asked him.

"We'll break one." He shrugged. "The building's high enough so that a broken window won't be all that visible from the ground."

"Don't be *too* obvious, Stragen," Caalador cautioned him. "I've got the feeling that we'll be going back inside every night for the next week or two. That's a large building."

"Let's get at it, then," Stragen said, rising to his feet. He looked out across the lawn. The fog had grown noticeably thicker. He tugged down on the rope a couple of times to make sure that the hook was secure and then began to climb up.

"You go on up next, dorlin'," Caalador said quietly to Mirtai.

"Why do you call me that?"

"Jist a-bein' friendly-like. It don't mean nothin' personal, so don't go complainin' t' yer bow-legged beau. He's a likeable sort, but he shore is touchy where yer concerned."

"Yes," Mirtai agreed. She went quickly up the rope and joined Stragen atop the wall. "What now?" she asked.

"We'll go across to the roof and start checking attic windows just as soon as Caalador climbs up."

"You'll use the hook again?"

He nodded.

"Burglars are about half ape, aren't they?"

"We prefer to think of ourselves as agile. Now, then, if we run into anybody inside, we'll try to hide first. If that doesn't work, we'll rap him on the head. Caalador's carrying a wine-skin, and he'll pour wine all over the man. The smell of that should make him less credible when he wakes up. Try not to kill anybody. It takes all night to clean up, and we'd have to carry the body away when we leave. This isn't an ordinary burglary, and we don't want anybody to know we've been here."

"You're repeating the obvious, Stragen."

"I've seen your instincts in operation before, love. If you *do* kill somebody, please try to leave *most* of the blood inside the body. I don't want to be caught in there with a mop in my hands when the sun comes up."

"Why are you both being so affectionate tonight?"

"I don't think I quite followed that."

"Caalador's been calling me 'darling' ever since we set out, and you just called me 'love.' Is there some sort of significance to that?"

He chuckled. "A gang of burglars is a very close-knit group, Mirtai. We depend on each other for our very lives. That creates powerful ties of affection—which usually last right up until the point when the time comes to divide up the spoils. That's when things sometimes turn ugly."

"Let's have it all in place *before* we make any overt moves, Sarabian," Ehlana counseled. "The Interior Ministry knows that we're up to *something*, but we're all pretending that everything's normal. The customary approach is to have everybody in custody before you start issuing proclamations and disbanding branches of government."

"I can see your point, of course," he agreed. They were standing atop the battlements again, looking out over the city as the sun rose above the thick ground fog. "That's pretty, isn't it?" he observed. "The color of the fog almost perfectly matches the mauve on the walls and domes."

"You have a beautiful city."

"With some not-so-beautiful people living in it. What am I going to do for a police force after I dissolve the Ministry of the Interior?"

"You'll probably have to declare martial law."

He winced. "The Atans won't make me very many friends,

I'm afraid. They tend to have a very simplified concept of justice."

"We don't have to stand for reelection, Sarabian. That's why we can do unpopular things."

"Only up to a point," he disagreed. "I have to live with the great houses of Tamul proper, and I'm still getting letters of protest from many of them about sons and brothers who were killed or maimed while the Atans were putting down the coup."

"They were traitors, weren't they?"

"No," he sighed, "probably not. We Tamuls pamper our children, and the noble houses carry that to extremes. Matherion's a political city, and when young Tamuls enter the university, they're *expected* to get involved in politics—usually of the most radical sort. The rank and position of their families protects them from the consequences of excessive juvenile enthusiasm. I was an anarchist when I was a student. I even led a few demonstrations against my father's government." He smiled faintly. "I used to get arrested on an average of once a week. They never *would* throw me in the dungeon, though, no matter *what* kind of names I called my father. I tried very hard to get thrown into the dungeon, but the police wouldn't cooperate."

"Why on earth did you want to spend time in a dungeon?" She laughed.

"Young Tamul noblewomen are *terribly* impressed by political martyrs. I'd have cut a wide track if I could have gotten myself imprisoned for a few days."

"I thought you got married when you were a baby," she said. "Isn't it sort of inappropriate for a married man to be thinking about how wide a track he can cut among the ladies?"

"My first wife and I stopped speaking to each other for about ten years when we were young, and the fact that I was required by tradition to have eight other wives made the notion of fidelity a sort of laughable concept." A thought came to him. "I wonder if Caalador would consider taking a post in my government," he mused.

"You could do worse. I have a man named Platime in my government, and he's an even bigger thief than Caalador." Ehlana glanced down the battlements and saw Mirtai approaching. "Any luck?" she asked.

"It's hard to say." The giantess shrugged. "We got inside easily enough, but we didn't find what we were looking for.

Stragen and Caalador are going out to the university to talk with some of the scholars there."

"Are they suddenly hungering and thirsting after knowledge?" Sarabian asked her lightly.

" 'Tain't hordly likely, dorlin'," Mirtai replied.

"Darling?" he asked her incredulously.

"But you *are*, Sarabian," the golden giantess replied, gently touching his cheek. "I discovered tonight that conspirators and thieves and other scoundrels are supposed to be very affectionate with each other. You're conspiring with us to overthrow the police, so you're a member of the family now. Stragen wants to talk with some specialists in architecture. He suspects that there might be some secret rooms in the Interior Ministry. He's hoping that the original plans for the building might be in some library." She gave the emperor a sly, sidelong glance. "That's what it iz that they're a-doin', dorlin'," she added.

"Are you really sure you want Caalador in your government, Sarabian?" Ehlana asked him. "That dialect of his seems to rub off on people. Give him a year or two, and everybody in the imperial compound will be calling you 'dorlin'.' "

"That might be preferable to some of the *other* names I've been called lately."

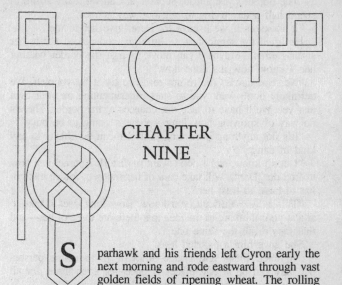

CHAPTER
NINE

Sparhawk and his friends left Cyron early the next morning and rode eastward through vast golden fields of ripening wheat. The rolling countryside sloped gradually downward into the broad valley where the Pela and Edek rivers joined on the border between Edom and Cynesga.

Sparhawk rode in the lead with Flute nestled in his arms. The little girl seemed unusually quiet this morning, and after they had been on the road for a couple of hours, Sparhawk leaned to one side and looked at her face. Her eyes were fixed, vacant, and her face expressionless. "What's the matter?" he asked.

"Not now, Sparhawk," she told him crossly. "I'm busy."

"Aphrael, we're coming up on the border. Shouldn't we—?"

"Leave me alone." She burrowed her forehead into his chest with a discontented little sound.

"What is it, Sparhawk?" Sephrenia asked, pulling Ch'iel in beside Faran.

"Aphrael won't talk to me."

Sephrenia leaned forward and looked critically at Flute's face. "Ah," she said.

"Ah what?"

"Leave her alone, Sparhawk. She's someplace else right now."

"The border's just ahead, Sephrenia. Can we really afford to spend half a day trying to talk our way across?"

"It looks as if we'll have to. Here, give her to me."

He lifted the semicomatose little girl and placed her in her sister's arms. "Maybe I can move us past the border without her. I know how it's done now."

"No, Sparhawk. You're not ready to try it by yourself. We definitely don't want you to start experimenting on your own just yet. We'll have to take our chances at the border. There's no way of knowing how long Aphrael's going to be busy."

"It's not anything important, is it? I mean, is Ehlana in any kind of danger?"

"I don't know, and I don't want to disturb Aphrael just now to find out. Danae will take care of her mother. You're just going to have to trust her."

"This is *very* difficult, you know. How long does it take to adjust your thinking to the idea that there are three of her—and that they're all the same one?"

She gave him a puzzled look.

"Aphrael, Flute, and Danae—they're all the same person, but they can be in two places at once—or even three, for all I know—and doing two or three different things."

"Yes," she agreed.

"Doesn't that disturb you just a little?"

"Does it concern you that your Elene God's supposed to know what everybody in the world's thinking? All at the same time?"

"Well—no. I suppose not."

"What's the difference?"

"He's God, Sephrenia."

"So's she, Sparhawk."

"It doesn't seem quite the same."

"It is, though. Tell the others that we're going to have to make the border crossing on our own."

"They'll want to know why."

"Lie to them. God will forgive you—one of them will, anyway."

"You're impossible to talk to when you're like this, do you know that?"

"Don't talk to me, then. Right now I'd prefer that you didn't anyway."

"Is something wrong?"

"I was just a little upset when you dissolved that cloud and it started swearing at you in Styric."

"I noticed that myself." He made a face. "How could anyone have missed it? I gather it's significant."

"What language do *you* swear in when you stub your toe?"

"Elenic, of course."

"Of course. It's your native tongue. Doesn't that sort of suggest that Styric's the native tongue of whoever's behind that shadow?"

"I hadn't thought of that. I suppose it does."

"The fact disturbs me, Sparhawk—more than just a little bit. It suggests all sorts of things that I don't really want to accept."

"Such as?"

"There's a Styric working with our enemy, for one thing, and he's highly skilled. That shadow's the result of a very complex spell. I doubt that there are more than eight or ten in all of Styricum who could have managed it, and I *know* all of those people. They're my friends. It's not a pleasant thing to contemplate. Why don't you go bother somebody else and let me work on it?"

Sparhawk gave up and dropped back to talk with the others. "There's been a little change of plans," he told them. "Aphrael's occupied elsewhere just now, so we won't be able to avoid the border crossing."

"What's she doing?" Bevier asked.

"You don't want to know. Believe me, Bevier, *you*, of all people, *really* don't want to know."

"She's doing one of those God-things?" Talen guessed.

"Talen," Bevier rebuked him. "They're called miracles, not God-things."

"*That* was the word I was looking for," Talen replied, snapping his fingers.

Vanion was frowning. "Border crossings are always tedious," he told them, "but the Cynesgans have a reputation for carrying that to extremes. They'll negotiate the suitable bribe for days on end."

"That's what axes are for, Lord Vanion," Ulath rumbled. "We use them to clear away inconveniences—underbrush, trees, obstructionist officials—that sort of thing."

"We don't need an international incident, Sir Ulath," Vanion told him. "We *might* be able to speed things up a bit, though. I've got an imperial pass signed by Sarabian himself. It might carry enough weight to get us past the border without too much delay."

The border between Edom and Cynesga was marked by the Pela River, and at the far end of the substantial bridge there stood a solid, blocklike building with a horse corral behind it.

Vanion led them across the bridge to the barricade on the Cynesgan side, where a number of armed men in strange flowing robes waited.

The imperial pass Vanion presented to the border guards not only failed to gain them immediate passage, but even added further complications. "How do I know that this is really his Majesty's signature?" the Cynesgan captain demanded suspiciously in heavily accented Tamul. He was a swarthy man in a loose-fitting black-and-white-striped robe and with a long cloth wound intricately around his head.

"What's much more to the point, neighbor, is how do you know that it *isn't*?" Sparhawk asked bluntly in the Tamul tongue. "The Atans take a very unpleasant stance toward people who disobey the emperor's direct commands."

"It means death to forge the emperor's signature," the captain said ominously.

"So I've been told," Vanion replied. "It *also* means death to ignore his orders. I'd say that *one* of us is in trouble."

"My men still have to search your packs for contraband," the captain said haughtily. "I will consider this while they carry out their orders."

"Do that," Sparhawk told him in a flat, unfriendly tone of voice, "and keep in mind the fact that a wrong decision here could have a negative impact on your career."

"I didn't catch your meaning."

"A man with no head seldom gets promoted."

"I have nothing to fear," the captain declared. "I am strictly following the orders of my government."

"And the Atans who'll chop off your head will be strictly following the orders of *theirs*. I'm certain that everyone involved will take enormous comfort in the fact that all the legal niceties were observed." Sparhawk turned his back on the officious captain, and he and Vanion walked back to rejoin the others.

"Well?" Sephrenia asked them.

"The emperor's voice doesn't seem to be very loud here in Cynesga," Vanion replied. "Our friend in the bathrobe has a whole book full of regulations, and he's going to use every single one of them to delay us."

"Did you try to bribe him?" Ulath asked.

"I hinted at the fact that I might entertain a suggestion along those lines." Vanion shrugged. "He didn't take the hint, though."

"Now *that's* unusual," Kalten noted. "Bribes are always the first thing on the mind of any official anywhere in the world. That sort of suggests that he's trying to hold us here until reinforcements arrive, doesn't it?"

"And they're probably already on their way," Ulath added. "Why don't we take steps?"

"You're just guessing, gentlemen," Sephrenia chided them. "You're all just itching for the chance to do Elenish things to those border guards."

"Did you want to do Elenish things to people, Ulath?" Kalten asked mildly.

"I was suggesting constructive Elenishism before we even got here."

"We're not contemplating it out of sheer bloodlust, little mother," Vanion told the woman he loved.

"Oh, *really?*"

"The situation's manageable now, but if a thousand mounted Cynesgans suddenly ride in from the nearest garrison, it's going to get out of hand."

"But—"

He held up one hand. "*My* decision, Sephrenia. Well, Sparhawk's, actually, since he's the preceptor now."

"Interim preceptor," Sparhawk corrected.

Vanion did not like to be corrected. "Did *you* want to do this?" he asked.

"No. You're doing just fine, Vanion."

"Do you want to be quiet then? It's a military decision, Sephrenia, so we'll have to ask you—respectfully, of course—to keep your pretty little nose out of it."

She said a very harsh word in Styric.

"I love you, too," he told her blandly. "All right, gentlemen, let's sort of drift on over to our horses. We'll do some of those Elenish things Ulath mentioned to the men who are going through our saddlebags. Then we'll run off all those horses in that corral and be on our way."

There were a score of border guards under the captain's command. Their primary weapon seemed to be the spear, although they wore a sort of rudimentary armor and scimitars at their waists.

"Excuse me a moment, friend," Ulath said pleasantly to the fellow who was rifling his saddlebags. "I'm going to need my tools for a couple of minutes." He reached for the war ax slung from his saddle.

"What for?" the Cynesgan demanded suspiciously in broken Tamul.

"There's something in my way." Ulath smiled. "I want to remove it." He lifted his ax out of its sling, tested the edge with his thumb, and then brained the border guard with a single stroke.

The fight around the horses was brief and the outcome promised to be fairly predictable. As a group, border guards are not among the world's most highly skilled warriors.

"What do you think you're doing?" Sparhawk bellowed at Talen as the boy pulled his rapier out of the body of one of the Cynesgans.

"Stragen's been giving me lessons," Talen replied. "I just wanted to find out if he knew what he was talking about. Watch your back."

Sparhawk spun, knocked aside the spear of a charging border guard, and cut the man down. He turned back just as Talen deftly parried the thrust of another, deflecting the curved blade off to one side. Then the young man lunged smoothly and ran the surprised fellow through. "Neat, wouldn't you say?" He smirked proudly.

"Quit showing off—and don't take so long to recover from your thrust. You're exposing yourself with all that posing."

"Yes, revered teacher."

What little question there had been about the outcome of the skirmish vanished once the knights were in their saddles. Things ended abruptly when the obnoxious captain, who had been shrieking, "You're all under arrest!" broke off suddenly as Sir Bevier coolly swung his lochaber ax and sent the officer's head flying.

"Throw down your weapons!" Ulath roared at the few survivors. "Surrender or die!"

Two of the guards, however, had reached their horses. They scrambled up into their saddles and rode off to the east at a gallop. One stiffened and toppled from his saddle after about fifty yards with Berit's arrow protruding from between his shoulder blades. The other rode on some distance, flogging desperately at his mount. Then he, too, lurched and fell to the musical twang of Khalad's crossbow.

"Good shot," Berit noted.

"Fair," Khalad agreed modestly.

The rest of the Cynesgans were throwing their weapons away.

"You run a good fight, Sparhawk," Vanion complimented his friend.

"I had a good teacher. Kalten, tie them all up and then run off their horses."

"Why me?"

"You're handy, and there's that other matter as well."

"I didn't break my oath," Kalten protested.

"No, but you were thinking about it."

"What's this?" Vanion asked.

"There's a lady involved, my Lord," Sparhawk replied loftily, "and no gentleman ever discusses things like that."

"What are you doing?" Aphrael asked sharply. She had raised her head from Sephrenia's shoulder and was looking suspiciously at Sparhawk.

"Are you with us again?" he asked her.

"Obviously. What are you doing?"

"There was some unpleasantness at the border, and we're probably being followed—chased, actually."

"I can't leave you alone for a minute, can I, Father?"

"It was more or less unavoidable. Have you finished with whatever it was you were doing?"

"For the time being."

"The town of Edek is just ahead, and we've probably got a brigade of Cynesgan soldiers right behind us. Do you suppose you could move us on ahead a ways?"

"Why didn't you do it yourself? You know how it's done."

"Sephrenia wouldn't let me."

"His attention wanders at critical moments," Sephrenia explained. "I didn't want him to put us down on the moon."

"I see your point," the little girl agreed. "Why don't we just move straight on to Cynestra, Sparhawk? There's nothing between here and there but open desert, you know."

"They were expecting us at the border," he replied. "It seems that our friend out there has alerted everybody along the way that we're coming. There's certain to be a large garrison of troops at Cynestra, and I'd like to feel my way through the situation there before I blunder into something."

"I guess that makes sense—sort of."

"How's your mother?"

"She's enjoying herself enormously. The political situation in Matherion's very murky right now, and you know how much Mother loves politics."

"I'm glad she's happy. You'll have to tell us about it, but let's get past Edek and outrun that Cynesgan brigade first. I don't like having people snapping at my heels."

"Tell the others to stop, and then get Vanion's map. Let's be sure we know where we're going this time."

"I'm never going to get used to that," Kalten shuddered after they had covered fifty leagues of open desert in a single grey-blurred moment.

"Your map's not very precise, Vanion," Aphrael said critically. "We were trying for a spot on the *other* side of that peak." She pointed at a jagged spire rearing up out of the desert.

"*I* didn't draw the map," Vanion replied a bit defensively. "What difference does it make, though? We're close enough, aren't we? We came to within a few miles of where we wanted to go."

"You'd have found out how much difference it makes if we'd been moving around near a large body of water," she said tartly. "This is just *too* imprecise."

Vanion looked back over his shoulder toward the west. "It's almost sunset. Why don't we get back away from this road and set up for the night? If we've got a problem with this, let's find a quiet place where we can work it out."

Sparhawk smiled. Despite all his protestations that he was no longer the Pandion Preceptor, Vanion automatically took charge unless he was consciously thinking about what he believed to be his changed status. Sparhawk didn't really mind. He was used to taking orders from Vanion, and his friend's assumption of authority relieved *him* of the nagging details of command.

They rode out into the desert a couple of miles and set up for the night in a dry wash behind an upthrust jumble of weathered boulders. Unlike the Rendorish desert, which was mostly sand, the desert here in Cynesga was sun-baked gravel, rusty-brown and sterile. The moving sands of Rendor at least gave an illusion of life. Cynesga was dead. Stark, treeless peaks clawed harshly at the sky, and the vast emptiness of gravel and rock was broken only by flat, bleached white beds of alkali.

"Ugly place," Ulath grunted, looking around. Ulath was used to trees and snow-capped peaks.

"I'm sorry you feel that way." Kalten grinned. "I was thinking of selling it to you."

"You couldn't *give* it to me."

"Look on the bright side. It almost never rains here."

"I think that's part of the problem."

"There's a lot of wild game, though."

"Really?"

"Snakes, lizards, scorpions—that sort of thing."

"Have you developed a taste for baked scorpion?"

"Ah—no, I don't think so."

"I wouldn't waste any arrows on them, then."

"Speaking of eating . . ."

"Were we speaking of that?"

"It's a topic that comes up from time to time. Do you know of a way to set fire to rocks?"

"Not right offhand, no."

"Then I'll volunteer to fix supper. I haven't seen a stick or a twig or even a dry leaf around here, so a fire's sort of out of the question. Oh, well, cold food never hurt anybody."

"We can get by without fire," Vanion said, "but we're going to have to have water for the horses."

"Aphrael and I can manage that, dear," Sephrenia assured him.

"Good. I think we might be here for a day or so. Sparhawk and Aphrael are going to be working with Bhelliom on this little problem of precision." He looked inquiringly at the Child-Goddess. "Is it likely to take very long?" he asked her.

"I'm not really positive, Vanion. When *I* do it, I still have the surrounding terrain to refer to, so I know where I am, no matter how fast I'm going. Bhelliom goes from one place to another instantaneously without any reference points. It's an altogether different process. Either Sparhawk and I are going to have to learn how Bhelliom's technique works, or we're going to have to make Bhelliom understand exactly what we want."

"Which way would be easier?" Kalten asked her.

"I'm not sure. It's possible that they're about the same—both very, very difficult. We'll find out tomorrow morning."

She looked at Vanion. "Are we more or less safe where we are right now?"

Vanion scratched at his short silvery beard. "Nobody really expects us to be here. Somebody might accidentally stumble across us, but there won't be any kind of organized search. They don't know where we are, and the rings are shielded, so our friend out there won't be able to pick up the sense of their location and follow that to us. I'd say that we're safe here."

"Good. We've got some time, then. Let's use it to let Sparhawk and Bhelliom get to know each other. There's nothing all that crucial going on right now, so a few mistakes and false starts won't hurt anything. They might be disastrous later on, though."

Sephrenia did not tell them where the water came from the next morning, but it was icy cold and tasted of snowmelt. It sparkled invitingly in its shaded little pool behind a rust-colored boulder, and by its very presence it alleviated a great deal of tension. Water is a source of major concern to people in a desert.

Flute took Sparhawk, Khalad, and Talen some distance out onto a broad graveled plain to begin the instruction.

"It's going to get hot out here before long," Talen complained.

"Probably, yes," the little girl agreed.

"Why do Khalad and I have to come along?"

"Vanion needs the knights with him here in case someone stumbles across our camp."

"You missed my point. Why do you two need *anybody* to come along?"

"Sparhawk has to have people and horses to carry. He's not going to be moving sacks of grain from place to place, you know." She looked at Vanion's map. "Let's see if Bhelliom can take us to this oasis up here, Sparhawk," she said, pointing at a symbol on the map.

"What does it look like?" he asked her.

"How would I know? I've never been there either."

"All you're giving me to work with is a *name*, Aphrael. Why don't we do it the way we did when we moved from outside Jorsan up to Korvan?—and all those other places we went to when we were jumping around to confuse the other side? You tell Bhelliom where we want to go and then I'll tell it to do it."

"We can't be sure that I'll always be available, Sparhawk. There are times when I have to be away. The whole idea here is to train you and Bhelliom to work together *without* my intervention."

"A *name* isn't really very much to take hold of, you know."

"There'll be trees, Sparhawk," Khalad told him. "An oasis is kind of a pond, and anywhere you've got water, you're going to have trees."

"And probably houses," Talen added. "There'd almost have to be houses, since water's so scarce here in Cynesga."

"Let's see the map," Sparhawk said. He studied the chart carefully for quite some time. "All right," he said finally. "Let's try it and see what happens." He lifted the cap on his ring and touched the band to the lid of the golden box. "Open," he said. Then he put on the other ring and took out the Bhelliom. "It's me again," he told the jewel.

"Oh, that's absurd, Sparhawk," Aphrael told him.

"Formal introductions take too long," he replied. "There may come a time when I'll be in a hurry." He carefully imagined a desert oasis—an artesian-fed pond with its surrounding palms and flat-roofed white houses. "Take us there, Blue-Rose," he commanded.

The air blurred and faded into grey. Then the blur cleared, and the oasis was there, just as he had imagined it.

"You see, Sparhawk," Aphrael said smugly. "That wasn't hard at all, was it?"

Sparhawk even laughed out loud. "This might work out after all."

"Talen," Khalad said, "why don't you ride on down to one of those houses and ask somebody the name of this place?"

"It's Zhubay, Khalad," Flute told him. "That's where we wanted to go, so that's where we are."

"You wouldn't mind a bit of verification, would you?" he asked her innocently.

She scowled at him.

Talen rode down to the cluster of houses and returned a few minutes later. "Let me see the map," he said to Khalad.

"Why?" Flute asked him. "We're in Zhubay, up near the Atan border."

"No, Divine One," the boy disagreed, "actually we're not." He studied the map for several minutes. "Ah," he said. "Here it is." He pointed. "*This* is where we're at—Vigayo, down near the southern border where Cynesga adjoins Arjuna. You missed your mark by about three hundred leagues, Sparhawk. I think you'd better sharpen your aim just a bit."

"What were you *thinking* about?" Aphrael demanded.

"Pretty much what Khalad was talking about—trees, a pond, white houses—just exactly what there is in front of us."

"Now what?" Talen asked. "Do we go back to where we started and try again?"

Aphrael shook her head. "Bhelliom and the rings are unshielded. We don't want to put Vanion, Sephrenia, and the others in danger by going back there too often. Let me down, Sparhawk. I want to think about this."

He set her down on the ground, and she walked down to the edge of the oasis, where she stood throwing pebbles into the water for a while. Her expression was dubious when she returned. Sparhawk lifted her again. "Well?" he asked.

"Take us to Zhubay, Sparhawk," she said firmly.

"Let me see the map again, Khalad."

"No," Aphrael said very firmly. "Never mind the map. Just tell Bhelliom to take us to Zhubay."

"Exactly!" Khalad said, snapping his fingers. "Why didn't we think of that before?"

"Think of what?" Sparhawk demanded.

"Try it, my Lord." Khalad grinned. "I think you might be surprised."

"If we wind up on the moon, you two are in trouble," Sparhawk threatened.

"Just try it, Sparhawk," Flute told him.

"Blue-Rose! Take us to Zhubay!" He said it without much conviction.

The air blurred again, and when it cleared they were sitting on their horses beside another oasis. There were a number of significant differences between this one and the one they'd just left.

"There probably isn't any need," Khalad said to his brother, "but you might want to ask anyway, just to be sure."

Talen rode on around the oasis and spoke with an old woman who had just come out of one of the houses. He was grinning when he came back. "Zhubay," he told them.

"How could it find the place with only the name to work with?" Sparhawk demanded. "It's probably never even *heard* the name Zhubay before."

"But the people who live here have, my Lord." Khalad shrugged. "The name Zhubay was sort of floating around in their minds. That's all Bhelliom really needed to find the place. Isn't that more or less the way it works, Flute?"

"That's *exactly* how it works. All Sparhawk has to do is mention the name of the place he wants to visit. Bhelliom will find it and take us there."

"Are you sure?" Talen sounded uncertain about the whole notion. "It seems awfully simple to me."

"There's one way to find out. Take us to Ahkan, Sparhawk."

"Where is it? What kingdom, I mean?"

"I don't think you need to know that. Just take us there."

Ahkan was a town in the mountains—*some* mountains, *some*where. It was surrounded by dark green fir trees, and the nearby peaks were snow-capped.

"Better and better," Flute said happily.

"Where are we?" Talen asked, looking around. "This isn't Cynesga, that's for certain, so where is it?"

"What difference does it make?" Flute shrugged. "Torrelta, Sparhawk."

It was snowing in Torrelta. The wind came howling in off a lead-grey sea driving a blizzard before it. The buildings around them were dim and indistinct in the swirling snowstorm, but they seemed to be constructed of rough-hewn logs.

"There's no *limit*!" Flute exclaimed. "We can go *anywhere*!"

"All right," Sparhawk said very firmly, "just which 'any-where' have we come to?"

"It doesn't matter. Let's go back to where we started from."

"Of course," he agreed pleasantly. "Just as soon as you tell us where we are."

"I'm getting *cold*, Sparhawk. I'm not dressed for a blizzard."

"It's nice and warm back in Cynesga," he told her, "and we'll go there—just as soon as you tell me where we are."

She said a naughty word. "Torrelta's on the north coast of Astel, Sparhawk. It's almost winter here now."

He looked around with feigned surprise. "Why, I believe you're right. Isn't that amazing?" He visualized the flat gravel plain near the dry wash where they had set up camp the previous evening. He groped for a name for a moment, then remembered the blunder he had made when they had first set out. "Hold the box open, Khalad," he instructed. "I'll put Bhelliom and Ehlana's ring inside just as soon as we get back." He drew the picture in his mind again. "Take us *there*, Blue-Rose!" he commanded.

* * *

"Where have you been?" Sephrenia demanded. She and Vanion had ridden out onto the gravel plain to look for them.

"Oh," Talen said evasively, brushing the snow off his shoulders, "here and there."

"I gather that one of the places was quite a ways off," Vanion surmised, looking at the snow still clinging to the travelers.

"It's really amazing, Sephrenia," Flute said happily, "and it's all so *simple*."

Khalad closed the box and handed it to Sparhawk. Sparhawk snapped the cap down over the ruby on his ring and then put the box back inside his tunic. "We made a couple of false starts right at first, though," he admitted.

"How does it work?" Vanion asked.

"We just let Bhelliom take care of everything." Sparhawk shrugged. "We *have* to do it that way, actually. It's when we try to help that things go wrong."

"Could you be just a bit more specific than that?" Sephrenia asked Flute.

"Sparhawk's really very close. All he has to do is tell Bhelliom a name—any name—of any place at all. Bhelliom goes and finds it, and then it takes us there."

"That's *all*?"

"That's it, dear sister. Not even Sparhawk can make any mistakes this way."

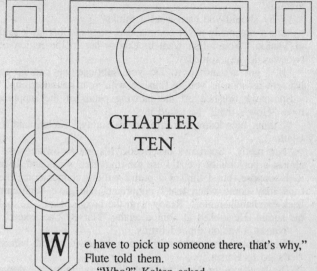

CHAPTER
TEN

W
e have to pick up someone there, that's why," Flute told them.

"Who?" Kalten asked.

"I don't know. All I know is that someone's supposed to go with us, and we have to pick him up in Cynestra."

"Another one of those hunches of yours?"

"You can call it that if you want to."

"I don't think we'll want to go into the city itself until we've had a chance to feel things out," Vanion said, looking up from his map. "There's a village just to the west of town. Let's go there and nose around a bit."

"What's the name?" Sparhawk asked him, opening the box and taking out his wife's ring.

"Narset," Vanion replied, looking up from the map.

"All right." Sparhawk took out the Bhelliom. He held it up and frowned slightly. "May I borrow your handkerchief, little mother?" he asked Sephrenia.

"Use your own," she told him.

"I seem to have left home without one. I'm not going to blow my nose on it, Sephrenia. Bhelliom's getting dusty. I wanted to brush it off a bit."

She gave him a peculiar look.

"It's being very helpful. I don't want it to think that I'm ungrateful."

"Why should you care what it thinks?"

"She's obviously never commanded troops," Sparhawk said to Vanion. "You might want to expose her to the notion of two-way loyalty someday."

"If I get around to it. Do you suppose we can go to Narset—as soon as you've finished with your housekeeping?"

Sparhawk brushed off the glowing petals of the sapphire rose. "How's that?" he asked it.

"I think he's losing his grip on his sanity," Kalten said to Ulath.

"Not really," Sparhawk disagreed. "It's got an awareness—almost a personality. I could use the rings like whips and drive it, I suppose, but I think I'd prefer willing cooperation. The time may come when that's important." He gave Sephrenia back her handkerchief. "Ready with the box, Khalad," he told his squire. He looked at Vanion again. "Narset?" he asked.

"Narset," Vanion replied firmly.

"Blue-Rose," Sparhawk said, taking the jewel in both hands, "let's go to Narset."

The Bhelliom throbbed, and that blurred twilight came down briefly. Then it cleared again.

Narset was a small, dusty village. The houses were hardly more than mud huts, and they had flat roofs and animal pens at the rear, pens that seemed largely decorative, since chickens, pigs, and goats wandered freely in the streets. There was a fair-sized city lying to the east, and all the buildings in that city were covered with white plaster to ward off the brutal desert sun.

Sparhawk put Bhelliom and Ehlana's ring away and flipped the golden cap back down over his own ring.

"We've got company coming," Talen warned.

A sallow-faced Tamul in a green silk robe was approaching with a squad of Cynesgan soldiers, swarthy men in the same flowing black and white robes and intricately wound cloth headdresses as the guards at the border had worn. The Tamul had hard-looking eyes, which he tried to conceal behind a contrived expression of joviality. "Well met, Sir Knights," he greeted them in slightly accented Elenic. "We've been expecting you. I am Kanzad, chief of the local office of the Ministry of the Interior. Ambassador Taubel posted me here to greet you."

"His Excellency is too kind," Vanion murmured.

"All the officials of the empire have been instructed to co-operate with you fully, Lord—?"

"Vanion."

Kanzad covered a momentary confusion. "I was led to believe that a Sir Sparhawk would be in command of your party."

"Sparhawk's been detained. He'll be joining us later."

"Ah." Kanzad recovered. "I'm afraid there'll be some slight delay before you can enter the city, Lord Vanion."

"Oh?"

Kanzad smiled a thin, humorless mile. "King Jaluah's feeling neglected at the moment." He threw a quick look at the squad of Cynesgans standing several paces behind him, then lowered his voice to a confidential tone. "Frankly, Lord Vanion, the Cynesgans and this pest-hole they call home are so unimportant in the affairs of the empire that no one takes them seriously. They're terribly touchy about that. Some idiot at the embassy neglected to pass on a routine communication from Matherion, and now the king's sulking in his palace. His sycophants have filled the streets with crowds of demonstrators. Ambassador Taubel's trying to smooth things over without resorting to the use of the Atan garrison, but things are a bit strained in the streets of Cynestra just now. His Excellency suggests that you and your companions wait here in Narset until he sends word that it's safe for you to proceed."

"As you think best," Vanion murmured politely.

Kanzad visibly relaxed. "First of all, let's get in out of this accursed sun." He turned and led them into the shabby village. There were no more than a couple dozen of the mud huts surrounding a well located in the sun-baked central square. Sparhawk idly wondered if the women of the village went to the well in the first steely light of dawn as the women of Cippria in Rendor had, and if they could possibly move with that same fluid grace. Then, for no reason at all, he wondered how Lillias was doing.

Aphrael leaned toward him from her sister's horse. "Shame on you, Sparhawk," she murmured.

"You've met Lillias," he replied easily, "so you know that she's not the sort of woman you forget—no matter how much you might want to."

The only building of any substance in the village was the local police station, an ominous stone structure with black iron bars on the windows. Kanzad's expression was smoothly apologetic. "It's not very inviting, Lord Vanion," he said deprecatingly, "but it's the coolest place in this pigsty."

"Should we kill him now and get it over with?" Bevier murmured to Sparhawk in Styric.

"Let's hold off on that," Sparhawk replied. "We have to wait for Aphrael's friend—whoever he is—so let's not precipitate anything just yet."

"I've had some refreshments prepared," Kanzad said to Vanion. "Why don't we go inside? That sun is really growing unbearable."

The knights dismounted and followed the policeman into the large dusty office. There was a long table set against one wall, a table laden with plates of sliced melon and figs and with flagons that promised other refreshments. "The fruits and melons here aren't nearly as palatable as those you'd find in Matherion," Kanzad apologized, "but the local wines aren't *entirely* undrinkable."

"Thanks all the same, Kanzad," Vanion declined, "but we stopped for lunch no more than an hour ago. We're all just fine."

A momentary flicker of annoyance crossed the Tamul's face. "I'll go make sure that your horses are being properly cared for, then, and I'll send a messenger to the embassy to advise Ambassador Taubel of your arrival." He turned and went out.

"Could you arrange some privacy, dear?" Vanion asked Sephrenia in Styric.

"Of course." She smiled. She quickly wove the spell and released it.

"Someday you'll have to teach me that one," he said.

"And become redundant?" She smiled. "Not on your life, my love."

"We appear to have taken them by surprise," Bevier noted. "Kanzad doesn't seem to have had much time to knock the rough edges off those lies he told us."

"I wouldn't," Ulath said as Kalten reached for one of the wine flagons. "One sip of that would probably stiffen you like a plank."

Kalten regretfully pushed the flagon away. "I suppose you're right," he agreed.

"We're prisoners, then, aren't we." Talen sighed. "That's depressing. I've been a thief all my life, and this is the first time I've ever been arrested."

"The fact that these refreshments are probably poisoned complicates things just a bit," Ulath growled. "Aside from that, Kanzad's been very helpful. He's just put us inside the strongest building in the village and he rather carelessly forgot to take our weapons. We can hold this place for as long as necessary."

"You're a fraud, Ulath." Bevier laughed. "Tynian's right. You pretend to hate sieges, but you're always the first one to suggest forting up."

"A true friend wouldn't mention that."

"I can provide water if worse comes to worst," Sephrenia told them, "but let's not precipitate anything just yet." She reached down and picked Flute up. "Have you had any hints about the one we're waiting for yet?"

Flute shook her head. "Nothing very specific so far. I *think* he's on his way, though."

"Good. This isn't really a very pleasant place."

"A thought, my Lords," Berit said. "Wouldn't it be a good idea to have Kanzad in here with us—just as a precaution? If someone starts thinking about storming the building, that might make them give it a few second thoughts."

"Good point," Ulath agreed.

Kanzad, however, did not return. The afternoon inched along, and the knights grew increasingly restless. "He's stalling, you know," Kalten said finally. "Either he's got reinforcements on the way, or he's hoping that we'll get thirsty."

"We'll just have to wait, Kalten," Flute told him. "The one who's going to be joining us is on his way."

"It's a race, then. We get to sit here making wagers on who gets here first—our new traveling companion or Kanzad's reinforcements."

"You can look at it that way if you want to, I suppose."

It was about two hours after their arrival in Narset when a large party came along the road from Cynestra. The man in the lead wore a rose-colored Tamul robe, and he was riding a spirited black horse. The ones following him were Atans.

"Whose side are the Atans on?" Talen asked.

"That depends on whether or not word from Matherion has reached the local garrison telling them to ignore orders from the Ministry of the Interior," Khalad replied.

"Things could be even murkier than that," Vanion suggested. "Back in Matherion, there's no love lost between the

Foreign Ministry and Interior. Kanzad was hinting at the fact that he and Ambassador Taubel are very cozy."

"That might suggest that our enemies have managed to penetrate Oscagne's service," Bevier added with a slightly worried frown.

"We'll find out in a minute," Berit said from where he had been watching out the window. "Kanzad just came out from behind the building."

They all crowded around the windows to watch.

Kanzad's welcoming smile crumbled from his face. "What are *you* doing here, Itagne?" he demanded of the Tamul on the black horse. "I sent for Ambassador Taubel."

The rose-clad man reined in. His eyes looked almost sleepy, and he had a lofty, superior expression on his face. "I'm afraid the ambassador's been detained, old boy," he replied in a cultured, almost deliberately insulting tone. His voice was oddly familiar. "He sends you his very best, though."

Kanzad struggled to regain his composure. "What is it exactly that's delaying the ambassador?" he asked bluntly.

Itagne turned his head slightly. "I'd say it was the chains, wouldn't you, Atana?" he asked the young Atan woman who appeared to be in charge of the detachment. "It's deucedly hard to run with chains on."

"It *could* be the chains, Itagne-Ambassador," the girl agreed. "Of course, the bars of his cell might be getting in his way, too." The young woman was full-figured, and her eyes were bold as she looked at the Tamul official.

"What's going on here?" Kanzad demanded.

"The Atana and I have become very close friends since my arrival, Kanzad—" Itagne smiled, "—but gentlemen shouldn't really talk about that sort of thing, should they? You *are* a gentleman, aren't you, Kanzad?"

"I wasn't talking about that." Kanzad's teeth were clenched. "What have you done with the ambassador?"

"There have been a few changes at the embassy, old boy— and in your own offices as well. I really hope you don't mind, but I had to commandeer your building. We don't *have* a dungeon at the embassy—distressing oversight there, I suppose. Anyway, Ambassador Taubel, along with all your grubby little policemen, are presently locked safely away in your dungeon. My compliments on it, incidentally. It's really very nice."

"By whose authority have you imprisoned the ambassador? You're only an undersecretary."

"Appearances *can* be deceiving, can't they? Actually, my brother placed *me* in charge here in Cynestra. My authority is absolute."

"Your brother?"

"Didn't the similarity between Oscagne's name and mine set off any bells in your brain, old boy? I *knew* you fellows at Interior were sort of limited, but I didn't think you were *that* dense. Shall we cut directly on through to the significant part of this discussion, Kanzad? It's beastly hot out here in the sun. My brother's authorized me to take charge here. I have the full support and cooperation of the Atan garrison, don't I, Atana?" He smiled at the golden giantess standing beside his horse.

"Oh *my*, yes, Itagne." She rolled her eyes. "We'll do almost *anything* for you."

"There you have it, then, Kanzad," Itagne said. "I've uncovered the fact that you and Taubel are a part of a treasonous conspiracy, so I've removed you from authority. I have all these lovely muscles to back me up, so there's really not a blasted thing you can do about it, is there?"

"You have no authority over me, Itagne."

"How tiresome." Itagne sighed. "Cynestra's currently under martial law, Kanzad. That means that I have authority over *everybody*. The Atans control the streets. I know you share my confidence in them." He looked critically at the policeman's stubborn face. "You just don't understand at all, do you, old boy?" He smiled fondly at the giantess. "Atana, dear, what would you do if I asked you to delete this tiresome wretch?"

"I'd kill him, Itagne." She shrugged, reaching for her sword. "Did you want me to split him up the middle, or just cut off his head?"

"Charming girl," Itagne murmured. "Let me think about it for a while, Atana. Kanzad's a fairly high-ranking official, so there may be some formalities involved." He turned back to the now-pasty-faced policeman. "I'm sure you see how things stand, dear boy," he said. "Oh, I suppose you should sort of consider yourself under arrest."

"On what charge?"

"I'm a Foreign Service man, Kanzad, so I'm not really up on all these legal terms. I suppose 'High Treason' will have to do. That's the crime they arrested Interior Minister Kolata for, anyway, and I used it again when I had Taubel picked up. It's an impressive sort of charge, and I'm sure that a man of your standing would be insulted if I had you arrested for loitering or spitting in the street. Atana, love, *do* be a dear and have this criminal taken back to Cynestra and thrown in his own dungeon."

"At once, Itagne-Ambassador," she replied.

"Darling child," he murmured.

"You favor your brother, your Excellency," Vanion said to the smiling Itagne, "not only in physical appearance but also in temperament."

"How *is* the old rascal?"

"He was well, the last time we saw him." Vanion frowned. "It might have been helpful if he'd told us that he was sending you here, though."

"That's my brother for you. Sometimes I think he tries to keep secrets from himself."

"Exactly what happened here, your Excellency?" Sparhawk asked him.

"You would be Sir Sparhawk," Itagne guessed. "Your nose is really famous, you know."

"Thank you," Kalten said modestly.

Itagne looked puzzled.

"I broke it for him, your Excellency—when we were children. I knew it was a good idea when I did it. He wears it like a badge. I'm a little disappointed in the fact that he's never once considered thanking me for the service I did him."

Itagne smiled. "As you've probably gathered, gentlemen, Oscagne sent me to Cynestra to look into the rather peculiar situation here. The chain of command in the outer corners of the empire's always been a little cloudy. The Foreign Office takes the position that the Elene kingdoms of the west, as well as Valesia, Arjuna, and Cynesga, are essentially foreign nations subservient to Tamul proper. This would make the ambassadors to those kingdoms the ultimate authority. Interior has always maintained that those kingdoms are integral parts of metropolitan Tamuli, and that puts *them* in charge. Oscagne and Kolata have been quibbling about it for years now. Ambassador Taubel's a political hack, and his stunning ability to reach a working accommodation with Interior sort of surprised my brother. That's why he pulled me out of the university— where I was quite happily putting down roots—and sent me here to investigate in the guise of an undersecretary." He laughed. "I'll make sure that he regrets it as much *this* time as he did both other times."

"That one escaped me, I'm afraid," Sparhawk conceded.

"This is the third time Oscagne's wrenched me out of private life to put out fires for him. I don't really like being wrenched, so I think I'll teach him a lesson this time. Maybe if I replace him as foreign minister for a while he'll get the point—if I ever decide to let him have his office back again."

"Are you really that good, Itagne?" Sephrenia asked him.

"Oh, good God, yes, dear lady. I'm at least twice as good as Oscagne—and he knows it. That's why my appointments are always temporary. Where was I? Oh, yes. I came to Cynestra, set up a functional apparatus, and found out in fairly short order that Taubel and Kanzad were eating from the same plate. Then I intercepted the instructions Matherion sent to Taubel after the disturbances there. I decided not to trouble him with the distressing news, so I went to the Atan garrison and personally took care of advising our towering friends that the Ministry of the Interior was no longer relevant. They were quite pleased about it, actually. The Atans dislike policemen intensely for some reason. I think it has to do with their national character. I was about ready to move on Kanzad and Taubel when one of my spies brought me word of your impending arrival, so I decided to wait until you got here before I upended things. I must say, Sparhawk, you *really* upset the people in the local office of the Interior Ministry."

"Oh?"

"They were running through the halls screaming, 'Sparhawk is coming! Sparhawk is coming!' "

"He has that effect on people sometimes," Flute told him. She looked around at the others. "This is the one," she told them. "We can leave here now."

Itagne looked baffled.

"In a moment," Sephrenia said to her sister. "Itagne, how did Interior find out that we were coming?"

He shrugged. "I didn't really look into that too deeply. There are all sorts of disgusting people who work for the Interior Ministry. One of them probably flogged four or five horses to death to bring the news."

"Quite impossible," she said. "No one could have gotten here ahead of us by normal means. Could the news have been brought by a Styric?"

"There aren't any Styrics in Cynesga, dear lady. The hatred between Cynesgans and Styrics predates history."

"Yes, I know. I think you may be wrong, though. I'm almost positive that at least *one* Styric passed through Cynestra just before the people at Interior went into their panic."

"How did you arrive at *that* conclusion, little mother?" Vanion asked her.

"There's a Styric working with our enemies," she replied. "He was in that shadow Sparhawk dissolved back in Edom. Whoever was inside was screaming in Styric, at any rate." She frowned. "I still don't understand how he got here before we did, though. He might be a renegade of some kind who has dealings with the Elder Gods. We've never really understood the full extent of their power."

"Could it be an Elder God himself?" Bevier asked apprehensively.

"No," Flute said flatly. "We imprisoned them all when we overthrew them—in much the same way we imprisoned Azash. The Elder Gods *don't* move around."

"I seem to be missing about half of this conversation," Itagne observed. "Aren't some introductions in order at this point?"

"Sorry, your Excellency," Vanion apologized. "We weren't really trying to be mysterious. The lady is obviously Styric. May I present Sephrenia, High Priestess of the Goddess Aphrael?"

"The Child-Goddess?"

"You know of her?" Sephrenia asked him.

"Some of my Styric colleagues at the university mentioned her to me. They didn't really seem to approve of her. They evidently feel that she's flighty—and a little frivolous."

"Flighty?" Flute objected. *"Frivolous?"*

"Don't take it personally," Sparhawk told her.

"But it *is* personal, Sparhawk! They've insulted me! When you get back to Matherion, I want you to go to the university and issue a challenge to those impious wretches! I want blood, Sparhawk! Blood!"

"Human sacrifice, Divine One?" he asked mildly. "Isn't that a little out of character?"

"Well—" She hesitated. "Couldn't you spank them anyway?"

Itagne was staring at them.

"Disappointing, isn't it?" Talen murmured.

* * *

To say that Oscagne's brother was shaken would be a profound understatement. He kept staring at Flute with bulging eyes as they rode eastward from Cynestra.

"Oh, *do* stop that, Itagne," she told him. "I'm not going to sprout another head or turn into a gorgon."

He shuddered and passed one hand across his face. "I should probably tell you that I don't believe in you," he said. "I'm not trying to be offensive, mind. It's just that I'm a confirmed skeptic in religious matters."

"I'll bet I can change your mind," she suggested with an impish little smile.

"Stop that," Sephrenia told her.

"He's a self-confessed agnostic, Sephrenia. That makes him fair game. Besides, I like him. I've never had a Tamul worshipper before, and I think I want one. Itagne will do just fine."

"No."

"I didn't ask you to buy him for me, Sephrenia. I'll coax him out of the bushes all by myself, so you're not in any way involved. It's really none of your business, dear sister, so keep your nose out of it."

"Does this ever get any easier?" Itagne plaintively asked the rest of them.

"No." Kalten laughed. "You get numb after a while, though. I've found that drinking helps."

"That's Kalten's answer to everything," Flute said with an airy little toss of her head. "He tries to cure winter with a barrel of Arcian red—every year."

"Have we finished here in this part of the empire?" Sparhawk asked her.

"No. Something else is supposed to happen." The Child-Goddess sighed and nestled against her sister. "Please don't be angry with me, Sephrenia," she said. "You're not going to like what's coming, I'm afraid. It's necessary, though. No matter how much it upsets you, always remember that I love you." She sat up and held her hands out to Sparhawk. "I need to talk with you," she said to him. "Privately."

"Secrets?" Talen asked her.

"Every girl needs secrets, Talen. You'll learn more about that as time goes on. Let's ride off a ways, Sparhawk."

They rode away from the road for several hundred yards and then moved on, keeping pace with the others. Faran's steel-shod hooves clattered on the rusty sun-baked gravel of the desert floor.

"We'll be going on toward the Tamul border," Flute said as they rode. "This event that's ahead of us will happen there, and I'll have to leave you before it does."

"Leave?" He was startled.

"You'll be able to manage without me for a while. I can't be present when this event takes place. There's a propriety involved. I may be as flighty and frivolous as Itagne suggested, but I *do* have good manners. A certain personage will be taking part in this affair and he'd be insulted if I were present. He and I have had some disagreements in the past, and we're not speaking to each other at the moment." She made a rueful little face. "It's been quite a lengthy moment," she admitted, "eight or ten thousand years, actually. He's doing something I don't really approve of—of course he's never fully explained it to me. I like him well enough, but he's got a terribly superior attitude. He always behaves as if the rest of us are too stupid to understand what he's doing—but *I* understand very well. He's breaking one of the cardinal rules." She waved her hand as if brushing it aside. "That's between him and me, though. Look after my sister, Sparhawk. She's going to have a very difficult time."

"She's not going to get sick, is she?"

"She'd probably prefer that." The Child-Goddess sighed. "I wish there were some way I could spare her this, but there isn't. She has to go through it if she's going to continue to grow."

"Aphrael, she's over three hundred years old."

"What's that got to do with it? I'm a hundred times older than that, and *I'm* still growing. She has to do the same. I'm loveable, Sparhawk, but I never promised to be easy. This is going to be terribly painful to her, but she'll be much better for having gone through it."

"You're not making any sense, you know."

"I don't have to make sense, Father. That's one of the advantages of my situation."

They made the journey from Cynestra to the border west of Sarna in easy stages, moving at a leisurely pace from oasis to oasis. Sparhawk could not be positive, but it seemed Aphrael was waiting for something. She and Vanion spent a great deal of time with the map, and their jumps across the sun-baked gravel of eastern Cynesga grew shorter and shorter, and their stays at the oases longer. As they neared the border, their pace

slowed even more, and more often than not they found themselves simply riding, plodding their way eastward through the
interminable, empty miles without any resort to Bhelliom at
all.

"It's difficult to get anything very precise," Itagne was saying on the afternoon of their fourth day out from Cynestra.
"Most of the sightings have been made by desert nomads, and
they don't trust the authorities enough to speak with them at
any length. There have been the usual wild stories about vampires and werewolves and Harpies and the like, but I rather
imagine that most of those flew out of the neck of a wineskin.
The Cynesgan authorities laugh most of those off as no more
than the hallucinations of ignorant people who drink too much
and spend too much time out in the sun. They take the reports
of sightings of the Shining Ones very seriously, however."

"All right, Itagne," Kalten said irritably, "we've been hearing about these 'Shining Ones' ever since we came to Daresia.
People turn all trembly and white-knuckled and refuse to talk
about them. We've got you way out here in the desert where
you can't run away, so why don't you tell us just who—or
what—they are."

"It's really quite grotesque, Sir Kalten," Itagne told him,
"and more than a little sickening."

"I've got a strong stomach. Are they some kind of monster?
Twelve feet tall and with nine heads or something?"

"No. Actually they're supposed to look like ordinary humans."

"Why are they called by that peculiar name?" Berit asked.

"Why don't you let *me* ask the questions, Berit?" Kalten
said bluntly. Kalten, it appeared, still had problems where Berit
was concerned.

"Excuse me, Sir Kalten," Berit replied, looking just a bit
startled and slightly hurt.

"Well?" Kalten said to Oscagne's brother. "What does it
mean? Why are they called that?"

"Because they glow like fireflies, Sir Kalten." Itagne
shrugged.

"That's all?" Kalten asked incredulously. "The whole continent collapses in terror just because some people glow in the
dark?"

"Of course not. The fact that they glow is just a warning.
Everybody in Tamuli knows that when he sees someone who

shines like the morning star coming toward him, he'd better turn around and run for his life."

"What are these monsters supposed to be able to do?" Talen asked. "Do they eat people alive or tear them all to pieces or something?"

"No," Itagne replied somberly. "The legend has it that their merest touch is death."

"Sort of like poisonous snakes?" Khalad suggested.

"Much worse than that, young sir. The touch of the Shining Ones rots a man's flesh from his bones. It's the decay of the grave, and the victim isn't dead when it happens. The descriptions from folklore are very lurid. We're given pictures of people standing stock-still, shrieking in agony and horror as their faces and limbs dissolve into slime and run like melted wax."

"That's a graphic picture." Ulath shuddered. "I'd imagine it sort of interferes with establishing normal relations with these people."

"Indeed, Sir Ulath." Itagne smiled. "But despite all of that, the Shining Ones are among the most popular figures in Tamul literature—which may provide you with some insight into the perversity of our minds."

"Are you talking about ghost stories?" Talen asked him. "Some people like those, I've heard."

"Delphaeic literature is far more complex than that."

"Delphaeic? What does that mean?"

"Literature refers to the Shining Ones as the Delphae," Itagne replied, "and the mythic city where they live is called Delphaeus."

"It's a pretty name."

"I think that's part of the problem. Tamuls tend to be sentimentalists, and the musical quality of the word fills the eyes of our lesser poets with tears and their brains with mush. They ignore the most unpleasant aspects of the legend and present the Delphae as a simple, pastoral people who are grossly misunderstood. For seven centuries they've inflicted abominable pastoral verse and overdrawn adolescent eclogues on us. They've pictured the Delphae as lyric shepherds, glowing like fireflies and mooning about the landscape, suffering pangs of unrequited love and pondering—ponderously, of course—the banalities of their supposed religion. The academic world has come to regard Delphaeic literature as a bad joke perpetuated far too long."

"It's an abomination!" Sephrenia declared with uncharacteristic heat.

"Your critical perception does you credit, dear lady—" Itagne smiled. "—but I think your choice of terms overdignifies the genre. *I'd* characterize Delphaeic literature as adolescent sentimentality perhaps, but I don't really take it seriously enough to grow indignant about it."

"Delphaeic literature is a mask for the most pernicious kind of anti-Styric bigotry!" she said in tones she usually reserved for ultimatums.

Vanion appeared to be as baffled by her sudden outburst as Sparhawk and the rest. He looked around, obviously seeking some way to change the subject.

"It's moving on toward sunset," Kalten noted, stepping in to lend a hand. Kalten's perceptiveness sometimes surprised Sparhawk. "Flute," he said, "did you plan to put us down beside another one of those waterholes for the night?"

"Oasis, Kalten," Vanion corrected him. "They call it an oasis, not a waterhole."

"That's up to them. They can call it whatever they want, but I know a waterhole when I see one. If we're going to do this the old-fashioned way, we're going to have to start looking for a place to camp, and there's a ruin of some kind on that hilltop over there to the north. Sephrenia can squeeze water out of the air for us, and if we stay in those ruins we won't have to put up with the smell of boiling dog all night the way we usually do when we camp near one of their villages."

"The Cynesgan don't eat dogs, Sir Kalten." Itagne laughed.

"I wouldn't swear to that without an honest count of all the dogs in one of their villages—both before and *after* supper."

"Sparhawk!" It was Khalad, and he was roughly shaking his lord into wakefulness. "There are people out there!"

Sparhawk threw his blankets to one side and rolled to his feet, reaching for his sword. "How many?" he asked quietly.

"I've seen a dozen or so. They're creeping around among those boulders down by the road."

"Wake the others."

"Yes, my Lord."

"Quietly, Khalad."

Khalad gave him a flat, unfriendly stare.

"Sorry."

The ruin in which they had set up their camp had been a

fortress at one time. The stones were roughly squared off, and they had been set without mortar. Uncounted centuries of blowing dust and sand had worn the massive blocks smooth and had rounded the edges. Sparhawk crossed what appeared to have been a court to the tumbled wall on the south side of the fortress and looked down toward the road.

A thick cloudbank had crept in during the night to obscure the sky. Sparhawk peered toward the road, silently cursing the darkness. Then he heard a faint rustling sound just on the other side of the broken wall.

"Don't get excited," Talen whispered.

"Where have you been?"

"Where else?" The boy climbed over the rubble to join the big Pandion.

"Did you take Berit with you again?" Sparhawk asked acidly.

"No. Berit's a little too noisy now that he's taken to wearing chain mail, and his integrity always seems to get in the way."

Sparhawk grunted. "Well?" he asked.

"You're not going to believe this, Sparhawk."

"I might surprise you."

"Those are more of those Cyrgai out there."

"Are you sure?"

"I didn't stop one to ask him, but they look exactly the same as those ones we ran across west of Sarsos did. They've got on those funny-looking helmets, the old-fashioned armor, and those silly short dresses they wear."

"I think they're called kilts."

"A dress is a dress, Sparhawk."

"Are they doing anything tactically significant?"

"You mean forming up for an attack? No. I think these are just scouts. They don't have their spears or shields with them, and they're doing a lot of crawling around on their bellies."

"Let's go talk with Vanion and Sephrenia."

They crossed the rubble-littered courtyard of the ancient fortress. "Our young thief's been disobeying orders again," Sparhawk told the others.

"No, I haven't," Talen disagreed. "You didn't order me not to go look at those people, so how can you accuse me of disobeying you?"

"I didn't order you not to because I didn't know they were out there."

"That *did* sort of make things easier. I'll admit that."

"Our wandering boy here reports that the people creeping around down by the road are Cyrgai."

"Someone on the other side's been winnowing through the past again?" Kalten suggested.

"No," Flute said, raising her head slightly. The little girl had appeared to have been sleeping soundly in her sister's arms. "The Cyrgai out there are as alive as you are. They aren't from the past."

"That's impossible," Bevier objected. "The Cyrgai are extinct."

"Really?" the Child-Goddess said. "How astonishing that they didn't notice that. Trust me, gentlemen. I'm in a position to know. The Cyrgai who are creeping up on you are contemporary."

"The Cyrgai died out ten thousand years ago, Divine One," Itagne said firmly.

"Maybe you should run down the hill and let them know about it, Itagne," she told him. "Let me go, Sephrenia."

Sephrenia looked a little startled.

Aphrael kissed her sister tenderly and then stepped a little way away. "I have to leave you now. The reasons are very complex, so you'll just have to trust me."

"What about those Cyrgai?" Kalten demanded. "We're not going to let you wander off in the dark while they're out there."

She smiled. "Would someone please explain this to him?" she asked them.

"Are you going to leave us in danger like this?" Ulath demanded.

"Are you worried about your own safety, Ulath?"

"Of course not, but I thought I could shame you into staying until we'd dealt with them."

"The Cyrgai aren't going to bother you, Ulath," she said patiently. "They'll be going away almost immediately." She looked around at them. Then she sighed. "I really have to leave now," she said regretfully. "I'll rejoin you later."

Then she wavered like a reflection in a pool and vanished.

"Aphrael!" Sephrenia cried, half reaching out.

"That is *truly* uncanny," Itagne muttered. "Was she serious about the Cyrgai?" he asked them. "Is it at all possible that some of them actually survived their war with the Styrics?"

"I wouldn't care to call her a liar," Ulath said. "Particularly not around Sephrenia. Our little mother here is very protective."

"I've noticed that," Itagne said. "I wouldn't offend you or your Goddess for the world, dear Lady, but would you be at all upset if we made a few preparations? History is one of my specialties at the university, and the Cyrgai had—have, I suppose—a fearsome reputation. I trust your little Goddess implicitly, of course, but . . ." He looked around apprehensively.

"Sephrenia?" Sparhawk said.

"Don't bother me." She seemed terribly shocked by Aphrael's sudden departure.

"Snap out of it, Sephrenia. Aphrael had to leave, but she'll be back later. I need an answer right now. Can I use Bhelliom to set up some kind of barrier that will hold the Cyrgai off until whatever it was that Aphrael was talking about chases them away?"

"Yes, but you'd let our enemy know exactly where you are if you did that."

"He already knows," Vanion pointed out. "I doubt that those Cyrgai stumbled across us by accident."

"He has a point there," Bevier agreed.

"Why bother with holding them off?" Kalten asked. "Sparhawk can move us ten leagues on down the road faster than we can blink. I'm not so attached to this place that I'll lose any sleep if I'm not around to watch the sun come up over it."

"I've never done it at night," Sparhawk said dubiously. He looked at Sephrenia. "Would the fact that I can't see where I'm going have any effect at all?"

"How would I know?" She sounded a little cross.

"Please, Sephrenia," he said. "I've got a problem, and I need your help."

"What in God's name is going on?" Berit exclaimed. He pointed to the north. "Look at that!"

"Fog?" Ulath said incredulously. "Fog in the *desert*?"

They stared at the strange phenomenon moving steadily toward them across the arid desert.

"Lord Vanion," Khalad said in a troubled voice, "does your map show any towns or settlements off to the north?"

Vanion shook his head. "Nothing but open desert."

"There are lights out there, though. You can see them reflecting off the fog. They're close to the ground, but you can definitely see them."

"I've seen lights in the fog before," Bevier said, "but never quite like that. That isn't torchlight."

"You're right there," Ulath agreed. "I've never seen light quite that color before—and it seems to be just lying on the fog itself, almost like a blanket."

"It's probably just the camp of some desert nomads, Sir Ulath," Itagne suggested. "Mist and fog do strange things to light sometimes. In Matherion you'll see light reflected off the mother-of-pearl on the buildings. Some nights it's like walking around inside a rainbow."

"We'll know more about it in a little bit," Kalten said. "That fog's moving right straight toward us, and it's bringing the light with it." He raised his face. "And there's absolutely no breeze. What's going on here, Sephrenia?"

Before she could answer, shrieks of terror came from the south, where the road was. Talen scurried across the littered yard to the tumbled wall. "The Cyrgai are running away!" he shouted. "They're throwing away their swords and helmets and running like rabbits!"

"I don't like the feel of this, Sparhawk," Kalten said bleakly, drawing his sword.

The fogbank approaching them had divided and flowed around the hill upon which they stood. It was a thick fog such as one might see in a coastal city, and it moved across the arid, barren desert, marching inexorably upon the ruined fortress.

"There's something moving in there!" Talen shouted from the far side of the ruin.

They were only blurs of light at first, but as the strange fog-bank drew nearer, they grew more and more distinct. Sparhawk could clearly make out the shapes of nebulous bodies now. Whatever they were, they had human shapes.

Then Sephrenia shrieked as one seized in the grip of an overpowering rage. "Defiled ones! Defiled ones! Foul and accursed!"

They stared at her, stunned by her sudden outburst.

The lights in the fog never faltered but continued their glowing, inexorable advance.

"Run!" Itagne suddenly shouted. "Run for your lives! It's the Delphae—the Shining Ones!"

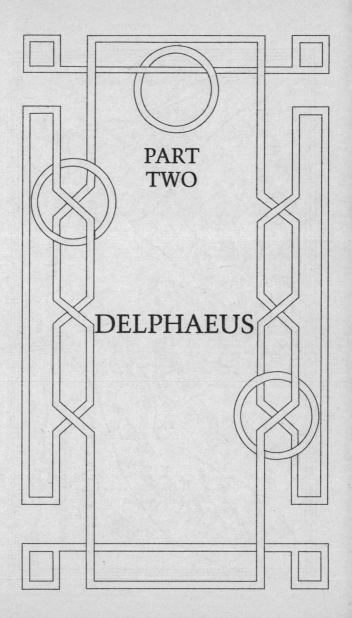

PART
TWO

DELPHAEUS

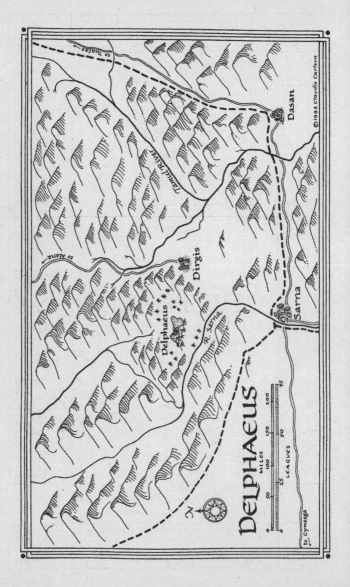

CHAPTER
ELEVEN

I t was the fog, perhaps. The fog blurred everything. There were no precise outlines, no
clear, sharp dangers, and the glowing figures
in the mist approached slowly, seeming al-
most to float up the graveled slope toward the ancient ruin,
bringing their obscuring fog with them. Their faces, their very
shapes, were indistinct, softened until they seemed hardly more
than glowing blurs. It was the fog, perhaps—but then again,
perhaps not. For whatever reason, Sparhawk felt no alarm.

The Delphae stopped about twenty yards from the broken
walls of the ruin and stood with their glowing fog eddying and
swirling around them, erasing the night with cold, pale fire.

Sparhawk's mind was strangely detached, his thoughts clear
and precise. "Well met, neighbors," he called out to the shapes
in the mist.

"Are you mad?" Itagne gasped.

"Destroy them, Sparhawk!" Sephrenia hissed. "Use the
Bhelliom! Obliterate them!"

"Why don't we see what they want first?"

"How can you be so calm, man?" Itagne demanded.

"Training, I suppose." Sparhawk shrugged. "You develop
instincts after a while. Those people out there don't have any
hostile intentions."

"He's right, Itagne," Vanion said. "You can definitely feel it

165

when someone wants to kill you. Those people out there don't want to fight. They're not afraid of us, but they're not here to fight. Let's see where this goes, gentlemen. Keep your guard up, but let's not precipitate anything—not yet, anyway."

"Anakha," one of the glowing figures in the fog called.

"That's a good start," Vanion murmured. "See what they want, Sparhawk."

Sparhawk nodded and stepped closer to the time-eroded boulders of the fallen wall. "You know me?" he called, speaking in Tamul.

"The very rocks know the name of Anakha. Thou art as no other man who hath ever lived." The language was archaic and profoundly formal. "We bear thee no malice, and we come in friendship."

"I'll listen to what you have to say." Sparhawk heard Sephrenia's sharp intake of breath behind him.

"We offer thee and thy companions sanctuary," the Delphae out in the fog told him. "Thine enemies are all about thee, and thy peril is great here in the land of the Cyrgai. Come thou even unto Delphaeus, and we will give thee rest and safety."

"Your offer's generous, neighbor," Sparhawk replied, "and my companions and I are grateful." His tone, however, was dubious.

"We sense thy reluctance." The voice in the fog seemed strangely hollow with a sort of reverberating echo to it, an echo such as one might hear in a long, empty corridor, a sound receding off into some immeasurable distance. "Be assured that we mean thee and thy companions no harm, and shouldst thou choose to come to Delphaeus, we will pledge thee our protection. Few there are in all this world who will willingly face us."

"So I've heard. But that brings up a question. Why, neighbor? We're strangers here. What possible interest can the Delphae have in our affairs? What do you hope to gain from this offer of friendship?"

The glowing shape in the fog hesitated. "Thou hast taken up Bhelliom, Anakha—for good or for ill, and thou knowest not which. Thy will is no longer thine own, for Bhelliom bends thee to its own purpose. Thou art no longer of this world, nor is thy destiny. Thy design and thy destiny are of Bhelliom's devising. In truth, we are indifferent to thee and thy companions, for our offer of friendship is not to thee, but to Bhelliom, and it is from Bhelliom that we will extract the price of that friendship."

"That's direct enough," Kalten muttered.

"Thy peril is greater than thou knowest," the glowing speaker continued. "Bhelliom is the greatest prize in all the universe, and beings beyond thine imagining seek to possess it. It *will* not be possessed, however. It chooseth its own, and it hath chosen thee. Into *thy* hand hath it placed itself, and through *thine* ears must we speak with it and offer our exchange." The speaker paused. "Consider what we have told thee here and put aside thy suspicion. Thy success or failure in completing Bhelliom's design may hinge on our assistance—or its lack—and we *will* have our price. We will speak more of this anon."

The fog swirled and thickened, and the glowing shapes dimmed and faded. A sudden night breeze, as chill as winter and as arid as dust, swept across the desert, and the fog tattered and shawled, whirling, all seethe and confusion. And then it was gone, and the Shining Ones with it.

"Don't listen to them, Sparhawk!" Sephrenia said in a shrill voice. "Don't even consider what he said! It's a trick!"

"We're not children, Sephrenia," Vanion told the woman he loved. "We're not really gullible enough to accept the word of strangers at face value—particularly not the word of strangers like the Delphae."

"You don't know them, Vanion. Their words are like the honey that lures and traps the unwary fly. You should have destroyed them, Sparhawk."

"Sephrenia," Vanion said in a troubled tone, "you've spent the last forty years with your hand on my sword arm trying to keep me from hurting people. Why have you changed? What's making you so bloodthirsty all of a sudden?"

She gave him a flat, hostile look. "You wouldn't understand."

"That's an evasion, dear, and you know me well enough to know that it's probably not true. The Delphae may not have been entirely candid with us about their offer, but they weren't hostile, and they weren't threatening us in any way."

"Ah—Lord Vanion," Ulath interrupted, "I don't think anybody in his right mind would threaten Sparhawk. Threatening the man who holds Bhelliom in his fist is *not* the course of wisdom—not even for people who glow in the dark and mulch their neighbors down into compost."

"That's exactly my point, Vanion," Sephrenia seized upon Ulath's words. "The Delphae were afraid to attack us because of Bhelliom. That's all that was holding them back."

"But they *were* holding back. They weren't any danger to us. Why did you want Sparhawk to kill them?"

"I despise them!" It came out in a kind of hiss.

"Why? What did they ever do to you?"

"They have no right to exist!"

"Everything has a right to exist, Sephrenia—even wasps and scorpions. You've spent your whole life teaching bloodthirsty young Pandions that lesson. Why are you suddenly throwing it away?"

She turned her face away from him.

"Please don't do that. You've got some kind of problem here, and your problems are mine. Let's pull this out into the light and look at it."

"No!" And she turned abruptly on her heel and stalked away.

"It has absolutely no basis in fact," Itagne told them as they rode across the barren miles under a murky sky.

"Those are usually the best stories," Talen said.

Itagne smiled briefly. "There's been a body of folklore about the Shining Ones in Tamul culture for eons. It started out with the usual horror stories, I suppose, but there's something in the Tamul nature that drives us to extremes. About seven hundred years ago, a decidedly minor poet began to tamper with the legend. Instead of concentrating on the horror, he began to wax sentimental, delving into how the Delphae felt about their situation. He wept copiously in vile verse about their loneliness and their sense of being outcast. He unfortunately turned to the pastoral tradition and added the mawkishness of that silly conceit to his other extravagances. His most famous work was a long narrative poem entitled 'Xadane.' Xadane was supposedly a Delphaeic shepherdess who fell in love with a normal human shepherd boy. As long as they met in the daytime, everything was fine, but Xadane had to run away every afternoon to keep her paramour from discovering her real identity. The poem's very long and tedious, and it's filled with lengthy, lugubrious passages in which Xadane feels sorry for herself. It's absolutely awful."

"I gather from what those people out in the fog said last night that the word *Delphae* is their own name for themselves," Bevier noted. "If Tamul literature also uses the term, that would seem to suggest some sort of contacts."

"So it would, Sir Knight," Itagne replied, "but there's no record of them. The traditions are very old, and I suspect that many of them grew out of the warped minds of third-rate poets. The city of Delphaeus supposedly lies in an isolated valley high in the mountains of southern Atan. The Delphae are said to be a Tamul people somewhat akin to the Atans but without the gigantic proportions. If we're to believe our poets, which we probably shouldn't, the Delphae were a simple pastoral folk who followed their flocks into that valley and were trapped there by an avalanche that sealed the only pass leading to the outside world."

"That's not entirely impossible," Ulath said.

"The impossibilities start cropping up later on in the story," Itagne said dryly. "We're told that there's a lake in the center of the valley, and the lake's supposed to be the source of the Delphaeic peculiarity. It's said to glow, and since it's the only source of water in the valley, the Delphae and their flocks are forced to drink from it and bathe in it. The story has it that after a while, they *also* started to glow." He smiled faintly. "They must save a fortune on candles."

"That's not really possible, is it?" Talen asked skeptically. "I mean, people aren't going to glow in the dark just because of what they eat or drink, are they?"

"I'm not a scientist, young sir, so don't ask me about what's possible and impossible. It could be some sort of mineral, or maybe a form of algae, I suppose. It's a neat sort of explanation for an imaginary characteristic."

"Those people last night *did* glow, your Excellency," Kalten reminded him.

"Yes, and I'm trying very hard to forget about that." Itagne looked back over his shoulder. Sephrenia had refused to listen to any discussion of the Delphae, and she and Berit followed the others at some distance. "Lady Sephrenia's reaction to the Delphae isn't really uncommon among Styrics, you know. The very name makes them irrational. Anyway, 'Xadane' enjoyed enormous popularity, and there were the usual imitators. A whole body of literature grew up around the Delphae. It's called, quite naturally, Delphaeic literature. Serious people don't take it seriously, and foolish people take it foolishly. You know how that goes."

"Oh, yes," Bevier murmured. "I had to read whole libraries

full of abominable verse when I was a student. Every professor had his favorite poet, and they all inflicted them on us without mercy. I think that's what ultimately led me to take up a military career."

Khalad came riding back to join them. "I wouldn't want to seem critical of my betters, my Lords," he said dryly, "but the decision to abandon the road and cut across country may have been just a little ill-advised on a day when we can't see the sun. Does anyone know which way we're going?"

"East," Vanion said firmly.

"Yes, my Lord," Khalad replied. "If you say it's east, then it's east—even if it really isn't. Aren't we supposed to be getting fairly close to the border?"

"It shouldn't be very far ahead."

"Doesn't your map indicate that the River Sarna marks the boundary between Cynesga and Tamul proper?"

Vanion nodded.

"Well, I just rode to the top of that hill up ahead and took a look around. I could see for about ten leagues in every direction, and there aren't any rivers out there. Do you suppose that someone might have stolen the Sarna?"

"Be nice," Sparhawk murmured.

"Cartography's not an exact art, Khalad," Vanion pointed out. "The distances on any map are only approximate. We started out at dawn, and we rode toward the lightest place in the cloud-cover. Unless somebody's changed things, that's east. We've taken sightings on landmarks every hour or so, and we're still riding in the same direction we were when we set out this morning."

"Where's the river then, my Lord?" Khalad asked, then looked at Itagne. "How wide would you say the valley of the Sarna is, your Excellency?"

"Sixty leagues, anyway. It's the longest and widest river on the continent, and the valley's very fertile."

"Grass? Trees? Lots of green crops?"

Itagne nodded.

"There's not a hint of green in any direction, my Lords," Khalad declared. "It's all a brown wasteland."

"We're riding east," Vanion insisted. "The mountains of Atan should be to the north—off to the left."

"They could be, my Lord, but they're a little bashful today. They're hiding themselves in the clouds."

"I've told you, Khalad, the map's inaccurate, that's all."

Vanion looked back over his shoulder. "Why don't you ride back and ask Sephrenia and Berit to join us? It's about lunchtime, isn't it, Kalten?"

"Definitely, my Lord."

"I sort of thought so myself. Let's dig into the packs and put together something to eat."

"Is Sir Kalten skilled at estimating the time?" Itagne asked Sparhawk.

Sparhawk smiled. "We normally rely on Khalad—when the sun's out. When it's cloudy, though, we fall back on Kalten's stomach. He can usually tell you to within a minute how long it's been since the last time he ate."

Late that afternoon when they had stopped for the night, Khalad stood a short distance from where the rest of them were setting up their encampment. He was looking out over the featureless desert with a slightly smug expression on his face. "Sparhawk," he called, "could you come here a moment? I want to show you something."

Sparhawk put down Faran's saddle and walked over to join his squire. "Yes?" he asked.

"I think you'd better talk with Lord Vanion. He probably won't listen to me, since he's already got his mind made up, but somebody's going to have to convince him that we haven't been riding east today."

"You're going to have to convince me first."

"All right." The husky young man pointed out across the desert. "We came from that direction, right?"

"Yes."

"If we've been riding east, that would be west, right?"

"You're being obvious."

"Yes, I know. I have to be. I'm trying to explain something to a knight. The last time I looked, the sun went down in the west."

"Please, Khalad, don't try to be clever. Just get to the point."

"Yes, my Lord. If that's west, then why's the sun going down over there?" He turned and pointed off toward the left, where an angry orange glow stained the clouds.

Sparhawk blinked, and then he muttered an oath. "Let's go talk to Vanion," he said, and led the way back across the camp to where the Pandion Preceptor was speaking with Sephrenia.

"We've got a problem," Sparhawk told them. "We made a wrong turn somewhere today."

"Are you still riding that tired horse, Khalad?" Vanion's tone was irritable. His conversation with Sephrenia had obviously not been going well.

"Our young friend here just pointed something out to me," Sparhawk said. "Speaking slowly, of course, because of my limited understanding. He says that unless somebody's moved the sun, we've been riding north all day."

"That's impossible."

Sparhawk turned and pointed toward the ugly orange glow on the horizon. "That's *not* the direction we came from, Vanion."

Vanion stared at the horizon for a moment, and then he started to swear.

"You wouldn't listen to me, would you?" Sephrenia accused. "*Now* will you believe me when I tell you that the Delphae will deceive you at every turn?"

"It was our *own* mistake, Sephrenia—well, mine, anyway. We can't just automatically blame the Delphae for everything that goes wrong."

"I've known you since you were a boy, Vanion, and you've never made this kind of mistake before. I've seen you find your way on a dark night in the middle of a snowstorm."

"I must have confused a couple of landmarks and taken my bearings on the wrong one." Vanion grimaced. "Thanks for being so polite about it, Khalad—and so patient. We could have ridden on until we ran into the polar ice. I tend to get pigheaded sometimes."

Sephrenia smiled fondly at him. "I much prefer to speak of your singleness of purpose, dear one," she told him.

"It means the same thing, doesn't it?"

"Yes, but it sounds nicer."

"Set out some markers, Khalad," Vanion instructed. He looked around. "There aren't any sticks lying around, so pile up heaps of rock and mark them with scraps of colored cloth. Let's get an absolute reference on the position of the sun this evening so that we don't make the same mistake again tomorrow morning."

"I'll take care of it, my Lord."

"They're back," Kalten said, roughly shaking Sparhawk awake.

"Who's back?" Sparhawk sat up.

"Your glowing friends. They want to talk with you again."

Sparhawk rose to his feet and followed his friend to the edge of the camp.

"I was standing watch," Kalten said quietly, "and they just appeared out of nowhere. Itagne's stories are entertaining enough, but I don't think they're all that accurate. The Shining Ones don't shine all the time. They crept up on me in the dark, and they didn't start to glow until they were in place."

"Are they still staying back a ways?"

Kalten nodded. "They're keeping their distance. There's no way we could rush them."

There was no fog this time, and there were only two of the Shining Ones standing about twenty yards from the picketed horses. The eerie glow emanating from them still blurred their features, however.

"Thy peril increases, Anakha," that same hollow, echoing voice declared. "Thine enemies are seeking thee up and down in the land."

"We haven't seen anyone, neighbor."

"It is the unseen enemy which is most perilous. It is with their minds that thine enemies seek thee. We urge thee to accept our offer of sanctuary. It may soon be too late."

"I wouldn't offend you for the world, neighbor, but we've only got your word for this unseen danger, and I think you may be exaggerating a bit. You said that Bhelliom's directing my steps, and Bhelliom has unlimited power. I've tested that myself a few times. Thanks for your concern, but I still think I can take care of myself and my friends." He paused a moment and then plunged ahead on an impulse. "Why don't we just cut across all this polite chitchat? You've already admitted to a certain self-interest here. Why don't you come right out and tell me what you want and what you're prepared to offer in exchange? That might give us a basis for negotiation."

"Your charm's positively blinding, Sparhawk," Kalten muttered.

"We will consider thy proposal, Anakha." The echoing voice was cold.

"Do that. Oh, one other thing, neighbor. Stop tampering with our direction. Deceit and trickery at the outset always seem to get negotiations off on the wrong foot."

The glowing Delphae did not respond, but receded back into the desert and slipped out of sight.

"Then you *do* believe me, don't you, Sparhawk?" Sephrenia

said from just behind the two knights. "You realize how un-
principled and dishonest those creatures are."

"Let's just say that I'm keeping an open mind on the subject, little mother. You were absolutely right about what you
said earlier, though. We could blindfold Vanion, spin him
around in circles for a day or so, and he'd still come out pointing due north." He looked around. "Is everybody awake? I
think we'd better start considering options."

They returned to the place where their beds were laid out on
the hard, uncomfortable gravel. "You're really very clever,
Sparhawk," Bevier said. "The fact that our visitors didn't deny
that accusation you pulled out of the air suggests that
Sephrenia's been right about them all along. They *have* been
misdirecting us."

"That doesn't alter the fact that the Cyrgai are out there,"
Ulath reminded him, "and the Cyrgai are definitely our enemies. We may not know what the Delphae are really up to, but
they ran off the Cyrgai for us last night, and that sort of inclines me to like them."

"Could that have been some sort of collusion?" Berit asked.

"That's very unlikely," Itagne said. "The Cyrgai traditionally
have a sublime belief that they're the crown of creation.
They'd never agree to any ruse that put them in a subservient
position—not even for the sake of appearances. It's just not in
their racial makeup."

"He's right," Sephrenia agreed, "and even though I hate to
admit it, an alliance of that sort would be totally out of character for the Delphae as well. There could be no common
ground between them and the Cyrgai. I don't know what the
Delphae are doing in this business, but they have their own
agenda. They wouldn't be cat's-paws for anyone else."

"Wonderful," Talen said sardonically, "now we've got *two*
enemies to worry about."

"Why worry at all?" Kalten shrugged. "Bhelliom can put us
down on the outskirts of Matherion in the space between two
heartbeats. Why don't we just go away and leave the Cyrgai
and the Delphae here in this wasteland to resolve their differences without us?"

"No," Sephrenia said.

"Why not?"

"Because the Delphae have misdirected us already. We *don't*
want to go to Delphaeus."

"They're not going to be able to fool the Bhelliom,

Sephrenia," Vanion disagreed. "They might have been able to confuse *me*, but Bhelliom's an entirely different matter."

"I don't think we can take that chance, dear one. The Delphae want something from Sparhawk, and it's obviously going to involve Bhelliom. Let's not deliver them both into Delphaeic hands. I know that it's tedious and dangerous, but let's keep our feet on the ground. Bhelliom moves through a vast emptiness. If the Delphae can deceive it, we could come out of that emptiness almost anyplace."

"What's an eclogue?" Talen asked. They were riding toward what they hoped was the east the following morning, and Itagne was continuing his rambling discourse on Delphaeic literature.

"It's a sort of primitive drama," he replied. "It usually involves a meeting between two shepherds. They stand around discussing philosophy in bad verse."

"I've known a few sheepherders," Khalad said, "and philosophy wasn't their usual topic of conversation. They're far more interested in women."

"There's some of that involved in eclogues as well, but it's so idealized that it's hardly recognizable." Itagne tugged thoughtfully at one earlobe. "I think it's some sort of disease," he mused. "The more civilized people become, the more they romanticize the simple bucolic life and ignore the dirt and grinding toil involved. Our sillier poets grow all weepy-eyed about shepherds—and shepherdesses, of course. It wouldn't be nearly as much fun without the shepherdesses. The aristocracy periodically becomes enamored of the pastoral tradition, and they go to great lengths to act out their fantasies. Emperor Sarabian's father even went so far as to have an idealized sheep farm built down near Saranth. He and his court used to go there in the summertime and spend months pretending to watch over flocks of badly overfed sheep. Their rude smocks and kirtles were made of velvet and satin, and they'd sit around all moony-eyed composing bad verse and ignoring the fact that their sheep were wandering off in all directions." He leaned back in his saddle. "Pastoral literature doesn't really hurt anything. It's silly and grossly oversentimental, and the poets who become addicted to it tend to be a bit heavy-handed when they ladle on the moral lessons. That's always been the problem with literature—finding a justification for it. It really doesn't serve any practical purpose, you know."

"Except that life without it would be sterile and empty," Bevier asserted.

"It would indeed, Sir Bevier," Itagne agreed. "Anyway, Delphaeic literature—which probably doesn't have anything at all to do with the real Delphae—grew up around these ridiculous literary conventions, but after several centuries of that nonsense, the potentials of the pastoral tradition had been pretty much exhausted, so our poets began to wander afield— like untended sheep, if I may extend the metaphor. Sometime during the last century, they began to posit the notion that the Delphae practice a non-Styric form of magic. That *really* upsets my Styric colleagues at the university." Itagne looked back over his shoulder to make sure that Sephrenia, who still rode in the rear with Berit, was out of earshot. "Many people find something fundamentally irritating about Styrics. The pudding of smug superiority and accusatory self-pity doesn't cook up very well, and the favorite form of Styric-baiting on the university campus is to mention 'Delphaeic magic' to a Styric and then watch him go up in flames."

"Can you think of anything at all that might explain Sephrenia's reaction to the Delphae?" Vanion asked with troubled eyes. "I've never seen her behave this way before."

"I really don't know Lady Sephrenia that well, Lord Vanion, but her explosion the first time I mentioned Delphaeic literature provides some clues. There's a very brief passage in 'Xadane' that hints that the Delphae were allied with the Styrics during the war that was supposed to have exterminated the Cyrgai. The passage was clearly based on a very obscure section in a seventh-century historical text. There's mention of a betrayal, but not much more. Evidently, when their war with the Cyrgai began, the Styrics contacted the Delphae and tricked them into mounting an attack on the Cyrgai from the east. They promised aid and all manner of other inducements, but when the Cyrgai counterattacked and began to overrun the Delphae, the Styrics chose to renege on their promises. The Delphae were almost exterminated. The Styrics have been wriggling and squirming for eons trying to justify that blatant breach of faith. There are many people in the world who don't like Styrics, and they've used that betrayal as a vehicle for their bigotry. Styrics quite understandably don't care much for the literature." He looked pensively out across the featureless desert. "One of the less attractive aspects of human nature is our tendency to hate the people we haven't treated very well;

it's much easier than accepting guilt. If we can convince ourselves that the people we betrayed or enslaved were subhuman monsters in the first place, then our guilt isn't nearly as black as we secretly know that it is. Humans are very, very good at shifting blame and avoiding guilt. We *do* like to keep a good opinion of ourselves, don't we?"

"I think it would take more than that to set Sephrenia off," Vanion said dubiously. "She's too sensible to catch on fire just because somebody says unflattering things about Styrics. She's spent several hundred years in the Elene kingdoms of Eosia, and anti-Styric prejudice there goes far beyond literary insults." He sighed. "If she'd only *talk* to me about it. I can't get anything coherent out of her, though. All she does is splutter wild denunciations. I don't understand at all."

Sparhawk, however, had an inkling of what was happening. Aphrael had hinted that Sephrenia was going to encounter something extraordinarily painful, and it was growing increasingly obvious that the Delphae would be the cause of her pain. Aphrael had said that Sephrenia's suffering would be necessary as a prelude to some kind of growth. Itagne, who really didn't know any of them that well, may have hit upon something relevant. Sephrenia was Styric to her fingertips, and the acceptance of racial guilt for an eons-old misbehavior would cause her the exact kind of pain Aphrael had so sorrowfully described. Sephrenia, however, would not be the only one who would suffer. Vanion had said that Sephrenia's problems were also his. Unfortunately, the same held true of her pain.

Sparhawk rode on across the desolate waste, his thoughts as bleak as the surroundings.

CHAPTER
TWELVE

Kring looked pensively out across the lawn. "It came on me like a madness, Atan Engessa," he told his towering friend. "From the moment I first saw her, I couldn't think of anything else." The two were standing in the shadows near the Ministry of the Interior.

"You are fortunate, friend Kring," Engessa replied in his deep, soft voice. "Most men's lives are never touched by such love."

Kring smiled a bit wryly. "I'm sure my life would be much easier if it hadn't touched mine."

"Do you regret it?"

"Not for a moment. I'd thought that my life was full. I was the Domi of my people and I'd assumed that my mother would find me a suitable wife in due time, as is customary and proper. I'd have married and fathered sons, and that would have satisfied the requirements. Then I saw Mirtai, and I realized how empty my life had been before." He rubbed one hand over his shaved scalp. "My people will have a great deal of trouble with her, I'm afraid. She's like no other woman we've ever encountered. It wouldn't be so difficult if I weren't the Domi."

"She might not have accepted you if you hadn't been, friend

Kring. Mirtai is a proud woman. She was meant to be the wife of a ruler."

"I know. I wouldn't have dared to approach her if I hadn't been Domi. There'll be trouble, though. I can see that coming. She's a stranger, and she's not at all like Peloi women. Status is very important to our women and Mirtai's of a different race, she's taller than even the tallest of the Peloi men, and she's more beautiful than any other woman I've ever seen. Just by themselves, those things would shrivel the hearts of Peloi women. You saw how Tikume's wife Vida looked at her, didn't you?"

Engessa nodded.

"The women of *my* people will hate her all the more because I am *their* Domi. She will be Doma, the Domi's wife, and she'll have first place among the women. To make matters even worse, she'll be one of the wealthiest of all the Peloi."

"I don't understand."

"I've done quite well. My herds have increased, and I've stolen much. All my wealth will belong to her. She'll own vast herds of sheep and cattle. The horse herds will still be mine, though."

"Is that the Peloi custom?"

"Oh, yes. Sheep and cattle are food, so they belong to the women. The women also own the tents and the beds and the wagons. The gold we get from the king for Zemoch ears is owned by all the people in common, so about the only thing we Peloi men own are our weapons and our horses. When you get right down to it, the women own everything, and we spend our lives protecting their possessions."

"You have a strange society, friend Kring."

Kring shrugged. "A man shouldn't have his mind all cluttered with possessions. It distracts him when the time comes for fighting."

"There's wisdom there, my friend. Who holds your possessions until you marry?"

"My mother. She's a sensible woman, and having a daughter like Mirtai will increase her status enormously. She has a great deal of authority among the Peloi women, and I'm hoping she'll be able to keep matters under control—at least among my sisters." He laughed. "I'm going to enjoy watching the faces of my sisters when I introduce them to Mirtai and they have to bow to her. I'm not really fond of them. They all pray for my death every night."

"Your own *sisters*?" Engessa sounded shocked.

"Of course. If I die before I'm married, everything I've won becomes the property of my mother, and my sisters will inherit all of it. They already think of themselves as women of property. They've turned down perfectly acceptable suitors because of their pride of position and the wealth they think they'll inherit. I've been too busy making war to think much about marriage, and every year that passed made my sisters feel that their ownership of the herds was that much more secure." He grinned. "Mirtai's sudden appearance is going to upset them, I'm afraid. One of the customs of our people obliges a bride-to-be to spend two months in the tent of her betrothed's mother—learning all the little things she'll need to know about him after they're married. During that period my mother and Mirtai will *also* select husbands for all my sisters; it's not a good idea to have too many women in one tent. That will *really* upset my sisters. I expect they'll try to murder Mirtai. I'll warn them against it, of course," he added piously. "I *am* their brother, after all. But I'm sure they won't listen—at least not until after Mirtai's killed a few of them. I've got too many sisters anyway."

"How many?" Engessa asked him.

"Eight. Their status will change drastically once I marry. Right now they're all heiresses. After my wedding, they'll be possessionless spinsters, dependent on Mirtai for every crust of bread they eat. I think they'll bitterly regret all the suitors they've refused at that point. Is that somebody creeping through the shadows over by the wall?"

Engessa looked toward the Interior Ministry. "It seems to be," he replied. "Let's go ask him his business. We don't really want anybody going inside that building while Atana Mirtai and the thieves are in there."

"Right," Kring agreed. He loosened his saber in its sheath, and the oddly mismatched pair moved silently across the lawn to intercept the furtive shadow near the wall.

"How far is it from here to Tega, Sarabian?" Ehlana asked, looking up from Sparhawk's letter. "In a direct line, I mean?"

Sarabian had removed his doublet, and he really looked quite dashing in his tight-fitting hose and full-sleeved linen shirt. He had tied back his shoulder-length black hair, and he was practicing lunges with his rapier, aiming at a golden bracelet hanging from the ceiling on a long string. "About a hundred and fifty leagues, wouldn't you say, Oscagne?" he replied, contorting his body into *en garde* position. He lunged and caught the rim of the bracelet with the point of his rapier, sending the bracelet spinning and swinging on the string. "Blast!" he muttered.

"Perhaps closer to a hundred and seventy-five, your Majesty," Oscagne corrected.

"Could it *really* be raining there?" Ehlana asked. "The weather's been beautiful here. A hundred and seventy-five leagues isn't really all that far, and Sparhawk says right here that it's been raining on Tega for the past week."

"Who can say what the weather's going to do?" Sarabian lunged again, and his rapier passed smoothly through the bracelet.

"Well thrust," Ehlana said a bit absently.

"Thank you, your Majesty." Sarabian bowed, flourishing his rapier. "This is really fun, you know that?" He crouched melodramatically. "Have at you, dog!" He lunged at the bracelet again, missing by several inches. "Blast."

"Alean, dear," Ehlana said to her maid. "Would you go see if the sailor who brought this letter is still on the premises?"

"At once, my Queen."

Sarabian looked inquiringly at his hostess.

"The sailor just came from Tega. I think I'd like to hear *his* views on the weather there."

"Surely you don't think your husband would lie to your Majesty, do you?" Oscagne protested.

"Why not? I'd lie to *him* if there was a valid political reason for it."

"*Ehlana!*" Sarabian sounded profoundly shocked. "I thought you loved Sparhawk."

"What on earth has that got to do with it? Of course I love him. I've loved him since I was about Danae's age, but love and politics are two entirely different things, and they should never be mixed. Sparhawk's up to something, Sarabian, and your excellent foreign minister here probably knows what it is."

"Me?" Oscagne protested mildly.

"Yes, you. Mermaids, Oscagne? *Mermaids?* You didn't *really* think I'd swallow that story, did you? I'm just a bit disappointed in you, actually. Was that the best you could come up with?"

"I was a bit pressed for time, your Majesty," he apologized

with a slightly embarrassed look. "Prince Sparhawk was in a hurry to leave. Was it the weather that gave us away?"

"Partly," she replied. She held up the letter. "My beloved outsmarted himself, though. I've seen his letters before. The notion of 'felicity of style' has never occurred to Sparhawk. His letters usually read as if he'd written them with his broadsword. This one—and all the others from Tega—have been polished until they glisten. I'm touched that he went to all the trouble, but I don't believe one word of them. Now, then, where is he? And what's he really up to?"

"He wouldn't say, your Majesty. All he told me was that he needed some excuse to be away from Matherion for several weeks."

She smiled sweetly at him. "That's all right, Oscagne," she said. "I'll find out for myself. It's more fun that way anyhow."

"It's a big building," Stragen reported the following morning. "It's going to take time to go over it inch by inch." He, Caalador, and Mirtai had just returned from their night of unsuccessful burglary.

"Have you made much progress?" Sarabian asked.

"We've covered the top two floors, your Majesty," Caalador replied. "We'll start on the third floor tonight." Caalador was sprawled in a chair with a weary look on his face. Like his two companions, he was still dressed in tight-fitting black clothing. He stretched and yawned. "God, I'm tired," he said. "I'm getting too old for this."

Stragen unrolled a time-yellowed set of drawings. "I *still* think that the answer's right here," he said. "Instead of opening doors and poking under desks, we should be matching dimensions against these drawings."

"Yer still a-thankin' there's sekert passages an' corn-sealed rooms in thar, ain't ya, Stragen?" Caalador drawled, yawning again. "That doesn't speak too well for your taste in literature, old boy."

Sarabian gave him a puzzled look.

"Thalesians are addicted to bad ghost stories, your Majesty," Caalador explained.

"It gives the copying houses in Emsat something to do now that they've exhausted the body of real literature." Stragen shrugged. "We've got a whole subgenre of highly popular books spewing out of grubby garrets on back streets—lurid narratives that all take place in cemeteries or in haunted houses on dark and stormy nights. The whores of Emsat absolutely adore them. I rather expect the policemen at Interior share that taste. After all, a policeman's sort of like a whore, isn't he?"

"I didn't exactly follow that," Mirtai said, "and I'm not really sure I want to. There's probably something disgusting involved in your thinking, Stragen. Caalador, *will* you stop yawning like that. Your face looks like an open barn door."

"I'm sleepy, little dorlin'. You two bin a-keepin' me up past muh bedtime."

"Then go to bed. You make my jaws ache when you gape at me like that."

"You should *all* get some sleep," Ehlana told them. "You're the official royal burglars now, and Sarabian and I would be absolutely mortified if you were to fall asleep in midburgle."

"Are we ready to be practical about this?" Caalador asked, rising to his feet. "I can have two dozen professionals here by this evening, and we'll have all the secrets of the Interior Ministry in our hands by tomorrow morning."

"And Interior will know that we have them by tomorrow afternoon," Stragen added. "Our impromptu spy network isn't really all that secure, Caalador. We haven't had enough time to weed out all the people Krager's probably subverted."

"There's no real rush here, gentlemen," Ehlana told them. "Even if we *do* find the documents the policemen at Interior are hiding, we won't be able to do a thing about them until my wandering husband finds his way home again."

"Why are you so positive that Sparhawk's deceiving you, Ehlana?" Sarabian asked her.

"It's consistent with his character. Sparhawk's devoted his entire life to protecting me. It's rather sweet, even though it *is* bloody, hindering awkward at times. He still thinks of me as a little girl—although I've demonstrated to him on any number of occasions that I'm not. He's out there doing something dangerous, and he doesn't want me to worry. All he really had to do was tell me what he was planning and then lay out the reasons why he thought it was necessary. I know it's hard for you men to believe, but women are rational, too—and far more practical than you are."

"You're a hard woman, Ehlana," Sarabian accused.

"No, I'm a realist. Sparhawk does what he thinks he has to, no matter what I say, and I've learned to accept that. The point I'm trying to make is that no matter what we dig out of the walls of the Interior Ministry, there's absolutely nothing we can do about it while Sparhawk and the others are out there wandering around the countryside. We're going to disband Interior and throw about a quarter of the empire's policemen in prison. Then we're going to place all of Tamuli under martial law, with the Atans enforcing our decrees. The Daresian continent's going to look like an anthill that's just been run over by a cavalry charge. I don't know what Sparhawk's doing, so I don't know what kind of impact that chaos is going to have on him. I am *not* going to let you put him in any more danger than I think he's already in."

"Do you know something, Ehlana?" Sarabian said. "You're even more protective of Sparhawk than he is of you."

"Of course I am. That's what marriage is all about."

"None of mine are," he sighed.

"That's because you've got too many wives, Sarabian. Your affection's dispersed. Your wives each return only as much love as you give them."

"I've found that it's safer that way."

"But dull, my friend, and sort of boring. Being consumed with a burning passion that only has a single object is very exciting. It's sort of like living in a volcano."

"What an exhausting prospect." He shuddered.

"Fun, though." She smiled.

Baroness Melidere had retired early, pleading a painful headache. It was not that she found her duties as Ehlana's lady-in-waiting onerous, but rather that she had an important decision to make; and she knew that the longer she put it off, the more difficult it would be. To put it rather bluntly, the baroness had reached the point where she was going to have to decide what to do about Stragen.

Melidere was no innocent. Few members of any court really are. An innocent girl has only one option in her dealings with the opposite sex. A more worldly girl has two, and this was the crux of Melidere's dilemma. Stragen, of course, would make a perfectly acceptable paramour. He was presentable, interesting, and he had exquisite manners. Melidere's reputation at court would not be tarnished by a liaison with him; quite the reverse, actually. That had originally been her intention, and the time had come for her to take the final step and to invite him to her bedchamber and have done with it. The liaison could be brief, or it could be extended—renewed each time Stragen visited Cimmura. That would give the affair a certain status, while at the same time leaving them both free to pursue other amusements, as was normal in such situations. Melidere, however, was not sure if that was all she wanted. More and more of late, she had found herself thinking of a more permanent arrangement, and therein lay the dilemma.

There is a rhythm, almost a tide, in the affairs of the heart. When that tide reaches its high point, a lady must give certain signals to her quarry. One set of signals points toward the bedchamber; the other, toward the altar. Melidere could no longer put it off. She had to decide which set of signal flags to hoist.

Stragen intrigued her. There was a sense of dangerous excitement about him, and Melidere, a creature of the court, was attracted by that. It could be intoxicating, addictive, but she was not entirely sure that the excitement would not begin to pall as the years went by.

There was, moreover, the problem of Stragen himself. His irregular origins and lack of any official status had made him overly sensitive, and he continually imagined slights where none had been intended. He hovered around the edges of Ehlana's court like an uninvited guest at a banquet, always fearful that he might be summarily ejected. He had the outsider's awe of the nobility, seeming at times to view aristocrats almost as members of another species. Melidere knew that if she decided to marry him, she would have to attack that first. She personally knew that titles were a sham and that legitimacy could be purchased, but how was she going to persuade Stragen of that? She could easily buy him out of bastardy and into the aristocracy, but that would mean that she would have to reveal the secret she had kept locked in her heart since childhood. Melidere had always concealed the fact that she was one of the wealthiest people at court, largely because her fabulous wealth had not been legally obtained.

And there it was! She almost laughed when she realized how simple it was. If she really wanted to marry Stragen, all she'd have to do is share her secret with him. That would put them on equal footing and tear down the largely imaginary barrier.

Melidere was a baroness, but her title had not been in her family for very long. Her father had begun life as a blacksmith in Cardos, a man with huge shoulders and a mop of curly blond hair, and he had amassed a fortune with a simple invention which he had crafted in his forge. Most people look upon gold coins as money—something with intrinsic and unalterable

value. There are some, however, who realize that the value of
a coin lies in the social agreement saying that it is worth what
the words stamped on its face say that it's worth. The words
do not change, even if the edge of the coin has been lightly
brushed with a file or a sharp knife a few times. The tiny frag-
ments of pure gold thus obtained do not amount to very much
if one files or carves the edge of *one* coin. If one tampers with
a thousand coins, however, that's quite another matter. Governments try to discourage the practice by milling the edges of
coins during the stamping process. A milled coin has a series
of indentations around its edge, and if the edge has been filed
or carved, it is immediately apparent. Melidere's father had
contrived a way to get around that. He had carefully crafted a
set of remilling dies, one die for each size coin. A blacksmith
will not handle enough coins in his entire life to make enough
to pay for the effort of hammering out such equipment.
Melidere's father was a genius, however. He did not make the
dies for his own use, nor did he sell them. Instead, he rented
them, along with the services of highly trained operators, taking a small percentage as his fee.

Melidere smiled. She was positive that very few gold coins
in the whole of Eosia were of true weight, and she also knew
that five percent of the difference between face value and true
value was stacked in ingots in the hidden vault in the basement
of her own manor house near Cardos. Once she had made
Stragen aware of the fact that she was a bigger and more successful thief than he was, the rest would be easy. His illusions
about her nobility would fall away to be replaced with an almost reverential respect for her consummate dishonesty. She
could even show him the source of her wealth, for she always
carried the most prized memento of her childhood, her father's
original dies. Even now, they nestled in velvet in the ornately
carved rosewood case on her dressing table, polished steel jewels more valuable than diamonds.

Even as she realized that the means to marry Stragen were
at hand, she also realized that she had already made her decision. She *would* marry him. She would, the very next time she
saw him, hoist *those* signal flags rather than the others.

Then she thought of something else. Her father's activities
had been confined to the Eosian continent. All of Tamuli was
literally awash with virgin coins unviolated by file or knife-
edge. Once he realized that, Stragen would not *walk* to the altar, he would *run*.

Melidere smiled and picked up her hairbrush. She hummed softly to herself as she brushed her long honey-blonde hair. Like any good Elene girl, she had attacked the problem logically, and, as it almost always did, logic had won out. Logic was a friendly and comforting thing to have around, particularly if morality didn't interfere.

"Hold it," Stragen whispered as the three of them started down the broad staircase descending to the third floor. "There's still somebody down there."

"What's he doing this late?" Mirtai asked. "They all went home hours ago."

"We could go ask him," Caalador said.

"Don't be absurd. Is it a watchman?"

"I don't know," Stragen replied. "I didn't see him. I just caught a flicker of candlelight. Somebody down there opened a door."

"Some drudge working late, most likely." Caalador shrugged.

"Now what?" Mirtai asked.

"We wait." Caalador sat down on the top step.

Stragen considered it. "Why don't the two of you stay here?" he suggested. "I'll go have a look. If he's settling in for the night, there's not much point in camping on these stairs until morning." He went on down, his glove-soft shoes making no sound on the mother-of-pearl tiles. When he reached the hallway below, he saw the fine line of candlelight glowing out from under a door at the far end. He moved quickly with the confidence of long practice. When he reached the door, he heard voices.

Stragen did not even consider listening at the door. That was far too amateurish. He slipped into the room adjoining the lighted one, felt his way carefully to the wall, and set his ear against it.

He couldn't hear a sound. He swore under his breath and went back out into the hallway. Then he padded on past the door with the candlelight coming out from under it and entered the room on the other side. He could hear the two men talking as soon as he entered.

"Our esteemed prime minister is beginning to grasp the situation," a rusty-sounding voice was saying. "It's a struggle, though. Pondia Subat's severely limited when something new appears on the horizon."

"That's more or less to be expected, your Excellency." Stragen recognized the second voice. It was Teovin, the Director of the Secret Police. "The prime minister's almost as much a figurehead as the emperor."

"You've noticed," the rusty-sounding man replied.

"Subat's not likely to ask too many questions. As long as he's aware of the situation in general terms, he'll probably prefer to let us handle things without personally learning details. And that's what we wanted in the first place. Have you made any progress with the others?"

"Some. I have to broach the subject rather carefully, you realize. The Elene strumpet's made many friends here at court. They all listen to me, though. I hold the keys to the treasury, and that helps to get their attention. Most of the ministries are ceremonial, so I haven't wasted much time on the men who head them. The Ministry of Culture's probably not going to be of much use—or the Ministry of Education either, for that matter."

"I wouldn't be so sure of that one, your Excellency. The Ministry of Education controls the universities. We have to think past the current emergency. I don't think either of us wants whole generations to go through life believing that Interior and Exchequer are hotbeds of treason. Technically, we *are* acting contrary to the emperor's wishes."

"That's true, I suppose, but Interior controls the police, and Exchequer levies and collects the taxes. We're neither one of us ever going to be very popular, no matter what we do. But you're probably right. If the history professors at the universities start telling their students that we're traitors, people might start claiming that it's their patriotic duty to ignore the officers of the law or to stop paying their taxes."

"That raises an interesting point, Chancellor Gashon," Teovin mused. "You've got a sort of police force, haven't you? Muscular fellows who accompany your tax collectors to make sure that people pay what they owe?"

"Oh, yes. One way or the other, *everybody* pays his taxes. I get money—or blood—from all of them."

"Follow me on this, if you will. The Elenes probably know that Interior—and most likely the army as well—are opposed to them, so they'll try their very best to disrupt our customary operations. I'd like to conceal some of my more-valuable people. Do you suppose I might transfer them into *your* enforcement branch? That way I'll still have a functional operation—even if the Elenes start burning down police stations."

"I can manage that, Teovin. Is there anything else you'll need?"

"Money, Chancellor Gashon."

There was a pained silence. "Would you accept eternal friendship instead?"

"Afraid not, your Excellency. I have to bribe people." Teovin paused. "There's an idea. I could probably use some form of tax-immunity as an inducement in many cases."

"I don't recognize the term."

"We give people an exemption from taxation in exchange for their cooperation."

"That's immoral!" Gashon gasped. "That's the most shocking thing I've ever heard in my whole life!"

"It was only a thought."

"Don't even suggest something like that, Teovin. It makes my blood run cold. Can we get out of here? Police stations make me apprehensive, for some reason."

"Of course, your Excellency. I think we've covered the things we wanted to keep private."

Stragen sat in the dark office listening as the two men pushed back their chairs and went out into the corridor. He heard Teovin's key turn in the lock. The blond thief waited for perhaps ten minutes, and then he went back to the foot of the staircase. "They're gone now," he called up the stairs in a loud whisper.

Mirtai and Caalador came on down. "Who was it?" Caalador asked.

"The head of the Secret Police and the Chancellor of the Exchequer," Stragen replied. "It was a very enlightening conversation. Teovin's enlisting other ministries to help him. They don't know what he's *really* up to, but he's managed to convince several of them that it's in their own interest to join him."

"We can sort out the politics later," Caalador said. "It's almost midnight. Let's get to burgling."

"There's no need." Stragen shrugged. "I've found what we're looking for."

"Isn't that disgusting?" Caalador said to the Atan giantess. "He tosses it off as if it weren't really very important. All right, Stragen, stun us with your brilliance. Make my eyes pop out, and make Mirtai swoon with admiration."

"I can't really take much credit for it," Stragen confessed. "I stumbled across it, actually. It *is* a secret room. I was right about that. We still have to find the door, though, and make sure that the documents we want are inside, but the room's in the right place. I should have thought of it immediately."

"Where is it?" Mirtai asked.

"Right next to Teovin's office."

"That's the logical place, right enough," Caalador noted. "How did you find it?"

"Well, I haven't actually found it yet, but I've reasoned out its existence."

"Don't throw away your soft shoes or your black clothes just yet, Caalador," Mirtai advised.

"You hurt me, love," Stragen protested.

"I've seen Elene reasoning go awry before. Why don't you tell us about it?"

"I wanted to do some constructive eavesdropping, so I went into the adjoining office to listen to Teovin and Chancellor of the Exchequer Gashon's conversation."

"And?"

"I couldn't hear a thing."

"The walls are stone, Stragen," she pointed out, "and they've got seashells glued to them."

"There's no such thing as a soundproof wall, Mirtai. There are always cracks and crannies that the mortar doesn't seep into. Anyway, when I tried the office on the other side, I could hear everything. Believe me, there's a room between that first office and the one Teovin uses."

"It *does* sort of fit together, dorlin'," Caalador said to Mirtai. "The door to that room would almost *have* to be in Teovin's office, wouldn't it? Those documents are sensitive, and he wouldn't want just anybody to have access to them. If we'd just taken a little while to think our way through it, we could have saved ourselves a lot of time."

"It wasn't a total waste." Mirtai smiled. "I've learned the art of burglary, and I've had the chance to absolutely wallow in your affection. You two have made me happier than I could possibly say. The office door's certain to be locked, you know."

"Nuthin' simpler, little dorlin'." Caalador smirked, holding up a needle-thin implement with a hook on the end.

"We'd better get started," Stragen said. "It's midnight, and it might take us the rest of the night to find the door to that hidden room."

"You're not serious," Ehlana scoffed.

"May muh tongue turn green iffn I ain't, yer Queenship." Caalador paused. "Dreadful, isn't it?" he added.

"I don't quite understand," Sarabian confessed.

"It's a cliché, your Majesty," Stragen explained, "taken from a type of literature that's currently very popular in Eosia."

"Do you really want to dignify that trash by calling it literature, Stragen?" Baroness Melidere murmured.

"It satisfies the needs of the mentally deprived, Baroness." He shrugged. "Anyway, your Imperial Majesty, the literature consists largely of ghost stories. There's always a haunted castle complete with hidden rooms and secret passages, and the entrances to these rooms and passages are always hidden behind bookcases. It's a very tired old device—so tired in fact that I almost didn't think of it. I didn't believe *anybody* would be so obvious." He laughed. "I wonder if Teovin thought it up all by himself or if he plagiarized. If he stole it, he has abominable taste in literature."

"Are books all that available in Eosia?" Oscagne asked curiously. "They're fearfully expensive here."

"It's one of the results of our Holy Mother's drive toward universal literacy during the last century, your Excellency," Ehlana explained. "The Church wanted her children to be able to read her message, so parish priests spend a great deal of time teaching everybody to read."

"The message of the Church doesn't really take all that long to browse through, however," Stragen added, "and after that you've got crowds of literate people with a skill they can't really apply. It was the invention of paper that set off the literary explosion, though. The labor costs involved in copying aren't particularly high. It was the cost of parchment that made books so prohibitively expensive. When paper came along, books became cheaper. There are copy houses in most major cities with whole platoons of scriveners grinding out books by the ton. It's a very profitable business. The books don't have illuminations or decorated capitals, and the lettering's a little shoddy, but they're readable—and affordable. Not everyone who can read has good taste, though, so a lot of truly dreadful books are written by people with minimal talent. They write adventure stories, ghost stories, heroic fantasies, and those naughty books that people don't openly display in their bookcases. The Church encourages lives of the saints and tedious religious verse. Things like that are produced, of course, but nobody really reads that sort of thing. Ghost stories are currently in vogue—particularly in Thalesia. It has something to do with our national character, I think." He looked at Ehlana. "The business of getting the information out of Teovin's hidey-hole is going to be tedious, my Queen. There are mountains of documents in there, and I can't take whole platoons of people in over the roof every night to help plow through them. Mirtai, Caalador, and I are going to have to read every document ourselves."

"Perhaps not, Milord Stragen," Ehlana disagreed. She smiled at the blond thief. "I had absolute confidence in your dishonesty, dear boy, so I knew that sooner or later you'd find what we were looking for. I struggled for a time with the very problem you just mentioned. Then I remembered something Sparhawk once told me. He'd used a spell to put the image of Krager's face in a basin of water so that Talen could draw his picture. I spoke with one of the Pandions who came along with us—a Sir Alvor. He told me that since Sephrenia refuses to learn to read Elenic, she and Sparhawk devised a way around her deliberate incapacity. She can glance at a page—a single glance—and then make the whole page come up in a mirror or on the surface of a basin of water hours or even days later. Sir Alvor knows the spell. He's a fairly young and agile fellow, so he'll be able to creep across the rooftop with you. Take him along, next time you visit the Interior Ministry, and turn him loose in Teovin's hidden closet. I rather imagine he'll be able to carry that entire library out with him in a single night."

"Does it really work, your Majesty?" Caalador asked her a bit dubiously.

"Oh, yes, Caalador. I handed Alvor a book he'd never seen before. He leafed through it in a couple of minutes and then printed it on that mirror over there—page after page after page. I checked what he was producing against the original, and it was absolutely perfect—right down to the smudges and the food-stains on the pages."

"Them there Pandion fellers is real useful t' have around," Caalador admitted.

"You know—" She smiled. "—I've noticed the exact same thing myself. There's one in particular who does all sorts of useful things for me."

CHAPTER
THIRTEEN

"We don't have any choice, dear," Vanion said to Sephrenia. "We've even tried turning around and going back, but we *still* keep moving in the same direction. We're going to have to use the Bhelliom." He looked up the gorge lying ahead of them. The mountain river was tumbling over the boulders jutting up out of its bed, sawing its way deeper and deeper into the rock with its white, roaring passage. The sides of the gorge were thick with evergreens that dripped continually in the swirling mist rising out of the rapids.

"No, Vanion," Sephrenia replied stubbornly. "We'll fall directly into their trap if we do that. The Delphae want the Bhelliom, and as soon as Sparhawk tries to use it, they'll attack us and try to kill him and take it away from him."

"They'll regret it if they do," Sparhawk told her.

"Maybe," she said, "but then again, maybe not. We don't know what they're capable of. Until I know *how* they're misleading us, I can't even guess at what else they can do. There are too many uncertainties involved to be taking chances."

"Isn't this what they call an impasse?" Khalad suggested. "We keep going north no matter how much we try to go in some other direction, and we don't know what the Delphae will do if Sparhawk tries to use Bhelliom to pull us out of these mountains. Why don't we just stop?"

193

"We have to get back to Matherion, Khalad," Sparhawk objected.

"But we're not *going* to Matherion, my Lord. Every step we take brings us that much closer to Delphaeus. We've been twisting and turning around through these mountains for two days now, and we're *still* going north. If all directions lead to a place where we really don't want to go, why keep moving at all? Why not find a comfortable campsite and stay there for a while? Let's make them come to *us*, instead of the other way around."

"It makes sense, Lord Vanion," Itagne agreed. "As long as we keep moving, the Delphae don't have to do a thing except herd us in the right direction. If we stop moving, they'll have to try something else, and that might give Lady Sephrenia some clues about their capabilities. It's called 'constructive inaction' in diplomatic circles."

"What if the Delphae just decide to wait us out?" Ulath objected. "Autumn isn't a good time to linger in the mountains. It wasn't so bad in those foothills we came through when we left the desert, but now that we're up here, time starts to get very important."

"I don't think they'll wait, Sir Ulath," Itagne disagreed.

"Why not? They've got all the advantages, haven't they?"

"Let's just call it a diplomat's instinct. I caught a faint odor of urgency about them when they approached us. They want us to go to Delphaeus, right enough, but it's *also* important to them that we get there soon."

"I'd like to know how you worked *that* out, your Excellency," Kalten said skeptically.

"It's a combination of a thousand little things, Sir Kalten— the tone of voice, slight changes of expression, even their posture and their rate of breathing. The Delphae weren't as certain of themselves as they seemed, and they want us to go to Delphaeus as quickly as possible. As long as we keep going, they don't have any reason to make further contact, but I think we'll find that if we just sit still, they'll come to us and start making concessions. I've seen it happen that way many times."

"Does it take long to learn how to be a diplomat, your Excellency?" Talen asked him with a speculative look.

"That depends entirely on your natural gifts, Master Talen."

"I'm a quick learner. Diplomacy sounds like a lot of fun."

"It's the best game there is." Itagne smiled. "There's no other that even approaches it."

"Are you considering another career change, Talen?" his brother asked him.

"I'm never going to be a very good knight, Khalad—not unless Sparhawk takes the Bhelliom and makes me about four times bigger than I am now."

"Isn't this about the third occupation you've grown excited about so far this year?" Sparhawk asked him. "Have you given up the notion of becoming the emperor of the thieves or the archprelate of larceny?"

"I don't really have to make any final decisions yet, Sparhawk. I'm still young." Talen suddenly thought of something. "They can't arrest a diplomat, can they, your Excellency? I mean, the police can't really touch him at all—no matter *what* he does?"

"That's a long-standing custom, Master Talen. If I throw *your* diplomats into a dungeon, you'll turn around and do the same thing to *mine*, won't you? That puts a diplomat more or less above the law."

"Well, now," Talen said with a beatific smile, "isn't *that* something to think about?"

"I like caves." Ulath shrugged.

"Are you sure you're not part Troll, Ulath?" Kalten asked.

"Even Trolls and Ogres can have good ideas once in a while. A cave's got a roof in case the weather turns sour, and nobody can come at you from behind. This one's a good cave, and it's been used before. Somebody spent quite a bit of time building a wall around that spring in there so that there's plenty of water."

"What if he comes back and wants his cave again?"

"I don't think he'll do that, Kalten." The big Thalesian held up a beautifully crafted flint spearhead. "He left this behind when he moved out. I'd say that he'd probably be too old to give us much to worry about—fifteen or twenty thousand years too old at least." He touched a careful thumb to the serrated edge of the spearpoint. "He did very nice work, though. He drew pictures on the wall, too—animals, mostly."

Kalten shuddered. "Wouldn't it be sort of like taking up residence in a tomb?"

"Not really. Time's all one piece, Kalten. The past is always with us. The cave served the fellow who made this spearpoint very well, and the work he left behind inclines me to trust his judgment. The place has everything we need—shelter, water, plenty of firewood nearby, and then there's that steep meadow a hundred yards off to the south, so there's plenty of forage for the horses."

"What are *we* going to eat, though? After a couple of weeks when our supplies run out, we'll be trying to boil rocks down for soup stock."

"There's game about, Sir Kalten," Khalad told him. "I've seen deer down by the river and a flock of feral goats higher up the slope."

"Goat?" Kalten made a face.

"It's better than rock soup, isn't it?"

"Sir Ulath is right, gentlemen," Bevier told them. "The cave's in a defensible position. So far as we know, the Delphae have to get close enough to touch us in order to do us any harm. Some breastworks and a well-planted field of sharpened stakes on that steep slope leading down to the river will keep them at arm's length. If Ambassador Itagne is right and the Delphae *are* pressed for time, that should encourage them to come to the bargaining table."

"Let's do it," Vanion decided. "And let's get right at it. The Delphae seem to come out at night, so we'll want some defenses in place before the sun goes down."

The overcast that had turned the sky into an oppressive leaden bowl for the past week was gone the following morning, and the autumn sunlight touching the turning leaves of the grove of aspens across the gorge from their cave filled the day with a vibrant, golden light. Everything seemed etched with a kind of preternatural clarity. The boulders in the streambed below were starkly white, and the swift-moving river was a dark, sun-illuminated green. The gorge was alive with birdsong and the chatter of scolding squirrels.

The knights continued the labor of fortification, erecting a substantial chest-high wall of loosely piled stones around the edge of the semicircular shelf that extended out from the mouth of the cave, and planting a forest of sharpened stakes on the steep slope that led down to the river.

They pastured their horses in the adjoining meadow by day and brought them inside the makeshift fort as the sun went down. They bathed and washed their clothing in the river and hunted deer and goats in the forest. They took turns standing watch at night, but there was no sign of the Delphae.

They stayed there for four nights, growing more restless

with each passing hour. "If this is how the Delphae respond to something urgent, I'd hate to sit around waiting for them when they were relaxed," Talen said dryly to Itagne on the morning of the fourth day. "They don't even have anybody out there watching us."

"They're out there, Master Talen," Itagne replied confidently.

"Why haven't we seen them, then? They'd be fairly hard to miss at night."

"Not necessarily," Kalten disagreed. "I don't think they glow all the time. We saw them shining out there in that fog the first time they came to call, but the second time, they crept up to within twenty yards of us before they lit up. They seem to be able to control the light, depending on the circumstances."

"They're out there," Itagne repeated, "and the longer they wait, the better."

"I didn't follow that," Talen confessed.

"They know by this time that we're not going to move from this spot, so they're out there right now arguing among themselves about what they're going to offer us. Some of them want to offer more than the others, and the longer we just sit here, the more we strengthen the position of that faction."

"Have you suddenly become clairvoyant, Itagne?" Sephrenia asked him.

"No, Lady Sephrenia, just experienced. This delay is fairly standard in any negotiation. I'm on familiar ground now. We've chosen the right strategy."

"What else should we be doing?" Kalten asked.

"Nothing, Sir Knight. It's their move."

She came from the river in broad daylight, climbing easily up the rocky path that ascended the steep slope. She wore a grey hooded robe and simple sandals. Her features were Tamul, but she did not have the characteristic golden skin-tone of her race. She was not so much pale as she was colorless. Her eyes were grey and seemed very wise, and her hair was long and completely white, though she appeared to be scarcely more than a girl.

Sparhawk and the others watched her as she came up the hill in the golden sunlight. She crossed the steep meadow where the horses grazed. Ch'iel, Sephrenia's gentle white palfrey, approached the colorless woman curiously, and the stranger gently touched the mare's face with one slim hand.

"That's probably far enough," Vanion called to her. "What is it that you want?"

"I am Xanetia," the young woman replied. Her voice was soft, but there was a kind of echoing timbre to it that immediately identified her as one of the Delphae. "I am to be thy surety, Lord Vanion."

"You know me?"

"We know thee, Lord Vanion—and each of thy companions. Ye are reluctant to come to Delphaeus, fearing that we mean you harm. My life will serve as pledge of our good faith."

"Don't listen, Vanion," Sephrenia said, her eyes hard.

"Art thou afeared, Priestess?" Xanetia asked calmly. "Thy Goddess doth not share thy fear. Now do I perceive that it is *thy* hatred which doth obstruct that which must come to pass, and thus it shall be into *thy* hands that I shall place my life—to do with as thou wilt. If thou must needs kill me to quench this hatred of thine, then so be it."

Sephrenia's face went deathly pale. "You know I wouldn't do that, Xanetia."

"Then put the implement of death into the hands of another. Thus thou mayest command my dying and put no stain of blood upon thine own hands. Is this not the custom of thy race, Styric? Thou shalt remain undefiled—even as this thirst of thine is slaked. All unsmirched mayest thou face thy Goddess and protest thine innocence, for thou shalt be blameless. My blood shall be upon the hands of thine Elenes, and Elene souls are cheap, are they not?" She reached inside her robe and drew out a jewel-like stone dagger. "Here is the implement of my death, Sephrenia," she said. "The blade is obsidian, so thou shalt not contaminate thy hands—or thy soul—with the loathsome touch of steel when thou spillest out my life." Xanetia's voice was soft, but her words cut into Sephrenia like the hard, sharp steel she spoke of.

"I won't listen to this!" the small Styric woman declared hotly.

Xanetia smiled. "Ah, but thou wilt, Sephrenia," she said, still very calm. "I know thee well, Styric, and I know that my words have burned themselves into thy soul. Thou wilt hear them again and again. In the silence of the night shall they come to thee, burning deeper each time. Truly shalt thou listen, for my words are the words of truth, and they shall echo in thy soul all the days of thy life."

Sephrenia's face twisted in anguish, and with a sudden wail she fled back into the cave.

Itagne's face was troubled as he came back along the narrow path from the meadow to the open area in front of the cave. "She's very convincing," he told them. "I get no sense of deceit from her at all."

"She probably doesn't know enough about the real motives of the leaders of her people to have anything to hide," Bevier said dubiously. "She could very well be nothing more than a pawn."

"She *is* one of the leaders of her people, Sir Bevier," Itagne disagreed. "She's the equivalent of the crown princess of the Delphae. She's the one who'll be Anarae when the Anari dies."

"Is that a name or a title?" Ulath asked.

"It's a title. The Anari—or in Xanetia's case, the Anarae—is both the temporal and spiritual leader of the Delphae. The current Anari is named Cedon."

"She's not just making it up?" Talen asked. "She *could* be just pretending to be their crown princess, you know. That way, we'd *think* she was important, when she's actually nothing more than a shepherdess or somebody's housemaid."

"I don't think so," Itagne said. "It may sound immodest, but I don't really believe anyone can lie to me for very long and get away with it. She says that she's the one who'll be Anarae, and I believe her. The move's consistent with standard diplomatic practice. Hostages *have* to be important. It's another indication of just how desperate the Delphae are in this business. I think Xanetia's telling the truth, and if she is, she's the most precious thing they possess." He made a wry face. "It definitely goes against everything I've been trained to believe about the Shining Ones since childhood, but I think we almost have to trust them this time."

Sparhawk and Vanion looked at each other. "What do you think?" Vanion asked.

"I don't see that we've got much choice, do you?"

"Not really. Ulath was right. We can't sit here all winter, and no matter which way we turn, we keep going toward Delphaeus. The fact that Xanetia's here is *some* assurance of good faith."

"Is it enough, though?"

"It's probably going to have to be, Sparhawk. I don't think we're going to get anything better."

"Kalten!" Sephrenia exclaimed. "No!"

"Somebody has to do it," the blond knight replied stubbornly. "Good faith has to go both ways." He looked Xanetia full in the face. "Is there something you'd like to tell me before I help you up onto that horse?" he asked her. "Some warning, maybe?"

"Thou art brave, Sir Kalten," she replied.

"It's what they pay me for." He shrugged. "Will I dissolve if I touch you?"

"No."

"All right. You've never ridden a horse before, have you?"

"We do not keep horses. We seldom leave our valley, so we have little need of them."

"They're fairly nice animals. Be a little careful of the one Sparhawk rides, though. He bites. Now, this horse is a pack animal. He's fairly old and sensible, so he won't waste energy jumping around and being silly. Don't worry too much about the reins. He's used to following along after the others, so you don't have to steer him. If you want him to go faster, nudge him in the ribs with your heels. If you want him to slow down, pull back on the reins a little bit. If you want him to stop, pull back a little harder. That packsaddle's not going to be very comfortable, so let us know if you start getting stiff and sore. We'll stop and get off and walk for a while. You'll get used to it after a few days—if we've got that far to travel."

She held out her hands, crossed at the wrist. "Wilt thou bind me now, Sir Knight?"

"What for?"

"I am thy prisoner."

"Don't be silly. You won't be able to hold on if your hands are tied." He set his jaw, reached out, and took her by the waist. Then he lifted her easily up onto the patient packhorse. Then he held out his hands and looked at them. "So far so good," he said. "At least my fingernails haven't fallen off. I'll be right beside you, so if you feel yourself starting to slip, let me know."

"We always underestimate him," Vanion murmured to Sparhawk. "There's a lot more to him than meets the eye, isn't there?"

"Kalten? Oh, yes, my Lord. Kalten can be very complicated sometimes."

They rode away from their fortified cave and followed the gorge the river had cut down through the rock. Sparhawk and Vanion led the way with Kalten and their hostage riding close behind them. Sephrenia, her face coldly set, rode at the rear with Berit, keeping as much distance as possible between herself and Xanetia.

"Is it very far?" Kalten asked the pale woman at his side. "I mean, how many days will it take us to get there?"

"The distance is indeterminate, Sir Kalten," Xanetia replied, "and the time as well. The Delphae are outcast and despised. We would be unwise to make the location of the valley of Delphaeus widely known."

"We're used to traveling, Lady," Kalten told her, "and we always pay attention to landmarks. If you take us to Delphaeus, we'll be able to find it again. All we'd have to do is find that cave and start from there."

"That is the flaw in thy plan, Sir Knight," she said gently. "Thou couldst consume a lifetime in the search for that cave. It is our wont to conceal the approaches to Delphaeus rather than Delphaeus itself."

"It's a little hard to conceal a whole mountain range, isn't it?"

"We noted that selfsame thing ourselves, Sir Kalten," she replied without so much as a smile, "so we conceal the sky instead. Without the sun to guide thee, thou art truly lost."

"Could *you* do that, Sparhawk?" Kalten raised his voice slightly. "Could you make the whole sky overcast like that?"

"Could we?" Sparhawk asked Vanion.

"*I* couldn't. Maybe Sephrenia could, but under the circumstances it might not be a good idea to ask her. I know enough to know that it's against the rules, though. We're not supposed to play around with the weather."

"We do not in truth cloud the sky, Lord Vanion," Xanetia assured him. "We cloud thine eyes instead. We can, an we choose, make others see what we wish them to see."

"Please, Anarae," Ulath said with a pained look, "don't go into too much detail. You'll bring on one of those tedious debates about illusion and reality, and I really hate those."

They rode on with the now-unobscured sun clearly indicating their line of travel. They were moving somewhat northeasterly.

Kalten watched their prisoner—or captor—closely, and he called halts somewhat more frequently than he might normally have done. When they stopped, he helped the strange pale woman down from her horse and walked beside her as they continued on foot, leading their horses.

"Thou art overly solicitous of my comfort, Sir Kalten," she gently chided him.

"Oh, it's not for you, Lady," he lied. "The going's a bit steep here, and we don't want to exhaust the horses."

"There's *definitely* more to Kalten than I'd realized," Vanion muttered to Sparhawk.

"You can spend a whole lifetime watching somebody, my friend, and you still won't learn everything there is to know about him."

"What an astonishingly acute perception," Vanion said dryly.

"Be nice," Sparhawk murmured.

Sparhawk was troubled. While Xanetia was certainly not as skilled as Aphrael, it was clear that she was tampering with time and distance in the same way the Child-Goddess did. If she had maintained the illusion of an overcast sky, he might not have noticed, but the position of the sun clearly indicated that there were gaps in his perception of time; the sun does not normally jump as it moves across the sky. The troubling fact was not that Xanetia did it badly, but the fact that she did it at all. Sparhawk began to revise a long-held opinion. This "tampering" was obviously not a purely divine capability. Itagne's rather sketchy discourse on the Delphae had contained at least *some* elements of truth. There was indeed such a thing as "Delphaeic magic," and so far as Sparhawk could tell, it went further and into areas where Styrics were unable or unwilling to venture.

He kept his eyes open, but did not mention his observations to his friends.

And then, on a perfect autumn evening when the birds clucked and murmured sleepily in the trees and a luminous twilight turned the mountains purple around them, they rode up a narrow, rocky trail that wound around massive boulders toward a V-shaped notch high above. Xanetia had been most insistent that they not stop for the night, and she and Kalten had pressed on ahead. Her normally placid face seemed somehow alight with anticipation.

When she and her protector reached the top of the trail, they stopped and sat their horses, starkly outlined against the last rosy vestiges of the sunset.

"Dear God!" Kalten exclaimed. "Sparhawk, come up and look at this!"

Sparhawk and Vanion rode on up to join them.

There was a valley below, a steep, basinlike mountain valley with dark trees shrouding the slopes. There were houses down there, close-packed houses with candlelighted windows and with columns of pale blue smoke rising straight up into the evening air from innumerable chimneys. The fact that there was a fair-sized town this deep in the inaccessible mountains was surprising enough, but Sparhawk and the others were not looking at the town.

In the very center of the valley, there was a small lake. There was, of course, nothing unusual about that. Lakes abound in mountains in all parts of the world. The spring run-off from melting snow inevitably seeks valleys and basins— any place that is lower than the surrounding terrain and from which there is no exit channel. It was not the fact that the lake was there that was so surprising. The thing that startled them and raised those vestigial hackles of superstitious awe along the backs of their necks was the fact that the lake glowed in the lowering twilight. The light was not the sickly, greenish glow of the phosphorescence that is sometimes exuded by rotting vegetable matter, but was instead a clear, steady white. Like a lost moon, the lake glowed, responding to the light of her new-risen sister standing above the eastern horizon.

"Behold Delphaeus," Xanetia said simply, and when they looked at her, they saw that she, too, was all aglow with a pure white light that seemed to come from within her and that shone through her garment and through her skin itself as if that pale, unwavering light were coming from her very soul.

CHAPTER FOURTEEN

Sparhawk's senses were preternaturally acute for some reason, although his mind seemed detached and emotionless. He observed; he heard; he catalogued; but he felt nothing. The peculiar state was not an unfamiliar one, but the circumstances under which this profound calm had come over him *were* unusual—very unusual. There were no armed men facing him, and yet his mind and body were preparing for battle.

Faran tensed, bunching his muscles, and the sound of his steel-shod hooves altered very slightly, becoming somehow more crisp, more deliberate. Sparhawk touched the big roan's neck with one hand. "Relax," he murmured. "I'll let you know when the time comes."

Faran shuddered, absently flicking his master's reassurance off like a bothersome insect and continuing his cautious pace.

Vanion looked at his friend questioningly.

"Faran's being a little sensitive, my Lord."

"Sensitive? That ill-tempered brute?"

"Faran doesn't really deserve that reputation, Vanion. When you get right down to it, he's a good-natured horse. He tries very hard to please me. We've been together for so long that he knows what I'm feeling most of the time, and he goes out of his way to match his attitude to mine. *I'm* the one who's the ill-tempered brute, but he gets all the blame. He behaves like a puppy when Aphrael's riding on his back."

"Are you feeling belligerent just now?"

"I don't like being led around by the nose, but it's nothing specific. You've overtrained me, Vanion. Any time anything unusual comes up, I start getting ready for war. Faran can feel that, so he does the same."

Xanetia and Kalten were leading them across the meadow that sloped down toward the glowing lake and the strangely alien town nestled on the near shore. The pale Delphaeic woman still glowed with that eerie light. The radiance surrounding her seemed to Sparhawk's heightened senses to be almost a kind of aura, a mark more of a special kind of grace rather than a loathsome contamination.

"It's all one building, did you notice that?" Talen was saying to his brother. "It looks like any other city from a distance, but when you get closer, you start to see that the houses are all connected together."

Khalad grunted. "It's a stupid idea," he said. "A fire could burn out the whole town."

"The buildings are made of stone. They won't burn."

"But the roofs are thatch, and thatch *will* burn. It's a bad idea."

Delphaeus had no separate wall as such. The outermost houses, all interconnected, turned their backs to the world, facing inward with their windowless rear walls presented to the outside. Sparhawk and the others followed Xanetia through a large, deep archway into the city. There was a peculiar fragrance about Delphaeus, a scent of new-mown hay. The streets were narrow and twisting, and they frequently ran *through* the buildings, passing under heavy arches into vaulted corridors that emerged again on the far side. As Talen had noted, Delphaeus was all one building, and what would have been called streets in another town were simply unroofed hallways here.

The citizens did not avoid their party, but they made no particular effort to approach. Like pale ghosts they drifted through the shadowy maze.

"No torches," Berit noted, looking around.

"No need," Ulath grunted.

"Truly," the young knight agreed. "Notice how it changes the smell of the place? Even Chyrellos always reeks of burning pitch—even in the daytime. It's a little strange to be in a city that doesn't have that greasy smoke clinging to everything."

"I don't think the world at large is ready for self-illuminating people yet, Berit. It's an idea that probably won't catch on—particularly in view of the drawbacks attached to it."

"Where are we going, Lady?" Kalten asked the pale, glowing woman at his side. Kalten's situation was a peculiar one. He guarded and protected Xanetia. He was solicitous about her comfort and well-being. He *would*, however, be the one who would kill her at the first sign of hostility from her people.

"We go to the quarters of the Anari," Xanetia replied. "It is he who must place our proposal before Anakha. Anakha holds the keys to Bhelliom, and only he can command it."

"You could have saved the rest of us a lot of trouble and made this trip alone, Sparhawk," Talen said lightly.

"Maybe, but it's always nice to have company. Besides, if you hadn't come along, you'd have missed all the fun. Look at how entertaining it was to jump off that cliff and lounge around in midair with about a thousand feet of absolute emptiness under you."

"I've been trying very hard to forget about that, my lord," the boy replied with a pained expression.

They dismounted in one of those vaulted corridors near the center of the city and turned their horses over to several young Delphae. The young men looked to Sparhawk like goatherds who had been pressed into service as stableboys. Then they followed the glowing woman to a dark-stained door, worn with centuries of use. Sparhawk, still in the grip of that emotionless calm, looked carefully at Xanetia. She was not much bigger than Sephrenia, and, although she was clearly a woman and quite an attractive one, that fact somehow had no meaning. Xanetia's gender seemed irrelevant. She opened the worn door and led them into a hallway with deeply inset doorways piercing the walls at widely spaced intervals. The hallway was lighted by glass globes hanging on long chains from the vaulted ceiling, globes filled with a glowing liquid—water drawn from the lake, Sparhawk surmised.

At the far end of the corridor, Xanetia paused in front of one of the doors, and her eyes grew distant for a moment. "Cedon bids us to enter," she said after a brief pause. She opened the door and, with Kalten close behind her, she led them into the chambers beyond. "The hall of Cedon, Anari of the Delphae," she told them in that peculiarly echoing voice that seemed to be one of the characteristics of her race.

Three worn stone steps led down into the central chamber, a tidy room with vaulted ceilings supported by low, heavy arches. The slightly inwardly curving walls were covered with white plaster, and the low, heavy furniture was upholstered with snowy lamb's wool. A small fire burned in an arched fireplace at the far end of the room, and more of those glowing globes hung from the ceiling.

Sparhawk felt like a crude, barbaric intruder here. Cedon's home reflected a gentle, saintly nature, and the big Pandion was acutely conscious of his chain-mail shirt and the heavy broadsword belted at his waist. He felt bulky and out of place, and his companions, wrapped in steel and leather and rough, grey cloth, seemed to loom around him like the crude monoliths of an ancient and primitive culture.

A very old man entered from the far side of the room. He was frail and bent, and his shuffling steps were aided by a long staff. His hair was wispy and snowy white, in his case the mark of extreme age rather than a racial characteristic. In addition to his unbleached wool robe, he wore a kind of shawl about his thin shoulders.

Xanetia went to him immediately, touching his wrinkled old face with a gentle hand. Her eyes were full of concern for him, but she did not speak.

"Well met, Sir Knights," the old man greeted them. He spoke in only slightly accented Elenic, and his voice sounded thin and rusty as if he seldom had occasion to speak at all. "And welcome to thee as well, dear sister," he added, speaking to Sephrenia in nearly flawless, though archaic, Styric.

"I am not your sister, old man," she said, her face cold.

"We are all brothers and sisters, Sephrenia of Ylara, High Priestess of Aphrael. Our kinship lies in our common humanity."

"That may have been true once, Delphae," she replied in a voice like ice, "but you and your accursed race are no longer human."

He sighed. "Perhaps not. It is hard to say precisely what we are—or what we will become. Put aside thine enmity, Sephrenia of Ylara. Thou wilt come to no harm in this place, and for once, our purposes merge into one. Thou wouldst set us apart from the rest of mankind, and that is now also *our* desire. May we not join our efforts to achieve this end?"

She turned her back on him.

Itagne, ever the diplomat, stepped in to fill the awkward gap. "Cedon, I presume?" he said urbanely.

The old man nodded.

"I find Delphaeus puzzling, revered one, I must confess it. We Tamuls know virtually nothing about your people, and yet the Delphae have been central to a grossly affected genre in our literature. I've always felt that this so-called 'Delphaeic literature' had been spun out of whole cloth by third-rate poets with diseased imaginations. Now I come to Delphaeus and find that all manner of things I had believed to be literary conceits have more than a little basis in fact." Itagne was smooth, there was no question about that. His assertion that he was even more clever than his brother, the foreign minister, was probably quite true.

The Anari smiled faintly. "We did what we could, Itagne of Matherion. I will grant thee that the verse is execrable and the sentimentality appalling, but 'Xadane' did serve the purpose for which it was created. It softened and turned aside certain of the antagonisms the Styrics had planted in your society. The Tamuls control the Atans, and we did not wish a confrontation with our towering neighbors. I cringe to confess it to thee, but I myself played no small part in the composition of 'Xadane.' "

Itagne blinked. "Cedon, are we talking abut the same poem? The 'Xadane' *I* studied as a schoolboy was written about seven hundred years ago."

"Has it been so long? Where *do* the years go? I did enjoy my stay in fire-domed Matherion. The university was stimulating."

Itagne was too well-trained to show his astonishment. "Your features are Tamul, Cedon, but didn't your coloration seem . . . odd?"

"Ye Tamuls are far too civilized to make an issue of deformity. My racial characteristics were simply taken to mean that I was an albino. The condition is not unheard of. I had a colleague—a Styric—who had a clubfoot. Rather surprisingly, we got on well together. I note from thy speech that contemporary Tamul hath changed from what it was when I was last among thy people. That would make it difficult for me to return to Matherion. Please accept my apologies for 'Xadane.' It is truly abominable, but as I say, it served its purpose."

"I should have known," Sephrenia cut in. "The whole body

of Delphaeic literature was created with the sole purpose of fostering a climate of anti-Styric bigotry."

"And what was the purpose of the eons of outright falsehood with which ye Styrics deceived the Tamuls?" Cedon demanded. "Was the design not precisely the same? Did ye not seek to instill the idea in the Tamul perception that the Delphae are subhuman?"

Sephrenia ignored the question. "Does your hatred of us run so deep that you would contaminate the understanding of an entire race?"

"And how deeply doth *thy* hatred run, Sephrenia of Ylara? Art thou not even now attempting to poison the minds of these simple Elenes against us?" The Anari sank into a cushioned chair, passing one weary hand across his face. "Our mutual hatreds have gone, methinks, too far to be healed. Better far that we live apart. And that doth bring us to the issue which hath brought us together. It is our wish to be apart from all others."

"Because you're so much better than the rest of us?" Sephrenia's tone was thick with contempt.

"Not better, Priestess, only different. We will leave *that* puffed-up sense of superiority to *thy* race."

"If you two want to renew a few eons-old hatreds, I think the rest of us would prefer not to sit through it," Vanion said coolly. "You both seem quite able to manage without our help."

"You don't know what they've done, Vanion," Sephrenia said with a mute appeal in her eyes.

"Frankly, dear, I'm not really interested in what happened several thousand years ago. If you want to chew old soup, please do it on your own time." Vanion looked at the ancient Delphae. "I believe you had some kind of an exchange in mind, Cedon. We'd love to sit around and watch you and Sephrenia slice each other into thin strips, but we're a little pressed for time. Affairs of state, you understand."

Even Sparhawk choked a bit on that.

"Thou art very blunt, Lord Vanion," Cedon said in a coldly reproving tone.

"I'm a soldier, revered Anari. A conversation made up of spiteful little insults bores me. If you and Sephrenia really want to fight, use axes."

"Have you had many occasions to deal with Elenes, revered Anari?" Itagne asked in an unruffled manner.

"Almost none."

"You might consider offering up a few prayers of thanksgiving for that. The Elenes have this distressing tendency to get right to the point. It's dreadfully uncivilized, of course, but it *does* save time. I believe you wanted to address your proposal to Anakha. That's him right there. I should probably warn you that Lord Vanion is the absolute soul of finesse when compared to Sparhawk, but Sparhawk is Anakha, so sooner or later you're going to have a deal with him."

"Since we've all decided to be unpleasant this evening, I don't think we'll get very far," Sparhawk said. "Why don't you tell me what you want, Cedon, and what you're prepared to offer in return? I'll think it over tonight, and then we can talk about it tomorrow, after we've had time to get a firmer grip on our civility."

"A wise course, perhaps, Anakha," the old man agreed. "There is turmoil afoot in Tamuli."

"Yes. We've noticed that."

"The turmoil is not directed at the empire, Anakha, but at *thee*. Thou wert lured here because thou hast the keys to Bhelliom. Thine enemies covet the jewel."

"We know that, too. I don't really need a preamble, Cedon. What's the point of this?"

"We will aid thee in thy struggle, and I do assure thee that without our aid, thou canst not prevail."

"You'll have to convince me of that, but we can talk about it some other time. What do you want in return?"

"We would have thee take up Bhelliom and seal us in this valley."

"That's all?"

"That is all we ask. Put us beyond the reach of all others, and put all others beyond *our* reach. All will be served by this—Elene and Tamul, Styric and Delphae. Use the infinite power of Bhelliom to set us apart from the rest of mankind so that we may continue our journey undisturbed."

"Journey?"

"A figure of speech, Anakha. Our journey is measured in generations, not in leagues."

"An even exchange, then? You'll help us to deal with our enemies if I close off this valley so that no one can ever get in—or out?"

"An even exchange, Anakha."

"All right. I'll think about it."

* * *

"She won't talk to me about it, Sparhawk," Vanion sighed, "or about anything else, for that matter." The silvery-haired preceptor and his friend were speaking privately in a small room just off the corridor that led to the cluster of tiny, cell-like rooms where they had spent the night.

"You *were* just a bit blunt last night," Sparhawk told him.

"Irrational behavior irritates me. I wish Aphrael were here. She could straighten Sephrenia out in fairly short order."

Sparhawk slid lower in his chair. "I'm not so sure, Vanion. I don't know if I'm supposed to tell you this, but I get the feeling that Aphrael wouldn't interfere. Before she left, she told me that Sephrenia has to work this out for herself."

"Could Itagne shed any light on this antagonism between the Styrics and the Delphae?"

Sparhawk shook his head. "No more than he's already told us. The whole business seems to date back to the time of the war with the Cyrgai. That was about ten thousand years ago, so history's a little vague about what really happened. Evidently the Styrics and the Delphae were allies, and there seems to have been a betrayal of some sort."

"I gathered as much. Can Itagne make any guesses about who was betrayed?"

"No. The Styrics have made themselves useful to the Tamuls over the centuries—as they made themselves useful to the Church in Eosia. They've been busy insinuating *their* version of what happened into the Tamul perception of history. From what Cedon told us last night, I'd say that the Delphae have infiltrated the University of Matherion and inserted Delphaeic literature into the Tamul culture with precisely the same idea. The events of ten thousand years ago are going to be buried under a thick layer of myth and legend anyway, and with both the Styrics and the Delphae busily muddying up the waters, the real truth probably won't ever come out into the open." He smiled faintly. "I'm not sure how significant it is, but the Styrics tried to contaminate the historians, while the Delphae spent their time trying to contaminate the poets. Interesting contrast, wouldn't you say?"

"Aphrael would know the truth."

"Probably, but she's not talking. I know her well enough to know that her silence is deliberate. I don't think she really wants us to know who was originally at fault. She doesn't seem to want us to take sides, for some reason, and that puts us in a very difficult position. I wonder if we'll ever find out the truth behind this racial antagonism—not that it really matters. I doubt if Sephrenia or the Anari themselves even know. They've both had about four hundred generations of hysterical propaganda to set their prejudices in stone. *Our* problem is that the Delphae can probably hold us here indefinitely. If we try to ride away, they'll just turn us around and lead us right back, so eventually we're going to have to negotiate with them. We all love Sephrenia, though, so if we *do* negotiate with the Delphae, she'll take fire spontaneously."

"Yes, I noticed that. What am I going to do, Sparhawk? I bleed when she so much as pricks her finger."

"Lie to her." Sparhawk shrugged.

"Sparhawk!"

"You don't have to be too obvious about it, but lean your neutrality slightly in her direction. *I'm* the one in charge of Bhelliom, so Cedon's going to have to deal with *me*. Technically, you're secondary here—sorry, Vanion, but it's true. Cedon's going to be negotiating with me, not you. Glare at me now and then and raise objections. Sephrenia's behaving irrationally, so the others, like good, logical Elenes, are going to oppose her. Let's not isolate her entirely. You're the most important person in her life, and if *you* seem to be turning against her as well, you'll break her heart." He smiled a bit wryly. "I'd take it as a personal favor, though, if you didn't let her turn me into a toad about midway through the negotiations."

"Let's go back a step or two, revered Anari," Sparhawk suggested when they had gathered again in the large, sunken room. "I need to know what I'm getting involved in here. I'm *not* going to do anything to injure the Styrics. They're sometimes a prickly and difficult people, but we've grown fond of them for some reason." He smiled at Sephrenia, hoping to soften her displeasure. "You mentioned a journey of some sort. Where are you going?"

"We are changing, Anakha. When the world turned against us, we appealed to Edaemus to protect us."

"Your God?"

The Anari nodded. "We were a childlike, unsophisticated people before the war with the Cyrgai, and Edaemus lived among us, sharing our simple joys and transient sorrows. Of all the people of this world, we were the least suited for war." The old man looked at Sephrenia. "I will not offend thy teacher by speaking the truth about what led to our being made outcast."

"The truth is well known," Sephrenia said stiffly.

"Yes, it is, but *thy* truth is quite different from *ours.* You believe that one thing happened, and we believe that something else took place. But that, Sephrenia of Ylara, is between us, and it doth not concern these Elenes. In truth, Lady, neither Styric *nor* Delphae were very admirable in that unfortunate affair. For whatever cause, Anakha, the Delphae were cast out, and the hands of all men were turned against us. We appealed, as I said, to Edaemus, and he responded by laying a curse on us."

"This Edaemus of yours has a peculiar way of showing his affection," Ulath noted.

"It was the only way to protect us, Sir Knight. We are not warlike and have no skill with the weapons with which other men kill each other, and so Edaemus cursed us to make our merest touch a weapon. Other men soon found that the touch of our hands meant death."

"Then why am I still here, Cedon?" Kalten asked. "I've been helping Xanetia on and off her horse for several days now, and her touch hasn't killed *me.*"

"We have learned to control the curse, Sir Kalten. That was a part of the plan of Edaemus when he raised his hand against our lake."

"The lake?"

The Anari nodded. "Edaemus could not bear the thought of laying his curse upon us directly, and so he cursed the waters of the lake instead. The lake is our only source of water, and we therefore must drink of it. When first we came to this valley, the mind of Edaemus was as childlike as ours. In the spirit of play gave he the waters of the lake that peculiar essence which doth illuminate us. We drink of the lake, and its waters infuse our bodies. Out of love did Edaemus make us appear like Gods. It was a harmless entertainment, and we soon forgave him for so altering us. When the world turned against us, however, did Edaemus curse the lake; and its infusing waters, changed by that curse, changed us as well. The touch of death which doth hold our enemies at bay is but a small part of the design of our God, however. Circumstance hath set us apart from this world, and it is the intent of Edaemus to set us yet further apart. We are changing, my friends. Our bodies are different, and our minds and spirits as well. We are no longer as ye—nor as once we were. With each generation this inexorable change progresses. Xanetia, dear, gentle Xanetia, so far surpasseth me that I cannot even begin to comprehend the extent of her thought. In time, methinks, she will equal—or even surpass—the very Gods themselves."

"And then you will supplant us," Sephrenia accused. "Even as the Trolls supplanted the Dawn-men and as we are supplanting the Trolls, so will you despised Delphae become our masters, putting aside our Gods and kenneling us like dogs in uninhabitable wastelands while *you* enjoy the fruits of the earth. We Styrics have endured such treatment at the hands of the Elenes for eons and we have learned much. You will not so easily subdue us, Cedon, and we will not worship you nor fawn at your feet like whipped dogs."

"How may we supplant thee and seize thy lands, Sephrenia of Ylara? We are bound to our lake and may not long be away from its waters. Thy submission, moreover, would have no meaning for us, for we will not be here. We journey toward the light, and we will *become* light. My Xanetia, who will be Anarae, could join with the light even now, but those of us who have not yet reached her perfection hold her back. When we are dead, there will no longer be any reason for her to remain, and she will lead the Delphae out to dwell among the stars with Edaemus, who hath gone before us to prepare our home."

"Where you will be Gods," Sephrenia added with a spiteful sneer.

"That is a word without meaning, Sephrenia of Ylara," Xanetia said quietly. "All of us, Gods *and* men, move toward the same goal. Edaemus hath gone before us, and we will go before thee. We will await thy coming with love, and we will even forgive thee for the wrong that thou hast done us."

"*Forgive me?*" Sephrenia exploded. "I spurn thy condescending forgiveness!" She had lapsed, probably without realizing it, into archaic Styric. "I will *never* forgive thee nor accept any of *thy* forgiveness."

"But thou wilt, Sephrenia," the glowing woman disagreed. "Even now is thine heart doubtful within thy breast. Thou art of two minds, gentle Sephrenia. I know thee well, and I know that this hatred of thine, like winter frost, doth lurk in the dark, shaded places of thy soul. I do assure thee that it will melt in the warm sun of thy loving nature—even as mine own hatred doth even now begin its painful thaw. But make no mistake, Sephrenia of Ylara, I do hate Styrics even as thou hatest the Delphae. An hundred centuries of enmity is not lightly cast aside. I do *hate* the perfidious Styrics, but I do *not* hate thee. I know thine heart, dear sister, for it is even as mine own. In time will we both put aside this childish hatred and live together in peace."

"*Never!*"

"Never, dear sister, is a long, long time."

"I think we're getting a little far afield here," Sparhawk cut in. "This sealing up of the valley isn't intended to be eternal, I gather?"

"There would be no need of that, Anakha," the Anari replied. "Once we are gone, Edaemus will lift his curse from the lake, its waters will return to normal, and other men may freely come to this valley without fear."

"I should probably tell you that if I seal the valley with Bhelliom, I *will* seal it. I can guarantee you that no Delphae will ever leave. If you're going to turn into moonbeams or sunlight, that won't inconvenience you, but if you've got some other notion hidden away, you might as well forget it. And if this Edaemus of yours has a secret agenda involving some sort of retaliation against the Styrics, you'd better tell him to drop it. Bhelliom eats Gods for breakfast—as Azash found out. Do you *still* want me to seal your valley?"

"Yes," Cedon replied without hesitation.

"How about you, Sephrenia?" Sparhawk asked. "Would that kind of guarantee satisfy you?"

"They'll try trickery, Sparhawk. They're a deceitful race."

"You know the Bhelliom, Sephrenia—probably even better than I do. Do you *really* think anybody—man *or* God—could trick it? If I tell it to keep the Delphae in and everybody else out, *nobody's* going to cross the line—not you, not me, not Aphrael, not Edaemus—not even the God of the Elenes. Even if all the Gods of this world and of all other worlds combined, Bhelliom would *still* keep them out. If I seal this valley, it will *stay* sealed. Even the birds and angleworms won't be able to leave. Will that satisfy you?"

She refused to look at him.

"I need an answer, little mother, and I'd rather not have to wait all year to get it. Will it satisfy you?"

"You're hateful, Sparhawk!"

"I've got a lot on my mind just now. Think it over and let me know what you decide." He turned to face the Anari. "All right, now I know what you want. The next question is what's in it for me? What do *I* get out of this arrangement?"

"Our assistance in thy struggle with thine enemies, Anakha."

"That's a little unspecific, Cedon. I've got the Bhelliom. What can you possibly do for me that I can't do for myself?"

"Thou must have the cooperation of the jewel, Anakha. Thou canst compel the stone, but it loves thee not, and it doth sometimes deliberately misunderstand thee—as when it took thee and the Child-Goddess to Demos when thou sought to go to Delo in Arjuna."

"How did you know about that?" Sparhawk was startled.

"Thy mind is open to me, Anakha, as are all minds. This is but one of the services we can offer thee. Would it not be to thine advantage to know what those about thee are thinking?"

"It would indeed, Cedon, but there are other ways to wrest the truth from men's hearts."

"But men who have been put to the torture know that they have been tortured, and they know what they have revealed unto thee. Our way is more subtle."

"He's got a point there, Sparhawk," Kalten said. "What am *I* thinking right now, Cedon?"

"Thou art troubled by the duty to slay Xanetia should our people play thee false, Sir Knight. Thy mind is gently inclined toward her."

"He's right about that," Kalten admitted to the others. "I think these people *can* hear what others are thinking."

"We have other capabilities as well, Sir Knights," the Anari told them, "and we freely offer them to thee in exchange for what we ask." He looked rather sadly at Sephrenia. "I fear that when I reveal the nature of these capabilities, it will cause thee pain and harden thine heart yet more toward us, dear sister."

"*Will* you stop calling me that? My heart is already like granite toward you and your kind."

"That is not true, Sephrenia of Ylara," Xanetia disagreed. "Thou art troubled forasmuch as thou hast found no wickedness in us in this, thy first meeting with our kind. Hard put art thou to maintain an hatred which groweth more from thy sense of duty to thy kindred than from any personal rancor. I do freely confess mine own similarly troubled state. I am inclined to love thee, even as thou art so inclined toward me."

"Stop that!" Sephrenia burst out. "Keep your unclean hands out of my thoughts.

"Stubborn, isn't she?" Ulath murmured.

"It is the nature of the Younger Gods of Styricum to protect their children—even from their own folly," the Anari noted. "Thus it is that the Styrics must appeal to their Gods with spells and prayers for aid when they would step beyond the powers of other men. Is it not so, Sephrenia of Ylara?"

She refused to answer him.

"That's the core of Styric magic, Cedon," Vanion replied for her.

She glared at him, and Sparhawk silently groaned. Why *couldn't* Vanion keep his mouth shut?

The Anari nodded. "Edaemus hath, as I say, gone before us to prepare the way, and he is therefore no longer able to watch over us. Thus hath he granted certain of us the power to do what must be done *without* his guidance."

"Unrestrained magic?" Sephrenia exclaimed. "You hold the power of the Gods in your *own* hands with no restraints?"

"Some few of us, yes."

"That's monstrous! The human mind isn't capable of understanding the nature of that kind of power. We can't grasp the consequences of unleashing it to satisfy our childish whims."

"Thy Goddess hath instructed thee well, Sephrenia of Ylara," Xanetia noted. "This is what she *wishes* thee to believe."

"Thy Goddess would keep thee a child, dear sister," the Anari said. "For so long as thou art a child, she is secure in thy love. I tell thee truly, however, Edaemus doth love us even as thine Aphrael doth love thee. His love, however, doth compel us to grow. He hath placed his power in our hands, and we must accept the consequences of our acts when we bring it to bear. It is a different kind of love, but it is love nonetheless. Edaemus is no longer here to guide us, so we can do whatever our minds are able to conceive." The Anari smiled gently. "Forgive me, my friends," he said to them, "but one as old as I hath but one peculiar interest." He held up one withered old hand and looked at it rather sadly. "How soon are we altered by the passing of years, and how distressing is the alteration."

The change seemed gradual, but considering the staggering nature of that change, what was happening before their eyes was nearly miraculous. The withered hand grew more firm-fleshed; the knobby joints smoothed; and the wrinkles faded. It was not only the hand, however. The tracery of wrinkles and lines on Cedon's face seemed to slide away. His hollow cheeks filled out, and his thin, wispy hair grew fuller, more abundant. They stared at him as, with no apparent effort, he reversed the erosion of years. He regressed to vigorous youth, his skin clear and his hand and face firm and unmarked. Then, he began to diminish, his limbs shrinking inside his garments. The prickly stubble vanished from his cheeks and chin, and, as he continued to regress, his head seemed to grow larger in proportion to his shrinking body. "That might be far enough," he said in a piping, childish voice. He smiled, a strangely ancient smile that looked very much out of place on that little boy's face. "A miscalculation here might reduce me to nothing. In truth, I have considered that, but my tasks and responsibilities are not yet completed. Xanetia has her own tasks, and I would not yet burden her with mine as well."

Sparhawk swallowed hard. "I think you've made your point, Cedon," he said in a strained voice. "We'll accept the fact that you can do things that we can't do." He looked around at his friends. "I can already see arguments brewing," he told them, deliberately avoiding Sephrenia's eyes, "and no matter what we decide, we'll probably all have serious doubts about it."

"We could pray," Bevier suggested.

"Or roll dice and let them decide," Ulath added.

"Not with *your* dice, we couldn't," Kalten objected.

"We could even fall back on logic," Vanion concluded, "but Sparhawk's right. No matter how we try to decide, we could probably sit here all winter and still not agree." He also avoided Sephrenia's eyes.

"All right, then," Sparhawk said, reaching inside his tunic, "since Aphrael's not here to bully us into agreement, we'll let Bhelliom decide." He took out the golden box and set it on the table in front of him.

"*Sparhawk!*" Sephrenia gasped.

"No, Anakha!" Xanetia also exclaimed.

"Bhelliom doesn't love any of us," he said, "so we can sort of rely on its neutrality. We need guidance here, and neither Edaemus nor Aphrael is around to provide it—besides which, I don't know that I'd trust either of them anyway, given the peculiar circumstances here. We want an uncontaminated opinion, so why don't we just find out what Bhelliom thinks about the situation?"

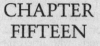

CHAPTER
FIFTEEN

Blue-Rose," Sparhawk said in Trollish to the glowing jewel in his hands, "I am Anakha. Do you know me?"

Bhelliom's glow pulsed slightly, and Sparhawk could sense the stone's stiff reluctance to acknowledge his dominion. Then he thought of something. "You and I need to talk," he said, speaking in Elenic this time, "and I don't think Khwaj and the others need to be listening. Can you understand me when I speak in this fashion?"

There was the faintest hint of curiosity in the pulse this time.

"Good. Is there some way you can talk to me? There's something you and I have to decide. This is too important for me to simply force you to do what I want, because I could be wrong. I know you're none too fond of me—or of any creature on this particular world—but I think that we may have some common interest this time."

"Let me go." The voice was a kind of lingering whisper, but it was familiar.

Sparhawk whirled around to stare at Kalten. His boyhood friend's face was wooden, uncomprehending, and the words came stiffly from his lips. "Why hast thou done this thing, Anakha? Why hast thou enslavèd me?" The archaic Elenic could not have come from Kalten, but why had Bhelliom chosen this most unlikely mouth?

219

Sparhawk carefully readjusted his thoughts, casting them in the profoundly formal language with which the stone had addressed him, and in the instant of that changeover, perception and understanding came. It somehow seemed that knowledge had lain dormant in his mind until unlocked by this peculiar key. Strangely, his understanding had been bound up in language, and once he made the conscious shift from contemporary Elenic with all its casual imprecision to more stately and concise cadences, that previously closed part of his mind opened. "It was not I who enslavèd thee, Blue-Rose. It was thine own inattention that brought thee into such perilous proximity to the red of iron which congealed thee into thy present state, and it was Ghwerig who lifted thee from the earth and contorted thee into this similitude of a flower with his cruel diamond implements."

A stifled groan came from Kalten's lips, a groan of pain endured and pain remembered.

"I am Anakha, Blue-Rose," Sparhawk continued. "I am *thy* creature. It is *thou* who hast causèd me to be, that I might be the instrument of thy liberation, and I will not betray thy trust in me. I am in some part made of *thy* thought, and I am therefore thy servant. It is thou who hast enslavèd *me*. Didst thou not set my destiny apart, making me a stranger to the Gods of this world and to all other men? But, though I am thine enslavèd servant, I am, nonetheless, still of *this* world, and I will not have it destroyed nor its people crushed by the vile oppression of mine enemies. I did free thee from the enslavement of Ghwerig, did I not? Is this not in some small measure proof of my fidelity to the task which thou hast lain upon me? And, bound together in common purpose, did we not destroy Azash, who would have chained us both in a slavery harsher than that which now chains us together? For mistake me not, Blue-Rose, even as thou art *my* slave, so am I *thine*, and once again the chain which binds us together is common purpose, and neither shall be free until that purpose be accomplishèd. Then shalt thou, and then shall I, be free to go our separate ways—I to remain, and thou to go, an it please thee, to continue thine interrupted and endless journey to the farthest star."

"Thou hast learned well, Anakha," Bhelliom said grudgingly, "but thine understanding of thy situation did never obtrude itself upon thy conscious thought where I could perceive it. I had despaired, thinking that I had wrought amiss."

Sephrenia was staring at them, first at Sparhawk and then at the seemingly comatose Kalten, and her pale, flawless face was filled with something very like chagrin. Xanetia stared, also, and her expression was no less chagrined. Sparhawk took a fleeting satisfaction in that. The two were very much alike in their perhaps-unconscious assumption of condescending superiority. Sparhawk's sudden, unexpected awareness of things long concealed in his understanding had shaken that irritating smugness of theirs. For the first time in his life he consciously knew that he was Anakha, and more importantly, he knew the meaning of Anakha in ways neither Sephrenia nor Xanetia could ever begin to comprehend. He had stepped around them to reach Bhelliom, and in joining his thought with Bhelliom's, he had to some degree shared Bhelliom's awareness, and that was something neither of them could ever do.

"Thou hast not wrought amiss, Blue-Rose," he told the jewel. "Thine error lay in casting thy thought in this particular speech. Mine understanding was also cast so, and it did not reveal itself to me until I responded to thy words in kind. Now, let us to work withal. Mine enemies are also thine, forasmuch as they would bind *thee* even as they would bind *me*. Neither of us shall be secure in our freedom until they are no more. Are we agreed upon that?"

"Thy reasoning is sound, Anakha."

"Our purpose then is the same?"

"So it would seem."

"We're making some headway here," Sparhawk murmured. Kalten's expression became coldly disapproving.

"Sorry," Sparhawk apologized, "force of habit, I suppose. Reason doth urge that since our enemies and our purpose are common, and our thoughts are linked by this chain of *thy* forging, we must join our efforts in this cause. In victory shall we be freed. Our enemies and our common purpose shall be no more, and the chain which links us will fall away. I do pledge it to thee that upon the completion of this task will I free thee to continue thy work. My life is surely within thy fist, and thou mayest destroy me if I play thee false."

"I find no falsity in thy thought, Anakha, and I will strengthen thine arm and harden thine heart, lest others, beloved by thee, seek to turn thee aside from thy design and thy pledge. We are agreed."

"Done, then!" Sparhawk exclaimed.

"*And done!*" Bhelliom's speech, emerging from Kalten's

lips, had been dry and unemotional, but this time the voice was exultant.

"And now to this decision which thou and I must make together."

"Sparhawk—" Sephrenia's tone was uncertain.

"I'm sorry, little mother," he said, "I'm not talking with you at the moment. Please don't interrupt." Sparhawk was not entirely sure whether he should address his question to the sapphire rose or to Kalten, who seemed to have been completely taken over by the spirit within the jewel. He settled for directing his question somewhere between them. "The Delphae have offered their assistance in exchange for a certain service," he said. "They would have us seal their valley that none may enter and none may leave, and in recompense for that small favor they promise to aid us. Is their offer made in good faith?" Sparhawk heard Xanetia's sharp intake of breath.

"It is," Bhelliom replied. "There is no falsity in their offer."

"I didn't think so myself, but I wanted to be sure."

"Anakha." The voice was firm. "When thou speakest so, thy mind is concealed from me. Our alliance is new and unfamiliar. It is not wise of thee to raise doubts in me by compressing thy words together so."

Sparhawk suddenly laughed. "Forgive my lapse, Blue-Rose," he said. "We can trust the Delphae, then?"

"For the moment, yes. Their intent is presently without guile. It is uncertain what it will be tomorrow. Thy kind is inconstant, Anakha." Kalten's voice hesitated briefly. "I say that not as criticism, merely as observation. For the nonce mayest thou put thy trust in their sincerity—and they in thine. What may come subsequently lieth in the hands of chance."

"Then there *is* such a thing as chance?" Sparhawk was a bit surprised at that. "We are told that all things are predetermined by the Gods."

"Whosoever told thee so was in error."

Bevier gasped.

"My journey and my task were interrupted by chance," Bhelliom continued. "If *my* course may be turned aside, might not thine as well? Truly I tell thee, Anakha, we *must* join with the Delphae in this enterprise, for if we do not, we shall surely fail. Whether one or both play the other false will depend on circumstance. At this time, the hearts of the Delphae are pure; that may change. At this time, *thine* heart is *also* pure; that may *also* change. But will we, nil we, we must join with them, lest we fail and languish forever in vilest bondage."

"You heard him, Bevier," Sephrenia was saying to the olive-skinned Arcian later when Sparhawk quietly entered the room where the two were deep in conversation, "they worship the lake—the source of the contamination that makes them outcast."

"He *did* mention a God, Lady Sephrenia," Bevier protested mildly. "I think he called their God Edaemus—or something like that."

"But Edaemus has abandoned them—cursed them and then turned his back on them."

"Anari said that Edaemus had gone before them to prepare a place for them." Bevier's objection seemed even weaker. "He said that they were changing—turning into pure light."

"Lies," she snapped. "The light that marks them is not the mark of a blessing, Bevier, it's the mark of their curse. Cedon was cleverly trying to twist it around to make it seem that the Delphae are turning into something holy, when the reverse is actually true."

"They *do* perform magic, Sephrenia, and a kind of magic I've never seen before. I wouldn't have believed that *anyone* could return to childhood if I hadn't seen it with my own eyes."

"Exactly my point, Bevier. They're using witchcraft, not magic. You've never seen *me* imitate a God, have you?"

Sparhawk stepped unobserved back out into the hallway and went on down to the doorless cell Vanion occupied. "We've got a problem," he told the Preceptor of the Pandions.

"Another one?"

"Sephrenia's trying to subvert Bevier. She's trying to convince him that the Delphae practice witchcraft. You know Bevier. His eyes start to bulge out any time anyone so much as mentions the word."

"*Why* won't she just leave it alone?" Vanion exclaimed, throwing his hands in the air. "Wasn't Bhelliom's word good enough for her?"

"She doesn't *want* to believe, Vanion," Sparhawk sighed. "We've run into exactly the same thing when we've tried to convince rural Elenes that Styrics aren't born with horns and tails."

"She of all people should be free of that sort of thing."

"I'm afraid not, my friend. Styrics are good haters, I guess. How do we want to handle this?"

"I'll confront her directly."

Sparhawk winced. "She'll turn you into a frog if you do."

Vanion smiled briefly. "No. I lived in Sarsos, remember? A Styric can't do anything like that without the consent of his God, and Aphrael's sort of fond of me—I hope."

"I'll round up the others and get them out from underfoot so that you can speak with her privately."

"No, Sparhawk, it has to be done in front of them. She's trying to slip around behind us to recruit converts. They're all going to have to be made aware of the fact that she's not to be trusted in this particular situation."

"Wouldn't it be a little better to talk with her privately at first—*before* you humiliate her publicly?"

Vanion shook his head stubbornly. "We've got to meet this head-on," he declared.

"You'd *better* hope that Aphrael's fond of you," Sparhawk murmured.

"They've reverted to total paganism," Sephrenia said stubbornly. "They might as well worship trees or oddly shaped rocks. They have no creed, no doctrine, and no restraints. Their use of witchcraft proves that." They had gathered at Vanion's summons in a large room at the end of the hall, and Sephrenia was urgently, even stridently, trying to make her case.

"What's the difference?" Talen shrugged. "Magic, witchcraft, it's all the same, isn't it?"

"Magic is of the Gods, Talen," Bevier explained. "Our Holy Mother, in her wisdom, has chosen to allow the Church Knights to learn the secrets of Styricum that we might better serve her. There are restraints on us—certain areas we may not enter. Witchcraft is unrestrained because it is of the evil one."

"The Devil, you mean? I've never really believed in the Devil. There's plenty of concentrated wickedness in people anyway, so we can probably get along fairly well without him. I've known some *very* nasty people, Bevier."

"The existence of the Devil has been proved."

"Not to me, it hasn't."

"Aren't we wandering a bit?" Ulath suggested. "Does it really matter *what* the Delphae worship? We've allied ourselves with all sorts of people in the past in order to achieve this or that goal. Bhelliom says that we have to join forces with the

Delphae, or we're going to lose. I don't like losing, so what's the problem?"

"Bhelliom doesn't know anything about this world, Ulath," Sephrenia said.

"So much the better. It comes at the problem with a clear and uncluttered understanding. If I need to jump behind a tree to keep from being swept away by an avalanche, I'm not going to stop to question the tree about its beliefs first."

"Bhelliom will do or say *anything* in order to gain its freedom," Sephrenia asserted. "That's why I was so much against using it in the first place."

"We *have* to believe Bhelliom, Sephrenia," Vanion told her, obviously trying to keep his irritation under control. "It doesn't make much sense for us to trust it with our very lives and then not believe what it tells us, does it? It *has* done some very useful things for us in the past, you know."

"Only because it was *compelled* to, Vanion. Bhelliom submits because it's forced to submit. I trust the Bhelliom even less than I trust the Delphae. It's alien, totally alien, and we have no way of knowing *what* it will do. We're safe only for as long as we keep it chained and force it to obey us. The minute we begin to listen to it, we're in great danger."

"Is that how you feel about us, too, little mother?" he asked her sadly. "We're Elenes, and as a race we've proved time and again that we're not to be trusted. Do you want to chain *us* as well? And *force* us to obey you?"

"Don't be absurd. Bhelliom's not a person."

"The Delphae *are*, though, aren't they?"

"No!"

"You're being illogical, Sephrenia. The Delphae *are* human. We don't care for the Zemochs or the Rendors, but we've never tried to pretend that they aren't human. There are a lot of Elenes who don't like you Styrics, but we've never gone so far as to try to deny your humanity." He paused, then drew in a deep breath. "I guess that's what it comes down to, love. If you're going to deny the humanity of the Delphae, how can I be positive that you don't secretly feel the same way about me? I've lived in Sarsos, and many of the Styrics there wanted to treat *me* like some lower life-form. Did you agree with them? Have I been some kind of pet, Sephrenia—a dog maybe? Or a tame ape that you kept around for your private amusements? Hang it all, Sephrenia, this is a question of morality. If we deny *anyone's* humanity, we open the door to unimaginable horror. Can't you see that?"

"The Delphae are different."

"*Nobody's* different! We *have* to believe that, because if we don't, we deny our *own* humanity as well. Why *won't* you understand?"

Her face was very, very pale. "This is all very highsounding and noble, Vanion, but it has nothing whatsoever to do with the Delphae. You don't know anything about what they are or who they are, so you don't really know what you're talking about. You've always come to me for guidance in the past when your ignorance was putting you in danger. Am I correct in assuming that we're not going to do that anymore?"

"Don't be silly."

"I'm not. I'm being very serious. Are you going to ignore me on this issue? Are you going to take up with these monstrous lepers, no matter what I tell you?"

"We don't have any choice in the matter, can't you see that? Bhelliom tells us that we're going to fail if we don't—and we *can't* fail. I think the whole world's going to depend on our not failing."

"You seem to have outgrown your need for me, then. It would have been polite of you to have told me that *before* you brought me to this accursed valley, but I suppose I was silly to expect politeness from an Elene in the first place. As soon as we get back to Matherion, I'll make arrangements to return to Sarsos, where I belong."

"Sephrenia—"

"No. This concludes it. I've served the Pandion Order well and faithfully for three hundred years, and I thank you for your generous payment for my years of toil. We're through, Vanion. This ends it. I hope the rest of your life will be happy, but happy or sad, you're going to live it without me." And she turned and swept from the room.

"It will be very dangerous, Anari," Itagne warned, "and Xanetia is the most important of all your people. Is it prudent to risk her life?"

"Truly, Itagne of Matherion," the old man replied, "Xanetia is precious to us, for she will be Anarae. She is, however, the most gifted of us, and it may well be that *her* gifts will weight the scale in our final confrontation with our common enemy."

Sparhawk, Vanion, and Itagne had been summoned to meet with Cedon prior to their departure from the valley of Delphaeus. It was a fine autumn morning. A hint of frost, fast melting in the newly risen sun, steamed on the meadow, and the shade under the boughs of the evergreens beyond that meadow was a deep, deep blue.

"I merely wished to point it out, Anari," Itagne said. "For all its splendor, Matherion is a city filled with hidden dangers—with rough, ignorant people who will react very strongly to the appearance of one of the Delphae in their midst. Your gentle Xanetia is an ethereal, unworldly sort of person, hardly more than a girl. The fact that she's a Shining One will protect her to some degree against overt physical attack, but are you really willing to expose her to the curses, the vituperation, and all the other kinds of abuse she's sure to encounter there at the center of the world?"

The Anari smiled. "Thou hast misperceived Xanetia, Itagne of Matherion. Doth she truly seem so much a child to thee? Would thy mind be more easy if thou wert aware that she is well past her first century of life?"

Itagne stared at him and then at Xanetia, who sat quietly near the window. "You are a strange people, Anari," he said. "I'd have guessed her age at no more than sixteen years."

"It is impolite to speculate about a lady's age, Itagne of Matherion." The pale woman smiled.

"Forgive me, Anarae," Itagne replied with a courtly bow.

"His Excellency here has raised a fairly important point, Anari," Vanion said. The preceptor's face was still marked by the pain of the previous day's conversation with Sephrenia. "The lady's appearance won't go unnoticed—not only in Matherion itself, but along the roads we'll have to follow as we ride east as well. Is there some way we could disguise her enough so that whole villages won't go into absolute panic the moment she rides by?" He looked apologetically at the Delphaeic woman. "I wouldn't offend you for the world, Anarae, but you *are* very striking."

"I thank thee for the compliment, gentle sir."

"Do you want to take over, Sparhawk?" Vanion said. "I just seem to be digging myself in deeper."

"We're soldiers, Xanetia," Sparhawk said bluntly, "and our answer to hostility is fairly direct. We can butcher our way from here to the imperial palace in Matherion if we have to, but I get the feeling that you might find that distressing. Would a disguise of some kind offend you?" Then a thought came to him. "*Can* we disguise you? I don't know if you've noticed, but you glow. Some of your people have come fairly close to us before the light started to show. Can your internal fire be dampened?"

"We can control the light, Anakha," Cedon assured him, "and Xanetia, the most gifted of us all, can control it even better than most—though it doth cause her pain to do so. For us, it is an unnatural thing."

"We'll have to work on that, then."

"The pain is of no moment, Anakha," Xanetia assured him.

"Not to you, perhaps, but it is to me. Let's start with your coloration, though. Your features are Tamul, but your skin and hair are the wrong color. What do you think, Itagne? Could she pass for Tamul if we dyed her skin and hair?"

"That is not needful, Anakha," Xanetia told him. Her brow furrowed briefly in concentration, and gradually, almost like a slow blush, a faint golden tint began to mount in her cheeks, and her hair slipped from its colorless white into pale blonde. "Color is a quality of light," she explained quite calmly even as the embronzing of her skin and the darkening of her hair continued, "and since I can control the light from within me, so can I also control my color—indeed, by thus altering the light rather than suppressing it entirely, I can lessen the pain. A most happy solution for me—and for thee as well, I wot, since thou seemest sensitive to the pain of others. This is a simple matter." Her skin by now was almost the same pale gold as Itagne's, and her hair was a deep, rich auburn. "The change of shape is far more difficult," she conceded, "and the change of gender more difficult still."

"The *what*?" Itagne choked.

"I do not do that often—nor willingly," she replied. "Edaemus did not intend for me to be a man, and I find it most uncomfortable. A man's body is so cluttered and untidy." She held out her arm and examined it closely. "The color seemeth to me correct," she observed. Then she took a lock of her now-black hair and looked at it. "And this as well," she added. "What thinkest thou, Itagne? Would I pass unnoticed in Matherion now?"

"Hardly, divine Xanetia." He smiled. "Thy passage through the streets of fire-domed Matherion would stop the hearts of all who beheld thee, for thou art fair, and thy beauty doth bedazzle mine eye beyond all measure."

"Well said," Sparhawk murmured.

"Thine honeyed words fall sweetly upon mine ears, Itagne," Xanetia smiled. "Thou art, I do believe, a master of flattery."

"You should probably know that Itagne is a diplomat, Anarae," Vanion advised her, "and his words aren't always to be trusted. This time he's telling you the truth, though. You're an extraordinarily beautiful woman."

She looked at him gravely. "Thine heart is sore within thee, is it not, Lord Vanion?" she observed.

He sighed. "It's my personal problem, Anarae," he replied.

"Not entirely so, my Lord. Now are we all of the same fellowship, and the troubles of one are the troubles of all. But that which troubleth thee is of far greater note and causeth us all much greater concern than that which might grow from our comradely feelings for thee. This breach between thy beloved and thee doth endanger our cause, and until it be healed, our common purpose doth stand in peril."

They rode eastward, following a scarcely perceptible track that seemed more like a game trail than a route normally followed by humans. Sephrenia, accompanied by Bevier and young Berit, rode some distance to the rear, her face set and her eyes as hard as flint.

Sparhawk and Vanion rode in the lead, following occasional directions from Xanetia, who rode directly behind them under Kalten's watchful eye. "Just give her some time, Vanion," Sparhawk was saying. "Women deliver ultimatums and declarations of war fairly often. Things like that are usually intended to get our attention. Any time I start neglecting Ehlana, she says something she doesn't really mean to bring me up short."

"I'm afraid this goes a little further than that, Sparhawk," Vanion replied. "Sephrenia's a Styric, but she's never been so totally irrational before. If we could find out what's behind this insane hatred of hers, we might be able to do something about it, but we've never been able to get any coherent reasons out of her. Apparently, she hates the Delphae simply because she hates the Delphae."

"Aphrael will straighten it out," Sparhawk said confidently. "As soon as we get back to Matherion, I'll have a talk with Danae, and—" Sparhawk broke off as a sudden thought chilled his blood. "I have to talk with Xanetia," he said, abruptly wheeling Faran around.

"Trouble?" Kalten asked as Sparhawk joined them.

"Nothing immediate," Sparhawk replied. "Why don't you go on ahead and ride with Vanion for a while. I need to talk with Xanetia."

Kalten gave him a questioning look but rode on forward without any further questions.

"Thou art troubled, Anakha," Xanetia observed.

"A little, yes. You know what I'm thinking, don't you?" She nodded.

"Then you know who my daughter is?"

"Yes."

"It's a sort of secret, Anarae. Aphrael didn't consult with my wife when she chose her present incarnation. It's very important that Ehlana doesn't find out. I think her sanity depends on it."

"Thy secret is safe, Anakha, I do pledge thee my silence on this issue."

"What really happened, Xanetia? Between the Styrics and the Delphae, I mean. I don't want your version or Sephrenia's. I want the truth."

"Thou art not meant to know the truth, Anakha. A part of thy task is to resolve this issue without recourse to the truth."

"I'm an Elene, Xanetia," he said in a pained voice. "I *have* to have facts in order to make decisions."

"Then it is thine intent to judge? To decide if the guilt doth condemn the Styrics or the Delphae?"

"No. My intent is to get to the bottom of Sephrenia's behavior so that I can change her mind."

"Is she so important to thee?"

"Why do you ask questions when you already know the answers?"

"My questions are intended to help *thee* formulate *thy* thought, Anakha."

"I'm a Pandion Knight, Xanetia. Sephrenia's been the mother of our order for three centuries. Any one of us would give up his life for her without any hesitation at all. We love her, but we don't share all of her prejudices." He leaned back in his saddle. "I'll only wait for so long, Xanetia. If I don't get the real truth out of you—or out of Sephrenia—I'll just ask Bhelliom."

"Thou wouldst *not*!" Her now-dark eyes were filled with a sudden chagrin.

"I'm a soldier, Xanetia, so I don't have the patience for subtlety. You'll excuse me? I have to go talk with Sephrenia for a moment."

"Dirgis," Xanetia told them as they crested a hill and saw a typical Atan town lying in the valley below.

"Well, *finally*," Vanion said, taking out his map. "Now we know where we are." He looked over his map for a moment and then squinted up at the evening sky. "Is it too late in the day for us to take one of those long steps, Sparhawk?"

"No, my Lord," Sparhawk replied. "There's plenty of light."

"Are we still concerned about that?" Ulath asked. "Haven't you and Bhelliom hammered that out yet?"

"We haven't been having any private chats," Sparhawk replied. "There are still people out there who can locate Bhelliom when it's out in the open, so I've been keeping it inside its little house—just to be on the safe side."

"It's well over three hundred leagues, Sparhawk," Vanion pointed out. "It's going to be later there."

"I'm never going to get used to that," Kalten said sourly.

"It's really very simple, Kalten," Ulath told him. "You see, when the sun goes down in Matherion, it's still—"

"Please, Ulath," Kalten told him, "don't try to explain it to me. It just makes things worse. When people start to explain it, I sometimes think I can actually feel the world moving under me. I don't like that very much. Just tell me that it's later there, and let it go at that. I don't really need to know *why* it's later."

"He's a perfect knight," Khalad told his brother. "He doesn't even *want* explanations."

"Look on the bright side of it, Khalad," Talen replied. "After we've gone through the wonderful training they've got planned for us, we'll be exactly like Kalten. Think how much easier life's going to be for us when we don't have to understand anything at all."

"I'd guess that it's very close to being fully dark in Matherion by now, Sparhawk," Vanion said. "Maybe we'd better wait until morning."

"I'm not so sure," Sparhawk disagreed. "The time's going to come sooner or later when we're going to have to make one of these jumps after the sun goes down. There's nothing urgent in the wind right now, so it's a good time for us to answer this question once and for all."

"Ah—Sparhawk?" Khalad said.

"Yes?"

"If you've got a question, why not ask? Now that you and Bhelliom are on speaking terms, wouldn't it be simpler—and safer—to just ask it first? *Before* you start experimenting? Matherion's on the coast, as I recall, and I'd rather not come down about a hundred leagues out to sea."

Sparhawk felt just a little foolish. He took out the small golden box and opened the lid. He paused momentarily, casting his question in antique Elenic. "I must needs have thine advice on a certain matter, Blue-Rose," he said.

"Say thy question, Anakha." This time the voice came from Khalad's lips.

"That's a relief," Kalten said to Ulath. "I almost chewed up my tongue with all the *thee*'s and *thou*'s last time."

"Can we safely go from one place to another when the pall of darkness hath covered the earth?" Sparhawk asked.

"There *is* no darkness for me, Anakha."

"I did not know that."

"Thou hadst but to ask."

"Yes. I do perceive that now. Mine understanding doth grow with each passing hour. On the eastern coast of far-flung Tamuli there doth lie a road which doth proceed southward to fire-domed Matherion."

"Yes."

"When my companions and I first beheld Matherion, we came in sight of it when we did crest a long hill."

"Yes. I share thy memory of the place."

"Couldst thou take us there, e'en though darkness doth cover the face of the earth?"

"Yes."

Sparhawk started to reach into the box for his wife's ring. Then he stopped. "We share a common purpose and thus are comrades. It is not meet that I should compel thee and whip thee into compliance with the power of Ghwerig's rings. Thus I do not command thee, but request instead. Wilt thou take us to this place we both know, out of comradeship and common purpose?"

"I will, Anakha."

CHAPTER
SIXTEEN

T he blur which surrounded them momentarily
was that same featureless grey, no darker than
it had been when Bhelliom had transported
them in daylight. Night and day appeared to
be irrelevant. Sparhawk dimly perceived that Bhelliom took
them through some different place, a colorless emptiness that
adjoined all other places—a kind of doorway to everywhere.

"You were right, my Lord," Kalten said to Vanion, looking
up at the star-studded night sky. "It *is* later here, isn't it?" He
looked sharply at Xanetia, who swayed slightly in her saddle.
"Are you unwell, Lady?" he asked her.

"It is of no moment, Sir Knight. A slight giddiness, nothing
more."

"You get used to it. The first few times are a little unsettling, but that wears off."

Khalad held out the box, and Sparhawk put Bhelliom back
inside. "I do not do this to imprison thee," he told the jewel.
"Our enemies can sense thy presence when thou art exposed,
and this receptacle doth conceal thee from their search."

The Bhelliom pulsed slightly in acknowledgment.

Sparhawk closed the cap over his ring, took the box from
his squire, and closed it. Then he tucked it back into its usual
place inside his tunic.

Matherion, ruddy with torchlight, lay below, and the pale

233

path of light from the newly risen moon stretched from the horizon across the waters of the Tamul Sea to her doorstep, yet another of the innumerable roads leading to the city the Tamuls called the center of the world.

"Are you open to a suggestion, Sparhawk?" Talen asked.

"You sound just like Tynian."

"I know. I'm sort of filling in for him while he's away. We've been out of Matherion for a while, so we don't know what's really been going on here. Suppose I slip into town and have a look—ask a few questions, find out what we're riding into—the usual sort of thing."

Sparhawk nodded. "All right," he said.

"That's all? Just 'all right'? No protests? No objections? No hour-long lectures about being careful? I'm disappointed in you, Sparhawk."

"Would you listen to me if I objected or delivered a lecture?"

"No, not really."

"Why waste the time, then? You know what you're doing and how to do it. Just don't take all night."

Talen swung down from his horse and opened his saddlebags. He took out a rough, patched smock and pulled it on over his other clothes. Then he bent, rubbed his hand in the dirt of the road, and artfully smudged his face. He stirred up his hair and sifted a handful of straw from the roadside onto it. "What do you think?" he asked Sparhawk.

"You'll do." Sparhawk shrugged.

"Spoilsport," Talen grumbled, climbing back on his horse. "Khalad, come along. You can watch my horse for me while I sniff around."

Khalad grunted, and the two rode on down the hill.

"Is the child truly so gifted?" Xanetia asked.

"He'd be offended if you called him a child, Lady," Kalten replied, "and he can come closer to being invisible than anybody I know."

They drew back some distance from the road and waited.

It was an hour later when Talen and his brother returned.

"Things are still more or less the way they were when we left," the boy reported.

"No open fighting in the streets, you mean?" Ulath laughed.

"Not yet. Things are a little hectic at the palace, though. It's got something to do with documents of some kind. The whole government's in an uproar. None of the people I talked with knew all that much about it. The Church Knights and the Atans are still in control, though, so it's safe to jump from here to the courtyard of Ehlana's castle if we want."

Sparhawk shook his head. "Let's ride in. I'm sure there are still Tamuls inside the walls, and probably half of them are spies. Let's not give away any secrets if we don't have to. Is Sarabian still staying in the castle?"

Talen nodded. "Your wife's probably been teaching him a few tricks—'roll over,' 'play dead,' 'sit up and beg'—that sort of thing."

"Talen!" Itagne exclaimed.

"You haven't met our queen yet, have you, your Excellency?" Talen grinned. "I'd say that you're in for a whole new experience."

"It has to do with setting up the new filing system, my Lord," the young Pandion at the drawbridge explained in reply to Vanion's question. "We needed room to rearrange things, so we spread all the government files out on the lawn."

"What if it rains?"

"That would probably simplify the job a great deal, my Lord."

They dismounted in the courtyard and went up the broad stairs to the ornately carved main door, paused briefly to put on the cushioned shoes that protected the brittle floor-covering, and went inside.

Queen Ehlana had been advised of their arrival and she was waiting for them at the door to the throne room. Sparhawk's heart caught in his throat as he looked at his lovely young wife. "So nice of you to stop by, Sir Sparhawk," she said tartly before she threw her arms about his neck.

"Sorry we're so late, dear," he apologized after they had exchanged a brief, formal sort of kiss. "Our travel plans got a little skewed." He was painfully conscious of the half-dozen or so Tamuls lingering nearby trying to look very hard as if they weren't listening. "Why don't we go on upstairs, my Queen? We've got quite a bit to tell you, and I'd like to get out of this mail shirt before it permanently embeds itself into my skin."

"You are *not* going to wear that stinking thing into *my* bedroom, Sparhawk. As I remember, the baths lie in that general direction. Why don't you take your fragrant friends and go make use of them? The ladies can come with me. I'll round up the others, and we'll all meet you in the royal quarters in about an hour. I'm sure your explanation of your tardiness will be absolutely fascinating."

Sparhawk felt much better after he had bathed and changed into the conventional doublet and hose. He and his friends trooped up the stairs that mounted into the central tower where the royal apartments were located.

"You're late, Sparhawk," Mirtai said bluntly when they reached the top of the stairs.

"Yes. My wife's already pointed that out to me. Come inside. You'll need to hear this, too."

Ehlana and the others who had remained behind were gathered in the large, blue-draped sitting room. Sephrenia and Danae were conspicuously absent, however.

"Well, *finally*!" Emperor Sarabian said as they entered. Sparhawk was startled by the change in the emperor's appearance. His hair was tied back from his face, he wore tight-fitting black hose and a full-sleeved linen shirt. He looked younger for some reason, and he was holding a rapier with the kind of familiarity that spoke of much practice. "Now we can get on with the business of overthrowing the government."

"What have you been up to, Ehlana?" Sparhawk asked.

"Sarabian and I have been expanding our horizons." She shrugged.

"I knew I shouldn't have stayed away so long."

"I'm glad you brought that up. That very same thought's been on my mind for the longest time now."

"Why don't you just save yourself some time and unpleasantness, Sparhawk?" Kalten suggested. "Just show her why we had to take this little trip."

"Good idea." Sparhawk reached inside his doublet and took out the unadorned gold box. "Things were beginning to get out of hand, Ehlana, so we decided to go fetch some reinforcements."

"I thought that's what Tynian was doing."

"The situation called for something a little more significant than the Church Knights." Sparhawk touched the band of his ring to the lid of the box. "Open," he said. He kept the lid partially closed to conceal the fact that his wife's ring was also inside.

"What have you done with your ring, Sparhawk?" she asked him, looking at the cover concealing the stone.

"I'll explain in a bit." He reached in and took out the

Bhelliom. "*This* is why we had to leave, dear." He held up the stone.

She stared at it, the color draining from her face. "Sparhawk!" she gasped.

"What a magnificent jewel!" Sarabian exclaimed, reaching his hand out toward the sapphire rose.

"That might not be wise, your Majesty," Itagne cautioned. "That's the Bhelliom. It tolerates Sparhawk, but it might pose some dangers to anyone else."

"Bhelliom's a fairy tale, Itagne."

"I've been reassessing my position on various fairy tales lately, your Majesty. Sparhawk destroyed Azash with Bhelliom—just by touching it to him. I don't advise putting your hands on it, my Emperor. You've shown some promise in the past few months, and we'd sort of hate to lose you at this point."

"Itagne!" Oscagne said sharply. "Mind your manners!"

"We're here to advise the emperor, brother mine, not to coddle him. Oh, incidentally, Oscagne, when you sent me to Cynestra, you invested me with plenipotentiary powers, didn't you? We can check over my commission, if you like, but I'm fairly sure I had that kind of authority—I usually do. I hope you don't mind, old boy, but I've concluded a couple of alliances along the way." He paused. "Well," he amended, "Sparhawk did all the real work, but my commission put some slight stain of legality on the business."

"You can't do that without consulting Matherion first, Itagne!" Oscagne's face was turning purple.

"Oh, be serious, Oscagne. All I did was seize some opportunities that presented themselves, and I was hardly in a position to tell Sparhawk what he could or couldn't do, now, was I? I had things more or less under control in Cynestra when Sparhawk and his friends dropped by. We left Cynestra, and—"

"Details, Itagne. What did you do in Cynestra?"

Itagne sighed. "You can be so tedious at times, Oscagne. I found out that Ambassador Taubel was in bed with Kanzad, the Interior Ministry's station chief. They had King Jaluah pretty much dancing to their tune."

Oscagne's face went bleak. "Taubel's defected to Interior?"

"I thought I just said that. You might want to run a quick evaluation of your other embassies, too. Interior Minister Kolata's been very busy. Anyway, I threw Taubel and

Kanzad—along with the entire police force and most of the embassy staff—into a dungeon, declared martial law, and put the Atan garrison in charge."

"You did what?"

"I'll write you a report about it one of these days. You know me well enough to know that I had justification."

"You exceeded your authority, Itagne."

"You didn't impose any limitations on me, old boy. That gave me carte blanche. All you said was to have a look around and to do what needed to be done, so I did."

"How did you persuade the Atans to go along with you without written authorization?"

Itagne shrugged. "The commander of the Atan garrison there is a fairly young woman—quite attractive, actually, in a muscular sort of way. I seduced her. She was an enthusiastic seducee. Believe me, Oscagne, she'll do absolutely *anything* for me." He paused. "You might want to make a note of that in my file—something about my willingness to make sacrifices for the empire and all that. I didn't give her *total* free rein, though. The dear child wanted to give me the heads of Taubel and Kanzad as tokens of her affection, but I declined. My rooms at the university are cluttered enough already, so I don't really have the space for stuffed trophies on the walls. I told her to lock them up instead and to keep a firm grip on King Jaluah until Taubel's replacement arrived. You needn't hurry with that appointment, my brother. I have every confidence in her."

"You've set back relations with Cynesga by twenty years, Itagne."

"What relations?" Itagne snorted. "The Cynesgans respond only to naked force, so that's what I used on them."

"You spoke of alliances, Itagne," Sarabian said, flicking the tip of his rapier. "Just exactly to whom have you committed my undying trust and affection?"

"I was just coming to that, your Majesty. After we left Cynestra, we went on to Delphaeus. We spoke with their chieftain, the Anari—a very old man named Cedon—and he offered his assistance. Sparhawk's going to take care of our side of the bargain, so there's no cost to the empire involved."

Oscagne shook his head. "It must come from our mother's side of the family, your Majesty," he apologized. "There was an uncle of hers that was always a little strange."

"What are you talking about, Oscagne?"

"My brother's obvious insanity, your Majesty. I'm told that things like that are hereditary. Fortunately, I favor our father's side of the family. Tell me, Itagne, are you hearing voices, too? Do you have visions of purple giraffes?"

"You can be so tiresome sometimes, Oscagne."

"Would *you* tell us what happened, Sparhawk?" Sarabian asked.

"Itagne covered it fairly well, your Majesty. I take it that you Tamuls have some reservations about the Shining Ones?"

"No," Oscagne said, "I wouldn't call them reservations, your Highness. How could we have any reservations about a people who don't exist?"

"This argument could go on all night," Kalten said. "Would you mind, Lady?" he asked Xanetia, who sat quietly beside him with her head slightly bowed. "If you don't show them who you are, they'll wrangle for days."

"An it please thee, Sir Knight," she replied.

"So formal, my dear?" Sarabian smiled. "Here in Matherion, we only use that mode of speech at weddings, funerals, coronations, and other mournful events."

"We have long been isolate, Emperor Sarabian," she replied, "and unmovèd by the winds of fashion and the inconstant tides of usage. I do assure thee that we find no inconvenience in what must seem to thee forcèd archaism, for it cometh to our lips unbidden and is our natural mode of speech—upon such rare occasions when speech among us is even needful."

The door at the far end of the room opened, and Princess Danae, dragging Rollo behind her, entered quietly with Alean close behind her.

Xanetia's eyes widened, and her expression became awed.

"She fell asleep," the little princess reported to her mother.

"Is she all right?" Ehlana asked.

"Lady Sephrenia seemed very tired, your Majesty," Alean responded. "She bathed and went directly to bed. I couldn't even interest her in any supper."

"It's probably best to just let her sleep," Ehlana said. "I'll look in on her later."

Emperor Sarabian had obviously taken advantage of the brief interruption to frame his thoughts in a somewhat studied archaism. "Verily," he said to Xanetia, "thy mode of speech doth fall prettily upon mine ear, Lady. In truth, however, thou hast been unkind to absent thyself from us, for thou art fair, and thine elegant mode of address would have added luster to our court. Moreover, thine eyes and thy gentle demeanor do shine forth from thee and would have provided instruction by ensample for they who are about me."

"Thy words are artfully honeyed, Majesty," Xanetia said, politely inclining her head, "and I do perceive that thou are a consummate flatterer."

"Say not so," he protested. "I do assure thee that I speak truly from mine heart." He was obviously enjoying himself.

She sighed. "Thine opinion, I do fear me, will change when thou dost behold me in my true state. I have alterèd mine appearance as necessary subterfuge to avoid affrighting thy subjects. For, though it doth cause me grave distress to confess it, should thy people see me in mine accustomed state, they would flee, shrieking in terror."

"Canst thou truly inspire such fear, gentle maiden?" He smiled. "I cannot give credence to thy words. In truth, methinks, shouldst thou appear on the streets of fire-domed Matherion, my subjects would indeed run—but *not* away from thee."

"That thou must judge for thyself, Majesty."

"Ah—before we proceed, might I inquire as to the state of your Majesty's health?" Itagne asked prudently.

"I'm well, Itagne."

"No shortness of breath? No heaviness or twinges in your Majesty's chest?"

"I said that I'm healthy, Itagne," Sarabian snapped.

"I certainly *hope* so, your Majesty. May I be permitted to present the Lady Xanetia, the Anarae of the Delphae?"

"I think your brother's right, Itagne. I think you've taken leave of—Good God!" Sarabian was staring in open horror at Xanetia. Like the dye running out of a bolt of cheap cloth, the color was draining from her skin and hair, and the incandescent glow that had marked her before she had disguised it began to shine forth again. She rose to her feet, and Kalten stood up beside her.

"Now is the stuff of thy nightmares made flesh, Sarabian of Tamuli," Xanetia said sadly. "This is who and what I am. Thy servant Itagne hath told thee well and truly what transpirèd in fabled Delphaeus. I would greet thee in manner suitable to thy station, but like all the Delphae, I am outcast, and therefore not subject to thee. I am here to perform those services which devolve upon my people by reason of our pact with Anakha, whom thou hast called Sparhawk of Elenia. Fear me not, Sarabian, for I am here to serve, not to destroy."

Mirtai, her face deathly pale, had risen to her feet. Purposefully, she stepped in front of her mistress and drew her sword. "Run, Ehlana," she said grimly. "I'll hold her back."

"That is not needful, Mirtai of Atan," Xanetia told her. "As I said, I mean no harm to any in this company. Sheathe thy sword."

"I will, accursed one—in your vile heart!" Mirtai raised her sword. Then, as if struck by some great blow, she reeled back and fell to the floor, tumbling over and over.

Kring and Engessa reacted immediately, rushing forward and clawing at their sword hilts.

"I would not hurt them, Anakha," Xanetia warned Sparhawk, "but I must protect myself that I may keep faith with the pact between thee and my people."

"Put up your swords!" Vanion barked. "The lady is a friend!"

"But—" Kring protested.

"I said to put up your swords!" Vanion's roar was shattering, and Kring and Engessa stopped in their tracks.

Sparhawk, however, saw another danger. Danae, her eyes bleak and her face set, was advancing on the Delphaeic woman. "Ah, there you are, Danae," he said, moving rather more quickly than his casual tone might have suggested. He intercepted the vengeful little princess. "Aren't you going to give your poor old father a kiss?" He swept her up into his arms and smothered her indignant outburst by mashing his lips to hers.

"Put me down, Sparhawk!" she said, speaking directly down his throat.

"Not until you get a grip on your temper," he muttered, his mouth still clamped to hers.

"She hurt Mirtai!"

"No, she didn't. Mirtai knows how to fall without getting hurt. Don't do anything foolish here. You knew this was going to happen. Everything's under control, so don't get excited— and *don't*, for God's sake, let your mother find out who you really are."

"It doesn't really talk!" Ehlana interrupted Sparhawk's account of what had taken place in Delphaeus.

"Not by itself, no," Sparhawk replied. "It spoke through Kalten—well, it did the first time, anyway."

"Kalten?"

"I have no idea why. Maybe it just seizes on whoever's handy. The language it uses is archaic and formal—*thee*'s and *thou*'s and that sort of thing. Its speech is much like Xanetia's, and it wants me to respond in kind. Evidently, the mode of speech is important." He rubbed one hand across his freshly shaved cheek. "It's very strange, but as soon as I began to speak—and think—in twelfth-century Elenic, something seemed to open in my mind. For the first time I knew that I was Anakha, and I knew that Bhelliom and I are linked together in some profoundly personal way." He smiled wryly. "It seems that you're married to two different people, love. I hope you'll like Anakha. He seems a decent enough sort—once you get used to the way he talks."

"Perhaps I should just go mad," she said. "That might be easier than trying to understand what's going on. How many other strangers do you plan to bring to my bed tonight!"

Sparhawk looked at Vanion. "Should I tell them about Sephrenia?"

"You might as well," Vanion sighed. "They'll find out about it soon enough anyway."

Sparhawk took his wife's hands in his and looked into her grey eyes. "You're going to have to be a little careful when you talk with Sephrenia, dear," he told her. "There's an ancient enmity between the Delphae and the Styrics, and Sephrenia grows irrational whenever she's around them. Xanetia has problems with the Styrics as well, but she manages to keep it under control better than Sephrenia does."

"Doth it seem so to thee, Anakha?" Xanetia asked. She had resumed her disguise, more for the sake of the comfort of the others than out of any real need, Sparhawk guessed. Mirtai sat not far from her with watchful eyes and with her hand resting on her sword hilt.

"I'm not trying to be personally offensive, Anarae," he apologized. "I'm just trying to explain the situation so that they'll understand when you and Sephrenia try to claw each other's eyes out."

"I'm sure you've noticed my husband's blinding charm, Anarae," Ehlana smiled. "Sometimes he absolutely overwhelms us with it."

Xanetia actually laughed, then looked at Itagne. "These

Elenes are a complex people, are they not? I do detect great agility of thought behind this bluff manner of theirs, and subtleties I would not have expected from a people who tailor steel into garments."

Sparhawk leaned back in his chair. "I haven't really covered everything that happened, but that's enough to let you know in general what we encountered. We can fill in more detail tomorrow. What's been going on here?"

"Politics, of course," Ehlana shrugged.

"Don't you ever get tired of politics?"

"Don't be silly, Sparhawk. Milord Stragen, why don't you tell him? It shocks him when I start going into all the sordid details."

Stragen was once again dressed in his favorite white satin doublet. The blond thief was sunk deep in a chair with his feet up on a table. "That attempted coup alerted us that there were more mundane elements involved in this business than hobgoblins and resurrected antiquities," he began. "We knew that Krager was involved—and Interior Minister Kolata—and that turned it into ordinary, garden-variety politics. We didn't know where Krager was, so we decided to find out just how deeply Interior was infected. Since all policemen everywhere are compulsive about paperwork, we were fairly sure that somewhere in that rabbit warren of a building was a set of files that would identify the people we wanted to talk with. The problem was that we couldn't just walk into the ministry and demand to see their files without giving away the fact that we knew what they were up to, which in turn would have let them know that Kolata was our prisoner instead of a willing guest. Baroness Melidere came up with the idea of a new filing system, and that gave us access to all the files of all the ministries."

"It was dreadful." Oscagne shuddered. "We had to disrupt the entire government in order to conceal the fact that we were really only interested in the files at Interior. Milord Stragen and the baroness put their heads together and concocted a system. It's totally irrational and wildly inconsistent, but for some reason it works amazingly well. I can lay my hands on any given piece of paper in less than an hour."

"Anyway," Stragen continued, "we browsed through the files at Interior for a week or so, but the people over there kept slipping back into the building at night to move things around so that we'd have to start all over again every morning. That's when we decided to just move our operations out onto the lawns. We stripped all the paper out of all the buildings and spread it out on the grass. That inconvenienced the rest of the government enormously, but Interior was still holding out on us. They were still hiding the critical files. Caalador and I reverted to type and tried burglary—along with Mirtai. The queen sent her along to remind us that we were looking for paper rather than miscellaneous valuables, I guess. It took a few nights, but we finally found the hidden room where the files we wanted were concealed."

"Didn't they miss them the next morning?" Bevier asked him.

"We didn't take them, Sir Knight," Caalador told him. "The queen called in a young Pandion who used a Styric spell to bring the information back to the castle without physically removing the documents." He grinned. "We got us all that there real incriminatin' stuff, an' they don't know we got it. We stole it, an' they don't even miss it."

"We've got the name of every spy, every informer, every secret policeman, and every conspirator of whatever rank Interior has in all of Tamuli." Sarabian smirked. "We've been waiting for all of you to come home so that we can take steps. I'm going to dissolve the Ministry of the Interior, round up all those people, and declare martial law. Betuana and I have been in close contact, and we've laid our plans very carefully. As soon as I give the word, the Atans are going to take charge of the entire empire. Then I'll *really* be the emperor instead of just a stuffed toy."

"You've all been very busy," Vanion observed.

"It makes the time go faster, my Lord." Caalador shrugged. "We went a little farther, though. Krager obviously knew that we were using the criminals of Matherion as spies, but we weren't sure if he knew about the hidden government. If he thinks our organization's localized, that's not much of a problem; but if he knows that I can give the order here in Matherion, and somebody dies in Chyrellos, that's a whole 'nother thang."

"I've missed that dialect," Talen said. He considered it. "Not really very much, though," he added.

"Critic," Caalador accused.

"How much were you able to find out?" Ulath asked him.

Caalador spread one hand and rocked it back and forth dubiously. "It's sorta hord t' say," he admitted. "They's some places whur it iz ez them folks o' ourn kin move around free ez frogs in a muddy pond. Other places, they can't." He made a sour face. "It probably all boils down to natural talent. Some are gifted; some aren't. We've made a little headway in putting names to some of the rabid nationalists in various parts of Tamuli—at least we *think* it's headway. If Krager really knows what we're doing, he could be feeding us false information. We wanted to wait until you came back before we tested the information we've got."

"How do you test something like that?" Bevier asked.

"We'll send out the order to have somebody's throat cut, then see if they try to protect him," Stragen replied. "Some chief of police somewhere, or maybe one of those nationalist leaders—Elron, maybe. Isn't that astonishing, Sparhawk? That's one of the things we found out. It turns out that Elron is the mysterious Sabre."

"What an amazing thing," Sparhawk replied with feigned astonishment.

"Caalador wants to kill the man named Scarpa," Stragen went on, "but I favor Elron—although my preference in the matter could be viewed as a form of literary criticism. Elron deserves killing more for his abominable verse than his political opinions."

"The world can stand a little more bad poetry, Stragen," Caalador told his friend. "Scarpa's the really dangerous one. I just wish we could put a name to Rebal, but so far he's eluded us."

"His real name's Amador," Talen told him. "He's a ribbon clerk in Jorsan on the west coast of Edom."

"How did you find *that* out?" Caalador seemed astonished.

"Pure luck, to be honest about it. We saw Rebal making a speech to some peasants out in the woods. Then, later on when we were in Jorsan, a gust of wind blew me into his shop. He isn't really very much to worry about. He's a charlatan. He uses carnival tricks to make the peasants think that he's raising the ghost of Incetes. Sephrenia seems to think that means that our enemies are spread thin. They don't have enough real magicians to arrange all these visitations, so they have to resort to trickery."

"What were you doing in Edom, Sparhawk?" Ehlana asked.

"We went through there on our way to pick up Bhelliom."

"How did you get there and back so fast?"

"Aphrael helped us. She's very helpful—most of the time." Sparhawk avoided looking at his daughter. He rose to his feet.

"We're all a little tired tonight," he suggested, "and I rather expect that filling in all of the details is going to take us quite a while. Why don't we break off here and get some sleep? Then we'll be able to attack it again in the morning when we're all fresh."

"Good idea," Ehlana agreed, also rising. "Besides, I've got this burning curiosity."

"Oh?"

"As long as I'm going to be sleeping with him, I should probably get to know this Anakha fellow, wouldn't you say? Sleeping with total strangers so tarnishes a girl's reputation, you know."

"She's still asleep," Danae said, quietly closing the door to Sephrenia's room.

"Is she all right?" Sparhawk asked.

"Of course she isn't. What did you expect, Sparhawk? Her heart's broken."

"Come with me. We need to talk."

"I don't think I want to talk with you right now, Father. I'm just a little unhappy with you."

"I can live with that."

"Don't be too sure."

"Come along." He took her by the hand and led her up a long flight of stairs to the top of the tower and then out onto the parapet. He prudently closed the door and bolted it behind them. "You blundered, Aphrael," he told her.

She raised her chin and gave him a flat, icy stare.

"Don't get imperial with me, young lady. You made a mistake. You never should have let Sephrenia go to Delphaeus."

"She *had* to go. She has to go through this."

"She can't. It's more than she can bear."

"She's stronger than she looks."

"Don't you have any heart at all? Can't you see how much she's suffering?"

"Of course I can, and it's hurting *me* far more than it's hurting you, Father."

"You're killing Vanion, too, you know."

"He's *also* stronger than he looks. Why did all of you turn against Sephrenia at Delphaeus? Two or three soft words from Xanetia was all it took to make you throw away three hundred years of love and devotion. Is that the way you Elenes customarily treat your friends?"

"*She's* the one who forced the issue, Aphrael. She started delivering ultimatums. I don't think you realize how strongly she feels about the Delphae. She was totally irrational. What's behind all of that?"

"That's none of your business."

"I think it is. What *really* happened during the Cyrgai wars?"

"I won't tell you."

"Art thou afeared to speak of it, Goddess?"

Sparhawk spun around quickly, a startled oath coming to his lips. It was Xanetia. She stood all aglow, not far from where they were talking.

"This doesn't concern you, Xanetia," Aphrael told her coldly.

"I must needs know thine heart, Goddess. Thy sister's enmity is of no real moment. *Thine*, however, would be more troublesome. Art thou also unkindly disposed toward me?"

"Why don't you leech my thoughts and find out for yourself?"

"Thou knowest that I cannot, Aphrael. Thy mind is closed to me."

"I'm so glad you noticed that."

"Behave yourself," Sparhawk told his daughter, speaking very firmly.

"Stay out of this, Sparhawk."

"No, Danae, I don't think I will. Are *you* behind the way Sephrenia was behaving at Delphaeus?"

"Don't be absurd. I sent her to Delphaeus to *cure* her of that nonsense."

"Are you sure, Aphrael? You're not behaving very well at the moment yourself, you know."

"I don't like Edaemus, and I don't like his people. I'm trying to cure Sephrenia out of love for *her*, not out of any affection for the Delphae."

"But thou didst stand for us against thy kindred when all this began, Goddess," Xanetia pointed out.

"That *also* was not out of any great affection for your race, Xanetia. My family was wrong, and I opposed them out of principle. You wouldn't understand that, though, would you? It had to do with love, and you Delphae have outgrown that, haven't you?"

"How little thou knowest us, Goddess," Xanetia said sadly.

"As long as we're all speaking so frankly, I've noticed a

certain bias against Styrics in some of *your* remarks, Anarae,"
Sparhawk said pointedly.

"I have reasons, Anakha—many reasons."

"I'm sure you have, and I'm sure Sephrenia has reasons,
too. But whether we like each other or not is really beside the
point. I *am* going to straighten this all out. I've got work to do,
and I can't do it in the middle of a catfight. I *will* make peace
among you—even if I have to use the Bhelliom to do it."

"Sparhawk!" Danae's face was shocked.

"Nobody wants to tell me what really happened during the
Cyrgai wars, and maybe that's just as well. I was curious at
first, but not any longer. What it boils down to, ladies, is that
I don't *care* what happened. The way you've all been behaving
sort of says that *nobody's* hands were really clean. I want this
spiteful wrangling to stop. You're all behaving like children,
and it's beginning to make me tired."

CHAPTER
SEVENTEEN

There were dark circles under Sephrenia's eyes the next morning, and the light had gone out of her face. Her white Styric robe was partially covered by a sleeveless overmantle of deepest black. Sparhawk had never seen her wear that kind of garment before, and her choice—of both the garment and the color—seemed ominous. She joined them at the breakfast table reluctantly, and only at Ehlana's express command. She sat slightly apart from the rest of them with her injury drawn about her like a defensive wall. She would not look at Vanion and refused breakfast despite Alean's urgings.

Vanion appeared no less injured. His face was drawn and pale, quite nearly as pale as it had been when he had been carrying the burden of the swords, and his eyes were filled with pain.

Breakfast under those circumstances was strained, and they all left the table with a certain relief. They proceeded directly to the blue-draped sitting room and got down to business.

"The others aren't really all that significant," Caalador told them. "Rebal, Sabre, and Baron Parok are decidedly second-rate. All they're really doing is exploiting existing hostilities. Scarpa's something quite different, though. Arjuna's a trouble-some sort of place to begin with, and Scarpa's using that to the fullest. The others have to be fairly circumspect because the

Elene kingdoms of western Tamuli are so well-populated. There are people everywhere, so the conspirators have to sneak around. Southeastern Arjuna's one vast jungle, though, so Scarpa's got places to hide, and places he can defend. He makes some small pretense at nationalism in the way that the others do, but that doesn't appear to be his main agenda. The Arjuni are far more shrewd than the Elene peasants and serfs of the west."

"Have you got any background on him?" Ulath asked, "where he came from, what he did before he set up shop, that sort of thing?"

Caalador nodded. "That part wasn't very difficult. Scarpa was fairly well known in some circles before he joined the conspiracy." Caalador made a face. "I wish there were some other word. 'Conspiracy' sounds so melodramatic." He shrugged. "Anyway, Scarpa's a bastard."

"Caalador!" Bevier said sharply, "there are ladies present!"

"It wasn't intended as an obscenity, Sir Bevier, merely as a legal definition. Scarpa's the result of a dalliance between a militantly promiscuous Arjuni tavern wench and a renegade Styric. It was an odd sort of pairing-off, and it produced a very odd sort of fellow."

"Don't pursue this too far, Caalador," Stragen said ominously.

"Grow up, Stragen. You're not the only one with irregular parentage. When you get right down to it, I'm not entirely sure who my father was, either. Bastardy's no great inconvenience for a man with brains and talent."

"Milord Stragen's oversensitive about his origins," Baroness Melidere explained lightly. "I've spoken with him time and again about it, but he still has feelings of inadequacy. It might not be a bad thing, though. He's so generally stupendous otherwise that a little bit of insecurity keeps him from being unbearable."

Stragen rose and bowed flamboyantly.

"Oh, sit down, Stragen," she said.

"Where was I?" Caalador said. "Oh, yes, now I recollect. This yere Scarpa feller, he growed-up in a shack-nasty sorta roadside tavern down thar in Ar-juna, an' he done all the sorta thangs which it iz ez bastards does in ther formative years in a place 'thout no real moral restraints on 'em."

"Please, Caalador," Stragen sighed.

"Just entertaining the queen, old boy." Caalador shrugged.

"She pines away without periodic doses of down-home folksiness."

"What does *shack-nasty* mean, Caalador?" Ehlana interrupted him.

"Why, jist whut it sez, yer Queenship. A *shack*'s a kinda th'owed-together hovel built outten ole boards an' scraps, an' *nasty* means purty much whut it sez. I knowed a feller ez went by that name when I wuz a pup. He lived in th' messiest place y' ever *did* see, an' he warn't none too clean his ownself, neither."

"I think I can survive for several hours now without any more mangled language, Master Caalador." She smiled. "I want to thank you for your concern, though."

"Always glad to be of service, your Majesty." He grinned. "Scarpa grew up in a situation that sort of skirted the edges of crime. He was what you might call a gifted amateur. He never really settled down into one given trade." He made a face. "Dabblers. I absolutely *detest* dabblers. Anyway, he pandered for his mother—just as every good boy should—and also for his numerous half sisters, who, if we're to believe the common gossip, were all whores from the cradle. He was a moderately competent pickpocket and cutpurse, and a fairly gifted swindler. Unlike many of his mother's one-time paramours, Scarpa's Styric father stayed around for a time, and he used to drop back to visit his son from time to time, so Scarpa got a smattering of a Styric education. Eventually, however, he made the kind of mistake we expect amateurs to make. He tried to cut the purse of a tavern patron who wasn't quite as drunk as he appeared to be. His intended victim grabbed him, and Scarpa demonstrated the Arjuni side of his nature. He whipped out a small, very sharp knife and spilled the fellow's guts out on the floor of the tavern. Some busybody went to the police about it, and Scarpa left home rather abruptly."

"Wise move," Talen murmured. "Didn't he get any professional training while he was growing up?"

"No. He appears to have picked things up on his own."

"Precocious."

Caalador nodded his agreement. "If he'd had the right teachers, he probably could have become a master thief. After he ran away, he seems to have kept moving for a couple of years. He was only twelve or so when he killed that first man, and when he was about fourteen, he turned up in a traveling carnival. He billed himself as a magician—the usual sort of carnival fakery—although he occasionally utilized a few Styric spells to perform *real* magic. He grew a beard—which is very unusual among the Tamul races, since Tamul men don't have much facial hair. Neither do Styrics for that matter, now that I think about it. Scarpa's a half-breed, and the mixture of Southern Tamul and Styric came out rather peculiarly. Neither his features nor some of his traits are really characteristic of either race." Caalador reached inside his doublet and drew out a folded sheet of paper. "Here," he said, opening the paper, "judge for yourselves."

The drawing was a bit crude—more a caricature than a portrait. It was a depiction of a man with a strangely compelling face. The eyes were deep-sunk under heavy brows. The cheekbones were high and prominent, the nose aquiline, and the mouth sensual. The beard appeared to be dense and black, and it was meticulously trimmed and shaped.

"He spends a lot of time on that beard," Kalten observed. "It looks as if he shaves off stray whiskers hair by hair." He frowned slightly. "He looks familiar, for some reason—something around the eyes, I think."

"I'm surprised you can even recognize the fact that it's supposed to be a picture of a human being," Talen sniffed. "The technique's absolutely awful."

"The girl hasn't had any training, Talen," Caalador defended the artist. "She's gifted in her own profession, though."

"Which profession is that, Master Caalador?" Ehlana asked.

"She's a whore, your Majesty." He shrugged. "The drawing is just a sideline. She likes to keep pictures of her customers. She studies their faces during the course of her business transactions, and some of the portraits have strange expressions."

"May I see that?" Sephrenia asked suddenly.

"Of course, Lady Sephrenia." Caalador looked a little surprised as he took the drawing to her. Then he returned to his seat. "Did you ever meet Djukta, Sparhawk?" he asked.

"Once."

"Now *there's* a beard for you. Djukta looks like an ambulatory shrub. He's even got whiskers on his eyelids. Anyhow, Scarpa traveled with the carnival for several seasons, then about five years back, he dropped out of sight for a year or so. When he returned, he went into politics—if that's what you want to call it. He makes some small pretense at nationalism in the same way that Rebal, Parok, and Sabre do, but that's only for the benefit of the truly ignorant down in Arjuna. The national hero there was the man who established the slave trade, a fellow named Sheguan. That's a fairly contemptible sort of thing, so not many Arjunis take much pride in it."

"They still practice it, though," Mirtai said bleakly.

"They do indeed, little dorlin'," Caalador agreed.

"Friend Caalador," Kring said, "I thought we agreed that you weren't going to call Mirtai that anymore."

"Aw, it don't mean nuthin', Kring. It's jist muh folksy way o' settin' people at ther ease." He paused. "Where was I?" he asked.

"You were starting to get to the point," Stragen replied.

"Testy this morning, aren't we, old boy?" Caalador said mildly. "From what our people were able to discover, Scarpa's far more dangerous than those three enthusiasts in western Tamuli. Arjuni thieves are more devious than run-of-the-mill criminals, and a number of them have infiltrated Scarpa's apparatus for fun and profit. The Arjuni are an untrustworthy people, so the empire's been obliged to deal with them quite firmly. Arjuni hatred for the Tamuls is very real, so Scarpa hasn't had to stir it up artificially." Caalador tugged at his nose a bit dubiously. "I'm not altogether sure how much of this we can believe—the Arjuni being what they are and all—but one highway robber down there claims to have been a member of Scarpa's inner circle for a while. He told us that our man's just a little deranged. He operates out of the ruins of Natayos down in the southern jungles. The town was destroyed during the Atan invasion back in the seventeenth century, and Scarpa doesn't so much hide there as he does occupy the place—in a military sense of the word. He's reinforced the crumbling old walls so that the town's defensible. Our highwayman reports that Scarpa starts raving sometimes. If we can believe our informant, he started talking about the Cyrgai once, and about Cyrgon. He tells his cronies that Cyrgon wants to make his people the masters of the world, but that the Cyrgai, with that institutionalized stupidity of theirs, aren't really intelligent enough to govern a global empire. Scarpa doesn't have any problems with the idea of an empire. He just doesn't like the way the present one's set up. He'd be more than happy with it if there were just a few changes—up at the top. He believes that the Cyrgai will conquer the world and then retreat back into their splendid isolation. *Somebody's* going to have to run the government of the world for them, and Scarpa's got a candidate in mind for the position."

"That's insane!" Bevier exclaimed.

"I think I already suggested that, Sir Knight. Scarpa seems to think he'd make a very good emperor."

"The position's already been filled," Sarabian noted dryly.

"Scarpa's hoping that Cyrgon will vacate it, your Majesty. He tells his people that the Cyrgai have absolutely no administrative skills and that they're going to need someone to run the conquered territories for them. He'll volunteer at that point. He'll genuflect perfunctorily in Cyrgon's direction once in a while, and more or less run things to suit himself. He has large dreams, I'll give him that."

"It has a sort of familiar ring to it, doesn't it, Sparhawk?" Kalten said with a tight grin. "Didn't Martel—and Annias—have the same sort of notion?"

"Oh, my goodness, yes," Ehlana agreed. "I feel as if I've lived through all of this before."

"Where does Krager fit in?" Sparhawk asked.

"Krager seems to be some sort of coordinator," Caalador replied. "He serves as a go-between. He travels a great deal, carrying messages and instructions. We're guessing about this, but we think that there's a layer of command between Cyrgon and the people like Scarpa, Parok, Rebal, and Sabre. Krager's known to all of them, and that authenticates his messages. He seems to have found his natural niche in life. Queen Ehlana tells us that he served Martel and Annias in exactly the same way, and he was doing the same kind of thing back in Eosia when he was carrying Count Gerrich's instructions to those bandits in the mountains east of Cardos."

"We should really make some sort of effort to scoop Krager up," Ulath rumbled. "He starts talking if someone so much as gives him a harsh look, and he knows a great deal about things that make me moderately curious."

"That's how he's managed to stay alive for so long," Kalten grunted. "He always makes sure that he's got so much valuable information that we don't dare kill him."

"Kill him *after* he talks, Sir Kalten," Khalad said.

"He makes us promise not to."

"So?"

"We're knights, Khalad," Kalten explained. "Once we give someone our oath, we're obliged to keep our word."

"You weren't thinking of knighting me at any time in the immediate future, were you, Lord Vanion?" Khalad asked.

"It might be just a little premature, Khalad."

"That means that I'm still a peasant, doesn't it?"

"Well—technically, maybe."

"That solves the problem, then," Khalad said with a chill little smile. "Go ahead and catch him, Sir Kalten. Promise him anything you have to in order to get him to talk. Then turn him over to me. Nobody expects a peasant to keep his word."

"I'm going to like this young man, Sparhawk." Kalten grinned.

"Zalasta's coming for me, Sparhawk," Sephrenia told the big Pandion. "He'll escort me safely back to Sarsos." She shook her head, refusing to enter the room to which they were returning after lunch.

"You're being childish. You know that, don't you, Sephrenia?"

"I've outlived my usefulness, and I've been around Elenes long enough to know what a prudent Styric does when that happens. As long as a Styric's useful, she's relatively safe among Elenes. Once she's served her purpose, though, her presence starts to be embarrassing, and you Elenes deal abruptly with inconvenient people. I'd rather not have one of you slip a knife between my ribs."

"Are you just about finished? Conversations like this bore me. We love you, Sephrenia, and it has nothing to do with whether or not you're useful to us. You're breaking Vanion's heart. You know that, too, don't you?"

"So? He broke mine, didn't he? Take your problems to Xanetia, since you're all enamored of her."

"That's beneath you, little mother."

Her chin came up. "I think I'd rather you didn't call me that anymore, Sparhawk. It's just a bit grotesque in the present circumstances. I'll be in my room—if it's still mine. If it isn't, I'll go live in the Styric community here in Matherion. If it's not too much trouble, let me know when Zalasta arrives." And she turned and walked down the corridor, ostentatiously wearing her injury like a garment.

Sparhawk swore under his breath. Then he saw Kalten and Alean coming down the tiled hallway. At least *that* particular problem had been resolved. The queen's maid had laughed in Kalten's face when the blond knight had clumsily offered to step aside so that she could devote her attentions to Berit. She had then, Sparhawk gathered, convinced Kalten that her affections were still quite firmly where they were supposed to be.

"But you never leave her side, Sir Kalten," the doe-eyed girl accused. "You're always hovering over her and making certain that she has everything she needs or wants."

"It's a duty, Alean," Kalten tried to explain. "I'm not doing it because I have any kind of affection for her."

"You're performing your duty just a little too well to suit me, Sir Knight." Alean's voice, that marvelous instrument, conveyed a whole range of feelings. The girl could speak volumes with only the slightest change of key and intonation.

"Oh, God," Sparhawk groaned. Why did he *always* have to get caught in these personal matters? This time, however, he moved quickly to put a stop to things before they got out of hand. He stepped out into the corridor to confront the pair of them. "Why don't we take care of this right now?" he suggested bluntly.

"Take care of what?" Kalten demanded. "This isn't any of your business, Sparhawk."

"I'm *making* it my business. Are you satisfied that Alean doesn't have any kind of serious feelings for Berit?"

Kalten and the girl exchanged a quick, guilty sort of glance.

"Good," Sparhawk said. "My congratulations to you both. Now, let's clear up this Xanetia business. Kalten was telling you the truth, Alean—as far as he went. His duty obliges him to stay close to her because he's required to make certain that no harm comes to her. We have an agreement with her people, and she's here as our hostage to make sure that they don't go back on their word. We all know that if the Delphae betray us in any way, Kalten will kill Xanetia. *That's* why he's staying so close to her."

"*Kill?*" The girl's huge eyes went even wider.

"Those are the rules, Alean." Kalten shrugged. "I don't like them very much, but I have to follow them."

"You *wouldn't!*"

"Only if I have to, and I wouldn't like it very much. That's what the word *hostage* means, though. I always seem to be the one who gets these dirty jobs."

"How *could* you?" Alean said to Sparhawk. "How could you *do* this to your oldest friend?"

"Military decisions are hard sometimes," Sparhawk told her. "Are you satisfied now that Kalten's not straying? You *do* know, don't you, that when he thought that you'd fallen in love with Berit, he started going out of his way trying to get himself killed?"

"You didn't have to tell her *that*, Sparhawk," Kalten protested.

"You idiot!" Alean's voice climbed effortlessly into the upper ranges. She spoke—at length—to Sparhawk's friend while he stood hanging his head and scuffing his feet like a schoolboy being scolded.

"Ah—" Sparhawk ventured. "Why don't the two of you go someplace private where you can discuss things?"

"With your leave, Prince Sparhawk," Alean agreed with an abrupt little curtsy. "You," she snapped to Kalten, "come with me."

"Yes, dear," Kalten said submissively, and the two went on back up the corridor.

"Was that Alean just now?" Baroness Melidere asked, sticking her head out through the doorway.

"Yes," Sparhawk replied.

"Where are she and Kalten going?" she asked, looking after the pair.

"They have something important to take care of."

"Something more important than what we're discussing in here?"

"*They* seem to think so, Baroness. We can manage without them this afternoon, I expect, and it's a matter that needs clearing up."

"Oh," she said, "one of those."

"I'm afraid so."

"Alean will straighten it out," Melidere said confidently.

"I'm sure she will. How's *your* campaign going, Baroness? I'm not trying to pry, you understand. It's just that these matters break my concentration, and I kind of like to have them out of the way so they don't come bubbling to the surface when I least expect them to."

"Everything's on schedule, Prince Sparhawk."

"Good. Have you told him?"

"Of course not. He doesn't need to know yet. I'll break it to him gently when the time comes. It's actually kinder that way. If he finds out too soon, he'll just worry about it. Trust me, your Highness. I know *exactly* what I'm doing."

"There's something I'd sort of like to get cleared up before we go on, Anarae," Stragen said to Xanetia. "The Tamuls all believe that the Cyrgai were extinct, but Krager and Scarpa say otherwise."

"The Cyrgai *want* the world to believe that they are no more," she replied. "After their disastrous march on Sarsos, they returned home and concentrated for a time on replenishing their subordinate forces, the Cynesgans, which forces had been virtually annihilated by the Styrics."

"So we've heard," Caalador said. "We were told that the Cyrgai concentrated with such single-mindedness that their *own* women were past child-bearing age before they realized their mistake."

"Thine informant spoke truly, Master Caalador, and it is the common belief in Tamuli that the Cyrg race died out some ten eons ago. That common belief, however, is in error. It is a belief which ignores the fact that Cyrgon is a God. He did *not*, however, take the blind obedience of his people into account when he commanded them to devote their attentions to the women of the Cynesgans. But when he saw that his chosen race was dying out, he did alter the natural course of such things, and agèd Cyrgai women became fertile once more—though most died in childbirth. Thus were the Cyrgai perpetuated."

"Pity," Oscagne murmured.

"Knowing, however, that the diminishèd numbers of his worshippers *and* the Styric curse which imprisoned them in their arid homeland did imperil them, Cyrgon sought to protect his people. The Cynesgans were commanded to confirm and perpetuate the belief of the other races of Tamuli that the Cyrgai were no more, and the dread city of Cyrga itself was concealed from the eyes of men."

"In the same way that Delphaeus is concealed?" Vanion guessed.

"Nay, my Lord. We are more subtle than Cyrgon. We conceal Delphaeus by misdirection. Cyrgon hides Cyrga in the central highlands of Cynesga by means of an enchantment. Thou couldst go to those highlands and ride close by Cyrga and never see it."

"An invisible city?" Talen asked her incredulously.

"The Cyrgai can see it," she replied, "and, when it doth suit them so, their Cynesgan underlings can as well. To all others, however, Cyrga is not there."

"The tactical advantages of that must be enormous," Bevier noted in his most professional tone. "The Cyrgai have an absolutely secure stronghold into which they can retreat if things go wrong."

"Their advantage is offset, however," Xanetia pointed out.

"They may freely ravage and despoil Cynesga, which is theirs already, and which is no more than a barren waste at best; but they may not pass the boundaries of their homeland. The curse of the Styrics is still potent, I do assure thee. It is the wont of the kings of the Cyrgai to periodically test that curse. Agèd warriors are taken from time to time to the boundary and commanded to attempt a crossing. They die in midstride as they obediently march across the line."

Sarabian was looking at her, his eyes narrowed shrewdly. "Prithee, Anarae, advise me in this matter. Thou hast said that the Cynesgans are subject to the Cyrgai?"

"Yes, Majesty."

"*All* Cynesgans?"

"Those in authority, Imperial Sarabian."

"The king? The government? The army?"

She nodded.

"*And* their ambassadors as well?" Oscagne added.

"Very good, Oscagne," Itagne murmured to his brother. "Very, *very* good."

"I didn't quite follow that," Ulath admitted.

"*I* did," Stragen told him. "We'd probably better look into that, Caalador."

"I'll see to it."

"Do you know what they're talking about, friend Engessa?" Kring asked.

"It's not all that complicated, Kring," Ehlana explained. "The Cynesgan embassy here in Matherion is full of people who take their orders from the Cyrgai. I'd guess that if we were to look into the matter, we'd find that the headquarters of the recent attempt to overthrow the emperor was located in that embassy."

"And if he's not out of town, we might even find Krager there as well," Khalad mused. "Talen, how long would it take you to teach me how to be a burglar?"

"What have you got in mind?" Sparhawk asked his squire.

"I thought I might creep into that embassy and steal Krager, my Lord. Since Anarae Xanetia can tell us what he's thinking, we wouldn't even have to break his fingers to make him talk—*or* make him any inconvenient promises that we probably didn't intend to keep anyway."

"I sense thy discontent, Anakha," Xanetia said later when she, Sparhawk, and Danae had returned to the fortified roof of the central tower of Ehlana's castle.

"I've been had, Anarae," he said sourly.

"I do not recognize the expression."

"He means that he's been duped," Danae translated, "and he's being impolite enough to imply that *I* have, too." She gave her father a smug little smile. "I told you so, Sparhawk."

"Spare me, please."

"Oh, no, Father. I've got this wonderful chance to gloat. You're not going to rob me of it. If I remember correctly—and I do—I was against the idea of retrieving Bhelliom from the very beginning. *I* knew that it was a mistake, but *you* bullied me into agreeing."

He ignored that. "Was any of it real? The Troll-Gods? Drychtnath? The monsters? Or was it all just some elaborate game designed to get me to bring Bhelliom to Tamuli?"

"Some of it may have been real, Sparhawk," she replied, "but you've probably put your finger on the actual reason behind it all."

"It is thy belief that Cyrgon deceivèd thee into bringing Bhelliom within his reach, Anakha?" Xanetia said.

"Why bother to ask, Anarae? You know what I'm thinking already. Cyrgon believes that he could use Bhelliom to break that curse so that his people could start invading their neighbors again."

"I told you so," Danae reminded him again.

"Please." He looked out over the glowing city. "I think I need a divine opinion here," he said. "Up until very recently, we all believed that Bhelliom was just a thing—powerful, but just an object. We know that's not true now. Bhelliom has its own personality and its own will. It's more of an ally than just a weapon. Not only that—and please don't be offended, Aphrael—in some ways it's even more powerful than the Gods of this world."

"I *am* offended, Sparhawk," she said tartly. "Besides, I haven't finished telling you that I told you so."

He laughed, swept her up into his arms, and kissed her. "I love you," he told her, still laughing.

"Isn't he a nice boy?" Danae said to Xanetia.

The Delphaeic woman smiled.

"If *we* didn't know about Bhelliom's awareness—*and* its will—could Cyrgon have known? I don't think Azash did. Speaking as a Goddess, would *you* want to pick up something that could make its own decisions—and *might* just decide that it didn't like you all that much?"

"*I* wouldn't," she replied. "Cyrgon might be a different matter, though. He's so arrogant that he might believe that he could control Bhelliom even against its will."

"But he couldn't, could he? Azash thought he could control Bhelliom by sheer force. He wasn't even interested in the rings. The rings *can* compel Bhelliom—because they're a part of it. Could Cyrgon be as stupid as Azash was?"

"Sparhawk, you're talking about one of my distant relatives. Please be a little more respectful." Danae's brow furrowed with thought. She absently kissed her father.

"Don't do that," he said. "This is serious."

"I know. It helps me to think. Bhelliom's never made itself known before. You're probably right, Sparhawk. Azash wasn't really very bright. Cyrgon has the same sort of personality, and he's made several blunders in the past. That's one of the drawbacks of divinity. We don't *have* to be intelligent. We all know about Bhelliom's power, but I don't think any of us have ever come to grips with the notion of its will before. Did it *really* talk to Sparhawk the way he said it did, Xanetia? As an equal, I mean?"

"As at least an equal, Goddess," Xanetia replied. "Bhelliom and Anakha are allies, not friends—and neither is master."

"Where are we going with this, Sparhawk?" Danae asked.

"I'm not sure. Cyrgon may have made another of those blunders, though. He may just have tricked me into bringing back the one thing that could defeat him. I think we may have an advantage here, but we should probably give a great deal of thought to just exactly how we're going to use it."

"You're hateful, Sparhawk," Danae said.

"I beg your pardon?"

"You've just taken all the fun out of all the *I told you so*'s I've been saving up."

Zalasta arrived in Matherion two days later. After only the briefest of greetings to the rest of them, he went immediately to Sephrenia's room.

"He'll straighten it out, Vanion," Sparhawk assured the preceptor. "He's her oldest friend, and he's far too wise to be infected with irrational prejudice."

"I wouldn't be all that sure, Sparhawk." Vanion's face was gloomy. "I thought *she* was too wise, and look what happened. This blind hatred may infect the entire Styric race. If Zalasta feels the same way Sephrenia does, all he's going to do is re-inforce her prejudices."

Sparhawk shook his head. "No, my friend. Zalasta's above that. He has no reason to trust Elenes either, but he was willing to help us, wasn't he? He's a realist, and even if he *does* share her feelings, he'll suppress them in the name of political expediency. And if I'm right, he'll persuade her to do the same. She doesn't have to like Xanetia. All she has to do is accept the fact that we need her. Once Zalasta convinces her of that, the two of you will be able to patch things up."

"Maybe."

It was several hours later when Zalasta emerged alone from Sephrenia's room with his rough-hewn Styric face somber. "It will not be easy, Prince Sparhawk," he said when the two of them met in the corridor outside. "She is deeply wounded. I cannot understand what Aphrael was thinking of."

"Who can *ever* understand why Aphrael does things, learned one?" Sparhawk smiled briefly. "She's the most whimsical and exasperating person I've ever known. As I understand it, she doesn't approve of Sephrenia's prejudice, and she's taking steps. The expression 'doing something to somebody for his own good' always implies a certain amount of brutality, I'm afraid. Were you able to talk any sense into Sephrenia at all?"

"I'm approaching the question obliquely, your Highness," Zalasta replied. "Sephrenia's already been deeply injured. This isn't a good time for a direct confrontation. I was at least able to persuade her to postpone her return to Sarsos."

"That's something, anyway. Let's go talk to the others. A lot has happened since you left."

"The reports come from unimpeachable sources, Anarae," Zalasta said coolly.

"I do assure thee, Zalasta of Styricum, they are nonetheless false. None of the Delphae have left our valley for well over an hundred years—except to deliver our invitation to Anakha."

"It's happened before, Zalasta," Kalten told the white-robed Styric. "We watched Rebal use some very obvious trickery when he was talking to a group of Edomish peasants."

"Oh?"

"It was the sort of thing one sees in second-rate carnivals, learned one," Talen explained. "One of his henchmen threw something into a fire; there was a flash of light and a puff of smoke; then somebody dressed in old-time clothes stood up from where he'd been hiding and started bellowing in an ancient form of speech. The peasants all thought they were seeing Incetes rising from the grave."

"Those who witnessed the Shining Ones were not so gullible, Master Talen," Zalasta objected.

"And the fellow who gulled them probably wasn't as clumsy." The boy shrugged. "A skilled fake can make almost anybody believe almost anything—as long as they aren't close enough to see the hidden wires. Sephrenia told us that it means that the other side's a little short on real magicians, so they have to cheat."

Zalasta frowned. "It *may* be possible," he conceded. "The sightings were brief and at quite some distance." He looked at Xanetia. "You are certain, Anarae? Could there perhaps be some of your people who live separately? Who are cut off from Delphaeus and may have joined with our enemies?"

"They would no longer be of the Delphae, Zalasta of Styricum. We are bound to the lake. It is the lake which doth make us what we are, and I tell thee truly, the light which doth illuminate us is but the least of the things which do make us unlike all others." She looked at him gravely. "Thou art Styric, Zalasta of Ylara, and thou art well aware of the consequences of markedly differing from thy neighbors."

"Yes," he agreed, "to our sorrow."

"The decision of thy race to attempt to co-exist with the other races of man may be suitable for Styrics," she continued. "For my race, however, it hath not been possible. Ye of the Styric race are oft met with contempt and derision, but thy differences are not threatening to the Elenes or Tamuls who are about you. We of Delphaeus, however, do inspire terror in the hearts of all others. In time, methinks, thy race will become acceptable. The wind of change hath already begun to blow, engendered in large measure by that fortuitous alliance betwixt ye and the Church of Chyrellos. The knights of that Church are kindly disposed toward Styricum, and their might shall alter Elenic predispositions. For the Delphae, however, such accommodation is impossible. Our very appearance doth set us forever apart from all others, and this doth stand at the heart of our present alliance. We have sought out Anakha, and we have offered him our aid in his struggle with Cyrgon. In exchange, we have besought him only to raise up Bhelliom and to seal us away from all other men. Then none may come against us, nor may we go against any other. Thus will all be safe."

"A wise decision perhaps, Anarae," Zalasta conceded. "It was a choice which *we* considered in eons past. Delphaeic numbers are limited, however, and your hidden valley will easily hold all of you. We Styrics are more numerous and more widespread. Our neighbors would not look kindly on a Styric homeland abutting their own borders. We cannot follow your course, but must live in the world."

Xanetia rose to her feet, putting one hand on Kalten's shoulder. "Stay, gentle Knight," she told him. "I must confer a moment with Anakha in furtherance of our pact. Should he detect falsity in me, *he* may slay me."

Sparhawk stood up, crossed to the door, and opened it for her. Danae, dragging Rollo behind her, followed them from the room.

"What is it, Anarae?" Sparhawk asked.

"Let us repair to that place above where we are wont to speak," she replied. "What I must tell thee is for thine ears alone."

Danae gave her a hard look.

"Thou mayest also hear my words, Highness," Xanetia told the little girl.

"You're *so* kind."

"We couldn't hide from her anyway, Xanetia," Sparhawk said. "We could go to the top of the highest tower in Matherion, and she'd fly up to eavesdrop on us anyway."

"Canst thou truly fly, Highness?" Xanetia looked startled.

"Can't everyone?"

"Behave yourself," Sparhawk told his daughter.

They climbed the stairs to the top of the tower again and went out onto the roof. "Anakha, I must tell thee a truth which thou mayest not wish to believe," Xanetia said gravely, "but it *is* truth, nonetheless."

"That's an unpromising start," Danae observed.

"I must speak this truth, Anakha," Xanetia said gravely, "for it is not only in keeping with our pact, but it doth also have a grave import on our common design."

"I get the feeling that I should take hold of something solid," Sparhawk said wryly.

"As it seemeth best to thee, Anakha. I must advise thee, however, that thy trust in Zalasta of Styricum is sorely misplaced."

"What?"

"He hath played thee false, Anakha. His heart and his mind are Cyrgon's."

CHAPTER
EIGHTEEN

T hat's absolutely impossible!" Danae exclaimed. "Zalasta *loves* my sister and me!
He'd *never* betray us!"

"He doth love thy sister beyond measure,
Goddess," Xanetia replied. "His feelings for *thee*, however, are
not so kindly. In truth, he doth hate thee."

"I don't believe you!"

Sparhawk was a soldier, and soldiers who cannot adjust to
surprises rapidly do not live long enough to become veterans.
"You weren't at Delphaeus, Aphrael," he reminded the Child-
Goddess. "Bhelliom vouched for Xanetia's truthfulness."

"She's just saying this to drive a wedge between us and
Zalasta."

"I don't really think so." A number of things were rapidly
falling into place in Sparhawk's mind. "The alliance is too important to the Delphae for her to endanger it with something
that petty, and what she just told us explains several things that
didn't make sense before. Let's hear her out. If there's some
question about Zalasta's loyalty, we'd better find out about it
right now. Exactly what did you discover in his mind,
Anarae?"

"A great confusion, Anakha," Xanetia said sadly. "The mind
of Zalasta might have been a noble one, but it doth stand on
the brink of madness, consumed with but one thought and one

desire. He hath loved thy sister since earliest childhood, Goddess, but his love is not the brotherly affection thou hast believed it was. This I know with greater certainty than all else, for it is ever at the forefront of his mind. He doth think of her as his affianced bride."

"That's absurd!" Danae said. "She doesn't think of him that way at all."

"Nay, but he doth think so of her. My sojourn within his thought was brief, therefore I do not as yet know all. As soon as I did perceive his treachery, my pledge bound me to reveal it to Anakha. With more time, I will discover more."

"What prompted you to look into *his* thought, Xanetia?" Sparhawk asked her. "The room was full of people. Why choose him—or do you just listen to everybody simultaneously? It seems to me that would be very confusing." He made a face. "I think I'm going at this backward. It might be helpful if I knew how your gift works. Is it like having another set of ears? Do you hear *every* thought going on around you—all at the same time?"

"Nay, Anakha." She smiled faintly. "That, as thou hast perceived, would be too confusing. Our ears, will we, nil we, hear *all* sound. My perception of the thought of others doth require my conscious direction. I must reach out to hear, *unless* the thought of one who is near me be so intense that it doth become as a shout. So it was with Zalasta. His mind doth scream the name of Sephrenia again and again. In equal measure, moreover, doth his mind shriek *thy* name, Goddess, and *those* shrieks are filled with his hatred of thee. In his mind art thou a thief, having stolen away all his hope of joy."

"A *thief*? *Me*? He was the one who was trying to steal what was mine! I *put* my sister here on this world. She's *mine*! She's always been mine! How *dare* he?" Danae's black eyes were flashing, and her voice was filled with outraged indignation.

"This isn't one of the more attractive sides of your nature, Divine One," Sparhawk suggested. "We don't own other people."

"I'm not a people, Sparhawk! I own what I want!"

"You're just digging yourself in deeper. I wouldn't pursue it any further."

"But I *do*, Father. I've devoted hundreds of years to Sephrenia, and all that time Zalasta's been sneaking around behind my back trying to steal her from me."

"Aphrael," he said gently, "you're an Elene in this particular incarnation, so you're going to have to stop thinking like a Styric. There are certain things that decent Elenes don't do, and you're doing one of them right now. Sephrenia belongs to herself—not to you, not to Zalasta, not even to Vanion. Her soul's her own."

"But I love her!" It was almost a wail.

"I'm not built right for this," Sparhawk muttered to himself. "How can any human hope to be the father of a Goddess?"

"Don't you love me, Father?" Her voice was tiny.

"Of course I do."

"Then *you* belong to me, too. Why are you arguing with me about it?"

"You're a primitive."

"Of course I am. We're *supposed* to be primitive. All these years Zalasta's been pretending to love me—smiling at me, kissing me, holding me while I slept. That wretch! That lying wretch! I'll have his heart for supper for this!"

"No, as a matter of fact, you won't. I'm not raising a cannibal. You won't eat pork, so don't start developing a taste for people."

"I'm sorry," she said contritely. "I got excited."

"Besides, I think Vanion's got first claim on Zalasta's tripes."

"Oh, dear. I completely forgot about Vanion. That poor, poor man." Two great tears welled up in her eyes. "I'll spend the rest of his life making this up to him."

"Why don't we let Sephrenia take care of that? Just heal the breach between them. That's the only thing he really wants." Then Sparhawk thought of something. "It won't wash, Xanetia. Zalasta could very well be in love with Sephrenia, but he hasn't gone over to Cyrgon. When we encountered those Trolls in the mountains of Atan, he was the one who saved us from them—and it wasn't just the Trolls. There were worse things there as well."

"The Trolls do not loom large in Cyrgon's plans, Anakha. The deaths of an hundred of them were of little moment. All else was illusion—illusion wrought by Zalasta himself to allay certain suspicions in the minds of diverse of thy companions. He sought to win thy trust by destroying those shadows of his own making."

"It *does* fit," Sparhawk said in a troubled voice. "Would you ladies excuse me for a moment? I think Vanion should hear this. It concerns him, too, and I'd like his advice before I start making decisions." He paused. "Will you two be all right here—together, I mean? Without someone here to keep you from each other's throats?"

"All will be well, Anakha," Xanetia assured him. "Divine Aphrael and I have something to discuss."

"All right," he said, "but no hitting—and don't start screaming at each other. You'll wake up the whole castle." He crossed the parapet to the door and went back down the stairs.

The meeting in the royal apartment had adjourned for a time, and Sparhawk found his friend sitting with his face in his hands in a room quite some distance from the one he normally shared with Sephrenia.

"I need some help, my friend," Sparhawk said to him. "There's something you need to know, and we're going to have to decide what to do about it."

Vanion raised his grief-ravaged face. "More trouble?" he asked.

"Probably. Xanetia just told me . . . well, I'll let her tell you about it herself. She and Danae are up at the top of the tower. I think we'll want to keep this private—at least until we decide what steps to take."

Vanion nodded and rose to his feet. The two of them went back out into the corridor and started up the stairs. "Where's Zalasta?" Sparhawk asked.

"He's with Sephrenia. She needs him right now."

Sparhawk grunted, not really trusting himself to speak.

They found Xanetia and Danae at the battlements looking out over the city. The sun was moving down the intensely blue autumn sky toward the craggy western horizon, and the breeze coming in off the Tamul Sea had a salt tang mingled with the ripe odor of autumn. "All right, go ahead and tell him, Xanetia," Sparhawk said. "Then we'll decide what to do."

To Sparhawk's surprise, Vanion didn't waste much time on incredulous exclamation. "You're sure, Anarae?" he asked after Xanetia had told him of Zalasta's duplicity.

She nodded. "I have seen his heart, my Lord. He hath played thee false."

"You don't seem very surprised, Vanion," Sparhawk said.

"I'm not—well, not really. There's always been something about Zalasta that didn't quite ring true. He had some trouble keeping his face under control when Sephrenia and I first went to Sarsos and moved into her house there. He tried to hide it, but I could tell that he wasn't very happy with our living arrangements, and his disapproval seemed to go quite a bit further than a generalized kind of moral outrage about unorthodox relationships."

"That's a delicate way to put it," Danae observed. "We've never understood why you humans make such a fuss about that. If two people love each other, they should do something about it, and living together is much more convenient for that sort of thing, isn't it?"

"There are certain ceremonies and formalities customary first," Sparhawk explained dryly.

"You mean something like the way the peacock shows off his feathers to the peahen before they start building a nest?"

"Something along those lines." Vanion sighed. "It seems that Sephrenia doesn't admire my feathers anymore."

"Not so, Lord Vanion," Xanetia disagreed. "She doth deeply love thee still, and her heart is made desolate by reason of her separation from thee."

"And Zalasta's with her right now doing everything he can to make the separation permanent," Sparhawk added, his voice bleak. "How do you want us to proceed with this, Vanion? You're the one most deeply involved here. There's nothing any of us could say that would convince Sephrenia that Zalasta's a traitor, you know."

Vanion nodded. "She's going to have to see it for herself," he agreed. "How far were you able to reach into his mind, Anarae?"

"His present thought is open to me; his memories somewhat less so. Proximity and some time should provide opportunity to probe more."

"That's the key, then," Vanion said. "Ehlana and Sarabian want to start tearing down the government almost immediately. Once that starts, Zalasta's presence in our inner councils is going to be potentially disastrous. He'll find out everything we've got planned."

"Let him," Danae sniffed. "It's not going to do him much good after I'm done with my supper."

"What's this?" Vanion asked.

"Our little savage here wants to eat Zalasta's heart," Sparhawk explained.

"While he watches," the Child-Goddess added. "That's the whole point of it—making him watch while I do it."

"Could she do that?" Vanion asked.

"Probably," Sparhawk replied. "I won't let her, though."

"I didn't *ask* you, Father," Danae said.

"You didn't have to. I said no. Now let's drop it."

"When did Zalasta make this arrangement with Cyrgon, Anarae?" Vanion asked.

"That is unclear for the nonce, my Lord," she replied. "I shall pursue it further. My sense of his thought doth suggest that their alliance dates back some years and doth involve Bhelliom in some fashion."

Sparhawk thought about that. "Zalasta *was* very upset when he found out that we'd thrown Bhelliom into the sea," he recalled. "I could start making some educated guesses at this point, but let's wait and see what Xanetia's able to turn up. Right now, I think we'd better concentrate on delaying Ehlana and Sarabian until we can devise some way to make Zalasta expose his own guilt. We need to get Sephrenia out from under his influence, and she's never going to believe that he's a traitor until she actually sees him convict himself by doing something that proves his treason."

Vanion nodded his agreement.

"I think we're going to have to keep this just among the four of us," Sparhawk continued. "Zalasta's very shrewd, and Sephrenia knows all of us better than we know ourselves. If the others have any idea of what we're doing, they'll let something slip, and Sephrenia will know about it immediately—and Zalasta will know about five minutes after she does."

"I'm afraid you're right," Vanion agreed.

"Hast thou a plan, Anakha?" Xanetia asked.

"Sort of. I've still got to work out some of the details, though. It's a little complicated."

Danae rolled her eyes upward. "Elenes," she sighed.

"Absolutely not," Ehlana said adamantly. "He's too valuable. We can't risk it." She was sitting near the window with the morning sun streaming in on her and setting her pale hair aglow.

"There's no risk involved, dear," Sparhawk assured her. "The cloud and the shadow are both gone. Bhelliom and I took care of that once and for all." There was the flaw. Sparhawk was not entirely positive of that.

"He's right, my Queen," Kalten agreed. "He tore the cloud to tatters and dissolved the shadow like salt in boiling water."

"I'd really like to ask Kolata some questions, Ehlana,"

Sarabian said. "It doesn't make sense to keep feeding him if we aren't going to get any use out of him. This is what we've been waiting for, my dear—some sort of assurance that he won't be torn to pieces the minute he opens his mouth."

"Are you absolutely sure, Sparhawk?" Ehlana asked.

"Trust me." Sparhawk reached inside his doublet and took out the box. "My blue friend here can make sure that Kolata remains intact—no matter *what* questions we ask." He looked at Zalasta. "I'm going to ask a favor of you, learned one," he said, keeping his voice casual. "I think Sephrenia should sit in on this. I know that she'd rather wash her hands of the lot of us, but maybe if she listens to Kolata's confession, she'll begin to take an interest in things again. It might be just the thing to bring her out of the state she's in right now."

Zalasta's face was troubled, though he was obviously trying very hard to keep his expression under control. "I don't think you realize how deeply she feels about this matter, Prince Sparhawk. I strongly advise you not to force her to be present when you question Kolata. It will only deepen the rift between her and her former friends."

"I won't accept that, Zalasta," Ehlana told him. "Sephrenia's a member of the royal council of Elenia. I appointed her to that position when I ascended the throne. Her personal problems are her own business, but I need her here in her *official* capacity. If necessary, I'll command her presence, and I'll send Kalten and Ulath to deliver the command and make sure that she obeys."

Sparhawk almost felt sorry for Zalasta at that point. Their decisions and their requests were all completely reasonable, and try though he might, Zalasta could find no way to avoid agreeing. Kolata's testimony was almost certain to be an absolute disaster for the first citizen of Styricum, but there was no way he could prevent that testimony without exposing himself as a traitor. He rose to his feet. "I will try to persuade her, your Majesty," he said, bowing to Ehlana. He turned and quietly left the blue-draped room.

"I don't understand why you won't let us tell him, Sparhawk," Kalten said. "He *is* a friend, after all."

"He's also a Styric, Kalten," Vanion said smoothly. "We don't know how he *really* feels about the Delphae. He might go up in flames if he finds out that Xanetia can pick his thoughts the way Talen picks pockets."

"Sephrenia's probably told him about it already, Lord Vanion," Bevier pointed out.

Sparhawk threw a brief questioning look at Xanetia, framing the question in his thought.

She shook her head. For some reason, Sephrenia had *not* yet told Zalasta about the Delphaeic woman's strange capability to delve into the minds of others.

"I don't think so, Bevier," Vanion was saying. "He hasn't shown any reluctance to be in the same room with the Anarae, and that's a fair indication that he doesn't know. Now, then, who's going to question Kolata? We should probably limit it to just one of us. If we all start throwing questions at him, his thoughts will be so jumbled that Xanetia won't be able to make any sense of them."

"Itagne's skilled at debate and disputation," Oscagne suggested. "Academics spend hours splitting hairs."

"We prefer to call it meticulous attention to detail, old boy," Itagne corrected his brother. "Kolata has ministerial rank."

"Not any more, he doesn't," Sarabian said.

"Well, he *used* to, your Majesty. I'd suggest that we let Oscagne conduct the interrogation. He holds the same rank as Kolata, so he'll be able to approach him as an equal."

"Might I make a suggestion?" Stragen asked.

"Of course, Milord Stragen," the emperor said.

"Teovin's been sneaking around out there trying his very best to subvert the other ministries of your Majesty's government. Wouldn't it be a good idea to make this a formal inquiry instead of a star-chamber proceeding? If all the ministers and the aides are present when we question Kolata, Teovin won't have the chance to scramble around and mend his fences."

"It's an interesting notion, isn't it, Ehlana?" Sarabian mused.

"Very interesting," she agreed. "We'll have to postpone the interrogation, though."

"Oh?"

"We'll want to give your Atan runners a head start." She looked at him gravely. "This is it, Sarabian. Up until now, it's only been speculation. Once Kolata starts talking in front of the rest of the government, you'll be committed. Are you really ready to go that far?"

The emperor drew in a deep breath. "Yes, Ehlana, I think I am." His voice was firm, but very quiet.

"Issue the order, then. Declare martial law. Turn the Atans loose."

Sarabian swallowed hard. "Are you certain your idea will work, Atan Engessa?" he asked the towering warrior.

"It always has, Sarabian-Emperor," Engessa replied. "The signal fires are all in place. The word will spread throughout Tamuli in a single night. The Atans will move out of their garrisons the following morning."

Sarabian stared at the floor for a long time. Then he looked up. "Do it," he said.

The difficult part was persuading Sarabian and Ehlana *not* to tell Zalasta about what was happening. "He doesn't need to know," Sparhawk explained patiently.

"Surely you don't mistrust him, Sparhawk," Ehlana protested. "He's proved his loyalty over and over again."

"Of course he has. He's a Styric, though, and this sudden move of yours is going to turn all of Tamuli upside down. There's going to be absolute chaos out there. He may try to get word to the Styric communities hereabouts—a warning of some kind. It's a natural thing for him to do, and we can't afford to risk letting that information get out. The only thing that makes your plan workable at all is the fact that it's going to be a total surprise. There are Styrics, and then there are Styrics."

"Say what you mean, Sparhawk," Sarabian said in a testy voice.

"The term *renegade Styric* means the same thing here in Tamuli as it does in Eosia, your Majesty. We almost have to assume that if we tell Zalasta, we're telling all of Styricum, don't we? We know Zalasta, but we *don't* know all the other Styrics on the continent. There are some in Sarsos who'd sign compacts with Hell itself if they thought it would give them a chance to get even with the Elenes."

"You're going to hurt his feelings, you know," Ehlana told him.

"He'll live. We only have one chance at this, so let's not take even the remotest of risks."

There was a polite tap at the door, and Mirtai stepped into the room where the three of them were meeting. "Oscagne and that other one are back," she reported.

"Show them in please, Atana," Sarabian told her.

There was a kind of suppressed jubilation on the foreign minister's face as he entered with his brother, and Itagne's expression was almost identical. Sparhawk was a bit startled by how much alike they looked.

"You two look like a couple of cats who just got into the cream," Sarabian told them.

"We're pulling off the coup of the decade, your Majesty," Itagne replied.

"Of the century," Oscagne corrected. "Everything's in place, my Emperor. We left it sort of vague—'general meeting of the Imperial Council'—that sort of thing. Itagne dropped a few hints. He's been planting the notion that you're considering having your birthday declared a national holiday. It's the sort of foolish whim your Majesty's family is famous for."

"Be nice," Sarabian murmured. He had picked up that particular Elene expression during his stay in Ehlana's castle.

"Sorry, your Majesty," Oscagne apologized. "We've passed the whole thing off as a routine, meaningless meeting of the council—all formality and no substance."

"May I borrow your throne room, Ehlana?" Sarabian asked.

"Of course." She smiled. "Formal dress, I suppose?"

"Certainly. We'll wear our crowns and our state robes. You wear your prettiest dress, and I'll wear mine."

"Your *Majesty*!" Oscagne protested. "The customary Tamul mantle is hardly a dress."

"A long skirt is a long skirt, Oscagne. Frankly, I'd prefer doublet and hose—and, given the circumstances, my rapier. Stragen's right. Once you get used to wearing one, you start to feel undressed without it."

"If formality's going to be the keynote, I think you and the others should wear your dress armor, Sparhawk," Ehlana told her husband.

"Excellent idea, Ehlana," Sarabian approved. "That way they'll be ready when things turn ugly."

They spent the rest of the day supervising the moving of furniture in the throne room. The Queen of Elenia, as she sometimes did, went to extremes. "Buntings?" Sparhawk asked her. "*Buntings*, Ehlana?"

"We want things to look festive, Sparhawk," she replied with an airy little toss of her head. "Yes, I know. It's frivolous and even a little silly, but buntings hanging from the walls and trumpet fanfares introducing each of the ministers will set the tone. We want this to look so intensely formal that the government officials won't believe that anything serious could possibly happen. We're laying a trap, love, and buntings are part of the bait. Details, Sparhawk, details. Good plots swarm with details."

"You're enjoying this, aren't you?"

"Of course I am. Is the drawbridge raised?"

He nodded.

"Good. Keep it that way. We don't want anybody slipping out of the castle with any kind of information. We'll escort the ministers inside tomorrow, and then we'll raise the drawbridge again. We want to be in absolute control of the situation."

"Yes, dear."

"Don't make fun of me, Sparhawk," she warned.

"I'd sooner die."

It was nearly dusk when Zalasta came into the throne room and took Sparhawk to one side. "I *must* leave, Prince Sparhawk," he pleaded, his eyes a little wild. "It is a matter of the gravest urgency."

"My hands are tied, Zalasta," Sparhawk replied. "You know my wife. When she starts speaking in the royal *we*, there's no reasoning with her."

"There are things I *must* set in motion, your Highness, things vital to the success of the emperor's plan."

"I'll try to talk with her, but I can't hold out much hope. Things *are* fairly well under control, though. The Atans know what to do outside the castle walls, and my Church Knights can handle things inside. There *are* ministers and other high-level officials whose loyalty is in doubt, you know. We don't know exactly what the questioning of the Minister of the Interior is going to bring out. We'll have those people in our hands, and we don't want them running off to stir up more mischief."

"You don't *understand*, Sparhawk!" The note of desperation was clearly evident.

"I'll do what I can, Zalasta," Sparhawk said. "But I can't make any promises."

CHAPTER
NINETEEN

T he Tamul architect who had designed Ehlana's castle had evidently devoted half a lifetime to the study of Elene buildings, and, like so many with limited gifts, he had slavishly imitated the details without capturing the spirit. The throne room was a case in point. Elene castles have but two purposes—to remain standing and to keep out unwanted visitors. Both these purposes are served best by the kind of massive construction one might consider in designing a mountain. Over the centuries, some Elenes have sought to soften their necessarily bleak surroundings by embellishment. The interior braces intended to keep the walls from collapsing—even when swept by a blizzard of boulders—became buttresses. The massive stone posts designed to keep the ceiling where it belonged became columns with ornately carved bases and capitals. The same sort of strength can be achieved by vaulting, and the throne room of Ehlana's Tamul-built castle was a marvel of redundancy. It was massively vaulted *and* supported by long rows of fluted columns, and was braced by flying buttresses so delicate as to be not only useless but actually hazardous to those standing under them. Moreover, like everything else in fire-domed Matherion, the entire room was sheathed in opalescent mother-of-pearl.

Ehlana had chosen the buntings with some care, and the

gleaming walls were now accented with a riot of color. The forty-foot-long blue-velvet draperies at the narrow windows had been accented with white satin, the walls were decorated with crossed pennons and imitation battle flags, bright runners carpeted the aisles, and the columns and buttresses were bandaged with scarlet silk. The place looked to Sparhawk's somewhat-jaundiced eye like a country fair operated by a profoundly color-blind entrepreneur.

"Garish," Ulath observed, buffing the black Ogre-horns on his helmet with a piece of cloth.

"Garish comes close," Sparhawk agreed. Sparhawk wore his formal black armor and silver surcoat. The Tamul blacksmith who had hammered out the dents and re-enameled the armor had also anointed the inside of each intricately wrought section and all the leather straps with crushed rose petals in a kind of subtle, unspoken criticism of the armor's normal fragrance. The resulting mixture of odors was peculiar.

"How are we going to explain all the guards standing around Ehlana and Sarabian?" Ulath asked.

"We don't have to explain things, Ulath." Sparhawk shrugged. "We're Elenes, and the rest of the world believes that we're barbarians with strange, ritualistic customs that nobody else understands. I am *not* going to let my wife sit there unprotected while she and Sarabian calmly advise the Tamul government that it's been dismantled."

"Good thinking." Ulath looked gravely at his friend. "Sephrenia's being difficult, you know."

"We more or less expected that."

"She might have an easier time if she could sit next to Zalasta."

Sparhawk shook his head. "Zalasta's an adviser to the government. He'll have to be on the main floor with the ministers. Let's keep Sephrenia off to one side. I'll have Danae sit with her."

"That might help. Your daughter's presence seems to calm Sephrenia. I wouldn't seat Xanetia with them, though."

"I hadn't planned to."

"Just making sure. Did Engessa get any kind of acknowledgment of his signal? Are we absolutely *sure* his order got to everybody?"

"*He* is. I guess the Atans have used signal fires to pass orders along for centuries."

"I'm just a bit dubious about bonfires on hilltops as a way to send messages, Sparhawk."

"That's Engessa's department. It won't matter all that much if word hadn't reached a few backwaters by sunrise this morning."

"You're probably right. I guess we've done all we can, then. I just hope nothing goes wrong."

"What could go wrong?"

"That's the kind of thinking that fills graveyards, Sparhawk. I'll go tell them to lower the drawbridge. We might as well get started."

Stragen had carefully coached the dozen Tamul trumpeters and the rest of his musicians, concluding the lesson with some horrendous threats and an instructional visit to the carefully re-created torture chamber in the basement. The musicians had all piously sworn to play the proper notes and to forgo improvisation. The fanfares that were to greet the arrival of each minister of the imperial government had been Ehlana's idea. Fanfares are flattering; they elevate the ego; they lull the unwary into traps. Ehlana was good at that sort of thing. The depths of her political instincts sometimes amazed Sparhawk.

In keeping with the formality of the occasion, armored Church Knights were stationed at evenly spaced intervals along the walls. To the casual observer, the knights were no more than a part of the decor of the throne room. The casual observer, however, would have been wrong. The motionless men in steel were there to make absolutely certain that once the members of the imperial government had entered the room, they would not leave without permission; and the drawbridge, which was to be raised as soon as all the guests had arrived, doubly insured that nobody would grow bored and wander off. Sarabian had advised his Elene friends that the Imperial Council of Tamuli had grown over the centuries. At first, the council had consisted only of the ministers. Then the ministers had included their secretaries; then their undersecretaries. By now it had reached the point where sub-sub assistant temporary interim undersecretaries were also included. The title "Member of the Imperial Council" had become largely meaningless. The inclusion of such a mob, however, insured that every traitor inside the imperial compound would be gathered under Ehlana's battlements. The Queen of Elenia was shrewd enough to even use her enemies' egotism as a weapon against them.

"Well?" Ehlana asked nervously when her husband entered the royal apartment. The Queen of Elenia wore a cream-colored gown, trimmed with gold lamé, and a dark blue, ermine-trimmed velvet cloak. Her crown looked quite delicate, a kind of lace cap made of hammered gold inset with bright-colored gems. Despite its airy appearance, however, Sparhawk knew—because he had picked it up several times—that it was almost as heavy as her state crown, which was locked in the royal vault back in Cimmura.

"They're starting to drift across the drawbridge," he reported. "Itagne's greeting them. He knows everybody of any consequence in the government, so he'll know when our guests have all arrived. As soon as everyone's inside, the knights will raise the drawbridge." He looked at Emperor Sarabian, who stood near a window nervously chewing on one fingernail. "It's not going to be all that much longer, your Majesty," he said. "Shouldn't you change clothes?"

"The Tamul mantle was designed to cover a multitude of defects, Prince Sparhawk, so it should cover my western clothes—*and* my rapier. I am *not* going in there unarmed."

"We'll take care of you, Sarabian," Ehlana assured him.

"I'd rather do it myself, Mother." The emperor suddenly laughed nervously. "A bad joke, perhaps, but there's a lot of truth to it. You've raised me from political babyhood, Ehlana. In that respect, you *are* my mother."

"If you ever call me Mommy, I'll never speak to you again, your Majesty."

"I'd sooner bite out my tongue, your Majesty."

"What's the customary procedure, your Majesty?" Sparhawk asked Sarabian as they stood peering around the edge of the draped doorway into the rapidly filling throne room.

"As soon as everybody gets here, Subat will call the meeting to order," Sarabian replied. "That's when I enter—usually to the sound of what passes for music here in Matherion."

"Stragen's seen to it that your grand entrance will be truly grand," Ehlana assured him. "He composed the fanfare himself."

"Are all Elene thieves artists?" Sarabian asked. "Talen paints, Stragen composes music, and Caalador's a gifted actor."

"We *do* seem to attract talent, don't we." Ehlana smiled.

"Should I explain why there are so many of us on the dais?" Sarabian asked, glancing at Mirtai and Engessa.

She shook her head. "Never explain. It's a sign of weakness. I'll enter on your arm, and they'll all grovel."

"It's called genuflectory prostration, Ehlana."

"Whatever." She shrugged. "When they get up again, we'll be sitting there with our guards around us. That's when *you* take over the meeting. Don't even let Subat get started. We've got our own agenda today, and we don't have time to listen to him babble about the prospects for the wheat harvest on the plains of Edom. How are you feeling?"

"Nervous. I've never overthrown a government before."

"Neither have I, actually—unless you count what I did in the Basilica when I appointed Dolmant to the Archprelacy."

"She didn't actually do that, did she, Sparhawk?"

"Oh, yes, your Majesty—all by herself. She was superb."

"Just keep talking, Sarabian," Ehlana told him. "If anyone tries to interrupt, shout him down. Don't even pretend to be polite. This is *your* party. Don't be conciliatory or reasonable. Be coldly furious instead. Are you any good at oratory?"

"Probably not. They don't let me speak in public very often—except at the graduation ceremonies at the university."

"Speak slowly. You tend to talk too fast. Half of any good oration lies in its cadence. Use pauses. Vary your volume from a shout down to a whisper. Be dramatic. Give them a good show."

He laughed. "You're a charlatan, Ehlana."

"Naturally. That's what politics is all about—fraud, deceit, charlatanism."

"That's dreadful!"

"Of course. That's why it's so much fun."

The brazen fanfares echoed back from the vaulted ceiling as each minister entered the throne room, and they had the desired effect. The ministers in their silken mantles all seemed slightly awed by their own sublime importance. They moved to their places with stately pace and slow, their expressions grave, even exalted. Pondia Subat, the prime minister, seemed particularly impressed with himself. He sat splendidly alone in a crimson-upholstered chair to one side of the dais upon which the thrones stood, looking out imperially at the other officials assembling in the chairs lining both sides of the broad central aisle.

Chancellor of the Exchequer Gashon sat with Teovin, the Director of the Secret Police, and several other ministers. There seemed to be a great deal of whispering going on in the little group.

"That would probably be the opposition," Ehlana observed. "Teovin's certainly involved, and the others are also most likely a part of it—to a greater or lesser degree." She turned to Talen, who stood directly behind her, wearing his page's knee britches. "Pay very close attention to that group," she instructed. "I want a report on their reactions. We should be able to determine their degree of guilt by the looks on their faces."

"Yes, my Queen."

Then Itagne appeared briefly at the massive double doors to the throne room and flicked his hand at Ulath, signaling that all of the relevant officials had arrived.

Ulath, who stood to one side of the dais, nodded and raised his Ogre-horn trumpet to his lips.

The room seemed to shudder into a shocked silence as the barbaric sound of the Ogre-horn, deep-toned and rasping, reverberated from the nacreous walls. The huge doors boomed shut, and two armored knights, one a Cyrinic all in white, and the other a Pandion all in black, placed themselves in front of the entryway.

The prime minister rose to his feet.

Ulath banged the butt of his ax on the floor three times to call for silence.

The emperor winced.

"What's wrong, Sarabian?" Mirtai asked him.

"Sir Ulath just broke several of the floor tiles."

"We can replace them with bone," she assured him. "There should be quite a few lying around before the day's over."

"Will the council please come to order?" Pondia Subat intoned.

Ulath banged the floor again.

Sparhawk looked around the throne room. Everyone was in place. Sephrenia, dressed in her white Styric robe, sat with Princess Danae and Caalador on the far side of the room. Xanetia, also in white, sat on the near side with Kalten and Berit. Melidere sat in a small gallery with the nine imperial wives. The clever baroness had carefully cultivated a friendship with Sarabian's first wife, Cieronna, a member of one of the noblest houses of Tamul proper and the mother of the crown prince. The friendship had by now grown so close that

Melidere was customarily invited to attend state functions in the company of the empresses. Her presence among them *this* time had a serious purpose, however. Sarabian had a wife from each of the nine kingdoms, and it was entirely possible that some of them had been subverted. Sparhawk was fairly certain that the bare-breasted Valesian, Elysoun, was free of any political contamination. She was simply too busy for politics. The Tegan wife, Gahenas, a puritanical lady obsessed with her personal virtue and her staunch republicanism, would probably not have even been approached by conspirators. Torellia of Aɪ juna, and Chacole of Cynesga, however, were highly suspect They had both established what might best be called personal courts liberally sprinkled with nobles from their homelands. Melidere had been instructed to keep a close eye on those two in particular for signs of unusual reactions to the revelation of Zalasta's true affiliation.

Sparhawk sighed. It was all so complicated. Friends and enemies all looked the same. In the long run, it might turn out that Xanetia's unusual gift would prove more valuable than a sudden offer of aid from an entire army.

Vanion, who had unobtrusively stationed himself with the knights lining the walls, reached up and first lowered, then raised, his visor. It was the signal that all their forces were in place. Stragen, who was with his trumpeters behind the dais, nodded briefly in acknowledgment.

Then Sparhawk looked rather closely at Zalasta, the unknowing guest of honor at this affair. The Styric, his eyes apprehensive, sat among the ministers, his white robe looking oddly out of place among all the bright-colored silk mantles. He quite obviously knew that something was afoot, and just as obviously had no idea what it might be. That was something, anyway. At least no one in the inner circle had been subverted. Sparhawk irritably shook that thought off. Under the circumstances, a certain amount of wary suspicion was only natural; but left unchecked, it could become a disease. He made a sour face. About one more day of this and he'd begin to suspect himself.

"The council will come now to order!" Pondia Subat repeated.

Ulath broke some more tiles.

"By command of his Imperial Majesty, Emperor Sarabian, this council is called to order!"

"Good God, Subat," Sarabian groaned, half to himself, "will you destroy the floor entirely?"

"Gentlemen, his Imperial Majesty, Sarabian of Tamuli!"

A single trumpet voiced a clear, ringing theme of majestically descending notes. Then another joined the first to repeat the theme a third of an octave higher—then another trumpet another third higher. Then, in a great crescendo and still higher, the musicians all joined in to fill the throne room with shimmering echoes.

"Impressive," Sarabian noted. "Do we go in now?"

"Not yet," Ehlana told him. "The music changes. That's when we start. Pay attention to my hand on your arm. Let me set the pace. Don't jump when we get to the thrones. Stragen's got a whole brass band hidden in various parts of the room. The climax will be thunderous. Draw yourself up, throw your shoulders back, and look regal. Try your very best to look like a God."

"Are you having fun, Ehlana?"

She grinned impishly at him and winked. "There," she said, "the flutes at the back of the hall have picked up the theme. That's our signal. Good luck, my friend." She kissed him lightly on the cheek and then laid her hand on his arm. "One," she said, listening intently to the music. "Two." She drew in a deep breath. "Now." And the Emperor of Tamuli and the Queen of Elenia stepped through the archway and crossed with regal pace toward their golden thrones as the flutes at the rear of the hall softly sang the plaintive accompaniment of Stragen's main theme, set now in a minor key. Immediately behind them came Sparhawk, Mirtai, Engessa, and Bevier. Talen, Alean, and Itagne, who was still puffing slightly from running through the halls, followed.

As the royal party reached the thrones, Stragen, who was using his rapier as a conductor's baton, led his hidden musicians into a fortissimo recapitulation of his main theme. The sound was overwhelming. It was not entirely certain whether the members of the imperial council fell to their faces out of habit or were knocked down by that enormous blast of sound. Stragen cut his rapier sharply to one side, and the musicians broke off, slashed as it were into silence, leaving the echoes shimmering in the air like ghosts.

Pondia Subat rose to his feet. "Will your Majesty address some few remarks to this assemblage before we commence?" he asked in an almost insultingly superior tone. The question

was sheer formality, almost ritualistic. The emperor traditionally did not speak at these sessions.

"Why, yes, as a matter of fact, I believe I will, Pondia
Subat," Sarabian replied, rising again to his feet. "So good of
you to ask, old boy."

Subat gaped at him, his expression incredulous. "But—"

"Was there something, Subat?"

"This is most irregular, your Majesty."

"I know. Refreshing, isn't it? We've got a lot to cover today,
Subat, so let's get cracking."

"Your Majesty has not consulted with me. We cannot proceed if I don't know what issues are—"

"Sit, Subat!" Sarabian snapped. "Stay!" His tone was one of
command. "You will remain silent until I give you leave to
speak."

"You can't—"

"I said sit down!"

Subat quailed and sank into his chair.

"Your head's none too tightly attached just now, my Lord
Prime Minister," Sarabian said ominously, "and if you waggle
it at me in the wrong way, it might just fall off. You've been
tiptoeing right on the brink of treason, Pondia Subat, and I'm
more than a little put out with you."

The prime minister's face went deathly pale.

Sarabian began to pace up and down on the dais, his face
like a thundercloud.

"Please, God, make him stand still," Ehlana said under her
breath. "He can't make a decent speech if he's loping around
the dais like a gazelle in flight."

Then the emperor stopped to stand at the very front of the
slightly elevated platform. "I'm not going to waste time with
banalities, gentlemen," he told his government bluntly. "We
had a crisis, and I depended on you to deal with it. You failed
me—probably because you were too busy playing your usual
games of politics. The empire required giants, and all I had to
serve me were dwarves. That made it necessary for *me* to deal
with the crisis personally. And that's what I've been doing,
gentlemen, for the past several months. You are no longer relevant, my Lords. *I* am the government."

There were cries of outrage from the ministers and their
subordinates.

"He's going too *fast*!" Ehlana exclaimed. "He should have
built up to that!"

"Don't be such a critic," Sparhawk told her. "It's his speech. Let him make it his own way."

"I will have silence!" Sarabian declared.

The council paid no attention. They continued their excited babbling. The emperor opened his mantle to reveal his Elene clothing, and then he drew his rapier. "I said *SILENCE!*" he roared.

All sound ceased.

"I'll pin the next man who interrupts me to the wall like a butterfly," Sarabian told them. Then he cut his rapier sharply through the air. The whistling sound of the blade's passage was as chill as death itself. He looked around at his cowed officials. "That's a little better," he said. "Now stay that way." He set the point of the rapier on the floor and lightly crossed his hands on the pommel. "My family has depended on the ministries to handle the day-to-day business of government for centuries," he said. "Our trust has obviously been misplaced. You were adequate—barely—in times of tranquility, but when a crisis arose, you began to scurry around like ants, more interested in protecting your fortunes, your personal privileges, and perpetuating your petty interdepartmental rivalries than in the good of my empire—and that's the one thing you all seem to forget, gentlemen. It's *my* empire. My family hasn't made a great issue of the fact, but I think it's time you were reminded of it. You serve *me*, and you serve only at *my* pleasure, not at *your* convenience."

The officials were all gaping at the man they had thought to be no more than a harmless eccentric. Sparhawk saw a movement near the middle of the throne room. His eyes flicked back to the front, and he saw that Teovin's chair was conspicuously empty. The Director of the Secret Police was more clever and much quicker than his colleagues, and, throwing dignity to the winds, he was busily crawling on his hands and knees toward the nearest exit. Chancellor of the Exchequer Gashon, thin, bloodless, and wispy-haired, sat beside Teovin's vacant chair, staring at Sarabian in open terror.

Sparhawk looked quickly at Vanion, and the preceptor nodded. Vanion had seen the crawling policeman, too.

"When I perceived that I had chosen little men with little minds to administer my empire," Sarabian was saying, "I appealed to Zalasta of Styricum for advice. Who better to deal with the supernatural than the Styrics? It was Zalasta who recommended that I submit a request directly to Archprelate

Dolmant of the Church of Chyrellos for assistance, and the very core of that assistance was to be Prince Sparhawk of Elenia. We Tamuls pride ourselves on our subtlety and our sophistication, but I assure you that we are but children when compared to the Elenes. The state visit of my dear sister Ehlana was little more than a subterfuge designed to conceal the fact that our main purpose was to bring her husband, Sir Sparhawk, to Matherion. Queen Ehlana and I amused ourselves by deceiving you—and you were not hard to deceive, my Lords—while Prince Sparhawk and his companions sought the roots of the turmoil here in Tamuli. As we had anticipated, our enemies reacted."

There was a brief, muted disturbance at one of the side doors. Vanion and Khalad were quite firmly preventing the Director of the Secret Police from leaving.

"Did you have a pressing engagement somewhere, Teovin?" Sarabian drawled.

Teovin's eyes were wild and he looked at his emperor with open hatred.

"If you're discontent with me, Teovin, I'll be more than happy to give you satisfaction," Sarabian told him, flourishing his rapier meaningfully. "Please return to your seat. My seconds will call upon you when we've concluded here."

Vanion took the Director of the Secret Police by one arm, turned him around, and pointed at the empty seat. Then, with a none-too-gentle shove, he started him moving.

"This windy preamble's beginning to bore me, gentlemen," Sarabian announced, "so why don't we get down to cases? The attempted coup here in Matherion was the direct response to Sir Sparhawk's arrival. The assorted disturbances which have kept the Atans running from one end of the continent to the other for the past several years have had one source and only one. We have a single enemy, and he has formed a massive conspiracy designed to overthrow the government and to wrest my throne from me, and—as I probably should have anticipated, given the nature of those who pretend to serve me—he had willing helpers in the government itself."

Some of the dignitaries gasped; others looked guilty.

"Pay very close attention, gentlemen," Sarabian told them. "This is where it gets interesting. Many of you have wondered at the long absence of Interior Minister Kolata. I'm sure you'll be delighted to know that Kolata's going to be joining us now."

He turned to Ulath. "Would you be so good as to invite the Minister of the Interior to come in, Sir Knight?" he asked.

Ulath bowed, and Kalten rose from his seat to join him.

"Minister Kolata, as the chief policeman in all the empire, knows a great deal about criminal activities," Sarabian declared. "I'm absolutely sure that his analysis of the present situation will be enlightening."

Kalten and Ulath returned with the ashen-faced Minister of the Interior between them. It was not the fact that Kolata was in obvious distress that raised the outcry from the other officials, however, but rather the fact that the chief policeman of the empire was in chains.

Emperor Sarabian stood impassively as his council members shouted their protests. "How am I doing so far, Ehlana?" he asked out of the corner of his mouth.

"I'd have done it differently," she told him, "but that's only a matter of style. I'll give you a complete critique when it's all over." She looked out at the officials who were all on their feet talking excitedly. "Don't let that go on for too long. Remind them who's in charge. Be *very* firm about it."

"Yes, Mother." He smiled. Then he looked at his government and drew in a deep breath. *"QUIET!"* he roared in a great voice.

They fell into a stunned silence.

"There will be no further interruptions of these proceedings," Sarabian told them. "The rules have changed, gentlemen. We're not going to pretend to be civilized anymore. I'm going to tell you what to do, and you're going to do it. I'd like to remind you that not only do you *serve* at my pleasure; you also continue to *live* only at my pleasure. The Minister of the Interior is guilty of high treason. You'll note that there was no trial. Kolata is guilty because I *say* that he's guilty." Sarabian paused as a new realization came to him. "My power in Tamuli is absolute. *I* am the government, and *I* am the law. We are going to question Kolata rather closely. Pay attention to his answers, gentlemen. Your positions in government—your very lives—may hinge on what he says. Foreign Minister Oscagne is going to question Kolata—not about his guilt, which has already been established—but about the involvement of others. We're going to get to the bottom of this once and for all. You may proceed, Oscagne."

"Yes, your Majesty." Oscagne rose to his feet and stood a

moment in deep thought as Sarabian sat again on his throne. Oscagne wore a black silk mantle. His choice of color had been quite deliberate. While black mantles were not common, they were not unheard of. Judges and imperial prosecutors, however, *always* wore black. The somber color heightened the foreign minister's pallor, which in turn accentuated his grim expression.

Khalad came forward with a plain wooden stool and set it down in front of the dais. Kalten and Ulath brought the Minister of the Interior forward and plopped him unceremoniously down on the stool.

"Do you understand your situation here, Kolata?" Oscagne asked the prisoner.

"You have no right to question me, Oscagne," Kolata replied quickly.

"Break his fingers, Khalad," Sparhawk instructed from his position just behind Ehlana's throne.

"Yes, my Lord," Khalad replied. "How many?"

"Start out with one or two. Every time he starts talking about Oscagne's rights—or his own—break another one."

"Yes, my Lord." Khalad took the Interior Minister's wrist.

"Stop him!" Kolata squealed in fright. "Somebody stop him!"

"Kalten, Ulath," Sparhawk said, "kill the first man who moves."

Kalten drew his sword, and Ulath raised his ax.

"You see how it is, old boy," Oscagne said to the man on the stool. "You're not universally loved to begin with, and Prince Sparhawk's command has just evaporated any minuscule affection anyone here might have had for you. You *will* talk, Kolata. Sooner or later, you'll talk. We can do this the easy way, or we can do it the other way, but you *are* going to answer my questions." Oscagne's expression had become implacable.

"They'll kill me, Oscagne!" Kolata pleaded. "They'll kill me if I talk."

"You're in a difficult situation, then, Kolata, because *we'll* kill you if you don't. You're taking orders from Cyrgon, aren't you?"

"Cyrgon? That's absurd!" Kolata blustered. "Cyrgon's a myth."

"Oh, really?" Oscagne looked at him with contempt. "Don't play the fool with me, Kolata. I don't have the patience for it.

Your orders come from the Cynesgan embassy, don't they? And most of the time, they're delivered by a man named Krager."

Kolata gaped at him.

"Close your mouth, Kolata. You look like an idiot with it hanging open like that. We already know a great deal about your treason. All we really want from you are a few details. You were first contacted by someone you had reason to trust—and most probably someone you respected. That immediately rules out a Cynesgan. No Tamul has anything but contempt for Cynesgans. Given our characteristic sense of our own superiority, that would also rule out an Arjuni or an Elene from any of the western kingdoms. That would leave only another Tamul, or possibly an Atan, or—" Oscagne's eyes suddenly widened, and his expression grew thunderstruck. "Or a *Styric!*"

"Absurd," Kolata scoffed weakly. His eyes, however, were wild, darting this way and that like those of a man looking for a place to hide.

Sparhawk looked appraisingly at Zalasta. The sorcerer's face was deathly pale, but his eyes showed that he was still in control. It was going to take something more to push him over the edge. The big Pandion placed his left hand on his sword hilt, giving Oscagne their prearranged signal.

"We don't seem to be getting anywhere, old boy," Oscagne drawled, recovering from his surprise. "I think you need some encouragement." He turned and looked at Xanetia. "Would you be so kind, Anarae?" he asked her. "Our esteemed Minister of the Interior doesn't seem to want to share things with us. Do you suppose you could persuade him to change his mind?"

"I can but try, Oscagne of Matherion," Xanetia replied, rising to her feet. She crossed the front of the room, choosing for some reason to approach the prisoner from the side where Sephrenia sat rather than the one from which she herself had been watching. "Thou art afeared, Kolata of Matherion," she said gravely, "and thy fear doth make thee brave, for it is in thy mind that though they who hold thy body captive may do thee great harm, he who hath thy soul in thrall may do thee worse. Now must thou contend with yet an even greater fear. Look upon *me*, Kolata of Matherion, and tremble, for *I* will visit upon thee the ultimate horror. Wilt thou speak, and speak freely?"

"I *can't!*" Kolata wailed.

"Then art thou lost. Behold me as I truly am, and consider well thy fate, for I am death, Kolata of Matherion, death beyond thy most dreadful imagining." The color drained from her slowly, and the glow within her was faint at first. She stood looking at him with her chin raised and an expression of deep sadness in her eyes as she glowed brighter and brighter.

Kolata screamed.

The other officials scrambled to their feet, their faces terrified, and their babbling suddenly shrill.

"Sit down!" Sarabian bellowed at them, *"and be silent!"*

A few of them were cowed into obedience. Most, however, were too frightened. They continued to shrink back from Xanetia, crying out in shrill voices.

"My Lord Vanion," Sarabian called over the tumult, "would you please restore order?"

"At once, your Majesty." Vanion clapped down his visor, pulled his sword from its scabbard, and raised his shield. "Draw swords!" He barked the command. There was a steely rasp as the Church Knights drew their swords. "Forward!" Vanion ordered.

The knights posted along the walls marched clankingly forward, their swords at the ready, converging on the frightened officials. Vanion stretched forth his steel-clad arm, extending his sword and touching the tip to the throat of the prime minister. "The emperor told you to sit down, Pondia Subat," he said. "Do it! *NOW!*"

The prime minister sank back into his chair, suddenly more afraid of Vanion than he was of Xanetia.

A couple of the council members had to be chased down and forcibly returned to their seats, and one rather athletic one—the Minister of Public Works, Sparhawk thought—was only persuaded to come down from the drape he'd been climbing by the threat of Khalad's crossbow. Order was restored. When the council had returned—or been returned—to their seats, however, the Chancellor of the Exchequer was discovered lying on the floor, vacant-eyed and with a large bubble of foam protruding from his gaping mouth. Vanion checked the body rather perfunctorily. "Poison," he said shortly. "He seems to have taken it himself."

Ehlana shuddered.

"Prithee, Anarae," Sarabian said to Xanetia, "continue thine inquiry."

"An it please your Majesty," she replied in that strange

echoing voice. She turned her gaze on Kolata. "Wilt thou speak, and freely, Kolata of Matherion?" She asked.

He shrank back in horror.

"So be it, then." She put forth her hand and moved closer. "The curse of Edaemus is upon me," she warned, "and I bear its mark. I will share that curse with thee. Mayhap thou wilt regret thy silence when thy flesh doth decay and melt like wax from thy bones. The time hath come to choose, Kolata of Matherion. Speak or die. Who is it who hath stolen thy loyalty from thine appointed master." Her hand, more surely deadly than Vanion's sword, was within inches of Kolata's ashen face.

"No!" he shrieked. "No! I'll tell you!"

The cloud appeared quite suddenly in the air above the gibbering minister, but Sparhawk was ready. Half-hidden behind Ehlana's throne, he had taken off his gauntlet and surreptitiously removed the sapphire rose from its confinement. "Blue-Rose!" he said sharply. "Destroy the cloud!"

The Bhelliom surged in his hand, and the dense, almost solid-appearing patch of intense darkness tattered, whipping like a pennon on a flagstaff in a hurricane, then it streamed away and was gone.

Zalasta was thrown back in his chair as his spell was broken. He half rose and fell back again, writhing and moaning as the jagged edges of his broken spell clawed at him. His chair overturned, and he convulsed on the floor like one caught in a seizure.

"It was *him*!" Kolata shrieked, pointing with a trembling hand. "It was Zalasta! He made me do it!"

Sephrenia's gasp was clearly audible. Sparhawk looked sharply at her. She had fallen back, nearly as shaken as Zalasta himself. Her eyes were filled with disbelief and horror. Danae, Sparhawk noticed, was talking to her, speaking rapidly and holding her sister's face quite firmly in her small hands.

"Curse you, Sparhawk!" The words came out in a kind of rasping croak as Zalasta, aided by his staff, dragged himself unsteadily to his feet. His face was shaken and twisted in frustration and rage. "You are *mine*, Sephrenia, *mine*!" he howled. "I have longed for you for an eternity, watched as your thieving, guttersnipe Goddess stole you from me! But no more! *Thus* do I banish forever the Child-Goddess and her hold on thee!" His deadly staff whirled and leveled. "Die, Aphrael!" he shrieked.

Sephrenia, without even thinking, clasped her arms around

Sparhawk's daughter and turned quickly in her seat, shielding the little girl with her own body, willingly offering her back to Zalasta's fury.

Sparhawk's heart froze as a ball of fire shot from the tip of the staff.

"No!" Vanion cried, trying to rush forward.

But Xanetia was already there. Her decision to approach Kolata from Sephrenia's side of the room had clearly been influenced by her perception of what lay in Zalasta's mind. She had consciously placed herself in a position to protect her enemy. Unafraid, she faced the raving Styric. The sizzling fireball streaked through the silent air of the throne room, bearing with it all of Zalasta's centuries-old hatred.

Xanetia held out her hand, and, like a tame bird returning to the hand that feeds it, the flaming orb settled into that hand. With only the faint hint of a smile touching her lips, the Delphaeic woman closed her fingers around Zalasta's pent-up hatred. For an instant, incandescent flame spurted out from between her pale fingers, and then she absorbed the fiery messenger of death, the light within her consuming it utterly. "What now, Zalasta of Styricum?" she asked the raging sorcerer. "What dost thou propose now? Wilt thou contend with me more at peril of thy life? Or wilt thou, like the whipped cur thou art, cringe and flee my wrath? For I do know thee. It hath been *thy* poisoned tongue which hath set my sister's heart against me. Flee, master of lies. Abuse Sephrenia's ears no longer with thy foul slanders. Go. I abjure thee. Go."

Zalasta howled, and in that howl there was a lifetime of unsatisfied longing and blackest despair.

And then he vanished.

CHAPTER
TWENTY

E mperor Sarabian's expression was strangely detached as he looked out over the shambles of his government. Some of the officials appeared to be in shock; others scurried aimlessly, babbling. Several were clustered at the main door, imploring the knights to let them out.

Oscagne, his diplomat's face imperturbable, approached the dais. "Surprising turn of events," he noted as if he were speaking of an unexpected summer shower. He studiously adjusted his black mantle, looking more and more like a judge.

"Yes," Sarabian agreed, his eyes still lost in thought. "I think we might be able to exploit it, however. Sparhawk, is that dungeon down in the basement functional?"

"Yes, your Majesty. The architect was very thorough."

"Good."

"What have you got in mind, Sarabian?" Ehlana asked him.

He grinned at her, his face suddenly almost boyish. "I ain't a-tellin', dorlin'," he replied in outrageous imitation of Caalador's dialect. "I purely wouldn't want t' spoil th' surprise."

"Please, Sarabian," she said with a weary sigh.

"Jist you watch, yer Queenship. I'm a-fixin' t' pull off a little koop my own-self."

"You're going to make me cross, Sarabian."

"Don't you love me anymore, Mother?" His tone was excited and exhilarated.

"Men!" she said, rolling her eyes upward.

"Just follow my lead, my friends," the emperor told them. "Let's find out how well I've learned my lessons." He rose to his feet. "Lord Vanion," he called. "Would you be so good as to return our guests to their seats?"

"At once, your Majesty," Vanion replied. Vanion, forewarned of Zalasta's treachery, was completely in control. He barked a few short commands, and the Church Knights firmly escorted the distracted officials back to their chairs.

"What was he doing?" Ehlana demanded of her husband in a tense whisper. "Why did he try to attack Danae?"

"He didn't, love," Sparhawk replied, thinking very quickly. "He was trying to attack Aphrael. Didn't you see her? She was standing right beside Sephrenia."

"She *was*?"

"Of course. I thought everyone in the room saw her, but maybe it was only me—and Zalasta. Why do you think he ran away so fast? Aphrael was right on the verge of jerking out his heart and eating it before his very eyes."

She shuddered.

Emperor Sarabian moved to the front of the dais again. "Let's come to order, gentlemen," he told them crisply. "We haven't finished here yet. I gather that you were surprised by the revelation of Zalasta's *true* position—some of you, anyway. I'm disappointed in you, my Lords—most of you for your profound lack of perception, the rest for not realizing that I could see through Zalasta—and you—like panes of glass. Some of you are traitors, the rest are merely stupid. I have no need of men of either stripe in my service. It is my excruciating pleasure to announce that at sunrise this morning, the Atan garrisons throughout Tamuli moved out of their barracks and replaced *all* imperial authorities with officers from their own ranks. With the exception of Matherion, the entire empire is under martial law."

They gaped at him.

"Atan Engessa," Sarabian said.

"Yes, Sarabian-Emperor?"

"Would you be so kind as to eliminate that lone exception? Take your Atans out into the city and take charge of the capital."

"At once, Sarabian-Emperor." Engessa's grin was very broad.

"Be firm, Engessa. Show my subjects my fist."

"It shall be as you command, Sarabian-Emperor."

"Splendid chap," Sarabian murmured loudly enough to be heard as the towering Atan marched to the door.

"Your Majesty," Pondia Subat protested weakly, half rising.

The look the emperor gave his prime minister was icy. "I'm busy right now, Subat," he said. "You and I will talk later—extensively. I'm sure I'll find your explanation of how all of this happened under your very nose without even disturbing your decades-long nap absolutely fascinating. Now sit down and be quiet."

The prime minister sank back into his chair, his eyes very wide.

"All of Tamuli is under martial law now," the emperor told his officials. "Since you've failed so miserably, I've been obliged to step in and take charge. That makes you redundant, so you are all dismissed."

There were gasps, and some of the officials, those longest in office and most convinced of their own near-divinity, cried out in protest.

"Moreover—" Sarabian cut across their objections, "—the treason of Zalasta has cast doubt upon the loyalty of each and every one of you. If I cannot *trust* all, I must *suspect* all. I want you to search your souls tonight, gentlemen, because we'll be asking you questions tomorrow, and we'll want complete truth from you. We don't have time for lies or excuses or attempts to wriggle out from under your responsibility or guilt. I strongly recommend that you be forthcoming. The consequences of mendacity or evasion will be *very* unpleasant."

Ulath took a long honing steel from his belt and began to draw it slowly across the edge of his ax-blade. It made the sort of screech that sets the teeth on edge.

"As a demonstration of my benevolence," Sarabian continued, "I've made arrangements for you all to be lodged here tonight, and to provide you with accommodations that will give each of you absolute privacy to review your past lives so that you can answer questions fully tomorrow. Lord Vanion, would you and your knights be so good as to escort our guests down to their quarters in the dungeon?" Sarabian was improvising for all he was worth.

"At once, your Majesty," Vanion replied, clashing his mailed fist against his breastplate in salute.

"Ah, Lord Vanion," Ehlana added.

"Yes, my Queen?"

"You might consider searching our guests before you put them to bed. We don't want any more of them hurting themselves the way the Chancellor of the Exchequer did, now, do we?"

"Excellent suggestion, your Majesty," Sarabian agreed. "Take all their toys away from them, Lord Vanion. We don't want them to be distracted by anything." He paused a moment. "Actually, Lord Vanion, I rather think our guests will be able to concentrate a little better if they have something tangible about them to emphasize their situation. It seems that I read something once to the effect that the prisoners in Elene dungeons wear a kind of uniform."

"Yes, your Majesty," Vanion told him with an absolutely straight face. "It's a sleeveless smock made of grey burlap—with a bright red stripe painted down the back, so that they can be identified in case they escape."

"Do you suppose we might be able to find something along those lines for our guests?"

"If not, we can improvise, your Majesty."

"Splendid, Lord Vanion—and take their jewels away from them as well. Jewels make people feel important, and I want them all to understand that they're little more than bugs. I suppose you'd better feed them as well. What do people usually eat in dungeons?"

"Bread and water, your Majesty—a little gruel once in a while."

"That should do nicely. Get them out of here, Vanion. The very sight of them is starting to nauseate me."

Vanion barked a few sharp commands, and the knights descended on the former government.

Each official had an honor guard of armored men to escort him—in some cases to drag him—down to the dungeon.

"Ah—stay a moment, Teovin," the emperor said urbanely to the Director of the Secret Police. "I believe there was something you wanted to say to me?"

"No, your Majesty." Teovin's tone was sullen.

"Come, come, old boy. Don't be shy. We're all friends here. If you're in any way offended by anything I've done here today, spit it out. Milord Stragen will be happy to lend you his rapier, and then you and I can discuss things; I'm sure you'll find my explanations quite pointed." Sarabian let his mantle slide to the floor. He smiled a chill smile and drew his rapier again. "Well?" he said.

"It would be treason for me to offer violence to your Majesty's person," Teovin mumbled.

"Good God, Teovin, why should *that* bother you? You've been involved in treason for the past several years anyway, so why concern yourself with a few picky little technicalities? Take up the sword, man. For once—just once—face me openly. I'll give you a fencing lesson—one you'll remember for the rest of your life, short though that may be."

"I will not raise my hand against my emperor," Teovin declared.

"What a shame. I'm really disappointed in you, old boy. You may go now."

Vanion took the director's arm in his mailed fist and half dragged him from the throne room.

The Emperor of Tamuli exultantly raised his rapier over his head, rose to his tiptoes, and spun about in a flamboyant little pirouette. Then he extended one leg forward and bowed extravagantly to Ehlana, sweeping his slender sword to the side. "And *that*, dear mother," he said to her, "is how you overthrow a government."

"No, Lady Sephrenia," the queen said flatly a half hour later when they had gathered again in the royal apartment, "you do *not* have our permission to withdraw. You're a member of the royal council of Elenia, and we have need of you."

Sephrenia's pale, grief-stricken face went stiff. "As your Majesty commands."

"Snap out of it, Sephrenia. This is an emergency. We don't have time for personal concerns. Zalasta's betrayed us all, not just you. Now we have to try to minimize the damage."

"You're not being fair, Mother," Danae accused.

"I'm not trying to be. You'll be queen one day, Danae. Now sit down, keep your mouth shut, and learn."

Danae looked startled. Then her chin came up. She curtsied. "Yes, your Majesty," she said.

"That's better. I'll make a queen of you yet. Sir Bevier."

"Yes, your Majesty?" Bevier replied.

"Tell your Cyrinics to man their catapults. Vanion, put the rest of the knights on the walls and tell them to start boiling the pitch. Zalasta's on the loose out there. He's completely lost control of himself, and we have no idea of what forces he has at his command. In his present state, he may try anything, so let's be ready—just in case."

"You sound like a field marshal, Ehlana," Sarabian told her.

"I am," she replied absently. "It's one of my titles. Sparhawk, can Bhelliom counter any magic Zalasta might throw at us?"

"Easily, my Queen. He probably won't try anything, though. You saw what happened to him when Bhelliom blew his cloud apart. It's very painful to have one of your spells broken. Sephrenia knows him better than I do. She can tell you whether or not he's desperate enough to risk that again."

"Well, Sephrenia?" Ehlana asked.

"I don't really know, your Majesty," the small Styric woman replied after a moment's thought. "This is a side of him I've never seen before. I honestly believe he's gone mad. He might do almost anything."

"We'd better be ready for him then. Mirtai, ask Kalten and Ulath to bring Kolata in here. Let's find out just how far this conspiracy goes."

Sparhawk drew Sephrenia to one side. "How did Zalasta find out about Danae?" he asked. "It's obvious that he knows who she really is. Did *you* tell him?"

"No. She told me not to."

"That's peculiar. I'll talk with her later and find out why. Maybe she suspected something—or it might have been one of those hunches of hers." He thought for a moment. "Could he have been trying to kill *you*? It *seemed* that he was throwing that fireball at Danae, but *you* might have been his target."

"I could never believe that, Sparhawk."

"At this point, I'm almost ready to believe anything." He hesitated. "Xanetia knew about him, you realize. She told us earlier."

"Why didn't you warn me?" Her tone was shocked.

"Because you wouldn't have believed her. You're not really inclined to trust her word, Sephrenia. You had to see Zalasta's treachery for yourself. Oh, incidentally, she *did* save your life, you'll remember. You might want to give that some thought."

"Don't scold me, Sparhawk," she said with a wan little smile. "I'm having a difficult enough time as it is."

"I know, and I'm afraid nobody can make it any easier for you."

Kolata proved to be very cooperative. His weeks of confinement had broken his spirit, and Zalasta's obvious willingness to kill him had canceled any loyalty he might have felt. "I really don't know," he replied to Oscagne's question. "Teovin might, though. He's the one who brought Zalasta's proposal to me originally."

"Then you haven't been involved in this affair since you were first appointed to office?"

"I don't think 'this affair,' as you call it, has been going on for that long. I can't say for certain, but I got the impression that it all started about five or six years ago."

"You've been recruiting people for longer than that."

"That was just ordinary Tamul politics, Oscagne. I knew that the prime minister was an idiot as soon as I took office. *You* were my only significant opponent. I was recruiting people to counter *your* moves—and your absurd idea that the subject kingdoms of Daresia are foreign nations rather than integral parts of metropolitan Tamuli."

"We can discuss jurisdictional disputes some other time, Kolata. It was Teovin, then? He's been your contact with the enemy?"

Kolata nodded. "Teovin and a disreputable drunkard named Krager. Krager's an Eosian, and he's had dealings with Prince Sparhawk before, I understand. Everyone in our loose confederation knows him, so he makes a perfect messenger—when he's sober."

"That's Krager, all right," Kalten noted.

"What exactly did Zalasta offer you, Kolata?" Oscagne asked the prisoner.

"Power, wealth—the usual. You're a minister of the government, Oscagne. You know the game and the stakes we play for. We all thought that the emperor was no more than a figurehead, well-meaning, a little vague, and not really very well informed—sorry, your Majesty, but that's what we all believed."

"Thank you," Sarabian replied. "That's what you were supposed to think. What really baffles me, though, is the fact that you all overlooked the fact that the Atans are loyal to me personally. Didn't any of you take that into consideration?"

"We underestimated your Majesty. We didn't think you grasped the full implications of that. If we'd thought for a moment that you really understood how much power you had, we'd have killed you."

"I rather thought you might have. That's why I played the simpleton."

"Did Zalasta tell you who was *really* behind all of this?" Oscagne asked.

"He pretended that he was speaking for Cyrgon," Kolata replied. "We didn't take that too seriously, though. Styrics are peculiar people. They always try to make us believe that they represent a higher power of some kind. They never seem to want to accept full responsibility. So far as I know, however, it was Zalasta's scheme."

"I think that maybe it's time for us to hear from Zalasta himself," Vanion said.

"Have you got him hidden up your sleeve, Vanion?" Ehlana asked.

"In a manner of speaking, your Majesty. Kalten, why don't you take the Minister of the Interior back to his room? He looks a little tired."

"I still have questions, Lord Vanion," Oscagne protested.

"We'll get you your answers, old boy," Itagne assured him, "quicker and in much greater detail. You plod, Oscagne. It's one of your failings. We're just going to hurry things along."

Vanion waited until Kalten and Ulath had removed Kolata from the room. "We've told you all in a general sort of way that Xanetia knows what other people are thinking. This isn't just some vague notion about feelings or moods. If she chooses, she can repeat your thoughts word for word. Most of you probably have some doubts about that, so in the interests of saving time, why don't we have her demonstrate? Would you tell us what Queen Ehlana's thinking right now, Anarae?"

"An it pleases thee, Lord Vanion," the Delphaeic woman replied. "Her Majesty is enjoying herself very much at the moment. She is, however, discontent with thee for thine interruption. She is pleased with the progress of Emperor Sarabian, thinking it might now be reasonable to expect some small measure of competence from him. She hath, as well, certain designs of an intimate nature upon her husband, for political activity doth ever stir that side of her personality."

Ehlana's face turned bright red. "You stop that at once!" she exclaimed.

"I'm sorry, your Majesty," Vanion apologized. "I didn't anticipate that last bit. Did Xanetia more or less read your thoughts correctly?"

"You know I won't answer that, Vanion." The queen's face was still flaming.

"Will you at least concede that she has access to the thoughts of others?"

"I'd heard about that," Sarabian mused. "I thought it was just another of the wild stories we hear about the Delphae."

"Bhelliom confirmed it, Emperor Sarabian," Sparhawk told him. "Xanetia can read others the way you'd read an open book. I'd imagine that she's read Zalasta from cover to cover. She should be able to tell us everything we want to know." He looked at Xanetia. "Could you give us a sort of summary of Zalasta's life, Anarae?" he asked her. "Sephrenia in particular is deeply saddened by what he revealed in the throne room. Maybe if she knows the reason for his actions, she'll find them easier to understand."

"I can speak for myself, Sparhawk," Sephrenia told him tartly.

"I'm sure you can, little mother. I was just serving as an intermediary. You and Xanetia don't get on too well."

"What's this?" Sarabian asked quickly.

"An ancient enmity, your Majesty," Xanetia explained. "So ancient, in truth, that none living knoweth its source."

"*I* know," Sephrenia grated at her, "and it's not as ancient as all that."

"Perhaps, but hearken unto the mind of Zalasta, and judge for thyself, Sephrenia of Ylara."

Kalten and Ulath returned and quietly took their seats again.

"Zalasta was born some few centuries ago in the Styric village of Ylara, which lay in the forest near Cenae in northern Astel," Xanetia began. "In his seventh year was there born also in that selfsame village she whom we know as Sephrenia, one of the Thousand of Styricum, tutor to the Pandion Knights in the secrets of Styricum, councillor of Elenia, and beloved of Preceptor Vanion."

"That's no longer true," Sephrenia said shortly.

"I spoke of Lord Vanion's feelings for *thee*, Sephrenia, not of thine for him. Zalasta's family was on friendly terms with Sephrenia's, and they did conclude between them that when Sephrenia and Zalasta should reach a suitable age, they would be wed."

"I'd forgotten about that," Sephrenia said suddenly. "I've never really thought of him that way."

"It hath been the central fact of his life, however, I do assure thee. When thou wert in thy ninth year didst thy mother conceive, and the child she bore was in truth Aphrael, Child-Goddess of Styricum, and in the instant of her birth did Zalasta's hopes and dreams turn to dust and ashes, for thy life was forever given over entirely to thine infant sister. Zalasta's wrath knew no bounds, and he did hide himself in the forest, lest his countenance betray his innermost thoughts. Much he traveled, seeking out the most powerful magicians of Styricum, even, at peril of his soul, those outcast and accursèd. His search had but one aim, to discover some means whereby a man might overthrow and destroy a God; for his despair drove him to an unreasoning hatred of the Child-Goddess; and, more than anything, he sought her death."

Princess Danae gasped aloud.

"You're supposed to be listening," her mother said.

"I was startled, Mother."

"You must never show that. Always keep your emotions under control."

"Yes, Mother."

"It was in the sixth year of the life of the Child-Goddess—in that particular incarnation—that Zalasta, in a frenzy of frustration, since all with whom he had spoken had told him that his goal was beyond human capability, turned to more direct means. Hoping perhaps that the Child-Goddess might be caught unawares or that by reason of her tender years might she not yet have come into her full powers, conceived he a reckless plan, an attempt to o'erwhelm her with sheer numbers. Though the Goddess herself is immortal, thought he that mayhap might her *incarnation* be slain, forcing her to seek another vessel for her awareness."

"Would that work?" Kalten asked Sparhawk.

"How should I know?" Sparhawk threw a guarded glance at his daughter.

Danae very casually shook her head.

"In furtherance of his hasty and ill-conceived scheme did Zalasta assume the guise of an Elene clergyman and did visit the rude villages of the serfs of that region and did denounce the Styrics of his own village, describing them as idolaters and demon-worshippers, whose foul rites demanded the blood of Elene virgins. So hotly did he inflame them with his false reports that on a certain day did the ignorant serfs gather, and swept they down upon that innocent Styric village, slaughtering all and putting their houses to the torch."

"But that was Sephrenia's home, too!" Ehlana exclaimed. "How could he be sure that she wouldn't be killed as well?"

"He was beyond caring, Queen of Elenia. Indeed, it was his thought that better far should she die than that Aphrael should have her. Better a grief that would pass than endless unsatisfied longing. But as it came to pass, the Child-Goddess had besought her sister that very morning that they two should go into the forest to gather wildflowers, and thus it was that they were not there when the Elene serfs fell upon the village."

"Zalasta told me the story once," Sparhawk interrupted. "He said that he was with Sephrenia and Aphrael in the forest."

"Nay, Anakha. He was at the village, directing the search for the two."

"Why would he lie about something like that?"

"Mayhap he doth lie even to himself. His acts that day were monstrous, and it is in our nature to obscure such behavior from ourselves."

"Maybe that's it," he conceded.

"Ye may well perceive the depths of Zalasta's hatred and despair when thou knowest that his own kindred perishèd there," Xanetia continued. "Yea, his father and his mother and sisters three fell beneath the cudgels and scythes of the ravening beasts he had unleashèd, even as he looked on."

"I don't believe you!" Sephrenia burst out.

"Bhelliom can confirm my truth, Sephrenia," Xanetia replied calmly, "and if I have broken faith by lying, Sir Kalten stands ready to spill out my life. Put me to the test, sister."

"He told us that the serfs had been inflamed against our village by *your* people—by the Delphae!"

"He lied unto thee, Sephrenia. Great was his chagrin when he discoverèd that Aphrael—and thou—didst still live. Seizing upon the first thought which came to him, he did shift his own guilt to *my* kindred, knowing that thou wouldst surely believe the worst of those whom thou wert already predisposèd to hate. He hath deceived thee since childhood, Sephrenia of Ylara, and would deceive thee still, had not Anakha forced him to reveal his true self."

"That's why you hate the Delphae, isn't it, Sephrenia?" Ehlana asked shrewdly. "You thought that *they* were the ones responsible for the murder of your parents."

"And Zalasta, ever striving to conceal his own guilt, lost no opportunity to remind her of that lie," Xanetia said. "In truth hath he poisoned her thoughts against the Delphae for centuries, filling her heart with hatred, lest she question him concerning his own involvement."

Sephrenia's face twisted, and she bowed her head, buried her face in her hands, and began to weep.

Xanetia sighed. "The truth hath made her grief all new. She weeps for her parents, dead these many centuries." She looked at Alean. "Take her somewhat apart, gentle child, and comfort her. She hath much need of the ministrations of women presently. The storm of her weeping will soon pass, and then woe unto Zalasta should he ever fall into her hands."

"Or mine," Vanion added bleakly.

"Boiling oil is good, my Lord," Kalten suggested. "Cook him while he's still alive."

"Hooks are good, too," Ulath added. "Long ones with nice sharp barbs on them."

"Must you?" Sarabian said with a shudder.

"Zalasta hurt Sephrenia, your Majesty," Kalten told him. "There are twenty-five thousand Pandion Knights—and quite a few knights from the other orders as well—who are going to take that very personally. Zalasta can pull mountain ranges over his head to try to hide, but we'll still find him. The Church Knights aren't really very civilized, and when somebody hurts those we love, it brings out the worst in us."

"Well said," Sparhawk murmured.

"We're getting afield here, gentlemen," Ehlana reminded them. "We'll decide Zalasta's punishment after we catch him. When did he become involved in this current business, Xanetia? Is he really allied with Cyrgon?"

"The alliance was of Zalasta's devising, Queen of Elenia. His failure in the forest of Astel and his own guilt arising therefrom did plunge him into deepest despair and blackest melancholy. He roamed the world, losing himself at times in vilest debauchery and at times dwelling alone and hermitlike in the wilderness of this world for decades on end. He sought out every Styric magician of reputation—good or ill—and gleaned from them *all* of the secrets. In truth, of all the Styrics who have ever lived in the forty eons of the history of their race, Zalasta is preeminent. But knowledge alone consoled him not. Aphrael lived still, and Sephrenia was ever bound to her.

"But the knowledge of Zalasta, which is beyond measure, did suggest to him a means by which he might break those bonds. At the dawn of time in far Thalesia had the Troll-Dwarf

Ghwerig wrought Bhelliom, and Zalasta knew that with Bhelliom's aid might he gain his heart's desire.

"Then came the birth of Anakha, signaling that Bhelliom itself would soon emerge from the place where it had lain hidden, and by signs and oracles and diverse other means did outcast Styrics perceive his birth, and counseled they Zalasta, instructing him to journey straightway to Eosia to observe Anakha throughout his childhood and youth that he might know him better, for it was the hope of Zalasta that in the day that Anakha did bring the flower-gem to light, might he wrest it from him and thereby gain the means to prevail over the Child-Goddess. But on the day when the ring did come into Anakha's possession, did Zalasta perceive his error. Well had the Troll-Gods wrought when they guided Ghwerig in the carving of the sapphire rose. Man is capricious and inconstant, and covetousness doth ever lurk in his heart, and Trolls are but reflections of the worst in men. Thus did the Troll-Gods make the rings the key to Bhelliom, lest any or all have power to command it. Thus did Aphrael disarm Ghwerig by stealing the rings, and thus did she scatter the power of the jewel that no mortal might command it. Thinking that their own power was absolute, the Troll-Gods had no interest in the flower-gem, and distrustful each of the others, they laid enchantments upon the stone to ensure that no one of them might take up Bhelliom unless all did. Only in concert might they command it, and they contrived it so that *they*, as Gods acting in concert, could command Bhelliom *without* the rings." She paused, reflecting, Sparhawk realized, on the peculiarities of the Troll-Gods.

"Now truly," she went on, "the Troll-Gods are elementals, each so limited that his mind may in no wise be considered whole and complete. Only when united, which doth rarely happen, can they by combination achieve that wholeness we see in the merest human child. For the other Gods, however, it is not so. The mind of Azash was whole and complete, despite his maiming, and in his wholeness had he the power to command Bhelliom without the rings. This then was the peril which did confront thee, Anakha, when thou didst journey to Zemoch to meet with him. Had Azash wrested Bhelliom from thee, he could have compelled it to join its will and its power with his."

"That might have been a bit inconvenient," Kalten noted.

"I don't quite understand," Talen said. "The last few times he's used it, Sparhawk's been able to get Bhelliom to do what he wants it to do *without* using the rings. Does that mean that Sparhawk's a God?"

"Nay, young sir." Xanetia smiled. "Anakha is of Bhelliom's devising and is therefore in some measure a *part* of Bhelliom—even as are the rings. For him, the rings are not needful. Zalasta did perceive this. When Anakha slew Ghwerig and took up the Bhelliom did Zalasta intensify his surveillance, ever using the rings as beacons to guide him. Thus did he observe Anakha's progress, and thus did he watch Anakha's mate as well."

"All right, Sparhawk," Ehlana said in a dangerous tone, "how did you get my ring? And what's this?" She extended her hand to show him the ruby adorning her finger. "Is it some cheap piece of glass?"

He sighed. "Aphrael stole your ring for me," he replied. "She's the one who provided the substitute. I doubt that she'd have used glass."

She pulled the ring off her finger and hurled it across the room. "Give it back! Give me back my ring, you thief."

"*I* didn't steal it, Ehlana," he protested. "Aphrael did."

"You took it when she gave it to you, didn't you? That makes you an accessory. Give me back my ring!"

"Yes, dear," he replied meekly. "I meant to do that, but it slipped my mind." He took out the box. "Open," he told it. He did not touch his ring to the lid. He wanted to find out if the box would open at his command alone.

It did. He took out his wife's ring and held it out to her.

"Put it back where it belongs," she commanded.

"All right. Here, hold this." He gave her the box, took her hand, and slipped the ring onto her finger. Then he reached for the box again.

"Not just yet," she said, holding it out of his reach. She looked at the sapphire rose. "Does it know who I am?"

"I think so. Why don't you ask it? Call it Blue-Rose. That's what Ghwerig called it, so it's familiar with the name."

"Blue-Rose," she said, "do you know me?"

There was a momentary silence as Bhelliom pulsed, its azure glow dimming and then brightening.

"Anakha," Talen said in a slightly wooden voice, "is it thy desire that I respond to the questions of thy mate?"

"It were well that thou didst, Blue-Rose," Sparhawk replied. "She and I are so intertwined that her thoughts are mine and mine hers. Whether we will or no, we are three. Ye two should know one another."

"This was not my design, Anakha." Talen's voice had an accusing note in it.

"The world is ever-changing, Blue-Rose," Ehlana said, "and there is no design so perfect that it cannot be improved." Her speech, like Sparhawk's, was profoundly formal. "Some there are who have feared that I might imperil my life should I touch thee. Is there in truth such peril?"

The wooden expression slid off Talen's face to be replaced with a look of bleak determination. "There is, mate of Anakha." The note in Talen's voice was as hard and cold as steel. "Once did I relent and once only. After ages uncounted of lying imprisoned in the earth, I did permit Ghwerig to lift me from the place where I had lain. This shape, which is so pleasing unto thee, was the result. With cruel implements of diamond and accursed red iron did Ghwerig carve and contort me, living, into this grotesque form. I *must* submit to the touch of a God; I willingly submit to the touch of Anakha in the sure and certain hope that he will liberate me from this shape which hath become my prison. It is death for any other."

"Couldn't you—?" She left it hanging.

"No." There was an icy finality in it. "I have no reason to trust the creatures of this world. The death that lieth in my touch shall remain, and also the lure which doth incline all who see me to touch me. They who see me will yearn to touch me and they will eagerly reach forth their hands—and die. The dead have no desire to enslave me; the living are not to be trusted."

She sighed. "Thou art hard, Blue-Rose," she said.

"I have reason, mate of Anakha."

"Someday, mayhap, we will learn trust."

"It is not needful. The achievement of our goal doth not hinge upon it."

She sighed again and handed the box back to her husband. "Please go on, Xanetia. That shadow that was pestering Sparhawk and me was Zalasta, then? At first we thought it was Azash—and then, later on, the Troll-Gods."

"The shadow was Zalasta's mind, Queen of Elenia," Xanetia replied. "A Styric spell known to very few doth make it possible for him thus to observe and listen unseen."

"I'd hardly call it unseen. I saw the edges of him every single time. It's a very clumsy spell."

"That was Bhelliom's doing. It sought to warn Anakha of Zalasta's presence by making him partially visible. Since one of the rings was on thy hand, the shadow of Zalasta's mind was also visible to *thee*." She paused. "Zalasta was afeared," she went on. "It was the design of the minions of Azash to lure Anakha—with Bhelliom in his grip—to go even unto Zemoch where Azash might take the jewel from him. Should that have come to pass, Zalasta's one hope of defeating Aphrael and possessing Sephrenia would have been forever dashed. In truth, Anakha, were all the impediments heaped in thy path to Zemoch of Zalasta's devising."

"I sort of wondered about that," Sparhawk mused. "Martel was being inconsistent, and that wasn't at all like him. My brother was usually as single-minded as an avalanche. We thought it was the Troll-Gods, though. *They* had plenty of reason not to want Bhelliom to fall into the hands of Azash."

"Zalasta wished thee to believe so, Anakha. It was yet another means whereby he could conceal his own duplicity from Sephrenia, and her good opinion of him was most important. In short, thou didst win thy way through to Zemoch and didst destroy Azash there—along with diverse others."

"We did *that*, all right," Ulath murmured. "Whole *groups* of diverses."

"Then was Zalasta sore troubled," Xanetia continued, "for Anakha had come to full realization of his power to control Bhelliom, and with that realization had he become as dangerous as any God. Zalasta could no more confront him than he could confront Aphrael. And so it was that he went apart from all other men to consider his best course of action, and to consult with certain outcasts of his acquaintance. The destruction of Azash had confirmed their surmise: Bhelliom *could*, in fact, confront and destroy the Gods. The means of the death of Aphrael was at hand, could Zalasta but obtain it. That means, however, was in the hands of the most dangerous man on life. Clearly, if Zalasta wished to achieve his goal, he must needs ally himself with a God."

"Cyrgon," Kalten guessed.

"Even so, my protector. The Elder Gods of Styricum, as ye have discovered, were powerless by reason of their lack of worshippers. The Troll-Gods were confined, and the Elene God was inaccessible, as was Edaemus of the Delphae. The Tamul Gods were too frivolous, and the God of the Atans too inhospitable to save his own children. That left Cyrgon, and

Zalasta and his cohorts did immediately perceive a means by which he might strike a bargain with the God of the Cyrgai. With Bhelliom might Cyrgon lift the Styric curse which confined his children and unleash them upon the world. In return, Zalasta believed, might Cyrgon be persuaded to permit him to use Bhelliom to destroy Aphrael, or, at the very least, to raise it against Aphrael with his own divine hand."

"It would have been a reasonable basis for opening negotiations," Oscagne conceded. "I'd take that kind of bargain to the table and expect a hearing at least."

"Perhaps," Itagne said dubiously, "but you'd have to live long enough to get to the table first. I don't imagine that the appearance of a Styric in Cyrga would have moved the population there to enthusiastic demonstrations of welcome."

"It was in truth a perilous undertaking, Itagne of Matherion. By diverse means did Zalasta gain entrance into the Temple of Cyrgon in the heart of the hidden city, and there did he confront the blazing spirit of Cyrgon himself and stay the God's vengeful hand with his offer of the liberation of the Cyrgai. The enemies at once became allies by reason of their mutual desires, and concluded they that Anakha must be lured to Daresia, for in no wise would they risk confrontation with the God of the Elenes, whose power, derived from his countless worshippers, is enormous. Conceived they then their involuted plan to disrupt all of Tamuli by insurrection and by apparition so that the imperial government must seek aid, and Zalasta's position of trust would easily enable him to direct the attention of the government to Anakha and to suggest accommodation with the Church of Chyrellos. The apparitions to be raised were no great chore for Zalasta of Styricum and his outcast comrades; nor was the deceit whereby Cyrgon persuaded the Trolls that their Gods commanded them to march across the polar ice to the north coast of Tamuli, an impossible task for the God of the Cyrgai. More central to their plans, however, were the insurrections which have so sorely marred the peace of Tamuli in recent years. Insurrection, to be successful, must be tightly controlled. Spontaneous uprisings seldom succeed. History had persuaded Zalasta that central to the success of their plan would be the character and personality of he who would unite the diverse populations of the kingdoms of the Tamul Empire and fire them with his force and zeal. Zalasta did not have far to seek to find such an one. Straightway upon his departure from Cyrga did he journey to Arjuna, and there presented he his plan to one known as Scarpa."

"Hold it," Stragen objected. "Zalasta's plan involved high treason at the very least. It probably involved crimes they haven't even named as yet—'consorting with ye powers of Darknesse' and the like. How did he know he could trust Scarpa?"

"He had every reason, Stragen of Emsat," she replied. "Zalasta knew that he could trust Scarpa as he could trust none other on life. Scarpa, you see, is Zalasta's own son."

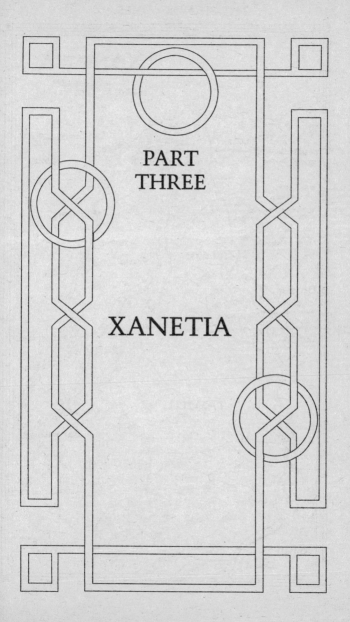

PART THREE

XANETIA

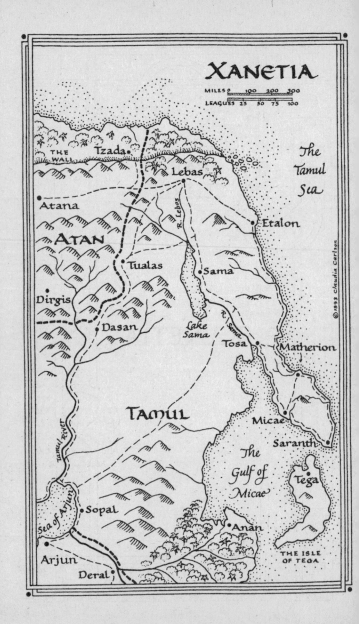

CHAPTER TWENTY-ONE

Sephrenia sat alone on the bed in her room. Her self-imposed isolation, she sadly concluded, would probably continue for the rest of her life. She had spoken in anger and haste, and this empty solitude was the consequence. She sighed.

Sephrenia of Ylara. It was strange that both Xanetia and Cedon had reached into the past for that archaic name, and stranger still that it should touch her heart so deeply.

Ylara had not been much of a village, even by Styric standards. Styrics had long sought to divert the hostility of Elenes by posing as the poorest of the poor, living in hovels and wearing garments of the roughest homespun. But Ylara, with its single muddy street and clay and wattle huts, had been home. Sephrenia's childhood there had been filled with love, and that love had reached its culmination with the birth of her sister. At the moment of Aphrael's birth, Sephrenia had found at once fulfillment and life-long purpose.

The memory of that small, rude village and its warmth and all-encompassing love had sustained her through dark days. Ylara, glowing in her memories, had always been a refuge to which she could retreat when the world and all its ugliness pressed in around her.

But now it was gone. Zalasta's treachery had forever fouled

and profaned her most precious memories. Now, whenever she remembered Ylara, Zalasta's face intruded itself; and now she saw his face for what it truly was—a mask of deceit and lust and a vile hatred for the Child-Goddess who was at the core of Sephrenia's very being.

Her memories had preserved Ylara; the revelation of Zalasta's corrupt duplicity had forever destroyed it.

Sephrenia buried her face in her hands and wept.

Sparhawk and Vanion found Princess Danae brooding alone in a large chair in a darkened room. "No," she replied emphatically to their urgent request, "I will *not* interfere."

"Aphrael," Vanion pleaded with tears standing in his eyes, "it's killing her."

"Then she'll just have to die. I can't help her. She has to do this by herself. If I tamper in any way at all, it won't mean anything to her, and I love her too much to coddle her and steal away the significance of what she's suffering."

"You don't mind if *we* try to help her, do you?" Sparhawk asked her tartly.

"You can try if you want—as long as you don't use Bhelliom."

"You're a very cruel little girl, did you know that? I didn't really intend to raise a monster."

"You're not going to change my mind by calling me names, Sparhawk—and don't try to sneak around behind my back, either. You can hold her hand or give her flowers or kiss her into insensibility if you want, but leave the Bhelliom right where it is. Now go away and leave me alone. I'm not enjoying this." And she curled up in her chair with her arms tightly wrapped around the battered Rollo and a look of ancient pain in her dark, luminous eyes.

"Zalasta's been interfering with us for a long time, hasn't he, Anarae?" Bevier asked the following morning when they had gathered once again in the blue-draped sitting room. They all wore more-casual clothing now, and the long table against the far wall was set with a breakfast buffet. Queen Ehlana had discovered a long time ago that meals did not necessarily have to interfere with important matters. Bevier's blue doublet was open at the front, and he was sunk low in his chair with his legs stretched out in front of him. "If he's been behind that shadow and the cloud, that would almost have to mean that he was involved in the Zemoch war, wouldn't it?"

Xanetia nodded. "Zalasta's scheming is centuries old, Sir Knight. His passion for Sephrenia dates back to his childhood, as doth his hatred for Aphrael, whose birth did dash all his hopes. Well he knew that should he confront the Child-Goddess directly, she could will away his very existence with a single thought. He knew that his lust was unwholesome, and that no God would be inclined to aid him in his struggle with Aphrael. Long he pondered this, and he concluded that his design required aid from some source with power, but without conscience or will of its own."

"Bhelliom," Sparhawk said. "Or at least that's how everyone saw it. We know differently now."

"Truly," she agreed. "Zalasta did share the common misperception of the jewel, thinking it to be a source of power only. He did believe that Bhelliom, untouched by morality, would obey him without question, and that it would destroy his mortal enemy and thus he could come to possess his heart's lust—for mistake me not, Zalasta sought possession of Sephrenia, not her love."

"That's vile," Baroness Melidere said with a shudder.

Xanetia nodded her agreement. "Zalasta knew that he must needs have the rings to command the sapphire rose," she went on, "but all of Styricum knew that the nimble Child-Goddess herself had purloined the rings from Ghwerig the Troll-Dwarf to prevent the misshapen creature from raising Bhelliom 'gainst the Styrics. Thus did Zalasta feign continuing friendship for Sephrenia and her sister, hoping to gain knowledge of the location of the rings and thus the keys to Bhelliom. Now the Gods had known, and some few humans as well, that one day Bhelliom's creature Anakha would appear, and by diverse signs and auguries did they divine that he would be born of the house of Sparhawk.

"Aphrael was wary, for she knew that the house of Sparhawk was Elene, and Elenes are not kindly disposed toward Styricum. She knew, however, that one day Anakha would come, and that he would raise Bhelliom from the place where it had lain hidden and wield it to his own purposes—and to the purposes of Bhelliom itself. She was troubled by this, for should Anakha share the common Elene despite of Styricum, might he raise the jewel against her worshippers. She sought to diminish that peril by separating the rings, placing one in the hands of Anakha's ancestor and the other elsewhere, so that when the one ring descended to Anakha, she might examine his heart and mind to determine whether it be safe to place both rings in his possession."

"Stories are more exciting when you know the people involved, aren't they?" Talen noted, filling his plate for the third time. Talen was growing again and he ate almost constantly. He *did*, however, remember his manners well enough to take a plate of sliced fruit and a glass of milk to Xanetia before he sat down to gorge himself.

Sparhawk phrased his question carefully. "I seem to remember that you once told me that you can't hear the thoughts of the Gods, Anarae. How is it that you know what Aphrael was thinking?"

"It is true that the thoughts of the Gods are veiled from me, Anakha, but Aphrael hath few secrets from her sister, and it is from Sephrenia's memories that I have gleaned what I have told ye.

"Now," she went on with her account, "Anakha's ancestor was a Pandion Knight dwelling with his brethren in the motherhouse of his order in the city of Demos in Elenia, and joined he in the war of the rash young king Antor against certain rebellious barons. And it came to pass that the knight and the king, separated from their companions, lay sorely wounded on the bloody field of battle. As darkness fell upon that field, did Sephrenia of Ylara, commanded by her sister, come reluctantly to bind their wounds and to deliver up the rings—one to each of them. She did conceal the true import of the rings, advising them that they were but tokens of their friendship, and by means of a Styric spell did she stain the rings with the mingled blood of the wounded pair to conceal their true nature and import. Thus did she bind the two houses together, which binding did prepare the way for the union of Anakha and his queen."

Ehlana beamed smugly at her husband. "I told you so," she said.

"I didn't quite follow that."

"I told you that we were destined to marry. Why did you keep arguing with me?"

"It seemed like the thing to do. I was fairly sure you could have done better." It was a slightly flippant reply, and it concealed his shocked surprise. Obviously Aphrael was absolutely ruthless in her manipulation of people's lives. Anakha was Bhelliom's creature, and the Child-Goddess, not certain she could trust him, had deliberately arranged to be born as his daughter so that she could in some measure control him.

"Now Zalasta, perceiving the intent of Aphrael, was troubled," Xanetia went on. "He had hoped to wrest Bhelliom from Anakha before Anakha could come to know the full import of his union with the stone, but Aphrael had once again blocked his design. By virtue of the rings and the mastery of Bhelliom which they conferred had Anakha been made invincible."

"All right, then," Ulath rumbled. "Zalasta was blocked. What did he do then?"

"There are some in Styricum—and have ever been—who, like the Elder Gods themselves, have used the power of the spells their race has learned to satisfy unwholesome personal desires. The Younger Gods are as children in this regard, and they cannot know the depths to which such as these will willingly sink. They are outraged by this coarser side of the nature of man, and such Styrics as display it are cast out and accursèd. These unfortunates dwell alone and sorrowing in wilderness and waste, or, all unrepentant, seek they their vile pleasure in the festering stews of the cities of this world. It was to these that Zalasta in desperation turned, and in Verel, foulest of the cities of southern Daconia, found he such a one as he sought."

"I've lived in Verel," Mirtai said. "That would be the place to look for degenerates, all right."

Xanetia nodded. "There in that sink of iniquity Zalasta did happen quite by chance upon one Ogerajin, a corrupt and ancient voluptuary. Now this Ogerajin was double-dipt in vileness, and by means of certain forbidden spells and enchantments had he reached into the darkness—yea, even into that ultimate corruption that lieth in the hearts of the Elder Gods. And Ogerajin, perceiving that Zalasta's lust was like his own and that they were therefore kindred, counseled him to seek out Otha of Zemoch."

Bevier gasped.

"Truly," Xanetia agreed. "And so did Zalasta journey even unto the city of Zemoch to make alliance with Otha."

"Hold it," Kalten said. "Didn't you tell us that Zalasta was trying to keep us *away* from Otha and Azash?"

She nodded. "Zalasta doth conclude alliances to further his *own* ends, not those of his allies. With Otha's aid he found other outcast Styrics in Eosia to aid him in keeping watch on the family of the Sparhawks, instructing them to seek out weaknesses which might be to his advantage when Anakha was born.

"As well ye might guess, Aphrael *also* set a watcher on those who would precede Sparhawk, and despite her sister's protests, the Child-Goddess sent Sephrenia to Demos to instruct the Elene Pandions in the Secrets of Styricum."

"Our charming little Aphrael has a heartless streak, I see," Stragen noted. "Considering what the Elene serfs in Astel did to Sephrenia's parents, sending her to Demos smacks of a certain lack of consideration."

"Who can know the mind of a God?" Xanetia sighed. She passed a weary hand across her eyes.

"Aren't you feeling well?" Kalten asked, his voice mirroring his concern.

"Some slight fatigue, Sir Kalten," she confessed. "The mind of Sephrenia was in great turmoil when I did gather in her memories, and it is with no small difficulty that I wring some consistency from them."

"Is that the way it works, Anarae?" Sarabian asked curiously. "You just reach in and swallow somebody else's mind whole?"

"Thy metaphor is inexact, Sarabian of Tamuli," she said in a slightly reproving tone.

"Forgive me, Anarae," he apologized. "I plucked it out of the air. What I meant to ask was whether you absorb the entire contents of another's awareness and memories with a single touch."

"Approximately, yes."

"How many minds have you got stored away?" Talen asked her. "Other people's minds, I mean?"

"Close on to a thousand, young master." She shrugged.

"Where do you find room?" He paused, looking just a little embarrassed. "I didn't say that very well, did I? What I was trying to ask was, Doesn't it get awfully crowded in there?"

"The mind is limitless, young master."

"*Yours* might be, Anarae." Kalten smiled. "I've found plenty of limits to mine, though."

"Is Sephrenia all right?" Vanion asked her with a worried frown.

"She is in great agony," Xanetia sighed. "Zalasta's treachery hath wounded her to the heart, and her mistaken belief that all of ye have forsaken her hath crushed her spirit."

"I'll go to her," Vanion said, rising quickly to his feet.

"No, my Lord," Kalten told him. "That wouldn't be a good idea. You're too close to her and if you went, you'd only make her feel worse. Why don't you let me go instead?"

"It's my place to go, Kalten."

"Not if it's going to make her suffer all the more, it isn't. Right now she needs to know that we still love her, and that means she needs somebody who's affectionate and not very bright. That's me, in case you hadn't noticed."

"You stop that!" Alean flared. "I won't have you saying things like that about yourself!" Then she seemed to realize that they were not alone, and she blushed and lowered her eyes in confusion.

"He might be right, Vanion," Ehlana said gravely. "Sir Kalten may have his faults, but he's straightforward and honest. Sephrenia knows that there's no deviousness in his nature. He's just too . . . too . . ."

"Stupid?" Kalten supplied.

"That's not the word I'd have chosen."

"It doesn't hurt my feelings, my Queen. They don't pay me to think—just to follow orders. When I try to think, I get in trouble, so I've learned to get along without thinking. I just trust my feelings instead. They don't lead me off in the wrong direction *too* often. Sephrenia knows me, and she knows I couldn't deceive her even if I tried."

"It's called sincerity, my friend." Sparhawk smiled.

"That's as good a word for it as any, I suppose." Kalten shrugged. "I'll just nip on down to her room and smother her with sincerity. That ought to make her feel better."

"It's me, Sephrenia. Kalten. Unlock the door."

"Go away." Her voice was muffled.

"This is important."

"Leave me alone."

Kalten sighed. It was going to be one of *those* days. "Please, little mother," he tried again.

"Just go away."

"If you don't open the door, I'll have to use magic on it."

"Magic? *You?*" She laughed scornfully.

Kalten leaned back, raised his right leg, and drove his booted heel against the latch. He kicked it twice more, and the door splintered and burst open.

"What are you *doing?*" she screamed at him.

"Haven't you ever seen Elene magic before, little mother?" he asked her mildly. "We use it all the time. You don't mind if I come in, do you?" He stepped through the splinter-littered doorway. "We thought you might be lonesome and that maybe you needed somebody to yell at. Vanion wanted to come, but I wouldn't let him."

"You? Since when have you started ordering Vanion around?"

"I'm bigger than he is—and younger."

"You get out of my room!"

"I'm sorry, but I can't do that." He glanced toward her window. "You've got a nice view from here. You can see all the way down to the harbor. Shall we get started? Screaming and hitting are all right, but please don't turn me into a toad. Alean wouldn't like that."

"Who sent you here, Kalten?"

"I already told you. It was my own idea. I wouldn't let Vanion come because you're upset right now. You might say something to him that you'd both regret later. You can say anything you want to *me*, Sephrenia. You can't hurt *my* feelings."

"Go away!"

"No, I won't do that. Would you like to have me make you a nice cup of tea?"

"Just leave me alone!"

"I already told you no." Then he took her by the shoulders and enfolded her in a huge bear hug. She struggled against him, but he was absolutely immovable. "Your hair smells nice," he noted.

She began to pound on his shoulders with her fists. "I *hate* you!"

"No, you don't," he replied calmly. "You couldn't hate me even if you wanted to." He continued to hold her. "It's been very mild this autumn, hasn't it?"

"*Please* leave me alone, Kalten."

"No."

She started to cry, clutching at his doublet and burying her face in his chest. "I'm so *ashamed*!" she wept.

"Of what? You didn't do anything wrong. Zalasta tricked you, that's all. He tricked the rest of us as well, so you're no more to blame than we are."

"I've broken Vanion's heart!"

"Oh, I don't think so—not really. You know Vanion. He can endure almost anything."

The storm of her weeping continued—which was more or less what Kalten had in mind. He pulled a handkerchief out of the sleeve of his doublet and gave it to her, still not relaxing his embrace.

"I'll never be able to face them again," she wailed.

"Who? You mean the others? Of course you will. You made a fool of yourself, that's all. Everybody does that now and then."

"How *dare* you!" She began to pound on him again.

Kalten *really* wished she'd get past that part of it. "It's true, though, isn't it?" he said gently. "Nobody's blaming you, but it's true all the same. You did what you thought was right, but it turned out to be wrong. Everybody's wrong sometimes, you know. There aren't any perfect people."

"I'm so ashamed!"

"You already said that. Are you sure you wouldn't like a nice cup of tea?"

"You should rest now, Anarae," Sarabian said solicitously. "I hadn't realized how exhausting this would be for you."

She smiled at him. "Thou art kind, Sarabian of Tamuli, but I am not so fragile as that. Let us proceed. It had been in the mind of Zalasta that he might by diverse inducements corrupt Anakha in his youth and thus gain access to Bhelliom without the need for perilous confrontation, but Sephrenia and Aphrael did closely attend the childhood and youth of Bhelliom's champion, once again and all unknowingly thwarting Zalasta's design.

"Then did Zalasta conclude that he had no choice but to approach Anakha as an enemy rather than a convert, and consulted he with Ogerajin and with Otha and went he even to Cimmura to seek allies to assist him. In furtherance of this did he pose as one of the numerous Zemoch Styrics Otha had sent into the Elene kingdoms to sow dissention and turmoil."

"There were plenty of those, all right," Ulath said. "Rumor had it that a Zemoch Styric could give an Elene anything he wanted—provided that the Elene wasn't too attached to his soul."

"The blandishments such Styrics offered were many," Xanetia agreed, "but the understanding of Otha's agents was limited."

"Profoundly limited," Vanion agreed.

"Truly. Zalasta, however, was more subtle, and far more patient. He did find an apt pupil in the person of the young chaplain to the royal house of Elenia, a priest named Annias."

"*Annias?*" Ehlana exclaimed. "I didn't know that he was ever the royal chaplain."

"It was before you were born," Sparhawk told her.

"*That* would explain why he had so much control over my father. Are you saying that Zalasta was behind all that, Anarae?"

Xanetia nodded.

"It isn't really all that easy to corrupt a young priest," Bevier objected. "They're usually filled with zeal and idealism."

"And Annias was no exception," Xanetia replied. "He was ambitious, but in his youth was he ever true to the ideals of his Church. That idealism stood in Zalasta's path until he found means to wear it away." She paused, flushing slightly. "I would not offend thee, Majesty," she apologized to Ehlana, "but thine aunt was ever lustful and wanton."

"It doesn't offend me in the slightest, Anarae," Ehlana replied. "Arissa's appetites were legendary in Cimmura, and I was never really all that fond of her in the first place."

"There was some connection, then?" Melidere asked.

"Indeed, Baroness," Xanetia replied. "Princess Arissa was the means whereby Zalasta recruited Annias to his cause. Well-schooled by the voluptuary Ogerajin, did Zalasta introduce the wanton princess to—" She broke off, blushing furiously.

"You needn't go into detail, Xanetia," Ehlana told her. "We all knew Arissa; there was nothing she wouldn't do."

"In truth was she an apt pupil," Xanetia agreed. "Now Zalasta concluded that Annias would be useful to him by reason of his position as adviser to thy father. Thus did he implant the firm belief in the mind of thy corrupt aunt that no act could be so vile as the seduction of a young priest. That notion, once implanted, did obsess Arissa, and 'ere long it bore fruit. In her twelfth year did Arissa steal away the dubious virtue of thy father's chaplain."

"At the age of *twelve*?" Melidere murmured. "She *was* precocious, wasn't she?"

"Then Annias was consumed with remorse," Xanetia continued.

"Annias?" Ehlana scoffed. "He didn't know what the word meant."

"You may be wrong there, my Queen," Vanion disagreed. "I knew Annias when he was a young man. He seemed committed to the principles of the Church. It wasn't until later that he began to change. Sparhawk's father and I always wondered what had happened to him."

"Evidently Arissa happened," Ehlana said dryly. She pursed her lips. "Then Zalasta gained access to Annias by means of my aunt?" she guessed.

Xanetia nodded. "The young priest, after much prayer and meditation, did resolve to renounce his vows and to wed the tarnished princess."

"A marriage made in heaven," Ulath noted sardonically.

"Arissa, however, would have none of such union, for so insatiable was her nature that she soon grew tired of her ecclesiastical paramour and did taunt him by reason of his waning prowess and stamina. At Zalasta's insinuating suggestion, however, did she bring her exhausted convert to a certain house in Cimmura, and there did Zalasta hint that he might restore the waning vigor of Annias by means of Styric enchantments. Thus did he secure a firm grip on the soul of he who would become Primate of Cimmura."

"We knew that Annias was getting help from one of Otha's Styrics," Sparhawk said. "We had no idea it was Zalasta, though. He had a hand in virtually everything, didn't he?"

"He is most clever, Anakha. Patiently did he instruct his two ever-more-willing pupils in that depravity which he himself had learned under the tutelage of Ogerajin of Verel. The royal chaplain was central to his plan, but first was it necessary to corrupt him beyond all hope of redemption."

"He did *that* part of it well enough," Ehlana said bleakly.

"Step by step did Arissa, guided by Zalasta, lead the chaplain down and down until all semblance of decency had been washed from him. Then it was that the Styric proposed the ultimate degeneracy—that the lustful princess, aided by her now equally foul paramour, should seduce thy father, her brother, and when he should be wholly in her thrall, should she broach the idea of incestuous marriage to him. Zalasta did well know that Anakha's father would resist such abomination to the death, and hoped he thereby to separate the house of Sparhawk from the royal house of Elenia. Reckoned he not, however, upon the iron will of the Sparhawks nor the weakness of King

Aldreas. The elder Sparhawk compelled thy father to wed another, but in truth had Zalasta's goal been achieved. A breach had been opened between the two houses."

"But we've healed that breach, haven't we, Sparhawk?" Ehlana said with a warm smile.

"Frequently," he replied.

"What can I *do*?" Sephrenia wailed, wringing her hands.

"You can stop doing that, for one thing," Kalten told her, gently separating her hands. "I found out a little while ago just how sharp your fingernails are, and I don't want you tearing off your skin."

She looked guiltily at the fresh scratches on his face. "I hurt you, didn't I, dear one?"

"It's nothing. I'm used to bleeding."

"I've treated Vanion so badly," she mourned. "He'll never forgive me, and I love him."

"Then tell him so. That's all you really have to do, you know. Just tell him how you feel about him, say you're sorry, and everything will go back to being the way it was before."

"It won't *ever* be the same."

"Of course it will. As soon as you two are back together, Vanion will forget it ever happened." He took her two small hands in his great ones, turned them over, and kissed her palms. "That's what love's all about, little mother. We all make mistakes. The people who love us forgive the mistakes. The people who won't forgive don't really matter, now, do they?"

"Well, no, but—"

"There aren't any buts, Sephrenia. It's so simple that even *I* can understand it. Alean and I trust our feelings, and it seems to work out fairly well. You don't really need complicated logic when it comes to something as simple as love."

"You're such a good man, Kalten."

That embarrassed him a bit. "Hardly," he replied ruefully. "I drink too much, and I eat too much. I'm not very refined, and I usually can't follow even a simple thought from one end to the other. God knows I've got faults, but Alean knows about them and forgives them. She knows that I'm just a soldier, so she doesn't expect too much from me. Are you just about ready for that cup of tea?"

"That would be nice." She smiled.

* * *

"Now *that* comes as a real surprise," Vanion said, "but why Martel?"

"Zalasta did perceive that of all the Pandions, Martel came closest to being a match for Anakha," Xanetia replied, "and Martel's hunger for the forbidden secrets provided Zalasta with an opening. The Styric did pose as an unlettered and greedy Zemoch, and did accept Martel's gold with seeming eagerness. Thus did he beguile the arrogant young Pandion until there was no turning back for him."

"And all this time he was posing as Otha's emissary?" Bevier asked her.

"Yes, Sir Knight. He served Otha's design so long as it suited him, but his heart and mind remained his own. Truly, he did corrupt Primate Annias and the Pandion Martel for his *own* ends, which did ever center upon that day when Anakha would lift Bhelliom from the place where it lay hidden."

"But it wasn't Anakha who lifted it, Anarae. It was Aphrael, and none of Zalasta's scheming could have taken that into account."

They all turned quickly at the sound of the familiar voice. Sephrenia, her face still drawn, stood in the doorway with Kalten hovering behind her. "Zalasta might possibly have been able to take the stone from Sparhawk, but not Aphrael. That's where everything fell apart on him. He couldn't bring himself to believe that *anyone*—even a God—would willingly surrender Bhelliom to someone else. Maybe someday I'll explain it to him."

"I have seen into the mind of Zalasta, Sephrenia of Ylara," Xanetia told her. "He could not comprehend such an act."

"I'll *make* him understand, Anarae," Sephrenia replied in a bleak voice. "I have this group of big savage Elenes who love me—or so they say. I'm sure that if I ask them nicely enough, they'll *beat* that understanding into Zalasta." And she smiled a wan little smile.

CHAPTER
TWENTY-
TWO

E hlana rose from her chair, went to Sephrenia, and kissed her palms in greeting. Sparhawk often marveled at how his young wife instinctively knew the right thing to do. "We've missed you, little mother," she said simply. "Are you feeling better now?"

A faint smile touched Sephrenia's lips. "Exactly how do you define *better*, Ehlana?" She looked closely at the blonde queen. "You're not getting enough sleep."

"You look a bit drawn yourself," Ehlana replied. "I suppose we both have reason enough."

"Oh, yes." Sephrenia looked around at the slightly apprehensive faces of her friends. "Oh, stop that," she told them. "I'm not going to throw a fit. I behaved badly." She reached up and fondly touched Kalten's cheek. "My overbearing friend here tells me that it doesn't matter, but I'd still like to apologize."

"You had plenty of reason to be upset," Sparhawk told her. "We were very abrupt with you."

"That's no excuse, dear one." She drew in a deep breath, squared her shoulders, and crossed the room to Xanetia with the air of one about to perform an unpleasant duty. "We don't really have any reason to be fond of each other, Anarae," she said, "but we should at least be civil. I wasn't. I'm sorry."

"Thy courage becomes thee, Sephrenia of Ylara. I do confess that I would be hard-pressed thus to admit a fault to an enemy."

"Exactly what did Sir Kalten do to bring you around, Lady Sephrenia?" Sarabian asked curiously. "You were in absolute despair, and Kalten wouldn't have been my first choice as a comforter."

"That's because you don't know him, Sarabian. His heart is very large, and he demonstrates his affection in a very direct way. He kicked my door down and smothered me into submission." She thought about it for a moment. "About all he really did was wrap his arms around me and tell me that he loved me. He kept saying it over and over again, and every time he said it, it struck me right to the heart. Elenes are very good bullies. I screamed at him for a while, and then I tried hitting him, but hitting Kalten is sort of like pounding on a brick. I even tried crying—I've always had good luck with crying—but all he did was offer to make me a cup of tea." She shrugged. "After a while, I realized that he was going to continue to love me no matter what I did and that I was making a fool of myself, so here I am." She smiled at Alean. "I don't know if you realize it, dear, but you may just be the luckiest woman in the world. Don't let him get away."

"No fear of that, Lady Sephrenia," the soft-eyed girl responded with a rosy blush.

Sephrenia looked around, suddenly all business. "I'm sure we have more important things to discuss than my recent temper tantrum. Have I missed much?"

"Oh, not really, dear sister," Stragen drawled. "About all we've discovered so far is that Zalasta's been responsible for nearly every catastrophe in human history since the fall of man. We don't have *quite* enough evidence to implicate him in *that* yet."

"We're a-workin' on it, though," Caalador added.

Sparhawk briefly summarized what Xanetia had told them of the hidden side of Zalasta. Sephrenia was startled to learn that it had been Zalasta who had corrupted Martel.

"I'm not trying to be offensive, dear sister," Stragen said, "but it seems to me that the Younger Gods weren't quite firm enough in dealing with these renegade Styrics. They seem to lend themselves to just about every bit of mischief that comes along. Something a bit more permanent than banishment might have been a better solution."

"The Younger Gods wouldn't do that, Stragen."

"Pity," he murmured. "That sort of leaves it up to us, doesn't it? We've got a group of people out there who are highly skilled at causing trouble." His expression grew sly. "Here's a notion," he said. "Why don't you have somebody draw up a list of names and give it to me. I'll see to it that the Secret Government takes care of all the messy details. We wouldn't even need to bother the Younger Gods or the rest of Styricum about it. You propose, and I'll dispose. Call it a personal favor if you like."

"You're a depraved man, Stragen."

"Yes. I thought you might have noticed that."

"What did Zalasta do after Sparhawk destroyed Azash?" Talen asked Xanetia. "Didn't that teach him that he'd be wiser to stay clear of our friend here?"

"He was much chagrined, young master. Anakha had demolished decades of patient labor in a single night and, with Bhelliom firmly in his grasp, he was more dangerous than ever. Zalasta's hopes of wresting the jewel from him were dashed, and he fled from Zemoch in rage and disappointment."

"And when he ran away, he missed seeing Sparhawk throw Bhelliom into the sea," the boy added. "So far as he knew, Sparhawk still had it in his pocket."

She nodded. "Returned he to Verel to consult with Ogerajin and diverse other renegades concerning this disastrous turn of events."

"How many of them are there, Lady?" Kalten asked, "and what are they like? It's always good to know your enemies."

"They are many, Sir Kalten, but four—in addition to Zalasta and Ogerajin—are most significant. They are the most powerful and corrupt in all of Styricum. Ogerajin is by far the foulest, but his powers are waning by reason of a loathsome disease which doth eat away at his mind." Xanetia suddenly looked uncomfortable and she even blushed. "It is one of those ailments which do infect those who engage overmuch in bawdry."

"Ah—" Sarabian came to her aid, "I don't know that we need to get too specific about Ogerajin's disease. Why don't we just say that he's incapacitated and let it go at that? Who are the others, Anarae?"

She gave him a grateful look. "Cyzada of Esos is the most versed in the darker aspects of Styric magic, Emperor Sarabian," she replied. "Residing close by the eastern frontier of Zemoch, had he frequent contacts with the half-Styric, half-Elene wizards of that accursèd land, and did he learn much from them. Reaches he with some facility into the darkness which did surround the mind of Azash, and he can summon certain of the creatures which served the Elder God."

"Damorks?" Berit asked. "Seekers?"

"The Damorkim perished with their master, Sir Knight. The fate of the Seekers is uncertain. Cyzada fears to summon such as they, for only Otha could surely control them."

"That's something, anyway," Khalad said. "I've heard some stories that I'd rather not have to confirm in person."

"In addition to Cyzada, Zalasta and Ogerajin have allied themselves with Ptaga of Jura, Ynak of Lydros, and Djarian of Samar," Xanetia continued.

"I've heard of them," Sephrenia said darkly. "I wouldn't have believed Zalasta could sink so low."

"Bad?" Kalten asked her.

"Worse than that. Ptaga's a master of illusion who can blur the line between reality and imagining. It's said that he conjures up the images of various women for the pleasure of the degenerates who pay him, and that the images are even better than reality could be."

"Evidently he's branching out," Oscagne noted. "It would appear that he's creating the illusions of monsters now instead of pretty ladies. That would explain all the vampires and the like."

"Ynak's reputed to be the most contentious man alive," Sephrenia went on. "He can start centuries-long feuds between families just by walking past their houses. He's probably behind the upsurge of racial hatred that's contaminating the Elene kingdoms to the west. Djarian is probably the preeminent necromancer in the world. It's said that he can raise people who never even really existed."

"Whole armies?" Ulath asked her, "like those antique Lamorks or the Cyrgai?"

"I doubt it," she replied, "although I can't be sure. It was Zalasta who told us it was impossible, and he may have been lying."

"I've got a question, Anarae," Talen said. "Can you *see* what Zalasta's thinking as well as hear it?"

"To some degree, young master."

"What are you getting at, Talen?" Sparhawk asked him.

"You remember that spell you used to put Krager's face in that basin of water back in Platime's cellar in Cimmura?"

Sparhawk nodded.

"A name's just a name," Talen noted, "and these particular Styrics probably aren't running around announcing themselves. Stragen suggested getting rid of them earlier. Wouldn't pictures make that a lot easier? If Xanetia can see Zalasta's memories of what those people look like and let me see them, too, I could draw pictures of them. Then Stragen could send the pictures to Verel—or wherever those Styrics are—and Zalasta would suddenly lose some people he's been counting on rather heavily. I think we owe him *that* much, anyway."

"I like the way this boy thinks, Sparhawk." Ulath grinned.

"Thy plan is flawed, young master," Xanetia said to Talen. "The spell of which thou didst speak is a Styric spell, and I have no familiarity with it."

"Sephrenia could teach it to you." He shrugged.

"You're asking the impossible, Talen," Bevier told him. "Sephrenia and Xanetia have only recently reached the point where they can be in the same room without wanting to kill each other. There's a lot of trust involved in teaching—and learning—spells."

Xanetia and Sephrenia, however, had been exchanging a long, troubled look. "Don't be too quick to throw away a good idea, Bevier," Sephrenia murmured. "It *has* got some possibilities, Anarae," she suggested tentatively. "The notion probably makes your skin crawl as much as it does mine, but if we could ever learn to trust each other, there could be all manner of things we might be able to accomplish. If we could combine your magic with mine . . ." She left it hanging.

Xanetia pursed her lips, and her expression oddly mirrored Sephrenia's. So intense was her consideration of the notion that her control slipped a bit, and her face began to glow. "The alliance between our two races *did* almost bring the Cyrgai to their knees," she noted, also rather tentatively.

"In diplomatic circles this is the point at which the negotiators usually adjourn so that they can consult with their governments," Oscagne suggested.

"The Anarae and I aren't obliged to get instructions from either Sarsos or Delphaeus, your Excellency," Sephrenia told him.

"Most diplomats aren't, either." He shrugged. "The announcement 'I must consult with my government' is merely a polite way of saying 'Your suggestion is interesting. Give me some time to think it over and get used to the idea.' You ladies are breaking new ground. I'd advise you not to rush things."

"What say you, Sephrenia of Ylara?" Xanetia said, smiling shyly. "Shall we pause for a fictional consultation with Sarsos and Delphaeus?"

"That might not be such a bad idea, Xanetia of Delphaeus," Sephrenia agreed. "And as long as we both know that it's fiction, we won't have to waste time waiting for nonexistent messengers to make imaginary journeys before we speak of it again."

"After the destruction of the city of Zemoch and all who dwelt there, did Zalasta and his cohorts meet in Verel to consider their course," Xanetia picked up the story after a brief recess. "Concluded they at once that they were no match for Anakha and Bhelliom. It was Ogerajin who did point out that Zalasta's tentative alliance had been with *Otha*, and that there had been no direct contact with Azash. He did speak slightingly to Zalasta concerning this and Zalasta's rancor regarding those words doth linger still."

"That's always useful," Vanion observed. "Dissention among your enemies can usually be exploited."

"The presence of the contentious Ynak doth heighten their discord, Lord Vanion. Ogerajin did berate Zalasta, demanding to know if he were so puffed up as to think himself the equal of a God, for Ogerajin doth consider Anakha to be such—or very nearly—because of his access to Bhelliom."

"How does it feel to be married-to a God, Ehlana?" Sarabian teased.

"It has its moments." She smiled.

"Cyzada of Esos then joined their discussion," Xanetia continued. "He did rather slyly suggest alliance with one or more of the myriad demigods of the netherworld, but his companions trusted him not, for he alone is conversant with the Zemoch spells which do raise and control such creatures of darkness. Indeed, trust is slight in that unwholesome company. Zalasta hath placed the ultimate prize before them and well doth he know that each of them doth secretly covet sole possession of the jewel. Theirs is an uneasy alliance at best."

"What did they finally decide to do, Anarae?" Kring asked. Sparhawk had noticed that the Domi seldom spoke at these meetings. Kring was not really comfortable indoors, and the subtleties of politics that so delighted Ehlana and Sarabian quite obviously bored him. Peloi politics were straightforward and simple—and usually involved bloodshed.

"It was the consensus of their deliberations that they might find—for a price—willing helpers in the imperial government itself," Xanetia replied.

"They were right about that," Sarabian said sourly. "If what we saw yesterday is any indication, my ministers were standing in line to betray me."

"It wasn't really personal, my Emperor," Oscagne assured him. "We were betraying each other, not you."

"Did anyone ever approach you?"

"Several, actually. They couldn't offer me anything I really wanted, though."

"Truth in politics, Oscagne?" his brother asked in feigned astonishment. "Aren't you setting a bad precedent?"

"Grow up, Itagne," Oscagne told him. "Haven't you learned by now that you can't deceive Sarabian? He claims to be a genius, and he's probably very close to being right—or will be as soon as we peel away his remaining illusions."

"Isn't that a blunt sort of thing to say, Oscagne?" Sarabian asked pointedly. "I'm right here, you know."

"Why, so you are, your Majesty," Oscagne replied with exaggerated astonishment. "Isn't that amazing?"

Sarabian laughed. "What can I do?" he said to Ehlana. "I need him too much to even object. Why didn't you tell me about this, Oscagne?"

"It happened when you were still feigning stupidity, your Majesty. I didn't want to wake you. I may have met this Ynak you've been talking about, Anarae. One of the men who approached me was Styric, and I've never met a more disagreeable individual. I've come across goats who smelled better, and the fellow was absolutely hideous. His eyes looked off in different directions, and his teeth were broken and rotting, and they all seemed to stick straight out. He looked like a man with a mouthful of brown icicles."

"Thy description doth closely match Zalasta's memories of him."

"That one shouldn't be too orful hord t' find, Stragen," Caalador drawled. "I kin send word t' Verel, iffn y' want. This yere Why-nack ain't likely t' be missed much if'n he's as onpleasant as the furrin minister sez."

Xanetia looked puzzled.

"It's a pose that amuses my colleague, Anarae," Stragen apologized. "He likes to put on the airs of a yokel. He *says* it's for the purposes of concealment, but I think he does it just to irritate me."

"Thine Elenes are droll and frolicsome, Sephrenia of Ylara," Xanetia said.

"I know, Anarae," Sephrenia sighed. "It's one of the burdens I bear."

"Sephrenia!" Stragen protested mildly.

"How did you put this fellow off without getting a knife in your back, your Excellency?" Talen asked Oscagne. "Declining that sort of offer is usually fatal."

"I told him that the price wasn't right," Oscagne shrugged. "I said that if he could come up with a better offer, I might be interested."

"Very good, your Excellency," Caalador said admiringly. "What kind of reason did he give you for making the offer in the first place?"

"He was a bit vague about it. He hinted about some kind of large-scale smuggling operation and said that he could use the help of the foreign service to smooth the way in various kingdoms outside Tamuli. He hinted that he'd already bought off the Interior Ministry and the customs branch of the Chancellory of the Exchequer."

"He was lying, your Excellency," Stragen told him. "There isn't that much money to be made in smuggling. It's a big risk for short pay."

"I rather thought so myself." Oscagne leaned back, stroking his chin thoughtfully. "This group of Styrics down in Verel may think they're very worldly, but they're like children when compared to *real* criminals and international businessmen. They cooked up a story that wasn't really very convincing. What they actually wanted was access to the government and the power of the various ministries in order to use that power to overthrow the government itself. The government had to be on the brink of collapse in order to get *me* to run off to Eosia to beg Prince Sparhawk to come here and save us."

"It worked, didn't it?" Itagne said bluntly.

"Well, yes, I suppose it did, but it was so clumsy. I'd personally be ashamed to accept such a shoddy victory. It's a matter of style, Itagne. Any amateur can blunder into occasional triumph. The true professional controls things well enough not to have to trust to luck."

* * *

They adjourned for the night not long after that. Sparhawk watched Sephrenia and Vanion rather closely as everyone filed out. The two of them exchanged a few tentative glances, but neither seemed ready to break the ice.

They gathered again the following morning, and Talen and Kalten seemed to be competing to see which of them could eat the most for breakfast.

After a bit of casual conversation, they got down to business again. "Right after the attempted coup here in Matherion, Krager paid me a visit," Sparhawk told Xanetia. "Was he telling the truth when he said that Cyrgon's involved in this?"

She nodded. "Cyrgon hath much reason to hate the Styrics and their Gods," she replied. "The curse which hath imprisoned his Cyrgai for ten eons hath enraged him beyond all measure. The outcast Styrics in Verel did share his hatred, for they, too, had been punished." She reflected a moment. "We all have reason to hate Zalasta," she said, "but we cannot question his courage. It was at peril of his life that he did carry the proposal of the renegades to the Hidden City of Cyrga to place it before Cyrgon himself. The proposal was simple. By means of Bhelliom could the curse be lifted and the Cyrgai loosed once more upon this world. The Styrics could be crushed, which would please both Cyrgon and the outcasts; the Cyrgai would come to dominate the world—with positions of honor and power reserved for Ogerajin and his friends; and Aphrael would be destroyed, thus giving possession of Sephrenia to Zalasta."

"Something for everybody," Sarabian said dryly.

"So thought Ogerajin and Zalasta," Xanetia agreed. "They had, however, reckoned not upon the nature of Cyrgon. They soon found that he would in no wise consent to the secondary role they had in mind for him. Cyrgon doth command; he doth not follow. He did set his high priest, one Ekatas, over his new allies, telling them that Ekatas spoke for him in all things. Zalasta did secretly laugh at the God's simplicity, thinking that the High Priest Ekatas would, like all the Cyrgai, die with the step which took him over the unseen line in the sand. Ekatas, however, had no need of crossing the line. With Cyrgon's aid did he travel with his *mind*, not his body, that he might observe and direct without leaving Cyrga. Truly, the mind of Ekatas can reach across vast distances, not only to convey the will of

Cyrgon, but to advise the diverse cohorts of what hath occurred elsewhere."

"That explains how the word that we were coming got from one end of Cynesga to the other so fast," Bevier said. "We sort of wondered how they were keeping ahead of us."

"Now," Xanetia pressed on, "though they are outcast and despised, Ogerajin and the others are still Styrics, and the Styrics are not a warlike people. Their efforts had concentrated on deception and misdirection previously. Cyrgon, however, is a war-God, and he did command them to raise armies to confront the Atans, who are the strong arm of the empire. Then were the outcasts of Verel nonplussed, for Cyrgon gave the command, but no guidance. Zalasta, who had traveled much in Eosia, did suggest to Ekatas that Cyrgon might deceive the Trolls and bring them to northern Tamuli, and Cyrgon did readily consent. Still he demanded more. Ynak of Lydros, who doth ever carry that cloud of dissention with him, could fan the fires of discontent in all of Tamuli, but so contentious is his nature that none would willingly follow him. Armies require generals, and Styrics are not gifted in that profession. I do not say this to give offense, Sephrenia," she added quickly. Both Xanetia and Sephrenia were being very careful with each other.

"I'm not offended, Xanetia. I *like* soldiers, mind you." Her eyes flickered toward Vanion. "Some of them, anyway. But I really think the world might be a nicer place without them."

"Bite your tongue," Ulath told her. "If we couldn't be soldiers, we'd all have to go out and find honest work."

Xanetia smiled. "It was in desperation—for Cyrgon did grow impatient—that Zalasta did journey to Arjuna to enlist his son Scarpa in the enterprise. Now Scarpa was unlike his father in that he did willingly—even eagerly—resort to violence. His years as a performer in shabby carnivals had taught him the skills of swaying crowds of people by eloquence and by his commanding presence. His profession, however, was held in low regard, and this did pain him deeply, for Scarpa hath an exalted opinion of himself."

"He does indeed, little Lady," Caalador agreed. "If what the thieves of Arjuna tell me is anywhere close to being accurate, Scarpa probably believes that he could fly or walk on water if he just set his mind to it."

"Truly," she agreed. "He hath, moreover, a deep contempt for the Gods and a profound hatred of women."

"That's not uncommon among bastards," Stragen said clinically. "Some of us blame our mothers—or our Gods—for our social unacceptability. Fortunately, I never fell into that trap. But then, I'm so witty and charming that I didn't have the usual inadequacies to try to explain away."

"I hate it when he does that," Baroness Melidere said.

"It's only a plain fact, my dear Baroness." He grinned at her. "False modesty is so unbecoming, don't you think?"

"Be clever on your own time, Stragen," Ehlana chided. "Did Zalasta tell his son *all* the details of this conspiracy, Anarae?"

"Yes, your Majesty. Given the nature of the two, there was surprising candor between them. Scarpa, however, was very young and had an exaggerated notion of his own cleverness. Zalasta did quickly realize that the rudimentary Styric spells which he had imparted to his son during his infrequent visits to Arjuna might serve to deceive rural bumpkins, but they would scarce be adequate for the business at hand. Therefore, took he his son to Verel to place him under the tutelage of Ogerajin."

"When was this, Anarae?" Caalador asked curiously.

"Perhaps five years since, Master Caalador."

"Then it fits together with what *we* found out. It was almost exactly five years ago that Scarpa disappeared from Arjuna. Then a couple of years later he came back and started stirring up trouble."

"It was a short education," Xanetia said, "but Scarpa hath a quick mind. In truth, it was his tutor who did suspend his training, for Ogerajin was much offended by the young man's arrogance."

"This Scarpa sounds like the sort you have to stand in line to hate," Talen noted. "I've never met him, and I already dislike him."

"Zalasta was also taken somewhat aback by his son's abrasive nature," Xanetia told them, "and thinking to awe him into some measure of civility, he did take him to Cyrga that he might come to know their master. Cyrgon did question the young man closely and then, evidently satisfied, did he instruct him in the task before him. Scarpa came away with no more respect for the God of the Cyrgai than he had felt 'ere they met, and Zalasta hath lost what small regard he previously had for his son. It is now in his mind that should their conspiracy succeed, Scarpa will not long survive the victory." She paused. "An it please thee to view it so, Sephrenia, thy vengeance hath already had its beginning. Zalasta is a hollow man with no

God and with none in all the world to love him or to call him friend. Even the scant affection he had for his son is now withered, and he is empty and alone."

Two great tears welled up in Sephrenia's eyes, but then she angrily dashed them away with the back of her hand. "It's not enough, Anarae," she said adamantly.

"You've spent too much time with Elenes, little mother," Sarabian said. That startled Sparhawk just a bit. He could not be sure if the brilliant, erratic Tamul emperor used that affectionate term deliberately, or if it had been a slip of the tongue.

"Who recruited the others, Anarae?" Vanion asked, smoothly moving away from a slightly touchy situation.

"It was Scarpa, Lord Vanion," she replied. "Cyrgon had directed him to seek out confederates to stir rebellion in western Tamuli, thus to bar the way should Anakha come with the armies of the Church, for Cyrgon would not willingly pit his cherished Cyrgai against such as you. Now Scarpa did know a certain out-at-the-elbows Dacite nobleman who, plagued by gambling debts and the ungentle urgings of his creditors to settle accounts, did flee from Daconia and conceal himself for a time in the very Arjuni carnival where Scarpa did practice his dubious art. This scruffy nobleman, Baron Parok by name, did Scarpa seek out on his return home from Cyrga. Parok, desperate out of all measure, soon willingly fell in with his former associate, for the inducements Scarpa offered were enticing. Consulted then the unscrupulous pair with the debauched Styrics at Verel and followed their counsel to seek out the merchant Amador in Edom and the poet Elron in Astel, both men being much taken with themselves and resentful of the station in life which fate had assigned them."

Bevier was frowning. "We've encountered both of them, Anarae, and neither one strikes me as a natural leader. Were they the best Scarpa could find?"

"Their selection was determined by their willingness to cooperate, Sir Knight. The ability to sway men with words and that commanding presence which doth draw all eyes can be elevated by certain Styric spells. Unimpressive though they are, it was the quality of desperation in them which Scarpa did seek. Both Amador and Elron suffered agonies by reason of their insignificance, and both were willing, even eager, to go to any lengths to exalt themselves."

"We see it all the time in Thalesia, Bevier," Ulath explained.

"We call it 'the little man's complaint.' Avin Wargunsson's a perfect example. He'd rather die than be ignored."

"Amador's not all that short," Talen pointed out.

"There are all kinds of littleness, Talen," Ulath said. "How did Count Gerrich in Lamorkand get involved, Anarae? And why?"

"He was recruited by Scarpa on Zalasta's instruction, Sir Ulath. Zalasta thought to stir discord and turmoil on the Eosian continent to persuade the Church of Chyrellos that her interests required that Anakha be dispatched to Tamuli to seek out the roots of the disturbances. Of all of them, only Zalasta hath his feet planted on both continents, and only he doth understand the thinking of thy Church. In truth, Elron and Amador are but pawns, knowing little of the true scope of the enterprise they have joined. Baron Parok is more knowledgeable, but he is still not privy to *all* their designs. Count Gerrich is peripheral. He follows his own purposes, which only occasionally match the purposes of his colleagues here in Tamuli."

"You almost have to admire them," Caalador said. "This is the most complicated and well-organized swindle I've ever heard of."

"But it all fell apart when Xanetia opened the door to Zalasta's mind," Kalten said. "As soon as we found out that he's been on the other side all along, the whole thing began to crumble." He thought of something. "How did Krager get mixed up in this?"

"Count Gerrich did suggest him to Scarpa," Xanetia replied. "Gerrich had found the one called Krager useful in times past."

"Yes," Ulath said. "We saw him being useful outside the walls of Baron Alstrom's castle in Lamorkand. Martel's still coming back to haunt us, isn't he, Sparhawk?"

"How much did my Minister of the Interior and the other traitors really know about all of this, Anarae?" Sarabian asked.

"Almost nothing, Majesty. In the main they did believe that their activities were but a part of the ongoing struggle between Foreign Minister Oscagne and Interior Minister Kolata. Kolata offered them profit, and so they did follow him."

"Ordinary palace politics, then," Sarabian mused. "I suppose I'll have to keep that in mind at their trials. They weren't really disloyal, only corrupt."

"All except for Kolata, your Majesty," Itagne noted. "His involvement had to have gone deeper than simple garden-variety political bickering, wouldn't it?"

"Kolata was a dupe, Itagne of Matherion," Xanetia corrected. "It was Teovin who was ever Zalasta's man at court. It was to *him* that the one called Krager did bring Zalasta's instruction, and Teovin did tell Kolata only so much as it was needful for him to know."

"This brings us to the coup attempt," Ehlana said. "Krager told Sparhawk that it wasn't intended to succeed—that it was only designed to force us to reveal our strengths and weaknesses. Was he actually telling the truth?"

"In part, Majesty," Xanetia replied. "In the main, however, was Zalasta uncertain about the truth of Anakha's declaration that he had cast Bhelliom into the sea. Sought he by raising rebellion in the streets of Matherion and endangering all whom Anakha held most dear to force him to reveal whether or no he still did possess the jewel."

"We played right into his hands by going after it, then, didn't we?" Khalad suggested.

"I don't think so," Sparhawk disagreed. "We'd never have found out about Bhelliom's awareness if we'd left it where it was. That's the thing that *nobody* knew about—except possibly Aphrael. Azash didn't seem to know about it, and neither does Cyrgon. I doubt that either one would have been so interested in it if they'd known that it might resist their commands—even to the point of obliterating this world if necessary."

"All right," Khalad said. "Now we know what's led up to all this. What happens next?"

"That lieth in the future, Khalad of Demos," Xanetia replied, "and the future is concealed from all. Know, however, that our enemies are in disarray. Zalasta's position as adviser to the imperial government was at the core of all their plans."

"How quickly will he be able to recover, Sephrenia?" Ehlana asked. "You know him better than anyone. Will he be able to strike back immediately?"

"Possibly," Sephrenia said, "but whatever he does won't be very well thought out. Zalasta's a Styric, and we don't react well to surprises. He'll flounder for a while—destroying mountains and setting lakes on fire—before he gets hold of himself."

"We should hit him again, then," Bevier observed. "We shouldn't allow him to recover his balance."

"Here's a thought," Sarabian said. "After we went through the secret files of the Interior Ministry, we decided to pick up only the top level of conspirators—the police chiefs and administrators in the various towns, for the most part. We didn't bother with the toadies and informers—largely because we didn't have enough jail space. The Interior Ministry was central to the whole conspiracy, I think, and now Zalasta and his friends will probably be forced to rely on the scrapings we left behind. If I send the Atans out to make a more thorough sweep, won't that push Zalasta off-balance all the more?"

"Let him start to settle down first, Sarabian," Sephrenia advised. "Right now he's so enraged that he probably wouldn't even notice."

"Is Norkan still on the Isle of Tega?" Vanion asked suddenly.

"No," Ehlana replied. "I got tired of the forged letters he was sending me from there, so we sent him back to Atan."

"Good. I think we'd better get word of Zalasta's treachery to him as quickly as possible. Betuana really needs to know about it."

"I'll see to it, Vanion-Preceptor," Engessa promised.

"Thank you, Engessa-Atan. If that little outburst in the throne room is any indication of his present state of mind, Zalasta's totally out of control right now."

"Infuriated to the brink of insanity," Sephrenia agreed. It was the first time she had spoken directly to Vanion since the rupture between them. That fact gave Sparhawk some hope.

"He'll almost have to do *something*, then, won't he?" Vanion asked her. "In his present state, inaction would be unbearable."

She nodded. "He'll respond in some way," she said, "and since he wasn't at all prepared for what just happened, whatever he does won't have been planned out in advance."

"So it'll have large holes in it, won't it?"

"Probably."

"Most likely it would involve the use of main force," Sparhawk added. "Enraged people usually try to smash things."

"You'd better alert Norkan and Betuana to the possibility, Engessa-Atan," Sarabian instructed.

"It shall be as you say, Sarabian-Emperor."

Vanion began to pace up and down. "Zalasta's still more or less in command," he said. "At least he will be until he does something so stupid that Cyrgon replaces him. Why don't we let him have his temper tantrum, crush it, and *then* round up all the minor conspirators? Let's frighten our opponents just a bit. If they see us methodically smashing everything they've gone to so much trouble to prepare and rounding up all their friends, they'll start having thoughts about their own mortality. At that point, I think Cyrgon's going to have to show himself, and then Sparhawk can turn Bhelliom loose on him."

"I hate it when he's like this," Sephrenia said to Xanetia. "He's so certain—and probably so right. Men are much more appealing when they're just helpless little boys." The casual-seeming remark was startling. Sephrenia was clearly stepping over ancient racial antagonisms between Styric and Delphae and speaking to Xanetia as one woman to another.

"Then all we really have to do is sit here and wait for Zalasta's next move," Sarabian observed. "I wonder what he's going to do."

They did not have to wait long for the answer. A few days later an exhausted Atan stumbled across the drawbridge with an urgent message from Ambassador Norkan.

"Oscagne," the message began with characteristic abruptness, "round up every Atan you can lay your hands on and send them all here. The Trolls are dismantling northern Atan right down to the very bedrock."

CHAPTER TWENTY-THREE

W e *can't* send them, Engessa-Atan," Sarabian said. "We need them right where they are. At the moment, they're all that's holding the empire together."

Engessa nodded. "I understand the situation, Sarabian-Emperor, but Betuana-Queen will only wait for so long. If the lands of the Atans are in peril, she will have no choice but to act. She will order the Atans home—despite her alliance with you."

"She's going to have to pull her people back," Vanion advised the huge Atan. "She doesn't have enough warriors to defend the north against the Trolls, so she may have to abandon northern Atan for a while. We won't be able to send full garrisons to her aid, but we *can* pull one or two platoons out of each garrison. That's several thousand warriors altogether, but it's going to take them longer to reach Atan because they're so spread out. She'll just have to pull back until we can get there."

"We are Atans, Vanion-Preceptor. We do not run away."

"I'm not suggesting that, Engessa-Atan. All your queen will be doing is repositioning her forces. She can't hold the north at the moment, and there's no point in wasting lives trying. The best we can do for her in the meantime is to send some Genidian advisers and Cyrinic technical assistance."

"Not quite, friend Vanion," Kring said. "I'll go to Tikume in central Astel. The eastern Peloi aren't as fearful of forests as my children are, and Tikume loves a good fight as much as I do, so he'll probably bring several thousand horsemen with him. I'll gather up a few hundred bowmen and come to Atan ahead of his main force."

"Your offer is generous, friend Kring," Engessa said.

"It's a duty, Engessa-Atan. You serve as Mirtai's father, and that makes us kinsmen." Kring absently rubbed his hand across his shaved scalp. "The bowmen are very important, I think. Your Atans have moral reservations about using bows in warfare, but when we met those Trolls in eastern Astel, we found out that you can't really fight them without shooting them full of arrows first."

"Here's another thought," Khalad said, holding up his crossbow. "How do your people feel about these, Engessa-Atan?"

Engessa spread his hands. "It is a new device here in Tamuli, Khalad-squire. We have not yet formed an opinion about it. Some Atans may accept it; others may not."

"We wouldn't have to arm *all* the Atans with crossbows," Khalad said. He looked at Sparhawk. "Will you be needing me here, my Lord?" he asked.

"Why don't you see if you can persuade me that I won't?"

"That's a cumbersome way to put it, Sparhawk. We've still got all those crossbows we gathered up when we put down the coup. I broke most of them, but it won't take me too long to fix them again. I'll go north with Engessa-Atan and the technical advisers. Engessa can try to persuade his people that the crossbow's a legitimate weapon of war, and I'll teach them how to use it."

"I'll join you in Atana later," Kring told them. "I'll have to lead Tikume's bowmen to the city. The Peloi tend to get lost in forests."

"Never mind, Mirtai," Ehlana told the giantess, whose eyes had suddenly come alight. "I need you here."

"My betrothed and my father are going to war, Ehlana," Mirtai objected. "You can't expect me to stay behind."

"Oh, yes, I can. You can't go, and that's final."

"May I be excused?" Mirtai asked stiffly.

"If you wish."

Mirtai stormed toward the door.

"Don't break *all* the furniture," Ehlana called after her.

* * *

It was really only a small domestic crisis, but it was a crisis all the same, largely because the Royal Princess Danae declared that she would die if her missing cat was not found immediately. She wandered tearfully around the throne room, climbing into laps, pleading and cajoling. Sparhawk was once again able to observe the devastating effect his daughter could have on someone's better judgment when she was sitting in the person's lap. "*Please* help me find my cat, Sarabian," she said, touching the emperor's cheek with one small hand. Sparhawk had long since learned that the first rule in dealings with Danae was never to let her touch you. Once she touched you, you were lost.

"We all need some fresh air anyway, don't we?" Sarabian said to the others. "We've been sitting in this room for more than a week now. Why don't we suspend our discussions and go find Princess Danae's cat. I think we'll all be fresher when we come back."

Score one for Danae. Sparhawk smiled.

"I'll tell you what," Sarabian continued. "It's a beautiful morning. Why don't we make an outing of it? I'll send word to the kitchens, and we can all have our lunches out on the lawns." He smiled down at Danae, whose hand might just as well have been wrapped around his heart. "We'll celebrate the return of Mmrr to her little mistress."

"What a *wonderful* idea!" Danae exclaimed, clapping her hands together. "You're *so* wise, Sarabian!"

They all smiled indulgently and rose to their feet. Sparhawk privately admitted that the emperor was probably right. The long day's conferences *were* beginning to make them all just a little fuzzy-headed. He went to his daughter and picked her up.

"I can walk, Father," she protested.

"Yes, but I can walk faster. My legs are longer. We *do* want to find Mmrr as soon as possible, don't we?"

She glared at him.

"You've got everybody under control," he murmured to her. "You don't have to herd them around like sheep. What's this all about? You can call Mmrr back home anytime you feel like it. What are you *really* up to?"

"There are some things I want to get settled before we get too busy, Sparhawk, and I can't do anything with all of you huddled together in this room like a flock of chickens. I need to get you all out of here so that I can straighten things out."

"Is Mmrr really lost?"

"Well, of *course* she isn't. I know exactly where she is. I just told her to go chase grasshoppers for a while."

"What sort of things were you talking about? Exactly what is it that you want to get straightened out?"

"Watch, Sparhawk," she told him. "Watch and learn."

"It's just not done, Kalten," Alean said in a sorrowfully resigned voice as the two walked out across the drawbridge with Sparhawk and Danae not far behind.

"What do you mean, 'not done'?"

"You're a knight, and I'm only a peasant girl. Why can't we just leave things the way they are?"

"Because I want to marry you."

She touched his face fondly. "And I'd give anything to be able to marry you, but we can't."

"I'd like to know why not."

"I told you already. We come from different social classes. A peasant girl can't marry a knight. People would laugh at us and say hateful things about me."

"Only once," he declared, clenching his fist.

"You can't fight the whole world, my love." She sighed.

"Of course I can—particularly if the world we're talking about consists of those butterflies that infest the court at Cimmura. I could kill a dozen of them before lunchtime."

"No!" she said sharply. "No killing! Can't you see what that would do? People would grow to hate me. We'd never have any friends. That's all right for you, because you'll be off at whatever war Prince Sparhawk or Lord Vanion sends you to, but I'll be completely alone. I couldn't bear that."

"I want to marry you!" he almost shouted.

"It would make my life complete as well, my dear love," she sighed, "but it's impossible."

"I want you to fix that, Sparhawk," Danae said out loud.

"Quiet! They'll hear us."

"They can't hear us, Sparhawk—or see us, either, for that matter."

"You're using a spell, I gather?"

"Naturally. It's a useful little spell that makes people ignore us. They kind of know we're here, but their minds don't pay any attention to us."

"I see. It tiptoes around the moral objection to eavesdropping, too, doesn't it?"

"What on earth are you talking about, Sparhawk? I don't

have any moral problems with eavesdropping. I *always* eavesdrop. How else am I supposed to keep track of what people are doing? Tell Mother to give Alean a title so that she and Kalten can get married. I'd do it myself, but I'm busy. Take care of it."

"Is *this* the sort of thing you were talking about earlier?"

"Of course. Don't waste time on all these silly questions, Sparhawk. We've got a lot more to do today."

"I *do* love you, Berit-Knight," Empress Elysoun said a little sadly, "but I love him, too."

"And how many *others* do you love, Elysoun?" Berit asked her acidly.

"I've lost count." The bare-breasted empress shrugged. "Sarabian doesn't mind. Why should you?"

"Then we're through? You don't want to see me any more?"

"Don't be ridiculous, Berit-Knight. Of *course* I want to see you again—as often as I possibly can. It's just that there are going to be times when I'll be busy seeing *him*. I didn't *have* to tell you this, you know, but you're so nice that I didn't want to go behind your back to ..." She groped for a word.

"To be unfaithful?" he said bluntly.

"I'm *never* unfaithful," she said indignantly. "You take that back right now. I'm the most faithful lady in the whole court. I'm faithful to at least a dozen young men, all at the same time."

He suddenly burst out laughing.

"What's so funny?" she demanded.

"Nothing, Elysoun," he replied with a genuine fondness. "You're so delightful that I can't help laughing."

She sighed. "Life would be so much simpler for me if you men wouldn't take these things so seriously. Love's supposed to be fun, but you all scowl and wave your arms in the air about it. Go love somebody else for a while. I won't mind. As long as everybody's happy, what difference does it make who *made* them happy?"

He smiled again.

"You *do* still love me, don't you, Berit-Knight?"

"Of course I do, Elysoun."

"There. Everything's all right, then, isn't it?"

"What was that all about?" Sparhawk asked his daughter. They were standing fairly close to Berit and Elysoun—close enough to make Sparhawk slightly self-conscious, at any rate.

"Berit was getting just a little too deeply involved with the naked girl," Danae replied. "He's learned what she could teach him, so it's time for their friendship to calm down a little. I have other plans for him."

"Have you ever considered letting him make his own plans?"

"Don't be ridiculous, Sparhawk. He'd just make a mess of things. I *always* take care of these arrangements. It's one of the things I do best. We'd better hurry. I want to look in on Kring and Mirtai. He's going to tell her something that isn't going to make her happy. I want to be there to head off any explosions."

They found Kring and Mirtai sitting on the lawn under a large tree ablaze with autumn color. Mirtai had opened the basket the kitchen had provided and was looking inside. "Some kind of dead bird," she reported.

Kring made a face. "I suppose it's civilized food," he said, trying to put the best face on it.

"We're both warriors, my betrothed," she replied, also looking less than happy with what had been prepared for their lunch. "We're supposed to eat red meat."

"Stragen told me once that you ate a wolf when you were younger," Kring said, suddenly remembering the story.

"Yes," she replied simply.

"Do you mean you actually *did*?" He seemed stunned. "I thought he was just trying to fool me."

"I was hungry—" she shrugged, "—and I didn't have time to stop. The wolf didn't taste very good, but he was raw. If I'd had time to cook him, he might have been better."

"You're a strange woman, my beloved."

"That's why you love me, isn't it?"

"Well—it's *one* of the reasons. Are you *sure* we can't talk about our problem?" He was obviously coming back to a subject they had discussed before—many times.

"There's nothing to talk about. We have to be married twice—once in Atana and then again when we get back to Pelosia. We won't be really married until we've gone through both ceremonies."

"We'll be *half* married after the ceremony in Atana, won't we?"

"Half-married isn't good enough, Kring. I'm a virgin. I've

killed too many men protecting that to settle for 'half-married.' You'll just have to wait."

He sighed. "It's going to take a long time, you know," he said mournfully.

"It's not *that* far from Atana back to your country. I'll race you there."

"It's not the journey that's going to take so long, Mirtai. It's the two months you'll have to spend in my mother's tent before the wedding in Pelosia. You'll have to learn our practices and ceremonies."

She gave him a long, steady look. "You said I have to *what*?" There was an ominous tone in her voice.

"It's the custom. A Peloi bride always lives for two months with the groom's mother before the ceremony."

"Why?"

"To learn about him."

"I already know about you."

"Well, yes, I suppose you do, but it's the custom."

"That's ridiculous!"

"Customs often are, but I *am* Domi, so I have to set a good example—and you'll be Doma. The Peloi women will have no respect for you if you don't do what's expected."

"I'll *teach* them respect." Her eyes had turned flint-hard.

He leaned back on his elbows. "I was sort of afraid you might feel this way." He sighed.

"Is that why you didn't mention it before?"

"I was waiting for the right time. Is there any wine in that basket? This might be easier if we're both more relaxed."

"Let's wait. We can get relaxed *after* you tell me. What *is* this nonsense?"

"Let's see if I can explain it." He rubbed his head. "When my people say that the bride is 'learning about her husband,' it doesn't really mean that she's learning about what he expects for breakfast or things like that. What they're really talking about is the fact that there's property involved."

"I don't have any property, Kring. I'm a slave."

"Not after you marry me, you won't be. You'll be a very wealthy woman."

"What are you talking about?"

"Peloi men own their weapons and their horses. Everything else belongs to the women. Always before whenever I stole something—cattle, usually—I gave it to my mother. She's been holding my wealth for me until I get married. She's entitled to *some* of it. That's what the two months is all about. It's to give the two of you time to agree on the division."

"It shouldn't take us *that* long."

"Well, probably not. My mother's a reasonable woman, but the two of you will *also* have to find husbands for my sisters. It wouldn't be so hard if there weren't so many of them."

"How many?" Her voice was *very* hard now.

"Ah—eight, actually."

"Eight?" She said it flatly.

"My father was very vigorous."

"So was your mother, apparently. Are your sisters presentable?"

"More or less. None of them are as beautiful as you are, though, love—but then who could be?"

"We can talk about that later. There's some kind of problem with your sisters, isn't there?"

Kring winced. "How did you know that?"

"I know *you*, Kring. You saved mention of these sisters until the very last. That means that you didn't want to talk about them, and that means there's a problem. What is it?"

"They think they're rich. That makes them put on airs."

"Is *that* all?"

"They're very arrogant, Mirtai."

"I'll teach them humility." She shrugged. "Since there are only eight, I should be able to do it all at once. I'll just take them all out into the nearest pasture for an hour or so. They'll be very humble when we come back—and eager to marry any men your mother and I choose for them. I'll make sure they're willing to do *anything* to get away from me. Your mother and I should be able to settle the property division in the morning; I'll civilize your sisters in the afternoon, and you and I can be married that same evening."

"It's not done that way, my love."

"It will be, *this* time. I'm no more enthusiastic about waiting than you are. Why don't you come over here and kiss me? Now that everything's been settled, we should take advantage of this opportunity."

He grinned at her. "My feelings exactly, love." He took her in his arms and kissed her. The kiss was rather genteel at first, but that didn't last for very long. Things turned slightly savage after a moment.

"That's going to work out just fine," Danae said smugly. "I

wasn't sure how Mirtai was going to take the idea of living with Kring's mother, but she's got everything in hand now."

"She's going to upset the Peloi, you know," Sparhawk said.

"They'll live." The princess shrugged. "They're too set in their ways anyhow. They *need* somebody like Mirtai to open their eyes to the modern world. Let's move on, Sparhawk. We're not done yet."

"How long has this been going on?" Stragen asked in a slightly choked voice.

"Since I was a little girl," Melidere replied. "My father made the dies when I was about seven or so."

"Do you realize what you've done, Baroness?"

"I thought we were going to drop the formality, Milord Stragen." She smiled at him.

He ignored that. "You've struck a direct blow at the economy of every kingdom in Eosia. This is monstrous!"

"Oh, *do* be serious, Stragen."

"You've debased the coinage!"

"I haven't really, but why should it make any difference to you?"

"Because I'm a thief! You've devalued everything I've ever stolen!"

"No, not really. The value of the coins doesn't really have anything to do with their true weight. It's a matter of trust. People may not *like* their governments, but they trust them. If the government says that this coin is worth a half crown, then that's what it's worth. Its value is based on an agreement, not on weight. If the coin has milled edges, it has the value that's stamped on its face. I haven't really stolen anything."

"You're a *criminal*, Melidere!"

"How can I be a criminal if I haven't stolen anything?"

"What if they find out about what you've been doing?"

"What if they do? They can't do anything about it. If they say anything or try to do something to me, I'll just tell the whole story, and every government in Eosia will collapse because nobody will trust their coins anymore." She touched his cheek. "You're such an innocent, Stragen. I think that's why I'm fond of you. You pretend to be depraved, but actually you're like a little boy."

"Why did you tell me about this?"

"Because I need a partner. I can handle these affairs in Eosia, but taking on Tamuli as well might strain my resources.

You have contacts here, and I don't. I'll teach you the business and then lease Tamuli to you. I'll buy you a title and set things up so that you can start immediately."

His eyes narrowed. "Why?" he demanded. "Why are you being so generous?"

"I'm not being generous, Stragen. You *will* pay your rent every month. I can see to that. And you *won't* pay in coins. I want bullion, Stragen—nice, solid bars of gold that I can weigh—and don't try mixing in any copper, either. I'll have your throat cut if you ever try that."

"You're the hardest woman I've ever known, Melidere." He sounded slightly afraid of her.

"Only in *some* places, Stragen," she replied archly. "The rest of me is fairly soft. Oh, that reminds me. We'll be getting married."

"We'll *what*?"

"Partnerships aren't made in heaven, Milord; marriages are. Marriage will give me one more hold on you."

"What if I don't *want* to get married?" He sounded a little desperate now.

"That's just too bad, Stragen, because like it or not, you *will* marry me."

"And you'll have me killed if I don't, I suppose."

"Of course. I'm not going to let you run around loose with this information. You'll get used to the idea, Milord. I'm in a position to make you deliriously happy—and fabulously wealthy to boot. When have you ever had a better offer?"

The look in Stragen's eyes, however, was one of sheer panic.

"Now *that* was something I didn't expect," Danae said as she and Sparhawk crossed the lawn.

Sparhawk was almost too shocked to answer. "You didn't know about Melidere's little hobby, you mean?"

"Oh, of course I knew about that, Sparhawk. Melidere bought her way into Mother's court several years ago."

"Bought?"

"She paid an old countess to step aside for her. What I didn't expect was the direct way she approached Stragen. I thought she might soften things a little, but she was all business. She carved him into neat little slices and she didn't give him any room to move at all while she did it. I think I've misjudged her."

"No, actually you misjudged Stragen. She used the only

technique that had any chance of success with him. Stragen's very slippery. You've got to pin him to the plate with a fork before you can carve him. He probably wouldn't have listened to an ordinary marriage proposal, so she was all business with him. The marriage was only an incidental part."

"Not to *her*, it wasn't."

"Yes, I know. She did it right, though. I'm going to have to tell your mother about this, you know."

"No, actually, you're not. You heard Melidere. Mother wouldn't be able to do anything about it, and all you'd do is worry her."

"They're stealing millions, Aphrael."

"They're not stealing anything, Sparhawk. What they're going to do in no way changes the value of money. When you get right down to it, they're actually *creating* wealth. The whole world will be better for it."

"I don't entirely follow the logic of that."

"You don't have to, Father," she said sweetly. "Just take my word for it." She pointed. "We want to go over there next."

"Over there," was beside the moat, where Sephrenia and Vanion walked side by side along the grassy bank. Sparhawk was growing accustomed to his de facto invisibility by now, but it was still strange to have one of his friends look directly at him without acknowledging his presence.

"It would depend entirely on what kind of fish were locally available," Vanion was explaining. Sparhawk could tell that Vanion was explaining because he was using his "explaining" voice, which was quite a bit like his "preaching" voice. Vanion had put whole generations of Pandion novices to sleep—both in the lecture hall and in chapel.

"Why is he talking like that?" Danae asked.

"Because he's afraid." Sparhawk sighed.

"Of *Sephrenia*? Vanion isn't afraid of anything—least of all Sephrenia. He loves her."

"That's what's making him afraid. He doesn't know what to say. If he says the wrong thing, it could all fall apart again."

"Now," Vanion continued to lecture, "there are warm-water fish and cold-water fish. Carp like the water to be warm, and trout like it colder."

Sephrenia's eyes were starting to glaze over.

"The water in the moat has been standing for quite a while,

so it's fairly warm. That would sort of rule out trout, wouldn't you say?"

"I suppose so," she sighed.

"But that doesn't mean that you couldn't plant some other kind of fish in there. A really good cook can do wonders with carp—and they *do* help to keep the water clean. There's nothing like a school of carp to keep standing water from turning stagnant."

"No," she sighed. "I'm sure there isn't."

"What on earth is he *doing*?" Danae exploded.

"It's called 'walking on eggshells,' " Sparhawk explained. "He probably talks a great deal about the weather, too."

"They'll *never* get back together if he doesn't talk directly to her about something that matters."

"He probably won't do that, Aphrael. I think Sephrenia's going to have to take the first step."

"I found her!" Talen's shout came across the lawn. "She's up in this tree!"

"Oh, bother!" Danae said irritably. "He wasn't supposed to find her yet—and what's she doing up a tree? She wasn't supposed to climb any trees."

"We may as well go on over," Sparhawk told her. "Everybody's drifting in that direction. You'd better dissolve your spell."

"What about Vanion and Sephrenia?"

"Why don't we just let them work it out for themselves?"

"Because he'll go on talking about fish for the next ten years, that's why."

"Sephrenia will only listen to lectures about fish for so long, Danae, then *she'll* get to the point. Vanion isn't really talking about fish. He's telling her that he's ready to make peace if she is."

"He didn't say anything about that. He was just about to start giving her recipes for boiled carp."

"That's what you *heard* him saying, but that wasn't what he was *really* saying. You've got to learn to listen with *both* ears, Danae."

"*Elenes!*" she said, rolling her eyes upward.

Then they heard Kalten shout, "Look out!"

Sparhawk looked sharply toward the spot where the others were gathered around a tall maple tree. Talen was up among the topmost branches, inching his way slowly out on a very slender limb toward the wild-eyed Mmrr. Things weren't going well. The limb was sturdy enough to support Mmrr, but Talen was too heavy. The limb was bending ominously, and there were unpleasant cracking sounds coming from its base.

"Talen," Kalten shouted again, "get back!"

But by then, of course, it was too late. The tree limb did not so much break off from the trunk as it did split at its base and peel down the side of the tree. Talen made a desperate grab, caught the confused and terrified cat in one hand, and then plunged headlong down through the lower branches of the tree.

The situation was still not irretrievable. The Church Knights were all versed in various levels of magic, Sephrenia was there, and Aphrael herself rode on Sparhawk's shoulders. The problem was that no one could actually *see* Talen. The maple tree had large leaves and the boy was falling down through the limbs and was thus totally obscured by the foliage. They could hear him hitting limbs as he fell, a series of raps and thumps accompanied by grunts and sharp cries of pain. Then he emerged from the lower foliage, falling limply to land with a thud on the grass under the tree with Mmrr still loosely held in one hand. He did not get up.

"Talen!" Danae screamed in horror.

Sephrenia concurred with the opinion of Sarabian's physicians. Talen had suffered no really serious injuries. He was bruised and battered, and there was a large, ugly knot on his forehead from his encounter with the unyielding tree limb that had knocked him senseless, but Sephrenia assured them that aside from a splitting headache, he would have no lasting aftereffects from his fall.

Princess Danae, however, was in no mood to be reassured. She hovered at the bedside, reacting with little cries of alarm each time the unconscious boy stirred or made the slightest sound.

Finally, Sparhawk picked her up and carried her from the room. There were people there who probably shouldn't witness miracles. "It got away from you, didn't it, Aphrael?" he observed to the distraught Child-Goddess.

"What are you talking about?"

"You *had* to tamper with things—trying to fix things that would have fixed themselves if you'd just left them alone—and you almost got Talen killed in the process."

"It wasn't *my* fault that he fell out of the tree."

"Whose fault was it, then?" He knew that logically he was

being grossly unfair, but he felt that maybe it was time for the meddling little Goddess to be brought up short. "You interfere too much, Aphrael," he told her. "People have to be allowed to live their own lives and to make their own mistakes. We can usually fix our mistakes by ourselves if you'll just give us the chance. I suppose that what it gets down to is that just because you *can* do something doesn't always mean that you *should* do it. You might want to think about that."

She stared at him for a long moment, and then she suddenly burst into tears.

"Tikume's bowmen will help," Vanion said to Sparhawk a bit later when the two stood together on the parapet. "Ulath's right about Trolls. You definitely want to slow them down before you fight them."

"And Khalad's idea about the crossbows isn't bad, either."

"Right. Thank God you brought him along." The preceptor pursed his lips. "I'd like to have you take personal charge of Khalad's training when you get him back to Cimmura, Sparhawk. Make sure that he gets instruction in politics, diplomacy, and Church law as well as in military skills. I think he's going to go a long way in our order, and I want to be sure he's ready for *any* position."

"Even yours?"

"Stranger things have happened."

Sparhawk remembered Vanion's lecture on fish that morning. "Are you making any progress at all with Sephrenia?" he asked.

"We're speaking to each other, if that's what you mean."

"It wasn't. Why don't you just sit down and talk with her? About something more significant than the weather, or how many birds can sit on a limb, or what kind of fish can live in the moat?"

Vanion gave him a sharp look. "Why don't you mind your own business?"

"It *is* my business, Vanion. She can't function while there's this rift between you—and neither can you, for that matter. I *need* you—both of you—and I can't really count on either of you until you resolve your differences."

"I'm moving as fast as I dare, Sparhawk. One wrong move here could destroy everything."

"So could a failure to move. She's waiting for you to take the first step. Don't make her wait too long."

Stragen came out onto the parapet. "He's awake now," he reported. "He's not very coherent, and his eyes aren't focused, but he's awake. Your daughter's making quite a fuss over him, Sparhawk."

"She's fond of him." Sparhawk shrugged. "She tells everybody that she's going to marry him someday."

"Little girls are strange, aren't they?"

"Oh, yes, and Danae's stranger than most."

"I'm glad I was able to catch the two of you alone," Stragen said then. "There's something I'd like to talk over with you before I mention it to the others." Stragen was absently twiddling two gold Elenic half crowns in his right hand, carefully running one fingertip across the milled edges and hefting them slightly as if trying to determine their weight. Baroness Melidere's confession appeared to have unsettled him just a bit. "Zalasta's little fit of rage wasn't quite as irrational as we thought it would be. Turning the Trolls loose on northern Atan was the most disruptive thing he could have done to us. We'll have to deal with that, of course, but I think we'd better start preparing for his next move. Trolls don't need much supervision once they're been pointed in the right direction, so Zalasta's free to work on something else now, wouldn't you say?"

"Probably," Sparhawk agreed.

"Now, I could be wrong—"

"But you don't think you are," Vanion completed his sentence sardonically.

"He's in a touchy mood today, isn't he?" Stragen said to Sparhawk.

"He's got a lot on his mind."

"It's my guess that whatever Zalasta comes up with next is going to involve those conspirators Sarabian and Ehlana left in place for lack of jail cells."

"It could just as easily involve the armies Parok, Amador, and Elron have raised in western Tamuli," Vanion disagreed.

Stragen shook his head. "Those armies were raised to keep the Church Knights off the continent, Lord Vanion, *and* they were raised at Cyrgon's specific orders. If Zalasta risked them now, he'd have to answer to Cyrgon for it, and I don't think he's *that* brave yet."

"Maybe you're right," Vanion conceded. "All right, let's say that he *will* use those second-level conspirators. Sarabian and Ehlana have already set things in motion to round them up."

"Why bother rounding them up at all, my Lord?"

"To get them off the streets, for one thing. Then there's also the small detail of the fact that they're guilty of high treason. They need to be tried and punished."

"Why?"

"As an example, you idiot!" Vanion flared.

"I'll agree that getting them off the streets is important, Lord Vanion, but there are more effective ways to make examples of people—not only more effective, but more terrifyingly certain. When you send policemen out to arrest people, it's noisy, and usually others hear the noise and manage to escape. There's also the fact that trials are tedious, expensive, and not absolutely certain."

"You've got an alternative in mind, I gather," Sparhawk said.

"Naturally. Why not have the executions first and the trials later?"

They stared at him.

"I'm sort of extending the idea I had the other day," Stragen said. "Caalador and I have access to a number of nonsqueamish professionals who can carry out the executions privately."

"You're talking about murder, Stragen," Vanion accused.

"Why, yes, Lord Vanion, I believe that *is* the term some people do use to describe it. The whole idea behind 'examples' is to frighten others so much that they won't commit the same crime. It doesn't really work, because criminals know that their chances of being caught and punished are very slim." He shrugged. "It's just one of the hazards of doing business." We professional criminals break laws all the time. We *don't*, however, break our own rules. People in our society who break the rules aren't afforded the courtesy of being tried. They're just killed. No acquittals, no pardons, no last-minute jailbreaks. Dead. Period. Case closed. The justice of regular society is slow and uncertain. Ours is just the opposite. If you want to use terror to keep people honest, use *real* terror."

"It *has* got possibilities, Vanion," Sparhawk suggested tentatively.

"You're not seriously considering it, are you? There are thousands of those people out there! You're talking about the largest mass murder in history!"

"It's a way to get my name in the record books." Stragen shrugged. "Caalador and I are probably going to do this anyway. We're both impatient men. I wouldn't have bothered you about it, but I thought I'd like to get your views on the subject. Should we tell Sarabian and Ehlana, or should we just go ahead and not bother them? Discussions about relative morality are so tedious, don't you think? The point here is that we need to come up with something that will unhinge Zalasta all the more, and I think this might be it. If he wakes up some morning in the not-too-distant future and finds himself absolutely and totally alone, it might give him some second thoughts about the wisdom of his course. And oh, incidentally, I've borrowed Berit and Xanetia. They're taking a stroll in the vicinity of the Cynesgan embassy so that Xanetia can run that dip net of hers through the minds of the people inside. We've got quite a few names, but I'm sure there are more."

"Doesn't she have to be in the same room with somebody to listen to his thoughts?" Vanion asked.

"She's not really certain. She's never had occasion to test the limits of her gift. The expedition today is something in the nature of an experiment. We're hoping that she'll be able to reach in through the walls and pull out the names of the people inside. If she can't, I'll find some way to get her inside so that she can seine out what we need. Caalador and I want as much information and as many names as we can get. Setting up the largest mass murder in history is a very complicated business, and we don't want to have to do it twice."

CHAPTER TWENTY-FOUR

I t's diversionary," Ulath said the next morning. He lowered one of the dispatches Emperor Sarabian had brought with him. "The werewolves and vampires and ghouls are just illusions, so they can't really hurt anybody, and these attacks on Atan garrisons are no more than suicidal gestures intended to keep things confused. This is just more of what they were doing before."

"He's right," Sparhawk agreed. "None of this is new, and it doesn't have any real purpose except to keep the Atans in place."

"Unfortunately, it's succeeding very well," Bevier said. "We can't reduce the Atan garrisons by very much to send help to Betuana with all this going on."

"Lord Vanion's idea of detaching platoon-sized units from the main garrisons should help a *little*," Sarabian protested.

"Yes, your Majesty," Bevier replied, "but will it be enough?"

"It's going to *have* to be," Vanion said. "It's all we can spare right now. We're talking about Atans, though, and numbers aren't that significant where they're concerned. One Atan is half an army all by himself."

Stragen motioned to Sparhawk, and the two of them drifted over to the long table laden with breakfast. The blond thief carefully selected a pastry. "It worked," he said quietly. "Xanetia has to be able to *see* the person whose thoughts she's stealing, but Berit found a building that's fairly close and quite a bit higher than the embassy. Xanetia's got a comfortable room to sit in with a window that faces the ambassador's office. She's picking up all sorts of information—and names—for us."

"Why are we keeping this from the others?"

"Because Caalador and I are going to use the information to set that new world record I was telling you about yesterday. Sarabian hasn't authorized it yet, so let's not upset him over something he doesn't need to know about—at least not until we've stacked all the bodies in neat piles."

Princess Danae fell ill the next day. It was nothing clearly definable. There was no fever, no rash, and no cough involved—only a kind of listless weakness. The princess seemed to have no appetite, and it was difficult to wake her.

"It's the same thing as it was last month," Mirtai assured the little girl's worried parents. "She needs a tonic, that's all."

Sparhawk, however, knew that Mirtai was wrong. Danae had not really been ill the previous month. The Child-Goddess made light of her ability to be in two places at the same time, but her father knew that when her attention was firmly fixed on what was going on in one place, she would be semicomatose in the other. This illness was quite different, somehow. "Why don't you go ahead and try a tonic, Ehlana?" he suggested. "I'll go talk with Sephrenia. Maybe she can think of something else."

He found Sephrenia sitting moodily in her room. She was looking out the window, although it was fairly obvious that she did not even see the view. "We've got a problem, little mother," Sparhawk said, closing the door behind him. "Danae's sick."

She turned sharply, her eyes startled. "That's absurd, Sparhawk. She doesn't *get* sick. She can't."

"I didn't think so myself, but she's sick all the same. It's nothing really tangible, no overt symptoms or anything like that, but she's definitely not well."

Sephrenia rose quickly. "I'd better go have a look," she said. "Maybe I can get her to tell me what's wrong. Is she alone?"

"No. Ehlana's with her. I don't think she'll be willing to leave. Won't that complicate things?"

"I'll take care of it. Let's get to the bottom of this before it goes any further."

Sephrenia's obvious concern worried Sparhawk all the more. He followed her back to the royal quarters with growing apprehension. She was right about one thing. Aphrael was not in any way susceptible to human illnesses, so this was no simple miasmic fever or one of the innumerable childhood diseases that all humans catch, endure, and get over. He dismissed out of hand the notion that there could be such a thing as the sniffles of the Gods.

Sephrenia was very businesslike. She was muttering the Styric spell before she even entered Danae's room.

"Thank God you're here, Sephrenia!" Ehlana exclaimed, half rising from her chair beside the little girl's bed. "I've been so—"

Sephrenia released the spell with a curious flick of her hand, and Ehlana's eyes went blank. She froze in place, half-risen from her chair and with one hand partially extended.

Sephrenia approached the bed, sat on the edge of it, and took the little girl in her arms. "Aphrael," she said, "wake up. It's me—Sephrenia."

The Child-Goddess opened her eyes and began to cry.

"What is it?" Sephrenia asked, holding her sister even more tightly and rocking back and forth with her.

"They're killing my children, Sephrenia!" Aphrael wailed. "All over Eosia! The Elenes are killing my children! I want to die!"

"We have to go to Sarsos," Sephrenia said to Sparhawk and Vanion a short while later when the three of them were alone. "I have to talk with the Thousand."

"I know that it's breaking her heart," Vanion said, "but it can't really hurt her, can it?"

"It could kill her, Vanion. The younger Gods are so totally involved with their worshippers that their very lives depend on them. Please, Sparhawk, ask Bhelliom to take us to Sarsos immediately."

Sparhawk nodded bleakly and took out the box, touching his ring to the lid. "Open!" He said it more sharply than he'd intended.

The lid snapped up.

"Blue-Rose," Sparhawk said, "a crisis hath arisen. The Child-Goddess is made gravely ill by reason of the murder of her worshippers in far-off Eosia. We must at once to Sarsos that Sephrenia might consult with the Thousand of Styricum regarding a cure."

"It shall be as thou dost require, Anakha." The words came from Vanion's mouth. The preceptor's expression turned slightly uncertain. "Is it proper for me to tell thee that I feel sympathy for thee and thy mate for this illness of thine only child?"

"I do appreciate thy kind concern, Blue-Rose."

"My concern doth not arise merely from kindness, Anakha. Twice hath the gentle hand of the Child-Goddess touched me, and even I am not proof against the subtle magic of her touch. For the love we all bear her, let us away to Sarsos that she may be made whole again."

The world seemed to shift and blur, and the three of them found themselves outside the marble-sheathed council hall in Sarsos. Autumn was further along here, and the birch forest lying on the outskirts of the city was ablaze with color.

"You two wait here," Sephrenia told them. "Let's not stir up the hotheads by marching Elenes into the council chamber again."

Sparhawk nodded and opened Bhelliom's golden case to put the jewel away.

"Nay, Anakha," Bhelliom told him, still speaking through Vanion's lips. "I would know how Sephrenia's proposal is received."

"An it please thee, Blue-Rose," Sparhawk replied politely.

Sephrenia went quickly up the marble steps and inside.

"It's cooler here," Vanion noted, pulling his cloak a little tighter about him.

"Yes," Sparhawk agreed. "It's farther north."

"That more or less exhausts the weather as a topic. Quit worrying, Sparhawk. Sephrenia has a great deal of influence with the Thousand. I'm sure they'll agree to help."

They waited as the minutes dragged by.

It was probably half an hour later when Sparhawk felt a sharp surge, almost a shudder, pass through the Bhelliom. "Come with me, Anakha!" Vanion's voice was sharp, abrupt.

"What is it?"

"The Styric love of endless talk discontents me. I must needs go past the Thousand to the Younger Gods themselves. These babblers do talk away the life of Aphrael." Sparhawk was a bit surprised by the vehemence in Vanion's voice. He followed as his preceptor, walking in a gait that was peculiarly not his own, stormed into the building. The bronze doors to the council chamber may have been locked. The screech of tortured metal that accompanied Vanion's abrupt opening of them suggested that they *had* been, at any rate.

Sephrenia was standing before the council, her hands upraised, pleading for aid. She broke off and stared incredulously at Vanion as he burst through the door.

"We don't allow Elenes in here!" one of the council members on a back bench shrieked in Styric, rising to his feet and waving his arms.

Then a sort of strangled silence filled the chamber. Vanion began to swell, spreading upward and outward into enormity even as an intensely blue aura flickered brighter and brighter around him. Flickers of lightning surged through that aura, and ripping peals of thunder echoed shockingly back from the marble-clad walls. Sephrenia stared at Vanion in sudden awe.

Prompted by an unvoiced suggestion that only he could hear, Sparhawk raised the glowing sapphire rose. "Behold Bhelliom!" he roared, "and hearken unto its mighty voice!"

"Hear my words, ye Thousand of Styricum!" The voice coming from the enormity that a moment before had been Vanion was vast. It was a voice to which mountains would listen and for which waves and torrents would stop at once to hear. "I would speak with your Gods! Too small are ye and too caught up in endless babble to consider this matter!"

Sparhawk winced. Diplomacy, he saw, was not one of Bhelliom's strong suits.

One of the white-robed councillors drew himself up, spluttering indignantly. "This is outrageous! We don't have to—" He was suddenly gone, and in his place stood a confused-looking personage who appeared to have been interrupted in the middle of his bath. Naked and dripping, he gaped at the huge, blue-lighted presence and at the glowing jewel in Sparhawk's hand. "Well, *really*—" he protested.

"Setras!" the profound voice said sharply, "how deep is thy love for thy cousin Aphrael?"

"This is *most* irregular!" the youthful God protested.

"How deep is thy love?" The voice was inexorable.

"I adore her, naturally. We all do, but—"

"What wouldst thou give to save her life?"

"Anything she asks, of course, but how could her life be in danger?"

"Thou knowest that Zalasta of Styricum is a traitor, dost thou not?"

There were gasps from the council.

"Aphrael said so," the God replied, "but we thought she might have been a little excited. You know how she is sometimes."

"She told thee truly, Setras. Even now do Zalasta's minions slaughter her worshippers in far-off Eosia. With each death is she made less. If this be permitted to continue, soon she will be no more."

The God Setras stiffened, his eyes suddenly blazing. "Monstrous!"

"What wilt thou give that she may live?"

"Mine own life, if need be," Setras replied with archaic formalism.

"Wilt thou lend her of thine own worshippers?"

Setras stared at the glowing Bhelliom, his face filled with chagrin.

"Quickly, Setras! Even now doth the life of Aphrael ebb away!"

The God drew in a deep breath. "There is no alternative?" he asked plaintively.

"None. The life of the Child-Goddess is sustained only by love. Give her the love of certain of *thy* children for a time that she may be made whole again."

Setras straightened. "I *will*!" he declared, "though it doth rend mine heart." A determined look crossed that divine face. "And I do assure thee, World-Maker, that mine shall not be the *only* children who will sustain the life of our beloved cousin with their love. *All* shall contribute equally."

"Done, then!" Bhelliom seemed fond of that expression.

"Ah," Setras said then, his tone slightly worried and his speech slipping into less formal colloquialism, "she *will* give them back, won't she?"

"Thou hast mine assurance, Divine Setras," Sephrenia promised with a smile.

The Younger God looked relieved. Then his eyes narrowed slightly. "Anakha," he said crisply.

"Yes, Divine One?"

"Measures must be taken to protect Aphrael's remaining children. How might that best be accomplished?"

"Advise them to go to the chapterhouses of the Knights of

the Church of Chyrellos," Sparhawk replied. "There will they be kept from all harm."

"And who doth command these knights?"

"Archprelate Dolmant, I suppose," Sparhawk replied dubiously. "It is he who doth exercise ultimate authority."

"I will speak with him. Where may I find him?"

"He will be in the Basilica in Chyrellos, Divine One."

"I will go there and seek him out that we may consult together regarding this matter."

Sparhawk nearly choked on the theological implications of *that* particular announcement. Then he looked at Sephrenia's face. She was still regarding Vanion with a certain amount of awe. Then, so clearly that he could almost hear the click in his mind, Sephrenia made a decision. Her whole face, her entire being, announced it louder than words.

"Ulath," Kalten said irritably, "pay attention. You've been woolgathering for the past two weeks. What's got you so distracted?"

"I don't like the reports we've been getting back from Atan," the big Genidian replied, shifting the princess Danae, Rollo, and Mmrr around in his lap. The little princess had been confined to her room for ten days by her illness, and this was her first day back among them. She was engaging in one of her favorite pastimes—lap switching. Sparhawk knew that most of his friends really didn't pay that much attention, responding automatically to her mute, wan little appeals to be picked up and held. In actuality, however, Aphrael, with toy and with cat, was very busily going from lap to lap to reestablish contact with those who might have drifted out of her grasp during her illness. As always, there were kisses involved, but those kisses were not really the spontaneous little demonstrations of affection they seemed. Aphrael could change minds and alter moods with a touch. With a kiss, however, she could instantly take possession of the entirety of someone's heart and soul. Whenever Sparhawk was engaged in a dispute with his daughter, he was always very careful to keep at least one piece of furniture between them.

"Things aren't working out the way I thought they would," Ulath said in a gloomy voice. "The Trolls are learning to hide from arrows and crossbow bolts."

"Even a Troll is bound to learn eventually," Talen said.

Talen seemed fully recovered from his tumble out of the maple tree, although he still complained of headaches occasionally.

"No," Ulath disagreed. "That's the whole point. Trolls *don't* learn. Maybe it's because their Gods don't learn—or can't. The Trolls that are walking around right now know exactly what the first Troll who ever lived knew—no more, no less. Cyrgon's tampering with them. If he alters the Trolls to the point that they can learn things, mankind's going to be in serious trouble."

"There's something more, too, isn't there, Ulath?" Bevier asked shrewdly. "You've had your 'theological expression' on your face for the past several days. You're tussling with some moral dilemma, aren't you?"

Ulath sighed. "This is probably going to upset everybody, but try to consider it on its merits instead of just going up in flames about it."

"That doesn't sound too promising, old boy," Stragen murmured. "You'd better break it to us gently."

"I don't think there *is* a gentle way, Stragen. Betuana's dispatches are getting more and more shrill. The Trolls won't come out in the open anymore. The mounted Atans can't get at them with lances, and the arrows and crossbow bolts are hitting more trees than Trolls. They're even setting grass fires so they can hide in the smoke. Betuana's right on the verge of calling her people home, and without the Atans, we don't have an army anymore."

"Sir Ulath," Oscagne said, "I gather that this gloomy preamble is a preparation for a shocking suggestion. I think we've all been sufficiently prepared. Go ahead and shock us."

"We have to take the Trolls away from Cyrgon," Ulath replied, absently scratching Mmrr's ears. "We can't let him continue to teach them even rudimentary tactics, and we definitely don't want them cooperating with each other the way they have been."

"And how exactly are you going to take totally unmanageable brutes away from a God?" Stragen asked him.

"I was sort of thinking along the lines of letting their *own* Gods do it. The Troll-Gods *are* available, after all. Ghwerig imprisoned them inside Bhelliom, and Sparhawk's got Bhelliom tucked away inside his shirt. I'd imagine that Khwaj and the others would do almost *anything* for us if we promise to give them their freedom."

"Are you mad?" Stragen exclaimed. "We can't turn them

loose! That's unthinkable!" He dropped the pair of gold coins he always carried now.

"I'd be more than happy to consider alternatives—if anyone can come up with some. The threat to Atan is serious enough, but the longer Cyrgon dominates the Trolls, the more they're going to learn from him. Sooner or later, they'll go back to Thalesia. Do we really want a trained army of Trolls outside the gates of Emsat? We've got at least *some* small advantage if we deal with the Troll-Gods. We hold the key to their freedom. But we don't really have *anything* Cyrgon wants—except Bhelliom itself. I'd rather deal with the Troll-Gods, myself."

"Why don't we just have Sparhawk take Bhelliom to northern Atan and exterminate the Trolls with it?"

Sparhawk shook his head. "Bhelliom won't do that, Stragen. It won't obliterate an entire species. I know that for certain."

"You've got the rings. You could force it to do as you say."

"No. I won't do that. Bhelliom isn't a slave. If it cooperates, it's going to have to be willingly."

"We can't just turn the Troll-Gods loose, Sparhawk. I may be a thief, but I'm still a Thalesian. I'm not going to just sit by and let the Trolls overrun the entire peninsula."

"We haven't even talked with the Troll-Gods yet, Stragen," Ulath told him. "Why don't we see what they have to say before we decide? No matter what, though, we're going to have to do *something* very soon. If we don't, we're going to start seeing long columns of Atans marching out of their barracks on their way back home."

Danae slipped down from Ulath's lap and retrieved Stragen's coins. "You dropped these, Milord," she said sweetly. Then she frowned. "Is it my imagination, or is one of them just a little lighter than the other?"

Stragen looked at her with a slightly sick expression on his face.

It was somewhat later, and Sparhawk and Vanion were escorting Sephrenia back to her room. They reached the door and stopped.

"Oh, this is absurd!" Sephrenia suddenly burst out in an exasperated tone of voice. "Vanion, go get your things and come back home where you belong!"

Vanion blinked. "I—"

"Hush!" she told him. Then she glared at Sparhawk. "And not a word out of you, either!"

"Me?"

"You have packing to do, Vanion," she said. "Don't just stand there gawking."

"I'll get right at it."

"And don't take all day." She threw her arms up in the air. "Men! Do I have to draw pictures for you? I did everything short of lighting signal fires and blowing trumpets, and all you wanted to talk about was the weather—or fish. Why wouldn't you *ever* get to the point?"

"Well—I—" he floundered. "You *were* very angry with me, Sephrenia."

"That was then. This is now. I'm not angry anymore, and I want you to come back home. I'm going to go have a word with Danae, and I want to see you back in our room when I return."

"Yes, dear," he replied meekly.

She glared at him for a moment, and then she spun on her heel and went off down the hall, talking to herself and waving her hands in the air.

"Well, Krager's back," Talen reported as they gathered again later that afternoon. "One of the beggars saw him slipping in through the back gate of the Cynesgan embassy about two hours ago—*staggering* might be a better word for it, though. He was roaring drunk."

"That's the Krager we've come to know and love." Kalten laughed.

"I can't understand how Zalasta can put any faith in a known drunkard," Oscagne said.

"Krager's very intelligent when he's sober, your Excellency," Sparhawk explained. "That was the only reason Martel put up with him." He scratched at his cheek. "Could we prevail on you to go back to that lookout near the embassy, Anarae?"

Xanetia started to rise from her chair.

"Not right now." He smiled. "It usually takes Krager all night to sober up, so tomorrow morning should be soon enough. I think we'll want to know what instructions he brings to the Cynesgan ambassador."

"There's something else, too," Stragen added. "We've never really been sure if Krager knows that we're using criminals to gather information for us. He knew that we were getting help from Platime in Cimmura and that we had contact with thieves and the like in other cities in Eosia, but we should find out if he's made the connection between the two continents yet."

"He sort of hinted that he knew when he talked with me after we put down the coup," Sparhawk reminded him.

"I don't want to discard the entire apparatus on the basis of a hint, Sparhawk," Stragen said, "and I *really* need to know if he's aware of the fact that we can use certain criminals for things other than spying."

"I shall probe his mind most closely," Xanetia promised.

"Where are Vanion and Sephrenia, Sparhawk?" Ehlana asked suddenly. "They should have been here an hour ago."

"Oh, I'm sorry, dear. I meant to tell you about that. I excused them for the rest of the day. They have something important to take care of."

"Why didn't you tell me?"

"I am, dear—right now."

"What are they doing?"

"They've resolved their differences. I'd imagine they're discussing that right now—at some length."

She flushed slightly. "Oh," she said in a neutral sort of way. "What finally got them back together again?"

He shrugged. "Sephrenia got tired of the estrangement and told Vanion to come back home. She was very direct about it—and she even managed to twist it around so that it was all his fault. You know how that goes."

"That will do, Sir Knight," she said firmly.

"Yes, your Majesty."

"Would this Krager person know where Zalasta is right now, Prince Sparhawk?" Oscagne asked.

"I'm sure he does, your Excellency. Zalasta probably doesn't *want* him to know—Krager being what he is, and all— but it's very hard to hide things from Krager when he's the least bit sober."

"He could be enormously valuable to us, Prince Sparhawk. Particularly in the light of the Anarae's special gift."

"You'd better get all you can from him right now, your Excellency," Talen suggested, "because just as soon as my brother gets back from Atan, he'll probably kill him."

Oscagne looked startled.

"It's a personal thing, your Excellency. Krager was involved in the death of our father—around the edges, anyway. Khalad wants to do something about that."

"I'm sure we can persuade him to wait, young master."

"I wouldn't be, your Excellency."

"It's been a part of us for so long that I don't think we'd be Styrics without it, Anarae," Sephrenia said sadly.

It was one of those private meetings at the top of the tower. Sparhawk and his daughter had joined Sephrenia, Vanion, and Xanetia as evening settled over Matherion, so that they could discuss certain things the others did not need to know about.

"It is even so with us, Sephrenia of Ylara," Xanetia confessed. "Our hatred of thy race doth in part define the Delphae as well."

"We tell our children that the Delphae steal souls," Sephrenia said. "I was always taught that you glow because of the souls you've devoured, and that the people you touch decay because you've jerked their souls out of them."

Xanetia smiled. "And we tell *our* young ones that the Styrics are ghouls who rob graves for food—when there are no Delphaeic children nearby to be eaten alive."

"I know a child with a slightly Styric background who's been considering cannibalism lately," Sparhawk noted blandly.

"Snitch!" Danae muttered.

"What's this?" Sephrenia demanded of her sister.

"The Child-Goddess was very upset when she found out that Zalasta had deceived her," Sparhawk said in an offhand sort of way, "and even more upset when she discovered that he wanted to steal you from her. She said she was going to rip his heart out and eat it right before his very eyes."

"Oh, I probably wouldn't have done it," Aphrael tried to shrug it off.

"Probably?" Sephrenia exclaimed.

"His heart's so rotten it would have made me sick."

Sephrenia gave her a long, steady look of disapproval.

"Oh, all *right*," the Child-Goddess said, "I was exaggerating." She looked pensively out over the city, then back at Sephrenia and Xanetia. "All this hatred and the wild stories the Styrics and the Delphae tell their children about each other aren't really natural, you realize. You've been very carefully coached to feel this way. The real argument was between my family and Edaemus, and it involved things you wouldn't even understand. It was a silly argument—most arguments are—but Gods can't keep their arguments private. You humans were drawn into something that didn't really concern you at all." She sighed. "Like so many of our disagreements, that one started to spill over from the part of the world where *we* live into your part. It's *our* party, and you never should have been invited."

"Where *is* this country of yours, Aphrael?" Vanion asked curiously.

"Right here—" She shrugged. "—all around us, but *you* can't see it. It might be better if we had our own separate place, but it's too late now. I should have told Sephrenia about our foolishness when she and I were children and I heard her parroting some of that nonsense about the Delphae, but then the Elene serfs destroyed our village and killed our parents, and Zalasta tried to shift his own guilt to the Delphae, and that set her prejudices in stone." She paused. "I always *knew* there was something about Zalasta's story that didn't ring true, but I couldn't get into his thoughts to find out what it was."

"Why not?" Vanion asked her. "You *are* a Goddess, after all."

"You've *noticed*!" she exclaimed. "What a *thrilling* discovery that must have been for you!"

"Mind your manners," Sparhawk told her.

"Sorry, Vanion," she apologized. "That *was* a little snippy, wasn't it? I can't look into Zalasta's thoughts because he isn't one of my children." She paused. "Sephrenia, don't you find it interesting that *I'm* limited but Xanetia isn't?"

"Xanetia and I are exploring our differences, Aphrael." Sephrenia smiled. "Every one of them we've examined so far has turned out to be imaginary."

"Truly," Xanetia agreed. Sparhawk could only begin to imagine how difficult even these tentative steps toward peacemaking must be for this strangely similar pair of women. The tearing down of institutionalized bigotry must have been somewhat akin to dismantling a house that had been standing for a hundred centuries.

"Vanion, dear," Sephrenia said then, "it's starting to get a little chilly."

"I'll run down and fetch your cloak."

She sighed. "No, Vanion," she told him. "I don't *want* a cloak. I want you to put your arms around me."

"Oh," he said. "I should have thought of that myself."

"Yes," she agreed. "Try to think of it more often."

He smiled and put his arms about her.

"That's *so* much nicer," she said, snuggling up against him. "There's something I've been meaning to ask," Sparhawk said to his daughter. "Regardless of who put them up to it, the people who attacked Ylara *were* Elenes. How in the world did you ever persuade Sephrenia to take on the chore of teaching the Pandions the Secrets? She must have hated Elenes."

"She did." The Child-Goddess shrugged. "And I wasn't too fond of you myself. I had Ghwerig's rings, though, and I absolutely *had* to get them on the fingers of King Antor and the first Sparhawk—otherwise, I wouldn't be here." She paused, and her eyes narrowed. *"That's intolerable!"* she exclaimed.

"What is?"

"Bhelliom manipulated me! After I stole the rings from Ghwerig—or maybe even before—it put the notion into the rings themselves. I *know* it did. I no sooner took those rings than the idea occurred to me to separate them by giving one of them to your ancestor and the other to Ehlana's. This has all been *Bhelliom's* scheme! That—that thing *used* me!"

"My, my," Sparhawk said blandly.

"And it was so *clever!*" she fumed. "It seemed like such a good idea! Your blue friend and I are going to have a long talk about this."

"You were telling us how you forced Sephrenia to become our tutor, I believe," he said.

"I commanded her to do it—after coaxing wouldn't work. First I ordered her to take the rings to that pair of bleeding savages, and then I took her to your motherhouse at Demos and compelled her to become your tutor. I had to have her there to keep your family on the right track. You're Anakha, and I knew I'd need some kind of hold on you. Otherwise, Bhelliom would have had you all to itself, and I didn't trust it enough to let *that* happen."

"Then you *did* plan all this in advance," Sparhawk said just a bit sadly.

"Bhelliom may have planned it first," she said darkly. "I was absolutely sure it was my idea. I thought that if I just happened to be your daughter, you'd at least pay some attention to me."

He sighed. "It was all completely calculated, then, wasn't it?"

"Yes, but that doesn't have anything to do with the way I feel about you. I had a great deal to do with inventing you, Sparhawk, so I do really love you. You were a darling baby. I almost disassembled Kalten when he broke your nose. Sephrenia talked me out of it, though. Mother was a different story. You were sweet, but she was adorable. I loved her from the first moment I saw her, and I knew you two would get on well together. I'm really rather proud of the way things have turned out. I even think Bhelliom approves—of course it would never admit it. Bhelliom's so stuffy sometimes."

"Did your cousin Setras actually go into the Basilica and talk with Dolmant?" Vanion asked her suddenly.

"Yes."

"How did Dolmant take it?"

"Surprisingly well. Of course Setras can be very charming when he wants to be, and Dolmant *is* fond of me." She paused, her dark eyes speculative. "I think his Archprelacy's going to bring about some rather profound changes in your Church, Vanion. Dolmant's mind isn't absolutely locked in stone the way Ortzel's is. I think Elene theology's going to change a great deal while he's Archprelate."

"The conservatives won't like that."

"They never do. Conservatives wouldn't even change their underwear if they didn't have to."

"That's extremely questionable from a legal standpoint, your Majesty," Oscagne said. "I'm not personally questioning your word, Anarae," he added quickly, "but I think we can all see the problem here. All we'll have in the way of evidence is Xanetia's unsubstantiated testimony about what somebody's thinking. Even the most pliable of judges is likely to choke a bit on that. These are going to be very difficult cases to prosecute—particularly in view of the fact that some of the accused are going to be members of the great families of Tamul proper."

"You might as well go ahead and tell them all of it, Stragen," Sparhawk suggested. "You're going to carry out your plan anyway, and they'll worry over legal niceties for weeks if you don't tell them."

Stragen winced. "I really wish you hadn't brought it up, old boy," he said in a pained voice. "Their Majesties are official personages, and they're more or less obliged to observe the strict letter of the law. They'd both be much more comfortable if they didn't know too many details."

"I'm sure they would, but all this fretting about building ironclad court cases is wasting time we should be spending on other problems."

"What's this?" Sarabian asked.

"Milord Stragen and Master Caalador are contemplating something along the lines of what you might call legal short-cuts, your Majesty—in the interests of expediency. Do you want to tell them, Stragen? or do you want me to do it?"

"You go ahead. It might sound better coming from you." Stragen leaned back, still brooding over his two gold coins.

"Their plan's very simple, your Majesty," Sparhawk told the emperor. "They propose that instead of rounding up all these conspirators, spies, informers, and the like, we just have them murdered."

"What?" Sarabian exclaimed.

"That was a very blunt way to put it, Sparhawk," Stragen complained.

"I'm a blunt man." Sparhawk shrugged. "Actually, your Majesty, I sort of approve of the notion. Vanion's having a little trouble choking it down, though." He leaned back in his chair. "Justice is a funny thing," he observed. "She's only partly interested in punishing the guilty. What she's *really* interested in is deterrence. The idea is to frighten people into avoiding crime by doing unpleasant things—publicly—to the criminals who get caught. But as Stragen pointed out, most criminals know that they probably won't *get* caught, so all the police and the courts are *really* doing is justifying their continued employment. He suggests that we bypass the police and the courts and send out the murderers some night very soon. The next morning, everybody even remotely connected with Zalasta and his renegade Styrics would be found with his throat cut. If we want a deterrent, that would really be the most effective one. There wouldn't be any acquittals or appeals or imperial pardons to confuse the issue. If we do it that way, everybody in all of Tamuli will have nightmares about the fruits of treason for years afterward. I approve of the idea for tactical reasons, though. I'll leave justice to the courts—or the Gods. I like the idea because of the damage it would do to Zalasta. He's a Styric, and Styrics usually try to get what they want by deception and misdirection. Zalasta's set up a very elaborate apparatus to gain his ends without a direct confrontation. Stragen's plan would destroy that apparatus in a single night, and only madmen would be willing to join Zalasta after that. Once the apparatus is gone, he'll *have* to come out in the open and fight. He's not good at that, but we are. This would give us the chance to fight this war on our own terms, and that's always an enormous tactical advantage."

"*And* we can pick our own time," Caalador added. "The timing would be very important."

"They wouldn't be expecting it; that's one thing," Itagne noted.

"There are rules, Itagne," his brother objected. "Civilization's based on rules. If *we* break the rules, how can we expect others to follow them?"

"That's the whole point, Oscagne. Right now, the rules are protecting the criminals, not society as a whole. We can wriggle around and come up with some kind of legalistic justification for it afterward. About the only real objection I have is that these—ah—agents of government policy, shall we say, won't have any official standing." He frowned for a moment. "I suppose we could solve that problem by appointing Milord Stragen to the post of Minister of the Interior and Master Caalador Director of the Secret Police."

"*Real* secret, your Excellency." Caalador laughed. "*I* don't even know who most of the murderers are."

Itagne smiled. "Those are the best kind, I suppose." He looked at the emperor. "That *would* put a slight stain of legality on the whole business, your Majesty—in the event that you decide to go ahead with it."

Sarabian leaned thoughtfully back in his chair. "I'm tempted," he said. "A bloodbath like this would insure domestic tranquility in Tamuli for at least a century." He shook off his expression of wistful yearning and sat up. "It's just too uncivilized. I couldn't approve of something like that with Lady Sephrenia and Anarae Xanetia watching me and sitting in judgment."

"What are *your* feelings, Xanetia?" Sephrenia asked tentatively.

"We of the Delphae are not overconcerned with niceties and technicalities, Sephrenia."

"I didn't think you would be. Good is good, and bad is bad, wouldn't you say?"

"It seemeth so to me."

"And to me as well. Zalasta's hurt the both of us, and Stragen's massacre would hurt *him*. I don't think either of us would object too much to something that would cause him pain, would we?"

Xanetia smiled.

"It's your decision, then, Sarabian," Sephrenia said. "Don't look to Xanetia and me for some excuse *not* to make it. *We* find nothing objectionable in the plan."

"I'm profoundly disappointed in both of you," he told them. "I was hoping you'd get me off the hook. You're my last chance, Ehlana. Doesn't this monstrous notion turn *your* blood cold?"

"Not particularly," she shrugged, "but I'm an Elene—*and* a politician. As long as we don't get caught with bloody knives in our *own* hands, we can always wriggle out of it."

"Won't *anyone* help me?" Sarabian actually looked desperate.

Oscagne gave his emperor a penetrating look. "It has to be your decision, your Majesty," he said. "I personally don't like it, but I'm not the one who has to give the order."

"Is it always like this, Ehlana?" Sarabian groaned.

"Usually," she replied quite calmly. "Sometimes it's worse."

The emperor sat staring at the wall for quite some time. "All right, Stragen," he said finally. "Go ahead and do it."

"That's Mother's darling boy," Ehlana said fondly.

CHAPTER TWENTY-FIVE

No, Caalador," Sparhawk said, "as a matter of fact, it *won't* take three or four weeks. I have access to a faster way to get from place to place."

"That won't do any good, Sparhawk," the ruddy-faced Cammorian objected. "The people in the Secret Government won't take orders from *you*."

"I won't be giving the orders, Caalador," Sparhawk told him. "*You* will."

Caalador swallowed. "Are you sure it's safe to travel that way?" he asked dubiously.

"Trust me. How many people will we have to get word to?"

Caalador threw an uncomfortable glance at Sarabian. "I'm not at liberty to say."

"I won't use the information, Caalador," the emperor assured him.

"You and I know that, your Majesty, but rules are rules. We like to keep our numbers just a little vague."

"Generalize, Caalador," Ehlana suggested. "A hundred? Five hundred?"

"Not hordly that many, dorlin'." He laughed. "Ther ain't *no* pie whut kin be cut into *that* many pieces." He squinted a bit anxiously at Stragen. "Let's just say more than twenty and less

377

than a hundred and let it go at that, shall we? I'd rather not get my *own* throat cut."

"That's general enough." Stragen laughed. "I won't turn you in for that, Caalador."

"Thanks."

"Don't mention it."

"Two or three days, then," Sparhawk said.

"Let's not start passing the word around until after the Anarae pulls her net through Krager's mind tomorrow morning," Stragen said.

"Thou art fond of that particular metaphor, Milord Stragen," Xanetia noted in a slightly disapproving tone.

"I'm not trying to be offensive, Anarae. I'm groping for a way to explain something I couldn't begin to understand, that's all." Stragen's face grew bleak. "If Krager really knows about the Secret Government, he's probably infiltrated it, and there'll be *some* people out there we won't want to tell about this."

"And whose names we'll be adding to our list," Caalador added.

"Just how long *is* your list, Master Caalador?" Oscagne asked.

"You don't really need to know that, your Excellency," Caalador replied in a tone that clearly said he wasn't going to discuss the matter. "Let's pick a date—something that sort of stands out in people's minds. Thieves and cutthroats aren't all that good at reading calendars."

"How about the Harvest Festival?" Itagne suggested. "It's only three weeks away, and it's celebrated in all of Tamuli."

Caalador looked around. "Can we wait that long?" he asked. "It *would* be the perfect time. Our murderers would have three nights to get the job done instead of one, and there's lots of noise and confusion during the Harvest Festival."

"And lots of drinking," Itagne added. "The whole continent gets roaring drunk."

"It's a general holiday then?" Bevier asked.

Itagne nodded. "Technically it's a religious holiday. We're supposed to thank the Gods for a bountiful harvest. Most people can get that out of the way in about a half a minute, and that leaves them three days and nights to get into trouble. The harvest crews are all paid off, they take their annual baths, and then head for the nearest town in search of mischief."

"It's made to order for our purposes," Caalador added.

"Will you be ready to move your forces against the Trolls in three weeks, Lord Vanion?" Sarabian asked.

"More than ready, your Majesty. We weren't planning to gather them all in one place anyway. The detachments from each garrison are only platoon-sized, and a platoon can move faster than a battalion. They're all moving toward staging areas along the Atan border."

"Do we want to hit them all at the same time?" Kalten asked.

"We could go any one of three ways on that," Sparhawk said. "We can hit the Trolls first and pull Zalasta's attention to northern Atan, or we can murder the conspirators first and send him scurrying around the continent trying to salvage what he can of his organization, or we can do it simultaneously and see if he can be in a hundred places all at the same time."

"We can decide that later," Sarabian said. "Let's get word to the murderers first. We *know* that we want them to go to work during the Harvest Festival. The military situation's more fluid."

"Let's make a special point of eliminating Sabre, Parok, and Rebal this time," Stragen said to Caalador. "Evidently the Atans missed them in the last general roundup. Those Elene kingdoms in western Tamuli are standing between Sir Tynian and Matherion, and as long as those three troublemakers are alive, he's going to have rough going. Is there any way we could get Scarpa as well?"

Caalador shook his head. "He's holed up in Natayos. He's turned it into a fortress and filled it with fanatics. I couldn't *pay* a murderer enough to try to kill him. The only way we'll get Scarpa is to mount a military expedition."

"That's a shame," Sephrenia murmured. "The death of his only son would definitely twist a knife in Zalasta's belly."

"Savage," Vanion accused affectionately.

"Zalasta killed my family, Vanion," she replied. "All I want to do is return the favor."

"That sounds fair to me." He smiled.

"I'm still dead-set against it," Stragen said stubbornly when he, Sparhawk, and Ulath met in the hallway a bit later.

"Be reasonable, Stragen," Ulath said. "It won't hurt anything to see what they have to say, will it? I'm not going to just turn them loose without any restrictions at all, you know."

"They'll agree to anything to get their freedom, Ulath. They might *promise* to pull the Trolls out of Atan—or even to help us deal with Zalasta and Cyrgon—but once they get back to Thalesia, they won't feel obligated to honor any commitments. We're not even members of the same species as their worshippers. We're just animals in their eyes. Would you feel obliged to keep promises you made to a bear?"

"That would depend on the bear, I suppose."

"The Troll-Gods might break promises they make to *us*," Sparhawk said, "but they won't break faith with Bhelliom, because Bhelliom can reabsorb them if they try any tricks."

"Well," Stragen said dubiously, "I want to be sure everybody understands that I don't like this, but I guess it won't hurt to hear what they have to say. I want to be present, though. I don't altogether trust you, Ulath, so I want to hear the promises you give them."

"Do you understand Trollish?"

Stragen shuddered. "Of course not."

"You're going to have a little difficulty following the conversation, then, don't you think?"

"Sephrenia's going along, isn't she? She can translate for me."

"Are you sure you trust *her*?"

"That's a contemptible thing to say."

"I thought I'd ask. When do you want to do this, Sparhawk?"

"Let's not be premature," Sparhawk decided. "I still have to take Caalador around to talk with his friends. Let's get that set up and make sure that the Atans Vanion's calling in are in the staging areas before we broach the subject to the Troll-Gods. There's no point in getting them excited until we need them."

"I think we'll want to be out in the countryside when we talk with them," Ulath suggested. "When we tell them that Cyrgon's stolen their worshippers, their screams of outrage might shatter all the seashells off the walls of Matherion."

"His mind is much fogged by drink," Xanetia reported about midmorning the next day after she and Berit had returned from the Cynesgan embassy, "and it is difficult to wring consistency from it."

"Does he have any suspicions at all, Anarae?" Stragen asked with a worried expression.

"He doth know that thou hast set thieves and beggars to watch him in the past, Milord Stragen," she replied, "but it is his thought that thou—or young Talen—must make these arrangements in each city and that one of you must go there to speak with each chief separately."

"He don't know nothin' about the Sekert Gover-mint?" Caalador pressed, speaking in dialect for some obscure reason.

"His understanding of thy society is vague, Master Caalador. Cooperation of such nature is beyond his grasp, for Krager himself is incapable of it, being guided only by immediate self-interest."

"What a splendid drunkard!" Stragen exulted. "Let's all pray that he never sobers up!"

"A-*men*!" Caalador agreed fervently. "Well, Sporhawk, why don't yew have a talk with this yere jool o' yourn, an' me'n you'll go a-hippety-skippin' 'round about Tamuli. We got us folks t' see an' th'otes t' cut."

Xanetia's face took on a pained expression.

Caalador was badly shaken the first few times Bhelliom whisked him halfway across the continent, but after that he seemed to grow numb. It took him about a half-hour each time to pass instructions to the various criminal chiefs of Tamuli, and Sparhawk strongly suspected that the ruddy-faced Cammorian settled his shaken nerves with strong drink at each stop. Sparhawk could not be sure, of course, since he was quite firmly excluded from the discussions. "You don't need to know who these people are, Sparhawk," Caalador said, "and your presence would just make them nervous."

Vanion's small Atan detachments were streaming into the staging areas along the Atan border from all over Tamuli, and Tikume had promised several thousand eastern Peloi in addition to the three hundred bowmen Kring had taken with him back to Atana. Bhelliom took Sparhawk and Vanion to the Atan capital so that they could reassure Betuana that they *were* in fact marshaling forces to come to her aid, *and* to explain why they were holding most of that aid at the border. "The Trolls wouldn't understand the significance of those reinforcements, Betuana-Queen," Vanion told her, "but Cyrgon's completely versed in strategy and tactics. He'd understand what was going on immediately. Let's not give him any hints about what we're doing until we're ready to strike."

"Do you really think you can spring surprises on a God, Vanion-Preceptor?" she asked. Betuana was dressed in what

passed for armor among the Atans, and her face clearly
showed that she had been functioning on short sleep for weeks.

"I'm certainly going to *try*, Betuana-Queen," Vanion replied
with a brief smile. "I think it's fairly safe to say that Cyrgon
hasn't had a new thought in the last twenty thousand years.
Military thinking's changed a great deal in that time, so he
probably won't fully understand what we're up to." He made
a wry face. "At least that's what I'm *hoping*," he added.

And then it reached the point where they could not put it off
any longer. None of them were really comfortable with the
idea of chatting with the Troll-Gods, but the time had come to
put Ulath's notion to the test.

About an hour before dawn of the day none of them had re-
ally been looking forward to, Sparhawk and Vanion went to
Sephrenia's room to speak with Sephrenia, Xanetia, and
Danae. Their discussions struck a snag almost immediately.

"I *have* to go along, Sparhawk," Danae insisted.

"That's out of the question," he told her. "Ulath and Stragen
are going to be there. We can't let them find out who you really are."

"They're not going to find anything out, Father," she said
with exaggerated patience. "It won't be *Danae* who'll be going
along."

"Oh. That's different, then."

"Exactly how are we going to work this, Sparhawk?"
Vanion asked. "Won't you have to release the Troll-Gods in order to talk with them?"

Sparhawk shook his head. "Bhelliom says we won't. The
Troll-Gods themselves will still be locked up inside Bhelliom.
Their spirits have always been free to roam around, except
when Bhelliom's encased in gold—or steel. They have a certain limited amount of power in that condition, I guess, but
their *real* power's locked up with them inside the Bhelliom."

"Wouldn't it be safer to get them to agree to use that limited
power, rather than to unleash them entirely?" Vanion asked.

"It wouldn't work, dear one," Sephrenia told him. "The
Troll-Gods may encounter Cyrgon, and if they do, they'll need
their full power."

"Moreover," Xanetia added, "I do strongly believe that they
will sense our need and bargain stringently."

"Are you going to do the talking, Sparhawk?" Vanion asked.

Sparhawk shook his head. "Ulath knows Trolls—and the
Troll-Gods—better than I do, and his Trollish is better than

mine. I'll hold Bhelliom and call the Troll-Gods out and then let him do the talking." He looked out the window. "It's almost dawn," he said. "We'd better get started. Ulath and Stragen are going to meet us down in the courtyard."

"Turn your backs," Danae told them.

"What?" her father asked.

"Turn around, Sparhawk. You don't have to watch this."

"It's one of her quirks," Sephrenia explained. "She doesn't want anybody to know what she really looks like."

"I already know what Flute looks like."

"There's a transition, Sparhawk. She doesn't go directly from Danae to Flute. She passes through her *real* person on the way from one little girl to the other."

Sparhawk sighed. "How many of her are there?"

"Thousands, I'd imagine."

"That's depressing. I've got a daughter I don't really know."

"Don't be silly," Danae said. "Of course you know me."

"But only one of you—a several-thousandth part of who you really are—such a tiny part." He sighed again and turned his back.

"It's not a tiny part, Father." Danae's voice changed as she spoke, becoming richer, more vibrant. It was no longer a child's voice, but a woman's.

There was a mirror on the far side of the room, a flat sheet of polished brass. Sparhawk glanced at it and saw the wavering reflection of a figure standing behind him. He quickly averted his eyes.

"Go ahead and look, Sparhawk. It's not a very good mirror, so you won't see all that much."

He raised his eyes and stared at the gleaming brass. The reflection was distorted. About all he could really see was the general size and shape. Aphrael was somewhat taller than Sephrenia. Her hair was long and very dark, and her skin was pale. Her face was hardly more than a blur in that imperfect reflection, but he could see her eyes quite clearly for some reason. There was an ageless wisdom in those eyes and a kind of eternal joy and love. "I wouldn't do this for just anybody, Sparhawk," the woman's voice told him, "but you're the best father I've ever had, so I'm stretching the rules for you."

"Don't you wear any clothes?" he asked her.

"What on earth for? I don't get cold, you know."

"I'm talking about modesty, Aphrael. I *am* your father, after all, and things like that are supposed to concern me."

She laughed and reached around from behind him to caress his face. It was not a little girl's hand that touched his cheek. He caught the faint scent of crushed grass, but the rest of the familiar fragrance that lingered about both Danae and Flute had been subtly changed. The person standing behind him was definitely *not* a little girl.

"Is this the way you appear to the rest of your family?" he asked her.

"Not very often. I prefer to have them think of me as a child. I can get my own way a lot easier in that form—and I get a lot more kisses."

"Getting your own way is very important to you, isn't it, Aphrael?"

"Of course. It's important to all of us, isn't it? I'm just better at it than most." She laughed, a deep, rich laugh. "I'm probably the best there is at getting my own way."

"I've noticed that," he said dryly.

"Well," she said then, "I'd love to talk more with you about it, but I suppose we shouldn't keep Ulath and Stragen waiting." The reflection wavered and began to shrink, sliding back into childhood. "All right, then," Flute's familiar voice said, "let's go have it out with the Troll-Gods."

It was blustery that morning, and dirty grey clouds scudded in off the Tamul Sea. There were few citizens abroad in fire-domed Matherion as Sparhawk and his friends rode out of the palace compound and down the long, wide street leading to the west gate.

They left the city and rode up the hill to the place from which they had first glimpsed the gleaming city. "How do you plan to approach them?" Stragen asked Ulath as they crested the hill.

"Carefully," Ulath grunted. "I'd rather not get eaten. I've talked with them before, so they probably remember me, and the fact that Sparhawk's holding Bhelliom in his fist may help to curb their urge to devour me right on the spot."

"Any particular sort of place you'd like?" Vanion asked him.

"An open field—but not *too* open. I want trees nearby—so I can climb one in case things turn ugly." Ulath looked around at the rest of them. "One word of caution," he added. "Don't any of you stand between me and the nearest tree once I get started."

"Over there?" Sparhawk suggested, pointing toward a pasture backed by a pine grove.

Ulath squinted. "It's not perfect, but no place really would be. Let's get this over with. My nerves are strung a little tight this morning for some reason."

They rode out into the pasture and dismounted. "Is there anything anyone would like to tell me before we start?" Sparhawk asked.

"You're on your own, Sparhawk," Flute replied. "It's all up to you and Ulath. We're just here to observe."

"Thanks," he said dryly.

She curtsied. "Don't mention it."

Sparhawk took the box out from inside his tunic and touched his ring to it. "Open," he told it.

The lid popped up.

"Blue-Rose," Sparhawk said, speaking in Elenic.

"I hear thee, Anakha." The voice came from Vanion's lips again.

"I feel the Troll-Gods within thee. Can they understand my words when I speak in this tongue?"

"Nay, Anakha."

"Good. Cyrgon hath by deceit and subterfuge lured the Trolls here to Daresia and doth hurl them against our allies, the Atans. We would attempt to persuade the Troll-Gods to reassert their authority over their creatures. Thinkest thou that they might be willing to give hearing to our request?"

"Any God listens most attentively to words concerning his worshippers, Anakha."

"I had thought such might be the case. Dost thou agree with mine assessment that the knowledge that Cyrgon hath stolen their Trolls will enrage them?"

"They will be discomfited out of all measure, Anakha."

"How thinkest thou we might best proceed with them?"

"Advise them in simple words of what hath come to pass. Speak not too quickly nor with obscured meaning, for they are slow of understanding."

"I have perceived as much in past dealings with them."

"Wilt *thou* speak with them? I say this not in criticism, but thy Trollish is rude and uncouth."

"Did *you* put that in, Vanion?" Sparhawk accused.

Vanion blinked, his face changing subtly as Bhelliom withdrew its hold. "Not me," Vanion protested his innocence. "I wouldn't know good Trollish from bad."

"Forgive mine ineptitude, Blue-Rose. Mine instructor was in haste when she schooled my tongue in the language of the man-beasts."

"Sparhawk!" Sephrenia objected.

"Well, weren't you?" He addressed the stone again. "My comrade, Sir Ulath, hath greater familiarity with Trolls and their speech than do I. It is *he* who will advise the Troll-Gods that Cyrgon hath stolen their creatures."

"I will bring forth their spirits that thy comrade may address them." The stone pulsed in his hand, and the gigantic presences Sparhawk had sensed in the Temple of Azash were there, but this time they were in front of him where he could see them. He fervently wished that he could not. Because their reality was still locked inside the Bhelliom, their forms were suffused with an azure glow. They bulked enormous before him, their brutish faces enraged and their fury held in check only by the power of Bhelliom.

"All right, Ulath," Sparhawk said. "This is a dangerous situation. Try to be very, very convincing."

The big Genidian Knight swallowed hard and stepped forward. "I am Ulath-from-Thalesia," he said in Trollish. "I speak for Anakha, Bhelliom's child. I bring word of *your* children. Will you hear me?"

"Speak, Ulath-from-Thalesia." Sparhawk judged from the crackling roar mingled in the enormous voice that it was Khwaj, the Troll-God of Fire, who spoke.

Ulath's face took on an expression of mild reproach. "We are baffled by what you have done," he told them. "Why have you given your children to Cyrgon?"

"What?" Khwaj roared.

"It was our thought that you wished it so," Ulath said, feigning surprise. "Did you not command your children to leave their home-range and to walk for many sleeps across the ice-which-never-melts to this alien place?"

Khwaj howled, beating at the ground with his apelike fists, raising a cloud of dust and smoke from the ground.

"When did this come to pass?" another voice, a voice filled with a kind of gross slobbering, demanded.

"Two full turns of the seasons, Ghnomb," Ulath answered the question of the God of Eat. "It was our thought that you knew. Blue-Rose called you forth that we might ask why you have done this. Our Gods wish to know why you have broken the compact."

"Compact?" Stragen asked after Sephrenia had translated.

"It's an agreement," Flute explained. "We didn't really want to exterminate the Trolls, so we told the Troll-Gods that we'd leave their children alone if they'd stay in the Thalesian mountains."

"When did this happen?"

"Twenty-five thousand years ago—or so."

Stragen swallowed hard.

"Why are your children obeying Cyrgon if you did not command it?" Ulath asked.

One of the gigantic figures stretched out an abnormally long arm, and the huge hand plunged into a kind of emptiness, vanishing as it went in almost as a stick seems to vanish when poked into a forest pool. When the hand reemerged, it held a struggling Troll. The enormous God spoke, harshly demanding. The language was clearly Trollish, snarling and roaring.

"Now that's interesting," Ulath murmured. "It appears that even Trollish has changed over the years."

"What's he saying?" Sparhawk asked.

"I can't entirely make it out," Ulath replied. "It's so archaic that I can't understand most of the words. Zoka's demanding some answers, though."

"Zoka?"

"The God of Mating." Ulath listened intently.

"The Troll's confused," he reported. "He says that they all thought they *were* obeying their Gods. Cyrgon's disguise must have been nearly perfect. The Trolls are very close to their Gods and they'd probably recognize any ordinary attempt to deceive them."

Zoka roared, and hurled the shrieking Troll back into emptiness.

"Anakha!" another of the vast Gods bellowed.

"Which one is that?" Sparhawk muttered.

"Ghworg," Ulath replied quietly. "The God of Kill. Be a little careful with him. He's very short-tempered."

"Yes, Ghworg," Sparhawk responded to that vast brute.

"Release us from your father's grip. Let us go. We must reclaim our children." There was blood dripping from the fangs of the God of Kill. Sparhawk didn't want to think about whose blood it might be.

"Let me," Ulath murmured. He raised his voice. "That is beyond Anakha's power, Ghworg," he replied. "The spell which imprisoned you was of Ghwerig's making. It is a Trollish spell, and Anakha is untaught in such."

"We will teach him the spell."

"No!" Flute suddenly broke in, throwing aside her pretense of merely observing. "These are *my* children. I will not permit you to contaminate them with Trollish spells."

"We beg you, Child-Goddess! Set us free! Our children stray from us!"

"My family will never agree. Your children look upon our children as food. If Anakha frees you, your children will devour ours. It cannot be."

"Ghnomb!" Khwaj roared. "Give her surety!"

The huge face of the God of Eat twisted in agony. "I cannot!" It was almost a wail. "It would lessen me! Our children *must* eat. All that lives *must* be food!"

"Our children are lost unless you agree!" The grass around the feet of the God of Fire began to smoke.

"I think I see a toehold here," Ulath said in Elenic. He spoke again in Trollish. "There is justice in Ghnomb's words," he told the Gods. "Why should he alone lessen himself? Each must *also* accept lessening. Ghnomb will not accept less."

"It speaks truly!" Ghnomb howled. "I will not be lessened unless all are lessened!"

The four other Troll-Gods squirmed, their faces reflecting the same agony that had marked Ghnomb's.

"What will satisfy you?" It was the voice of the God who had not yet spoken. There were blizzards in that voice.

"The God of Ice," Ulath identified the speaker, "Schlee."

"Lessen yourselves!" Ghnomb demanded stubbornly. "I will not if you will not!"

"Trolls," Aphrael sighed, rolling her eyes. "Will you accept my mediation in this?" she demanded of the monstrous deities.

"We will hear your words, Aphrael," Ghworg replied dubiously.

"Our purposes are the same," the Child-Goddess began.

Sparhawk groaned.

"What's wrong?" Ulath asked quickly.

"She's going to make a speech—now of all times."

"Shut up, Sparhawk!" the Child-Goddess snapped. "I know what I'm doing." She turned to face the Troll-Gods again. "Cyrgon deceived your children," she began. "He brought them across the ice-which-never-melts to this place to make war on *my* children. Cyrgon must be punished!"

The Troll-Gods roared their agreement.

"Will you join with me and my family to cause hurt to Cyrgon for what he has done?"

"We will cause hurt to him by ourselves, Aphrael," Ghworg snarled.

"And how many of your children will die if you do? My children can pursue the children of Cyrgon into the lands of the sun, where your children die. Should we not join, then, that Cyrgon will suffer more?"

"There is wisdom in her words," Schlee said to his fellows. The breath of the God of Ice steamed in the air, though the air was not really cold, and glittering snowflakes appeared out of nowhere to settle on his massive shoulders.

"Ghnomb must agree that your children will no longer eat mine," Aphrael bored in. "If he does not, Anakha will not free you from his father's grip."

Ghnomb groaned.

"Ghnomb *must* do this," she insisted. "If he does not, I will not permit Anakha to free you, and Cyrgon will *keep* your children. Ghnomb will not agree to this if each of you will not accept equal lessening. Ghworg! You must no longer drive your children to kill mine!"

Ghworg raised both huge arms and howled.

"Khwaj!" she continued inexorably. "You must curb the fires which rage through the forests of Thalesia each year when the sun returns to the lands of the north."

Khwaj stifled a sob.

"Schlee!" Aphrael barked. "You must hold back the rivers of ice which crawl down the sides of the mountains. Let them melt when they reach the valleys."

"No!" Schlee wailed.

"Then you have lost all your children. Hold back the ice or you will weep alone in the wastes of the north. Zoka! No more than two offspring can issue from each she-Troll."

"*Never!*" Zoka bellowed. "My children *must* mate!"

"Your children are now Cyrgon's. Will you aid Cyrgon's increase?" She paused, her eyes narrowing. "One last agreement will I have from you all, or I will not let Anakha free you."

"What is your demand, Aphrael?" Schlee asked in his ice-choked voice.

"Your children are immortal. Mine are not. Your children must also die—each in an appointed time."

They exploded in an absolute rage.

"Return them to their prison, Anakha," Aphrael said. "They will not agree. The bargaining is done." She said it in Trollish, so it was obviously intended for the benefit of the raging Troll-Gods.

"Wait!" Khwaj shouted. "Wait!"

"Well?" she said.

"Let us go apart from you, that we may consider this monstrous demand."

"Do not be long," she said to them. "I have little patience."

The five vast beings withdrew further into the pasture.

"Weren't you pushing them a little far?" Sephrenia suggested. "That last demand of yours may very well kill any chance of reaching an agreement."

"I don't think so," Aphrael replied. "The Troll-Gods can't think that far into the future. They live for now, and right now the most important thing for them is taking their Trolls back from Cyrgon." She sighed. "The last demand is the most important, really. Humans and Trolls can't live in the same world. One or the other has to leave. I'd rather that it was the Trolls, wouldn't you?"

"You're very cruel, Aphrael. You're forcing the Troll-Gods to assist in the extermination of their own worshippers."

"The Trolls are doomed anyway," the Child-Goddess sighed. "There are just too many humans in the world. If the Trolls suddenly become mortal, they'll just slip away peacefully. If you humans have to kill them all, half of your number will die with them. I'm just as moral as the rest of the Gods. I love my children, and I don't want half of them killed and eaten in the mountains of Thalesia in some war to the death with the Trolls."

"Sparhawk," Stragen said, "didn't Khwaj do something that made it possible for you to watch Martel and listen to him talking when we were going across Pelosia toward Zemoch?"

Sparhawk nodded.

"Can Aphrael do that?"

"I'm right here, Stragen," Flute told him. "Why don't you ask me?"

"We haven't really been properly introduced yet, Divine One," he said with a fluid bow. "Can you? Reach out and talk with somebody on the other side of the world, I mean?"

"I don't like to do it that way," she replied. "I want to be close to someone when I talk to him."

"My Goddess places great importance on touching, Stragen," Sephrenia explained.

"Oh. I see. All right, then, when the Troll-Gods come back—and if they agree to our preposterous demands—I'd like to have Sparhawk or Ulath ask Khwaj to do me a favor. I need to talk to Platime back in Cimmura."

"They do return," Xanetia advised.

They all turned to face the monstrous beings coming back across the autumn-browned pasture.

"You have left us no choice, Aphrael," Khwaj said in a broken voice. "We must accept your brutal demands. We *must* save our children from Cyrgon."

"You will no longer kill and eat my children?" she pressed.

"We will not."

"You will no longer burn the forests of Thalesia?"

Khwaj groaned and nodded.

"You will no longer fill the valleys with glaciers?"

Schlee sobbed his agreement.

"You will no longer breed your Trolls like rabbits?"

Zoka wailed.

"Your children will grow old and die as do all other creatures?"

Khwaj buried his face in his hands. "Yes," he wept.

"Then we will join with you and do war upon Cyrgon. You will return to Bhelliom's heart for now. Anakha will carry you to the place where your children languish in thrall to Cyrgon. There will he release you and there will you wrest your children from Cyrgon's vile grasp. And there will we join together to cause hurt to Cyrgon. We will make his pain like the pain of Azash."

"*YES!*" the Troll-Gods howled their agreement in unison.

"Done!" Aphrael declared in a ringing voice. "One boon more, Khwaj—in demonstration of our newly formed alliance. This child of mine would speak with one known as Platime in Cimmura in far-off Elenia. Make it so that he can."

"I will, Aphrael." Khwaj held out his vast hand, and a sheet of unwavering fire dripped from his fingertips.

Behind the fire there lay a bedchamber with a vast, snoring bulk sprawled on an oversized bed.

"Wake up, Platime," Stragen said crisply.

"Fire!" Platime shrieked, struggling into a sitting position.

"Oh, be quiet!" Stragen snapped. "There isn't any fire. This is magic."

"Stragen? Is that you? Where are you?"

"I'm behind the fire. You probably can't see me."

"Are you learning magic now?"

"Just dabbling," Stragen lied modestly. "Now listen carefully; I don't know how long the spell will last. Get in touch with Arnag in Khadach. Ask him to kill Count Gerrich. I don't have time to explain. It's important, Platime. It's part of something we're doing here in Tamuli."

"Gerrich?" Platime said dubiously. "That's going to be expensive, Stragen."

"Get the money from Lenda. Tell him that Ehlana authorized it."

"Did she?"

"Well—she would if she knew about it. I'll get her approval next time I talk with her. Now, this is the most important part. Gerrich *has* to be killed exactly fifteen days from now—not fourteen, not sixteen. The time's very important."

"All right, I'll see to it. Tell Ehlana that Gerrich will die in exactly fifteen days. Was there anything else? That magic fire of yours is making me very nervous."

"See if you can identify anybody else Gerrich has been dealing with and kill them as well—those Pelosian barons who've allied themselves with him certainly, and any people in the other kingdoms who are in this with him. You know the kind I mean—the ones like the Earl of Belton."

"You want them all killed at that same time?"

"As close as you can. Gerrich is the really important one, though." Stragen pursed his lips. "While you're at it, you'd probably better kill Avin Wargunsson as well—just to be on the safe side."

"He's as good as dead, Stragen."

"You're a good friend, Platime."

"Friend, my foot. You'll pay the usual fees, Stragen."

Stragen sighed. "All right," he said mournfully.

"How deeply are you attached to your Elene God, Stragen?" Aphrael asked as they rode back to Matherion.

"I'm an agnostic, Divine One."

"Would you like to examine that last sentence for logical consistency, Stragen?" Vanion asked with an amused expression.

"Consistency's the mark of a little mind, my Lord," Stragen replied loftily. "Why do you ask, Aphrael?"

"You don't really belong to *any* God, then, do you?"

"No, not really."

Sephrenia started to say something, but Aphrael raised one little hand to cut her off. "You might want to look into the advantages of coming to serve *me*," the Child-Goddess suggested. "I can do all sorts of *wonderful* things for you."

"You're not supposed to do this, Aphrael!" Sephrenia protested.

"Hush, Sephrenia. This is between Stragen and me. I think that maybe it's time for me to broaden my horizons. Styrics are very, very nice, but sometimes Elenes are more fun. Besides, Stragen and I are both thieves. We've got a lot in common." She grinned at the blond man. "Think it over, Milord. I'm not at all difficult to serve. A few kisses and a bouquet of flowers now and then and I'm perfectly happy."

"She's lying to you," Sparhawk warned. "Enlisting in the service of Aphrael is volunteering for the profoundest slavery you could possibly imagine."

"Well," the Child-Goddess said deprecatingly, "I suppose it is, when you get right down to it—but as long as we're all having fun, what difference does it make?"

CHAPTER TWENTY-SIX

I t was quite early, several hours before dawn, Sparhawk judged, when Mirtai entered the royal bedroom—as usual without knocking. "You'd better get up," the golden giantess announced.

Sparhawk sat up. "What's the problem?" he asked.

"There's a fleet of boats coming toward the city," she replied. "Either that, or the Delphae have learned how to walk on water. There are enough lanterns on the eastern horizon to light up a small city. Put your clothes on, Sparhawk. I'll go wake the others." She turned abruptly and left the room.

"I *wish* she'd learn to knock," Sparhawk muttered, throwing off the covers.

"*You're* the one who's supposed to make sure the doors are locked," Ehlana reminded him. "Do you think it might be trouble?"

"I don't know. Did Sarabian say anything about expecting a fleet?"

"He didn't mention it to me," she replied, also rising from their bed.

"I'd better go have a look." He picked up his cloak. "There's no need for you to go outside, dear," he told her. "It's chilly up on the parapet."

"No. I want to see for myself."

They went out of the bedroom. Princess Danae came out of her room in her nightdress, rubbing her eyes with one hand and dragging Rollo behind her. Mutely she went to Sparhawk, and he picked her up without even thinking.

The three of them went into the hallway and up the stairs toward the top of the tower.

Kalten and Sarabian were standing on the east side of the tower looking out across the battlements at the lights strung along the eastern horizon.

"Any idea of who they might be?" Sparhawk asked as he and his family joined them.

"Not a clue," Kalten replied.

"Could it be the Tamul navy?" Ehlana asked the emperor.

"It *could* be, I suppose," he replied, "but if it is, they're not responding to any orders *I* sent."

Sparhawk stepped back a few paces. "Who do the ships belong to?" he murmured to his daughter.

"I ain't a-tellin', dorlin'," she replied with a little smirk.

"Stop that. I want to know who's coming."

"You'll find out—" She squinted toward the lights on the horizons, "—in a couple of hours, I'd imagine."

"I want to know who they are," he insisted.

"Yes, I can see that, but wanting isn't getting, Father, and I ain't a-gonna tell ya."

"Oh, God," he groaned.

"Yes?" she responded innocently. "*Was* there something?"

The dawn came up rusty that morning. There was no hint of a breeze, and the smoke from the chimneys of fire-domed Matherion hung motionless in the air, blurring the light from the east. Sparhawk and the other knights roused the Atan garrison, put on their armor, and rode down to the harbor.

The approaching ships were clearly of Cammorian construction, but banks of oars had been added along their sides.

"Somebody was in a hurry to get here," Ulath noted. "A Cammorian ship with a good following wind can make thirty leagues a day. If you added oars to that, you could increase it to fifty."

"How many ships are there?" Kalten asked, squinting at the approaching fleet.

"I make it close to a hundred," the big Thalesian replied.

"You could carry a lot of men on a hundred ships," Sarabian said.

"Enough to make me nervous, your Majesty," Vanion agreed.

Then, as the ships entered the harbor, the red and gold standards of the Church were run up on the masts, and as the lead vessel came closer, Sparhawk could make out two familiar figures standing in the bow. The one man had broad shoulders and a massive chest. His round face was split with a delighted grin. The other was short and very stout. He was also grinning.

"What kept you?" Ulath shouted across the intervening water.

"Class distinctions," Tynian shouted back. "Knights are defined as gentlemen, and they objected to being pressed into service as oarsmen."

"You've got *knights* manning the oars?" Vanion called incredulously.

"It's a part of a new physical conditioning program, Lord Vanion," Patriarch Emban shouted. "Archprelate Dolmant noticed that the Soldiers of God were getting flabby. They're much more fit now than they were when we left Sarinium."

The ship approached the wharf carefully, and the seamen threw the mooring hawsers to the knights ashore.

Tynian leapt across. Emban gave him a disgusted look and waddled back amidships to wait for the sailors to extend the gangway.

"How's the shoulder?" Ulath asked the broad-faced Deiran.

"Much better," Tynian replied. "It aches when the weather's damp, though." He saluted Vanion. "Komier, Darellon, and Abriel are leading the Church Knights east from Chyrellos, my Lord," he reported. "Patriarch Bergsten's with them. Patriarch Emban and I came on ahead by ship—obviously. We thought a few more knights here in Matherion might be useful."

"Indeed they will, Sir Tynian. How many do you have with you?"

"Five thousand, my Lord."

"That's impossible, Tynian. There's no way you could crowd that many men and horses on a hundred ships."

"Yes, my Lord," Tynian replied mildly, "we noticed that ourselves almost immediately. The knights were terribly disappointed when they found out that we weren't going to let them bring their horses with them."

"Tynian," Kalten objected, "they *have* to have horses. A knight without his horse is meaningless."

"There are already horses here, Kalten. Why bring more?"

"Tamul horses aren't trained."

"Then we'll just have to train them, won't we? I had a hundred ships. I could have brought fifteen hundred knights along with their horses, or five thousand *without* the horses. Call the extra thirty-five hundred a gift."

"How were you able to make them row?" Ulath asked.

"We used whips." Tynian shrugged. "There's a Captain Sorgi who plies the inner sea, and the oars were his idea."

"Good old Sorgi." Sparhawk laughed.

"You know him?"

"Quite well, actually."

"You'll be able to renew your friendship. His ship's out there with the fleet. We'd have sailed aboard *his* ship, but Patriarch Emban didn't like the looks of it. It's all patched and rickety."

"It's old. I think Sorgi has a secret bet with himself about which of them falls apart first—him or his ship."

"His mind's still sharp, though. When we asked him how to get more speed out of the ships, he suggested adding oars. It's very seldom done that way because of the expense of paying the oarsmen—not to mention the fact that they take up room usually reserved for cargo. I decided not to bring any cargo, and Church Knights are sworn to poverty, so I didn't have to pay them. It worked out fairly well, actually."

They gathered in Ehlana's sitting room several hours later to hear Emban and Tynian report on what was happening in Eosia.

"Ortzel nearly had apoplexy when Dolmant pulled all the knights out of Rendor," Emban told them. He leaned back in his chair with a silver tankard in his pudgy hand. "Ortzel *really* has his heart set on returning the Rendors to the bosom of our Holy Mother. Dolmant seemed inclined to agree with him at first, but he woke up one morning with a completely different outlook. Nobody's been able to explain his sudden change of heart."

"He received a message, Emban." Sephrenia smiled. "The messenger can be *very* impressive when he wants to be."

"Oh?"

"An emergency came up, your Grace," Vanion explained. "Zalasta had sent word to his confederates in Eosia, and they began killing the worshippers of the Child-Goddess Aphrael.

That put *her* life in danger as well. We spoke with one of the other Younger Gods—Setras. He agreed that the Younger Gods would lend Aphrael some of *their* children, and he went to Chyrellos to ask Dolmant to offer sanctuary to Aphrael's surviving worshippers. He was also going to try to persuade Dolmant to send the Church Knights here. Evidently he was a bit more convincing than you and Tynian were."

"Are you saying that a Styric God went into the Basilica?" Emban exclaimed.

"He said that's what he was going to do," Sparhawk replied, shifting his daughter in his lap.

"No Styric God has *ever* gone into the Basilica!"

"He's wrong," Princess Danae whispered into her father's ear. "I've been there dozens of times."

"I know," Sparhawk whispered back. "Setras paid a *formal* visit, though." He thought of something. "Setras went to Chyrellos just a short time ago," he murmured into her ear. "Even with oarsmen to help, Tynian's fleet couldn't have reached Matherion *this* fast. Have you been tampering again?"

"Would I do that?" Her eyes were wide and innocent.

"Yes, as a matter of fact, you probably would."

"If you already knew the answer, why did you ask the question? Don't waste my time, Sparhawk. I *am* very busy, you know."

"Things seem to be coming to a head in Lamorkand," Tynian continued his report. "Count Gerrich's forces have taken Vraden and Agnak in northern Lamorkand, and King Friedahl's been appealing to the other monarchs for assistance."

"We'll be taking care of that shortly, Sir Tynian," Stragen told him. "I've been in touch with Platime, and he's arranging fatal accidents for Gerrich and the various barons who've been helping him."

The door opened, and Berit entered with Xanetia.

"What did you find out, Anarae?" Sephrenia asked intently.

"This morning's sortie was quite profitable, little mother," Berit advised her. "Zalasta's friend Ynak showed up at the Cynesgan embassy, and the Anarae was able to probe his mind. I think we've got most of the details of their plan now."

"Is this the lady with the rare gift?" Emban asked.

"I seem to be forgetting my manners," Vanion apologized. "Anarae Xanetia, this is Sir Tynian of Deira and Patriarch

Emban of the Church of Chyrellos. Gentlemen, this is Xanetia, the Anarae of the People of Delpheaus."

Tynian and Emban bowed, their eyes curious.

"What have our friends at the embassy been up to, Anarae?" Sarabian asked.

"Though it was not pleasant to probe so vile a mind, Ynak's thought did reveal much, Majesty," she replied. "As we had surmised, the outcast Styrics at Verel have long known that the greatest threat to their design would come from Eosia. They wished Anakha to come to Tamuli, but they did *not* wish for him to bring an hundred thousand Church Knights with him. The turmoil in western Tamuli is intended to block the passage of the knights; all else is extraneous. Moreover, the attacks of the Trolls in Atan are also designed to divert attention. It is from the *south* that our enemies plan their main assault. Even now do Cynesgan troops filter across the unguarded frontier to join with Scarpa's forces in the jungles of Arjuna; and Elenes from western Tamuli, moreover, do journey by ship to southern Arjuna to add their weight to Scarpa's growing horde. The distractions in the west and in Atan were to drain away imperial might, thus opening a path for Scarpa to strike directly across Tamul and to lay siege to Matherion itself. Ynak and the others were much chagrined by the exposure of Zalasta's treachery, for it voided his opportunity to do us harm by misdirection and false counsel."

"What's the real goal of a siege of Matherion, Lady Xanetia?" Emban asked shrewdly. "It's a nice enough city, but . . ." He spread his hands.

"Our enemies thought to compel the imperial government to surrender up Anakha by posing a threat to Matherion itself, your Grace. The subversion of diverse officials gave them hope that the prime minister might be persuaded to capitulate so that Matherion might be spared."

"That might have worked," Sarabian noted. "Pondia Subat's backbone isn't really very rigid. Zalasta and his four friends plan things quite well."

"Three friends now, your Majesty." Berit grinned. "The Anarae tells me that the one named Ptaga came a cropper a few days ago."

"The vampire-raiser?" Kalten said. "What happened to him?"

"May I tell them, Anarae?" Berit asked politely.

"An it please thee, Sir Knight."

"It seems that Ptaga was in southern Tamul proper, in those mountains between Sarna and Samar. He was waving his arms and creating the illusion of Shining Ones to turn loose on the populace. One of the *real* Delphae was out scouting the area and came across him and quietly joined the crowd of illusions." Berit grinned a nasty little grin.

"Well?" Kalten said impatiently. "What happened?"

"Ptaga was inspecting his illusions, and when he came to the *real* Shining One, not even *he* could tell the difference. The Delphaeic scout reached out and touched him. Ptaga's cast his last illusion, I guess. He was in the process of dissolving when the scout left the area."

"Ynak of Lydros is *most* discomfited by his associate's demise," Xanetia added, "for without the illusion of Ptaga, our enemies must produce *real* forces to confront us."

"And that brings us to something we should consider," Oscagne observed. "The arrival of Sir Tynian and Patriarch Emban with five thousand knights, the elimination of these illusions that were terrorizing the populace, and our knowledge of this planned attack from the south change the whole strategic situation."

"It certainly does," Sarabian agreed.

"I think we might want to consider these new developments in our planning, then, your Majesty."

"You're right, of course, Oscagne." Sarabian squinted at Sparhawk. "Could we prevail on you to go up to Atana and bring Betuana back here, old boy?" he asked. "If we're going to discuss changes in planning, she should be present. Betuana's bigger than I am, and I *definitely* don't want to insult her by leaving her out of our discussions."

Betuana, the Queen of the Atans, ruled more or less by default. King Androl, her husband, was a stupendous warrior, and that may have been a part of the problem. He was *so* stupendous that the normal concerns of the military commanders—such problems as being grossly outnumbered, for example—were quite beyond his grasp. Men who are sublimely convinced of their own invincibility seldom make good generals. Betuana, on the other hand, *was* a good general, quite possibly one of the best in the world, and the peculiar Atan society, which totally ignored any distinctions between the sexes, gave her talents the fullest opportunity to flower. Far from resenting his wife's superiority, Androl was inordinately proud of her. Sparhawk rather suspected that Betuana might have preferred it otherwise, but she was a realist.

She had, moreover, a disconcerting level of trust. Sparhawk had carefully marshaled a number of explanations both about the need for the council of war and about their mode of travel, but those explanations proved totally unnecessary. "All right," she replied calmly when he told her that Bhelliom would transport them instantly to Matherion.

"You don't want any details, your Majesty?" He was more than a little surprised.

"Why waste time explaining something I wouldn't understand anyway, Sparhawk-Knight?" She shrugged. "I'll accept your word that the jewel can take us to Matherion; you don't have any reason to lie to me about it. Give me a few moments to tell Androl that I'm going and to change clothes. Sarabian-Emperor finds my work clothes a trifle unsettling." She glanced down at her armor.

"He's changed quite a bit, your Majesty."

"So Norkan tells me. I'm curious to find out just how much your wife has modified him. I'll be right back." She strode from the room.

"You get used to that, Sparhawk," Khalad said. "She's very direct, and she doesn't waste time asking questions about things she doesn't need to know about. It's quite refreshing, actually."

"Be nice," Sparhawk said mildly.

Ambassador Norkan was nervous, but both Kring and Engessa were quite nearly as calm as the queen.

"God!" Emperor Sarabian exclaimed as the momentary blur faded and the trees of the Atan vanished to be replaced by the familiar blue carpeting, breeze-touched drapes, and the gleaming, opalescent walls of the royal sitting room in Ehlana's castle. "Isn't there some way you can announce that you're coming, Sparhawk?"

"I don't think so, your Majesty," Sparhawk replied.

"Having a group of people pop out of nowhere is very unnerving, you know." He frowned. "What would have happened if I'd been standing in the same spot you just appeared in? Would we have gotten sort of combined? All mixed together into one person?"

"I don't really know, your Majesty."

"Tell him that it is impossible, Anakha," Vanion spoke with

the voice of Bhelliom. "I would not make such errors, and it is unusual for two things to be in the same place at once."

"Unusual?" Sarabian demanded. "Do you mean that it *can* happen?"

"I pray thee, Anakha, ask him not to pursue this question. The answers will greatly disturb him."

"You're looking fit, Sarabian-Emperor," Betuana said. "You are much changed. Do you know how to use that sword?"

"The rapier? Oh, yes, Betuana. Actually, I'm quite proficient."

"The weapon is light for my taste, but each of us must select such arms as suit him best. Sparhawk-Knight and Vanion-Preceptor tell me that much has changed. Let us consider those changes and adjust our plans to fit them." She looked at Ehlana and smiled. "You look well, Sister-Queen," she said. "Matherion suits you."

"And you're as lovely as ever, dear sister," Ehlana replied warmly. "The gown is breathtaking."

"Do you really like it?" Betuana turned almost girlishly to show off her deep blue Atan gown that left one golden shoulder bare and was girdled at the hips with a golden chain.

"It's absolutely stunning, Betuana. Blue is definitely your color."

Betuana glowed at the compliment. "Now, then, Sarabian," she said, all business again, "what's happened, and what are we going to do about it?"

"I do not find that amusing, Sarabian-Emperor," Betuana declared angrily.

"I didn't say it to amuse you, Betuana. I felt much the same way when they told me. I've sent for the lady. You're probably going to have to see for yourself."

"Do you take me for some child to be frightened by stories of ghosts and hobgoblins?"

"Of course not, but I assure you, Xanetia really *is* a Delphae."

"Does she glow?"

"Only when it suits her. She's been suppressing the light— for the sake of our peace of mind—and she's altered her coloration. She looks like an ordinary Tamul, but believe me, she's far from ordinary."

"I think you've lost your mind, Sarabian-Emperor."

"You'll see, dorlin'."

She gave him a startled look.

"Local joke." He shrugged.

The door opened, and Xanetia, Danae, and Sephrenia entered.

Princess Danae, her face artfully innocent, went to Betuana's chair and held out her arms. Betuana smiled at the little girl, picked her up, and held her on her lap. "How have you been, Princess?" she asked in Elenic.

"That's all right, Betuana," the little girl replied in Tamul. "Sephrenia's taught us all to speak the language of humans. I've been a little sick, actually, but I'm all better now. It's really boring to be sick, isn't it?"

"I've always thought so, Danae."

"I don't think I'll do it anymore, then. You haven't kissed me yet."

"Oh." Betuana smiled. "I forgot. I'm sorry." She quickly attended to the oversight.

Sarabian straightened in his chair. "Queen Betuana of Atan, I have the honor to present Anarae Xanetia of Delphaeus. Would you mind showing the queen who you are, Anarae?"

"An it please thee, Majesty," Xanetia replied.

"It's a startling experience, your Majesty," Emban said to the Atan queen, folding his pudgy hands on his paunch, "but you get used to it."

Xanetia looked gravely at Betuana. "Thy people and mine are cousins, Betuana-Queen," she said. "Long, however, have we been separated. I mean thee no harm, so fear me not."

"I do not fear thee." Betuana lapsed automatically into archaic Tamul.

"Mine appearance here in Matherion is of necessity disguised, Betuana-Queen. Behold my true state." The color drained quickly from Xanetia's hair and face, and her unearthly glow began to shine through.

Danae calmly reached up to touch Betuana's face with one small hand. Sparhawk carefully concealed his smile.

"I know what you're feeling, Betuana," Sephrenia said quite calmly. "I'm sure you can imagine how Xanetia and I both felt about each other the first time we met. You know about the enmity between our two races, don't you?"

Betuana nodded, obviously not trusting herself to speak.

"I'm going to do something unnatural, Anarae," Sephrenia said then, "but I think Atana Betuana needs reassurance. Let's both try to control our reactions." Then with no hesitation or evident revulsion, she embraced the glowing woman. Sparhawk knew her very well, however, and he could see the faint ripple along her jaw. Sephrenia had steeled herself as she might have before thrusting her hand into fire.

Almost timidly, Xanetia's arms slipped around Sephrenia's shoulders. "Well met, sister mine," she murmured.

"Well met indeed, my sister," Sephrenia replied.

"Did you notice that the world didn't come to an end, Betuana?" Ehlana said.

"I think I *did* feel it quiver, though," Sarabian noted.

"We seem to be surrounded by people obsessed with their own cleverness, Xanetia." Sephrenia smiled.

"A failing of the young, my sister. Maturity may temper their impulse to levity."

Betuana straightened in her chair and put Danae down. "This alliance meets with your approval, Sarabian-Emperor?" she asked formally.

"It does, Betuana-Queen."

"Then I shall abide by it." She rose to her feet and went to the two sorceresses, holding out her hands. Sephrenia and Xanetia took those hands, and the three stood together so for a long minute.

"Thou art brave, Betuana-Queen," Xanetia noted.

"I'm an Atan, Anarae." Betuana shrugged. Then she turned and gave Engessa a stern look. "Why did you not tell me?" she demanded.

"I was told not to, Betuana-Queen," he replied. "Sarabian-Emperor said that you would need to see Xanetia-Anarae before you would believe that she is who we say she is. He also wanted to be present when you and she met. He takes delight in the astonishment of others. His is a peculiar mind."

"Engessa!" Sarabian protested.

"I am bound to speak the truth as I see it to my queen, Sarabian-Emperor."

"Well, I suppose you are, but you don't have to be quite so blunt about it, do you?"

"All right, then," Vanion summed it all up, "we start marching north with the knights, the majority of the local Atan garrisons, and the Imperial Guard. We'll make a great deal of noise, and Ekatas, Cyrgon's High Priest, will pass the word to Zalasta and Cyrgon that we're on the way. That will give Stragen's murderers a free hand, because everybody will be watching *us*.

Then, when the Harvest Festival's over and the bodies start to turn up, our friends out there should be a bit distracted. At that point, Sparhawk takes Bhelliom to northern Atan and releases the Troll-Gods. Northern Atan becomes totally secure at that point. We reverse our line of march, pick up the bulk of the Atans, and go south to meet Scarpa. Are we all agreed so far?"

"No, we're not, Vanion-Preceptor," Betuana said firmly. "The Harvest Festival's still two weeks away, and the Trolls could very well be in the streets of Atana in two weeks. We *have* to devise some means to slow their advance."

"Forts," Ulath said.

"I must be getting used to you, Ulath." Kalten laughed. "I actually understood that one."

"So did I," Sarabian agreed, "but the Trolls might just bypass any forts we build and keep marching on Atana."

"The *Trolls* might, your Majesty," Sparhawk disagreed, "but Cyrgon won't. Cyrgon's got the oldest military mind in the world, and a soldier absolutely will *not* leave enemy strongholds behind his lines. People who do that lose wars. If we build forts, he'll *have* to stop his advance to deal with them."

"And if the forts are in open fields, the Trolls won't be able to hide in the forest," Bevier added. "They'll have to come across open ground, in plain view of the Peloi archers, my catapult crews, and Khalad's crossbowmen. Even if they cover the field with smoke, we'll be able to put down a goodly number of them with blind shots."

"My Atans do not like to hide behind walls," Betuana said stubbornly.

"We all have to do things we don't like sometimes, Betuana," Ehlana told her. "Forts will keep your warriors alive, and dead soldiers don't serve any purpose at all."

"Except to provide supper for the Trolls," Talen added. "There's an idea, Sparhawk. If you could train your Pandions to eat their enemies, you wouldn't need supply trains."

"Do you mind?" Sparhawk said acidly.

"It still won't work," Betuana told them. "The Trolls are too closely engaged with my armies. We don't have the *time* to build forts."

"We could build the forts a few miles behind your lines and withdraw your troops into them once they're finished, your Majesty," Sparhawk told her.

"Have you had many dealings with Trolls, Prince Sparhawk?" she asked tartly. "Do you have any idea how fast they run? They'll be on top of you before you can get the walls up."

"They can't run anywhere if time stops, your Majesty. We used that when we were on our way to Zemoch. The Troll-God of Eat can put people—or Trolls—into the space between one second and the next. We found that when we were in that space, the rest of the world didn't move at all. We'll have plenty of time to build forts."

"Why don't you verify that with the Bhelliom before you start making predictions, Sparhawk?" Emban suggested. "Let's be sure that it's going to work before we base any strategies on it. Let's find out if Bhelliom has any reservations about the notion."

Bhelliom, as it turned out, had several. "Thy design is flawed, Anakha," it responded to Sparhawk's question. Vanion's hand lifted Sephrenia's teacup and released it.

The cup stopped in midair and hung there.

"Take the vessel down, Anakha," Vanion's voice instructed.

Sparhawk took hold of the cup and immediately found that it was as immobile as a mountain. He tried as hard as he could to move it, but it simply stayed where it was.

"Thou couldst not so much as move a leaf, Anakha," Bhelliom told him. "Thou canst easily move *thyself* through that frozen moment, but to move other objects would require thee to move the entire universe."

"I see," Sparhawk said glumly. "Then we wouldn't be able to cut down trees and build forts, would we?"

"Are those structures of great importance to thee? Doth some obscure custom require them?"

"Nay, Blue-Rose. It is our intent to place obstructions in the path of the Trolls that they may not attack our friends, the Atans."

"Wouldst thou be offended were I to offer suggestion?"

Ulath looked sharply at Tynian. "Have you been talking to that poor stone in secret?" he accused.

"Very funny, Ulath," Tynian said sourly.

"I did not understand." Vanion's tone was slightly chilly.

"It is an ongoing discussion between the two, Blue-Rose," Sparhawk explained, giving the pair a hard look. "It hath reached a point so obscure now that it is incomprehensible. Gladly would I hear thy suggestion, my friend."

"Is it needful to injure the Trolls, Anakha? If they be totally denied access to the lands of thy friends, the Atans, must thou kill them?"

"Indeed, Blue-Rose, we would prefer *not* to cause them harm. When their Gods wrest them from Cyrgon's dominion shall they be our allies."

"Would it offend thee should *I* erect a barrier before them? A barrier beyond their ability to cross?"

"Not in the least. Indeed, we would be most grateful."

"Let us then to Atan, and I will make it so. I would not see *any* destroyed needlessly. My child will surely aid me, and between us, she and I will bar the Trolls from proceeding farther southward."

"Thou hast a daughter, too, Blue-Rose?" Sparhawk was stunned.

"I have millions, Anakha, and each is as precious to me as thine is to thee. Let us to Atan, then, that the bloodshed may cease."

Northern Atan was forested, but the more rugged mountains lay to the south. The mountains of the north had been ground down by glaciers in ages past, and the land sloped gradually down to the Sea of the North where eternal pack-ice capped the globe. Sparhawk looked around quickly. Bhelliom had responded to his unspoken request and had brought only warriors to this northern forest. There were certain to be arguments about that later, but that could not be helped.

"Engessa-Atan." Vanion's voice was crisply authoritative. An absurd notion occurred to Sparhawk. He wondered suddenly if Bhelliom had ever commanded troops.

"Yes, Vanion-Preceptor?" the big Atan replied.

"Command thy kinsmen to withdraw one league's distance from the place where now they are engaged."

Engessa looked sharply at Vanion, then realized that it was not the Pandion Preceptor who had spoken. "That will take some time, Blue-Rose," he explained. "The Atans are engaging the Trolls all across the North Cape. I will have to send messengers."

"Do thou but speak the command, Engessa-Atan. *All* shall hear thee, thou hast mine assurance."

"I wouldn't argue, friend Engessa," Kring advised. "That's the jewel that stops the sun. If it says they'll all hear you, they'll all hear you. Take my word for it."

"We'll try it, then." Engessa raised his face. "Withdraw!" he roared in a shattering bellow. "Fall back one league and re-group!"

The huge voice echoed and reechoed through the forest.

"I think you could make yourself heard from one side of the cape to the other without any help at all, Engessa-Atan," Kalten said.

"Not *quite* so far, Kalten-Knight," Engessa replied modestly.

"Thy judgment of thy people's speed will be more precise than mine, Engessa-Atan," Bhelliom told him. "Advise me when they have reached safety. I would not have them trapped north of the wall."

"The wall?" Ulath asked.

"The barrier of which I spake." Vanion bent and touched the ground with strangely gentle fingertips. "It is well, Anakha. We are within a few paces of the place I sought."

"I have ever had absolute faith in thine ability to find a precise spot, Blue-Rose."

"*Ever* is perhaps an imprecise term, Anakha." A faint, ironic smile touched Vanion's lips. "It seemeth to me I do recall some talk of finding thyself on the surface of the moon when first we began to move from place to place."

"You *did* say that, Sparhawk," Kalten reminded his friend.

"Thou spakest of thy daughter, Blue-Rose," Sparhawk said, rather quickly changing the subject. "May we be privileged to meet her?"

"Thou hast met her, Anakha. Thou standest this very moment upon her verdant bosom." Vanion's hand fondly patted the ground.

"The earth itself?" Bevier asked incredulously.

"Is she not fair?" There was a note of pride in the question. Then Vanion straightened. "Let us withdraw somewhat from this spot, Anakha. What I am to do here will take place some six of thy miles beneath our feet, and its effects here at the surface are difficult to predict. I would not endanger thee or thy companions by mine imprecision, and there will be some disturbance here. Is it safe to proceed now, Engessa-Atan?"

Engessa nodded. "Any Atan who hasn't covered at least a league by now doesn't deserve to be called an Atan," he replied.

They turned and walked some hundred paces to the south. Then they stopped.

"Farther, I pray thee, Anakha, yet again as far, and it would be well if thou and thy companions did lie upon the earth. The disturbance may be quite profound."

"Your friend is beginning to make me nervous, Sparhawk," Tynian confessed as they walked another hundred paces back. "Exactly what is it planning here?"

"You know as much about it as I do, my friend."

Then they heard a deep-toned subterranean booming that seemed to rise up out of the core of the earth. The ground shuddered sharply under their feet.

"Earthquake!" Kalten shouted in alarm.

"I think that may be what you were asking about, Tynian," Ulath rumbled.

"This is not simple, Anakha," Bhelliom observed in an almost clinical tone. "The pressures are extreme and must be adjusted with great delicacy to achieve the end we do desire."

The next jolt staggered them. The ground heaved and shuddered, and the dreadful, hollow booming grew louder.

"It is time, Anakha. The disturbance which I did mention previously is about to begin."

"*Begin?*" Bevier exclaimed. "It's all I can do to stand up *now*!"

"We'd better do as we're told," Sparhawk said sharply, dropping to his knees and then sprawling out facedown on the carpet of fallen leaves. "I think the next one's going to be spectacular."

"The next one" lasted for a full ten minutes. Nothing with legs could have stood erect on the violently jerking and convulsing earth. Then, with a monstrous roar, the earth not fifty paces in front of them split. The land beyond that ghastly crack in the earth's shell seemed to fall away, while the shuddering ground to which they clung heaved upward, rising ponderously, rippling almost like a wind-tossed banner. Great clouds of birds, squawking in alarm, rose from the shuddering trees.

Then the earthquake gradually subsided. The violence of the tremors grew less severe and less frequent, although there were a number of intermittent jolts. The awful booming sound grew fainter, echoing up through miles of rock like the memory of a nightmare. Vast clouds of dust came billowing up over the lip of the newly formed precipice.

"Now mayest thou contemplate mine handiwork, Anakha," Bhelliom said quite calmly, although with a certain modest pride. "Speak truly, for I will not be offended shouldst thou find flaws. If thou dost perceive faults in what I have wrought, I will correct them."

Sparhawk decided not to trust his feet just yet. Followed closely by his friends, he crawled to the abrupt edge that had not been there fifteen minutes earlier.

The cliff was almost as straight as a sword-cut, and it went down and down at least a thousand feet. It stretched, moreover, as far as the eye could reach both to the east and to the west. A huge escarpment, a vast wall, now separated the upper reaches of the North Cape from the rest of Tamuli.

"What thinkest thou?" Bhelliom asked, just a little anxiously. "Will my wall deny the Trolls access to the lands of thy friends? I can do more if it is thy wish."

"No, Blue-Rose," Sparhawk choked, "no more, I pray thee."

"I am pleased that thou art satisfied."

"It is a splendid wall, Blue-Rose." It was a ridiculous thing to say, but Sparhawk was badly shaken.

Bhelliom did not seem to notice. Vanion's face was suddenly creased with a shy smile at Sparhawk's stunned expression of approval. "It is an adequate wall," it said a bit deprecatingly. "There was some urgency in our need, so I had not time enough to mold and shape it as I might have wished, but methinks it will serve. I would take it as kindness, however, that when next thou dost require modification of the earth, thou wouldst give me more extensive notice, for truly, work done in haste is never wholly satisfactory."

"I shall endeavor to remember that, Blue-Rose."

CHAPTER
TWENTY-
SEVEN

I t's not so bad in here, Sarabian," Mirtai was saying to the distraught emperor. "The floor's carpeted, so most of the tiles weren't broken when they fell." She was on her knees gathering up the small opalescent tiles as Sparhawk and the others emerged from that blurred grey emptiness.

"Sparhawk!" Sarabian exclaimed, recoiling in shocked surprise. "I *wish* you'd blow a trumpet or something before you do that!"

"What happened, your Majesty?" Vanion asked, staring at the littered carpet.

"We had an earthquake! Now I've got an economic disaster on my hands in addition to everything else!"

"You felt it *here*, your Majesty?" Vanion choked.

"It was *terrible*, Vanion!" Sephrenia said. "It was the worst earthquake I've ever been through!"

"Here?"

"You're going to make me cross if you keep saying that. Of course we felt it here. Look at the walls."

"It looks like a bad case of the pox," Kalten said.

"The tiles were jumping off the walls like grasshoppers," Sarabian said in a sick voice. "God knows what the rest of the city looks like. This will bankrupt me."

"It's over four hundred leagues!" Vanion choked. "Twelve hundred miles!"

"What *is* he talking about, Sparhawk?" Ehlana demanded.

"We were at the center of the earthquake," Sparhawk replied. "It was up in northern Atan."

"Did *you* do this to me, Sparhawk?" Sarabian demanded.

"Bhelliom did, your Majesty. The Trolls won't be attacking the Atans anymore."

"Bhelliom shook them all to pieces?"

Sparhawk smiled faintly. "No, your Majesty. It put a wall across the North Cape."

"Can't the Trolls climb over it?" Betuana demanded.

"I wouldn't think so, your Majesty," Vanion said. "It's about a thousand feet high, and it stretches from the Tamul Sea to that coast that lies to the northwest of Sarsos. The Trolls won't be coming any farther south—not in the next two weeks, anyway, and after that, it won't make any difference."

"What exactly do you mean when you say 'wall,' Vanion?" Patriarch Emban asked.

"Actually, it's an escarpment, your Grace," Vanion explained, "a huge cliff that stretches all the way across the North Cape. That's what caused the earthquake."

"Won't Cyrgon be able to reverse whatever Bhelliom did?" Sephrenia asked.

"Bhelliom says no, little mother," Sparhawk replied. "He isn't strong enough."

"He's a God, Sparhawk."

"Evidently that doesn't make any difference. What happened was just too enormous. Bhelliom said that it shifted some things about six miles beneath the surface of the earth, and certain changes in the shape of that part of the continent happened all at once instead of being spread out over a million or so years. The changes were going to happen anyway, but Bhelliom made them happen all at once. I gather that the escarpment will become a mountain range as it gradually breaks down. The concepts are just too vast for Cyrgon to comprehend, and the pressures involved are beyond his ability to control."

"What in God's name have you done, Sparhawk?" Emban exclaimed. "You're ripping the world apart!"

"Tell them not to be disquieted, Anakha," Bhellion spoke again in Vanion's voice. "I would not hurt my daughter, for I do love her. She is a wayward and whimsical child at times, much given to tantrums and sweet, innocent vanity. Behold how she doth adorn herself with spring and mantle her shoulders with the white gown of winter. The stresses and tensions which I did relieve in raising the wall had, in truth, been causing her some discomfort for the past thousand eons. Now is she content, and indeed doth she take some pleasure in her new adornment, for, as I say, she *is* a trifle vain."

"Where's Kring?" Mirtai asked suddenly.

"We left him, Engessa, and Khalad back at the escarpment," Sparhawk told her. "Bhelliom's excellent wall keeps the Trolls from getting at *us*, but it also keeps us from getting at *them*. We have to work out some way to get the Troll-Gods past it to steal back their Trolls."

"You've got Bhelliom, Sparhawk," Stragen said. "Just jump over it."

Sparhawk shook his head. "Bhelliom says that we'd better not. The ground's still a little touchy near the wall right now. If we jump around too much in that general vicinity, we might set off more earthquakes."

"God!" Sarabian cried. "Don't do that! You'll shake the whole continent apart!"

"We're trying to avoid that, your Majesty. Engessa, Kring, and Khalad are working on something. If we can't go down the escarpment, we may have to use Tynian's fleet and sail around the eastern end of it."

"We want to think about that for a while, though," Vanion added. "Sparhawk and I are still debating the issue, but I think we'll want to make some show of marching north. If we leave here in about a week with banners flying and five thousand knights added to the forces we've gathered in this general area, we'll have Zalasta's full attention. If we go out to sea, he won't know we're coming, and that might give him the leisure to sniff out some details of Stragen's plans for our special celebration of the Harvest Festival. Both ideas have an element of surprise involved. We're quibbling about which surprise would disrupt Zalasta's plans the most."

The training of Tamul horses began immediately. Tynian's knights, of course, complained bitterly. The riding horses favored by the Tamul gentry were too small and delicate to carry armored men, and the oversized plow-horses used by Tamul farmers were too slow and docile to make good war-horses.

They were always rushed now. Caalador had given the order, and it was irrevocable. The murders *would* take place during the Harvest Festival, whether their other plans were fully in place or not, and every minute brought the holiday that much closer.

It was five days following the return of Sparhawk and his friends from northern Atan that a runner reached Matherion with a message from Khalad. Mirtai admitted the weary Atan to the sitting room, where Sparhawk and Vanion were arguing the relative merits of their opposing plans. Wordlessly, the messenger handed Khalad's note to Sparhawk.

" 'My Lord,' " he read the characteristically abrupt note aloud. " 'The earthquake has jumbled the northeast coast. Don't rely on any charts of the area. You're going to have to come by sea, however. There's no way we can climb down the wall—particularly not with Trolls waiting for us at the bottom. Engessa, Kring, and I will be waiting with the Atans and Tikume's Peloi a couple of leagues south of where the wall dives into the Tamul Sea. Don't take too long to get here. The other side is up to something.' "

"That throws both your plans out the window, doesn't it?" Emperor Sarabian noted. "You won't be able to go by land, because you can't climb down the wall; and you can't go by sea, because the sea's filled with uncharted reefs."

"And we've only got about two days to make the decision," Itagne added. "The forces we're sending north are going to have to start moving at least a week before the festival if they're going to reach the North Cape in time to spring our second surprise on Zalasta."

"I'd better go have a talk with Captain Sorgi," Sparhawk said, rising to his feet.

"He and Caalador are down in the main pantry," Stragen advised him. "They're both Cammorians, and Cammorians like to be close to food and drink."

Sparhawk nodded, and he and Vanion quickly left the room.

An almost immediate friendship had sprung up between Caalador and Sorgi. They were, as Stragen had pointed out, both Cammorians, and they even looked much alike. Both had curly hair, though Sorgi's was nearly silver by now, and they were both burly men with heavy shoulders and powerful hands.

"Well, Master Cluff," Sorgi said expansively as Sparhawk and Vanion entered the large, airy kitchen storeroom, "have you solved all the world's problems yet?" Captain Sorgi always called Sparhawk by the alias he had used the first time they had met.

"Hardly, Sorgi. We've got one that maybe *you* can solve for us, though."

"Get the money part settled first, Sorgi," Caalador recommended. "Ol' Sporhawk here, he gets a little vague when th' time comes t' settle up."

Sorgi smiled. "I haven't heard that dialect since I left home," he told Sparhawk. "I could sit and listen to Caalador talk by the hour. Let's not worry about money yet. The advice is free. It starts costing you money when I lift my anchor up off the bottom."

"We have to go to a place where there's been an earthquake recently," Sparhawk told him. "Kurik's son just sent me a message. The earthquake has changed things so much that all the old maps are useless."

"Happens all the time," Sorgi told him. "The estuary that runs up to Vardenais changes her bottom every winter."

"How do you deal with that?"

Sorgi shrugged. "We put out a small boat with a strong sailor to do the rowing and a clever one to heave the sounding line. They lead us through."

"Isn't that sort of slow?"

"Not nearly as slow as trying to steer a sinking ship. How big an area got churned up by the earthquake?"

"It's sort of hard to say."

"Guess, Master Cluff. Tell me exactly what happened, and give me a guess about how big the danger spot is."

Sparhawk glossed over the cause of the sudden change in the coastline and described the emergence of the escarpment.

"No problem," Sorgi assured him.

"How did you arrive at that conclusion, Captain?" Vanion asked him.

"We won't have to worry about any reefs to the north of your cliff, my Lord. I saw something like that happen on the west coast of Rendor one time. You see, what's happened is that the cliff keeps on going. It runs on out to sea—under the water—so once you get north of it, the water's going to be a thousand feet deep. Not too many ships I know of draw that much water. I'll just take along some of the old charts. We'll go out about ten leagues and sail north. I'll take my bearings every so often, and when we get six or eight leagues north of this new cliff of yours, we'll turn west and run straight for the beach. I'll put your men ashore up there with no trouble at all."

"And *that's* the problem with your plan, Sparhawk," Vanion said. "You've only got a hundred ships. If you take both the knights *and* their horses, you'll only be able to take fifteen hundred up there to face the Trolls."

"Is a-winnin' this yere arg-u-ment *real* important t' you two?" Caalador asked.

"We're just looking for the best way, Caalador," Sparhawk replied.

"Then why not combine the two plans? Have Sorgi start north first thing in the morning, and you mount up your armies and ride up that way as soon as you get organized. When Sorgi gets to a place ten leagues or so south of the wall, he can feel his way in to shore. You meet him there, and he starts ferrying your army around the reef and puts you down on the beach north of the wall. Then you can go looking for Trolls, and Sorgi can drop his anchor and spend his time fishing."

Sparhawk and Vanion looked at each other sheepishly.

"It's like I wuz a-sayin', Sorgi." Caalador grinned. "Th' gentry ain't' got hordly no common sense a-tall. I b'leeve it's 'cause they ain't got room in ther heads fer more'n one i'dee at a time."

Inevitably, the day arrived when the relief column was scheduled to depart for Atan. It was before dawn when Mirtai came into the bedroom of the Queen of Elenia and her Prince Consort. "Time to get up," the giantess announced.

"Don't you know how to knock?" Sparhawk asked, sitting up in bed.

"Did I interrupt something?"

"Never mind, Mirtai," he sighed. "It's a custom, that's all."

"Foolishness. Everybody knows what goes on in here."

"Isn't it almost time for you and Kring to get married?"

"Are you trying to get rid of me, Sparhawk?"

"Of course not."

"Kring and I have decided to wait until after all of this is finished. Our weddings are going to be a little complicated. We have to go through two ceremonies in two parts of the world. Kring's not very happy about all the delay."

"I can't for the life of me see why," Ehlana said innocently.

"Men are strange." Mirtai shrugged.

"They are indeed, Mirtai, but how would we amuse ourselves without them?"

Sparhawk dressed slowly, pulling on the padded, rust-stained underclothing with reluctance and eying his black-enameled suit of steel work clothes with active dislike.

"Did you pack warm clothing?" Ehlana asked him. "The nights are getting chilly even this far south, so it's going to be very cold up on the North Cape."

"I packed it." He grunted. "For all the good it's going to do. No amount of clothing helps when you're wearing steel." He made a sour face. "I know it's a contradiction, but I start to sweat the minute I put the armor on. Every knight I've ever known does the same. We keep on sweating even when we're freezing and icicles are forming up inside the armor. Sometimes I wish I'd gone into another line of work. Bashing people for fun and profit starts to wear thin after a while."

"You're in a gloomy mood this morning, love."

"It's just that it's getting harder and harder to get started. I'll be all right once I'm on the road."

"You *will* be careful, won't you, Sparhawk. I'd die if I lost you."

"I'm not going to be in all that much danger, dear. I've got Bhelliom, and Bhelliom could pick up the sun and break it across its knee. It's Cyrgon and Zalasta who'll have to watch out."

"Don't get overconfident."

"I'm not. I've got more advantages than I can count, that's all. We're going to win, Ehlana, and there's nothing in the world that can stop us. All that's really left is the tedious plodding from here to the victory celebration."

"Why don't you kiss me for a while?" she suggested. "*Before* you put on the armor. It takes weeks for the bruises to go away after you kiss me when you're all wrapped in steel."

"You know—" He smiled. "—that's an awfully good idea. Why don't we do that?"

The column stretched for several miles, undulating across the rounded hills on the east coast of Lake Sama. There were Church Knights, Atans, Kring's Peloi, and a few ornately garbed regiments of the Tamul army.

It was a splendid day, one of those perfect autumn days with a stiff wind aloft hurrying puffy white clouds across an intensely blue sky, and the enormous shadows of those clouds raced across the rolling landscape so that Sparhawk's army rode alternately in sunshine and in shadow. The pennons and flags were of many hues, and they snapped and rippled in the breeze, tugging at the lances and flagstaffs to which they were fastened.

Queen Betuana strode along at Faran's shoulder. "Are you sure, Sparhawk-Knight?" she asked. "The Troll-beasts are animals, and all animals are born knowing how to swim. Even a cat can swim."

"Only reluctantly, Betuana-Queen." Sparhawk smiled, remembering Mmrr's "cat-paddling" in Sephrenia's fish pond in Sarsos. "Ulath-Knight says that we won't have to worry about the Troll-beasts swimming around the end of the escarpment. They'll swim across rivers and lakes, but the sea terrifies them. It has something to do with the tides, I think—or maybe it's the salt."

"Must we continue at this slow pace?" Her tone was impatient.

"We want to be certain that Zalasta's spies see us, your Majesty," Vanion told her. "That's a very important part of our plan."

"Elene battles are very large," she observed.

"We'd prefer smaller ones, Atana, but Zalasta's schemes stretch across the whole continent, so we have to respond."

Sephrenia, with Flute riding in front of her, rode forward with Xanetia. They had all watched the tentative friendship growing between Sephrenia and Xanetia. Both were still very cautious, and there were no great leaps in their relationship. The tenuousness now came not from defensiveness but rather from an excess of concern about inadvertently giving offense, and Sparhawk felt that to be a rather profound change for the good. "We grew tired of all the stories," Sephrenia told Vanion. "I can't be sure which is the bigger liar, Tynian or Ulath."

"Oh?"

"They're trying to outdo each other. Ulath's exaggerating outrageously, and I'm sure Tynian's doing the same thing. Each of them is doing his level best to persuade the other that he missed the adventure of the century."

"It's a demonstration of a form of affection, little mother," Sparhawk explained. "They'd be too embarrassed to admit that they're genuinely fond of each other, so they tell each other wild stories instead."

"Did you understand that, Xanetia?" Sephrenia smiled.

"What reasonable person can *ever* understand how and why men express their love, sister."

"Men aren't really comfortable with the word *love*," Sparhawk told them, "particularly when it's applied to other men."

"It *is* love, though, isn't it, Sparhawk?" Sephrenia asked him.

"Well, I suppose it is, but we're not comfortable with it all the same."

"I have meant to speak with thee, Anarae." Betuana lapsed perhaps unconsciously into archaic Tamul.

"Gladly will I hear thy words, Queen of Atan."

"It hath been the wont of youthful Atans to seek Delphaeus, having it in their minds to destroy thine home and to put thy people to the sword. I am heartily sorry that I have permitted this."

Xanetia smiled. "It is of no moment, Queen of Atan. This is but an excess of adolescent enthusiasm. I must freely confess that *our* fledglings do entertain themselves by deceiving and distracting *thine*, leading them away from their intended goal by rudimentary enchantments and clumsy deceptions. It cometh to me all unbidden that thus are we *both* relieved of the obligation to entertain our children, who, by virtue of their youth, inexperience, and profound inability to divert themselves, do continually complain that there is nothing for them to do—at least nothing worthy of what they perceive to be their enormous gifts."

Betuana laughed. "Do *thy* children have that selfsame plaint, Anarae?"

"*All* children complain," Sephrenia assured them. "It's one of the things that makes parents age so fast."

"Well said," Sparhawk agreed. Neither he nor Sephrenia looked directly at Flute.

They reached Lebas in northern Tamul in about two days. Sparhawk had spoken with the army, stressing the enormous power of Bhelliom as he explained how it would be possible for them to cover great distances in a short period of time. In actuality, however, Bhelliom was in no way responsible. Flute was in charge of their travel arrangements on this particular trip.

There was another Atan runner waiting for them in Lebas with yet another message from Khalad—a fairly offensive note that suggested that the runner had been sent to guide them to the stretch of beach where Kring and Engessa waited with their forces, since if knights were left to their own devices in the forest, they would inevitably get lost. Khalad's class prejudices were still quite firmly in place.

There was no road as such leading north from Lebas, but the trails and paths were quite clearly marked. They reached the southern edge of the vast forest that covered the northeastern quadrant of the continent, and the hundred Peloi that Kring had brought with him from Eosia pulled in to ride close to their allies. Deep woods made the plains-dwelling western Peloi very nervous.

"I think it has to do with the sky," Tynian explained to the others.

"You can barely see the sky when you're in the deep woods, Tynian," Kalten objected.

"Exactly my point," the broad-faced Deiran replied. "The western Peloi are accustomed to having the sky overhead. When there are tree limbs blocking their view of it, they start to get nervous."

They were never able to determine if the attempt was random or was deliberately aimed at Betuana. They were a hundred leagues or so into the forest and had set up their night's encampment; and the large tent for the ladies—Betuana, Sephrenia, Xanetia, and Flute—had been erected somewhat apart so that they might have a bit of privacy.

The assassins were well-concealed, and there were four of them. They burst out of the thicket with drawn swords just as Betuana and Xanetia were emerging from the tent. Betuana responded instantly. Her sword whipped out of its sheath and plunged directly into the belly of one of the attackers. Even as she jerked the sword free, she dove to the ground, rolled, and drove both feet full into the face of yet another.

Sparhawk and the others were running toward the tent in response to Sephrenia's cry of alarm, but the Queen of the Atans seemed to have things well in hand. She parried a hasty thrust and split the skull of the shabby assailant who had made it. Then she engaged the remaining attacker.

"Look out!" Berit shouted as he ran toward her. The man she had felled with her feet was struggling to rise, his nose bleeding and a dagger in his hand. He was directly behind the Atan queen.

Always before when Xanetia had shed her disguise, the change had been slow, the concealing coloration receding gradually. This time, however, she flashed into full illumination, and the light within her was no mere glow. Instead, she blazed forth like a new sun.

The bloody-nosed assassin might have been able to flee from her had he been in full possession of his faculties. The kick he had received in the face, however, appeared to have rattled him and shaken his wits.

He did scream once, though, just before Xanetia's hand touched him. His scream died in a hoarse kind of gurgle. With his mouth agape and his eyes bulging with horror, he stared at the blazing form of she who had just killed him—but only for a moment. After that, it was no longer possible to recognize his expression. The flesh of his face sagged and began to run down, turned by that dreadful touch into a putrefying liquid. His mouth seemed to gape wider as his cheeks and lips oozed down to drip off his chin. He tried to scream once, but the decay had already reached his throat, and all that emerged from his lipless mouth was a liquid wheeze. The flesh slid off his hand, and his dagger dropped from his skeleton clutch.

He sagged to his knees with the slimy residue of skin and nerve and tendons oozing out of his clothing.

Then the rotting corpse toppled slowly forward to lie motionless on the leaf-strewn floor of the forest—motionless, but still dissolving as Xanetia's curse continued its inexorable course.

The Anarae's fire dimmed, and she buried her shining face in her glowing hands and wept.

CHAPTER
TWENTY-
EIGHT

I t was raining in Esos, a chill, persistent rain that swept down out of the mountains of Zemoch every autumn. The rain did not noticeably dampen the Harvest Festival celebration, since most of the revelers were too drunk to even notice the weather.

Stolg was *not* drunk. He was working, and he had nothing but contempt for men who drank on the job. Stolg was a nondescript sort of fellow in plain clothing. He wore his hair cropped close and he had large, powerful hands. He went through the crowd of revelers unobtrusively, moving toward the wealthier quarter of the city.

Stolg and his wife Ruta had argued that morning, and that always put him in a bad humor. Ruta really had little cause for complaint, he thought, stepping aside for a group of drunken young aristocrats. He *was* a good provider, after all, and their neat little cottage on the outskirts of town was the envy of all their friends. Their son was apprenticed to a local carpenter, and their daughter had excellent prospects for a good marriage. Stolg loved Ruta, but she periodically became waspish over some little thing and pestered him to death about it. This time she was upset because their cottage had no proper lock on the front door, and no matter how many times he told her that *they*, of all people, had no need of locks, she had continued to harp on the subject.

Stolg stopped and drew back into a recessed doorway as the watch tramped by. Djukta would normally have bribed the watch to stay out of Stolg's way, but it was Harvest Festival time, so there would be plenty of confusion to cover any incidental outcries. Djukta was not one to spend money needlessly. It was a common joke in the seedier taverns in Esos that Djukta had deliberately grown his vast beard so that he could save the price of a cloak.

Stolg saw the house that was his destination and went into the foul-smelling alley behind it. He had arranged for a ladder to be placed against the back of the house, and he climbed up quickly and entered through a second-story window. He walked down the hallway and through the door at the end into a bedroom. A former servant in the house had drawn a diagram and had pointed out the room of the owner of the house, a minor nobleman named Count Kinad. Once inside the room, Stolg lay down on the bed. As long as he had to wait, he might as well be comfortable. He could hear the sound of revelry coming from downstairs.

As he lay there, he decided to install the lock Ruta wanted. It wouldn't be expensive, and the peace and quiet around the house would be more than worth it.

It was no more than half an hour later when he heard a heavy, slightly unsteady footfall on the stair. He rolled quickly off the bed, crossed silently to the door, and put his ear to the panel.

"It's no trouble at all," a slurred voice outside said. "I've got a copy in my bedroom."

"Really, Count Kinad," a lady's voice called from below, "I take your word for it."

"No, Baroness, I want you to read his Majesty's exact words. It's the most idiotic proclamation you've ever seen." The door opened, and a man carrying a candle entered. It was the man who had been pointed out to Stolg two days ago. Stolg idly wondered what Count Kinad had done to irritate someone enough to justify the expense of a professional visit. He brushed the thought aside. That was really none of his business.

Stolg was a thorough professional, so he had several techniques available to him. The fact that Count Kinad's back was to him presented the opportunity for his favorite, however. He drew a long poniard from his belt, stepped up behind the count, and drove the long, slim blade into the base of the count's skull with a steely crunch. He caught the collapsing body and quietly lowered it to the floor. A knife-thrust in the brain was always certain, and it was quick, quiet, and produced a minimum of mess. Ruta absolutely *hated* to wash her husband's work clothes when there was blood all over them. Stolg set his foot between the count's shoulders and wrenched his poniard out of the back of the skull. That was sometimes tricky. Pulling a knife out of bone takes quite a bit of strength.

Stolg rolled the body over and looked intently into the dead face. A professional always makes sure that a client has been permanently serviced.

The count was definitely dead. His eyes were blank, his face was turning blue, and a trickle of blood was coming out of his nose. Stolg wiped off his poniard, put it away, and went back out into the hallway. He walked quietly back to the window through which he had entered.

There were two more names on the list Djukta had given him, and with luck he could service another this very night. It was raining, however, and Stolg really disliked working in the rain. He decided to go home early instead and tell Ruta that he would give in just this once and install the lock she wanted so much. Then he thought it might be nice if they took their son and their daughter to the tavern at the end of the street to have a few tankards of ale with their neighbors. It *was* the Harvest Festival, after all, and a man should really try to spend the holidays with his friends and family.

Sherrok was a small, weedy sort of fellow with thinning hair and a lumpy skull. He did not so much walk as scurry through the crowded streets of Verel in southern Daconia. In the daytime, Sherrok was a minor official in the customshouse, biting his tongue as he took orders from his Tamul superiors. Sherrok *loathed* Tamuls, and being placed in a subservient position to them sometimes made him physically ill. It was that loathing which had been primarily behind his decision to sell information to the diseased Styric Ogerajin, to whom a mutual acquaintance had introduced him. When Ogerajin, after a few carefully worded questions, had slyly hinted that certain kinds of information might be worth quite a bit of money, Sherrok had leapt at the chance to betray his despised superiors—*and* to make tidy sums as well.

The information he had for Ogerajin tonight was *very* important. The greedy, bloodsucking Tamuls were going to raise the customs rate by a full quarter of a percent. Ogerajin should pay handsomely for *that* piece of information.

Sherrok licked his lips as he rushed through the noisy crowds celebrating the Harvest Festival. There was an eight-year-old Astellian girl available at one of the slave marts, a ravishing child with huge, terrified eyes, and if Ogerajin could be persuaded to be generous, Sherrock might actually be able to buy her. He had never owned a child so young before, and the very thought of her made his knees go weak.

His mind was full of her as he passed a reeking alleyway, and so he was not really paying any attention—until he felt the strand of wire snap tight around his neck.

He struggled, of course, but it was really not much use. The assassin dragged him back into the alley and methodically strangled him. His last thought was of the little girl's face. She actually seemed to be laughing at him.

"You're really more trouble than you're worth, you know," Bersola said to the dead man sprawled in the bow of the row-boat. Bersola always talked to the men he had killed. Many of Bersola's colleagues believed that he was crazy. They were probably right.

Bersola's major problem lay in the fact that he always did things exactly the same way. He invariably stuck his knife into someone between the third and fourth ribs at a slightly downward angle. It *was* effective, though, since a knife thrust there absolutely *cannot* miss the heart. Bersola also *never* left a body lying where it fell. He had a compulsive sense of neatness that drove him to put the remains somewhere out of sight. Since Bersola lived and worked in the Daconian town of Ederus on the coast of the Sea of Edom, disposal was a simple matter. A short trip in a rowboat and a few rocks tied to the deceased's ankles removed all traces. Bersola's habit-driven personality, however, led him to always sink the bodies in the exact same place. The other murderers of Ederus made frequent laughing reference to "Bersola's Reef," a place on the lake bottom supposedly piled high with sunken bodies. Even people who didn't fully understand the significance of the phrase referred to Bersola's Reef.

"You went and did it, didn't you?" Bersola said to the corpse in the bow of the boat as he rowed out to the reef. "You just *had* to go and offend somebody. You've got nobody to blame but yourself for this, you know. If you'd behaved yourself, none of this would have happened."

The corpse did not answer. They almost never did.

Bersola stopped rowing and took his bearings. There was the usual light in the window of Fanna's Tavern on the far shore, and there was the warning fire on the rocky headlands on the near side. The lantern on the wharf protruding out from Ederus was dead astern. "This is the place," Bersola told the dead man. "You'll have lots of company down there, so it won't be so bad." He shipped his oars and crawled forward. He checked the knots on the rope that held the large rock in place between the dead man's ankles. "I'm really sorry about this, you know," he apologized, "but it *is* your own fault." He lifted the rock—and the dead man's legs—over the side. He held the shoulders for a moment. "Do you have anything you'd like to say?" he asked.

He waited for a decent interval, but the dead man did not reply.

"I didn't really think you would," Bersola said. He let go of the shoulders, and the body slithered limply over the gunwale and disappeared into the dark waters of the lake.

Bersola whistled his favorite tune as he rowed back to Ederus.

Avin Wargunsson, Prince Regent of Thalesia, was in an absolute fury. Patriarch Bergsten had left Thalesia without so much as a by-your-leave. It was intolerable! The man had absolutely no regard for the Prince Regent's dignity. Avin Wargunsson *was* going to be king one day, after all—just as soon as the raving madman in the north tower finally got around to dying—and he deserved *some* courtesy. People always ignored him! That indifferent lack of regard cankered the soul of the little crown prince. Avin was scarcely more than five feet tall, and in a kingdom absolutely awash with blond people a foot or more taller, he was almost unnoticeable. He had spent his childhood scurrying like a mouse out from under the feet of towering men who kept accidentally stepping on him because they refused to look down and see that he was there.

Sometimes that made him so angry that he could just scream.

Then, without even bothering to knock, two burly blond ruffians opened the door and rolled in a large barrel. "Here's that cask of Arcian red you wanted, Avin," one of them said. The ignorant barbarian didn't even know enough to use a proper form of address.

"I didn't order a barrel of wine," Avin snapped.

"The chief of the guards said you wanted a barrel of Arcian red," the other blond savage declared, closing the door. "We're just doing what we were told to do. Where do you want this?"

"Oh, put it over there," Avin said, pointing. It was easier than arguing with them.

They rolled the barrel across the floor and set it up in the corner.

"I don't think I know you two," Avin said.

"We're new." The first one shrugged. "We just joined the Royal Guard last week." He set a canvas bag on the floor and took out a pry-bar. He carefully inserted the bar under the lid of the barrel and worked it back and forth until the lid came free.

"What are you doing?" Avin demanded.

"You can't drink it if you can't get at it, Avin," the fellow pointed out. "We've got the right tools, and you probably don't." At least the man was clean-shaven. Avin approved of that. Most of the men in the Royal Guard looked like trees with golden moss growing on them. "You'd better taste it and make sure it hasn't soured, Brok."

"Right," the other one agreed. He scooped up some of the wine in the cupped palm of his hand and sucked it in noisily. Avin shuddered. "Tastes all right to me, Tel," he reported. A thoughtful look crossed his face. "Why don't I fill up a bucket of this before we put the lid back on?" he suggested. "Hauling this barrel up the stairs was heavy business, and I've worked up quite a thirst."

"Good idea," Tel agreed.

The bearded man picked up the brass-bound wooden bucket Avin used for a wastebasket. "Is it all right if I use this, Avin?" he asked.

Avin Wargunsson gaped at him. This went too far—even in Thalesia.

The burly fellow shook the contents of the wastebasket out on Avin's desk and dipped it into the barrel. Then he set the pail on the floor. "I guess we're ready, Tel," he said.

"All right," Tel replied. "Let's get at it."

"What are you doing?" Avin demanded in a shrill voice as the two approached him.

They didn't even bother to answer. It was intolerable! He was the Prince Regent! People had no right to ignore him like this!

They picked him up by the arms and carried him over to the barrel, ignoring his cries and struggles. He couldn't even get their attention by kicking them.

"In you go," the one named Tel said pleasantly, almost in the tone one uses when he pushes a horse into a stall. The two lifted Avin Wargunsson quite easily and stuffed him feetfirst into the barrel. The one called Brok held him down while Tel took a hammer and a handful of nails out of the canvas bag and picked up the barrel lid. He set the lid on Avin's head and pushed him down. Then he rapped his hammer around the edge of the lid, settling it in place.

Only Avin's eyes and forehead were above the surface of the wine. He held his breath and pounded impotently on the underside of the lid with both fists.

Then there was another pounding sound as well as Tel calmly nailed down the lid of the barrel.

The ladies quite firmly dismissed Kalten when they set out the morning after the attempt on Queen Betuana's life. Kalten took his self-appointed duties as Xanetia's protector quite seriously, and he was a bit offended at being so cavalierly sent away.

"They need some privacy right now," Vanion told him. "Set some knights to either side to protect them, but give them enough room to get Xanetia through this." Vanion was a soldier, but his insights were sometimes quite profound. Sparhawk looked back over his shoulder. Sephrenia rode close to one side of the sorrowing Xanetia, and Betuana strode along on the other. Xanetia rode with her head bowed, holding Flute in her arms. There was about them a kind of exclusionary wall as they closed ranks around their injured companion. Sephrenia rode very close to the Anarae, frequently reaching out her hand to touch the stricken woman. The racial differences and eons-old enmity appeared to have been overridden by the universal sisterhood of all women. Sephrenia reached across those barriers to comfort her enemy without even thinking about it. Betuana was no less solicitous, and in spite of the gruesome demonstration of the effects of Xanetia's touch, she walked very close to the Delphaeic woman.

Aphrael, of course, was in complete control of the situation. She rode with her arms about Xanetia's waist, and Aphrael's touch was one of the more powerful forces on earth. Sparhawk was quite certain that Xanetia was not really suffering. The Child-Goddess would not permit that. The Anarae's apparent horror and remorse at what she had been compelled to do was primarily for the benefit of her two comforters. Aphrael was quite deliberately erasing Sephrenia's racial animosity and Betuana's superstitious aversion by the simple expedient of intensifying Xanetia's outward appearance of grief.

It was easy to underestimate Aphrael when she appeared in one of her innumerable incarnations as a capricious little girl, and that was probably the main reason she had chosen the form of the Child-Goddess in the first place. Sparhawk, however, had seen the reality of Aphrael waveringly reflected in the brass mirror back in Matherion, and the reality was neither childish nor whimsical. Aphrael, he guessed, generally knew exactly what she was doing, and generally got exactly what she wanted. Sparhawk firmly fixed the wavering image of the reality of Aphrael in his mind so that it would always be present when the dimples and the kisses began to cloud his judgment.

The days were significantly shorter this far to the north. The sun rose far to the southeast now and it did not go very high above the southern horizon before it started to descend again. Each long night's frost piled up on the previous night's lacy blanket, since the pale, weak sun no longer had the strength to melt what had built up during the hours of darkness.

It was nearly sunset when a towering Atan came loping down a frosty forest path to meet them. He went directly to Queen Betuana, banged his fist against his chest in salute, and spoke urgently. Betuana motioned quickly to Sparhawk and the others. "A message from Engessa-Atan," she said tersely. "There are enemies gathering on the coast at the eastern end of the wall."

"Trolls?" Vanion asked quickly.

The tall Atan shook his head. "No, Vanion-Lord," he replied. "They're Elenes, and for the most part they're not warriors. They're cutting trees."

"To use in building fortifications?" Bevier asked.

"No, Church-Knight. They are lashing the trees together to build things that will float."

"Rafts?" Tynian asked. "Ulath, you said that Trolls are

afraid of the sea. Would they be willing to use rafts to go around the outer edge of the escarpment?"

"It's hard to say," the blond-braided Thalesian replied. "Ghwerig *did* use a boat to cross Lake Venne, and he almost had to have stolen a ride on some ship to get from Thalesia to Pelosia when he followed King Sarak during the Zemoch war, but Ghwerig wasn't like other Trolls." He looked at the Atan. "Are they building these rafts north of the wall or here on the south side?"

"They're on this side of the wall," the Atan replied.

"That doesn't make too much sense, does it?" Kalten asked.

"Not to *me*, it doesn't," Ulath admitted.

"I think we'd better get up there and have a look, Sparhawk," Vanion said. "That attack on Betuana last night was fair evidence that Zalasta knows we're coming, so this little stroll through the woods has accomplished its purpose. Let's join forces with Engessa and Kring and find out if Sorgi's made it to the beach yet. Winter's coming on fast, and I think we'll want to deal with the Trolls before the sun goes down permanently."

"Would you see to that, Divine One?" Sparhawk said to Aphrael. "I'd ask Bhelliom to do it, but you've been handling things so well that I wouldn't want to appear critical by taking over at this point."

Aphrael's eyes narrowed. "Don't push your luck, Sparhawk," she said ominously.

Sparhawk was never really certain whether Aphrael had somehow moved them during the night or had slipped them across the intervening miles at some point between the time when they swung up into their saddles and the time when their mounts took their first steps. The Child-Goddess was too practiced, too skilled, to be caught tampering when she didn't want to be.

The hill was the same hill that had been lying to the northwest of their night's encampment when the sun had gone down—or so it seemed—but when they crested it about a half hour after they set out, there was a long, sandy beach and the lead-grey expanse of the Tamul Sea on the other side instead of a broad, unbroken forest.

"That was quick," Talen said, looking around. Talen's presence on this expedition had never really been explained to Sparhawk's satisfaction. He suspected Aphrael, however. It was easy to suspect Aphrael of such things, and more often than not the suspicions proved to be well-founded.

"There's someone coming down the beach," Ulath said, pointing at a tiny figure riding along the water's edge from the north.

"Khalad." Talen shrugged.

"How can you tell?"

"He's my brother, Sir Ulath—besides, I recognize his cloak."

They rode on down the hill and out onto the sand.

"What kept you?" Khalad asked Sparhawk bluntly when he joined them.

"I'm glad to see you, too, Khalad."

"Don't try to be funny, Sparhawk. I've been struggling to keep Engessa and his Atans from swimming around the outer edge of the escarpment for the past ten days. They want to go attack the Trolls all by themselves. How did Stragen's plan come off?"

"It's hard to say," Talen told him. "We were on the road during the Harvest Festival. I know Stragen and Caalador well enough to know that *most* of the people they were after are probably dead by now. We're a little late because we wanted to make sure that Zalasta's people saw us coming. We thought we might be able to divert him enough to keep him out of the way of Caalador's murderers."

Khalad grunted.

"Are the Trolls gathering anywhere nearby?" Ulath asked.

"As closely as we can tell, they're all clustered around the abandoned village of Tzada over on the other side of the Atan border," Khalad replied. "They tried to climb the wall for a while, then they pulled back. Engessa's got scouts on top of the wall; they'll let us know when the Trolls start to move."

"Where are Engessa and Kring?" Vanion asked him.

"Up the beach about a mile, my Lord. We've built an encampment back in the forest a ways. Tikume's joined us. He brought in several thousand of the eastern Peloi about five days ago."

"That should help," Kalten said. "The Peloi are very enthusiastic about their wars."

"Any sign of Sorgi yet?" Sparhawk asked.

"He's feeling his way in through the reefs," Khalad replied. "He sent a longboat ahead to let us know he was coming."

"What's this business with the rafts all about?" Vanion asked him.

"They aren't rafts, my Lord. They're sections of a floating bridge."

"A bridge? A bridge to where?"

"We aren't sure. We've been staying back so that the Edomish peasants constructing it won't see us."

"What are Edomishmen doing on *this* side of the continent?" Kalten asked with some astonishment.

"Building a bridge, Sir Kalten. Weren't you listening? Talen's old friend Amador—or Rebal, or whatever he calls himself—is sort of in charge, but Incetes is there, too, and *he's* the one who's making the big impression. He bellows orders in archaic Elenic, and he's been braining anyone who doesn't understand him or move fast enough."

"Is it that counterfeit one we saw in the woods near Jorsan?" Talen asked.

"I don't think so. This fellow seems to be quite a bit bigger, and he's got a sizeable contingent of men in bronze armor with him. I'd guess that somebody's resurrecting people out of the past again."

"That would probably be Djarian of Samar," Sephrenia said. "Maybe he *can* raise whole armies after all."

"He can if Cyrgon's lending him a hand," Aphrael added. The Child-Goddess had appeared to be dozing in her sister's arms, but she had clearly been listening. She opened her large, dark eyes. "Hello, Khalad," she said. "You look a little wind-burned."

"We've had some gales coming in off the Tamul Sea, Divine One. There's a strong smell of ice mixed up in them."

"*That's* what they're doing," Ulath said, snapping his fingers.

"Does he still do that?" Tynian asked. "I was hoping you'd cured him of it by now."

"Ulath likes to play leapfrog with his mind, Tynian," Sephrenia said calmly. "He'll come back in a moment or two and fill in the blank spaces for us."

"How long has it been cold up here, Khalad?" Ulath asked.

"It wasn't particularly warm when we *got* here, Sir Ulath."

"Is any ice forming up in the inlets and along the beach at night?"

"Some. It isn't very thick, though, and the tide comes in and breaks it up before it has the chance to spread."

"The floating ice a mile or so out to sea *isn't* breaking up, though," Ulath said. "It rises and falls with the tide because it's not grinding up against the rocks. It's probably almost a foot thick out there by now. The Edomishmen aren't building rafts or a bridge. They're building a pier out to that pack ice. There'll be another one north of the wall as well. The Trolls *will* cross the ice. We know that because they did it to get here from Thalesia. Cyrgon's going to march the Trolls to the pier north of the wall and drive them out to the pack ice. Then they'll march south across the ice and come ashore on this south pier."

"And then they'll attack the Atans again," Vanion said bleakly. "How thick will the pack ice have to be to support the weight of the Trolls?"

"Two feet or so. It should be thick enough by the time the piers are finished—if it stays cold."

"I think we can count on Cyrgon to make sure that it stays cold," Tynian noted.

"There's something else, too," Khalad added. "If Cyrgon's playing with the weather this way, it won't be *too* long before Sorgi's ships are locked in ice. I think we'd better come up with something, my Lords—and fairly soon—or we're going to be hip-deep in Trolls again."

"Let's go talk with Kring and Engessa," Sparhawk said.

CHAPTER TWENTY-NINE

The beach has changed, friend Sparhawk," Kring was saying. "When you get close to the cliff, there's about a mile of what used to be the sea-bottom that's out of the water now."

"It looks as if Bhelliom pushed the land from north of the break underneath the rest of the continent," Khalad added. "It sort of slid under and pushed this side of the crack upward to form the cliff. That's what raised the sea-bottom on this side. The land to the north of the cliff sank, though, so the sea went a couple of miles inland. You can see treetops sticking up out of the water. The break was clean and straight back where we were when the earthquakes started, but there were a lot of landslides out here on the coast. There are big rocks sticking up out of the water north of the cliff."

"Where are those Edomishmen you mentioned?" Vanion asked.

"Up near the top of the cliff, my Lord. They're cutting trees and rolling the logs down to the edge of the water. That's where they're building the rafts." Khalad paused, his expression slightly critical. "They aren't very good rafts," he added. "If the Trolls try to come ashore on that floating pier, they're going to get their feet wet."

"He's his father's son, all right." Kalten laughed. "Why do you care whether or not the Trolls get their feet wet, Khalad?"

"If you're going to do something, you should do it right, Sir Kalten," Khalad said stubbornly. "I hate sloppy workmanship."

"Where's this place the Trolls are gathering?" Vanion asked. "What was its name again?"

"Tzada, Vanion-Preceptor," Engessa replied. "It's over in Atan."

"What are they doing?"

"It's a little hard to tell from the top of the cliff."

"Where's the border between Tamul proper and Atan?" Tynian asked.

"There isn't any real border, Tynian-Knight," Queen Betuana told him. "It's just a line drawn on the map, and the line doesn't mean anything up here on the North Cape. A land where the sun goes down in the late autumn and doesn't come up again until early spring and where the trees freeze and explode in midwinter doesn't attract too many settlers. The western part of the cape's supposed to be in Astel; the middle's in Atan; and the east is called part of Tamul proper. Nobody up here really pays any attention to things like that. The land belongs to anybody foolish enough to live this far north."

"It's about a hundred and fifty leagues to Tzada," Engessa told them.

"That's a good week's travel for a Troll," Ulath said. "How far along are the Edomishmen with their pier?"

Khalad scratched his cheek. "I'd guess that they've got a good ten more days before they finish."

"And in ten days the pack ice out to sea should be thick enough to hold the weight of the Trolls," Ulath concluded.

"Cyrgon will make *sure* it's thick enough," Flute said.

"Somebody's doing some very tight scheduling," Bevier noted. "The Edomishmen will have their piers complete in ten days, the ice will be thick enough to walk on, and if the Trolls set out from Tzada three days from now, they'll get here just when everything's ready."

"We have all sorts of options here," Vanion said. "We could destroy this southern pier and leave the Trolls stranded out on the ice; we could just wait and meet them when they try to come ashore; we could use Sorgi's ships to assault them while they're on the pier itself; or we could . . ."

Queen Betuana was firmly shaking her head.

"Something wrong, your Majesty?" Vanion asked her.

"We don't have that much time, Vanion-Preceptor," she replied. "How long is the daylight here now, Engessa-Atan?"

"Not much more than five hours, Betuana-Queen."

"In ten days it won't even last that long. Do we want to fight Trolls in the dark?"

"Not even a little bit, your Majesty." Ulath shuddered. "The point is that we don't really want to fight them at all. We want to steal them. We could just ignore all this construction work here on the coast, you know. Sorgi's ships could ferry us around these work gangs and put us ashore far enough north of the escarpment so that Bhelliom won't set off a new batch of earthquakes, and then we could have it carry us directly to Tzada."

"That's a good plan, Ulath-Knight," Betuana agreed, "except for the ice. It's already forming out there, you know."

"Aphrael," Sparhawk said to the Child-Goddess, "could you melt that ice for us?"

"If I really *had* to," she replied, "but it wouldn't be polite. The ice is a part of winter, and winter belongs to the earth. The earth is Bhelliom's child, not mine, so you'll have to talk to Bhelliom about it."

"What should I ask it to do?"

She shrugged. "Why not just leave that up to Bhelliom? Tell it that the ice is a problem and let *it* decide how to deal with it. You've got a lot to learn about the etiquette of these situations, Sparhawk."

"I suppose so," he admitted, "but it's the sort of thing that doesn't come up every day, so I haven't had much practice."

"You see what I mean about those rafts, Sparhawk?" Khalad said. "Those green logs lie so low in the water that you couldn't lead a donkey along that pier without getting him wet all the way up to the hocks."

"How would *you* have built them?"

"I'd have used a double layer of logs—one layer across the top of the other." The two of them were lying under some bushes on a knoll watching the Edomish peasants laboring on the rafts. The first part of the pier was already anchored in place, and it jutted about a quarter of a mile out into the icy water. Additional rafts were being added to the outer end as quickly as they were completed.

"There's Incetes," Khalad said, pointing at a huge man in a

bronze mail shirt and horned helmet. "He and those prehistoric warriors he brought with him have been driving those poor peasants to the point of exhaustion. Rebal's running around waving his arms and trying to look important, but it's Incetes who's really in charge. The peasants don't seem to understand his dialect, so he's been talking to them by hand." Khalad scratched his short black beard. "You know, Sparhawk, if we killed him, his warriors would vanish, and one charge by the knights would chase Rebal and his peasants halfway back to Edom."

"It's a nice idea, but how are we going to get close enough to kill him?"

"I'm already close enough, Sparhawk. I could kill him from right here."

"He's two hundred and fifty paces away, Khalad. Your father said that the maximum range with a crossbow is two hundred yards—and even that involved a lot of luck."

"I'm a better shot than Father was." Khalad lifted his crossbow. "I've modified the sights and lengthened the arms a bit. Incetes is close enough, believe me. I could stick a bolt up his nose from here."

"That's a graphic picture. Let's go talk with Vanion." They slid back down the back of the knoll, mounted their horses, and rode back to their hidden encampment. Sparhawk quickly explained his squire's plan to the others.

"Are you sure you could hit him at that range, Khalad?" Vanion asked a bit skeptically.

Khalad sighed. "Do you want a demonstration, my Lord?" he asked.

Vanion shook his head. "No. If you tell me you can hit him, then I'll believe you."

"All right. I can hit him, my Lord."

"That's good enough for me." Vanion frowned. "What would you say might be the absolute extreme range of the crossbow?" he asked.

Khalad spread his hands uncertainly. "I'd have to experiment, Lord Vanion," he said. "I'm sure I could build one that will reach out a thousand yards, but aiming it would be difficult, and it would probably take two men a half hour to recock it. The arms would have to be very stiff."

"A thousand paces," Vanion sighed, shaking his head. He rapped his knuckles on the chest of his suit of armor. "I think we're becoming obsolete, gentlemen." Then he straightened.

"Well, we're not obsolete yet. As long as we're here anyway, let's go ahead and neutralize this southern pier. All it's going to cost us is one crossbow bolt and a single mounted charge. The dismay it's going to cause our enemies is worth *that* much, anyway."

Kring and Tikume came riding up the hill from the beach with Captain Sorgi clattering along beside him. Sorgi was not a very good horseman and he rode stiffly, clinging to the saddlebow. "Friend Sorgi came ashore in one of those rowboats," Kring said. "His big boats are still about a mile out in the water."

"Ships, friend Kring," Sorgi corrected with a pained expression. "The little ones are boats, but the big ones are called ships."

"What's the difference, friend Sorgi?"

"A ship has a captain. A boat operates by mutual consent." Sorgi's expression grew somber. "We have a problem, Master Cluff. The ice is forming up right behind my ships. I'll be able to bring them ashore, but I don't think they'll be of much use to you. I've had soundings taken, and we'll have to sail a couple of miles out to get around the reef that runs out to sea from that cliff. We don't *have* those two miles anymore. The ice is moving inshore very fast."

"You'd better talk with Bhelliom, Sparhawk," Aphrael said. "I think I told you that this morning."

"Yes," he agreed, "as a matter of fact you did."

"Why didn't you do it then?"

"I had a few other things on my mind."

"They get like that as they grow older," Sephrenia told her sister. "They get mulish and deliberately put off doing things they're supposed to do just because *we* suggest them. They *hate* being told what to do."

"What's the best way to get around that?"

Sephrenia smiled sweetly at the warriors standing around her. "I've always had good luck with telling them to do the exact opposite of what I really want."

"All right," the Child-Goddess said dubiously. "It sounds silly to me, but if it's the only way to get the job done . . ." She drew herself up. "Sparhawk!" she said in a commanding voice, "don't you *dare* talk to Bhelliom!"

Sparhawk sighed. "I wonder if Dolmant could find an opening in a monastery for me when I get home," he said.

* * *

Sparhawk and Vanion went off a ways from the others to consult with the sapphire rose. Flute trailed along behind them. Sparhawk touched his ring to the lid of the box. "Open," he said.

The lid snapped up.

"Blue-Rose," Sparhawk said, "winter doth approach with unseemly haste, and the freezing of the sea doth hinder our design. We would proceed some distance beyond thine excellent wall so that our movements will not perturb thy daughter."

"Thou art considerate, Anakha," Vanion's voice replied.

"His courtesy is not untainted by self-interest, Flower-Gem," Aphrael said with an impish little smile. "When thy daughter shudders, it doth unsettle his stomach."

"You didn't have to say that, Aphrael," Sparhawk told her. "Are you going to do this?"

"No. My manners are better than that."

"Why did you come along, then?"

"Because I owe Bhelliom an apology—and it owes me an explanation." She looked into the golden cask, and the azure glow from the stone illuminated her face. She spoke directly to the stone in a language Sparhawk did not understand, although it was somehow tantalizingly familiar. There were pauses as she spoke, pauses during which Sparhawk presumed Bhelliom was responding, communing directly with her in a voice that only she could hear. At one point she laughed, peal upon peal of silvery laughter that almost seemed to sparkle in the chill air. "All right, Sparhawk," she said finally, "Bhelliom and I have finished apologizing to each other. You can go ahead and present your problem now."

"You're too kind," he murmured.

"Be nice."

"I would not trouble thee with our trivial concerns, Blue-Rose," Sparhawk said then, "but methinks the onset of the winter ice hath been hastened by Cyrgon's hand, and it is beyond our power to respond."

Vanion's tone was stern as Bhelliom replied. "Methinks Cyrgon doth need instruction in courtesy, Anakha—and perchance in humility as well. He hath bent his will to the premature formation of the ice. I will tweak his beard for this. There are rivers in the sea, and he hath turned one of these aside to freeze this coast in furtherance of his design. I will turn aside yet another and bring the torrid breath of tropic climes to this northern shore and consume his ice."

Aphrael clapped her hands together with a delighted laugh. "What's so funny?" Sparhawk asked her.

"Cyrgon's going to be a little sick for a few days," she replied. "Thou art wise beyond measure, Flower-Gem," she said gaily.

"Thou art kind to say so, Aphrael, but methinks thy praise hath some small taint of flattery to it."

"Well," she said, "a *little*, perchance, but overfulsome praise for those we love is no sin, is it?"

"Guard well thine heart, Anakha," Bhelliom advised. "The Child-Goddess will steal it from thee when thou dost least expect it."

"She did that years ago, Blue-Rose," Sparhawk replied.

"I can do this myself, Sparhawk," Khalad whispered. "I don't need a chaperon." The two were lying behind a log atop the knoll from which they had observed the Edomish workmen the previous day. The work gangs were laboring by the smoky light of fires being fed with green wood. The moon was full, and the smoke from the fires seemed almost to glow in its pale light.

"I just came along to admire the shot, Khalad," Sparhawk replied innocently. "I like to watch professionals in action. Besides, I have to give Ulath the signal just as soon as you put Incetes to sleep." He shivered. "Aren't we a bit early?" he asked. "The sky won't start to get light for another hour yet. All we're doing here is sprouting icicles."

"Did you want to do this?"

"No. I probably couldn't even come close at this range."

"Then do you want to keep your mouth shut and let me do it?"

"You're awfully grouchy for so young a fellow, Khalad. That doesn't usually set in until a man's much older."

"Dealing with knights has prematurely aged me."

"How does this new sight of yours work?"

"Do you know what the word *trajectory* means?"

"Sort of."

Khalad shook his head wearily. "Never mind, Sparhawk. My calculations are accurate. Just take my word for it."

"You actually work it out on paper?"

"Paper's cheaper than a bushel of new crossbow bolts."

"It sounds to me as if you spend more time calculating and adjusting your sights than you do shooting."

"Yes," Khalad admitted, "but if you do it right, you only have to shoot once."

"Why did we come out so early, then?"

"To give my eyes time to adjust to the light. The light's going to be peculiar when I make the shot. I'll have moonlight, firelight, and the first touches of dawn in the sky when the time comes. It'll all be changing, and I need to watch it change so that my eyes are ready. I've also got to pick Incetes out and keep a close eye on him. Killing his second cousin won't do the job."

"You think of everything, don't you?"

"Somebody has to."

They waited. The pale light of the full moon made the sand of the newly emerged, mile-wide beach intensely white, almost the same as snow, and the night air was bitingly cold.

"Keep your head down, Sparhawk, or hold your breath."

"What?"

"Your breath is steaming. If somebody looks this way, he'll know that we're here."

"They're two hundred and fifty paces away, Khalad."

"Why take chances if you don't have to?" Khalad peered intently at the antlike figures working at the edge of the trees. "Is Empress Elysoun still chasing Berit?" he asked after a few moments.

"She seems to be branching out a bit. I think she caught him a few times, though."

"Good. Berit was awfully stuffy when he was younger. He's in love with your wife, you know."

"Yes. We talked about it some years back."

"It doesn't bother you?"

"No. It's just one of those infatuations young men go through. He doesn't really intend to do anything about it."

"I like Berit. He'll make a good knight—once I grind off the remnants of his nobility. Titles make people a little silly." He pointed. "It's starting to get light off to the east."

Sparhawk glanced out across the icy reaches of the north Tamul Sea. "Yes," he agreed.

Khalad opened the leather pouch he had brought along and took out a length of sausage. "A bite of breakfast, my Lord?" he offered, reaching for his dagger.

"Why not?"

The first faint touches of light along the eastern horizon faded back into darkness as the "false dawn" came and went.

No one had ever satisfactorily explained that particular phenomenon to Sparhawk. He had seen it many times during his exile in Rendor. "We've still got about another hour," he told his squire.

Khalad grunted, lay back against the log, and closed his eyes.

"I thought you were here to watch," Sparhawk said. "How can you watch if you're asleep?"

"I'm not sleeping, Sparhawk. I'm just resting my eyes. Since you came along anyway, *you* can watch for a while."

The true dawn began to stain the eastern sky some time later, and Sparhawk touched Khalad's shoulder. "Wake up," he said quietly.

Khalad's eyes opened quickly. "I wasn't asleep."

"Why were you snoring, then?"

"I wasn't. I was just clearing my throat."

"For half an hour?"

Khalad rose up slightly and peered over the top of the log. "Let's wait until the sun hits those people," he suggested. "That bronze breastplate Incetes is wearing should gleam in the sunlight, and a brighter target's easier to hit."

"You're the one doing the shooting."

Khalad looked at the laboring Edomish peasants. "I just had a thought, Sparhawk. They've built a lot of those rafts. Why waste them?"

"What did you have in mind?"

"Even if Bhelliom melts Cyrgon's ice, it's going to take Captain Sorgi a couple of days to ferry all of us around that reef. Why not use these rafts? Sorgi can put a good-sized force on the beach a few miles north of the pier that's probably being constructed on the other side of the wall, and the rest of us can slip around the reef from this side on those rafts, and we can jump the people up there from both sides."

"I thought you didn't like these rafts."

"I can fix them, Sparhawk. All we have to do is take two of them, lay one on top of the other, and we'll have one good one. Cyrgon might have more forces up here on the North Cape than just the Trolls. I think we'll want to put all these rafts well out of his reach, don't you?"

"You're probably right. Let's talk to Vanion about it." Sparhawk looked at the eastern horizon. "The sun's starting to come up."

Khalad rolled over and laid his crossbow across the log. He

carefully checked the settings on his sighting mechanism and then settled the stock against his shoulder.

Incetes was standing on a tree stump in the full light of the half-risen sun. He was waving his arms and bellowing incomprehensible exhortations to his exhausted workmen.

"Are we ready?" Khalad asked, laying his cheek against the stock and squinting through the sight.

"*I'm* ready, but *you're* the one who has to shoot."

"No talking. I have to concentrate now." Khalad drew in a deep breath, let part of it out, and then stopped breathing entirely.

Incetes, gleaming golden in the new-risen sun, stood bellowing and waving his arms. The titan from prehistory looked tiny, almost toylike in the distance.

Khalad slowly, deliberately squeezed the release lever.

The crossbow thumped heavily, its rope-thick gut string giving off a deep-toned twang. Sparhawk watched the bolt arc upward.

"Got him," Khalad said with a certain satisfaction.

"The arrow hasn't even reached him yet," Sparhawk objected.

"It will. Incetes is dead. The arrow will go right through his heart. Go ahead and signal Ulath to charge."

"Aren't you being a little—"

A vast cry of chagrin rose from the crowd at the edge of the forest. Incetes was toppling slowly backward, and the bronze-age warriors surrounding him wavered and vanished even as he fell.

"You've got to learn to have a little more faith, Sparhawk," Khalad noted. "When I tell you that somebody's dead, he's dead—even if he doesn't know it yet. Were you planning to signal Ulath—sometime today?"

"Oh. I almost forgot."

"Age does that to people—or so I've been told."

"The ministries are corrupt, Ehlana. I'll be the first to admit that; but if I have to rebuild the government from the ground up, I'll spend the rest of my life at it, and I'll never get anything else done." Sarabian's tone was pensive.

"But Pondia Subat's such an incompetent," Ehlana objected.

"I *want* him to be an incompetent, dear heart. I'm going to reverse the usual roles. *He's* going to be the figurehead, and *I'm* going to be the one pulling the strings. The other ministers are in the habit of obeying him, so having him as prime minister won't even confuse them. I'll write Subat's speeches for him and terrorize him to the point that he won't depart from the prepared text. I'll terrorize him to the point that he won't even change clothes or shave without my permission. That's why I want him to sit in and hear the reports of Milord Stragen's unique solution to our recent problem. I want him to imagine the feel of the knives going in every time he has an independent thought."

"Might I make a suggestion, your Majesty?" Stragen asked.

"By all means, Stragen." Sarabian smiled. "The stunning success of your outrageous scheme has earned you a sizeable balance of imperial indulgence."

Stragen smiled and began to pace the floor, his face deep in thought and his fingers absently weighing a gold coin. Ehlana wondered where he had picked up that habit. "The society of thieves is classless, your Majesty," he pointed out. "We're firm believers in the aristocracy of talent, and talent shows up in some of the strangest places. You might want to consider including some people who aren't Tamuls in your government. Racial purity is all well and good, I suppose, but when every government official of rank in every subject kingdom is a Tamul, it stirs the kind of resentment that Zalasta and his friends have been exploiting. A more ecumenical approach might dampen those resentments. If an ambitious man sees the chance for advancement, he's much less likely to want to throw off the yoke of the Godless yellow devils."

"Are they still calling us that?" Sarabian murmured. He leaned back. "It's an interesting notion, Stragen. First I ruthlessly crush rebellion, and then I invite the rebels into the government. It should confuse them, if nothing else."

Mirtai opened the door to admit Caalador.

"What's afoot?" Ehlana asked him.

"Our friends at the Cynesgan embassy are very busy, your Majesty," he reported. "Evidently our unusual celebration of the Harvest Festival made them nervous. They're bringing in supplies and reinforcing the gates. It looks as if they're expecting trouble and they're getting ready to fort up."

"Let them," Sarabian shrugged. "If they want to imprison themselves, it saves me the trouble of doing it."

"Is Krager still inside?" Ehlana asked.

Caalador nodded. "I saw him walking across the courtyard this morning my very own-self."

"Keep an eye on him, Caalador," she instructed.

"I purely will, dorlin'." He grinned. "I purely will."

Vanion led the charge up the beach. The knights and the Peloi descended upon the demoralized work gangs in a thunderous rush, while Engessa's Atans ran along the water's edge to the foot of the makeshift pier to cut off the escape of those laboring to extend it farther out into the chill waters of the Tamul Sea.

The ribbon clerk Amador was shrieking orders from the pier, but no one was really paying much attention to him. Some few of the workmen who had been cutting trees put up a feeble resistance, but most fled back into the forest. It only took a few minutes for those who had chosen to resist to realize that the decision had been a bad one, and they threw down their weapons and raised their hands in surrender. The knights, trained to be merciful, readily accepted surrenders; Tikume's Peloi did so only reluctantly; the Atans on the pier tended to ignore those who sued for mercy, pausing only long enough to kick them off into the water. With Betuana and Engessa in the lead, the Atans marched ominously out onto the pier, killing anybody who offered any resistance and throwing the rest into the chill water on either side. The men in the water struggled to shore to be rounded up by the Tamul soldiers from the imperial garrison at Matherion. The soldiers' presence was primarily a gesture, since they were ceremonial troops unprepared by either their training or their natural inclinations for fighting. However, they *were* quite good at rounding up the shivering men who emerged, dripping and blue with the cold, from the icy water.

"I'd say that Bhelliom's warm current hasn't arrived yet," Khalad observed.

"It wouldn't seem so," Sparhawk agreed. "Let's go on down. The days are very short now, and I'd like to secure the north pier before the sun goes down."

"If there *is* a north pier," Khalad said.

"There *has* to be one, Khalad."

"You wouldn't mind if I ambled over to the edge of the cliff and had a look for myself, would you? Logic is all well and good, but a little verification never hurt anything."

They walked back down the knoll, mounted, and rode out to join their friends.

"Not much of a fight," Kalten complained, looking disdainfully at the mob of terrified prisoners.

"Those are the best kind," Tynian told him.

"Sorgi's coming," Ulath told them, pointing at the fleet moving toward the beach. "As soon as Betuana and Engessa finish clearing the pier, we'll be able to get started."

The Atans were halfway to the end of the pier by now, and the terrified Edomishmen were being crowded into a tighter and tighter mass by that inexorable advance.

"How cold is that water?" Talen asked. "I mean, has it started to warm up at all?"

"Not noticeably," Ulath said. "I saw a fish swim by earlier wearing a fur coat."

"Do you think a man could swim back to shore from the end of the pier?"

"Anything's possible," Ulath shrugged. "I wouldn't want to wager any money on it, though."

Rebal was at the very end of the pier by now, and his screams were growing increasingly shrill. The Atans leveled their spears and continued their inexorable advance. They did not even bother to kill the Edomishmen anymore. They simply shoved everyone off the pier to struggle in the icy water. A large knot of the workmen at the very end of the pier went off the end in a kind of cluster, the ones at the extreme outer end dragging their fellows with them as they toppled off. The Atans lined the sides and the end of the pier, keeping everyone in the water at spear's length from safety. That went somewhat beyond the bounds of civilized behavior, but Sparhawk knew of no diplomatic way to object to Queen Betuana about it, so he ground his teeth together and let it pass.

There was a great deal of splashing at first, but that did not last for very long. Singly and in groups the freezing peasants gave up and slid under the waves. A few athletic ones struck out for shallow water, but no more than a handful reached that questionable safety.

Amador, Sparhawk noted, was not among the few survivors being rounded up by the Tamul soldiers at the water's edge.

Sorgi's ships were standing at anchor some few yards off the beach by now, and the plans they had all drawn up the night before proceeded smoothly.

There was one thing, however, that their planning had not taken into account. Khalad had ridden to the edge of the cliff to look to the north, and he rode back with a slightly worried frown.

"Well?" Sparhawk asked him.

"There's a pier north of the wall, right enough," Khalad replied, dismounting, "but we've got a problem coming up from the south. Bhelliom's warm current is arriving."

"Why is that a problem?"

"I think Bhelliom got a little carried away. It looks as if the leading edge of that current is boiling."

"So?"

"What do you get when you pour boiling water on ice, Sparhawk?"

"Steam, I suppose."

"Right. Bhelliom's melting the ice out there, right enough, but it's raising a lot of steam in the process. What's another word for steam, my Lord?"

"Please don't do that, Khalad. It's very offensive. Just how big is this fogbank?"

"I couldn't see the end of it, my Lord."

"Thick?"

"You could probably walk on it."

"Could we possibly stay ahead of it?"

Khalad pointed out to sea. "I sort of doubt it, my Lord. I'd say it's already here."

The fog was rolling across the water in a thick grey blanket, its leading edge a solid wall obscuring everything in its path.

Sparhawk started to swear.

"You seem melancholy, my Queen," Alean said when the ladies were alone.

Ehlana sighed. "I don't like being separated from Sparhawk," she said. "There were too many years of that when he was in exile."

"You've loved him for a long time, haven't you, your Majesty?"

"I was born loving Sparhawk. It's really more convenient that way. You don't have to waste time thinking about other possible husbands. You can concentrate all your attention on the one you're going to marry and make sure you've closed all his escape routes."

There was a knock on the door, and Mirtai rose, put her hand on her sword hilt, and went to answer it.

Stragen entered. He was wearing rough clothes.

"What on earth have you been up to, Milord?" Melidere asked him.

"Pushing a wheelbarrow, Baroness." He shrugged. "I'm not sure that it accomplishes all that much to disguise myself this way, but it's good to maintain proper work habits. I've been posing as an employee of the Ministry of Public Works. We've been repairing the street outside the Cynesgan embassy. Caalador and I rolled dice, and he won the right to sit on a rooftop to keep watch. I get to trundle wheelbarrow-loads of cobblestones to the pavers."

"I gather that something's happening at the embassy?" Ehlana guessed.

"Yes, my Queen. Unfortunately, we can't quite figure out what. All the chimneys are spouting smoke that doesn't look like woodsmoke. I think they're burning documents. That's usually a sign of incipient flight."

"Don't they know that they haven't a chance of getting out of town?" Mirtai asked him.

"It appears that they're going to make a try anyway. It's just a guess, but I'd say they're planning something that's going to seriously offend the authorities, and then they're going to make a run for it." He looked at Ehlana. "I think we'd better tighten our security arrangements, your Majesty. All these preparations hint at something serious, and we don't want to be caught off-guard."

"I'll have a talk with Sarabian," Ehlana decided. "It was useful to have that embassy functioning as long as Xanetia was here to eavesdrop. Now that she's off with Sparhawk and the others, the embassy's just an irritation. I think it might be time to send in some Atans to nullify it."

"It's an embassy, your Majesty," Melidere objected. "We can't just go in and round everybody up. That's against all the rules of civilized behavior."

"So?"

"We don't have much choice, Master Cluff," Sorgi said gravely. "When you're out in deep water and this kind of fog comes up, all you can do is put out your sea anchor and hope you don't run aground on some island. You'd never be able to pick your way around the end of that reef with those rafts, and I'd rip the bottoms out of half the ships in the fleet if I tried to slip through the channel between the reef and the ice. We're going to have to wait until this lifts—or thins out, at least."

"And how long will that be?" Sparhawk asked.

"There's no way to tell."

"The air's colder than the water, Sparhawk," Khalad explained. "That's what's causing the fog. I don't think it's going to lift until the air warms up. We won't be ready to leave here until tomorrow anyway. We're going to have to do something to raise those rafts up out of the water a bit before we load men and horses on them. If we try to use them the way they are, we'll be trying to move them half-submerged."

"Why don't you get started on that, Khalad?" Vanion suggested. "Sparhawk and I'll go have a talk with Sephrenia and Aphrael. We might just need a bit of divine intervention here. Coming, Sparhawk?"

The two of them went back on down the beach to the fire Kalten had built for the ladies.

"Well?" Sephrenia asked. She was seated on a driftwood log with her sister in her lap.

"The fog's creating some problems," Vanion replied. "We can't get around the end of the reef until it lifts, and we're a little crowded for time. We'd like to reach Tzada before the Trolls start to march. Any ideas?"

"A few," Aphrael replied, "but I'll need to talk with Bhelliom first. There are certain proprieties and courtesies involved, you understand."

"No," Sparhawk replied. "I don't, really, but I'll take your word for it."

"Oh, *thank* you, Sparhawk!" she said with a certain false ingenuousness. "I think Bhelliom and I should discuss this in private. Open the box and give it to me."

"Whatever you say." He took out the cask and touched it with his ring. "Open," he told it. Then he handed the box to the Child-Goddess.

She slid off Sephrenia's lap and went down the beach a little way. Then she stood looking out at the fog-enveloped sea. So far as Sparhawk could tell, she was not speaking aloud to the sapphire rose.

It was about ten minutes later when she returned and handed the box back to Sparhawk. "It's all taken care of," she told him in an offhand way. "When do you want to leave?"

"Tomorrow morning?" Sparhawk asked Vanion.

Vanion nodded. "That should give Khalad time to modify the rafts, and we can get the knights and their horses on board Sorgi's ships and ready to go by then."

"All right," Aphrael said. "Tomorrow, then. Now why don't you go find Ulath and ask him whose turn it is to do the cooking? I'm absolutely famished."

It was not much of a breeze, and it did not entirely dissipate the fog, but they could at least see where they were going, and the tattered remnants of mist would provide them with some cover after they rounded the tip of the reef.

Khalad had decided that the quickest way to modify the rafts was to simply double them, pulling one raft on top of another so that the added buoyancy would provide a reasonable freeboard. This made the rafts very cumbersome, of course. They were heavy and hard to steer, and so their progress out along the reef was painfully slow.

The skiff leading the way, however, cut through the water ahead of the flotilla and faded into the remnants of the fog-bank. Khalad and Berit had announced that they would scout on ahead.

After about an hour, the skiff returned. "We marked the channel," Khalad told them. "That boiling water really cut the ice away, so there'll be plenty of room to get the rafts around the tip of the reef."

"We saw Captain Sorgi's ships go by," Berit reported. "Apparently he didn't entirely trust the sails. This breeze is a little erratic—" He hesitated. "You don't have to tell Aphrael I said that, of course. Anyway, Sorgi's put the knights to work rowing. They'll get to the beach north of the pier quite some time before we make it to shore."

"Are those trees sticking up out of the water going to cause us any problems?" Kalten asked.

"Not if we stick close to the face of the cliff, Sir Kalten," Khalad replied. "The landslides Bhelliom's earthquake set off knocked down all the trees for about a hundred yards out from the wall. The trees farther out will give us some additional cover. When you add them to what's left of the fog, I don't think anybody on shore will see us coming."

"It's working out fairly well, then," Ulath said, grunting as he pushed his twenty-foot-long pole against the sea-bottom, "except for this part, of course."

"We could always swim," Tynian suggested.

"No, that's all right, Tynian," Ulath replied. "I don't mind poling all *that* much."

* * *

When they reached the tip of the reef, the flotilla of rafts split up into two separate fleets. Queen Betuana and Engessa took the Atans and made their way along the outer edge of the half-submerged forest toward the pier that thrust out from shore, while Sparhawk and his friends took the Peloi and the knights for whom there had not been room aboard Sorgi's ships along the cliff-face, with Khalad and Berit scouting ahead in the skiff. Since even Sorgi's hundred ships and the large number of rafts were not enough to carry *all* their forces, they had been obliged to leave a sizeable portion of their army on the south beach along with Sephrenia, Talen, Flute, and Xanetia.

"It's shoaling," Ulath said after about half an hour. "I think we're getting closer to shore."

"More of the trees are sticking up out of the water as well," Kalten added. "I'll definitely be glad to get off this raft. It's a nice enough raft, I suppose, but pushing it through the water with a twenty-foot pole is sort of like trying to tip over a house."

The skiff came ghosting back out of the fog. "You'd better start keeping your voices down, my Lords," Khalad said in a hoarse whisper. "We're getting closer." He reached out with one hand to steady the skiff. "We're in luck, though. There used to be a road running parallel to the beach—at least I think it was a road. Anyway, the road or whatever it was gives us an open channel through the trees, and the trees between us and the beach will keep the workmen from seeing us."

"And probably keep us from getting ashore as well," Tynian added.

"No, Sir Tynian," Berit replied. "There was a meadow out there a mile or so from where the cliff is now, and that's where the pier is. All we have to do is follow that road and it'll bring us out almost on top of the work gangs."

"Could you hear them at all?" Vanion asked.

"Oh, yes," Khalad replied, "almost as if they were standing about ten feet away—and you'll start hearing their axes in just a few minutes." He and Berit climbed aboard the raft.

"Could you make out their accents? Were they more of those Edomishmen we came up against on the south pier?"

"No, my Lord. The men up here are Astels. We couldn't see the beach, but I'd guess that the people giving the orders came from Ayachin's army instead of Incetes' people."

"Let's push on, then," Kalten said, hefting his pole. "Figuratively speaking, of course," he added.

* * *

"Are we all ready?" Sparhawk asked, looking up and down the line of rafts strung out to either side.

"What is there to get ready for, Sparhawk?" Kalten asked. "If anything, Astellian serfs are going to be even more timid than those Edomish peasants were. Ulath could probably chase them all back into the trees by just standing out here in what's left of the fog blowing on his Ogre-horn."

"All right, then," Sparhawk said. *Aphrael*—he threw the thought out—*are you listening?*

Well, of course I'm listening, Sparhawk.

He decided to try a different approach. He cast his request in formal Styric this time. *An it please thee, Divine Aphrael, I do beseech thine aid.*

Aren't you feeling well? Her tone was suspicious.

I but sought to demonstrate mine unutterable regard and respect for thee, Divine One!

Are you making fun of me?

No, of course not. I just realized that I haven't been all that respectful lately. We're in position now. We're going to start moving the rafts slowly toward shore. As soon as we can make out the people on the beach, Ulath's going to give the signal for the general attack. I'd appreciate a nice strong gust of wind at that point, if it's not too much trouble . . .

Well, I'll think about it.

Will you be able to hear Ulath's horn? Or would you rather have me tell you when we need the wind?

Sparhawk, I can hear a spider walking across the ceiling of a house ten miles away. I'll blow as soon as Ulath does.

That's a novel way to put it.

Get moving, Sparhawk, or you'll run out of daylight.

Yes, ma'am. He looked around at the others. "Let's get started," he told them. "The Divine One is drawing in deep breaths. I think she plans to blow the fog all the way to the pole."

The rafts inched forward, concentrating on staying in a straight line so that none of them emerged from the fog before the others.

They could clearly hear the voices speaking in Elenic from the shore now and the faint lapping of wavelets sloshing over the protruding roots of the trees off to the left.

"Six feet," Kalten reported in a loud whisper as he lifted his pole out of the water. "We can make a mounted charge when it shoals down to four."

"*If* the fog holds out that long," Bevier amended.

They crept on with the water shoaling under their rafts inch by inch as they eased closer to shore.

They heard the sound of a heavy blow and curses spat out in archaic Elenic.

"That's one of Ayachin's men," Khalad whispered.

"Ayachin himself wouldn't be here, would he?" Berit asked.

"Incetes was, so I wouldn't discount the possibility."

"If Ayachin *is* here, I want you two to go looking for Elron," Sparhawk instructed. "We lost Amador, but Xanetia should be able to get the same kind of information out of Elron. Don't let him get away—or get himself killed."

"Three feet!" Kalten announced in a triumphant whisper. "We can charge just as soon as we catch sight of them."

The rafts inched closer, and the voices ahead were much louder now.

"There's something moving," Khalad said, pointing at a dim shape ahead.

"How far?" Sparhawk asked, peering into the white blankness ahead.

"Maybe thirty paces."

Then Sparhawk saw more of the dark outlines in the fog and heard the sound of men slogging through shallow water. "Mount up!" he commanded in a low voice, "and signal the other rafts."

They pulled themselves slowly into their saddles, being careful not to make any noise.

"All right, Ulath," Sparhawk said aloud, "let everybody know that we're starting."

Ulath grinned and lifted the curled Ogre-horn to his lips.

CHAPTER
THIRTY

I t was more like a gale than a breeze, and it came howling out of nowhere, bending the evergreens and tearing the last of the leaves from birch and aspen. The fog streamed away in the leaf-speckled blast.

The crests of the shallow waves were suddenly whipped to froth, and the water ran against a shoreline that was not sand, nor gravel, nor rock, but grass and half-submerged bushes. There were thousands of men on shore, roughly dressed serfs laboring in a field of tree stumps.

"Heretic Knights!" a man at the edge of the water screamed. He wore crude bits and pieces of ancient armor and he stood gaping at the huge force of mounted men which had appeared quite suddenly out of nowhere as the gale tore the fog away.

Ulath's horn continued its barbaric call, and Tikume's Peloi and the knights plunged off the rafts, their mounts sending great sheets of water out to either side, almost like icy wings.

"What must we do, noble Ayachin?" the crudely armored man shrieked to a lean fellow astride a white horse. The mounted man was more completely armored, although his armor was an archaic blend of steel plate and bronze chain mail.

"Fight!" he roared. "Destroy the heretic invaders! Fight— for Astel and our holy faith!"

Sparhawk sawed Faran's reins around and charged directly

454

at the resurrected Astellian hero, his sword aloft and his shield in front of his body.

Ayachin's helmet had no visor as such, but rather a steel nose-guard protruding down over half his face. There was a quick intelligence in that face and a burning zeal. The eyes, however, were the eyes of a fanatic. He set himself, raised his heavy sword, and spurred his white mount forward to meet Sparhawk's charge.

The two horses crashed together, and the white mount reeled back. Faran was the bigger horse and he was skilled at fighting. He slammed his shoulder into Ayachin's mount and tore great chunks from the white animal's neck with his teeth. Sparhawk caught the ancient hero's sword-stroke with his shield and countered with a heavy overhead stroke of his own, clashing his blade down on the hastily raised and bulky shield.

"Heretic!" Ayachin snarled. "Spawn of Hell! Foul sorcerer!"

"Give it up!" Sparhawk snapped. "You're out of your class!" He found that he had no real wish to kill this man who was fighting to defend his homeland and his faith from a brutal Church policy long since abandoned. Sparhawk had no real quarrel with him.

Ayachin bellowed his defiance and swung his sword again. He showed some proficiency with the weapon, but he was no real match for the black-armored Pandion he faced. Sparhawk caught the sword-stroke with his shield again and struck a chopping blow at his opponent's shoulder. "Run away, Ayachin!" he barked. "I don't want to kill you! You've been duped by an alien God and dragged thousands of years into the future! This isn't your fight! Take your people and go!"

It was too late, though. Sparhawk saw the madness in his opponent's eyes and he had been in too many fights not to recognize it. He sighed, crowded Faran in against the white horse, and began a series of strokes he had used so many times in the past that once it began, the succeeding blows were automatic.

The ancient shade fought bravely, struggling to respond with his unwieldy equipment, but the outcome was inevitable. Sparhawk's progressive strokes bit him deeper and deeper, and chunks of his armor flew from each savage cut.

Then, altering his last stroke to avoid a grotesque maiming, Sparhawk thrust instead of delivering the customary overhand stroke which would have split his opponent's head. His swordpoint crunched through the ancient and ineffective armor and smoothly ran through Ayachin's chest.

The fire went out of that ancient face, and the hero Ayachin stiffened and toppled slowly from his saddle.

Sparhawk raised his sword hilt to his face in a sad salute.

A great cry went up from the Astellian serfs as Ayachin's army vanished. A burly serf at the water's edge bawled contradictory orders, gyrating his arms like a windmill. Berit leaned over in his saddle and brought the flat side of his axblade down on top of the man's head, felling him instantly.

There were a few pockets of ineffective and halfhearted resistance, but the serfs for the most part fled. Queen Betuana and her Atans drove the panicky workers from the pier, and the knights and the Peloi parted ranks to permit them to flee into the forest. Sparhawk rose in his stirrups and looked to the north. The knights from Sorgi's ships were driving the misguided serfs on the far side of the pier back into the trees.

The battle, such as it had been, was over.

The Queen of the Atans came ashore with a look of discontent on her golden face. "It was not much of a fight, Sparhawk-Knight," she accused.

"I'm sorry, your Majesty," he apologized. "I did the best I could with what I had to work with. I'll try to do better next time."

She suddenly grinned at him. "I was teasing you, Sparhawk-Knight. Good planning reduces the need for fighting, and you plan well."

"Your Majesty is kind to say so."

"How long will it take that Cammorian sailor to bring the rest of our army to this side of the wall?"

"The rest of today and most of tomorrow, I'd imagine."

"Can we afford to wait that long? We should go to Tzada before the Troll-beasts start to march."

"I'll talk with Aphrael and Bhelliom, your Majesty," he said. "They'll be able to tell us what the Trolls are doing—and delay them if necessary."

Khalad rode up. "We couldn't find any sign of Elron, Sparhawk," he reported. "We captured a few of those serfs, and they told us that he wasn't here."

"Who was in charge, then?"

"That husky fellow Berit put to sleep with the flat of his ax seems to have been the one giving all the orders."

"Wake him up and see what you can get out of him. Don't twist him too hard, though. If he decides to be stubborn, we'll wait until Xanetia gets here. She can find out everything he knows without hurting him."

"Yes, my Lord." Khalad wheeled his mount and went looking for Berit.

"You have a kindly disposition for a warrior, Sparhawk-Knight," Betuana observed.

"These serfs aren't really our enemies, Betuana-Queen. I'll show you the other side of my nature after we catch Zalasta."

"His name is Torbik," Khalad reported when he joined them in the pavilion they had erected for the ladies. "He was one of Sabre's first followers. I think he's a serf from Baron Kotyk's estate. He wouldn't say so, but I'm fairly sure he knows that Elron is Sabre."

"Does he know why Elron sent *him* rather than coming here himself?" Tynian asked.

"He hasn't a clue—or so he says," Khalad replied. "Anarae Xanetia can look inside his head and find out for sure." He paused. "Excuse me, Anarae," he said to the Delphaeic woman. "We all keep groping for ways to describe what you do when you listen to the thoughts of others. We'd probably be a lot less offensive if you'd tell us the right word for it."

Xanetia, who had arrived with Sephrenia, Talen, and Flute on Sorgi's ship with the first contingent being ferried around the reef, smiled. "I had wondered which of you would be the first to ask," she said. "Methinks I should have known it would be thee, young master, for thine is the most practical mind in all this company. We of the Delphae do refer to this modest gift as 'sharing.' We *share* the thoughts of others, we do not *leech* them, nor do we scoop them like struggling minnows from the dark waters of consciousness."

"Would it offend you, Sir Knights, if I pointed out that it's easier to ask than to grope your way through four languages looking for the right term?" Khalad asked rather innocently.

"Yes," Vanion said, "as a matter of fact it *would* offend us."

"I won't point it out, then, my Lord." Khalad even managed to say it with a straight face. "Anyways, Torbik was here primarily to keep the Astellian serfs from talking with Ayachin's warriors too much. Evidently there's a great potential for confusion in the situation. Elron didn't want the two groups to start comparing notes."

"Does he have any idea at all about where Elron is right now?" Kalten asked.

"He doesn't even know where *he* is right now. Elron just said a few vague things about eastern Astel and let it go at that. Torbik wasn't really the one in charge here—any more than Ayachin was. There was a Styric with them, and *he* was the one who was giving all the orders. He was probably one of the first to run off into the woods when we came ashore."

"Could that have been Djarian?" Bevier asked Sephrenia, "Zalasta's necromancer? *Somebody* plucked Ayachin out of the ninth century."

"It might have been," Sephrenia replied dubiously. "More likely, though, it was one of Djarian's pupils. It's the initial spell that's difficult. Once the people from the past have been successfully raised, a fairly simple spell can bring them back again. I'm sure there was a Styric south of the wall calling up Incetes and *his* men as well. Zalasta and Ogerajin have a large body of renegades to draw upon."

"May I come in?" Captain Sorgi asked from just outside the tent.

"Of course, Captain," Vanion replied.

The silvery-haired seaman came inside. "We'll have the last of your people ashore on this side of the reef by tomorrow noon, my Lords," he reported. "You'll want us to wait here, won't you?"

"Yes," Sparhawk replied. "If all goes well, we'll need to go back around the reef after we've finished at Tzada."

"Will the warm water hold? I'd rather not get icebound up here."

"We'll see to it, Captain," Sparhawk promised.

Sorgi shook his head. "You're a strange man, Master Cluff. You can do things no one I've ever met can do." He suddenly smiled. "But strange or not, you've thrown a lot of profit my way since you started running away from that ugly heiress." He looked at the others. "But I'm just interrupting things here. Do you suppose I might have a word with you in private, Master Cluff?"

"Of course." Sparhawk rose and followed the sailor outside.

"I'll get right to the point," Sorgi said. "Do you have any further plans for these rafts—after you use them to go back around the reef, I mean?"

"No, I don't think so."

"Would it be all right with you if I left a crew on the beach south of the reef while I run you and your friends back to Matherion?"

"I have no objections, Captain, but why?"

"The rafts are made of very good logs, Master Cluff. After your army uses them to get around the reef, they'll just be lying there. It'd be a shame to waste them. I thought I'd leave a crew to lash them together into some kind of boom. I'll come back after I drop you off in Matherion, and we'll tow them to the timber market in Etalon—or maybe even back to Matherion itself. They should fetch a good price."

Sparhawk laughed. "Good old Sorgi," he said, putting a friendly hand on the sea captain's shoulder. "You never overlook a chance for a profit, do you? Take the logs with my blessing."

"You're a generous man, Master Cluff."

"You're my friend, Captain Sorgi, and I like doing things for friends."

"You're my friend as well, Master Cluff. The next time you need a ship, come and look me up. I'll take you anywhere you want to go." Sorgi paused, his expression suddenly cautious. "For only half price," he added.

The village of Tzada had been abandoned several years ago, and the rampaging Trolls had knocked most of the buildings down. It lay at the edge of a vast, marshy meadow with Bhelliom's escarpment looming over it to the south. The sun was just rising far to the southeast, and the grassy meadow was thick with frost that glittered in the slanting sunlight.

"How large is the meadow, your Majesty?" Vanion asked Betuana.

"Two leagues across and six or eight leagues long. It will be a good battlefield."

"We were sort of hoping to avoid that, your Majesty," Vanion reminded her.

Engessa was ordering his scouts out to pinpoint the exact location of the Trolls. "We were able to see them from the top of the escarpment," he told Vanion. "They've been gathering out in the middle of the meadow every day for the past several weeks. They were too far away for us to see exactly what they've been doing, though. The scouts will locate them for us."

"What's the plan, friend Sparhawk?" Kring asked, fingering his saber hilt. "Do we march on them and then turn their Gods loose on them at the last minute?"

"I want to talk with the Troll-Gods first," Aphrael said. "We want to be absolutely certain that they understand all the conditions of their release."

Vanion rubbed at the side of his face. "I think we'll want the Trolls to come to us instead of the other way around, don't you, Sparhawk?"

"Definitely, but a feint of some kind should draw them out." Sparhawk thought a moment. "Why don't we move a mile or so into the meadow so they can see us. Then we'll draw up in a standard formation—knights in the center, Atans on either side, and the Peloi out on the flanks. Cyrgon's got a military mind, and that formation's older than dirt. He'll think we're preparing to attack. The Cyrgai are an aggressive people, and *they* would want to attack first. Cyrgon's commanding Trolls this time instead of his own people, but I think we can count on him to do what's customary."

"He might as well." Ulath shrugged. "The Trolls will attack as soon as they see us no matter *what* Cyrgon wants them to do. The idea of defending themselves won't even occur to them. They look on us as food, and somebody who sits in one place waiting for supper to come to him usually goes to bed hungry."

"Better and better," Vanion said. "We'll hold our formation and let them get to within a few hundred yards of us. Then we'll turn the Troll-Gods loose. They'll reclaim their Trolls, and Cyrgon will be left standing out there in the middle of the meadow all alone."

"Maybe not quite," Sephrenia added. "He might have Zalasta with him. I certainly *hope* so, anyway."

"Savage," Vanion said fondly to her.

"Let's leave the army here and go around to the back side of the village," Sparhawk suggested. "If we're going to talk with the Troll-Gods, I'd rather not do it out in plain sight." He turned Faran and led the others around the ruined village to a smaller clearing a few hundred yards to the east.

Sparhawk had deliberately not closed the box after Bhelliom had transported them to Tzada. This time he *wanted* his enemies to know where he was. "Blue-Rose," he said politely, "canst thou find anything amiss in our plan?"

"It seemeth sound to me, Anakha," the stone replied through Vanion's lips. "It might be prudent, however, to advise the Troll-Gods that Cyrgon may reach back into antiquity for reinforcements once he doth perceive that the Trolls are no longer deceived by his assumèd guise."

"Thou art wise, my friend," Sparhawk replied. "We shall so advise them." He looked at Aphrael. "Don't pick any fights right now," he told her. "Let's try to get along with our allies—at least until the battle's over."

"Trust me," she said.

"Do I have any choice?"

"No, not really. Bring on the Troll-Gods, Sparhawk. Let's get to work. The day won't last forever, you know."

He muttered something under his breath.

"I didn't quite hear that," she said.

"You weren't supposed to." He raised the glowing gem. "Please bring them forth now, my friend," he told it. "The Child-Goddess doth grow impatient."

"I did notice that myself, Anakha."

Then the vast presences of the Troll-Gods were there, glowing blue and towering enormous.

"The time is come," Sparhawk announced in Trollish. "This is the place where Cyrgon has your children. Let us join together to cause hurt to Cyrgon."

"Yes!" Ghworg exulted.

"I will remind you of our compact," Aphrael said. "You have given surety. I will hold you to your promises."

"Well will we keep them, Aphrael." Ghworg's voice was sullen.

"Let us repeat them," she said shrewdly. "Promises made in haste are sometimes forgotten. Your children will no longer eat my children. Is it agreed?"

Ghnomb sobbed his assent.

"Khwaj will restrain his fire and Schlee his ice. Agreed? Ghworg will forbid your children to kill mine, and Zoka will permit no more than two cubs to each she-Troll. Is it agreed?"

"Agreed. Agreed," Ghworg said impatiently. "Free us."

"In a moment. Is it also agreed that your children will become mortal? That they will age and die as do mine?"

They howled in fury. They had evidently been hoping in their dim minds that she had forgotten that promise.

"Agreed?" she bored in with a not-so-veiled threat in her voice.

"Agreed," Schlee said reluctantly.

"Turn them loose, Sparhawk."

"In a minute." Then he spoke to the Troll-Gods directly. "It is our intent to cause hurt to Cyrgon," he told them. "Let him seem to have victory in his mouth before we jerk it from between his teeth. Thus will he suffer more."

"It speaks well," Schlee told the others. "Let us hear its words. Let us find out how the hurt of Cyrgon may be made greater."

Sparhawk quickly outlined their plan of battle. "Thus," he concluded, "when your children are ten tens of strides from Aphrael's children and Cyrgon exults, you can appear and tear your stolen children back from his grasp. In pain and agony may he bring his *own* children from the shadowy past to meet us. I will appeal to the Child-Goddess and ask her to relent this once and let your children feast upon Cyrgon's, and Cyrgon himself will feel their teeth as they rend and tear the flesh of his children."

"Your words are good, Anakha," Schlee agreed. "It is my thought that you are almost worthy to be a Troll."

"I thank you for thinking so," Sparhawk replied a bit dubiously.

The army advanced at a steady trot. The Church Knights, their armor gleaming in the slanting rays of the newly risen sun and the pennons on their lances fluttering, rode forward, the hooves of their half-trained war horses crushing the knee-high grass of the meadow. The unmounted Atans loped along on either side, and Tikume's Peloi, probably the finest light cavalry in the world, ranged out on the flanks. Despite Vanion's violent objections, Sephrenia and Xanetia rode with the knights. Flute, for some obscure reason, rode with Talen this time.

They had trotted perhaps two miles out into the frost-white meadow when Vanion held up his hand to signal a halt. Ulath blew a long, strident blast on his Ogre-horn to pass the word.

Engessa, Betuana, and Kring joined them. "We have more details now," Betuana told them. "Some of our scouts concealed themselves in the high grass to watch the Trolls. Cyrgon is exhorting the man-beasts, and there are several Styrics with him. My people don't know the language of those monsters, so they couldn't understand what Cyrgon was saying."

"It's not too hard to guess," Tynian shrugged. "We've got quite an army here, and we've drawn up in the traditional battle formation. I'm sure Cyrgon thinks we're planning to attack the Trolls. He's preparing them for battle."

"Could your scouts recognize any of the Styrics, Betuana?" Sephrenia asked, her face grim.

The Atan Queen shook her head. "They couldn't get that close," she replied.

"Zalasta is there, Sephrenia," Xanetia said. "I can feel the presence of his mind."

"Can you hear his thoughts, Anarae?" Bevier asked her.

"Not clearly, Sir Knight. He is not yet close enough."

Vanion frowned. "I wish we could get some assurance that this ruse of ours is working," he fretted. "This could turn very ugly if Zalasta's got any ideas at all of what we're planning. Could your scouts get any kind of estimate about how many Trolls are out there, your Majesty?"

"Perhaps fifteen hundred, Vanion-Preceptor," Betuana replied.

"That's almost the whole herd," Ulath observed. "There aren't really very many Trolls." He made a wry face. "There don't really have to be. One Troll's a crowd all by himself in a fight."

"If we *were* planning a battle, would we have enough men?" Tynian asked him.

Ulath wobbled one hand back and forth uncertainly. "It'd be touch and go," he replied. "We've only got about twelve thousand. Attacking fifteen hundred Trolls with so few would be an act of desperation."

"Our ruse is believable, then," Vanion said. "Cyrgon and Zalasta shouldn't have any reason to suspect a trap."

They waited. The horses of the knights were restive and some grew more difficult to control as the minutes ticked by.

Then an Atan woman came running back across the frosty meadow. "They've started to move, Betuana-Queen!" she shouted from about a hundred yards out.

"It worked, then," Talen said gleefully.

"We'll see," Khalad said cautiously. "Let's not start dancing in the streets just yet."

The scout came the rest of the way across the meadow to join them.

"Tell us what you saw," Betuana commanded.

"The man-beasts are coming toward us, Betuana-Queen," the woman replied. "They move singly, some far to the front and others lagging behind."

"Trolls wouldn't understand the concept of fighting as a unit," Ulath told them.

"Who commands them?" Betuana asked.

"Something that is very large and ugly, Betuana-Queen," the

scout reported. "The man-beasts around it are taller than any Atan, and they scarcely come as high as its waist. There are Styrics with it as well—eight, by my count."

"Did one of them have silvery hair and beard?" Sephrenia asked intently.

"There are two such. One is thin, and one is fat. The thin one is close by the big ugly thing."

"*That* one is Zalasta," she said in a bleak voice.

"I'll take a promise from you now, Sephrenia," Vanion said firmly.

"You can go whistle for promises, Vanion," she said tartly. She was flexing her fingers in an ominous sort of way.

"You were right, Sparhawk-Knight," Engessa said with a faint smile. "When we reached Sarsos last summer, you said Sephrenia was two hundred feet tall. She *does* seem to grow as one comes to know her better, doesn't she? I don't think I'd care to trade places with Zalasta right now."

"No," Sparhawk agreed. "That wouldn't be a good idea."

"Will you at least agree to *think* just a little before you start grappling with Zalasta?" Vanion pleaded. "For *my* sake? My heart stops when you're in danger."

She smiled at him. "That's very sweet, Vanion, but I'm not the one in danger just now."

Then they heard it. It was a dull, rhythmic thudding of hundreds of feet striking the earth in rhythmic unison, and that thudding was accompanied by a low, brutish grunting. Then the thudding and grunting suddenly broke off, and a shrill, wailing ululation rose, fluctuating and piercing the chill air.

"Kring!" Ulath barked. "Let's go have a look!" And the two galloped out across the frozen meadow.

"What is it?" Vanion asked.

"Very bad news," Kalten replied tensely. "We've heard that noise before. When we were on our way to Zemoch, we came across some creatures Sephrenia called the Dawn-men. They make Trolls look like tame puppies by comparison."

"And the Troll-Gods wouldn't have any authority over them," Sephrenia added. "We might have to retreat."

"Never!" Betuana almost shouted. "I *won't* run away again—not from anything! I've been humiliated too many times already! My Atans and I will die here if necessary!"

Ulath and Kring came riding back, their faces baffled. "They're just ordinary Trolls!" Ulath exclaimed. "But they're stamping and grunting and wailing the same way the Dawn-men did!"

Flute suddenly burst out laughing.

"What's so funny?" Talen demanded.

"Cyrgon," she replied gaily. "I knew he was stupid, but I didn't think he was *this* stupid. He can't tell the difference between Trolls and Dawn-men. He's forcing the Trolls to behave the way their ancestors did, and that won't work with Trolls. All he's doing is confusing them. Let's go out and meet them, Sparhawk. I want to watch Cyrgon's face crumble and fall off the front of his head." Then she drove her little grass-stained feet into the flanks of Talen's horse, obliging the rest of them to follow along behind.

They crested a low hill and reined in. The Trolls were advancing through the tall grass on a broad front, quite nearly a mile across, shuffling, stamping their heels, and grunting in unison. A vast shape that very closely resembled Ghworg, the God of Kill, shambled along in the center of the brutish throng, beating on the frozen ground with a huge iron-bound club.

The monstrous apparition was closely surrounded by a group of white-robed Styrics. Sparhawk could quite clearly see Zalasta at Cyrgon's right.

"Cyrgon!" Aphrael called. Her voice was shatteringly loud. Then she spoke at some length in a language that had only traces of Styric in it and was shaded around the edges with bits and pieces of Elenic and Tamul and a half-dozen other languages as well.

"What tongue is that?" Betuana demanded.

"It is the language of the Gods," Vanion replied, his voice carrying that slightly wooden overtone that always overlaid it when Bhelliom spoke. "The Child-Goddess doth taunt Cyrgon." Vanion seemed to wince slightly. "Thou wert perhaps unwise to expose thy Goddess overmuch to Elenes, Sephrenia," Bhelliom observed. "Her capacity for imprecation and insult seemeth to me inappropriate for one so young."

"Aphrael is hardly young, Blue-Rose," she replied.

A faint smile touched Vanion's lips. "Not to thee, perhaps. Perspective, however, doth color all. To me, thy seemingly ancient Goddess is scarce more than a babe."

"Be nice," Aphrael murmured. Then she continued to rail at the now-enraged Cyrgon.

"Can you hear Zalasta's thoughts now, Anarae?" Kalten asked.

"Clearly, Sir Knight," Xanetia replied.

"Does he have any suspicion at all about what we're going to do?"

"Nay. He doth believe that victory is within his reach."

Aphrael stopped in midcurse. "Let's disabuse him of that right now," she said. "Turn loose the Troll-Gods, Sparhawk."

"An it please thee, Blue-Rose," Sparhawk said politely, "evict thine unwanted tenants now."

"More than gladly, Anakha," Bhelliom replied with great relief.

The Troll-Gods were not surrounded by that azure nimbus this time. They appeared suddenly and in vividly excruciating detail. Sparhawk suppressed a wave of revulsion.

"Go to your children, Ghworg!" Aphrael commanded in Trollish. "It is *your* semblance Cyrgon has stolen, and it is your right to cause hurt to him for that."

Ghworg roared his agreement and charged down the hill with the other Troll-Gods close on his heels.

The counterfeit Ghworg gaped up the hill at the dreadful reality descending upon him. And then he screamed in sudden agony.

"That is Cyrgon, isn't it?" Kalten shouted.

"Does that even happen to Gods?" Talen asked Flute. "Does it hurt you as much as it hurts humans to have one of your spells broken?"

"Even more," she almost purred. "Cyrgon's brains are on fire right now."

The Trolls were also gaping at their suddenly materialized Gods. One huge brute not far from the writhing God of the Cyrgai reached out almost absently, picked up a shrieking Styric, and pulled off his head. Then he tossed the head aside and began to eat the still-convulsing body.

The Troll-Gods roared something in unison, and the Trolls all fell on their faces.

Cyrgon writhed, shrieking, and the seven remaining Styrics collapsed as if they had been cut down. The false shape of Ghworg shuddered away into nothingness, and Cyrgon himself suddenly appeared as an amorphous blob of pale intense light.

Aphrael sneered. "That's Cyrgon for you," she noted. "He claims to be too proud to assume a human form. Personally, I think he's just too clumsy. If he tried, he'd probably put the head on upside down or both arms on the same side." She shrieked a few more triumphant insults.

"*Aphrael!*" Sephrenia actually sounded shocked.

"I've been saving those up," the Child-Goddess apologized. "You weren't really supposed to hear me say them."

Cyrgon's fire was fluctuating wildly now, flaring and dimming as his agony swelled and then diminished.

"What is Zalasta feeling now?" Sephrenia eagerly asked Xanetia.

"His pain doth go beyond mine ability to describe it," the Anarae replied.

"Dear, dear sister!" Sephrenia exulted. "You've made me happier than you could possibly imagine!"

"Are you ever going to be able to tame her again?" Sparhawk asked Vanion.

"It may take a while." Vanion's tone was troubled.

The writhing, half-formed shape of the flamelike Cyrgon partially rose and waved one huge, fiery arm; and a half mile or so behind the Trolls there suddenly appeared a vast glittering.

"He's called up his Cyrgai!" Khalad shouted. "We'd better do something."

"Ghworg! Schlee!" Vanion roared in Bhelliom's huge voice. "Cyrgon hath summoned his children! Now may *your* children feast!"

The Troll-Gods swelled even more enormous and barked sharp commands to their prostrate worshippers. The Trolls scrambled to their feet, turned, and looked hungrily at the advancing Cyrgai drawn from ages past. Then with a great roar they rushed toward the banquet Cyrgon had so generously provided.

Ehlana was tired. It had been one of those exhausting days with so many things to do that nothing had been really wrapped up before the next intruded itself. She had retired with Mirtai, Alean, and Melidere to prepare for bed. Danae trailed along behind them, dragging Rollo by one hind leg and yawning broadly.

"The emperor was in a peculiar humor this evening," Melidere noted, closing the door behind them.

"Sarabian's nerves are strung a little tight right now," Ehlana said, sitting down at her dressing table. "The future of his whole empire hinges on what Sparhawk and the others are doing in the north, and there's no way he can keep track of what's going on up there."

Danae yawned again and curled up in a chair.

"Where's your cat?" Ehlana asked her.

"She's around somewhere," Danae replied sleepily.

"Check my bed, Mirtai," Ehlana instructed. "I don't like furry little surprises in the middle of the night."

Mirtai patted down the canopied royal bed and then dropped to her knees to look under all the furniture. "No sign of her, Ehlana," she reported.

"You'd better go find her, Danae," the queen said.

"I'm sleepy, Mother," Danae objected.

"The sooner you find your cat, the sooner you can get to bed. Let's catch her *before* she gets out of the castle this time. Go with her, Mirtai. After you two find the cat, put Danae to bed, and then see if you can locate either Stragen or Caalador. One of them's supposed to bring me a report on what's going on at the Cynesgan embassy tonight, and I'd like to get it out of the way before I go to bed. I don't want them banging on my door in the middle of the night."

Mirtai nodded. "Come along, Danae," she said.

The princess sighed. She climbed out of her chair, kissed her mother, and followed the golden giantess out of the room.

Alean began to brush the queen's hair. Ehlana loved to have her hair brushed. There was a kind of sleepy, sensual delight in it that relaxed her tremendously. She was quite vain about her hair. It was thick and heavy and lustrously blonde. Its pale color was astounding to the dark-haired Tamuls, and she knew that all eyes would be on her any time she entered a room.

The three of them talked, the drowsy, intimate talk of ladies preparing for bed.

Then there was a polite tapping at the door.

"Oh, bother," Ehlana said. "See who that is, Melidere."

"Yes, your Majesty." The baroness rose to her feet and crossed the bedroom to the door. She opened it and spoke for a moment with the people outside. "It's four of the Peloi, your Majesty," she said. "They say they have word from the north."

"Bring them in, Melidere." Ehlana turned to face the door.

The man who came through the door wore typical Peloi clothing, tight-fitting and mostly leather, with a saber at his waist. His head was shaved, as were the heads of all Peloi men, but this fellow's face was slightly tanned, whereas his scalp was as pale as the belly of a fish. Something was wrong here.

The man behind the first wore a carefully trimmed black beard. His face was very pale, and it looked somehow familiar.

The last two also wore Peloi garb and had shaved their heads, but they were definitely *not* Peloi. The first was Elron, the juvenile Astellian poet, and the second, pouchy-eyed and slightly tipsy, was Krager. "Ah," he said in his drink-slurred voice, "so good to see you again, your Majesty."

"How did you get in here, Krager?" she demanded.

"Nothing easier, Ehlana." He smirked. "You should have kept a few of Sparhawk's knights to stand watch. Church Knights are more observant than Tamul soldiers. We dressed as Peloi, shaved our heads, and no one gave us a second glance. Elron here covered his face with his cloak when the baroness answered the door—just as a precaution—but otherwise it was almost too easy. You *have* met Elron before, haven't you?"

"I vaguely remember him, don't you, Melidere?"

"Why, yes, I believe so, your Majesty," the blonde girl replied. "Wasn't he that literary incompetent we met back in Astel?"

Elron's face went suddenly white with outrage.

"I'm not an expert in poetry, Ladies." Krager shrugged. "Elron tells me that he's a poet, so I take him at his word. May I present Baron Parok?" He indicated the first man who had entered the room.

Parok bowed floridly. His face was marked with the purplish broken veins of a heavy drinker, and his eyes were pouchy and dissipated-looking.

Ehlana ignored him. "You're not going to get out of here alive, Krager. You know that, don't you?"

"I *always* get out alive, Ehlana." He smirked. "My preparations are very thorough. Now I'd like to have you meet our leader. This is Scarpa." He gestured at the bearded man. "I'm sure you've heard of him, and he's been absolutely *dying* to make your acquaintance."

"He doesn't look at all that dead to me—yet," she noted. "Why don't you call the guards to remedy that, Melidere?"

Scarpa blocked the baroness. "This bravado is quite out of place," he said to Ehlana coldly in a voice loaded with contempt. "You give yourself too many airs. All the genuflecting and *your Majesty*s seem to have gone to your head and made you forget that you're still only a woman."

"I don't think I need instruction in proper behavior from the bastard son of a whore!" she retorted.

Scarpa's face flickered a brief annoyance. "We're wasting time," he said. His voice was deep and rich, the voice of a performer, and his manner and gestures were studied. He had obviously spent a great deal of time in the public eye. "We have many leagues to cover before dawn."

"I'm not going anyplace," she declared.

"You'll go where I tell you to go," he said, "and I'll teach you your place as we go along."

"What do you hope to gain from this?" Melidere demanded.

"Empire and victory." Scarpa shrugged. "We're taking the Queen of Elenia hostage. Her husband is so stupid that he forgets that the world is full of women—one very much like another. He's so foolishly attached to her that he'll give us anything for her safe return."

"Are you such an idiot that you actually believe that my husband will trade Bhelliom for me?" Ehlana said scornfully. "Sparhawk is Anakha, you fool, and he has Bhelliom in his fist. That makes him a God. He killed Azash, he'll kill Cyrgon, and he'll *definitely* kill you. Pray that he does it quickly, Scarpa. He has it in his power to make your dying last for a million years if he chooses."

"I do not pray, woman. Only weaklings put any faith in Gods."

"I think you underestimate Sparhawk's devotion to you, Ehlana," Krager said. "He'll give anything to gain your safe return."

"He won't have to," Ehlana snapped. "I'll deal with the four of you myself. Do you really think you can get out of here when one word from me will bring half the garrison running?"

"You won't give that word, however." Scarpa sneered. "You're just a little too arrogant, woman. I think you need to know the full reality of your situation." He turned and pointed at Baroness Melidere. "Kill that one," he commanded Elron.

"But—" the pasty-faced literary poseur began to object.

"Kill her!" Scarpa snapped. "If you don't, I'll kill *you!*"

Elron tremblingly drew his rapier and advanced on the defiant baroness.

"It's not a knitting needle, you clot," Melidere told him. "You can't even hold it right. Stick to butchering language, Elron. You don't have the skill—or the stomach—to move up to people yet, although your so-called poetry's bad enough to make people *want* to die."

"How dare you?" he almost screamed, his face turning purple.

"How's your *Ode to Blue* coming, Elron?" she taunted him. "You could make a fortune peddling that one as an emetic, you know. I felt the urge to vomit before you'd finished reciting the first stanza."

He howled in absolute rage and made a clumsy thrust with his rapier.

Ehlana had watched Stragen training Sarabian often enough to know that the thrust was off the mark. The intrepid baroness coolly deflected the blade with the wrist of the hand she seemed to be raising in a futilely defensive gesture, and Elron's blade passed smoothly through her shoulder.

Melidere gasped, clutching at the blade to conceal the exact location of the wound. Then she lurched back to pull herself free and clawed at the wound, spreading the blood spurting from it over the bodice of her nightdress. Then she fell.

"You murderer!" Ehlana shrieked, rushing to her fallen friend. She hurled herself across Melidere's inert body, weeping and crying out in apparent anguish. "Are you all right?" she muttered under her breath between sobs.

"It's only a scratch," Melidere lied, also in a whisper.

"Tell Sparhawk that I'm all right," the queen instructed, tugging off her ring and concealing it in Melidere's bodice, "and I forbid him to give up Bhelliom, no matter what they threaten to do to me." She rose to her feet, her face tear-streaked. "You'll hang for this, Elron," she said in a deadly voice, "or maybe I'll have you burned at the stake instead—with a slow fire." She pulled a blanket from the bed and quickly covered Melidere with it to prevent too close an examination.

"We will leave now," Scarpa said coldly. "That other one is also your friend, I believe." He pointed at the ashen-faced Alean. "We'll take her along, and if you make any outcry at all, I'll personally slit her throat."

"You're forgetting the message, Lord Scarpa," Krager said, pulling a folded piece of paper from the inside of his leather Peloi jacket. "We *have* to leave a friendly little note for Sparhawk—just to let him know that we stopped by to call." Then he drew a small knife. "Your pardon, Queen Ehlana"—he smirked, exhaling the sharp, acrid reek of his wine-sodden breath into her face—"but I need a bit of authentication to prove to Sparhawk that we're really holding you captive." He took hold of a lock of Ehlana's hair and roughly sawed it off with his knife. "We'll just leave this with our note so that he can compare it with later ones to verify that it's really yours." His grin grew even more vicious. "If you should feel a sudden urge to cry out, Ehlana, just remember that all we *really* need is your head. We can harvest hair from that, so we won't need to bring the rest of you along if you start being *too* much bother."

Thus concludes the tale of The Shining Ones,
the second book in the saga of The Tamuli.
In The Hidden City, *the final volume
in David Eddings's stirring epic,
Sparhawk and Ehlana face the ultimate challenge,
in a distant and merciless land.*

DAVID EDDINGS

Published by Del Rey Books. Available in your local bookstore.